Chris Bunch is the author of the Sten Series, the Dragonmaster Series, the Seer King series and many other acclaimed SF and fantasy novels. A notable journalist and bestselling writer for many years, he died in 2005.

Find out more about Chris Bunch and other Orbit authors by registering for the free monthly newsletter at www.orbitbooks.net

THE OMNIBUS EDITION

DRAGON MASTER

CHRIS BUNCH

Contains:

Storm of Wings
Knighthood of the Dragon
The Last Battle

www.orbitbooks.net

ORBIT

First published in Great Britain in 2007 by Orbit
Reprinted 2007 (three times), 2008, 2009, 2010, 2011

A CIP catalogue record for this book
is available from the British Library.

ISBN 978-1-84149-486-9

Typeset in Sabon by M Rules
Printed in the UK by CPI Mackays, Chatham ME5 8TD

Papers used by Orbit are from well-managed forests
and other responsible sources.

 MIX
Paper from
responsible sources
FSC
www.fsc.org   FSC® C104740

Orbit
An imprint of
Little, Brown Book Group
100 Victoria Embankment
London EC4Y 0DY

An Hachette UK Company
www.hachette.co.uk

www.orbitbooks.net

CONTENTS

STORM OF WINGS

Again, for L'il Karen

1

Hal Kailas heard the distant chittering of the dragon as he plodded home. He looked up eagerly, needing to see color beside the gray cobbles, stone houses, mountains, drab mine buildings, high-piled tailings, even the overcast sky.

The crimson and deep-green monster, he guessed a cow, although the beast was really too high for him to see the female's characteristic darker belly stripes, banked back and forth, horned head darting from side to side, looking down.

Somewhere in the crags just above the village, and Hal thought he knew just where from his solitary, but not lonely, hill explorations, the beast had its nest. The nest where dragons had hatched their young for over a century.

He wondered what had sparked its curiosity, what could spark any creature's interest in the village of Caerly. Nothing but gray, including, he thought morosely, all the people who lived there and went down the tin mine for their slender living.

He'd ducked his schooling this day, thinking that if he had to hear the tutor drone on once more about the workers' duty to support the way things are, which meant obediently going down the Tregonys' mine, and kissing their hands in gratitude, he'd go mad.

He dreamed, or rather tried to dream, for it seemed impossible, of the hillmen's legendary past. A past of fierce reivers and warriors, until the king of Deraine's army came through, and slew all those who didn't bend, kiss the sword, and become good little servitors to those nobles the king named as the region's overlords and exploiters.

Two hundred years gone, certainly. But there were still those who muttered about the injustice.

A wind blew cold across his face, and he pulled his wool coat, new only last birthday, closer about him.

Kailas was a bit past thirteen, tall for his age, but he had never been gawky. He had slender arms and legs, belying his strength. His brown hair was tousled, and he had green eyes in a somewhat long face.

The dragon shrilled loudly, and Hal started, for very close to him came an answering cry, higher, not as loud, from seemingly around the corner.

He rounded the corner, and saw four boys torturing a dragon kit. He guessed it to be fresh-hatched, for it was no more than a yard long. It must have fallen from its nest on to something that cushioned its landing.

Now the mother was frantically trying to recover it.

One of the boys was Nanpean Tregony, the local lord's son, and Hal knew the kit wouldn't be allowed to live beyond the hour. Tregony, a year older than Hal, good-looking, always ready with a smile for his elders, kept his cruel streak well hidden.

Hal knew better, having come on him laughing in hysterical glee after he'd soaked a kitten in lantern oil, and struck a spark.

None of the four noticed him. Tregony had a broken broom across the dragon's neck, pinning it to the cobbles, while the other three poked at it with sharp sticks.

Hal knew the other three as well, Tregony's toadies, like Nanpean a year or two older than Kailas, always sucking around him, hoping for favor from the mine owner's son.

The dragon screamed in pain, and an answering scream came from above, drowned by Tregony's jeering laughter. Tregony reached into a pouch inside his waistband, took out a slender, evil-looking spring knife. He touched a button, and its blade sprung out.

"Hold it still," he told one of his cohorts, passing him the broomstick. "And watch this, now," he said, and bent over the struggling kit.

Hal Kailas didn't have much of a temper . . . Or so he thought. But when he became truly angry, his voice sank to a whisper, and the world seemed to slow to a crawl, so that he had all the time in the world to do as he wished. That cold rage had made him more than a bit feared by the other village boys.

So it was now, on this gray, windy street.

He saw a length of wood, almost as long as he was tall, lying in a pile of scrap nearby. Hal soon had the wood, half as thick as his wrist, in both hands.

"Stop!" he shouted, and ran toward the four boys. One turned, was hit on the head, very hard, howled in panic, and started running.

Tregony jumped to one side.

"Kailas!" he shouted. "Get your peasant ass away from here, or my father'll roast you!"

Hal barely heard the words. He lifted the wood, and another boy raised his hands to fight back. Hal kicked him in the belly. The boy collapsed, near the dragon, and his face was ravaged by the kit's tiny claws as it flailed. The fourth boy was running after the first.

But Tregony had a bit of courage.

"Come on, then," he said, his face a smiling rictus. "Come on," he said again, waving the knife back and forth in front of him.

Hal had the stick in both hands, like a fighting stave wielded by men in paintings in his father's taproom, moving it up, down, keeping the knife away.

Tregony lunged, and Hal jerked sideways, had the stick like a spear at one end, and thrust hard. He caught Tregony along the neck, and the jagged end tore flesh. Hal pulled back, lunged once more, into Tregony's breastbone, heard ribs crack. Nanpean howled in agony, had hold of the spear's end, then stumbled back, fell hard against the stone wall beside him. He tried to get up and Hal kicked him, quite deliberately, in the face.

His eyes stared hard at Hal, then glazed, closed. For an instant Kailas thought he'd killed Tregony, then saw the steady rise and fall of the young man's chest.

Instantly he forgot him, knelt over the dragon, who was up on unsteady feet.

It shrieked fear, and, from above, his mother answered.

"Now for you," Hal muttered. "You little pain in the ass."

The dragon kit wriggled, wrapped in Hal's coat, as the boy reached for another handhold. He almost slipped, feet scrabbling on wet stone, then he was safe, inside a jagged crevice that led straight upward.

He looked down at Caerly a thousand feet below him, and was surprised he felt no vertigo, no particular fear beyond what any fool should feel high on this huge crag, only a few yards below a dragon's nest.

"Dammit!" he said, trying to sound like an adult. "Stay still! I'm on your side!"

The kit didn't seem to understand, squirming more frantically.

Across the valley, gray rain was sweeping toward him in the dusk, and he realized, unless he wanted to be trapped here by nightfall, he'd best keep moving.

He scanned the skies for the mother dragon, saw nothing. Hal wondered where the bull was, hoped not diving at the back of his head.

The musky scent of the nest came to him, something he'd heard others describe as nauseating. He found it quite otherwise, not attractive, but certainly not disgusting.

Realizing he was avoiding the last of the climb, he hitched his coat more securely to his waist, saw that the little dragon had ripped the cloth, knew he'd pay for what he was doing when winter winds struck, put his back to the crevice wall, and pushed upward with his feet.

He'd seen egg-gatherers walk their way up sheer cliffs like this, their grass baskets tied to their chests, tried to imitate them.

The rock wall behind him tore at his linen shirt, scratching his skin, but he ignored it, looking only up, only at that huge nest, looking like a pile of abandoned lumber and brush.

The nest had been built in an alcove of the crag, out of the way of wind and most weather. It was huge, thirty feet in diameter. As Hal got closer, he smelt carrion over the dragon-reek, and his stomach churned, wondering what he'd find inside the nest.

A shriek tore at his ears, and he jumped, almost losing his hold, and a wind pulled at him as the mother dragon dove past him, less than ten feet away.

"Go away, dammit!" he shouted. "I've got your baby! Go away or you'll kill us both!"

The baby dragon wiggled, squealed, and the mother heard. Hal had enough of a hold to let the kit's head snake out of the jacket.

The cow roared at him again, climbed, leathery wings, over a hundred feet across, slowly stroking down, lifting the monster high into the air.

The dragon caught the wind, banked, came back, mouth open, fangs menacing. The kit saw its mother, screeched, and again the cow turned away.

Hal scrambled up the last few feet, tumbled into the nest, landed on the decaying, half-eaten carcass of a lamb.

The nest was a litter of bones and debris. Here and there were tattered clothes, stolen from washlines below, bits of shabby rug that the dragons evidently fancied for either padding or decoration.

A deep roar sounded, and Hal saw the bull dragon, above its mate, fifty feet long, its spiked tail, a twenty-foot-long killing whip, lashing, head darting back and forth on the ten-foot-long neck.

"Here," he said, and unwrapped the kit, spilling it into the nest.

He pulled his coat and arm away, not quite fast enough as the kit caught him below the elbow with its fangs, tearing his arm open to the wrist.

The kit shrilled in evident triumph, and the bull dove at the nest.

Hal had one instant of pure awe, seeing the dragon, jaws yawning, foreleg talons extended, wing talons reaching, coming at him, and the thought flashed of how few people could have seen this and lived, realized if he didn't move quickly he might not be one of those survivors, and eeled over the edge of the nest, almost falling, then had a hold on a two-inch length of lumber sticking out of the brush.

The cow flared her wings and landed above him, in the nest, her interest only in her kit.

The bull had climbed, dropped a wing and came back at him, but Hal was tucked in the crevice, slithering down as fast as he could.

The dragon tried again for him, couldn't slow enough to reach into the cranny, screaming rage.

It was below him then, and Hal looked at its wide shoulder blades, at the carapace behind the dragon's long neck and horned head, thought, insanely, that could be a seat, and you could be flying yourself, if you could figure a way to make the dragon do your bidding, and he forced that away, climbing down and down.

The dragon's rage receded as he shinnied down the outcropping, and cold fear finally came, fear of what would greet him when he reached the ground and his parents' tavern.

"I hope that'll not leave the scar I fear," Hal's mother said, as she finished bandaging Hal's arm with the spell-impregnated bandage she'd gotten from the village witch.

"It'll be fine, Mother," Hal said.

"Then that'll be the only thing that shall," she said. She rubbed her eyes wearily. "Twenty years gone for us now."

"Lees," Hal's father, Faadi, said quietly, "that's not going to make our son feel any better about what happened . . . nor is it likely to offer any solutions to our problem."

"I'm sorry for what happened, Da," Hal said.

"Are you really?" his father asked.

Hal started to reply, thought, then shook his head. "No. Nossir, I'm not. That Nanpean ought not to be able to pain others, even a dragon."

"No," Faadi said. "He ought not. Any more than his father ought to be able to use his gold and power given by the king to rule our lives." He shrugged. "But that seems to be the way of the world."

"Some of Lord Tregony's men—" Lees began.

"Thugs," Faadi corrected. "Goons. Bullyboys. Hardly men of good or free will."

"Regardless," Lees said. "They wanted you, Hal."

"Naturally, we told them to go away or we'd call the warder," Faadi said.

"They laughed at that, and said that even if they didn't find you," Lees went on, "there'd be charges pressed, and our tavern would be theirs, and we'd be beggars on the road. We should know full well the warders and the magistrate are on their side, like they side with everyone of riches."

"Tomorrow, before dawn, I'll ride for the city, and hire the best advocate I can," Faadi said. "That'll put a bit of a stave in their wheel."

"But aren't those expensive?" Hal asked.

"We own this building clear," Faadi said. "That should pay at least some of his price. For the rest, he – or she – will have to take payments."

"Which will be a time in coming," Lees said. "Tregony's men also said that Tregony would order none of his miners – his miners, indeed, as if they were his slaves – to drink here. That's the greater part of our business."

"Not everyone in Caerly dances to the Lord's precise fluting," Faadi said.

"Most do."

"But there's others who'll still come here for their pint and pasty," Faadi said.

"I wish . . ." Hal said forlornly, his voice trailing away.

"What?" Faadi asked.

"Never mind," Hal said, trying to keep from crying. Lees put an arm around him.

"We'll fight them, Hal," she said firmly. "Fight them and win."

Hal wanted to believe her, but heard the doubt in her voice.

*

Later, in his attic room, Hal did cry, feeling like a stupid baby, knowing that wouldn't do any good at all.

He stared out the window, at the rainy street below, remembering his mother's words about being "beggars on the road."

No. That would never happen. Not to his parents.

The clock downstairs in the taproom rang midnight. There'd been no customers to run out to their homes. The whole village seemed to be holding its breath, waiting to see what Lord Tregony would do to the boy who dared hurt his only son.

Hal thought of what his father had said, about going to the city with his hat in his hand to hire an advocate who'd stand firm against Tregony's pocket magistrate.

No, he thought. That would never do. Not for his parents.

He thought about them, about their careful lives, careful budgeting, here in this tiny mining village in the back of beyond. And he considered his own life, what he would grow up to be.

He knew he'd never go down the mines like his fellows, What, then? Inherit the tavern, and have to listen to the sponges and the old gaffers, mumbling their drunken way toward the grave? Maybe become a tutor to teach the miners' children to barely read and write and bow and scrape before the boys followed their fathers underground, and the girls began to bear baby after baby until they were worn out at thirty?

No.

At least, he thought a bit forlornly, he didn't have to worry about saying goodbye to his friends, since he really didn't think he'd ever had any.

Moving very quietly, he dressed, wearing his best woolen pants, heaviest shoes, a sweater and his rather bedraggled and torn coat. He improvised a pack from another pair of pants, stuffed two shirts into it, along with a toothbrush and a bar of soap.

He started downstairs past his parents' bedroom, heard the sound of their fitful sleep.

In the taproom, he wrote a note that he wished would say everything in his heart, but couldn't.

He took bread, cheese, two pints of the tavern's ale, a small square of smoked ham. He saw a sheathed knife, ancient, a wall hanging, next to an antique sword, took it down, tested its edge.

It would serve, and he found a small sharpening stone in the taproom' s utensil drawer, added a knife, fork, spoon to it.

There were a handful of coins in the cash drawer and, feeling for the first time like a thief, he took a few of them.

He looked around the taproom, inviting, warm in the dying firelight, the only world he'd known.

Then he unlocked the front door, pulling his coat on, went down the steps, and off through the rain for a new and better world.

2

Hal looked up at the dragon crouched on the outcropping, put one foot in the step of his stilts and pushed off. He wobbled back and forth, then had his balance.

He glanced back at the dragon. It was, he thought, looking amusedly at Hal's clumsiness, although no one but Kailas would've given the monster that characterization. It was green and white, young, he guessed, perhaps two years old, thirty feet long, and had been hovering around the hopfields for three days now.

The workers had tried to ignore it, in the hopes it meant no harm, although no one knew just what would enrage one of the monsters.

This picking of the hops was too happy a festival for the workers who'd flocked out from the capital of Rozen with their families to allow a damned dragon to ruin things.

It was late summer, hot, dry, the hop flowers beginning to dry, perfect weather for picking. The workers used stilts to walk down the rows of pole-tied vines, as that was faster than using ladders, to reach the cones fifteen feet overhead.

The hops were baled and taken to the big kilns in the strange-looking circular oasthouses for drying, then pressed and carted away to the breweries.

For centuries, the poor of Rozen had taken this harvest as a holiday, streaming out of their cobbled streets and packed slums. The farm owners provided tents, and vied with each other, claiming to offer better food and stronger beer.

The work wasn't that hard, and there was the night to look forward to, when torches flared, friendships were renewed, and scandals and marriages made in the soft meadow grass.

This was Hal's first festival. He'd been talked into staying on for the hop picking after the peach season ended. The farm owner had vaguely spoke of hiring him full-time, having noted Hal's hard work.

Kailas didn't know if he'd accept, thought not. He'd been offered other steady work in the two years since he'd left the stony mining village, but had never accepted, not sure of the reason.

He'd done just about any job offered that paid quickly, in cash, and didn't try to change him, from road laborer to clerk to wagoneer. The only one that had drawn him, and that for a moment, was being a taleteller, carrying whatever stories and news heard from village to village, performing in a square or tavern for peasants who mostly couldn't read or write. But he realized he had no talent for the dramatics required to wring the last handclap and copper from his audience.

He'd roamed Deraine from north to south, and the road had taught its lessons – never turn down a meal or a warm place to sleep; those who're kindly to passing strangers generally have their own reason for charity; never beg, but offer work and mean it; the first one to make friends with you is most always the last person you want for a companion; it's better to look shabby and clean than rich and filthy, and other messages neither the village tutor nor his father's books had offered.

So he could, possibly, linger on this hopfarm for the winter, although autumn hadn't come yet.

But he could also be far to the south when the first snow came. Perhaps he'd go into one of the coastal cities, as he had a year ago. There, able to read and write, unlike most of his fellow wanderers, he could find work as a clerk or shipper's assistant, out of the tempests.

Last year he'd made the mistake of signing on to a fishing boat, and his bones were still frozen and his fingers prickered from the hooks that ended in his hand.

As Hal thought of the future, his hands worked swiftly, stripping the cones from the stems on the trellis overhead and dropping them into the sack around his neck, then stepping forward, stilt legs striking puffs of dust in the ground ten feet below.

He grinned at himself. When would he learn to let tomorrow take care of itself, and concentrate on the moment?

Such as Dolni, with her waist-length black hair, her smiling red lips, the simple frocks she wore, with nothing beneath. She was sixteen, the daughter of one of the farmer's cooks, with a merry laugh and eyes that promised much.

Late the night before, her arms had fulfilled the promise of her eyes, and it had been close to dawn before she pulled her dress on, pushed Hal away, saying she must be back in her bed before dawn, and perhaps tomorrow night – tonight! – there would be more.

Hal felt like puffing his chest, for hadn't she chosen him over the others she'd gone walking with on other nights of the harvest? Dolni vowed the others had done nothing with her, although they'd begged her for her favors.

Dolni may not have been the first Hal had bedded, but she was far and away the prettiest and the most passionate.

Hal stumbled, taken by his heated lust, almost fell, and brought himself back to work, just as the dragon, on the jutting crag at the far end of the field, snorted, and dove from its perch.

There were yelps of alarm, a scream, from other pickers. But the dragon was merely picking up speed – or, perhaps, harassing the spindly two-legs below, as its great wings caught the afternoon wind, and lifted it high into the air.

Hal stared up at it, banking, gliding.

Now there was where he longed to be, somehow aloft with that fabulous beast, caring nothing for what was below.

Except, perhaps, for Dolni, riding behind him, the sweet tinkle of her laughter ringing through the skies.

Perhaps they would fly north, toward the rumored Black Island, or, more logically, south, beyond Deraine, across the Chicor Straits to the walled city of Paestum, or beyond that small free city, over Sagene and its baronies.

That was too much even for his imagination, and he pulled himself back, and concentrated on his picking, vowing he'd have more full sacks by dusk than any other picker, no matter how experienced, how agile, and shine in Dolni's eyes.

It was hard telling what there was more of: food, or varieties of the various beers the district boasted.

There were barreled oysters, river crayfish, ham, chicken with hot peppers, spiced beef in pasties, kidney pie, cold cuts, breads, pickles, potato cakes, a dozen varieties of barely-steamed vegetables, corn relish, a dozen cheeses, desserts and more.

There was heavily-hopped pale beer, dark porter, heavy stout, lager, wheat beer, even strawberry beer.

All was set on long tables, and everyone was welcome to take as much as he wanted, unlike the meanness of the city.

Some pickers had brought instruments with them, and there were half a dozen guitars playing, a couple of lutes, some wood-winds, three or four small drums, wooden whistles, men and women singers, a chorus that couldn't quite decide whose song to join in.

Children bounced through the throng, intent on their own games. Dogs chased cats, and sometimes were sent howling when they caught them.

Hal Kailas pushed through the crowd, looking for only one thing: Dolni.

He finally saw her, just as she ran, hand in hand with a local farmer's son, notable only for his muscles and blond hair, up a hill and disappeared into a clump of brush.

Her laughter rang behind her.

Hal thought of going after her, but what would he say? He had no rights at all, he realized, just as he also realized those boys who'd gone before him had no rights.

He thought of swearing, knew that wouldn't do any good. If he had any brains, he thought forlornly, he would laugh at his own stupidity for thinking he was more than just one more conquest for the little roundheels. He tried, but the sound was most hollow.

Very well, then, he thought. I shall get drunk. Why that idea came he had no idea. He'd been taken by drink three times, and disliked not only how it made him feel the next morning, but the dizziness, foolishness and sickness it brought that night.

Nevertheless, he found a heavy wooden mug, and went to the barrels of beer. Dark would be the strongest, he guessed, and the most potent, and grimly ladled his mug full.

Maybe he'd hoped for unconsciousness, but after two and a half mugs, it hadn't come. In fact, the brew had made him feel more alert, more alive. He felt strength run through him, had a flashed thought of what vitality Dolni had missed, almost burst into tears.

He looked around for something to do, someone to impress, heard the faint honk of the dragon, saw it settling on to the jutting rock, folding its wings for the night.

An idea came.

If Dolni would not fly with him, he would fly by himself.

*

Both moons were up, as befitted a harvest, but the higher Hal climbed, even though he could easily make out handholds in the rock, the more he wished it was just a bit darker, for the light showed him entirely too much.

He could see, perhaps two hundred distant feet below, the fires of the festival, heard the sounds of laughter and music, could even pick out a couple of stumbling drunks who couldn't decide whether to fight or to hug each other.

Also, he could see, and now hear, very well, the rumbling snores – he hoped it was snores – of the dragon just around the outcropping and a bit below him.

The effects of the beer had worn off somewhat, and he thought, if he was anything other than a cursed fool, he'd go back the way he came. No one, after all, had seen him begin this stupid climb, or heard him boast of his intent, so he had no foolish pride to sustain.

But he climbed on, another ten feet, thinking that would surely be enough. He slipped across the crag, using an all too convenient crack, and came out in the full flood of the moonlight.

About thirty feet below him was the motionless dragon. He could see its sides heave in sleep, had a sudden wonder what dragons dreamed, or if they dreamed at all.

Meanwhile, without bidding or thought, his hands and legs were finding new holds, and he was moving down toward the monster. Closer, ever closer, and he was within ten feet of its broad back.

Well, he thought, this is as stupid a way to die as ever a man, let alone a boy, ever thought of, and jumped, legs reaching, just for that flat area behind the carapace that guarded the creature's shoulder blades.

He landed fair, and the dragon woke with a screech, wings flailing, trying to reach back with its talons, with its fangs, to tear away the interloper.

But Hal was out of its reach, and the nightmare launched itself out, into empty air.

Hal Kailas was truly flying as the dragon dove for speed, then climbed high, banking, rolling, and he was holding on to the back of the plate, rough scales perfect for handholds, the warmth of the beast beneath him, and he could look up – seeing down – at the fires below him, people looking up, hearing the dragon scream rage and fear, and faintly he heard shouts as men and women saw him, saw him riding the dragon, flying.

The dragon tucked a wing, and the world was rightside up. Above him were the moons, and all the stars, and below him the world he had little use for.

He tried a kick, a tap really, against the left side of the dragon's neck, and the beast turned as bidden. He kicked with his right foot, and another turn came.

He was not just flying, but he was in command of this wonderful monster, this beast of dreams.

"To the stars," he shouted to the dragon, but the creature tucked its head, and dove, shaking like a horse trying to rid itself of a rider.

The ground was rushing up at him, and Hal could do nothing but hold on, hoping the dragon wasn't about to kill himself just for revenge against this petty creature with the foolhardiness to try to ride him.

The dragon shook himself, the membrane of his wings rattling like great drums, and Hal lost his grip, and fell.

Now the ground, the dark ground, swirled up at him, and the torch fires wound about him as he spun. He kept his eyes open, took, for his last sight before death, that peaceful moon, far above.

Then he landed.

Landed easily in one of the huge wagons filled with bundled hops, and the air was driven out of him, and all was black for an instant.

Then he saw light, fires, heard people running toward him, and he fought his way to his feet, feeling every muscle in his body protest.

A bearded face came over the cart top.

"Whut th' *hells*—"

"Someone said," Hal said, in as careless a voice as he could manage, "dragons couldn't be ridden."

"Boy, you are the *godsdamnedest* fool I ever heard of!" a woman said as she pulled herself up beside the beard.

"Maybe," Hal said. He looked out, saw the pickers running toward him, heard more shouts, thought he saw Dolni, though, now, for some strange reason, it mattered not at all to him.

"Maybe I am," he said thoughtfully. "But I rode the dragon."

3

Autumn had arrived, but only on the calendar. It was hot and dry, the rains promised by the sages and tradition still absent. Dust swirled about Hal's feet as he tramped on, ever south toward the cities along the Chicor Straits.

His purse was full, if of more copper than silver, he had a new cloak rolled on his shoulders, and his pack held bread, cheese, and a flask of beer.

Kailas should have been content, for a wandering worker. But he felt aimless, with nothing north or south to particularly draw him, nor did any of the jobs he considered much interest him.

He heard the clatter of hooves, jumped out of the way as a fast coach drawn by eight thundered past.

Hal coughed his way through the dust cloud it left, the driver of course not bothering to slow for one more shabby wanderer, his unseen master hidden behind drawn curtains.

Such it would always be, Kailas thought, with only a bit of resentment. There would always be those who rode in coaches, like the Tregonys of the village he'd left, and those who walked in the dust or mud.

Like Hal.

He didn't really mind being a poor nomad – at his age, almost everything was an adventure. But he'd seen the older vagrants, tottering along, joints screaming, able to eat only mush, drunkenness their only solace, without kith or kin to care about them until the day they finally died in some roadside ditch.

That was not what he wanted.

But he was damned if he knew what he *did* want.

A shrilling came, and he looked up, saw a large dragon, all shades of green, following the road, about a hundred feet up. He was ready to duck for cover – other travelers had told him dragons haunted this lonely road, ready to swoop, kill and carry off any solitary vagabond.

But then he forgot his caution as he saw, on the dragon's back, a rider.

The dragon soared closer, and Hal could make out more of the man on its back. He was tall, very thin, long-faced, and had a well-trimmed gray beard. He wore brown leather boots, breeches and vest, a tan shirt under the vest, and a slouch hat crammed down on his head.

He held reins in one hand that ran to ringbolts mounted through spikes behind the dragon's mouth, and was sitting comfortably on some sort of pad on its shoulder blades.

He saw Hal, boomed laughter that seemed to ring across the land below.

Hal gaped like a ninny. He'd heard of men who had learned to ride dragons, didn't quite believe the tales even though he'd briefly been on one of the monsters a month gone.

But here was proof – the man appeared in complete control of the beast, touching reins, and the dragon pirouetted through the air.

The man reached in a bag, and scattered a handful of dust.

The dust sparkled in the air, then shimmered, and letters came, floating in the middle of nowhere:

!MAGICK!

!SORCERY!

!ATHELNY OF THE DRAGONS!

SEE THE

WONDROUS DISPLAY OF

ATHELNY'S ART AND SKILL!

RIDE A

DRAGON YOURSELF

NO DANGER BUT ONLY

FOR THE BOLDEST

Hal barely noted that the warning was in quite small letters.
Ride a dragon?

He tore off his cap, waved, shouted, danced in the dusty road.
Again the dragon swooped back, and its rider cupped his
hands, and shouted:

"Two villages away, boy! We'll see you there . . . if you've got
the silver!"

The dragon banked.

Hal shouted back: "You will! I'll be there!"

But, if Athelny – that must be him – heard, he neither flew nor
looked back.

Hal ran after him, then caught himself, slowing to a trot and
then a fast walk. Yes. He surely would be there.

He wondered what it cost for a ride.

It was one silver coin too much. Hal counted his purse for the
fourth time, wasn't able to improve his pelf.

The sign implacably read:

Ride the Dragon
10 Silver Barons

An outrageous sum – but there were people lining up to pay it.
Most were young bravos from the village, or merchants' children.
Hal noticed half a dozen giggling girls in the line.

He tried to remember where that silver coin he needed so desperately had strayed. A night's lodging and a long, luxuriant bath
after leaving the hopfields? That steak with half a bottle of
Sagene wine he'd treated himself to? That damned cloak he'd
thought a wonderful present to himself, when the weather suggested he wouldn't be needing it for awhile?

It was no use.

Even with his coppers, he was still short . . . and if he managed
to find a spare coin in his delvings, what would he do for food on
the morrow?

Glumly, he considered Athelny's show.

To someone from a big city, it might have appeared somewhat unimpressive: three wagons, one for sleeping, the other two
heavy freight wagons with flat tops and ties to keep the dragons

secure. Athelny had three wagoneers, plus two cunning-looking young men, not much older than Hal, obviously city sharpsters. They took tickets, made sure the passengers were securely tied in behind Athelny, jollied the crowd and joked with each other, just a little too loudly, about the rustics around them.

But none of this mattered to Hal, because Athelny had two real dragons, the green one he'd seen on the road, and a slightly younger one, in various dark reds.

The red dragon was sprightlier, constantly trying to take off with the other, the one Athelny was giving rides with. Earlier, the red one had shown his tricks in aerial acrobats, which Hal had seen the last of.

Both monsters were well-tended, scales brushed and oiled so they gleamed, wings shining, talons polished.

Hal had already noted Athelny's riding-pad, a flat saddle tied to two ringbolts drilled through the dragon's neck carapace. Now he saw a second saddle mounted behind the rider's, this one fitted with leather shoulder straps.

If these dragons were his, Hal thought, he wouldn't demean them by giving bumpkins rides for silver.

He would be the bold explorer, finding lands no one from Deraine would know, perhaps even visiting Black Island that the boastful Roche claimed as their own, reputedly the home of the biggest, most dangerous black dragons, a breed unto themselves.

His practical side jeered – and what would he use to feed his dragons, let alone himself?

There were two bullocks, lowing as if knowing their fate, tied behind the wagons, and one of the teamsters had said they would serve as dinner for man and beast.

"Pity they don't breath fire, like tavern talk would have it," one of the teamsters had told him. "That way, we could get 'em cooked in th' bargain."

Perhaps, his dream ran on, he could find a rich lord to sponsor his explorations.

If not, and he must make his way giving jaunts for his wages, he would cater to the rich, and charge accordingly, giving long flights to lords and their ladies. He'd learn about the country around him, and lecture and be thought wise.

And wasn't it you, not long ago, thinking of how much you despised those rich? I do, Hal thought. It's only their gold I lust for.

Suddenly he grinned.

Nice dreams, he thought, remembering the wanderer's weary joke: If I had some ham, I could have some ham and eggs, if I had some eggs. All I need is some money, some dragons and some wagons, and I'm as good – better, maybe – then Athelny.

Meantime, it's him up there, darting among the clouds, a squealing girl hanging tightly to him, and Hal down here, slumped against a wagon wheel, without the money for even a few seconds aloft.

"Why ain't you in line, since you was so innarested in dragons?"

It was the teamster he'd talked to earlier. Hal thought about it, told her the truth.

The woman nodded.

"Athelny charges fair coin for his pleasures, he does," She thought a moment. "Course, there's always a way for someone who's not afraid of work to earn a lift."

Hope came.

"Work's no stranger to me," he said.

The woman looked about. "I could be a shit, an' ask if you'd mind killin' those beeves we've got tied up . . . but I ain't.

"Tell you what. By th' way, m'name's Gaeta. I handle the business, day to day, for the show. Our wagons're filthy. I'll have Chapu – he's that fat one over there – drive 'em back to that river we forded.

"You'll find some rags and a bucket from the wagonbox over there."

Hal was on his feet, hurrying toward the wagon she'd pointed out before she finished.

"So you're the lad who's been shining m'wagons for the last half-day, eh?" Athelny asked. He had a bluff, hearty voice, and wanted the listener to think he was one of the upper classes, Hal thought.

Nothing wrong with that, his mind went on, as his fingers linked the two straps, once saddle cinches, that would hold him firm in the seat behind Athelny.

"Have to do you a return, then, and give you a proper ride," Athelny said. "If that's what you want. Or would you rather have the nice lift, the smooth sail, and the gentle landing such as I've been giving the girls of this burg all day?"

"Whatever you want, sir," Hal said.

"Thought you might want a little excitement, which is why I

changed saddles for Red. But if you get sick on me," Athelny promised, "you'll think cleaning those wagons was a jolly sport."

"I won't," Hal said, and told his stomach it'd best obey or he'd put nothing in it for the next year, damnit!

"Then hang on."

Athelny slid easily on to the pad in front of Hal, grabbed the reins and slapped them against the dragon's neck. The beast snorted, and its wings uncurled, thrashed, like distant thunder.

"You interested in flying one day?" Athelny asked over his shoulder.

"Yessir." Hal didn't mention his momentary flight over the hopfields.

"Then I'll tell you what's going on. M'dragon, Red, here'd be happier if he had a height to sail down from, instead of having to lift all by himself.

"Another thing that's makin' him a bit unhappy is how hot and muggy 'tis. You'd think, with the air thick like this, a dragon's wings'd have more to push against, and would take off easier.

"But not. Demned if I know why. Now, he'll start trundlin' forward, and then stroke hard, and here we are!

"Airborne!"

Indeed they were, and Hal saw the remnants of the crowd grow smaller, and then he could see the wagons, and then the village.

"We'll climb up for a time," Athelny said, still not having to raise his voice. They weren't moving very fast, so there was little wind rush.

"Now, we're up a couple of hundred. We'll give Red a bit of a relax here, and circle while we're still climbing.

"Not that he believes he needs it for what he knows we'll attempt. You've got to think for a dragon, sometimes, for he's not sure of what he wants. Then, other times . . ." Athelny didn't finish the sentence.

Hal barely noticed, looking down at the road he'd traveled so slowly this morning, hurry as he would, to reach the village. To either side there were trees, farmers' fields, and over there a lake he'd never suspicioned, growing from that small creek he'd forded.

Still farther out, in the blue haze of approaching dusk, were low hills, and unknown valleys.

"How far would we have to go up to see the ocean, sir?" he shouted.

"Don't b'lieve we could from here. Get as high as we could, where men and dragons have trouble breathing, their wings not lifting as they should, I still don't think we'd even see the province cap'tal, let alone any of the Strait Cities."

"Oh," Hal said, a bit disappointed.

"Why? You have people on the coast?"

"Nossir. I was just curious."

"Where are you from?"

Hal didn't feel like giving his biography.

"Not much of anywhere, sir. Some time back, up north."

Athelny turned, looked at him closely.

"You're just on the road, eh?"

He didn't wait for an answer, turned back.

"Now, we've got some height to us. Note how Red responds to the reins. Tap him on the left side of his neck, he turns left. On the right, unless he's in a mood, he goes right.

"Flying, when the weather's calm like this – and when your beast's well-trained and in a proper mood – is easy as walking.

"Other times . . . Well, that's why there's so few dragon-masters."

Dragonmaster. It was a new word.

"How many are there?"

Athelny shrugged.

"Good question. P'raps a dozen here in Deraine, maybe more. I've heard there's some just flyin' for rich lords' pleasure, around their estates or wandering afar, just exploring for the sights."

That was for him, Hal thought.

"Roche has more. Quite a few more. Their queen's interested in anything new. I've heard some say they've got a hundred fliers, though I think that's a bit many for easy belief.

"Sagene . . . maybe ten. Their barons don't seem interested in anything other than their own pleasures and arses. Though I've wondered if there might not be gold to be made across the Straits, showing what a good honest Deraine flier can do.

"Enough of such. Now, hang on, for what we're doing is a climbing turn, taking us back the way we came."

And so Red obeyed, and the village came into sight again.

"Now a diving turn . . ."

The ground grew closer.

"Hang on, for Red's going to loop."

Hal was hanging from his ropes, looking up at down, as he had riding the dragon in the hopfields.

He couldn't hold back, but let out a yelp of pure joy.

"Good boy," Athelny approved. "Mayhap you *are* cut out for a flier. Now we'll do a series of rolls."

The world barreled about Hal, and his stomach made a mild protest, which he ignored.

"Excellent, m'Red," Athelny approved. "You'll get the blood of one steer for that in your meal this night.

"Now, what do you think of this, son?"

Red suddenly dove, again reminding Kailas of his previous adventure. Just below them were the show's wagons, and there were dots getting larger, becoming horses, people, as they closed on the ground.

But it was all quite remote for a few seconds. Then the earth was rushing up at them, fast, faster. Athelny was pulling back hard on the reins, grunting with effort.

The dragon's wings were spread flat, braking the long dive, and rattling loudly.

Then the ground was below them, not fifty feet, as the dragon's dive flattened, and then, once more, Red climbed for the skies.

"Did you have your eyes closed?"

"Nossir."

"Then, did you notice how the world seemed to be coming up at you quicker there at the last?"

"I did, sir." Hal was pleased that his guts were silent now.

"Good. When that happens, means you're within a couple hundred feet, too close, and you'd best be recovering from your dive, or you're about to spread yourself neatly over the landscape.

"Which is not considered proper by any worthwhile flier."

Athelny put Red through a few more turns, these more gentle, then brought the dragon in on the grassy field, braking with its wings, and landing gently on its four legs.

Hal unfastened his straps, and Athelny slid off the beast, gave him a hand to the ground.

"Have you a job around here?"

"Not yet, sir. I was the one you waved at, when you were coming up the road. Tomorrow I guess I'll start looking."

"You still think you might want to learn to fly?"

"I'd do anything, sir."

"Hmm." Athelny was about to say something as Gaeta came up, rethought.

"Did this boy do a good job as it 'pears to me?"

"He did," Gaeta said.

"It'd be nice to have everything always this neat, wouldn't it?"

Gaeta shrugged.

"You're welcome to stay and eat with us," Athelny said.

"Thank you, sir. And . . . and if you're looking for somebody, I'll work harder'n anybody, sir."

"We'll see," Athelny said vaguely. "We'll see."

Hal's hopes sank.

But in the morning, when the show moved on, there was a place in one of the wagons for Hal's pack, a bench on the side for him to ride on, and leather harness for him to be rubbing neat's-foot oil into, even if there still was never a mention of what his job actually was, or what his wages might be.

4

"Stand, deliver and such," the bandit drawled casually, although his crossbow was aimed steadily at Hal's belly.

Hal half-raised his hands, dropping his reins across his horse's neck.

Half a dozen other thieves rode out of the brush, weapons ready. At their head was a lean, hard-looking rogue with a carefully waxed goatee.

It was a perfect place for an ambush – about two leagues outside the Sagene walled city of Bedarisi, close enough to safety for a rider to relax his guard a little.

The goateed man peered at Hal.

"Ah. 'Tis the younger who rides for the Deraine dragonmaster, eh, the one who came first through last summer?"

"I am he," Hal said.

"And you missed paying your toll when you rode out yesterday for Frechin, did you not?"

"Didn't see anyone to give it to, Cherso."

"We remember each other!" the man with the goatee said with some pleasure. "It's always a good sign when men doing business know each other's names. And the reason no one was out to greet you yesterday was we stopped a brandy merchant yesterday, and he decided to fight, and we had to take all." He smiled sweetly. "It was very good brandy, and so we were sleeping in."

Hal managed a half-smile, took a small pouch from inside his leather vest, tossed it across. Cherso looked at his followers.

"Note, this is a sensible lad, beyond his years, who knows when it's cheaper to pay, not like that merchant, whose bones'll never be seen by his loved ones."

Cherso opened the pouch, looked inside, frowned.

"Nothing in here but silver, lad."

"We've not had the best of seasons," Hal said truthfully. "There's more fliers from Deraine come across doing shows this year."

"Not to mention th' Roche," a pockmarked man said. "A shitpot load of 'em just came in from the east into Bedarisi. Had five great snakes, all tied in cages, biggest I've over seen."

"Plus so'jers to guard, so we just watched 'em pass," another said.

Hal grimaced. The men of Roche had also discovered flying shows. He'd not seen one yet, but the tales were their perfectly trained fliers, wearing common livery, and performing in formation, shamed most dragon shows, including Athelny of the Dragons, now with only a single beast.

Cherso caught Kailas' expression, tucked the pouch away.

"Now, I'll take your word for having a thin season, boy. For it's good when men can trust each other, and never take more than the other can give, is it not?"

Hal managed a smile.

"Perhaps if I had a better story you'd not be taking any tribute at all?"

"Now, now," Cherso said. "Leave us not press our luck. Each of us has to do what he must, and I think I'm being kindly, most kindly, taking this pittance not only for your safety, but for your master's and crew as well. I assume they'll be passing this way in the next few days?"

"They will," Hal said. "I've been papering Frechin, as you guessed, and Athelny said we'd be leaving in a day or so.

"You know, Cherso, if times get any harder, perhaps you and your men would consider taking your tribute in free rides?"

There was scornful laughter, and Cherso spat on the ground.

"Do we appear mad? Why should anyone want to get off nice

solid ground and ride a dragon? We're not fools who willingly court danger."

"But you're bandits."

"That's a trade we know well," Cherso said. "Some of our fathers, brothers, were men of the road as well."

He glanced away, not wanting the obvious rejoinder from Hal asking what rope or headsman's ax they'd encountered to end their careers.

"Speaking of which," he said, ostentatiously changing the subject, "these times we're living in are becoming a bit dangerous, if you haven't noticed."

"I've seen a lot more men with arms about this season," Hal said. "And merchants are travelling in convoys, and few families abroad."

"They sense trouble, as do I," Cherso said. "A man came out, two weeks gone, to talk to us about an amnesty."

"That doesn't seem like trouble to me," Hal said. "Are you going to take it?"

"Nary a chance," the pockmarked man said.

"Not under the conditions he set us," Cherso agreed. "It wasn't a blanket amnesty, such as a baron might offer when his daughter's married or his wizard achieves power over his enemy.

"Seems there's now a Council of Barons, and some say they're considering naming a king from amongst themselves. You heard aught about that?"

Hal shook his head. "I don't pay much attention to politics."

"Nor do we," Cherso said. "But mayhap we'd best start. This Council has offered an amnesty to men of arms – sorry, I meant men of the road like ourselves, freelances, and such – on condition they join the army they're putting together."

"Armies," the other bandit snorted. "Have to do all the fighting, share your loot with some fatass who sat on a hill lookin' proud in armor, and prob'ly get trampled in some charge anyway. Piddle on armies."

"Worst, they've got a wizard making anyone who takes the amnesty swear a blood oath to him, that if you do something sensible, such as desert after the first pay, you'll be eaten by flaming worms or somethings.

"Not that the barons' alliance will hold together long enough for them to backstab each other until a king wades out of the gore and grabs a crown, but the bastards might hang together long enough to sweep the countryside for us men of daring. As I said, not a good sign."

Hal gnawed at his lip, wondered if any of this would pertain to him, couldn't see how.

"A question for you," the pockmarked thief said. "Does Deraine have highwaymen like Sagene?"

"Not many," Hal answered.

"No men of spirit in your kingdom, eh?"

"No," Hal said, unoffended. "We have laws."

The pockmarked man grinned, tapped the hilt of his sheathed sword. "So do we."

That brought laughter from the other thieves. When it died, Cherso asked, "As I recall, you wintered last year in Paestum. Does your master plan the same?"

"Don't know yet," Hal said. "He was thinking of going into winter quarters early, and voyaging over to the Roche coast for a replacement for the dragon we lost last year.

"But the Roche denied his permit, and he's not taken me into his secrets about what his plans are now."

"Word of advice," Cherso said. "I wouldn't be too eager to spend time in Paestum these days. Far, far too close to Roche, and those bastards and their damned queen keep whining in the broadsheets about having been snookered out of their claim to the city."

"No matter to me," Hal said.

"Nor me," Cherso said, taking the bolt from his crossbow. "Life goes on, and we do the best we can with what we have."

Hal nodded.

"You'd best be getting on to Bedarisi, before dark," Cherso said. "I've heard there's some masterless men who have been lurking just beyond the walls, men without any law to guide them.

"Good luck to you, young dragon man. And we'll see you next spring."

As quietly as they'd come, the bandits were gone, and the road was clear.

Hal thought about what the bandit had told him. Armed men on the roads, a possible amnesty to raise an army, Cherso saying the Roche were growing ambitious. No, it should not pertain to him, at least as long as he kept a wary eye out and his back close to a wall.

It wouldn't hurt if he had a bit more money in the pouch tied to his inner thigh. Athelny wasn't a stingy man, but he had a weakness for the rattle of dice. It was always a race to see whether he'd get his hands on the cash box before Gaeta after a show.

She was the only one left of the troupe Hal had joined that dusty fall day – the others had found better wages with other shows – circuses, traveling bestiaries – or just gotten tired of the wanderer's life.

Hal was still with Athelny because he still wanted, after three years, to become a dragon rider. But so far his master had been stingy training Kailas in his art.

"You don't think I'm mad," he said once, somewhat in his cups, "for if I teach you all I know, wouldn't you just run off, find a dragon of your own and become my competitor?" He laughed in that strange, high-pitched way he had.

Hal had to admit there was truth to that. Athelny, not at all a bad man, had taught him some things. Hal could have found another flier, but he had no guarantee that master would be any more generous with his knowledge.

As for leaving the road, that was absurd, since Hal hadn't seen any trade more enticing, let alone the pure thrill of traveling new roads, seeing new villages and people, even returning to a place not visited for a year, and seeing the changes.

At least once a show, Athelny would give Hal a ride, and recently had let him sit in front, and start learning the basics of flying.

That also never ceased to thrill, from the awkward flapping journey upward, to the easy soaring on wind currents, like a sailing ship of the skies, to darting, carefully, through clouds, always expecting them to taste like the spun candy sold at village fairs, forgetting their dankness, sudden rain and occasional danger.

Even the danger drew him – watching, from aloft, a thunderstorm approach, barely diving down to shelter in time. Or, if there were low clouds, flying just above them, like flying above feathery snowfields. Dragons, too, seemed, as Hal had thought, to enjoy the joy of flight, cool wind across their savage faces, gliding down, silently, to startle a questing eagle, or suddenly appearing above a flock of ducks and hear them raucously dart groundward, away from the claws and fangs.

Athelny had only one dragon now, the green beast called Belle.

The young dragon named Red, Hal's favorite, had managed to break free one afternoon, when the show was camped in the high mountains. There were wild dragons in the heights, and Athelny had said it was mating season.

Dragons, when they came into season, were wildly promiscuous. Then they'd pick a mate from one of the bulls they'd mated with and remain with him through the four-month incubation period, and for a year after the kit was born.

They'd watched, Athelny whispering unconscious obscenities, as Red eagerly flew toward a female. Two males had attacked him. He'd fought hard, lashing with his talons and fangs, but the other two were older, bigger and more savage.

One dove on Red, and had his neck in its claws. He rolled, as Red tore at him, and Hal heard the young dragon's neck snap from hundreds of feet below.

The teamsters had started to object when Athelny ordered them to bury the dragon, but then they saw the terrible look in the flier's eyes and set to.

When Red's corpse was under the mound, and stones were heaped atop it, Athelny had sat, in some strange wake, beside the grave for a day and a night.

Hal, too, had felt aching sadness, such as he'd never felt for another human, and he wondered about himself.

Then the caravan had gone on, and Athelny had never mentioned Red's name again.

What he proposed next, with Roche having refused permission to go to Black Island for a replacement, Hal didn't know. Dragons were most expensive, more so these days. The story was that Roche was buying any trained or half-trained bull or cow, and would even purchase kits.

Athelny had told him he preferred his dragons to be no more than hatchlings when he bought them. "There's only one secret to raising dragons," he said. "You've got to be kind to the little buggers, even when they've ripped your damned arm open. Hate 'em, and they'll sense what you're feeling, and one day . . . Well, either they fly off, or else it won't be your arm that's bleeding."

Hal had his own scars now, mostly from Red, but some from the fairly placid Belle. And he had no trouble treating the beasts as Athelny had taught him – he could brook no man's hand being raised against a beast, even one as deadly as a dragon.

It was bad enough, Hal thought, trying to worry about

himself, without having to think about kings and queens and armies and such.

The hells with it, he said, deciding to listen to the bandit's advice and not worry about anything behind his horizon.

The Roche dragon fliers were set up just beyond the city gates, and clearly didn't have to worry about any lurking masterless men: Hal counted at least twenty heavily armed men in unfamiliar uniforms around the circled wagons. The Roche had their dragons loose, and were rehearsing.

Hal, never having seen their performance, joined the half-hundred idlers of Bedarisi watching.

He'd never seen anything like it, and certainly Athelny would never be able to put on a show to compare.

The five dragons were dark, greens, blues, browns, with only minor stripes of color. They were big, as big as any Hal had seen, save for a few monsters in the wild, and the Roche flyers had their animals under perfect control.

They flew in close formation, caracoling through various maneuvers – banking, diving, climbing, rolling across each other's back. Then came games – follow-my-leader, mock duels, even a flyer jumping from one dragon to another in midair.

There were two wizards with the show, and they circulated around the crowd, doing various illusions of dragons.

All the while, leather-lunged barkers kept reminding the crowd that this was only a hint of the wonders Roche was bringing to them, that tomorrow, and for three days and nights, this show of *Ky* Yasin's would bring them glories they'd never dreamed of.

Hal heard Yasin referred to as "the *Ky*" by one of the soldiers, gathered that was a title, not a first name.

Kailas was shaken – this was only a rehearsal? Athelny's troupe would be very lucky to attract enough Sagene to cover their expenses here in Bedarisi.

About half the soldiers formed up, as the magicians took a pair of tiny wicker baskets from a case, muttered spells, and the baskets grew until they were about five by ten feet.

Four soldiers, on command, jumped into each basket, and a dragon landed beside each one. Heavy straps connected the baskets with rings fastened through the dragons' outer scales. The beasts, with much shouting from their masters, crashed their wings, beating at the air, and slowly, slowly, climbed into the sky.

Then the dragons turned, and made a mock assault on the crowd. The soldiers fired arrows down into the turf as they passed, very low.

The crowd applauded spatteringly, but was mostly silent. It was very easy, especially considering the way Roche had been behaving of late, to see the obvious military use dragons might provide.

Again, Hal had heard of nothing like this from any flyer of Deraine or Sagene.

The dragons landed, and the soldiers piled out. The barkers changed their tune, and started soliciting for rides, half price because the show hadn't officially opened.

Several people got in line.

Hal was interested to note that the pair of dragons giving rides didn't carry passengers on their backs, but in the wicker baskets, three or four, depending on the size of the passenger, at a time.

Hal thought these dragons older and therefore calmer of temperament than the others.

Their takeoff and flight suggested he was right. These dragons gave very sedate rides up to about 500 feet, toured over Bedarisi, then made a long circle back to a gentle landing. There were no acrobatics or stunts.

Then the rehearsal was over, and the ground staff of the show busied themselves feeding the monsters and cleaning equipment.

It didn't appear as if they minded visitors in their camp, and so Hal left his horse tethered, and wandered about *Ky* Yasin's establishment.

Everything was luxury to Kailas – the flyers had small wagons to themselves, and servants. The transport wagons – two to each dragon – were new, and brightly kept. There were other wagons for the troops, staff, a cookhouse, equipage, and enough horses and oxen to have fitted out a regiment of soldiery.

Hal didn't have Gaeta's experience, but had helped her take care of the books long enough to have some idea of what it cost to run a show. He couldn't get the numbers for this troupe to come out right, unless the Roche were charging ten gold pieces or more for a ride, and he'd seen the priceboard – rides were even cheaper than with Athelny.

Perhaps Yasin was very rich, and subsidizing the troupe from his wealth.

Perhaps.

Or, Hal thought, and wondered where he'd developed such a subterfugous mind, perhaps Yasin and his flyers were advance scouts for a war being whispered about.

Perhaps.

He was mulling this about as he passed by a medium-sized wagon, whose door was open. He heard the sound of a man cursing, then another man laughing.

He knew that high-pitched laugh, and his heart dropped as he heard someone say, in heavily accented Sagene, "You see, *Ky* Athelny, as I promised, your luck was about to change."

Hal went up the steps, trying to concoct a story as he went.

Inside were four men around a table with small, numbered boards, dice, and piled gold and silver. One, short, very thin, wore the expensive silks of a Sagene nobleman; another, a comfortably fat man, wearing gray suede and moleskin breeches.

The third was a man no more than three years beyond Kailas' seventeen, with carefully close-trimmed beard and hair. He wore black leather breeches, with a matching jacket, unbuttoned to his waist, with a white collarless shirt, a red scarf around his neck and high boots. He was clearly a flier. The man, in spite of his youth, bore himself with authority that was almost arrogance. Hal wondered if he might not be *Ky* Yasin.

The fourth was Athelny. He had the smallest pile of money, mostly silver, of them all, in front of him. It was clear he'd gotten to the cash box, and, remembering how much had been in it when Hal rode out for Frechin with his posters the day before, wasn't winning.

Athelny had been drinking, but what of that? Wine never gave nor took away card sense or luck from him.

He looked up, saw Hal, looked first surprised, then guilty for an instant, then his long face flushed with anger. He tried to cover.

"'Tis a surprise indeed," he said, forcing his would-be upper class drawl, "to see you."

"Uh, yessir," Hal said. "I've just returned from Frechin, and thought you might wish a report."

"Later, lad," Athelny said. "I doubt me if these gentlemen, the noble Bayle Yasin, his manager, or Lord Scaer would be interested in our business."

"But, sir—"

"You may wait outside for me. I shan't be long."

Scaer, the small, thin man, looked at Athelny's pot, snickered, but said nothing.

"I . . . yessir," Hal managed, and went out.

He slumped down against the wagon, not knowing why he was so cast down. So Athelny was gaming? He'd done that before. So he was losing? He almost always did that, too, sometimes wiping them out so they had to steal grain for Belle, who grudgingly would accept fodder other than meat, and beg for their own dinners.

He tried not to listen to the game as it went on, but couldn't. Athelny won a few small rounds, then lost again and again.

Hal sparked awake after an hour, hearing Yasin say quietly:

"*Ky* Athelny, are you sure you wish to chase that wager? 'Twould appear you're bested on the face of things."

"I thank'ee for your wisdom," Athelny said, a bit sharply. "But there're two more draws.

"Lord Scaer, here is the sum total of my stake to say you do not hold the numbers you want me to think."

There was a laugh.

"Give out the counters, then," Scaer said.

Hal heard the clack of the wood, and a breath, sharply intaken.

"Fortune favors the bold, as they say," Scaer said. "To see your last counter will take a deal of gold."

"I'm out of *this* turn," Yasin said.

"As am I," another voice, obviously the Roche troupe's manager, said.

There was silence for a moment.

"I have naught but confidence," Athelny said. "I trust you'll take my note of hand?"

"I'm afraid not," Scaer said. "Meaning no offense, but men who're not of Bedarisi . . . Well . . ."

"All right," Athelny said. "Here. Give me paper and that pen." Scratching came.

"I trust this deed to my show will allow me to continue in this game?"

"*Ky* Athelny," Yasin said. "Are you sure that's what you wish to do?"

"The Derainian is of age," Scaer said. "Irregular though it is, I accept the bet. The counters, if you will."

Hal was on his feet, mouth dry in panic, fear. Athelny, at least as far as he knew, had never gone this far into madness.

He started up the steps, but there was nothing he could do as wood rattled once more.

"And there you have it," Scaer said.

There was a moan, that could only have come from Athelny.

"So now I own a flying lizard and some wagons," Scaer said, strange triumph in his voice.

"And what will you do with them?" Yasin asked.

"I'm damned if I know. Would you be interested in acquiring that beast?"

"We would not, I'm afraid," Yasin's manager said.

"I know not what I'll do with it either. Perhaps tether it in my park for children to marvel at. Or let it fly on a long rope, and let my guards practice their bowmanship."

"You can't—" Athelny blurted.

"Oh yes, I can," Scaer said. "And I'll arrange for my soldiers to come for the beast, and the rest of your gear, early tomorrow.

"I'm not a hard man, so that will give you time for you and your people to gather their personal belongings. In return, perhaps you'd give my stable master some tips on the care and feeding of dragons. Haw!"

There was a scrape of a chair, and Athelny stumbled out of the wagon, down the steps. He saw Hal, then looked away.

Hal, wanting to hit him, wanting to put a dagger in the guts of that damned Scaer, still not knowing what to do, followed.

They'd reached the patch of cleared ground, not much more than a pair of lots, just inside the walls of the city, where Athelny had set up his show, before the flier could face Hal, who'd walked behind him across the city, leading his horse.

"I'm . . . I'm sorry. It's just when I see the cards, and the silver, I can't seem to hold back, and all my . . . I'm sorry."

Hal thought of things he could say, maybe should say, but pity took him. He shook his head.

"What's done is done."

He called Gaeta, the other two teamsters and their only spieler, told them what had happened.

"What are we going to do?" one of the teamsters said dully.

Hal looked at Athelny, but the flier remained silent.

Something came to Kailas then. If no one took charge, then he must. He dug into his pants, took out his purse. He had saved a dozen gold coins, more in silver. He gave the spieler and the two teamsters a gold coin each.

"Get your things, and go. Cut a horse free if you wish, but you've got to do it before nightfall."

"Where will we go?" a teamster asked plaintively.

Hal shook his head.

"I'm damned if I know. Gaeta and I'll make for Paestum, try to find work to get across the Straits to home, I guess."

"What about him?" The other teamster jerked a shoulder at Athelny, who stood slumped, utterly defeated.

Before Hal could find an answer, ten soldiers doubled up to the lot.

Athelny saw them, shouted something Hal never understood, and ran for the wagon where Belle was tethered.

"Hey! You!" one of them shouted.

"That's his dragon!" Hal shouted back.

"Th' hells 'tis! It now b'longs t' Lord Scaer, an' we're here to make sure there's no trickery."

"There'll be none," Hal said, running toward the soldiers, suddenly sure what Athelny intended.

"That's for damned sure," the soldier said. "You there! Old man! Get away from that monster!"

"He's likely 'bout to sic' 'im on us," another soldier said.

"In a pig's arse he will!" the first said. "Get your bows ready! Fire on my command!"

Athelny had Belle loosed, and her wings were unfurled, clashing in anticipation.

"Stop there, you!" the soldier said. His fingers pulled an arrow from his belt quiver, and he nocked it, lifted the bow.

Hal dove at him, knocked him down, was about to get up, and another soldier had a sword at his throat.

"Stay easy," he ordered, and Hal obeyed.

"Now, Belle," Athelny shouted, pulling himself up on to the beast's neck. Belle's wings thundered again, and she stumbled clear of the ground, was lifting, trying for height.

The soldier had another arrow nocked, aimed, and his bowstring twanged.

Athelny shouted agony, and Hal saw the arrow sticking out of his side.

But he was able to pull himself up behind the carapace as Belle's wings beat stronger.

Other arrows went up, fell short of the dragon, and then it

was high in the air, outlined against the sun, setting a true course north, out of sight, flying north toward Paestum, toward Deraine, toward home.

Gaeta and Hal traveled together, taking the road toward Paestum Athelny would have flown above. They stopped at every village, asked every traveler.

Only one man, and he looked unreliable, said he'd seen a green dragon overhead, days earlier. But there was no one mounted aboard it.

No one reported finding a strange body, dead of an arrow wound along the road, either.

Two weeks later, little better than beggars, the two reached Paestum.

There were other dragon fliers there. But none of them had heard anything of Athelny or Belle.

Hal went to the cliffs at the edge of the city, just at sunset, and stared across the Straits.

He hoped, wished really, that somehow Athelny and Belle had made it across them to Deraine and whatever home Athelny had.

He suddenly realized in the two years he'd known the dragon-master he'd never heard Athelny speak of home or family.

All that he'd had, all that he'd wanted, was the dragons.

Perhaps, he thought sadly, perhaps Belle had taken him on to the land that Athelny might have dreamed of, the land of dragons far bigger, far fiercer than any known, far beyond Black Island and the ken of men.

Then Hal Kailas turned back, toward the city of Paestum.

Now there was another life to begin, a life he had no idea of or dreams for.

5

"You," the man carrying a spear and a half-shield called. "Over here!"

Hal pretended he wasn't the intended. The man shouted again, and pointed at Kailas.

Hal put on an innocent face – hard when you're ragged and hungry – and strolled casually across the oceanfront walk.

"City warder on special duty," the man said importantly. "Who're you?"

"Hal Kailas."

"Citizen of what country?"

"Deraine."

"You sure you're telling the truth? There's Roche about in Paestum claiming to be Deraine, which is why we're checking."

"Deraine," Hal repeated.

"From where?"

"Up country. Caerly, originally."

"Never heard of it."

Hal shrugged, anger starting to grow.

"They've never heard of you, either."

"Don't crack wise," the man growled, "or we'll find my serjeant and let him sort you out. What's your business in Paestum?"

"I was on the road, and decided it was time to get back home."

"You and what looks like a million others. Damned if I knew there were that many Deraine in Sagene," the man said, loosening a trifle.

Hal didn't answer.

"All right," the warder allowed. "Your accent's too backwoodsy for any Roche to imitate. On your way."

Hal didn't acknowledge, but moved quickly off into the crowd.

The waterfront was crowded, and not with a holiday throng. Men, women, children, some richly dressed, some ragged, some carrying elegant travel cases, others with improvised packs of breeches or sheets, eddied up and down the walkway, stopping at the gangways of the tied up ships. Most were looking for one thing – passage they could afford home before the war started.

Hal had been almost three months in Paestum. He and Gaeta had gone their separate ways, figuring their luck would be better alone than in company.

Hal had started looking for work with two dragon fliers he'd found in Paestum. Both were heading back for Deraine, though. The first told Hal he had no interest in hiring somebody who'd pick his brain and end up a competitor.

The other, more kindly, a man named Garadice, said he

would, normally, be willing to take on an apprentice, particularly one who'd worked for Athelny, which proved Hal had brains, was a hard worker, and had the ability to get along with difficult people. But he was heading for home, "and putting my head under the covers."

Hal asked, and the man explained why. He'd just gotten back from Roche.

"*Damned* scary. Everyone's running around talking about how they're not getting their rightful place in the world, and Deraine and Sagene are conspiring against 'em, always have, and Queen Norcia's the first to recognize it, and they'll get their own back, and then we'll see what we'll see.

"Don't like it none. Especially when I saw the army warrants combing the villages, enlisting for the army.

"Roche is getting like a damned armed camp. The smithies are churning out swords and spears, the farriers have horses lined up for shoeing, even the damned little old ladies are sewing uniforms for 'their boys.'

"Like I said, a place in the country where nobody comes, a good store of food and wine, and I'll take note of the world again in a year or so.

"Or maybe not."

Hal was driven to casual labor, unloading wagons, clerking for a day, cleaning anything that needed to be cleaned. But there were hundreds, maybe thousands like him, streaming into Paestum, willing to work for a meal, when Hal needed silver for his passage.

And every time he had some money, the price of the passage across the Straits, no more than two days' sail, had gotten dearer and dearer.

Hal had at least found a warm, dry place to sleep in a byre whose owner treated him like he was invisible, not minding him washing up in a trough or even stealing a dipper of milk in the mornings before he went out looking for work.

He was almost hungry and desperate enough to consider the army's recruiters. But not quite. He'd worked too hard to serve any master for longer than a moment, except Athelny. He didn't fancy regimentation, square-bashing or the yessir nossir three-bagsfull attitude the army demanded.

Somehow, some way, he'd find a way aboard one of those damned ships with their heartless captains, get across to Deraine and regroup.

As the days passed, he started paying close attention to the rumors, taletellers and broadsheets.

The rumors first said there were raiders abroad, hitting lonely farms and small villages along the Roche-Sagene border. The rumors were confirmed, and the story was they were actually Roche warriors in mufti.

Queen Norcia denied these rumors, saying it was very like Deraine and Sagene to come up with these lies when they couldn't keep their citizens safe, and perhaps they needed Roche to bring order back.

Rumors said there were Roche infiltrators in Paestum, waiting for the moment to rise and support an attacking army. Frighteningly, these rumors were neither confirmed nor denied by the criers and broadsheets.

Hal gloomily decided it couldn't get much worse.

But it did.

The situation deteriorated by the day.

A company of raiders was wiped out by government cavalry. Strangely enough, the cavalry was a mixed unit of Derainian and Sagene soldiers, strange because it was unknown for the two rival countries, always rivals, to cooperate.

The massacre supposedly happened not many leagues south of Paestum.

Next it was revealed the raiders weren't brigands but Roche military, making provocative raids into Sagene.

The Roche government, rather than disavow the dead bandits, agreed they were Roche dragoons, on an official mission, and had been ambushed well inside the Roche borders.

This was shrilly denied by every official in Sagene, Paestum and Deraine.

Next an official statement from Roche, sent out in Queen Norcia's own hand, said the situation was intolerable, and reparations would be required from both Sagene and Deraine.

The Council of Barons and Deraine's King Asir icily refused.

Queen Norcia increased her demands: reparations, plus a conference, in Roche, which would determine the proper governing of Paestum. At the very least, Deraine must agree to a power-sharing with Roche for the free city.

Failure to meet these "reasonable" demands could have only one response.

Norcia announced her military was being called up, and

rumor had it Roche troops were already massing on the border, ready to march against Paestum.

Deraine refused the "offer," King Asir calling it blackmail "no decent man would ever respond to," and force would be met with force, if necessary, although he hoped there was still a chance of peace.

Hal looked up, wondering if that dragon, high above the city, was Roche. Other dragons, all flying in and out to the east, had been overflying Paestum.

No one knew what they were doing, but hearsay had it there were Roche troops hidden not far across the nearby border.

Hal remembered *Ky* Yasin and his flying show, and wondered just where the flier was, and if he might not be wearing a uniform or commanding those dragons overhead.

But it wasn't his concern, since he'd just figured a way that was almost unbeatable to stow away on a fishing boat bound for Deraine.

There were dangers of smothering under a load of fish, being caught and thrown overboard or simply drowning in a fishwell, but what of it? Staying here in Paestum was already dangerous, between the threat of starving, and onrushing war.

His planning was cut short by a stocky warder, flanked by a dozen grinning fellows. All had swords at their waists, carried ready truncheons, and looked as if they were in a transport of delight.

"You, lad. Who's your master?"

"Uh . . . I have none."

"Your work?"

"None, at present."

"You now have both. This is your official announcement that you've been accepted into His Majesty's Army, and your service will be required to defend the walls of Paestum."

"But I'm a civilian, and have no interest in carrying a damned spear," Hal protested.

"That's tough treacle. King Asir has authorized conscription for all Derainians in this present emergency, and you're one of the first to be honored and permitted to become one of the heroes of Paestum.

"Lads, take charge of our new recruit, and escort him to the barracks for outfitting."

6

Hal stared down from the battlement as scouts and dragoons of the oncoming Roche army sacked the outskirts of Paestum.

Overhead, two dragons soared, banking back and forth in the stormy winds coming onshore. Hal supposed they were observing for the Roche commanders, comfortably behind the lines, planning the assault.

Centuries ago, when Deraine had seized by force of arms the seaside city on the border of Sagene and Roche that became Paestum, they'd made it impregnable with high stone walls, sixteen feet thick, covering the peninsula the town occupied from both sea and land assault. Time passed, and Paestum, the most prosperous trading port along the Chicor Straits, had built up to those walls and beyond. After all, it was unlikely there'd be war again, certainly not between the three most powerful countries in the known world.

These suburbs had given fine cover for the Roche army as it entered the city. Cavalry, dragoons and lancers, had been the first to attack the Deraine lines on the outskirts, under the cover of a sorcerous fog. The untrained Deraine, in a moil of confusion, hesitated, and Roche smashed two waves of experienced assault troops into them.

The Deraine fell back, not quite breaking, through the outskirts of Paestum into the ancient fortress.

Hal had been very grateful that he'd been guarding the wall with his newly-issued unsharpened sword, dented shield, and leather armor. That had been – what, he thought dully – three, no four days ago. Or maybe more.

Hal had been assigned to a cavalry formation that lacked only one thing – their horses. He was supposed to be on guard half the day, the rest on other duties including eating and sleeping time. But there'd been continual panics, cries to man the parapets and such, so he didn't remember the last time he'd had two hours of quiet, let alone sleep.

Now Roche was bringing up its main force – Hal had seen, before the storm roared in on them, caterpillar-like columns in their brightly-colored, if campaign-stained, uniforms moving steadily toward the city.

Two soldiers manned a dart thrower in the nearby tower, a pedestal-mounted bow, arms of rigid iron bars. Tension came from hair skeins. The soldiers wound it back to full cock, aimed, and sent a long bolt flashing high at one dragon. The bolt missed by a dozen feet, and the dragon's rider pulled it higher. The next dart fell well below the beast, and the two continued circling.

Roche, fearless and confident, had sent four dragons against the men on the walls after the city was invested. They'd torn several men off the parapets to their deaths, then the dart throwers had been brought up under cover of night.

The bolts, a yard long, iron-headed, tore into the dragon formation when they attacked the next day. Two dragons had been hit hard, and, screaming, snapping at the huge arrows stuck in their bodies, had pinwheeled to the ground. Crossbowmen finished off the one that still floundered in the muck, its rider already sprawled in death beside it. The other dove into a burning building, and both animal and rider had howled down into death.

After that, the dragon fliers were more cautious, flying at greater altitude, doing no more than observing.

Hal looked up at them, wishing he were up there, even in this building storm, a storm that everyone said had been brought by magic, the magic of Roche, so that Deraine wouldn't be able to reinforce Paestum from across the Straits.

Hal didn't know, didn't care about that. But he figured the Roche couldn't try to climb the walls while this wind blew, and squally rain sheeted down.

He scanned his sector again. No movement, save the occasional scuttle of looters. Then he smelt smoke, and saw flames rising from one house, then another.

The Roche had fired the abandoned homes and businesses of the suburbs. Whether deliberately or by accident Hal didn't know. Probably looters had done it, in drunken accident, for nothing happened for an hour or so.

He heard shouts from behind him, looked across, saw a procession coming up the ramp to the next parapet. He was grateful they weren't coming to him – he'd already learned one of a soldier's greatest lessons: that anyone of higher rank showing up can only mean trouble.

The group consisted of four men, wearing the gaudy green and yellow uniform of the King's Protectors of Paestum, the supposedly elite regiment that guarded Paestum's governor, high-ranking officials, nobility and interesting things like the treasury.

Behind them were two young men, heavy-laden with boxes and cases, wearing expensive civilian garb.

Following was the reason for this procession: an impressively-bearded man, wearing dark robes and tall red cap, stalking along with dignity, followed by four more guards.

Hal decided this might be interesting. Interesting things attracted attention, so the first thing he did was plan his retreat – half a dozen steps to the nearest tower and its stairs, then inside against any danger.

That settled, he watched the show, about a hundred feet away, as the magician's acolytes opened box after box, spread out rugs and set up braziers. Incense went into the braziers, and the magician touched each brazier, lips moving.

In spite of the wind and occasional rain, the incense smoked into life. A crosswind took the smoke under Hal's nose, and he coughed. It was a smell not to his liking, of spices far too strong and unknown.

One of the acolytes and a guard turned and scowled in his direction. Hal put on an innocent air, and walked his rounds until they lost interest.

Evidently, magicians needed silence to work their crafts.

Ribbons were laid out in intricate patterns atop the carpets, and the two acolytes took up stations, each holding a long taper.

Two gestures by the wizard, and the tapers smoked into flame.

The sorcerer picked up a huge book, very ancient and decrepit, opened it, and began chanting.

Hal shivered, for the chanting came very clear to him, in spite of the wind, and grew louder. He didn't know the words as the chant grew louder and louder, the voice deeper in pitch, almost sounding as if no human throat could produce these sounds.

The magician gestured three times toward the Roche lines, and each time thunder slammed against Hal, though he saw no lightning.

The wind backed, then cut, and a flash of sunlight came through the clouds.

The wizard must be casting a counterspell against the storm conjuration.

The dark clouds that had raced overhead broke for certain, a sunny rift growing like a huge arrow over Paestum.

Then the wizard screamed. Hal jolted, saw the man stagger, hurl his grimoire high in the air in a spasm, tear at his robes.

Fire gouted from the tapers, took the two acolytes, curled like a living thing, and reached a red and black hand for the sorcerer.

He was shrieking, possibly a spell, but the fire-magic was stronger, taking him, and his body roared into flames. He pirouetted, fell, clawing at his body as it burnt.

Hal dove for his cover, out of sight, heard more screams, chanced peering out, saw all of the men on the parapet, soldiers and acolytes, writhe and die in agony.

Then the storm wind began once more.

The next day, at dawn, the Roche attacked.

They struck three times that day, with long ladders covered by archers sheltering in the ruins. Each time they were driven back, the last with cauldrons of boiling pitch.

All was quiet for two days, then Roche soldiers built a heavy wooden passageway to the walls. Flaming pitch was poured down to fire it, but the passage's roof was covered with animal hides, constantly soaked with water.

It crept toward the part of the wall Hal was guarding, butted against it.

Dull thudding began, and word came – Roche was digging a mine under the wall to collapse it.

"Arright, you stumblebums, pay attention," Sancreed Broda grated. The fifty soldiers were instantly silent.

Broda was a puzzlement, and a terror, to them all, officer to recruit. He was old, hard, with a scarred face and ropy-muscled body. He wasn't a member of Hal's cavalry unit, nor was he in uniform. He wore leather breeches so stiff with dirt they could have stood of their own accord, a yellow shirt that might have been white once, some time before the war started, and a leather jerkin even dirtier than his pants. On his feet were some sort of slippers, and a silk scarf was knotted around his long gray hair. He was armed with a hammer, and Hal had seen him use it twice on Roche who'd gotten to the top of "his" wall, grinning madly through yellow, rotting teeth.

No one knew why he was in charge, only that he was, and the gods help anyone who questioned that, although no one had seen him do anything worse than growl at the men under his command.

"This 'ere's a real official docyment from our rulers, gods bless 'em and give 'em royal assaches," Sancreed went on. "It's got all kindsa praise for you lummocks, on account of you're standin' in the most dangerous spot in Paestum, the thin whatever-color-you-yoinks-are line between barb'rism an' civilization, bullshit, bullshit, bullshit . . . I'm givin' you the short version, 'cause we've got to figger out what to do next, ignorin' these eejiots, 'less you feel like dyin'.

"Anyway, everybody's real proud of you, for holdin' firm, even with those friggin' Roche diggin' away under our feet."

He stopped and, without realizing it, everyone listened. All heard the sound from below them of the Roche diggers.

"Now, what you're s'posed to do, an' everybody'll think worlds of you, accordin' to these royal farts back in th' palace," Broda said, his voice withering in scorn, "is go walkin' back and forth atop th' wall 'til the mine's fired, then die real noble in the wreckage, keepin' the Roche back 'til other troops drive 'em back.

"Heroes to a friggin' man," he sneered. "They'd prob'ly name boulevards after your dead young asses if we go an' win this stupid damn war.

"Now, that ain't gonna happen. There'll be four volunteers up on the walls, making sure none of the bassids come up at us. That's you, you, you and you. Get up those ramps.

"The rest of you are gonna pull back, into that old warehouse there. Out of th' weather an' all.

"When they put fire to their mine, you won't be doin' anything like gettin' dead, but comin' out after 'em. Maybe a bit of a su'prise for the bassids.

"'At's fine. You officers can take charge of your troops, an' get 'em under cover now. Half sleep. Get rested, get fed, 'cause I think it'll get shitty in not too long.

"Yeah. One other thing. Four volunteers to listen for when th' diggin' stops. You, you, you and you. Follow me."

Hal was one of the four. He obediently followed Broda into the base of the tower. The old man picked up a bundle of torches, used flint and steel to fire one, went down narrow, spider-webbed steps. There was dank stone all around Hal, and above him.

The sound of digging got louder.

"You wants to keep it quiet when you're down here," Broda said. "Mebbe th' fools think they're doin' all this shit in silence, an' we don't know squat about what's goin' on."

He snorted.

The steps ended in a small cellar. The thudding sounded like it was not quite below them, but very close.

"Right," Broda said. "Here's your posts. Two on, two off. You're listenin' for the diggin' to stop. Like I told you afore, which you likely forgot, when they stop diggin' is when they'll be gettin' ready, pullin' back an' firin' their pit props an' whatever other flam'bles packed in to collapse th' tunnel an' let th' wall cave in atop.

"You're to wait for that silence, an' when it comes, haul ass outa here and find me. Don't hang about, bein' cute and waitin' for th' smell of smoke or like that.

"*Nobody* gets to play a godsdamned hero," he grated, and Hal thought his eyes glowed in the darkness. "If you go and do something dumb like get killed, you'll answer to me. Understand?"

For some reason, none of the four soldiers thought what Broda had said either absurd or stupid.

They waited for another day and a half. Hal swore that if he made it through this, he'd live in a tree or under a bush, and never go under a roof again, let alone this far underground, with the rats and people who wanted to kill him, deadly moles, digging ever closer.

He could have stayed in his village, become a miner, and died when a shaft collapsed around him if he wanted a fate like this, he thought.

He wasn't meant for this. He was ... well, he would be, a dragon flier. Let him live through this, let him at least die in the light of day. He thought of praying, couldn't think of any particular god he believed in.

But his fellow listener evidently did, mumbling supplications to many gods, more than Hal thought a priest could honor.

Irritated, driven out of his own funk by the other, he kicked him and told him to shut up.

The other soldier, even younger than Hal, obeyed.

Hal was wondering how long it was until the end of their shift, when they could go up those stairs for a bowl of what everyone had started calling siege stew.

Some said it was made of rats, that all the real meat in Paestum was being hoarded by the rich. Hal didn't believe that, although he'd noticed very few dogs about the last few days.

Quite suddenly, there was silence.

The two soldiers looked at each other, eyes wide against their smoke-darkened faces. His partner started for the stairs.

"Wait," Hal hissed. "Maybe they're only changing diggers."

But the sound of picks and shovels didn't come.

"The hells with you," the other soldier snarled, and was gone.

Hal thought the other right, and went up the stairs behind him, into the spitting rain and dawn light, exulting that he had lived, would live, as long as he made it through the attack that would come.

They found Broda, who grunted, told them to wait, and went down the steps they'd boiled up.

A long time passed, and Broda came back into sight, trying to look as if he wasn't in a hurry.

"'At's right," he said. "They're comin'. You, boy. Go wake up th' other so'jers and tell 'em to get ready."

Two hours later, Hal was smelling smoke as the underground fire built, and then he heard a grinding sound, stones moving against each other.

The drawn-up soldiers moaned, without realizing it.

But Hal saw no sign of movement.

The smell grew stronger and the grinding came now and again.

"Look," someone shouted, and everyone stared up, seeing the wall sway slightly.

"Awright," Broda shouted. "It'll be comin' in a tit. Get y'selfs ready!"

The wall moved more, teetering inward, then with a grinding roar, toppled outward in a boil of dust and ricocheting stones. The wall was down, stones taller than a man bouncing away, sliding.

"Here they come!" someone shouted unnecessarily, and, stumbling over the high-piled rubble, coming toward them, was a wave of Roche infantrymen.

First were spearmen, archers behind.

Deraine bows twanged, and the archers dropped, fell back, but there were grim rows of men with swords behind them.

"Now!" Broda shouted, and Hal was moving forward, when his brain told him to run, that the points of those spears was death. One lunged at him, and he took the strike on his shield, pushed it out of the way as he numbly remembered someone telling him to do, and drove his sword into the Roche's chest.

Then there was another man with a sword, and he parried, ducked, and kicked the man in the kneecap. The man screeched, bent, and Hal booted him out of the way, into another man's spear.

There was a man pushing against him, chest against Hal's shield, and he smelt foul breath, drove his knee up into the man's crotch, killed him as he fell back.

Hal had his back against a high stone, and two men were coming at him, and then they were both down with arrows in their chests.

Hal didn't know who to thank, saw Broda standing in a circle of bodies, hammer dripping blood.

Chanting came, high-pitched, and something grew out of nothing, a green-skinned demon, dripping slime, crouching, claws scraping the ground.

Someone screamed in terror, and Hal realized he was the one screaming. The demon looked about, pupilless eyes finding a victim, and it leapt toward Sancreed Broda.

The old man moved surprisingly fast, rolled aside, and struck up at the nightmare. It brushed his hammer aside, and claws ripped.

Broda howled in pain, chest torn open, tried for another smash, fell back, dead.

Hal Kailas felt that hard, cold rage build within him.

The demon looked for another target, saw Hal, just as Hal saw, beyond the fiend, a very young man with very long, very blond hair. He had no weapon but a wand, and his lips were moving as the wand moved, pointing at Kailas.

Just before the demon leapt, Hal, having all the time in the world, scooped up a fist-sized rock, and threw it at the magician's head.

The man howled, clawed at the ruins of his face, wand flying away as the demon disappeared.

Hal jumped over a waist-high boulder, and drove his sword into the young wizard's body.

A Roche warrior with a long, two-handed sword was rushing him, and Hal braced. Before the man reached him an eerie wail began, and other apparitions, taller than a man, completely red, body a terrible parody of humanity, with scythe-like claws at the ends of their arms and legs appeared, leaping on to Roche soldiers and tearing at them.

The Roche soldiers paused, confused, terrified, and things that looked like hawks but weren't dove out of nowhere, claws ripping.

The Roche soldiery broke, turned and ran, even as their wizards' counterspell disappeared the red demons and hawks.

But panic had full hold on the Roche, and they didn't stop or look back.

Charging past Hal came wave after wave of Derainian infantry, counterattacking, and he was pulled along with their attack, beyond the shattered walls, and cavalry galloped out of a city gate after the enemy.

Roche magic couldn't recover the advantage, and the attackers were in full flight, through the ruined suburbs back toward their camps, and the siege was broken.

Hal stopped, letting the others run on, killing, pillaging the corpses.

It was not for him.

He turned back, to find Sancreed Broda's body, and get someone to make a pyre. Somehow he knew there'd be no family, no friends to provide the last rites for the terrible old man who'd saved his and many other lives.

Above him, above Paestum's shattered wall, a dragon screamed once, circling in the clean morning sky.

7

The ten horsemen rode at a walk into the glade below a forested hill. Hal made a swooping motion with his hand, then at the ground. Obediently, the other nine dismounted.

He pointed to two men, then to his right, two more to his left. They moved off to provide security for his flanks.

He chose one more, his normal second in command, a prematurely wizened city boy named Jarth Ordinay, and, taking a long ship's glass from his saddlebag, crept up the hill toward the hill crest, hoping for no surprises.

There were no ambushers or wizards waiting.

He went on his hands and knees, and crawled into the heart of a clump of brush, through to the other side, Ordinay, well-trained, about five feet behind him. He had an arrow and a strung bow ready.

The hill rolled down, past a nearly dry stream to open fields that had been well tilled once, but were now choked with brambles.

The morning was hot, still, and the loudest thing the buzzing of a swarm of bees nearby.

Half a mile from Hal was the Roche army.

Its tents were struck, rolled into the baggage wagons, and men were forming up across its front. Behind the infantry, massed cavalry were trotting out toward the flanks.

Hal swept the breaking camp with his glass, found a handful of still-standing tents. There were banners in front of them. Hal read them easily. A year and a half in the cavalry had made him an expert at heraldry.

Duke this, Baron that, Lords the other and his brother, no surprise, seen them before during the campaign, then he started a bit, at one banner he'd never seen before.

It was, he was fairly sure, that of the queen of Roche herself. He couldn't believe she'd decided to take the field, then saw, below the main banner, a longer pennant.

No. Not the queen, but some lord of her household.

That would be, assuming Deraine victory, almost as good.

That also meant that Roche had great hopes for the forthcoming battle.

He slithered back, out of the brush, motioned to Jarth, and they went back to the horses. The flank guards saw his return and, unordered, came back in.

"They're just where the wizard said they'd be," Hal whispered, reporting in the event he didn't make it back to the main Deraine lines. "I'd guess ten, maybe fifteen thousand. Armored infantry, heavy cavalry, maybe a regiment of light cavalry.

"They're getting ready for the march, headed west, again, like we expected.

"They've got flankers out, heavy cavalry, so we'd best skitter back home, for fear of getting pinchered."

The men mounted. Their horses, as well trained as the men, had stayed still, rein-tethered.

Hal led them out of the glade, through the trees, into the open. Fifty yards distant was the ruins of a road.

"At the walk," he said in a low voice, and the horses moved slowly toward the ruined byway.

In unknown territory, using any road, no matter how shattered, could be suicidal. But Hal had taken his patrol nearby less than an hour before, and thought it unlikely there'd been a trap laid in the interim.

He was more worried about being between the two armies – the Deraine army was only half a dozen miles distant.

One reason he'd survived since the siege of Paestum was staying as far away from famous battles as possible. That was why he'd been promoted serjeant, and his troops called him Lucky behind his back.

When he took a patrol out, it was very seldom he didn't bring everyone back, generally without serious wounds.

That was an uncommon boast for these times – after the siege, King Asir had brought a great army across the Chicor Straits, made alliance with Sagene's Council of Barons, and gone after Queen Norcia's army.

They found it, and the two forces smashed each other until they were both tottering, each unable to land the death blow.

They'd broken apart, brought in replacements during their winter quarters, and began skirmishing, each looking for the advantage rather than going toe-to-toe again.

There'd been half a dozen major battles, ten times that in minor brushes that produced no grander results than adding to the casualty lists in the eighteen months since Hal had been dragooned into the army.

One side would move south, the other after it, then the other way around.

Caught in the smash were the Sagene civilians, their villages and farms. A great swathe was cut along the Roche-Sagene border. Here, all was desolation, save the occasionally staunchly garrisoned castle. What trade there was, what merchants there were, stayed close to the army, doing business as they could, when they could.

But the lands weren't empty. There were wanderers, deserters from both sides, and – most to be feared – those who'd turned renegade.

They knew all men's hands were turned against them, so gave and asked no mercy from any group of soldiers they encountered.

That was one of the jobs of the light cavalry, tracking and destroying the bandits, one reason that Hal Kailas' face showed hard lines, and his smile came but seldom these days.

But it was better, in terms of surviving, than his present

task, scouting for the main force as they closed once more for battle.

Everyone knew this encounter was unlikely to be decisive, was not likely to end the war.

Everyone except the high commands on both sides.

Victory would only be won by one army breaking through and laying waste to the other's homeland, yet maintaining its own supply lines.

Sagene and Deraine had more men, more horses. Roche's soldiers were better trained, generally better led. Plus they had more dragons, more magicians.

Just recently, the Roche dragons had changed their tactics. They still scouted overhead, but, just as they'd done in the siege of Paestum, had begun attacking riders and patrols who ventured beyond the safety of the Deraine catapults.

The few Deraine dragons were only used for observation, and what they reported was frequently wrong, and even more frequently disregarded.

Hal sometimes wondered if the end would be all three countries hammered back into barbarism.

All he could hope for, and it was a measure of his strength that he still could hope, was to survive until the war ended. All too many soldiers had given up, dully realized their doom was to be killed, wounded or captured, nothing more.

But an end to this war seemed far in the future.

Hal broke his thoughts, not only because they were veering into gloom, but because anyone who thought of anything other than the minute he was living in was likely to add to the butcher's bill.

He turned in his saddle, looking back at his patrol, scanning the hillsides for movement, then the skies.

As he did, a flight of four dragons, in vee-formation, broke out of the clouds and dove on the patrol.

Hal swore – some Roche magician must have sensed them, and sent out the fliers.

"Dragons!" he shouted. "Spread out, and ride hard for our lines!"

The green-brown dragons swept past above them, then banked back, and dove toward the ground. They flared their wings no more than fifteen feet above the ground, and, almost wingtip to wingtip, beat toward Hal's onrushing patrol, hoping to panic horses and horsemen. But this was not the first, nor the fifth, time Hal had been attacked by dragons.

"Jink!" Kailas shouted, and, obediently, the riders kicked their mounts one way, then another. The dragons tried to turn with them, couldn't, and the ten men rode safely under their attackers. One man – Hal didn't see who – had courage enough to fire an arrow at a dragon.

"Full gallop," and the riders kicked their horses hard, bending low in the saddle, trying to keep from looking back at the closing doom.

It was hard, especially when a scream came. Hal chanced a look, saw a horse pinwheeling through the air, gouting blood from deep talon-wounds in its back, saddle torn away.

Its rider . . . Its rider was tumbling in the dust, getting to his feet, stumbling into a run, knowing no one would turn back for him, following the strictest orders.

Hal wheeled his mount into a curvet, came back at his afoot soldier, saw, out of the corner of his eye, a swooping dragon. He leaned out, arm hooked, and the man had it, was neatly flipped up behind him, and the dragon whipped past, close enough for Hal to have touched its right talon as it missed him.

Again he turned, and his horse was gasping, flanks lathered. Two dragons were coming at him, each not seeing the other, then avoiding collision at the last minute as Hal rode under a torn-apart tree.

A dragon smashed through branches above his head, climbed for height for another attack, and on the other side of the hill were the Deraine lines. Hal's patrol was strung out in front of him, riding for safety.

Two dragons came in for another attack, but the patrol was too close to the lines, and half a dozen catapults sent six-foot darts whipping through the air at them.

All missed, and the Roche dragons were climbing away.

One screamed in rage and disappointment, and Jarth Ordinay blatted an imitation up at him, one of his major talents.

They galloped past the outlying pickets, were in the forward lines, and now they could sit straight, breathe, and even show a cavalryman's panache, laughing at the past danger, easy in the saddle, safe for one more day.

"It has been in my mind for some time," Lord Canista, commander of the Third Deraine Light Cavalry, "that our king might be well served by your being promoted lieutenant and knighted, Serjeant."

Hal gaped. Being made an officer was impressive enough, the Deraine army having three ranks: lieutenant, generally knighted; captain, always knighted, and commander, who'd be a lord, duke or even prince.

Outside Canista's tent, all was a bustle as the army got ready once more for battle.

"First, that pennant you spotted belongs to one Duke Garcao Yasin, who's Lord Commander of Queen Norcia. The two, I was told, are close." Canista coughed suggestively. "Very, very close. So obviously this upcoming battle will be of great import to Roche." He noticed Hal's expression.

"You know of him?"

"Uh . . . nossir." Hal thought back, remembered the Yasin with the flying dragons back in Bedarisi had a first name of Bayle or something like it. "But I may've encountered a relative of his before the war. A dragon flier. Do you know if he's got a brother?"

"Of course not," Canista said, a bit impatiently. "And let us return to more important matters, such as your knighthood. You fight well. But more important . . . Well, did you know your troopers call you Lucky?"

"Uh . . . yessir." Hal was still considering this Baron Yasin. Assuming a relationship, and he had no way of knowing whether Yasin was a common name in Roche, that would certainly indicate the Roche fliers were, indeed, spies. He brought himself back, listened to Canista.

"That's more important . . . for a leader," the lord went on. "Any damned fool with no survival sense can become a great warrior . . . until he's cut down by some lucky sod from the rear.

"Deraine needs lucky officers, Kailas," Canista went on. "The gods know we haven't had many leading us thus far."

Hal looked blankly unopinionated at that.

"Well, I assume you have an opinion?"

"Sir, I'm a commoner."

"Everyone knows that," Canista said. "Where do you think all these damned knights' and barons' and dukes' and whatalls' fathers came from?

"Damned few of us were born to the purple. Time past, time enough for us to get snotty about things, one of our ancestors was good at sticking people with his sword, and lucky enough to do it mostly within the law, or not get caught, plus live through the experience.

"And their descendants are the ones who've ridden out in this war. And are getting themselves killed, like everyone else.

"Deraine will need a whole new generation of nobility, and where the hells do you think it'll come from? From commoners like you.

"It might interest you that my grandsire, ten, no eleven generations gone, was a blacksmith."

"Yessir," Hal said.

"Mmmph," Canista said. "At any rate, that's something for you to think on, if you want the responsibility. Actually, I'm speaking like a damned fool, for you already have the responsibility. Being knighted would just get you more.

"We've a battle afore us, so think on it. Afterwards, if we all live, you can give me your decision."

"Yessir." Hal clapped his right hand against his breastplate in salute, turned to leave.

"Wait, lad," Canista said. Hal turned back.

"Something I'm required to show you," he said, pulling a rumpled piece of paper from his small field desk, handing it to Hal.

Dragon Men!
Deraine Needs You!
Men . . . and Women
Who Wish to Fly
Mighty Dragons
As the Eyes
Of the Army
Are Bidden
By His Most Holy Majesty
To Volunteer
For the Newly-Forming
Dragon Flights!
Experienced Dragon Handlers
Will Do Deraine
The Greatest Service
By Volunteering
Fly High Above the Fray!
Defy Roche's Evil Monsters!
Extra Pay
Extra Privileges
Bask in the Adulation

Of the Nation!
Join Now!!
Experienced Men and Women Only!!

"I call this damned nonsense," Canista grumbled. "But some-one said you'd been around the horrid monsters back before you joined up.

"And doing the king's duty, I decided to show it to you, and give you the chance.

"Even though there's a war, a real war, to be fought down here on the ground, not zooming around peering at the foe and, often as not, making up lies to confuse poor honest lords such as myself!"

Hal barely heard the lord, looking at the sheet of paper, think-ing, dreaming.

To be out of the muck, away from the front lines and shouting officers, to be clean. Inadvertently, Hal scratched at a louse bite on his elbow, caught himself.

Gods, how he wanted that . . . to be above the clouds, above this endless cutting and killing, free, alone.

Then he caught himself.

"Thank you, sir," he said, handing the paper back.

"Good man! Not interested at all, I can see, like a proper sol-dier."

No. It was hardly lack of interest.

It was Hal's mind, suddenly reminding him of the twenty-five cavalrymen he was given charge of, plus another ten supporting troopers.

If he left, who would take care of them?

He thought of other sections, whose warrants had been killed or transferred, and their new commanders, who had caused more than their share of deaths learning the ways of war.

Could Hal give over men, who'd entrusted him with their lives, to some fool, fresh from Deraine's horse academies?

Never.

As long as they lived, Hal Kailas had to be there to lead and, if necessary, die with them.

8

"Water," the soldier gasped, reaching a clawed hand up for Hal's stirrup. "For the mercy of the gods, water!"

Hal saw the gaping wound across the man's stomach, his spilled guts, knew he could do no good, even if orders permitted him to halt.

The Roche soldier's hand fell away.

"Then grant peace," he croaked. "Please, for the sake of your mother's soul."

Hal couldn't bring himself to kill the wounded man, no matter what he wanted. But someone behind him in the column had no qualms. Hal heard the dull thud of a lance going home, the soldier's gasp, and then silence except for the clatter of horses' hooves and the creak of their harness.

This was the battle's fourth day, thus far a sweeping defeat for Roche.

Deraine, given the advance warning by Hal and, no doubt, other scouts, had time to find a strong position along a rocky ridgecrest. Then they'd waited for Roche.

Duke Yasin had taken position on a ridge a mile distant from Deraine's lines, a valley rich with grain between them. Deraine had made no offensive moves, and so Roche attacked first.

Yasin sent his infantry sweeping wide, trying to flank Deraine on the north. But the lines were firmly anchored with heavy cavalry, and Roche was driven back.

They attacked again, and were broken a second time.

Then it was time for the wizards. Roche sent sweeping winds against Deraine, but the spells were broken, and counterspells of dust devils sent back against Roche.

Yasin tried a night attack, with ghostly illuminations. But that barely penetrated the front line, before the Deraine second wave smashed into them.

The third day dawned hot, muggy, promising rain, but none came.

The drums started just before midday, all along the Roche line.

Hal's section had been assigned courier duty, since the light cavalry wasn't needed for scouting, so he was well forward, almost in the front lines, when Duke Yasin's army surged forward behind the drummers across the valley. Hal saw them coming, in wave after wave, and swallowed hard, very glad he wasn't one of the poor bastards in the forward line trying to keep his spearpoint from trembling, trying to gather strength from his equally frightened brothers.

Then sorcery came into play, and this no illusion. Red creatures surged into existence in the Roche line, creatures about the size of a small dog. They were fanged, and clawed, like enormous red ants, but each had the face of a leering man. They tore into the legs of the oncoming soldiers, and when they fell, others fastened their claws into the man's armor, and tore at his face and throat.

The screams rang loud above the drums, and the Deraine front line commanders ordered their troops forward.

The Deraine units obeyed, and the lines came together, and it was a knotted madness. Deraine pulled back, Hal thought beaten back, then realized they'd been ordered to withdraw, regroup, and come in again.

The ant-demons savaged the Roche soldiers but, having taken mortal form, could be killed, although their fangs still held to their final bite, heads dangling from men's arms, legs, bodies.

As suddenly as they came, they vanished, the Roche sorcerers having found the counterspell.

Deraine attacked again, and once more the lines smashed against each other. Deraine sent their reserves down into the valley, and that broke the Roche. They fell back, up the hill toward their own lines, pursued by Deraine infantry, killing as they went.

The heavy cavalry started forward, to finally break Roche and defeat them in detail. But Roche regained its positions, behind sharp-pointed abatis and piled brush, and the Deraine attack was called off.

The Roche, defeated, should have retreated, back within the safety of their own support lines. But they held on the ridgeline all that day and night.

Perhaps Duke Yasin was afraid to retreat, afraid to reveal his defeat to Queen Norcia. Or perhaps he had another plan in the works. Or perhaps he was simply too stubborn to know when he was beaten.

Regardless, the Third Light Cavalry, augmented with half a regiment of Sagene light, was assembled before dawn, and told to scout the Roche flanks and determine what they were up to.

Hal attended Lord Canista's orders assembly, staying, as deserved a young warrant, well in the back, behind the lords, keeping his doubts to themselves.

One knight, a very slender, very long-haired and mustached man in gleaming armor, did not.

"Sir," he said. "This is no more'n the second time we've ridden together in this strength."

"Third, actually, Sir Kinnear," Lord Canista said. "The other was before you joined us."

"Which means we're not experienced at fighting together. Plus light cavalry," Kinnear went on, "isn't supposed to do more than scout and raid."

"We have our orders," Canista said. "But I believe the reason for us going forth in such strength is the lords of the army wouldn't mind if we ran into some nice fat supply wagons and wreaked a bit of havoc."

"S'posing, sir, that we go a little too far, and supposing their damned heavies charge us?"

"We withdraw in an orderly fashion."

There was a murmur of amusement.

"S'posing, once again, we don't have that luxury," Kinnear persisted.

"According to *my* orders," Canista said, "the Sagene heavy cavalry will be in close support, and if they're outmanned, our own heavies will be committed."

"Sagene?" Kinnear said with a snort.

"I resent that," a Sagene knight, heavy, bearded, scowling said. "Are you accusing my people of cowardice?"

"No," Kinnear drawled, "just a certain ... tardiness to respond."

"You have been given a chance to withdraw your words," the Sagene knight said. "Now I must demand satisfaction!"

"Now or at any other time," Kinnear said, one hand on his sword.

"Both of you stop!" Canista snapped. "We have an enemy to face, and if either of you persist in your foolishness, I'll have you chained in your tents. After the battle, you're welcome to satisfy your honor by any means you deem necessary.

"But not before! We have a task set before us, gentlemen. Return to your troops and get them ready to ride, for the glory of Deraine and your regiments, and I wish you battleluck!"

Hal was close enough to Sir Kinnear to hear him mutter,

"This'll be damned disastrous. Too many troops to move with any sort of subtlety, not enough to stand firm if we're found out. *Damned* disastrous!"

Hal agreed, but there was, of course, nothing that could be done.

They went out at dawn, curving out from their lines, intending to skirt the enemy's right flank, and probe, very cautiously, for his intent.

The valley that had been yesterday's battleground was a welter of bodies. Some, thankfully, lay still, quite dead. Others writhed, screaming, or, energy almost gone, managing no more than animal moans.

There were healthy men from both sides afield – men looking for the wounded, dead, from their units, some to-be-blessed chirurgeons, some simply good hearted, trying to tend to the wounded, ease the pain of dying.

And there were others, skulking jackals, looting the dead and, not infrequently, making sure the wounded wouldn't object to being plundered, with a swift dagger.

Hal heard a bowstring twang, saw one such brigand screech, grab at his side, and go down. He turned, saw Jarth Ordinay reaching for another arrow.

"No," he ordered. "We may need them later."

Ordinay hesitated, then nodded, and put the arrow back in his saddle quiver.

Unconsciously Hal's section spread out as they closed on the edges of the ridge Roche supposedly still held, making themselves into less of a target.

Canista's cutting it a little close, Kailas thought. If I held the regiment, I would have taken us straight away from the lines until I was beyond the sight of the fighters, then come back on the Roche from the rear, trying to figure out their intentions from the deployment of their quartermaster wagons and other noncombatants who might not be able to kill you as readily as an infantryman or, worse, a heavy cavalry soldier.

Light cavalrymen wore no more armor than a breastplate and chainmail to mid-thigh and an open helmet. They were generally armed with no more than bow, sword and dagger, although when facing battle, as today, they would carry a light lance, not much more than a spear. They relied on their horses' speed, maneuverability and their own cunning to keep them alive.

Heavy cavalry was their nemesis – men in three-quarters armor to the knee with half-shields, riding great horses that looked suitable for pulling brewery wagons. They were armed with sword, dagger, lance, and frequently a mace or a hammer. They rode in close formation and if the light horsemen were brought to battle by the heavies and couldn't escape, they were almost certainly doomed.

These lumbering monsters were most highly regarded, their units draped with battle honors and their riders among the most noble of any kingdom.

Hal hoped to spend this day without seeing any of them, neither Roche nor on his own side, for that would portend disaster.

All he wanted was to obey orders, get in, get out and get back. Tomorrow, when the armies rumbled back on the move they could resume their patrolling and skirmishing duties.

Before he heard the first warning shout, he felt the earth begin shaking.

Riding out of the forest fringing the Roche lines, coming between the trees in close formation, came the Roche heavy cavalry. Hal was never sure if there were two or three regiments. Not that it mattered. Just one would have given the battle edge to Roche.

Lord Canista shouted to one of his aides to ride back for their promised support, the Sagene heavy cavalry. The young officer saluted, wheeled his horse, and galloped hard for the rear.

He'd gone no more than a quarter of a mile when a crossbowman rose from behind a bush, and shot him off his horse.

Other crossbowmen came up on line, ran toward Hal's unit, closing the jaws of the trap.

Canista shouted for the regiment to turn away from the attackers, and make for a knoll, dismount and fight on foot until their support arrived.

They never made it.

Half a company of Roche were charging Hal's section. He shouted for his men to turn into the attack, comb the lancers, then try for the knoll.

They obeyed, but the heavy cavalrymen held formation, and Hal's section couldn't break through. A knight was coming hard at Hal, and Kailas ducked under his lance, spitted him in the throat, above his gorget, with his sword. Another rider cut at him, missed, and Hal slashed, also going wide.

Then he was behind the first wave, saw another stream of riders thundering toward him.

He pulled at his horse's reins, as the animal screamed and reared. Hal slid off the back as his mount fell back, thrashing, a crossbow bolt in its throat, another between its ribs.

A Roche crossbowman was coming at him, long double-edged dagger held low. Hal parried, ran him through, felt another bolt whip past his face.

A dismounted cavalryman was coming at him, two-handed sword up. Hal went to his knees, drove his sword under the man's breastplate, into his guts.

Then something smashed into the back of his head, and he went flat, world spinning.

He didn't know how long he was out, seconds or minutes, but then he was back on his feet, sword bloody, staggering toward that knoll. Someone was stabbing at him with a spear, and he cut the spearhead away, killed that man.

There were three corpses in front of him, all three members of his section.

A man was standing over them in Roche uniform. Hal killed him, stumbled on.

There was a ditch, and he went down, sprawled face-first, hearing the whine of bolts above him.

A man jumped down, breathing hard, started to stab Hal, saw he wore the same uniform, clambered out and a spear took him in the shoulder. He spun, and another spear went into the back of his neck.

A Roche soldier ran up, not seeing Hal, and Hal's sword took him in the armpit.

There was blood, there was screaming, loud, dying away, and Hal was down in the dust, seeing the Roche heavy cavalry ride past him, back toward their lines, the crossbowmen who'd closed the trap trotting beside them, prodding a few prisoners ahead of them.

Then there was nothing but the sound of men dying.

Hal got back up, waiting to be killed. But there was no one on the field except the dead, dying and desperately wounded.

There was no sign of the promised Sagene heavy cavalry.

Hal considered his injuries. A slash across the back, no more than painful, but bloody enough to have made him look dead, lying in the ditch. An arrow stub stuck out of his upper thigh, and he pushed it through, snapped the arrowhead off. He almost fainted, then pulled the shaft free and tied up the bloody wound with his torn tunic. He was bruised here and there, but felt no broken bones.

He should have gone back to his own lines before the vultures and thieves came.

But he stopped, seeing a man who'd followed his orders, down in death.

A strange fascination came, and he wandered the battlefield, finding one, another, others of his section, all dead.

He saw the body of Lord Canista, half a dozen armored Roche sprawled around him.

A dozen yards away was the body of Sir Kinnear, lying back to back with the Sagene knight who'd challenged him. They, too, had taken their share and more with them.

Time blurred, and it was late afternoon, almost twilight.

He was kneeling beside the body of Jarth Ordinay, who was sprawled on his back, his dagger in the chest of one of the three men who'd died killing him.

Ordinay's face had a quiet, peaceful smile. The lines of premature aging were gone, and he looked the boy he'd been when the army took him.

Hal nodded solemnly, as if Ordinay had told him something, got up, and started back the way he'd come.

Somewhere he found a horse, a bloody slash along its neck, pulled himself into the saddle, and rode slowly back toward safety.

All dead, he mourned. All gone. All dead.

His mind wryly told him, now you can go ride the king's damned dragons if you want, can't you?

The hulk's sails caught the southerly wind, fair for Deraine, a dim line on the horizon. The ship plunged in the swell, yards clattering and sailors scurrying about.

Hal paid little attention to the bustle, eyes on Paestum's harbor they were sailing out of, and the distant border of Roche to his left.

He would be back, though, as a dragon flier.

Back, with a hard vengeance to take.

9

Deraine's capital, Rozen, had he been in another frame of mind, could have angered Hal Kailas. There were no buildings shattered by catapult stones, empty storefronts, shops with only one or two items for sale.

Deraine could almost have been a country at peace.

Almost.

But here was a column of uniformed recruits being chivvied along by a pair of shouting warrants; there another formation of trained soldiers, grim-faced under steel helms and laden with weaponry, and there were far fewer young men to be seen on the streets and in the cafes than in peacetime. Here were a knot of women wearing mourning bands, there other women and children scanning the posted list of those killed or wounded across the Straits.

Small patrols of warders, half civilian, half military, swept the streets.

Kailas paid them no mind, his orders secure in a belt pouch, his mind on other things, specifically the cup of iced custard he was wolfing.

He grinned. The hardened warrior, home at last, was supposed to head for the closest taproom and drink himself senseless on his favorite brew.

Kailas, who'd never thought himself much of a milk drinker, had developed a lust for the rich, cream-heavy Deraine liquid, despising the thin, frequently watered whey of Sagene. He'd had three big glasses, and was topping them off with this custard, flavored with cloves and cinnamon.

Kailas also thought of the other requirement of the homecoming soldier – a lovely girl under his arm, or at least a popsy.

He had no one.

Hal turned his mind away from loneliness, headed for the address he was supposed to report to.

Rozen was a city that had cheerfully "just grown" at the confluence of two rivers. The only coherency it had managed was the result of three fires four hundred years earlier. Then there'd been great architects, working under the king's close supervision, intending to build a city of splendor, the marvel of the world.

There were those great palaces and monuments, but two streets away might be a slum or a silversmith's street or even a knacker's yard.

Hal had been in Rozen twice, before he joined Athelny's circus, and hated it both times, feeling alone and forgotten – which he had been.

Now, an equally faceless figure in battered half-armor, sword-belt tied around his meager roll of belongings, he felt quite at home in the great city.

He felt as if he were watching a camera obscura, arranged for his solitary pleasure. Kailas felt outside this city's life, but it wasn't unpleasant at all.

He'd been offered leave after the destruction of his regiment, and had thought about it, but there was no one for him to go to. He had no desire to return to the tiny village he'd come from, nor any desire to visit his parents, and so he asked for orders to his next duty assignment.

He wondered if soldiering had changed his outlook from the other times he'd been in the capital. Perhaps he'd seen enough people die young and violently to not mind being an outsider. He decided to give the matter a bit more thought, perhaps over a pint, later, after he'd reported in.

His orders read for him to report to the Main Guildhall, which seemed odd, until he entered the huge building. It had been commandeered by the army, and now was a shouting bustle of recruiting booths.

It was near chaos: a warrant brayed about the virtues of the dragoons, a clerk talked quietly of the safety of the quartermaster corps, an archer chanted about his elite regiment. Other warrants shouted how smart Lord such-and-so's Light Infantry uniforms were, or how Sir whatever would not only outfit a recruit, but send money to his family. Every branch of the service was represented, from chiurgeons to an arrogant-looking pair of magicians to a brawny farrier to a pair of jolly teamsters. There were even a scattering of women, raising nursing, transport, support units.

Most of them had at least one, frequently more, recruits weighing the virtues and dangers of a corps.

Except for one, a stony-faced, leathery-looking serjeant, lean as death, wearing the coronet of a troop warrant over his two stripes.

Behind him, tacked to the wall, was a poster-size version of the leaflet Lord Canista had shown Hal a month ago, announcing the formation of dragon flights.

Civilians prospecting the various booths would look at the warrant, then at the poster, and hasten onward. Evidently dragon flying was thought an advanced form of suicide.

Hal walked up to the man, saluted.

"I'm one of yours, Serjeant." He passed the orders from his corps commander across.

"Fine," the man said, lowering the parchment. "M'name's Ivo Te. I was starting to think I've got plague."

Hal didn't answer. Te looked him over hard.

"You appear to have been rode hard and put away wet, young Serjeant."

"Polishing rags aren't easy to find in Sagene," Hal said.

"Don't I know it," Te said. "Until two months ago, I was top warrant with Eighth Heavy Cavalry."

"I was Third Light. We scouted for you a few times."

"You did," Te said. "I heard about your disaster. But it's nice to have someone else along who knows which end of a sword gets sharpened."

"There are others?"

"There are others," Te said grimly. "And, with one or two exceptions, a bigger lot of shitepokes, crap merchants, layabouts and deeks I've never met before."

Hal grinned. "That good?"

Te sighed. "It's going to be a long war, lad. A long war indeed."

The recruits for dragon school were housed in an inn not far from Guildhall. Hal had little time to assess them before a dozen wagons arrived and, under a steady storm of cursing by Serjeant Te, the forty prospective fliers and their dunnage were loaded aboard and the wagons creaked away for the secret training grounds, somewhere beyond the capital.

The base sat close to a forbiddingly high cliff, on Deraine's west coast. Below, gray surf boomed uninvitingly.

"Be a good place for a morning bath after a good, healthy run," Serjeant Te said briskly, and was glowered at all around.

Before the war, the base had been a religious retreat, gray-stone main buildings and cottages scattered about the huge estate. Hal saw at once why the retreat had been taken over – the religious types must have worshipped a horse god, or else their benefactors were of the galloping set. There were huge barns and corrals, and what must have been a race course at one time, now being leveled by teams of oxen towing rollers back and forth.

"Where are our dragons?" a very young, very redheaded, very confident woman asked.

"Not here yet, and that'll be Serjeant to you," Te growled.

"Then wot the 'ells will we do, waitin'? Play wi' ourselves?" a man who could have been the young brother of Hal's cocky second, Jarth Ordinay, asked, cheekily.

"The Lord Spense will find work for you," Te said. "For all of us."

Hal noted, with a sinking feeling, the serjeant's face didn't look pleased.

Te had good reason.

This was only the second dragon flying class held here at Seabreak – three more schools around Deraine, were also training dragon flights.

Hal asked how the first class had managed, if the school didn't have any dragons, and was told they'd taken their monsters with them to Sagene, just as his class would ... when the dragons materialized.

The trainees were detailed off to the four-person huts by shouting warrants. One, a Serjeant Patrice, saw Hal's evident status as a combat veteran, but, unlike Te, didn't appear to like it, and chose Kailas for special attention, which meant more close range shouting than for others.

Hal had learned, trying to sleep in the rain, to put his mind elsewhere, generally soaring with dragons, so it was easy to ignore Patrice.

The huts spread out in four rows, each in a different compass heading, meeting at a common assembly area.

Hal managed to get one as far from the assembly field as possible, knowing which huts would likely be chosen for details by the warrants.

He did manage a minute with Serjeant Te, and requested the diminutive Farren Mariah, and "anybody else you think livable" for hutmates.

The other two were Ev Larnell, a haunted-looking, thin man a couple of years younger than Kailas; and Rai Garadice, a cheerful, muscled youth the same age as Hal, whose name sounded familiar to Hal.

The thirteen women on the course had their own huts, interspersed with the men's. No one, at least so far, slept anywhere but in the hut assigned him or her. There hadn't been any regulations read out about sex, but everyone automatically sensed it was against the rules. It had to be, since it felt good.

The huts were single open rooms, twenty feet on a side, and there was a wooden bunk and a large open hanging closet for each student. In the center of the room was a stove, which would be welcome as fall became winter, and a wash basin near the door.

Studded amid the huts were privies, with a long door at the rear, and half-barrels to catch the waste. Patrice had told them his favorite detail was telling someone to jockey a wagon down the rows, collecting the barrel's contents. All this was said with Patrice's usual expression, an utterly humorless tight smile the trainees found strangely annoying.

They were allowed half an hour to unpack their gear, then fallen back out. Hal had a few moments to consider a few of the other trainees: the confident, redheaded woman, Saslic Dinapur; a stocky loud man named Vad Feccia; and an arrogant man named Brant Calabar, *Sir* Brant Calabar he was careful to let everyone know. He reminded Hal of his old enemy as a boy, Nanpean Tregony.

Then they were pushed into formation, the experienced soldiers already knowing the drill, the civilians becoming quick studies of the others, for an address by the school's commanding officer.

"This is not my first school command," Lord Pers Spense said. "I've taught at His Majesty's Horse Guards, and was chosen to be Master of the Ring; and half a dozen crack regiments had me as their guest instructor before the war.

"I know little of this dragon flying you men – and women," he added hastily, "are about to attempt, but doubt me that it can be that different from riding any beast, except that you will be high in the skies."

Spense was red-faced, probably balding under the dress helm he wore over a very flashy uniform Hal couldn't identify, but knew it wouldn't last beyond the first archer on the battleground. He was most stocky, hardly appearing to be anyone who was the first to push back from the dinner table.

Spense slapped a riding crop against his highly polished thigh boots.

"Therefore, we shall begin training all of you in what I call the School of the Soldier.

"Serjeant Teh," he went on, mispronouncing the name, "has informed me that some of you have already seen bully fighting against the barbarians, those savages who call themselves the Roche, with barely a hundred years or so since they crawled from the swamp.

"For you, it shall be good to refresh your memory of the most important part of soldiering: drill. For only with the confidence that drill inspires can you go forth into battle, knowing the man on your left will do just what you are doing, and so bring the savages to their knees."

The speech went on, and on. Hal didn't bother listening to more.

He knew why Serjeant Te had winced.

"You *will* run everywhere," Serjeant Patrice bayed, and so the column of trainees ran through the estate grounds, twice around the cookhall, and stopped, some panting hard, in a long line.

Hal, not by accident, found himself behind the redhead, Saslic Dinapur. They introduced themselves, wondered about the food.

"And why'd you join?" she asked.

"I was already in the army," Hal said. "Things . . . changed at my old posting." He didn't elaborate about the massacre. "And I was a oddjob boy for a dragon flier named Athelny, back before the war."

Saslic grinned.

"I met that old rascal once, when he came to the Menagerie, to ask something of my father. Even as a little girl, I thought he was a definite rogue."

"He was that," Hal agreed.

"Do you have any idea what he's doing now? I hope wealthy, perhaps married to some rich dowager, and raising dragons somewhere in the north."

"He's dead," Hal said. "Killed by a bastard . . . Sorry—"

"Don't apologize," Saslic interrupted. "I've heard – used – worse myself. And we are in the army, aren't we?"

"I guess so," Hal said. "But after Lord Spense's uh, enlightening talk, I'm not sure what century's."

Saslic laughed, a very pleasant sound Hal decided he could get used to.

"Anyway, about poor Athelny?"

"Killed by an archer of a Sagene nobleman who'd euchred Athelny out of his dragon," Hal said. "He flew off, north, toward Deraine, I guess, and we never found his body."

Saslic was quiet for a few moments, then said, softly, "A bad way to die . . . but a better funeral than most of us'll see."

"True," Hal agreed.

"Move up, there," a voice behind him grated. "Some of us want our dinner."

Hal turned, looked at the bluff Vad Feccia, thought of saying something, didn't, deciding to fit into this new world as easily as he could, turned back.

Feccia laughed, a grating noise, and Hal realized he'd made a mistake. The man probably thought Kailas was afraid of him. Oh well. Bullies could be sorted out at a later time.

"You said something about the Menagerie?" Hal asked Saslic.

Saslic nodded. "My father is one of the keepers at the King's Own Menagerie, and I helped. I really liked working around the dragons, wanted to learn how to fly them, and when this came up, well, I guess my father'll speak to me sooner or later for running off."

They entered the long building, which was divided into thirds, one the kitchen, the second a dining room for students, the third, closed off with a screen for the cadre. They got tin plates from a pile, had a glop of what looked like stew, some tired vegetables, a pat of butter and bread dumped on the plate as they passed down the line of bored-looking serving women.

"Oh dear," Saslic said.

Hal thought it looked quite a bit better than most of the rations the army fed its troops in Sagene, but he didn't tell Saslic that.

The two looked around the small hall for a seat at one of the benched tables, just as Sir Brant Calabar crashed to his feet.

"This is a damned outrage! Eating with commoners!"

Farren Mariah, evidently the man he objected to, looked up.

"'At's fine, mate. Yer can wait outside, an' I'll save yer indignity, an' polish off yer plate as a pers'nal favor."

Calabar clashed his plate down.

"Where I come from, a bastard like you'd warrant a whipping!"

A man at the table behind Calabar stood. He was slender, long-faced, with a large, beaked nose.

"Now, sir," he said, in a nasal tone Hal had heard lords in the army use, "best you show some manners here. We're all learners together, and there's surely no call to behave like a pig."

Calabar whirled.

"And who the blazes are you?"

"Sir Loren Damian," the man said. "Former equerry to His Most Royal Majesty, detached on special duty to this school, also Lord Dulmin of the Northern Reaches, Quinton of Middlewich, and other equally ponderous titles I shan't bore anyone with, but ones I suspect have precedent in the Royal List over yours."

"Oh," Calabar said in a very quiet voice, out-titled to the hilt.

"Now, be a good sort, and sit down, and eat your meal," Sir Loren said.

Calabar started to obey, then crashed out of the hall.

"Tsk," Damian said. "But I suppose he'll come around, when his belly calls, which it appears to do on a rather regular basis."

There was a bit of laughter. Sir Loren picked up his plate, and pointedly walked to the table Calabar'd stormed away from.

"May I join you, sir?"

"Uh ... surely, I mean, yes m'lord," Mariah managed.

"My title here is Loren," Damian said. "Most likely something resembling scumbucket to our warrants, I'd imagine."

He started eating.

Hal and Saslic found seats. Kailas saw Serjeant Te leaning against the entrance to the cadre's section, a bit of a smile on his face, wondered what it portended for Calabar or Damian, decided that was none of his concern, started eating.

The food was actually fairly awful.

"Forrard ... harch!" Serjeant Patrice bellowed. "Hep, twoop, threep, fourp ... hep, twoop, threep, fourp ... godsdammit, Kailas, get in step!"

Hal almost stumbled over his own feet getting them in the proper military order.

The forty trainees, in a column of fours, marched away from the assembly area, down one of the curving brick paths into an open area.

"Right flank . . . harch!"

Hal turned left, and almost knocked a heavy-set woman, Mynta Gart, spinning.

"Lords of below, Kailas, can't you do anything right?"

The class was in military ranks, and the warrant teaching it had trouble reading the handbook he was holding.

Hal was half-listening, looking at another trainee two rows away. The man kept looking back at him as if he knew him.

As the class was dismissed for a break, Hal recognized him and went up.

"You're Asser, aren't you?"

"I am that . . . and where do I know you from?"

"Hal Kailas. I was Athelny's dogsbody when you were barkering for him. You and . . . Hils, that was his name."

"Right!" Asser smiled delightedly. "I heard Athelny's dead. What're you doing here? Did that old fart ever give you a chance to ride a dragon like you wanted?"

Hal explained, considering Asser as he spoke. Once, a long time ago, he'd thought the young man most dapper, a city slick. But he saw him through different eyes now, no more than another one of those who doesn't sow, but has every hustle in the world for reaping.

"Hils," Asser said sadly. "He's dead, too. I guess he thought he could outrun the warders, and anyway didn't believe one of 'em would cut him down from behind. A pity. He was just about the smoothest bilker I ever knew, and him and me had a great partnership . . . for awhile."

"So what made you join up?" Hal asked.

"It was like you said . . . made's the word. The magistrate didn't believe I had no idea who Hils was, and told me I was either gonna volunteer or be headed for the poogie for five years or so.

"I heard about this dragon thing we're in, figured that'd be a good place to lay low."

"I've seen Roche's dragons," Hal said. "If I weren't a fool, I'd think maybe five years in prison might be a little safer."

"Haw," Asser snorted. "You don't think a smart lad like me'll ever go across the water, now do you?"

Hal didn't reply, excused himself, seeing an angry-looking Saslic motioning to him.

"What's the problem?"

"That frigging Feccia's a lying sod!"

"I'm not surprised," Hal said mildly. "In what category?"

"Probably all of them. But start with his claims to be a dragon rider, back as a civilian, although he's pretty damned vague about the details. But I caught him. Asked him some questions, which he didn't answer quite right. Then I asked him when he thought was the best time to separate a dragon pup from the doe."

"What?"

"And he went and gave me a vague answer, saying it varied, depending on circumstances." Dinapur shook her head. "What a jack! A pup my left nipple!"

"Not to mention a dragon doe," Hal said, starting to laugh. "You know, a man who's so damn dumb he doesn't even know a kit and a cow probably won't get very far around here."

"Who's going to call him? A trainee? I'm not going to peach on someone, and for sure the cadre don't know the difference."

"You're right," Hal said. "I wouldn't nark the idiot off either. I guess we'll just have to wait for his mouth to take care of himself."

"To the rear . . . harch! In the name of any god you want, Kailas, can't you learn how to drill? I thought you were some kind of combat hero!"

Hal thought of telling him killing someone, or keeping from being killed yourself, didn't have a lot to do with square-bashing, and no, he'd never had any instruction whatsoever on what foot you were supposed to start marching with. The army across the water was a little too busy to concern itself with left-right, left-right.

But he kept his mouth shut. So far, he'd stayed off the emptying shitter detail.

So far.

The day finally came when they turned in their civilian gear, and Hal his threadbare uniform, which they'd been washing when they could, as they could, and were issued new uniforms.

They were fairly spectacular, which Hal guessed meant higher ranks were particularly interested in dragon flights: black thigh boots, into which tight-fitting white breeches were bloused, a red tunic with white shoulderbelts and gold shoulderboards, and a smart-looking forage cap, also red, which Hal thought would blow away twenty feet off the ground. With the gaudy uniform went very practical, and completely unromantic, undergarments, both in padded winter issue and plain summer wear.

Someone, probably down the line from the uniform's designers, had a bit of practicality, thinking what it would be like, flying in winter, and gauntleted catskin gloves and a heavy thigh-length jacket that must have required an entire sheep to produce were issued.

Another practical item was a set of greenish-brown coveralls, perfect, as Serjeant Patrice said, "for cleaning the shitter."

Hal was starting to think the man had a problem with his bowels.

They were also issued weapons – long spears and swords. Hal couldn't see either having much use aboard a dragon, figured that Sir Spense had called for the issue so the class would look like his idea of proper soldiery.

The only practical weapon was a long, single-edged dagger, which looked as if it had been designed and forged by an experienced bar brawler.

He was a bit surprised Spense hadn't given out spurs.

"*Lord*, they let some raggedy-asses into uniform these days," Patrice said, grinning his risus sardonicus. "Now, the reason you're in these ten-deep ranks is we're practicing parade maneuvers, and there aren't enough of you idiots to form a proper parade.

"Forrard . . . harch!"

Hal stepped out correctly, determined for once he wasn't going to make a mistake.

"By the right . . . wheel!"

The way the maneuver should've been done was the right flanker performed a right turn, began marking time, the soldier next to him took one more step, and so forth until the entire ten-man rank had turned right. In the meantime, the second row was doing the same, one step behind.

It didn't work out that way as soldiers slammed into each other, got confused and started marking time when they should've been moving, and everything became absolute chaos.

"Halt, halt, godsdammit, halt," Patrice screamed, and chaos became motionless chaos. He considered the mess.

"I'm starting to think this whole son of a bitching class has got a case of the Kailases."

Hal, who for once had done exactly what he should've, felt injured.

Somewhere in the mess Calabar laughed.

"I heard laughter," Patrice said. "Is there something funny I've missed?"

Silence.

"Who laughed?"

More silence.

"I don't like being lied to," Patrice said. "And nobody confessing is lying, now isn't it?"

Still more silence.

"I asked for an answer."

The class got it, and raggedly boomed, "YES, SERJEANT."

"I have a good ear, I've been told," Patrice said. "Don't you think so, Sir Brant?"

An instant later, he shouted, "Not fast enough, Sir Brant. Front and center!"

Calabar trundled out of the ranks.

"Was that you who laughed?" Patrice cooed.

"Uh . . . uh . . . yessir."

"Don't call me sir! I know who my parents were! You get your young ass to your hut, secure your clothes bucket, and run on down to the ocean and bring me back a bucket of water.

"Move out!"

Patrice watched Calabar run off, then turned back to his victims.

"Now, shall we try it again, children?"

Serjeant Te took Hal aside.

"How're you holding up, Serjeant?"

"I didn't think we had any rank here, Serjeant Te."

"That appears to be one of the good Sir Spense's ideas. You've noticed that no one's been returned to his or her unit yet for failure, either."

"That's right."

Te nodded sagely. "Just a word, or mayhap a suggestion. It could be the good Sir Spense is truly in the dark, and afraid to throw anyone out until he has some idea of what might be required.

"As for Serjeant Patrice—"

"I don't mean to interrupt," Hal said. "But he's water to a duck's back."

Te grinned.

"Good. I didn't figure he'd get under your skin."

"Not a chance, Serjeant. Matter of fact, he's given me an idea on handling a problem of my own."

"I don't suppose," Rai Garadice asked Farren Mariah, "you'd be willing to tell us how you happened into dragon flying, since we've got a whole hour to waste before dear Serjeant Patrice takes us for a nice morning run."

The class was in a stable, looking out at the drizzle beyond.

Farren pursed his lips, then shrugged.

"I don't guess there's a'matter. The on'y dragons I've ever been around was oncet, when a show come to Rozen, I got a job cleanin' up the hippodrome a'ter 'em."

"Nice start for a career," Saslic said.

"You name the tisket, I've held it," Farren said. "Crier, runner, butcher's boy, greengrocer's assistant, glazier, changer's messenger, a ferryboat oarsman for a bit, maybe a couple things I don't think I oughta be jawin' about."

"None of this answers Rai's question," Hal said.

"Well . . . I went an' made a bet wi' a friend, don't matter wot, an' lost, an' the wager was the loser hadda take the king's coin."

"Hell of a bet," Saslic said.

"Yeh, well there weren't much goin' on around, so it din't matter," Farren said. "An' then, oncet I was in barracks, there was a certain misunderstanding, an' somebody'd told me about these flights, an' I thought maybe it'd be best to skip outa the line of fire."

"Misunderstanding?"

"Uh . . . the men around me thought I was a witch."

There was a jolt of silence.

"Are you?" Saslic asked gently.

"Course not. I just got a bit of the gift, not like my ma, or my uncle, or his family. And my gran'sire was s'posedly a great wizard, good enough for nobility to consult."

"Oh," Garadice said, forcing himself not to move away. Most people without the gift were quite leery of magicians.

"A wizard," Saslic said in a thoughtful tone. "Maybe we could have you rouse a spell that'd, say, cause Patrice to fall over yon cliff, or make his dick fall off."

"I couldn't do someat like that!" Mariah said, sounding shocked.

"Then what earthly good are you?" Saslic asked.

"Broadly speaking," the warrant droned, "if two cavalries of approximately equal mobility maneuver against each other in open country, neither side can afford the loss of time that dismounting to fight on foot entails. Hence, the same fundamental rules apply to all cavalry combats . . ."

Saslic looked at Hal, made a face, mouthed the plaintive words, "When are we gonna learn about dragons?"

Hal shrugged. Maybe some time before they reembarked for the wars.

Somehow Patrice made a mistake on the schedule, and the trainees had a whole two hours after eating before the mandatory late class, this one on Proper Horsemanship.

Not that anyone actually had time for relaxation, busy with boot-blackening, cleaning their weapons – "all this stabbin' and wot really rusts a blade out, eh?" was Farren Mariah's comment – or trying to remember what it was like to be around a dragon.

Since it was an unseasonably warm fall evening, most of them were gathered outside their huts, talking while they polished.

Mynta Gart saw Brant Calabar staggering away from the steps down to the rocky beach with yet another full bucket, said, "Guess our Serjeant Patrice is havin' himself a salt water bath."

"Good for his complexion, I'd bet," Saslic said.

"A better wash'd be to trail him overside for a league or so," Gart said. "And then cut loose the hawser."

"You sound like a sailor," Saslic said.

"That I am," Gart said proudly. "Will be again, once the fighting stops. Once had my own coaster, then got bit by that patriotic fever, and got made a mate on one of the king's patrol boats.

"Which was damn stupid of me, since what navy Roche has looks to be hiding in port until the war's over."

"So why'd you volunteer for dragon flying?" Hal asked.

"Why not? Used to be, when I was up on the north coast, I'd see wild dragons overhead, some heading, no doubt, for Black Island.

"Looked romantic and free to me." She looked around at the trainees.

"*Damn*, but I love this freedom."

"What about you, Kailas?" Feccia asked, when the rueful laughter died. "You have a personal invite from the king to bless us with your company?"

"Where I'm from," Hal said, "that's not a question *civil* men ask."

"Prob'ly wise," Feccia said. "I've heard villains are careful about things like that."

Something snapped inside Hal. He'd made a bit of a joke about solving his problem, and now was suddenly the time. Crossbelts and white polish sailing, he was on his feet and blurred across the ten feet to the bigger man.

His mouth was gaping, and Hal, anger giving him strength, yanked Feccia to his feet. He slapped him hard across the mouth twice, and blood erupted.

Hal let him stumble back, kicked him hard in the stomach, was about to hammer him, double-fisted, across the back of the neck when Ev Larnell pulled him back. Kailas spun, was about to go after Larnell when the red rage faded.

He dropped his hands.

"Sorry."

Hal turned back to Feccia, gagging, bent over, and jerked him erect.

"Now, listen, for I'll only say this once," he said, his voice barely above a whisper even as his fury died. "You'll not talk to me, nor about me to anyone else, unless you're ordered."

Feccia stared up at him, his expression that of a cow staring at the butcher's hammer. Hal backhanded him twice again, grated, "Did you understand?"

The man nodded dumbly, and Hal shoved him away. Feccia stumbled off, toward the jakes, stopped, vomited, then staggered on.

The anger was now cold, gone in Kailas.

The other trainees were looking at him, quite strangely.

Saslic suddenly grinned.

"Did anyone ever tell you you're lovely when you're angry, soldier?"

The tension broke, and there was a nervous laugh, and the trainees went back to their cleaning.

"You look like you've been in a fight, Feccia," Serjeant Patrice said through his grin. "You know fighting's forbidden here."

"Nossir," Feccia muttered, breathing coming painfully past

cracked ribs. His face was puffed, swollen and bruised. "Not fighting, Serjeant. Walked into a doorjamb, Serjeant."

"You sure?"

"Sure, Serjeant."

Patrice stepped back. "Damned surprise, this. Maybe you *might* end up making a soldier."

That night, in their hut, Hal decided to break his own rule, and asked Rai Garadice if his father happened to be a dragon flier.

"He is," Garadice said. "Trained me, even if he thought I was still too young to go on the circuit with him."

"I thought so," Hal said, and said he'd tried to find a job with Garadice just before the war started, and that he'd said he was going to go find a place in the country and let the world go past until it was tired of war.

"That was his intent," Rai said. "Then, after Paestum was besieged, he – what was it Gart said this afternoon? – got bit by patriotic fever, and tried to enlist.

"They told him he was too old, and go home.

"He moped around for awhile, and I thought he'd given up, then he started writing letters to everybody when the war started dragging on. Including, I think, to Saslic's father at the King's Menagerie, saying he knew a lot about dragons, and they could be the key to victory.

"I guess everybody thought he was a little bit mad, since nobody's yet figured out what good dragons are for, other than playing spy in the sky, or so I'm told.

"Anyway, they came to him, made him a lieutenant officer, put him out with twenty others, and now he's a dragon requisition officer, responsible for buying dragons from their owners, or taking young ones from their nests and taming them to be flown.

"I hope he might be with our dragons when they finally arrive."

"Be a damn relief," Farren put in from his corner, "if the king'd give him orders to boot this eejit Spense back into a horse ring, and get some bodies in wot know which end of a dragon poops and which end bites."

"So then we've got three dragon riders in one hut," Ev Larnell put in.

"You've got experience?" Garadice said.

"Course I do," Larnell said. "In my district, we had fairs, and we'd always have dragon riders to top the day."

"And you were one of them?"

"Sure," Larnell said.

"How'd you rig your harness?" Garadice asked.

There was a long silence from Larnell's end of the room, then, "Why, just like everybody, we used ropes as reins, to a heavy metal bit and a chain headstall."

"What about saddles?"

"Just like on a horse," Larnell said, and his voice was thin. "Except with long straps, under the front legs and coming forward from just in front of the back ones."

"Oh," Garadice said flatly.

Hal realized there was more than one phony in the class besides Feccia.

The next day, after the forenoon drill, Ev Larnell came to Hal. He licked his lips, and said, tentatively, "I need a favor."

"If I can."

"Last night . . . Well, I guess you and Garadice figured out that I've never really been on a dragon in my life."

Hal made a noncommittal noise.

"You're right," Larnell said, his voice getting desperate. "All I've done is seen 'em fly overhead, and I went to a show once, before I joined up."

"So why'd you lie?"

"Because . . . because I was scared."

"Of what?"

"I joined up when Paestum was surrounded by the Roche, and went to Sagene with the King's Own Borderers.

"We've fought in every battle so far, and generally in the vanguard. Kailas, every man, twice over, in my company's been killed or taken off, grave wounded.

"I'm the only one who's still alive from the first ones, and I know they're going to keep putting us in the thick of things, and then, when we're wiped out, bringing up fresh men, so it's like a whole new unit, and there's no need to give us rest.

"But I remember . . . I'll always remember. Remember what it's like, seeing all your friends, down in death, friends you were joking with an hour earlier. Then you determine you're not going to let anybody close, let anybody be your friend, and maybe that's worse." Larnell's voice was growing higher. "I just couldn't take it any more.

"I'm no shirker . . . I wouldn't run away. But I thought, if I claimed I knew something about dragons, it'd get me out of the lines. Give me a chance to think, to pull myself together.

"Don't tell on me," he pleaded, and his voice was that of a child, terrified of being reported to his parents.

Hal looked into his eyes, saw the wrinkles at the edges, thought Larnell had the gaze of a very old man.

"Look," Hal said after a moment. "I don't nark on people. I've said it before, I'll probably say it again.

"You want to fly dragons, that's good. But don't start things, like you did last night. Keep your mouth shut, and don't go looking to get exposed."

"I won't. I promise I won't. And thanks. Thank you."

He bobbed his head twice, scurried away.

Excellent, Hal thought. Now, you're all of what, twenty, and you're a priest confessor. And what if Larnell finishes training, and then breaks in combat, and puts somebody's ass in a sling?

If that happens, a part of his brain said coldly, you'll have to kill him yourself.

"Can I get you something from the canteen, Hal?" Vad Feccia asked, parading an ingratiating smile.

"No, thanks."

Feccia hesitated, then ran off.

Serjeant Te had witnessed the exchange.

"He's been acting a bit different since he had some kind of accident I heard about," he observed.

"He is that," Hal said shortly.

"Almost like a bully that's been whipped into line . . . Or the way a dog licks the arse of a bigger dog that got him on his back, pawing for mercy . . . except, of course, there's no fighting at this school."

Hal made no answer. Feccia had been very friendly with Kailas since the "fight," which Hal considered no more than a shoving match.

"Word of advice, young Serjeant," Te said. "A snake that turns once can do it again."

"I'd already figured that."

"Thought you might've."

"This 'un might be in'trestin'," Farren Mariah said. "You see what I'm wigglin' here?"

"Looks like," Hal said carefully, "a kid's toy. You going back to your childhood, Farren, playing the simpleton, hoping to get away from one of Patrice's little fun details?"

"Heh. Heh." Mariah said deliberately, if uninformatively. "What sort of kid's toy?"

"Uh . . ."

"Like the shitwagon coming down the line, 'bout halfway with its rounds," Rai Garadice said. The four hutmates were crouched in the door to their hut, Farren having cautioned them, without explaining, against being seen.

"Wood, wood, goodwood," Mariah said. By now, the others were used to his occasional rhyming slang. "Just so, just like, and keep thinking that.

"And who's ramblin' up the row toward the shitwagon?"

"Patrice."

"Heh. Heh. Heh," Farren said again, spacing his "hehs" deliberately.

"This center piece's carved by me, out of a bit whittledy from the wagon's arse. It's dipped in real shit – used my own, sackerficin' an sanctifyin', like they said – an' rubbed with some herbs I plucked on the last run beyont the grounds I know the meanin' of. Plus I said some words my gran'sire taught me when I was puttin' it together.

"Th' wheels're toothpicks, an' touched an' charmed by rubbin' against the real ones out there.

"Now, be watchin', that wagon, and I'll be chantin' away."

Garadice drew back, a little nervously. Farren grinned, seeing that.

"Careful m'magic don't slip, an' you go hoppin' out as a toady-frog.

> "*Wagon roll*
> *Wagon creak*
> *Full of stuff*
> *I'll not speak*
>
> *Wheel wiggle*
> *Wheel haul*
> *Wheel wobble*
> *Wheel FALL!!*"

At the last words, Farren twisted one of the toothpick wheels off the toy.

But no one noticed.

Outside, a wheel on the real privy carrier groaned, and gave way.

The cart teetered, and Serjeant Patrice had a moment to shout alarm. Then it crashed sideways, spilling a brown wave high into the air, to splash down over the warrant.

He tried to run, but the wagon was turning on its side, and more ordure washed over him.

There were shouts, screams, laughter as the students tumbled out of their huts.

"Paradise," Hal said, solemnly taking Farren by the ears and kissing him.

"Git away!" Mariah spluttered.

"You *are* a wizard," Ev Larnell said.

"It'll be a long night's cleanup he'll be having us doing," Rai said. "But worth every minute."

"Can I ask a question, Serjeant?" Hal asked Te, who'd taken charge of the formation due to Patrice's absence.

"Ask."

"You're assigned to this class, correct?"

"Aye."

"But I haven't seen you doing any teaching, or more than a morning run once a week or so."

"Aye."

"Can I ask why?"

Te smiled, the look of a cat with many, many, secrets, didn't respond.

"I've got a question of my own, Kailas."

"Yes, Serjeant."

"Do you have any ideas how that unfortunate accident could've happened to poor Serjeant Patrice?"

"No, Serjeant."

"Didn't think you would. Nobody else does either." Te smiled, and his skull face looked almost friendly.

"Go after your classmates, young Serjeant. Late class is coming up."

Hal, realizing he wasn't going to get an answer to his question, saluted, and doubled away.

As he ran, a possible answer came – just as a high-ranking officer didn't get where he was without having a bit of a political sense, the same had to be true of a troop serjeant.

Was Te aware of how screwed this school was, and making sure none of the blame would stick to his coat?

Some of the students had gotten in the habit of sitting behind the row of huts, in a quiet glade, between curfew and bed check, when the weather permitted. It gave them a chance to talk about the day, to try to decide if they were ever going to look at a dragon, let alone learn how to ride one.

Since fall was edging toward winter, most brought blankets to sit on and wrap around themselves.

One night, everyone had gone to bed except for Hal and Saslic.

It was clear, a chill in the air, and it seemed very natural for them to lean together, and look up at the almost-full moon.

"Do you suppose," Saslic asked softly, "that over in Roche there are a boy and girl dragon rider, looking up at the same moon . . . I wonder what they're thinking? Romantic things, maybe?"

Hal had been wondering about the Roche as well, except that his thoughts were running more toward some ideas he had for killing Roche dragon fliers, no matter their sex.

"Of course," he said hastily. "Romantic things, and about, umm, dancing in the moonlight, and . . ."

His voice trailed off, and he was looking into her eyes, great moonpools.

It seemed like a good idea to kiss her, and he was moving closer, her lips parting, and a voice whispered in their ear.

"How wonderfully romantic!"

Hal whirled, saw Serjeant Patrice, who'd crept up behind them on his hands and knees.

"We have a great deal of energy, do we, to be wanting to play stinkfinger when we ought to be in bed like good little boys and girls?"

"Uh . . ."

"On your feet, students, and at attention! Move!"

They obeyed.

"I suppose, with all this vim and vigor, you'd appreciate a task to occupy you for the rest of the night, wouldn't you, since you can't be sleepy?"

"Uh . . ." Hal managed.

"Is the shitwagon fixed yet, Serjeant?" Saslic said.

"No, more's the pity. Not that I'd detail you for that, since it makes noise, and I don't want any of your classmates disturbed from their slumber merely because of your . . . pastimes.

"You go change into your fatigue suits, children. And then meet me on the far side of where the horse ring used to be. There's at least one stable that wasn't cleaned thoroughly from the old days."

By false dawn, that stable was as clean as it had been on the day it'd been built, Hal and Saslic working by lantern light and with Patrice's occasional check-in.

"Very good," he approved, just as the drums of reveille began clattering. "Now, back to your huts, and change into class uniform. You've an easy fifteen minutes, and I don't want either of you late, or stinking of horse dung like you do now.

"Fifteen minutes, and I've planned a nice cross-country run for us before breaking our fasts."

Brooms were clattered down and the two pelted for their huts, knowing there was absolutely no way they'd be able to get clean, let alone dressed.

But then came the surprise.

Two huts – Hal's and Saslic's – gleamed with fire- and lamp-light.

"Come on, you eejiots," Farren shouted, and Mynta Gart beckoned from the other hut. "Water's heatin', and yer uniforms're ready."

Busy hands helped Hal out of his stinking fatigue suit, and buckets of soapy water were cascaded about him, as he stood, shivering, outside the hut. Across the way, Saslic was getting similar treatment.

Hal was too tired to even consider lascivious thoughts as his clothes were hurled at him, pulled on.

The only thought that did come, as he and the other students ran toward the shrilling of whistles in the assembly area, was that, with or without dragons, somehow the students had come together, and formed a team, cadre be damned.

The next day the dragons arrived, and everything changed.

10

There were twenty-five dragons, angrily hissing, long necks snaking around, trying to sink their fangs into anyone around. They were chain-lashed to wagons, each drawn by ten oxen.

Hal thought they were just entering their prime.

Saslic agreed, and said they were four, maybe five years old.

"A little young for riding, but easier to train," Rai Garadice added, then yelped in glee, broke formation, in spite of Serjeant Patrice's snarl, and ran into the arms of a medium-height, frothy-bearded man Hal recognized.

"Didjer happen to do a count?" Farren said. "Twenny-five of th' monskers. Assumin' that we, like the eejiots afore, take these mooncalves off to war as our personal mounts, a'ter they've finished trainin' us, that means that somebody's allowin' for either cas'lties or bustouts. So fifteen of us're doom't."

"Most likely both," Ev Larnell said gloomily.

"Yar, well, I don't plan on bein' either," Mariah put in snappily. "Fly the skies, spy the ground, that's my fambly motto."

"Since when?" Larnell asked suspiciously.

"Since right now," Farren said. "What's a good fambly 'less you can shake it, change it, turn it all about?"

There were very immediate changes. Garadice had brought five of his dragon-buying team, all experienced dragon fliers. He announced he had orders to take over command of the school, and everyone would now please help unload the dragons.

"Cadre included," he said.

Sir Pers Spense departed, and no one saw him leave.

Garadice appeared at the dinner formation, told all the students to gather around.

"I'm not one for speeches. I understand from the good Serjeant Te you've been getting marched back and forth a great deal, and it doesn't appear much was done about why you all volunteered.

"That'll change.

"Serjeant Te will take charge of whatever military drill needs doing, which I don't think is much, and the bulk of the time will be spent trying to teach you men and women not only how to fly, but how to stay alive once you reach the front.

"The battle has worsened, and no one is quite sure how dragons will fit in. So it'll be up to you to not only fight bravely, but determine the future of dragon flying.

"There are quite a few . . . well, I shouldn't say old fuds, but that's what they are, who think an army should forget nothing, and learn nothing.

"It'll be your job, and the few that have gone before, and, hopefully, the many that will follow, to make them learn differently.

"Now, go in to eat. I'm afraid tonight's meal is nothing but cold victuals, pickles, tomatoes and bread. I was forced to discharge the cooking staff, since I believe we should eat no worse than dragons, so until we bring in some better qualified people, we'll have to shift for ourselves, and some of you'll be detailed to help prepare and serve.

"Not that any of us will have much time to brood about food. We're all going to be very, very busy."

"Very well," Garadice said, propping a pair of half-moon spectacles on the bridge of his nose, "you might want to pay attention here."

He lifted an enormous folio on to the lectern. It was stuffed with papers, some printed, some scribbled on.

"This is what I think I know about dragons, from twenty years' experience.

"But if any of you know better, or even think you do, please interrupt me.

"Remember, we've only known about dragons for three hundred years or so, when they first appeared on our shores."

"Where did they come from?" Sir Loren Damian asked.

"Almost certainly from the far north, even beyond Black Island."

"Better, why'd they come south?" Farren asked.

"No one knows, precisely. Some have theorized the climate changed, and drove them south.

"Another theory is that they feed naturally on the great herds of oxen that roam the northern wildernesses. Perhaps a plague of oxen, or even overcrowding their natural grounds could have caused this migration."

"More like, somebody was chasin' 'em," Farren said.

"That's not unlikely." Garadice smiled. "Which may be one reason why the far north remains unexplored, besides the problem that Black Island, the logical jumping off place for any such exploration, is claimed by the kingdom of Roche."

The students were paired off, almost two to a dragon, and stable duties began. Somehow Vad Feccia ended as Hal's stable partner. Hal did most of the work, since Feccia seemed terrified of the monsters.

That didn't bother Hal. He cheerfully put Feccia to pumping the stirrup pump they were given, and sprayed his beast with soapy water, then scrubbed it with stiff-bristled, long-handled brushes.

"His" dragon seemed to like that, at least it only tried to sink its fangs into him at the beginning of the session and at the end.

Saslic determined the dragon's sex was probably female. "All to the good, Hal. Easier to train, easier to keep."

Saslic had a male dragon, which she'd named Nont, after, she said, "one of my imaginary friends when I was a little girl."

Hal didn't name his. He knew that it was going to be a long war, and this dragon might be the first of many, especially if his ideas bore fruition.

After washing, Hal oiled his dragon's scales, checked its talons for splitting, although he wasn't sure what he'd do if one was broken, carted out the amazing amount of waste a dragon could produce, changed the straw it slept on, odorous with the beast's pungent urine.

He then took it, on a very long lead, its wings bound, for a walk around the horse ring. He thought it was a good sign that "his" dragon wasn't very friendly to the other beasts.

The dragon was fed twice a day, generally a sheep or calf in the morning, perhaps some salt fish at night. Hal was grateful there was a butcher attached to Garadice's unit. As a special treat, a handful of rabbits might be tossed into the dragon's cage alive.

"There are four, most likely more, species of dragons. It's also possible that three of these are merely variations.

"The other class, known as the Black Island or black variation, is significantly larger in all dimensions than other dragons, is predominately black in coloration, and is considered untamable, and the deadliest of mankillers.

"As a side note, though," Garadice said, "a number of dragon fliers, back before the war, were able to obtain, tame and successfully ride dragons which had supposedly been gotten from

Black Island, so here, again, nothing is certain. Do these other species interbreed with the black dragons?

"I simply do not know."

New cooks had been brought in, Garadice permitted the issue of beer at the end of each week, and one afternoon was given over to free time.

None of this was important to Hal as Rai, who'd quickly been promoted to cadre, gave him a hand up into the rear saddle of a docile dragon cow for his first flight.

"Now, here's the way you steer this brute," he said, "which I suppose you know from your days with Athelny. Slap her with the reins on the left side of her neck, and, with training, she'll turn that way. Hit her on the right – and I don't mean hard, you're not supposed to be cruel – she'll go that way. Drag the reins back, and – with any kind of luck – the beast'll climb. Rap both reins on her neck, and she'll probably dive.

"Kick if you want her to fly faster, pull back on the reins again to slow her down.

"That's the hard way to do things. Some dragons – I remember the one my father gave me – obeyed by voice. Others I've seen can feel the rider bend in the saddle, and will turn with him.

"This lumbering cow is purely stupid, and thinks just getting off the ground is repayment enough for her daily meat.

"Strap yourself in, and let's go flying."

Hal obeyed, and Rai slid into the front saddle.

"Hup," he shouted, and the dragon stirred, got up from her crouch, and staggered forward, out of the pen. Her wings uncurled, beat, beat again, and, very simply, they were flying.

Rai let the dragon climb of her own will, giving no commands.

He looked back, saw Hal's look of pure glee, nodded.

"You *were* a flier, or anyway you've been up, not like some of us."

Hal didn't answer, intent on looking at that most magical of all sights, the ground lower away below him, and the horizon unroll.

"I'll not take her higher," Rai said. "I want you up front here as soon as possible, really learning something, not joyriding with your finger in your nose."

The classroom training was very much by guess and by the gods. Garadice and the other instructors taught map reading, use of a compass, survival skills in case they landed and were trapped in enemy territory.

There was an infantry training camp about half an hour's flight distant, and the trainees helped the class learn what horsemen, marching infantry, a command group looked like from the air.

Hal thought it mildly amusing that the soldiers, when the dragons landed, treated the prospective fliers with a mixture of awe and incredulity that any normal-looking man or woman would trust themselves to the monsters they loved.

He could see the use of most training, but it was evident that no one, instructor or student, was really sure how these dragons, and their fliers, would serve Deraine.

Hal, keeping his own council, was following Garadice's lead, and keeping a notebook that filled up with his own, rather bloody, thoughts on what use dragons might be put.

"Damnation, Kailas," the instructor shouted. "Don't saw at the reins – you're not trying to cut this poor beast's neck in half!"

Hal tried to be lighter with his controls, and the dragon ignored him. He tried leaning to suggest a command, and the dragon ignored him.

He felt sweat on his forehead, under his arms, in spite of the wintry day.

"This isn't producing much," the instructor said. "Bring him down toward the ground, and I'll take the reins.

"I do hope you do better next time," the instructor added, gloomily.

Hal nodded dumbly, terrified that he would be one of the ones found unsatisfactory, and returned to his unit. There were already half a dozen failures, after only two weeks.

Hal Kailas was afraid he'd be the seventh.

Saslic was a natural flier, and her dragon seemed to revel at every moment in the air, the pair quickly progressing to aerial acrobatics, turning, twisting in the stormy skies above the base.

She tried to help Hal on what he was doing wrong, but had to admit, finally, that it was just a matter of "feel," and he should maybe relax, and it would come to him in a flash.

Sir Loren Damian also learned easily, as he seemed to do everything, without effort and with a bit of a smile on his lanky face.

The other knight on the course, Calabar, was stodgy, but competent. One nasty habit he had was carrying a dogwhip with him, and belaboring his dragon at the slightest "failure."

Garadice told him he was heading for trouble, that dragons, like men, loved masters, if masters there had to be, who were easy in the saddle.

Calabar curled a lip and said, "In my experience, a master who gives a serf an ounce of slack is on the way to making a rebel, a bandit, and deserves a whipping as much as his disobedient thrall."

Asser seemed to be learning, then, one day, he was absent from roll call. Two days later, he was brought back, in manacles, by a pair of military warders, who'd caught him on the streets of Rozen.

Everyone expected him to be thrown out, and finally vanish. But he was kept on, although his evenings were spent with a shovel and broom under the tutelage of Serjeant Patrice. No one knew what story he told Garadice, but Farren said, a trace of envy in his voice, "Th' bastid must've a throat that's silver, pure silver."

"It seems fairly certain," Garadice read, "that the dragon's egg, which is about two feet long, is sat upon, in the nest, for about four months before hatching. The Kit is carefully tended by both parents for almost a year, until it is deemed ready to leave the nest. During this time, it's vulnerable only to two things: the weather, and man.

"Dragons seem to return to the same nest, year after year, refurbishing it with considerable skill before the cow deposits the egg."

He closed the book.

"Stop yawning, Mariah, or were you signaling for a break? Outside, all of you, breathe some rain, and wake up."

The class clattered out of the room, and down the hall to the main hall's entranceway, staring out at the rain, almost as gray as the stone and the sea beyond, that sheeted down.

"Damned glad to be inside on a day like this," Saslic said. "Look . . . way out there, to sea. That fisherman's in heavy weather."

Mynta Gart was staring at it.

"Sometimes, I think I wish . . ." Her voice trailed off.

"You were out there, getting bobbed around?" Hal suggested.

"Just so."

"The hells with that," Farren said. "Old Garry – sorry, Rai – goin' on about the dragon's egg, and nary a word about how they ring th' bell for each other, which might've kept me awake.

"D'yer know, I was brushin' that beast of mine, and his wanger came out shootin' out, like a dog's. Big as one of these damn' columns here. I skittered out of the way in a shot for fear he was feelin' lovelorn! Makes a man humble, feelin' inferior, even me, the grandest of lovers, an' ud put me off my feed for a week, were there anyone around here who's feelin' romantic-like about me.

"Which there ain't, an' I'm thinkin' about tryin' a new brand of soap."

Hal sat glumly in the stables, staring at the dragon across from him, which he was thinking of as his less and less. The next beast that would be his, the way things were going, would be another horse, back in the cavalry.

He wasn't supposed to be out of his hut, but the curfew regulations, like most of the others put out by Pers Spense, weren't being enforced, to Serjeant Patrice's annoyance.

"These men and women are adults, or had damned well better be if they're going to be trusted scouting for an entire army," Garadice had said flatly. "So we'll treat them like adults until they give damned good cause to warrant other considerations, in which case it will probably be best to just return them to their parent formations."

The penned dragon across from him had stared at Hal, wondering what he was doing here this deep in the night, but eventually the yellow eyes had closed, and the monster started breathing in a soft bubble.

Hal wasn't really seeing the dragon, but thinking over and over about what he was, what he must, be doing wrong, and why he couldn't seem to get it right.

About half the surviving class were now flying alone, well on their way toward graduation, while Kailas farted about like a stumblebum, having not a clue as to what he should be doing.

He started, hearing the stable door creak open, saw Saslic slip in, close the door behind her.

"What—"

She came over to him. "I couldn't sleep, and went to your hut. Farren said you'd gone out, probably to offer yourself as a sacrifice to the dragon god.

"I figured I'd find you here."

"Farren always makes life easier," Hal said. "Pull up a bucket and help me sulk."

Saslic stayed on her feet.

"You've got to stop worrying, Hal. You get all tensed up, and then you get jerky, and get more tense, like a kitten chasing its tail."

"I know," Kailas said. "But knowing and being able to do something about it seem to be two different things. Hells, I'm such a dunderbrain, I probably deserve being back on a horse, chasing bandits."

Saslic moved behind him, started rubbing his shoulders.

"I can feel the muscles knotted up," she said softly.

"Do you remember," she said after awhile, "the night we got caught, sitting out by Patrice?"

"I do."

"I had the idea you were going to kiss me before that asshole materialized."

"The thought was in my mind."

"Well?"

Hal stood, turned, and was holding her. She was small, light, and felt very good in his arms. He kissed her, and that felt better. She kissed him back, tongue writhing in his mouth, and he couldn't remember having felt that good in a long time.

Then they were lying, close together, in a hay manger. Her tunic was unbuttoned, and he was kissing the small buttons of her nipples, her fingers moving in his hair.

She broke from the kiss, and said, breathing hard, "You could be a gentleman, you know, and take off your breeches and tunic for a bedsheet. Straw isn't the easiest thing on a girl's bottom, you know."

They didn't stop making love until the drums of reveille began tapping.

"Dammit, Hal, quit trying to pull the poor dragon's head off," Rai snapped. "Gently! Feel what you want!"

Hal clenched his teeth, felt, again, his muscles clenching. Then his body remembered Saslic's gentle fingers, and all at once, he had it. He felt one with the dragon he was riding, and the monster responded, banking easily left, tucking a wing, and coming back on its own course.

"Now a right turn," Rai said, his voice suddenly excited.

Again the dragon banked, and this time Hal tapped it into a shallow dive, back toward the base, a gray blur in the grayness.

He didn't feel the cold wind coming off the sea, nor the spatter of rain that caught him as he sent the dragon curveting through the skies.

He did have it, and knew it, and wondered at his own clumsiness of bare minutes ago. It was, he thought, like watching a butterfly stagger out of its chrysalis onto a leaf, and, moments later, soar into the summer air.

He looked back over his shoulder, saw Rai grinning at him.

"See how easy it is?" the young Garadice said.

And it was easy.

"There probably has never been a creature so perfectly adapted for fighting as a dragon," Garadice read, "from its dual horns to the impressive fangs. Dragons, in territorial or mating battles, also use their neck spikes to tear at their opponent.

"The four claws are equally adept at ripping at their enemies with the three talons on each.

"The steering tail is also used to lash at an enemy, easily its most lethal weapon. The wing talons are used not only to impale prey, but to tear away wings, since a beast's wings are more delicate away from the forward, ribbed edge.

"Dragons have remarkable powers of healing and even regeneration, although a dragon that's entirely lost a wing or a limb is doomed.

"It's interesting that the beasts not only fight in earnest, but seem, from what I've observed, to play at fighting, although it appears as if that can become real combat quite easily, which is frequently to the death."

Dragon games, Hal thought, scribbling in his notebook. Men's games.

Like war . . .

Most students weren't slow as Hal had been, nor flashy like Saslic and Damian.

Mynta Gart plugged along, learning steadily, stolidly. Farren learned his new craft readily, always with a ready jest. So did Vad Feccia, in spite of his almost-fear of dragons, to Hal's minor disappointment.

Ev Larnell was quick to learn, even if he was hesitant to try out something new. Hal was glad he hadn't said anything to anyone about Ev's lie about being an experienced flier, although a couple of the cadre wondered aloud why he seemed to be slower than someone with his background should have been.

Other students couldn't seem to learn, were quietly but quickly removed from the school, their gear vanished with them, their mattresses rolled as if no one had ever slept there.

There were other losses . . .

Hal was walking his dragon in the horse ring, and heard a dragon scream. He saw Sir Brant Calabar lashing at his dragon's neck as the creature flapped clear of the ground, savagely yanking back on its reins.

The dragon's wings beat faster, and it climbed for altitude rapidly. But that evidently wasn't quick enough for Calabar, for he kept hitting the creature with his dogwhip. Hal could hear the man's shouting, couldn't make out the words.

The dragon was flying almost straight up, slowing.

Then it tucked a wing, and turned through a semi-circle, back toward the ground.

Calabar lost his hold, flailed, and, screaming, fell, 500 feet or more. He hit near in the middle of one of the exercise rings with a sodden thud, very final, like a bag of grain tossed from a high-bedded wagon.

Hal was the first to reach him. Calabar was motionless, his eyes glaring straight up. It didn't look as if he had an unbroken bone in his body.

His dragon circled overhead, screaming, and Hal thought his screams were triumphant.

Two more students died and were buried in the next week after Calabar. After their funerals, Garadice behaved as if they'd never been, and pushed the students even harder, spending more and more time in the air.

"Guess there was someat goin' about," Farren joked, and then everyone did as Garadice had, and the three had never lived.

That was the beginning of a ghastly tradition in the dragon flights.

One thing the students had to learn was there were days a dragon simply would not fly. No one seemed to know why, including Garadice, who said that was one problem with his pre-war shows: "You'd have the area filled, and your dragon would be sulking in his wagon, and you'd best leave him alone, or maybe feed him or her choice tidbits until the mood passed."

One student didn't listen to his advice, and kept chivvying her dragon. The brute started hissing, then, before she could jump back, snapped out, taking most of her arm off.

"Now, that's a way to get out of bein' kilt acrost the Straits I've naught considered, an' wi' a nice pension, I'd hope," Farren said, and everyone was a bit more careful around the beasts after that.

Hal, now that he had the flying problem in hand, but still refusing to name his dragon, spent more hours with the beast than most. He had to keep the lead on it, but let the rope and chain slack, and took the monster away from the base, into the trees around it. The dragon seemed to care little for the weather, paying little heed to winds or rain sweeping across its leathery hide.

Saslic caught him having a one-way conversation with the creature one time, and told him he'd gone right over the edge.

Kailas thought, then agreed with her, especially since he fancied the dragon had begun, by claw gestures and hisses, to talk back.

"Now," Serjeant Te said, "Serjeant Kailas has told us how his patrols were stalked by Roche dragons, which is a new tactic.

"We've orders for all of you to start learning the same tactic, which is why you see those dummies on straw horses across that field.

"Each of you is to take your dragon off, and try to bring it close to a dummy. Encourage your dragon – no, I don't have any ideas how – to grab the rider, and tear him from his horse. It's also all right to have him take the horse and rider, too.

"Be careful, and don't run into the ground.

"First man! Kailas! Get out there and give us a good example."

"A question, Serjean'?" Farren said.

"I'm listening."

"I ain't objectin' to killin' Roche . . . I s'pose that's why I'm here, a'ter all. But this grabbin' an' yankin' don't appear economical t' me. One expensive dragon, one expensive rider, riskin' all t' pull some plowboy off a horse, and takin' a chance of some archer yoinkin' you through th' throat. Or puttin' an arrer int' yer dragon, which ain't likely to make *him* happy, either."

Te hesitated, giving Hal enough time to remember the catapults that'd been fired at the Roche dragons who'd attacked his
patrol on the way back from that last scout of his.

"Orders're orders," Te said, without conviction. "But I'll pass
your word on to Lieutenant Garadice."

Farren looked at Hal, made a face. Kailas nodded slightly, ran
for his dragon.

Hal and Saslic made love whenever they could get away, which
wasn't that often. Their instruction was coming faster and faster,
and Kailas fancied he could hear the horror that was war breathing its fetid breath closer and closer.

The winter drove at them, and cut flying time. But Hal still managed to bundle himself in all that wonderfully warm issued gear
as often as possible, and prod his beast into the air, and up,
through the clouds to where a chill sun gleamed.

His dragon, not happy at first, warmed, and so they would fly,
sailing around the huge buttresses of clouds, sometimes through
them, and chancing being tossed by the winds hiding in the soft-
ness.

Then it was chancy, as he'd lower down into the solid cover,
losing altitude foot by foot, hoping there wasn't a hidden outcropping just below.

Once he broke out into the open, only a few feet above the
tossing waves, the cliffs of the base dim in the distance.

It was dangerous, but he was teaching himself.

And, as Saslic had said earlier, maybe vanishing in flight
wasn't the best way to die, but it made for as good a funeral as
anyone could wish.

"That's it," Garadice announced at one morning's formation, a
touch of spring in the air. "We've nothing more to teach you.

"You're dragon fliers."

There was a gape of astonishment, then the students began
cheering. The noise sounded like a great deal more than the nineteen who'd survived.

Garadice, at his own expense, had small golden dragons cast, and
gave one to each student, telling them to pin them on their
uniform, to be worn above any other decoration they won.

*

"I wish you all the luck in the world," Serjeant Patrice said. "And I'm proud to have helped make you into soldiers."

Saslic looked scornfully at his outthrust hand, refused to take it.

"No," she said, voice bitter. "Screw the way it works in romances. You're still nothing but a bully and a cheap prick to me."

She stalked away, to laughter. Patrice, face purpling, scurried back into the main hall.

And so the class broke up, each with a wagon carrying his or her distinctly unhappy dragon, creaking toward the Straits ports and Paestum, to report to different units.

Now, Hal thought, the real learning will begin.

11

It was a bit more than six months since Hal had been in Paestum, but the city had changed almost beyond recognition. The ruins from the siege had been mostly razed, and spreading far beyond the walls were caterpillering tents for the replacements and new units streaming across the Straits into Sagene.

When Hal had left, there'd been only *the* army. Now there were four, interspersed with Sagene armies down the Roche border, to meet the building threat of new Roche forces.

But the tactics hadn't changed, still the bloody head-smashing battles as the forces moved back and forth in the wasted, bloody landscape, hoping, each time, without luck, for a breakthrough into the heart of the enemy's country for the capital.

Hal, having a great deal of back pay in his purse, and nowhere to spend it, found a copyist involved with the replacement section who was bribable.

He was negotiating with him to keep Saslic, of course, plus Farren and possibly Ev Larnell, with him, whichever dragon flight he was assigned to, having learned there's no such word as "no" in the military if the pleader has sufficient rank or silver.

There were, at present, two flights assigned to each Deraine army, with Sagene having its own flights, roughly set up the same as Deraine's.

The transport ship had unloaded their dragons, and the new fliers were given a tented area to themselves, while they waited for orders to whichever dragon flight would need them. They were left largely in peace, no warrants rooting through their area for scut-details, since no one seemed to want to get too close to the monsters or the lunatics who rode them.

Contrasting with this were the jokes going around that no one had ever seen a dead dragon rider, and dragon riders were mainly concerned with qualifying for their king's old age pension, whereas an infantryman or cavalryman would certainly never live long enough to worry about it.

Hal was trying to figure out how much he'd have to increase the copyist's bribe to get "his" people assigned to the northernmost First Army area, near Paestum. Even though it was cold, rainy and swampy in spots, it was the area of the border he knew well, and thought that knowledge would improve his, and his friends', chances of surviving.

Then everything shattered.

Roche magicians managed to cloak the assembly of half a dozen armies, south, near the city of Frechin. They'd crossed the border, smashing a Sagene army.

Only the spring rains were holding them back from driving hard toward Sagene's capital of Fovant. But each day, the salient grew longer, a finger reaching into the heart of Sagene.

Deraine's First and Second Armies were stripped of any unit not vitally needed, all offensives against the Roche were put aside, and all replacements arriving in Paestum were detached on temporary duty to units in the Third Army, now engaged with the enemy.

So Hal's entire graduating class of novice fliers, and their beasts, were ordered south, at all possible speed. The Third Army needed them for scouts, spies and couriers.

The roads below were packed with troops, marching, riding, in wagons. Hal was very glad to be high above the roiling mud below. His dragon wanted to find a nice, dry cave and hole up until the weather changed, but he drove it onward, and eventually it gave up squealing protest when he led it out from the canvas aerie the detailed quartermasters set up every night when they camped.

South and south they went, but it never got warmer, and the fliers wore everything they were issued, and still shivered.

Some of them – Feccia among them – got in the habit of buying whatever brandy they could find in their flights. Hal took barely a nip on even especially frozen mornings. He'd already learned brandy as a friend could quickly become brandy as a creaking crutch, and wanted none of that.

Of course the villagers along the roads were either bought or looted out by the time Hal's detachment passed, but the dragons had the option of flying away from the march routes, finding villages who barely knew there was a war, eager to trade, sell or even patriotically give away their produce, eggs, or drink.

It didn't make much of an impression to the ground-bound soldiery, seeing dragons float back to their wagons at dusk, laden with plunder. The elderly infantry warrant who'd been put in charge of the formation seemed to have no objections to what was going on, and Hal shrugged, it not being his concern. It didn't, however, improve his mood to hear the infantry give them new labels: "Defenders of the Veal," "Champions of the Poultry Run," "Guardians of the Keg," "Omelet Defenders," and so forth.

At least he and Saslic were able to be together at least every third night or so, when one or another didn't have guard duty around the dragons.

Other fliers made similar arrangements, or, like Farren, chased after any women they encountered with the dignity of a hound in heat.

There were persistent rumors of bandits abroad, or cross-border partisans, but Hal never saw any, and these scoundrels were, according to the tales, either a day's march in front of or behind the yarn-spinner.

Before Bedarisi the open roads that had given the soldiers speed changed. Now the roads were packed with refugees, fleeing ahead of the advancing Roche armies.

Hal would always remember a few things from those days.

An old man, pushing an older woman in a barrow, and, from the time they first saw the pair until they vanished around a bend, she never stopped railing at him.

A middle-aged man, wearing nothing but long winter drawers, carrying only an ornate old clock taller than he was.

Three wagons full of young women, who claimed to be from

a religious school, and were full of laughter. But if they were religious, they had scandalous rites, although those men – and a few women – who hadn't made bed partners seemed to enjoy their company. Hal and Saslic visited their camp, across from the dragon fliers, for a glass of wine, and Saslic noted, behind the laughter, the fear in the women's eyes, and the way they kept glancing south, toward the oncoming Roche.

A wizard, with two acolytes, their robes stained with travel, trudging along. Farren landed his dragon, got provisions from one of the fliers' wagons, and walked for a third of a league beside them, then came back.

"Dreadful bad it is, in the south," he reported. "Or so the mage says. Roche cavalry ridin' here an' there, lootin', cuttin', murderin', rapin', and the Sagenes don't seem to be able to stop 'em.

"He says we'll have our jobs set for us, an' wished us luck."

Hal asked why the man's magic hadn't kept him from becoming another wanderer, and Mariah, serious for once, had said, "I guess magic don't al'as help the one who's castin' it. Sure fire it didn't make m' grandsire rich, just notable. Guess that the gods, whoreson bastids that they be, don't want wizards comin' up as kings or, worse yet, competin' wi' them.

"That gives us some sort of order, I guess, 'though, thinkin' from present circ'mstances, I wouldn't mind if they let an option out f'r one short amat'ur witch, who's doodlin' around in the wilderness wi' dragons at present, needin' all the help he can get."

One day they were stranded before a washed-out bridge, waiting for the pioneers to rebuild it. There was a small country inn on a promontory over the river, but its proprietor said, mournfully, he'd sold everything he had in the way of provender, and their chickens and ducks had been pirated away by either soldiers or refugees.

Mynta Gart flew away north-west on her dragon, and came back two hours later with a cargo net full of foodstuffs bought in distant villages.

She refused the proprietor's money, told him to build omelets, and the man's two daughters went through dozens of eggs at a time until the fliers thought they might cluck and peck at each other.

Now their forced march from Paestum caught up with them, and Hal could feel fatigue at his back. But he said nothing, and cut Vad Feccia off sharply when he whined about sore muscles, merely pointing to the road they'd pulled away from, at the long lines of infantry, plodding through the mire, a pace at a time, and with nothing but a groundsheet and what they had scrounged from the roadside or begged or stolen from passing wagons for rations.

They reached Bedarisi, the streets crowded with fleeing citizens. It took them two full days to work their way through the jammed streets to open country again.

Feccia suggested low-flying the dragons over the crowd, and hoping some terror would clear the way, but the old warrant forbade it.

Beyond the city, they saw their first Roche dragons, swooping and diving in the distance, spying the country, and felt the war close on them.

Two of their dragons saw them, and Hal was pleased with their response – angry hissing and snorts, their heads snaking back and forth, mouths open, fangs dripping. He hoped the fliers mirrored their attitude.

Now the roads, such as they were, country tracks worn wide and into sloppy ditches by the army's passings, were empty once more of everything except the military.

They stopped at an enormous post at an intersection of three of these tracks, a log stripped of leaves and branches, and buried vertically. On it were half a hundred wooden boards, each pointing to where a different formation might be found.

Far at the top, Farren saw a small painted dragon.

"Or else't a winged worm," he opined.

They turned the wagons down that track, and went on for several leagues, passing encampments, ration dumps, stables.

The track emptied into a wide meadow, with a pond at one end, and there they found the dragon flight.

Hal kept his face blank, but Farren, Feccia and some others gaped in shock.

Expecting lines of hopefully weatherproof huge stables for the dragons, and neat barracks to the side for the men, they saw, instead, some tattered tents, worse than the ones the former students had brought with them, patched here and there with other colored canvas or even cloth. Some of them had torn grommets, and were held to the ground, flailing in the strong wind, with branches for stakes.

The human quarters were even worse, everything from huge

packing crates to tiny infantry tents to sod-roofed shanties supported on logs and "found" lumber.

It looked like a proper base – one that had been struck by a tornado, and then reoccupied by trolls.

There were a handful of people about, most seemingly doing nothing except squelching back and forth on the open meadow in front of the squadron's buildings.

One woman was watering a dragon at the pond.

At both sides of the meadow were catapults, with infantrymen manning them.

A single dragon patrolled the air overhead, flying in endless circles around the meadow.

Hal ignored the moans – as an old soldier, he noted what must be the cooktent, a large, well-pitched tent, with smoke coming from chimneys at the front and back.

Seeing that, he knew that everything had not fallen apart.

"Do you want me to report in, sir?"

"I'd appreciate that," their escort warrant said. "Now we're away from my grounds, and on yours."

Hal caught himself, glanced at Sir Loren Damian, who grinned damply, but made no protest.

There was a guidon pitched in front of a bell tent, and Hal went to it, knocked on the ridgepole.

"Enter."

He pushed the outer flap aside, and walked into a tent crowded with four cots, one piled high with maps and swordbelts.

On another, a man snored loudly, a ragged cloak pulled over him.

Sitting at a field desk sat a man whose body and face were sculpted by exhaustion. Hal was tired, but this man was beyond that.

"Serjeant Hal Kailas," Hal said, clapping a hand to his breast. "With eighteen other dragon fliers and mounts, mobile, as ordered by First Army Headquarters."

The man blinked, rubbed his eyes, picked up a bottle of brandy, and uncorked it. He shook his head, and put the bottle away.

"I am assuming for the moment you're not a magician's imp, sent to taunt me with impossibilities."

"Nossir. I'm . . . we're for real."

"Just maybe there are gods," the man breathed, realized Hal was still holding the salute. "Sit down . . . or, anyway, find something to lean against.

"I'm Lieutenant Sir Lu Miletus. Someone said I was going to be a captain, but the orders seem to have gone awry.

"You said nineteen dragon fliers?"

"Yessir."

The man stood, extended a hand, and Hal clasped it. Miletus looked as if he'd been studying to become a priest or other ascetic before the war, with his lean, long-faced, somber expression. But Hal saw smile lines on his face.

"Nineteen," Miletus breathed again. "That just might put us back in the war. Any support people?"

"Nossir. We were told you'd have all necessary ground personnel."

"We did," Miletus said. "Until the dragons brought the cavalry on us. At least we didn't lose any of our beasts . . . all ten of them.

"And now, just a little late, we've got those arrow-throwers assigned to keep us safe from intruders."

He shook his head.

"Never mind. We've gotten so good at making do with very little we can probably win this godsdamned war with absolutely nothing."

He pulled on a muddy cloak.

"Let's go see how we can get your people settled, Serjeant. I'll tell you beforehand I'm going to make myself rather loathed, since I'm going to take away five of your dragons from their masters."

Hal kept his face still.

"My fliers – all six of them – have more experience . . . I assume that none of you are more than school-trained?"

"That's correct. Sir."

"Don't look so sour, man. What I'm doing is not only best for the flight, but it might keep some of you alive.

"Also, all of you are grounded until I personally give you permission."

He grinned, noting Hal's deliberately blank look. "And I don't mean to denigrate you by keeping you out of harm's way for the moment.

"You'll see. You'll see your training didn't really give you any help for what's out here.

"Now, let's get your men fed, and start finagling for quarters."

"Four of us are women, sir."

"I'd heard they'd finally gotten around to recognizing the other half," Miletus said. "Not to worry. I don't think any of my men have enough energy to raise a smile, if that was your concern."

The new ones were quartered here and there, some in existing tents, some in the smaller tents they'd brought with them.

The escort warrant and his men rode back the way they came, showing evident relief they wouldn't be required to get any closer to the war zone than they already had.

Miletus didn't, as far as Hal saw, quiz any of the replacements about who was the best flier, who the worst. Instead, he put them up, one by one, over the meadow, ordering them to do certain maneuvers.

Hal quickly found out neither war nor careless habits had driven the flight into slovenry.

They'd been hammered hard when the Roche crossed the lines, losing fliers and dragons to Roche magic, their catapults, which were brought up just behind the front lines, weather, and two to enemy dragons, who'd attacked their beasts until the Deraine dragons went out of control, whipping across the skies and losing their riders, then vanishing into the mists.

Bad enough ... but then the dragons had guided enemy cavalry through the shattered Deraine positions to the flight's base.

"Everyone," Miletus said tiredly, "became infantry, and we fought as well as we could." He looked around sadly "Which wasn't very, I'm afraid, although at least we drove them back.

"The closest thing we had to a hero was Chook, the cook."

Hal waited for an explanation, but none came.

"The Sagene command offered us infantry to guard the base, but I told them to keep the men on the lines, except for those catapult men. There isn't anything here worth another attack." He brightened. "At least not 'til your arrival."

He grinned. "I'm certain you find that reassuring."

Hal found a relatively dry bell tent, with four cots. Three of them were bare, the fourth occupied by a wiry man with amazing mustaches, who introduced himself as Aimard Quesney, and told him to take any bed he wanted.

"Won't I be disturbing anybody?"

"If you are, and anyone says anything, move out sprightly," Aimard said. "For they're all quite dead, and I'm getting tired of waiting for their ghosts."

"Small, but cozy," Saslic said, waving a hand around her hut. "Note the greenery on the roof, which'll go well with my face when I think about what I got myself into wanting to play soldier."

The hut was small, ten feet on a side. But shelves had been built along the walls by a skilled carpenter, and there were cleverly-hinged windows on either wall.

"Built for two," Saslic said. "But I hid the other cot before anyone could claim it."

"Why?" Hal asked.

"Did your mother have any sons with intelligence?"

"I don't guess so. Explain."

"I thought a certain northern fool might want to come visiting from time to time, and since I'm not into either threesies or witnesses, I thought we might like privacy."

"Oh."

"Speaking of which, why don't you slide the door shut? I noticed you coming back from the pond, looking cleaner than you have since we left Paestum, and thought you might be interested in messing about."

In the dimness, Hal saw her slide out of her coveralls, and lay back on the bed.

"Close, but perhaps we can manage," she murmured.

Later, as they lay together, Hal had a question.

"I know men aren't supposed to ask and all. But what's going to happen to us?"

Saslic kissed him on the nose.

"Why, we're going to get killed. Preferably nobly, in battle."

"Oh." Hal thought. "No. I'm going to live through this."

"Of course you are," Saslic drawled. "That's what everybody who filled up all these empty cots knew."

"No," Hal said stubbornly, trying to sound as if he were positive about things. "I'm going to survive."

"Well, good for you," Saslic said. "I'm not. Which is why I haven't bored either one of us talking about love, or after the war, or anything else beyond this moment. So remember me fondly when I'm gone, and name your first child after me.

"And as for immediate moments . . ."

She moved close, hooked a leg over his thighs, and pulled him on top of her.

"Remember, anything you don't see might kill you," Miletus said over his shoulder. "C'mon, Fabulous. Get your arse in the sky."

He tapped reins, and the dragon's wings flapped slowly, and it took a few steps forward. Then it was clear of the mucky ground, and climbed into the skies.

Hal, sitting behind Miletus, tried to keep the map he'd studied ready, and glanced at the compass clipped to his fur-lined jacket, then put it away, mindful of Miletus' orders to keep his eyes on the sky, not anywhere else.

He shivered at the chill spring wind blowing in his face, and decided, before next winter, if he lived that long, he'd have to have someone make him furry thigh boots like Miletus wore, and some sort of tie-down fur-lined cap.

They flew south-south-west, toward the salient.

"I'll skirt the edges of the battleground," Miletus shouted. "No point in giving their damned catapults a shot at a virgin, now is there?"

The lines were clearly demarked – two long scraggly rows of huts, with most of the vegetation in front cleared, the woods around cleared for firewood and building materials. Between them was open, rutted land torn by marchers and horsemen.

They flew down the lines, turned, went back the way they came, turned back to base.

Miletus slid out of the saddle, tossed the reins to one of his handlers, said, "Well? What did you see?"

"Not much of anything," Hal said honestly. "Smoke from fires, a couple of horsemen back of the lines."

"That's all?"

"Yessir."

Miletus shook his head.

"And you're a combat veteran. Kailas, if you expect to be alive in a month, you'd better learn to sharpen your eyes.

"First, you missed a flight of three dragons, ours, but they could well have been Roche, moving east, just west of that little bend in the lines that's marked as the Hook.

"Second, there was a Roche dragon circling a position about a mile north of them.

"Then there was that stationary cloud over that ruined village."

Kailas looked perplexed.

"There was a wind blowing, maybe seven, eight miles an hour. Clouds don't hang about when there's wind, correct?"

"Nossir."

"That'd suggest, if we were a proper scouting patrol, to take a look. Probably the cloud is magically cast, and there's most likely something underneath it the Roche would rather we not see.

"I'll send a couple of beasts up as soon as I finish with you.

"Then there was a column of cavalry, a company, perhaps more, riding toward the southern end of the salient, which would suggest someone's up to no good.

"Lastly, and you couldn't have known this, we passed over a scruffy little forest that was a nice open piece of land yesterday or the day before."

"Magic?"

"Probably not," Miletus said. "More likely camouflage nets. By the size of the area, I'd guess an encampment of a company, perhaps more, on the move.

"On patrol, it'd be your job to get lower and closer, and find out what sort of unit."

Hal had nothing to say.

"Your most important weapons are your eyeballs," Miletus said. "Keep looking, keep moving your head about. And don't forget to keep looking over your shoulder.

"The Roche love to creep up on you from the rear.

"When you can find one, buy a nice lady's scarf, the softest silk or lamb's wool you can find. That'll keep your neck from getting chafed.

"Pity there's no way to clamp a mirror somewhere on a beast's neck plate.

"Now you see what we face, and what you've got to learn.

"I'll sign you off for patrol – but only with an experienced flier, until he tells me you actually stand a chance of staying alive around here."

Chook was a large, jovial, nearly bald man, who claimed that his family owned the biggest – and, of course, the best – restaurant in Rozen, with a clientele of knights, dukes, even, once or twice, the king himself, "though he came in disguise, of course," plus a goodly contingent of the royal court's magicians.

No one knew if he was lying, but no one cared. Chook was

not only a superb cook, but could almost always make something close to edible out of the iron rations they mostly lived on these days.

He prided himself on his "beef in the grand tradition of Chook," which consisted of the smashed dried beef they were issued, the iron-hard crackers, powdered milk, and assorted liquids and spices from the huge wooden cabinet that was always kept locked.

It was this cabinet that'd made him into a hero. When the Roche cavalry attacked, he'd stayed in his mess tent, until four cavalrymen dismounted and, sabers ready, came looking for some food or drink to loot.

Chook told them to get out.

They laughed, started toward him.

The first two were bowled over by one of the long wooden benches he threw at them. The third slashed at the cook, who ducked around the stroke and hurled him against the glowing stove.

The fourth turned to run, and Chook threw, with unerring aim, the cleaver he used to behead any looted chickens. It buried itself, with a dull chunk, in the back of the man's head.

Miletus heard the sounds of sobbing, ran into the tent, saw the fourth corpse, the third man's head stuck into the open oven door, charring nicely, and the other two with ghastly saber wounds in their chests from their own blades.

Chook sat at a bench, crying bitterly.

If few were stupid enough to criticize his cooking before, for fear he'd throw a pot and lose his brilliance, no one at all dared after the slaughter.

"So what should I be most scared of?" Hal asked Aimard Quesney.

He raised an eyebrow almost as groomed as his mustaches.

"Odd for anyone to be owning to fear," he replied. "I thought we were all fearless knights of the air, and so on and so forth and I was the only one who . . ." And he broke into song:.

> "*There's a dragon leaving the border*
> *Limping its way toward its home*
> *With a shit-scared flier a-clinging*
> *With a grip that'd bruise to the bone.*"

He hiccuped, pushed the flagon of fairly decent wine at Hal, who shook his head.

"I'm on my first patrol tomorrow."

"Have a drink anyway," Aimard said. "Gods know I will." He swilled, ignoring his glass. "It's easier to die with a hangover. Besides, it gives you an excuse for drinking the next day."

The flight had a separate club/mess for the fliers, administered to by the legendary Chook. It was no more than a raggedy tent, with planed logs for benches, and a long bar their rather pathetic supply of alcohol sat behind. The canvas walls were pinned with cutouts from the broadsheets of Deraine and Sagene: sketches of beautiful ladies, pertinent letters, stories of society and such.

The best thing was that the mess was open around the clock, with either Chook or one of his assistants standing by.

"To be most afraid of," Quesney mused. "First, your own dragon, who'll be the most likely to kill you, chewing your leg off, or just dumping you off to see if you can walk on air like it can.

"Second, the weather closing in, and you getting lost in it, or blown into a mountain or forest.

"Third . . . leave third for a minute.

"Fourth, the Roche on the ground, with their catapults, crossbows and archers. If you're hit, try to steer your dragon as far away from the troops as you can, for they'll treat you most harshly should you fall into their hands.

"At least, try for some soldiers you haven't been spying on, and hope for their tender mercies.

"Fifth, our own soldiery, who'll be as quick to launch a bolt at you as the Roche. Perhaps, since we're losing, a bit more quickly.

"Sixth, our own command, who haven't the foggiest what a dragon's supposed to do, and so will punt us into the most unlikely places and situations.

"Now, to go back to third." Quesney paused.

"That, of course, is the enemy dragons."

"What will they do?" Hal asked.

"What they'll try to do is scare you away, back away from the lines and your scouting.

"If there's one in the vicinity, they might try to attack with one of their teams. That's if their dragons decide they want to attack you, which is very seldom.

"They'll try to tear you off your dragon, or tear at your dragon's wings and body, though that's rare enough. Generally they make great pains of themselves, and occasionally get lucky, and one of them'll be close enough to get in with that snaky head and have a bite of you."

"Has anybody thought of taking a magician up, and having him cast a spell against the Roche dragons?" Hal asked, thinking of some of the ideas in his notebook.

Quesney looked puzzled, shook his head.

"Doubt if you could find a wizard stupid enough to strap himself on the back of a dragon. And it'd take long enough to build a spell so that everyone concerned would be miles away by the time it swirls into life."

"What about an archer?"

"Never heard of such an idea. Can't imagine a bowman astute enough to be able to cling on, and aim while some nasty monster's hissing and snapping at him," Quesney said. "Why? Are you planning on starting a one-man war in the sky?"

Hal smiled, poured a glass of water.

"I don't like that idea," Quesney said. "Just flying's enough of a hazard.

"Start bringing in that kind of thing, and we'd be no better than those poor bastards down in the mud, now would we?"

Hal's stomach was roiling gently, but he had enough remove to think of laughing at himself. As a cavalryman, he'd led patrols into Roche territory a dozen, a hundred, who knew how many times?

But here he was, as his dragon climbed away from the flight's base, with Aimard Quesney to his left and, beyond him, Farren Mariah, on his first dragon patrol.

He determined he'd follow Miletus' suggestion, and kept his head moving, swiveling like his dragon's, who also seemed eager to spy something out.

The day was starting to warm, but there were huge thunderheads towering over the land. Quesney had said they were to fly east along the salient, toward where the lines had been before the Roche attack, until the weather broke, which it would, and then strike back for base.

Hal kept his reins loose, scanning the ground below. Nothing, for a long time, then movement. A column of infantry, heading away from the lines.

Hal jotted a note on the supposedly waterproof pad he had strapped to his knee.

Something moved at the corner of his eye, and he saw two dragons, not far distant, flying toward him.

They closed, and he saw, with relief, they were Deraine, passing no more than a hundred yards away, with a wave.

Hal's dragon, though, cared little about man's definitions, and hissed a loud challenge, which the evidently older and certainly wiser dragons ignored.

Smoke down below . . . He couldn't tell what it came from. But the plume was large enough to warrant a note.

The clouds were closing on them, and he kept glancing at Quesney, who seemed oblivious.

Far in the distance was a flight of three dragons. Quesney slid a glass out of his boot-top, focused, then lifted a small trumpet, and blatted two notes.

One, Aimard had said, meant return to base. Two was enemy in sight, other toots had other meanings.

So there were the Roche, perhaps half a mile distant, no, more, Hal thought, allowing for the rain-rich air's magnification.

Quesney waved an arm, pointed down, and Hal pulled his reins right, tapped them on the dragon's neck, and the beast's head lowered, and the three dove away from the enemy, who showed no sign of having seen them.

They landed at their base, handlers running out to meet them, just as the rain began.

In the next three days, Hal made five more patrols, finally being trusted with a solo mission. The other novices were cleared for patrol, and enough dragons were assigned so the flight was at full strength, at least in the air, and everyone had a monster of her or his own.

On the ground, the formation was still woefully undermanned: at full strength, a flight should have about eighty men. The fliers were at the top of the pyramid, below them two stablehands for each monster, teamsters, cooks, clerks, blacksmiths, orderlies, leathersmiths, veterinarians, and so forth. Hal wondered why there weren't any magicians assigned, and Miletus laughed hollowly. "I'm sure, eventually, we'll get them. As soon as every infantry and cavalry regiment have them, plus all headquarters, supply people and any other unit who's been around for 150 years or so."

Then the storm closed in on them.

So far, no one had died, and Hal had come the closest to Roche monsters.

No one thought this would continue.

Hal was going through his notebook, staring gloomily out at the driving rain.

Saslic curled on the back of his cot. Quesney snored gently on his own cot, mustaches waving.

"Hey," Saslic said. "Aren't you bored?"

"No," Kailas said. "Thinking."

"I am. You want to go have a beer?"

"Not especially."

"You want to go for a walk in the rain?"

"Why?"

"Fresh air's good for you. What're you thinking about, anyway?"

"Oh . . . crossbows . . . magicians . . . if there's any better way of passing on information than those stupid little trumpets. Things like that."

"Hmmph," Saslic said. "You're bound and determined to grow up to be a dragonmaster, aren't you?"

Hal grinned. "I haven't heard that word used since . . . since before the war. I don't know if it applies."

"Maybe it should," Saslic said. "Maybe if this godsdamned war drags on much longer, it'll come back."

"Meaning what?"

"Considering the way you seem to be thinking, somebody who's figured out a way to kill Roche dragons."

"Dragons," Hal said. "Maybe. Or maybe their fliers. A dragon without a mount isn't all that dangerous."

"Why are men so bloody-minded?" Saslic asked thin air. Receiving no answer, she got to her feet

"All right. Last offer. You want to go help me make up my bed?"

Hal lifted an eyebrow. Saslic giggled.

They pulled on their cloaks, and went out, into the storm.

Aimard Quesney opened one eye, grinned, then went back to snoring.

The weather broke for an hour, and Hal volunteered for a patrol. Miletus shook his head, muttered something about people too damned eager for a medal, and nobody else on the front would be in the air, but approved. Hal's dragon plodded through puddles, wings thrashing, then came clear of the ground.

By rights, Hal thought, a dragon base ought to be on a bluff somewhere, so the poor monsters didn't have to work that hard to get airborne. But in this sector there was little but rolling flatland for leagues around.

Hal circled the field, picking up height through scattered clouds, then turned his dragon toward the salient.

He was within a league of the lines when he snapped to full alert.

To his left, a flight of three Roche dragons. To his right, two more flights.

Something was very much afoot.

He could see no sign of any other Deraine beasts.

Ahead, he saw another three dragons climbing.

Hal thought quickly. Of course he couldn't proceed. But . . .

He had an idea, turned his dragon back the way he'd come, as if fleeing the watchful Roche, flew for the shelter of a cloud. Hidden, he dove for the ground, then banked back toward the salient. He flew no more than fifteen feet above the ground, his dragon's wings beating hard.

He climbed above trees, over abattis, tents, noted a Deraine flag near one pavilion, then was over broken ground.

Hal gigged his dragon for speed, and the beast's wings thrashed, like a ship's sails in a gale, and he was over the Roche positions, moving too fast for anything other than dimly heard shouts, and one arrow that missed by leagues.

A road junction was in front of him, and Hal's jaw dropped. The roads were packed with Roche troops, marching in close formation.

On another, parallel, rode columns of cavalry.

Below him, quartermaster wagons were being moved closer to the lines, unloaded for fresh supply dumps.

Their army was on the march.

He chanced overflying the junction, further into the salient, and every road, it seemed, had soldiers on the move.

The Roche must've used the break in fighting and the storm to rebuild their forces, and now were mounting an offense intended to end the deadlock, smash into open country, once and for all.

But no Deraine, evidently, had heard, seen or reported anything. No courier had come to the base with any reports of this . . .

Hal heard a screech, looked up and behind, saw a Roche flight, three huge monsters, diving on him. Their talons were reaching out for him, claws working in and out.

He jerked his dragon into a diving bank, turned back for his own lines, barely above spare treetops, his dragon flying as fast as its wings could beat.

Behind him, one dragon was closing fast, the other two hanging back, Hal's young beast having energy on the Roche brutes.

If there was some way of fighting back, Kailas thought, I'd let the bastard close, and try to take care of him.

But there was none, and the Roche flier was getting closer. His dragon was far bigger than Hal's, and he had a slight height advantage. Clearly his intent would be to savage Kailas as he overflew him, or else panic Hal's dragon into diving into the ground.

The two flashed over the lines, and Hal thought for an instant he was safe.

But the Roche must've known Hal had seen the troop movement, and must not be allowed to report.

The rain set in, drenching sheets, and Kailas hoped he could lose his pursuers in the gray dimness. But the Roche remained on his tail.

Long before they reached the base, Hal knew, at least that leading dragon would be on him.

There must be something . . .

Ahead, the ground rose to a stony hillside. Hal forced his dragon even lower, until the beast's talons were tearing across the scrub brush.

He looked back again, and the Roche flier was almost on him, having eyes only for his prey.

Hal forgot about him, saw two trees to his right, aimed his dragon at the gap between them, his monster screeching in unhappiness.

They shot through the gap, the dragon half-closing his wings, branches tearing, the dragon dipping, almost crashing, and Hal heard, behind him, an enormous crash.

The Roche flier hadn't been watching ahead, and his dragon had smashed into the trees, and pinwheeled, throwing its flier high into the air, arms flailing, trying to stay aloft, with no success.

The other two . . . The other two were far back, and Hal forgot about them, and went hard for his base.

The great hall of the half-ruined castle was silent, so quiet Hal could hear the patter of rain outside. Through a still-unshattered window, he could see couriers gallop in and out, wagons arrive, leave, marching men disappear out the gate.

It was the very model of an army headquarters.

There were seven men in the hall: Hal, Sir Lu Miletus, and three staff officers. Another wore a dark robe, breeches, and carried a magician's wand.

Standing behind a huge desk, easily dominating it, and the men around him, was the Third Army Commander, Duke Jaculus Gwithian. He was tall, perfectly white-haired, with a warrior's build. He wore dark brown, with a chain mail gorget. This far from the lines, it couldn't be for protection, more likely to remind everyone Duke Gwithian was a fighting leader. Complementing this was a low-slung leather belt, with a sheathed dagger with a jeweled handle.

His voice was a low, imposing rumble, full of certitude.

As far as Hal could tell, thus far on their first meeting, Duke Gwithian appeared to have less brains than a rabbit ensorcelled by a snake.

Frowning, he held a copy of Hal's report.

"I realize, Sir Lu," he said, "you place great trust in your . . . soldiers, which is a dictate of all commanders. However . . ."

Miletus waited, his face stone.

"What Duke Gwithian means, no doubt," one of the staff officers said, "is your man Kailas isn't the most experienced flier under your orders, isn't that correct?"

"I think any man who's flown that low, and seen what he saw doesn't need to have any more experience than a boarhound's pup to know what he's looking at," Miletus said, trying to keep his voice calm.

"Still," another staff officer added, "you must agree these circumstances are a bit . . . unusual. I mean, none of our wizards, none of our scouts, have reported such a move, and this young man sees . . . sees whatever he thinks he sees."

Hal, perhaps a year older than the staff officer, held his temper with difficulty.

"That is one worrisome point," Duke Gwithian agreed. "Certainly, I have the most powerful wizards, ones I cannot believe the Roche can flummox. Correct, Warleggan?"

The mage nodded frostily. He was slim to the point of emaciation, and his clean-shaven face appeared never to have smiled.

"I am hardly the one to agree with you, Duke Gwithian, not being given to vainglory. However, I do think that myself, and my more than competent aides, would certainly have detected signs, traces, of any spell the Roche thaumaturges could be working, and certainly a great spell such as this one would leave vast traces."

There was an uncomfortable silence, broken by Miletus.

"Sir Oubang," he said to the officer who hadn't spoken, "you specialize in analyzing the information from our scouts."

"I do."

"Has nothing been reported by our light cavalry?"

"Well, this is the one thing that troubles me slightly," the small, stout man said. "Actually, over the last two days, our scouting has been most minimal, due to a combination of circumstances.

"We've been shifting our light cavalry to the tip of the salient, expecting an eventual attack by the Roche. Other units have been relocated to the base of the salient, getting ready for . . . well, for an action of ours that should solve our current problems that I'm not at liberty to discuss the details of.

"So, contrary to what Sir Cotehele said, we really haven't had what I'd call a truly effective scouting screen out beyond the lines for over a week."

"Be that as it may," Cotehele said, a bit of anger in his voice, "I find it utterly impossible that no one, no one except this . . ." He didn't finish, but his look made it obvious what he thought of dragon fliers in particular, and Hal Kailas in particular. "This man, saw.

"There is, after all, such a thing as logic, is there not?"

"In war?" Miletus' voice dripped incredulity.

"Now, now, gentlemen," Duke Gwithian said soothingly. "Let's not let ourselves get worked up.

"This young man risked his life to make a report. I commend him for it. And we shall take this information under advisement, and assign the correct value to it.

"Sir Lu . . . and you, Serjeant Kallas, was it? I thank you for doing what you conceived as your duty.

"Be sure to avail yourselves of a good meal before you leave my headquarters.

"A meal . . ." And he looked at the two fliers' weather-worn garb. "And, if you feel there is time before returning to your – what is it, squadron? No, flight, that's it – making proper ablutions and drawing less shabby uniforms.

"Thank you."

Without waiting for the salute, Duke Gwithian walked out through a side door.

Hal was seething as he followed Miletus out of the hall.

"He didn't believe us, did he, sir?"

"Of course not," Miletus said. "He wouldn't've believed just you if you'd come back with a Roche prince's head on your dragon's headspike."

"So what are we going to do?"

"Eat his godsdamned meal – fast – and get our arses back to the flight," Miletus said grimly. "And get ready for the Roche attack."

12

Miletus gave his orders to the flight most cagily. He told them to be ready to move with an hour's notice, not saying which direction they might be moving. Of course most of the fliers, having heard Hal's report of the Roche on the move, assumed the worst.

Miletus made sure all the troops had their weaponry sharpened and ready for use, inspecting them in sections.

Nothing happened in the tag end of that day, and the weather stayed bad the next.

"Hard telling," Miletus said at nightfall, "whether the rain's been encouraged by Roche sorcerers or not. It keeps their movement cloaked, but it can't make their progress any easier.

"We'll go to half alert for the night. You fliers, you're exempt. It's not unlikely you'll be needed soon enough."

*

Hal woke well before dawn, hearing a sound like thunder, but somehow different, more like a series of great drumrolls. It came from the south, from the salient.

Faintly, he heard the sound of a wind roaring.

Few of the flight members needed awakening.

Chook and his assistants readied a hasty breakfast of bacon, fried bread and tea, and Miletus ordered the men and women to the cooktent in shifts.

But nothing happened for a time, no one disturbed their isolated camp. The sun came up, blearily, through haze. No couriers with orders rode down the single road that led away from the front.

Miletus had the fliers standing by their dragons, ready for anything.

It was mid morning when a pair of riders bulled through the brush past the pond and through the meadow. Their horses were slathered, panting, and the men were wild-eyed, and had thrown away their arms.

"They're attacking . . . they've broken through . . . magic . . . their damn wizards had an infernal spell . . . no warning . . . they're just behind us . . . ride for your lives!"

Miletus tried to stop them, but they galloped around him, and were gone.

He hesitated, then ordered the unit into motion. "There's but one road away from here, and we'll not be bottled up."

He looked at Hal.

"If I'm wrong, I hope you'll be a character witness at my court martial."

Before Kailas could answer, Miletus ordered all dragons into the air, scouting ahead of the flight's wagons and horses. He had his own beast chained to its wagon, and stayed on the ground with the soldiery.

Slowly, terribly slowly, the flight started moving. They were held back not only by the nearly ruined road, but by the herd of sheep being driven in the middle of the flight, the dragons' rations.

Hal saw a rider galloping hard toward the flight. The rider pulled up in front of Miletus, hands waving for a few moments. Then he wheeled his horse, and splashed back the way he'd come.

Miletus's trumpet blatted, and the fliers circled, landed in an open patch.

"The Roche have broken through our lines," Miletus said. "They're supposedly coming north, toward us. That rider ordered us to scout south, to try and evaluate the damage."

He looked to his non-flying adjutant.

"Eitner, take charge of the formation. Keep them moving as far as the main north-south road, then wait for us to return. If you're threatened, retreat north, and we'll find you somewhere."

"Sir."

"All dragons in the air! Scout separately, don't take any more risks than you must. Reassemble at that crossroads," Miletus ordered, then ran for the wagon with his dragon. His handlers were already unchaining the creature.

In ragged formation, spreading out as they flew, the dragons flapped south, climbing as they went.

First they came on the retreat – mounted men, riding hard for the north and safety. The roads were no better than cart-tracks, and were jammed with fleeing men. After the riders came wagons, then men on foot.

It was ugly. Soldiers weren't supposed to run like civilians. But the Third Army, and its attached units, were in full retreat.

Hal wondered what horror could have panicked an entire army, then saw it.

A thin greenish cloud was spreading slowly north, holding close to the ground, no more than fifty feet in the air.

Again he heard the rolling thunder, and the whistle of wind, even though none blew.

Something told Hal not to get close to the cloud.

He pulled his reins and the dragon climbed.

Hal looked down again, and saw, in the wake of the cloud, bodies of horses, men, oxen, lying motionless.

Behind the ghastly cloud came the Roche army. Flights of dragons, more than Hal could imagine, floated in front of the waves of cavalry, infantry behind them.

He'd seen enough, and turned his dragon back, over the panic, to the road junction Miletus had designated as the assembly point.

Other dragons from his flight were making the same track.

Hal spotted the flight, drawn up near the crossroads, which was a roiling chaos of units, groups of soldiers, single men, all fighting to get on that road north, north to Frechin, Bedarisi, safety.

He landed, and found Eitner. With him were two couriers.

He made his report as the other fliers streamed in, all with bad news.

Eitner also had some unpleasantries to pass along, learned from passing officers and one near-hysterical magician.

The Roche wizards had cast more than the great spell that'd masked their soldiers' movement to the lines. They had another spell, the one accompanied by the wind-whine and thunder. Eitner'd talked to men who'd paused in their flight long enough to tell him what it was like: suddenly the air had gone bad, not hard to breath, but as if all the goodness that gave life had gone out of it, even as it hazed into the ghastly green.

The green haze killed anyone and anything that lingered for more than a few minutes.

The fliers looked at each other, hoping she or he didn't look as frightened us the other.

"Be wonders if the spell'd work just on m'lice," Farren joked feebly, and no one bothered to respond.

"All right," Miletus ordered. "You, courier. Take the word back to your headquarters. You, stay with us. No. Get your ass out to the road, and grab anyone who's got a good mount and isn't completely crazy, and tell them they're drafted to carry messages for me.

"You fliers, get back in the air. Keep scouting the Roche progress."

"What about that cloud?"

"Just hope to hells our magicians come up with a counterspell, and keep away from it.

"I'll stay with the flight down here," he said. "I don't have any orders, but we'll do no one any good fighting as a rear guard. We'll try to bash our way into this column, and move north.

"I'll have men paint arrows on the wagon tops so you'll be able to find us. Stay up no more than an hour at a time. Scout away from the roads for abandoned animals, for your dragons, and make sure they're watered.

"Rest them before you take off again, and reassemble before dark."

He stopped, realizing he was caught up by the panic a bit himself if he was telling the fliers what every stablehand knew.

"Get gone," he said.

They flew back and forth all that long day, giving the reports of disaster, of broken, wiped out, decimated units, and the seemingly unstoppable Roche offensive to Miletus, who scrounged riders here and there, gave them dispatches for army headquarters. They rode off, and no one ever knew if they obeyed orders, or just continued their flight.

The Deraine and Sagene forces lost their blind panic, but continued retreating, and the Roche army kept after them.

The sodden roads, further torn by the retreating soldiers, slowed them some.

There were rumors to fuel the flight – this attack was personally led by Duke Garcao Yasin, that Queen Norcia was with her retinue with his headquarters.

That may have frightened some, but Kailas remembered Yasin's failure once before. He wondered if Yasin's brother was on the battlefield with some dragons, vaguely wanted to find him. But without any weapons, other than the instinctual ones of his beast, any encounter was more likely to result in Hal's destruction than anything else.

Eventually the day ended, and Hal found the flight, hasty-camped near the road, still filled with soldiers tramping steadily toward Frechin.

The next day, they retreated through Frechin. By now, the city was almost deserted, most of its inhabitants having fled before the rumored horrors of the Roche cavalry and their dragons.

On the other side of the city, Hal, flying very high, high enough to feel a bit dizzy in the thin air, looked back and down, saw Roche dragons swarming in the air as their army continued its advance.

"I think," Aimard Quesney said, tugging at his mustache, "our Rochey friends have stepped upon their fundament."

"Right," Mariah said. "They're comin' on, we're haulin' ass. Surefire screw-up there."

Half of the fliers were crouched around a dying fire, too worked up, too tired, for sleep.

"Shut up, Farren," Saslic said. "Make me feel better, Aimard."

"Well, this probably won't make *you* – or any of the rest of us – feel better."

"I do love your abstract wisdom," Sir Loren said wryly.

"Any wisdom these days is better'n none," Mynta Gart said.

"Would you people shut up and let him explain," Hal said. "I, for one, could use anything cheery, whether it's about me or the King of Deraine."

"Thank you, Serjeant Kailas. The Roche have come a cropper, as I was saying," Quesney said. "Now, this offensive of theirs is intended to win the war, correct?"

"An' here I went an' thought it were just a spring fancy," Farren said.

"The best way to do serious damage would be to make for Fovant. Once Sagene's capital falls, what're the odds their Council of Barons wouldn't sue for peace, together or separately?"

"No kidding," Saslic said. "That's what we were told is why they invaded Sagene in the first place, which brought all us down here."

"Oh," Hal said. "Of course. I got it."

"There's one other great mind among us besides myself," Quesney said smugly. "You may finish my thought, Serjeant."

"If they began the battle, opening the salient," Hal said slowly, "then they *were* going for Fovant. But then, with this new attack, their warlord – Yasin, or whoever it is – has lost sight of what he started out to do, and is chasing us around the country, instead of heading east like he should."

"Precisely," Quesney said. "Perhaps he's lost his head with all the destruction . . . Or, more likely, his queen changed orders on him.

"In either event," he said, stretching and yawning, "we'll most likely get obliterated. But Roche just lost the chance to win the war."

He disappeared toward his bedroll.

"What a *cheerful* man he is," Mynta Gart said sarcastically. "He'll make my dreams this night ever so lovely."

"I'll make them worse," Sir Loren said. "The Roche have learned something we haven't. When this war started, it was wham, a battle, then people regrouped, reformed, looked around, and then wham, another battle.

"Now they're keeping up the offensive, never really letting up.

"We'd better learn to do the same, pretty damned quickly."

Now the Roche unleashed yet another weapon.

Small groups of Roche infantry suddenly materialized here and there in the rear. There were mutters of magic, then Hal saw

two dragons, flying close together, with something hanging
between them.

He remembered the Roche flying show, before the war, in
Bedarisi, and their stunting with soldiers, riding in baskets strung
between two dragons, then giving rides.

An idea came, and he flew back to the flight, in the middle of
the ponderous retreat.

He landed, found Miletus, told him.

"*Damn,* but I wish I had more rank," Miletus said. "I'd grab
some smithy unit, and set them to fabricating . . . But I don't, so
I can't. But I'll send men back to that village we just passed
through. That temple had iron gates on it, that should work.
Our smiths can shape the metal this night, and we'll give your
idea a try on the morrow."

By sunrise, all fifteen dragons were equipped. The wrought-iron
gates had been cut into pieces, and each section bent into a hook.
Three hooks were brazed together into a grapnel. Ropes were
requisitioned from a retreating quartermaster unit, and harnesses
improvised. Slings hung from each dragon's neck and hindquarters, the hook at their bottom, hanging about twenty feet below
each beast.

The dragons didn't object too much to this latest weirdness
from their masters, snorting and hissing no more angrily than
usual in the dawn grayness.

Miletus gave the flight its orders, told them he'd give the word
for takeoff when he sighted some of the Roche dragon-trans-
ports, and took off.

Vad Feccia came to Hal, said his dragon wasn't behaving
properly, and perhaps he ought to stand down.

Hal told him to get back to his mount.

Asser looked at him with a wry face, quickly looked away.

They ate buttered bread and cheese, cut from a great wheel
Chook had liberated, waited. An hour after sunrise, Miletus flew
overhead, trumpet blasting.

They mounted their beasts, kicked them into a stumbling run,
and were in the air, following Sir Lu back toward Frechin, hooks
cradled behind them.

They'd only flown a few minutes when they sighted pairs of
dragons, twenty of them, soldier-carrying baskets between
them.

Hal forgot the others, tossed his grapnel overside and steered his dragon toward one pair. His monster honked protest for an instant, then screeched a challenge as his courage grew.

Hal closed fast on the pair. One beast was looking up at Hal, head whipping, the other was looking down, ready to flee. Their riders were shouting, kicking their mounts, and Hal steered his dragon just over their heads, going in the opposite direction.

His dragon jerked as the grapnel caught on one of the basket's support lines and tore it away.

The paired dragons banked away from each other, terrified, and the basket spilled soldiery, falling, flailing, to the ground 500 feet below.

Hal came back, tore at another dragon pair. These two held together, diving for the ground, and he let them go, climbing back for another target.

He ripped at a third, and this time his rope broke and he lost his grapnel as the Roche basket broke away from its dragons, and plummeted down.

Saslic's dragon, Nont, flashed past him, and he heard her yelling, face fierce in anger. Behind her came Sir Loren, his grapnel half awry, but still after the Roche beasts.

Hal forced his dragon up, reaching for height above the shattered Roche formation. He saw, in the distance, on-rushing dragons in threes, which could only be Roche.

He turned to meet them, hoping, without a grapnel, to give the others a chance to wreak further damage.

Then they were on him, shouting, dragons hissing, each trying to terrify the other, and the air was a swirling mass of monsters.

There was a dragon turning, just above him, its head darting. He leaned away, and it missed, tried to grab his mount's neck in its fangs, talons ripping at the air, reaching for Hal.

Hal had his dagger out, and thrust hard. It went home in the beast's eye, and it screamed deafeningly, rolled, dumping its rider, who fell, endlessly.

Then he was in empty sky, looked back, saw the Roche dragon-carriers and the other Roche monsters in the distance, no signs of his own flight.

Hal dove for the ground, found the main road, and followed it back to his flight.

There was jubilation – they'd finally found a way to strike back at the beasts.

"Now, let's find a way to kill the damned riders and leave the beasts alone," Saslic said. "They don't deserve what we're dealing out to them, any more than the poor damned horses deserve that green horror."

"I'm thinking about it," Hal said. "And I've got some ideas, if this war would slow down for a little and give me a chance to work them out."

There was one man separate from the others – Vad Feccia. He claimed his dragon was sick, unflyable. Hal noted that, put it aside for later.

There was one man missing – Asser. No one had seen him after they'd taken off that morning, and he was never seen again by the army. Hal didn't know if he'd been killed in the fight, or, more likely, if he'd flown north toward Paestum, toward safety as far as he could, then melted into the crowd and made it across the Straits to Deraine. He guessed he wasn't much as a hard man, for he sort of wished Asser luck.

Twice more that day Miletus sent them against the soldier-carriers. Once they tore a formation apart, the survivors flying back at full speed. The second time the dragon-carriers were escorted by thirty Roche dragons, and Hal's flight couldn't attack.

They were fighting back – but the retreat went on, to Bedarisi.

Bedarisi was an even bigger nightmare than Frechin, units on top of other units, soldiers looking for their fellows, others trying to avoid rejoining a fighting formation, bewildered civilians, officers without commands bawling orders, and always the walking wounded, staggering, looking for a chiurgeon or a wizard to treat them, forcing themselves to keep moving, afraid of what the Roche would do if they captured them.

Everyone was terrified the Roche would bring that greenish fog down once more, but it didn't materialize. Perhaps the Deraine sorcerers *had* found a counterspell.

It was bad enough that the Roche dragons were flying close to the city, and the suburbs were being harried by Roche light cavalry.

Hal remembered a ring road from before the war, led the unit around the city and found a place to set the flight up. Chook and his helpers went looking for a ration point or foodstuffs to buy or steal, and Miletus rode into the city center, looking for Third Army headquarters.

He came back in a few hours, looking very grim.

He'd not found Duke Gwithian's headquarters, but had encountered a lord who was somewhat in authority.

That nobleman had brayed that the army wouldn't need spies or fliers, but only men with swords, and for the flight to leave its dragons and work its way to the front lines forming before the city, and become infantrymen.

Ev Larnell was gray-faced, obviously sure he would never cheat the death he'd avoided.

"Damme," Farren said softly, "wot a waste of all that trainin'. Not to mention some pretty good folks as well."

13

"The Roche are expected to attack before dark," Miletus said. "Every man who can fight is to be on the lines."

He was about to continue when Rai Garadice gasped, and pointed. Everyone turned.

Smoke coiled above Bedarisi, and Hal thought for an instant the Roche killing fog was about to strike. But the smoke firmed, and became the huge figure of a man, armored, sword in hand, but helmetless.

Kailas recognized him. It was Duke Jaculus Gwithian, the Third Army Commander, the man who'd refused to admit the Roche were on the attack, standing more than 300 feet tall, noble, warlike, awe-striking.

He lifted his sword, pointed it south, and spoke, his voice a rumble that shook the ground, or so Hal thought.

"Soldiers of the king! I call on you in this most desperate hour. The enemy has driven us back, but from this hour, this minute, we shall retreat no more.

"I order you as soldiers, and also you of Sagene who fight alongside us. This shall be our finest hour.

"Here we will make our final stand. Not one man, not one woman shall fall back, shall flee.

"We call upon our courage, our gods, our heritage as free men and women to fight to the last man.

"This battle, shall Deraine and Sagene live on for an aeon, will be looked back by those who come after us with awe, and give inspiration for a thousand generations.

"Here we stood, moving back not one yard, not one inch, fighting for our king and, uh, our barons.

"Here we shall stand, like a rock against the tide, firm, to the last man.

"Here, in Bedarisi, a new legend is being born, a legend of—"

Suddenly the figure writhed, and changed, and became a rooster wearing armor, who crowed loudly.

Then the image changed once more, and was a Roche warrior, who looked down at Bedarisi, and began laughing, a grating, ominous laugh.

And then there was nothing.

"Dunno," Farren said skeptically, "what *that* was supposed t' do for my morale."

"That isn't important," Sir Loren said. "We've just got our marching orders . . . or, rather, our dying orders.

"We fight – and die – where we stand."

A few minutes later, they dimly heard the chortle of trumpets, and knew battle was closed.

"I suppose," Saslic said, rather weakly, "we'd best be going forward as Roche fodder."

"Or else runnin'," Farren said, pointing down at the road, where soldiers continued to trail past, "like those, who've gone an' decided they'll go for home and make those other gen'rations the image was talkin' about, to tell them about us."

"There's something we could try that might be a little better than a suicide stand with a sword," Hal said, surprising himself, for his ideas weren't quite formed.

"Anything's better than dying in the muck," Ev Larnell said.

"Agreed," Miletus said. "What do we need?"

"Fifteen brave men . . . or fifteen fools."

"Goin' beyont us fools?" Farren said.

"Sir, if you'll go with me out to the road," Hal said. "We'll go fishing."

"What am I for?" Miletus said, half smiling.

"To give me a little authority."

"After you . . . Serjeant."

It only took half an hour to find the prospective heroes.

There were thirty of them, crossbowmen, shambling along, beaten, with no officers at their head. But Hal, who'd let a group of archers and another of catapult men pass, since they were unarmed, noted that these thirty still had their bows in hand, and bolts in their quivers.

Men who're broken don't bother, generally, worrying about their arms.

"You men," Miletus called at Hal's nudge. "Form up over here."

A few lifted their heads, studied Miletus, looked back at the road.

"I said, over here!" Miletus shouted, and there was a hard snap to his voice.

The thirty came to a scuffling halt. The man at the head of the group was huge, mightily muscled with a gut to match.

"Who're you to order us . . . sir?"

"We need you," Hal said. "To fight. With us."

"Haw." The man spat. "We're done fightin'. Mebbe Paestum's worth fighting for, more likely Deraine, on our own ground."

"Not here, against dragons like you appear to be flying, and the Roche's damned magic, and Sagenies who won't stand up for themselves."

Hal ignored him, but unobtrusively took something from his belt pouch and held it in his fist.

"I need fifteen of you," he continued, "who aren't afraid to fly on – and fight from – the back of a dragon."

Utter silence, except for the shuffle of other soldiers moving steadily past. Then somebody catcalled, and somebody else laughed harshly. But Hal had seen a couple of men shed their fatigue, straighten, and look slightly interested. Very slightly interested.

"Fifteen men," Hal said again. "Who wouldn't mind taking down some Roche fliers."

The big man sneered.

"You want us to go up on them beasts, what, riding behind, and do what? I ain't had shit to do with dragons, but I'll wager they take more than one shitty little bolt to kill."

"I didn't say anything about dragons," Hal said. "We're going after their fliers."

A man, lean, with an intelligent look on his face stepped forward.

"Somebody just came up with this idea," he said. "Nobody ever thought about it before? You'd think *someone* would've tried it, and got himself killed. Or, more likely, some other people killed. Which might make you think this idea isn't all that great from the outset."

"This is the army, remember?" Hal said. "They barely admit to having dragons, let alone how to use them. And since when is any army quick with new ideas?"

That got a few smiles.

"Aw, sod off," the big man said. "I'm not about to get kilt followin' your foolishness, nor am I gonna let any of my friends get et up by monsters.

"Let's go, people. We're moving on."

"Stand where you are," Miletus said. "That's an order. You're still in the army!"

"Naw. Naw, I ain't. Call it uni . . . uni . . . whatever resignation."

"I gave you an order, man."

"And I told you to sod off," the big man said. "If you're hard of hearing, try this."

He started to pull the long sword at his side from its sheath. Hal stepped forward, and snapped a punch into the man's stomach.

The man's sour breath gushed out, and he stumbled forward and threw up. He fought for air, couldn't find it, and fell on his knees, then, moaning, on his face in the dust.

"Toss him on that bank," Hal ordered, picking up the sword, and putting his hand back into his pouch for an instant. "You, and you. I'll not trust a man like him at my back, on a dragon or in a brawl."

He indicated two men, who'd been fingering their crossbows.

"Now, fifteen of you," he went on. "Volunteers. We'll do it the army way. You men there . . . and you four . . . and you two. You just volunteered. The rest of you little boys can keep right on running."

He turned his back, and started back toward the flight. After a dozen yards, he looked back. A bit to his astonishment the fifteen, plus another three, were straggling at his heels.

Hal looked at Miletus beside him, and grinned.

"Not bad, Serjeant," Miletus said. "You're not a bad leader . . . or fighter, either. One punch! That was one enormous bruiser."

"It doesn't hurt," Hal said, "to have a bit of an equalizer." He reached in his pouch again, showed Miletus the paper-wrapped roll of coins that'd been hidden in his fist.

*

"You ever flown before?" Hal asked the intelligent-looking man.

"No, Serjeant," the man said, looking around curiously from his perch behind the dragon's shoulders on a hastily-improvised saddle. Other crossbowmen were being helped to mount as well. "Thought about going for a ride a couple of times, before the war, when a show'd come to our district. But either I didn't have the coin, or the courage, or enough drink, or, once, the head of the school I was teaching at heard I was thinking about it, and forbade it.

"Said that wouldn't be a good example for my students."

He looked at his ragged uniform, sword-belt, and crossbow across his knees.

"As if this is."

"The name's Kailas. Or Hal. Forget the serjeant. You?"

"Hachir."

"That's a good upcountry name."

Hachir grinned.

"Here's what we're intending," Hal said, although he'd already lectured the drafted crossbowmen, as he hoped each flier was doing to his assigned soldier. "First, you *can't* fall."

The man fingered the ropes that held him securely in place, nodded.

"Keep hold of your bolts, though. Without them, you might as well be riding for joy. Now, have you the strength to recock your bow after each shot?"

"I do," Hachir said. "Assuming I can get a foot in the stirrup, and I'm not being thrown about."

"Good." Hal made a mental note for something to try at another time.

"What we're going to do is simple," Hal said, sounding very confident. He'd learned that with his serjeant's stripes, remembering the number of times his patrol had been utterly lost, yet he'd reassured his fellow riders that they were in exactly the place they were supposed to be.

"I'm going to find some Roche dragons. I'll get as close as I can, and you take a shot. Try and hit the rider in the body. About the only place that'd be vulnerable on a dragon with your crossbow would be under the wing, right where it joins the body, or between the bellyplates, and that'd take, I think, a very sure aim."

"I'm not a bad shot," Hachir said, without boasting. "But I'll aim as you say."

He looked about him once more.

"The woman I'm affianced to will never believe this, and most likely whip me like a dog for making even more of a fool of myself than I did joining up."

Hal laughed, climbed up into his seat, and picked up the dragon's reins.

"Let's go see if we can change the way the war's going, just a little."

Miletus motioned Hal to take the formation lead as they circled over their wagons below. "Since you seem to have all the ideas today," he shouted when their two dragons came close.

Hal waved acknowledgement, shouted back to Hachir, "We'll try to get on top of the Roche before we attack them. Maybe that'll give us surprise."

The crossbowman grunted. Hal glanced back, afraid the man was getting sick, saw he was staring about him, wide-eyed, entranced, reminding Kailas of his first flight with Athelny.

He hoped that was a sign everything would be all right.

Just south of Bedarisi was a throng of dragons, too many to be from Deraine or Sagene. They paid little attention to the tiny formation of dragons a few miles distant, especially as the Deraine monsters appeared to have no interest except possibly flying into the sun.

The Roche dragons were intent on the battle being waged below, lines of infantry crashing together down blocked streets and through ruined buildings, and, to the east, the twisting mêlée of a cavalry fight.

Hal and his flight were a thousand feet above the Roche.

Hal signaled, pulled reins, and his dragon began a long, slanting dive toward the enemy. Behind him streamed the others. This time, even Vad Feccia hadn't backed out.

"Get ready," Hal said, and felt Hachir stir about behind him.

He bent over his dragon.

"That one, that one," he said in a croon, stroking the monster's neck, pulling the reins with his other hand until the dragon was looking at a beast circling at the edge of the Roche formation.

The creature seemed to understand what Hal intended, wings clattering as it turned, flying faster, closing on the Roche.

The rider saw Hal's onrushing dragon, and his eyes widened.

"Shoot!" Hal called, and the crossbow thwacked. The

bolt went just wide of the rider, ricocheting off the dragon's carapace.

"Shit!" Hachir shouted.

"Forget it! Try again!" Hal shouted, pulling the reins, finding another target, closing, wondering if his idea was that great.

"Now!" he shouted, wishing he had the crossbow in his own hands.

Once more, the bow fired, and this time the bolt buried itself in the rider's back. Hal heard him scream, saw him contort, fling himself backward, off the dragon.

"Again," Hal shouted, feeling a fierce grin across his face, and there was a dragon above them, its rider peering down. The crossbow fired, and the man clawed at his throat, collapsed across his mount's neck.

Hal saw a shadow, and reflexively snapped his reins, and his dragon dove, just as an enormous brute whipped past, talons clawing at Hal's dragon's wing.

"Godsdammit!" Hachir shouted, but Hal paid no mind, yanking his dragon into a tight, climbing turn.

"At his guts!"

Hachir pulled the trigger, and his bolt thunked home in the Roche dragon's side. The monster screamed, impossibly loudly, whipped on its back, talons clawing at the wound. Hal saw the rider hanging by his reins below the dragon's head, then the man lost his hold, and fell.

Hal forgot him, and looked for another dragon rider to kill.

He saw Ev Larnell's dragon, pursued by two Roche beasts. He slapped his dragon's reins, trying to go to the rescue, but his dragon was closing slowly, too slowly.

A Roche dragon had a bit of height on Larnell, tucked its wings, and dove. Hal thought it would ram Larnell, but it passed just above him.

A talon reached out, almost casually, took Larnell's head in its grasp, and tore it off.

Larnell's corpse sprayed blood like a fountain, and his dragon squealed in fear, dove away. The crossbowman behind him sat petrified, making no move to reach for the reins, and then the dragon was gone, far below.

There was nothing around Kailas but his fellows.

The Roche dragons were fleeing south, in a ragged mess.

Hal took his flight down, across the battleground, saw, on a knoll, the colors of Deraine and a handful of dismounted knights fighting desperately around the rallying point. Roche soldiers swarmed about the knoll.

There was nothing Hal could do except go back to the flight, get more bolts, and look for more dragons.

He couldn't tell what was happening on the ground below, who might be winning.

Hal looked for that knoll when he was airborne once more, couldn't be sure he found the right one, since there was nothing but high-piled bodies.

At dusk, he landed, dazed with fatigue, mourning Larnell, wondering if he'd still be alive if Hal had exposed him on that long ago day.

But the fliers had learned their lesson about how to mourn their dead.

Chook had found a flagon of brandy, and they, and their crossbowmen, toasted Larnell's memory.

And then they forgot him.

Hal and Hachir had killed five dragons or their riders that day.

The flight had taken out sixteen Roche beasts. Saslic had taken out three, as had Sir Loren. Rai Garadice had accounted for two.

By their last flight, no Roche dragons were in the air.

But that mattered little, at least at the moment. He asked of the battle, the real battle, down on the ground.

Deraine had held the Roche, driven them back slightly.

Duke Jaculus Gwithian, and his staff, were among the knights who stood their ground to the last man, neither asking nor giving quarter.

He may have been a dumb bastard, Hal thought. But he was surely a brave dumb bastard.

Aimard Quesney was sitting near the dragon lines, away from the others that night. Hal brought him a plate of food. He took it, set it down untasted.

"And so you've got what you wanted," Quesney said. His voice was flat, not pleased, not angry. "You've got your war and your killing.

"Be proud, Kailas. Be very proud. We've bloodied the land and the water, and now you're the first to take it to the skies."

Without waiting for a response, he walked away, into the darkness.

*

They were in the air at dawn the next day. Again, Miletus, even though he commanded the flight, let Hal control the fighting.

It didn't matter to Kailas – the situation was so desperate nothing mattered except killing Roche.

Again, the battle on the ground was mounted, and again Deraine held.

On the next morning, before the two sides could stumble together and hew away in exhaustion, they heard trumpets from the south and east.

This time the flight's mission was its original – to scout the land.

To the east, they found, proud in its finery, freshness and armor, a massed Sagene army. They barely had time to report the miracle before the Sagene smashed into the unprotected Roche flank.

They were the army that'd been assembled to defend Sagene's capital of Fovant, and the Roche attack on the Deraine soldiers had given them time to march east, and strike where they weren't expected.

The Roche fell back, across the wasteland their soldiers and green mist had created. But they didn't break, as the Deraine soldiers had, but fought stubbornly from hilltop to ravine to draw, killing one Deraine here, half a dozen Sagene there.

But they were pushed all the way back through that bloody summer, back across the border, and several miles into Roche territory.

Deraine and Sagene disengaged, numbly prepared fighting positions, and then collapsed in total exhaustion.

No one knew how many men died in the brutal series of battles. Some said half a million, others said a million, others even more.

"Serjeant Kailas," Miletus said. Hal was helping his hands groom his dragon. Hachir, still with the flight as were the other thirteen crossbowmen, was also helping.

"Sir?"

"I've got orders for you."

Hal waited.

"Since the crisis appears over, you, and six others – Dinapur, Feccia, Garadice, Gart, Mariah, Sir Loren, are reassigned."

"Where?"

"Back where you were supposed to have gone in the first place. The First Army," Miletus said. "Around Paestum."

That was what Hal had wanted, but he was just too tired to celebrate.

"I'll be sorry to leave you, sir," he said, telling the truth.

"Don't be," Miletus said. "Those bastards across the line're too tired to do anything for awhile. Things will be nice and quiet in these parts, and we can recover and maybe think about getting drunk and laid.

"Up north, where you're going, things are just starting to get interesting.

"I've sent dispatches to whatever Lord High Plunk will take over the Third Army about what you did . . . about your ideas.

"And I'm giving you a sealed dispatch, for your new Commander at the First Army, with the same details. Maybe he'll give you a medal, or make you a knight, or even give you a free drunk in Paestum.

"As for leaving us . . . we'll run into each other again, down the road.

"If we live.

"It's looking to be a *very* long war."

14

Again, Paestum had changed, becoming more and more a smooth-running machine to process troops toward the front and, as a byprocess, to relieve them of as much money as possible.

Hal was the ranking warrant of the seven fliers, still with the rank he'd had with the light cavalry. He'd wondered a time or two why no dragon flier ever seemed to get promoted. But he'd learned that if the army had a reason for doing what it did, it seldom chose to share its wisdom with the lower ranks.

Hal's orders read for the seven to report to the Eleventh Dragon Flight. He asked a provost, got instructions to its camp, two leagues west of the city.

All of them were heavy-pursed – there hadn't been much to

buy during the retreat and battles. But none seemed in the mood for revel, still tired from the fighting, and Hal didn't think his new commander would be entranced if a warrant decided to stop the war so his charges could get seduced and drunk.

He was very right.

The Eleventh Flight had commandeered a sprawling farm, almost a manor. Most of the buildings were cheery red brick, and the grounds were neat if overgrown, although the land had been fought through during the siege of Paestum, and there were still shattered remnants of outbuildings here and there.

It looked very peaceful in the summer sun.

Hal smiled when he heard the screech of a dragon from behind the manor house, answered by one of their dragons on the wagons.

But his smile vanished, seeing a formation of soldiers marching back and forth to the chant of an iron-lunged warrant.

"Drill," Farren said as he might have mentioned slow torture. "Drill, here?"

"Maybe," Saslic said, from her seat behind the wagon's driver, "maybe those are guards for the flight."

"Maybe," Farren said. "Or, more likely, we've fallen into the clutches of a martynet, who thinks the war's to be won by square-bashint."

Captain Sir Fot Dewlish dabbed delicately at his nose with a handkerchief that, Hal decided, was probably starched and ironed.

Sir Fot was a very dapper officer. His uniform had clearly been tailored, and equally clearly had never seen a muddy battlefield, any more than Sir Fot had.

He sat, very calm, very much at ease, at a desk that wasn't sullied with paper. Dewlish was about to say something when a clock gonged.

Both men turned to look at it. The clock was a bronze monstrosity of a dragon, holding a world in one claw, a clock in the other. It had been carefully painted in exact colors.

"That's our mascot," Dewlish explained. "The lower ranks quite revere him, and call him Bion."

Hal made a vaguely understanding noise. He rather wished there was a dragon on Dewlish's chest, indicating he was also a flier, instead of on the mantel.

"To continue," Dewlish said. "I cannot say, to be truthful,

I'm much impressed by your, or your fellows', appearance. I've always heard that some of the dragon flights permit their fliers to go around looking scruffy, and now believe it."

"There weren't a lot of tailors where we were, sir."

"Do not be impertinent!" Dewlish snapped. "Now, or ever."

"Sorry, sir."

"I'll make arrangements for you to go into Paestum, in turn, and visit my tailor. He's quite good, and fairly economical. I assume that your lot has some money?"

"Yes, sir."

"Good. Now, first let me acquaint you with the way I run this flight. I believe a good soldier keeps himself, or herself, quite smart." He frowned, as if not liking the idea of women being assigned to his flight, but said nothing.

"There is no room for slackers, Serjeant Kailas. Not here, at any rate.

"I believe that was the reason my late predecessor in charge of this flight suffered such terrible casualties."

Hal didn't reply.

"Fortunately, I understand you have had the benefit of being schooled, at least in your first days in dragon school — dreadful name, that — by an old friend of mine, a fellow heavy cavalryman, Sir Pers Spense."

"Uh . . . yessir. We were, sir."

"A pity how he ran afoul of these new thinkers in the army. Now he's over here, responsible for dealing with the recruits that arrive, before they're assigned to their new units.

"He tells me their discipline is shocking, most shocking, and he, and a loyal coterie, are doing their utmost to make them into proper soldiers of the king.

"Poor fellow. He wants, more than anything, to be reassigned to a proper station, perhaps in charge of one of the schools of heavy cavalry.

"But, like all of us, he soldiers on, without complaining."

Dewlish smiled at Hal, and Kailas guessed he was supposed to have some sort of response. He smiled back, more a twitch than anything else, in return.

"Now, Serjeant, I'll acquaint you with my manner of soldiering. I'll be wanting to address the new men, and, er, women, before evening meal. But you can give them the gist of my feelings, and, since it's still morning, help them to begin shaking things out, as I believe you fliers call it, informally.

"I believe, as I said, in running things firmly. All fliers will be neatly dressed at all times, including when flying. I especially despise those disreputable sheepskins you wear."

Hal was grateful it was still summer, hoped that Dewlish would trip over his spurs or a dragon before winter came.

"We assemble before dawn, for calisthenics, and a run, for I believe a sound body breeds sound fighters. Then three flights, of two dragons each, go out on morning patrol, to scout the assigned tasks from army headquarters that we receive during the night.

"Then the fliers return for noon meal and, after, drill, which shall be mounted, once I manage to obtain horses. Then the afternoon flight goes up, on its assigned tasks. Sometimes there will be an evening flight as well, returning just at dusk.

"Are there any questions?"

"Sir, won't the Roche figure out that we're passing over their lines at a certain time, and arrange their affairs to allow for that?"

Dewlish snorted.

"I do not believe those barbarians are capable of that kind of analysis. In any event, those are my orders, and, consequently, that is the way this flight will be run.

"I'm aware," he said, reaching into a desk drawer and taking out a rather thick envelope, "that your former commander allowed a great deal of independence.

"I received an interesting letter from him, suggesting that certain extraordinarily irregular changes you tried recently might be implemented in my command.

"First, the existing King's Regulations give us quite enough to do as it is.

"But second, and more important, just as I do not tell any officer how to run his command, so I brook no interference from others!"

He ostentatiously tossed Miletus' letter into a red leather wastebasket.

"As for certain other recommendations he made about you . . . well, I think a soldier must prove himself in person before any awards or such can be considered.

"That, I think, is all, Serjeant. My orderly officer will show you your quarters, which of course are rigidly segregated as to the sexes, which is only natural, and the stables for your beasts. The rank and file you brought with you will be integrated into the flight, which should speed up their learning my way of doing things, and your wagons will become part of my establishment.

"Oh yes. One other thing. I believe in a proper reward at the proper time for a man who has distinguished himself. And, on the other hand, I punish offenders uniformly, and with a very severe hand.

"That is all, Serjeant."

Hal stood, saluted smartly, and marched out, wondering what Farren Mariah would say when he found out about the new wind blowing changes.

Mariah offered four absolutely horrifying and anatomically impossible obscenities.

"Worst, the bastid ain't flyin', so that means he's prob'ly immortal," he mourned.

"We could always arrange an accident," Saslic said.

"Careful," Sir Loren warned. "This Dewlish doesn't impress me as someone who can take a joke like that."

"Who was joking?" Saslic said.

"One other thing," Hal said. "Dewlish isn't one for holding hands in the moonlight."

"So what?" Saslic said. "I wasn't considering holding his paw."

"For him . . . or for anybody else."

Saslic used two sentences, and Farren's eyes widened in admiration.

"That eunuch," she added. "I suppose we can't drink, either."

"I already checked," Rai Garadice gloomed. "Fliers are permitted two drinks daily, which are served before dinner in the main mess."

"I was wrong," Saslic decided. "He's not a eunuch, he's a godsdamned Roche secret agent, determined to ruin our morale."

Following a daily briefing, the fliers went out, morning and afternoon, over Paestum, to the Roche positions on the coast, south for a time, then home.

The First Army's orders were always the same: "Scout the Roche lines east of Paestum, and to their rear for any signs of troop build-up."

Of course, since clocks could be set by the time the dragons overflew the lines, there was seldom anything to be seen, other than cavalry skirmishing, or an occasional infantry patrol in contact with the enemy.

Once Hal saw movement, extensive movement, in a forest just inland, and asked permission of Dewlish to take another patrol back over the area at once, to catch whoever was moving about down there by surprise.

Permission, of course, was refused – Dewlish said if it was anything of significance, it would be reported by the afternoon flight.

Nothing was seen.

"What the hell are we going to do about him?" Hal snarled.

"You keep telling me I can't arrange an accident," Saslic complained.

"Even if I did, who would you go to?"

"Probably take care of matters myself," Saslic said. "Buy some poison next time I'm in Paestum. Lord knows if Dewlish ever fell over dead, there'd be no end of suspects.

"The fliers all want him skinned alive, and the rest of the flight think that's too easy a fate."

"Rest easy, children," Sir Loren said. "Concentrate on practicing your flying and getting ready for the next time our peerless leaders decide it's time to go out and get killed.

"Besides, nothing lasts forever. Not even Sir Fot Dewlish."

"You c'n afford to be, what do they call it, c'mplacent," Mariah said. "You're ahead of him in the Royal List, so he gives you little agony."

"True," Sir Loren said, grinning. "And you lesser beings can work out your own fate."

"Can I push him in the pond?" Farren asked Hal.

"With my blessing," Hal said.

"Now, now. Us high-ranking knights deserve a little respect," Sir Loren said.

"And that's what you're getting," Hal said. "Very damned little respect."

Frustrated, Hal took to doing just as Sir Loren suggested – flying his dragon either morning or afternoon around the base area if he wasn't scheduled for a patrol, and doing acrobatics in the sky.

Thinking about the crossbowmen they'd used over Bedarisi, Hal started teaching his dragon to respond to shouts and pressure from his thighs. That would leave his hands free for other actions, which he was still devising. One thing he'd vaguely noted back then, through the haze of exhaustion, was that his dragon flew more slowly, couldn't climb as fast, with Hachir behind him.

His dragon, still nameless, seemed to like curveting about, either high above the farm, or else flying very low, very fast along the country roads, hopefully terrifying any travelers and, sometimes, sending a wagon careening into a ditch.

The first time it happened, Hal expected the farmer who'd emerged dripping from the green water to complain to Dewlish, but nothing happened.

One of the stablemen said the locals were all terrified of the dragon fliers, swearing they'd made pacts with demons for their powers, and wanting nothing to do with any of them.

"Which's a great laugh f'r us, 'cept when we figger ain't none of us getting' laid by th' local lassies. Though," he said and looked sly, "I've hopes for th' future, puttin' the word about one of th' gifts th' demons give us is double-length dicks."

On the way back from a patrol, Hal landed near an infantry base, and traded some of the wine he'd bought in Paestum for a crossbow and a selection of bolts.

He set up targets at various ranges, and began mastering the weapon. He rated himself a fair shot with a conventional bow, learned when he was with the cavalry, and had little trouble adjusting to the more modern weapon.

But firing at motionless bales of straw on the ground did little to teach him how to hit a moving target in the air. He found a Roche banner, and a length of rope, and convinced Saslic to tow the line behind her dragon, Nont, and let him shoot at the banner.

The first time out, he almost shot Nont in the tail. Saslic had words with him when they landed, made him vow that if he was going to miss, miss to the rear, not forward.

"One more like that – especially if it happens to tweak me – and it'll be a long, long time before this playground'll be open for you," she said.

Two problems were immediately obvious – he wasn't good enough to always hit the banner on the first shot, and reloading the crossbow, while rocking in the saddle, was a good way to suddenly start practicing air-walking; and his bolts were unretrievable.

The crossbowmen he'd traded for the first weapon became his

very, very good, if a bit alcoholic, friends, since he had to stop almost every day for new bolts.

Since his stops meant the other dragon in his patrol had to fly about for a time, he was afraid Dewlish would find out his extracurricular pastime, and forbid it, like he arbitrarily had forbidden the fliers associating with their stablehands when not on duty, keeping alcohol in their quarters, and ever appearing out of uniform.

He thought of acquiring more crossbows, but the thought of going flying with a stack of weaponry clattering about behind him, possibly hung on hooks drilled in the dragon's plating made him laugh, wryly.

"How strong're you?" Farren asked without preamble.

"Strong enough, I suppose," Hal said.

"Look 'ere," Farren said, taking a roll of paper from under his arm. "I remember, back as a lad, seein't a toy like this, use't to shoot at the poor larks flyin' about. I took the toy away from the little savage what wielded it, and warmed his butt with the thing.

"It looked sorta like this."

The sketch was of a crossbow. But conventional crossbows had nothing but a length of wood from the butt to the foot stirrup, with perhaps a guard around the trigger. This had a curved grip just behind the trigger, and a second grip in front of it.

"Now, you can't see too good f'rm my sketch, but the fore handle kinda slides, don't remember how, but it's got fingers, up here, t' grab the string and cock the bow.

"Now, this, over here, on the side's a box, wi' I guess some kinda spring inside, for it held bolts. You sorta clamped it on the bow, and worked this fore handle back, cockin' the piece, an' a bolt drops down, and the wretch pointed it an' shot.

"On'y problem is it'd be kinda light for killin' people 'stead of larks.

"Anything innit?"

Hal studied the sketch.

"Maybe. I don't know. I think I need to talk to somebody who knows more about weaponry than I do."

That day, the flight took its first casualty since Hal and the others had joined it.

The afternoon patrol was swarmed by ten Roche dragons, just before it was supposed to turn north. One of the Roche monsters had an archer sitting behind. No one knew if the lost flier – one of Dewlish's – had been hit by an arrow, or ripped from his mount by a dragon.

The dragon came home, bare-saddled, blood drenched down its sides.

Hal waited for Dewlish to react, to change the patrol order, possibly even to investigate Hal's idea of crossbowmen, but, other than a mawkish funeral speech, the commander did nothing.

The sign over the small backstreet house featured an ornately carved dagger, with lettering under it:

Joh Kious
Fine steel
By Appointment
To the Royal Household

Hal entered, and was dazzled. He had never dreamed of, let alone seen, so many different tools of destruction.

There were swords, daggers, maces, morningstars, javelins, short and long spears, arrows of various wickednesses.

Between them were bits of armor, a few ceremonial, most grimly practical. From the rear came the cheerful sound of hammers beating against steel.

The man behind the counter was slender, in his fifties, placid-looking, with an easy smile.

"Uh . . . Sir Kious?"

"There's no sir to it, my friend. Merchants tend not to get much from their supposed betters, except their gold."

Kious had a bit of a sharp tongue, though his accent was soft and country.

"How may I be of service? I've just recently opened this branch across the water to help in our efforts against the Roche."

Hal produced Farren's sketch, explained it, asked if Kious could build one, suitable for combat use. Kious thought a moment, noted the dragon emblem on Kailas' chest.

"Might I ask you to do something, sir?" Kious asked. "Try to pull my arm down straight when I hold it up like this."

Hal obeyed. Kious might have been slender, but was surprisingly strong. Hal put some of his war muscle into it, and succeeded.

"Well," Kious said. "I've built some crossbows, though not for years, and certainly not of this type. I assume you want an adequate poundage, which is why I tested your strength.

"Are you planning on using this in the air?"

"I am." Hal explained his intent.

"That somewhat increases the problem," Kious said and went on in a scholarly fashion. "You would want, oh, about 150 pounds draw weight to be sure of dropping your man. But sitting down, cocking a 150-pound bow, especially more than once, with this rather ingenious arrow-box . . . that could be a strain.

"But if we decrease the poundage of the prod – that's the bow itself – and increase the draw length – possibly use compound stringing – that will give us the arrow speed we want.

"Hmm. Hmm. Hmm. An interesting project. I'll require a deposit of . . . oh, twenty-five gold coins, sir. The total cost will be . . . oh, seventy-five gold, and that will include a goodly supply of arrows. I notice your wince, sir, and must tell you, I would charge at least double, more likely triple, were you a civilian wanting this for sport.

"And I assume you want it to be ready yesterday, as do the other warriors who've come to me."

Hal grinned.

"Of course I do," he said. "If I'd wanted it tomorrow, I would've come to you tomorrow."

Kious smiled, a bit painfully.

"At least a month, sir. And that will be setting aside some ceremonial daggers I'm quite entranced by, and am already late on.

"But gore takes precedence.

"So if you'll step into the back, sir, we can take appropriate measurements for the bow length and such."

Dewlish summoned him to his office a day later. Hal barely noticed the other man present, other than he was older, slim, white haired with a bristling white mustache, since the CO was purse-lipped, red-faced.

Hal wondered what he'd done wrong this time.

"This man is here to see you," Dewlish said. "I expect you to handle yourself in a soldierly manner.

"That is all."

Hal blinked as Dewlish stormed out the back door of the office.

The other man got up, held out an open palm. Hal, completely bewildered, touched it.

"I'm Thom Lowess," he said. "I'd suppose your commander doesn't like taletellers."

"I, uh . . . I don't know, sir." A taleteller? For him? Hal had no idea what this was all about, but a thought came that Dewlish might like taletellers very well – if they were interested in glorifying him.

"Perhaps we could find a more, um, congenial place to talk?" Lowess said, picking up a slender leather case.

Hal checked the dragon clock.

"The fliers' mess is open. We could go there."

"Good. It's always good to lubricate someone before you tell them what you want."

Lowess tasted the glass of wine set in front of him, nodded approval as Hal sipped beer.

"Very good. This is a thirsty business I'm in," he said, opening his case and taking out a notepad and pen. "I'm sure you're aware of my trade, and hope you don't, like too many soldiers, spit at its mention."

"Not at all, sir," Hal said. "Matter of fact, at one time I thought of becoming a teller. But I really don't have the gift."

"Things have changed since the war," Lowess said. "Some of us still work the villages, telling our stories. But others have been commissioned by the Royal Historian, to visit the armies, and bring back stories for the others to spread abroad in their wanderings. It's our bit for the war . . . and, of course, for recruiting.

"By the way, it's Thom, not sir."

Hal nodded, waited for an explanation.

"I've made it my specialty to interview heroes," Lowess went on.

"I beg your pardon?"

"Please don't be modest, Serjeant . . . Hal, if I may?"

"You may, but I'm still lost."

"Actually," Lowess said, "I'm the one who's lost. I've heard of your exploits in the south, yet I see no medals on your chest. Are you very modest?"

"Medals, sir?"

"I would think," Lowess said dryly, "that a man who's destroyed ten Roche dragons should have some sort of awards, should he not?"

"I've been given nothing," Hal said. "Nor asked for anything, to be honest. And I've only taken out five dragons – no, six, counting that poor transport brute.

"And I didn't destroy them, actually, but just flew close on the five, so a crossbowman, a soldier named Hachir, could take care of them . . . or their riders."

"Very interesting . . . and still very modest," Lowess said. "I'd like the full story, if you don't mind."

"It'll sound like bragging."

"No, it won't," Lowess said firmly. "If it makes you feel any easier, I have the courtesy rank of captain, which is why your Sir Fot wasn't able to run me off, and can give you an order to tell all, if that would make it easier.

"Or I could merely buy you another beer.

"By the way, there's little use in evading me. I understand there are others in this flight who were with you on that detached duty with the Third Army, and I'll be talking to them before I take my leave."

Hal took a deep breath.

"I don't have any choice, do I?"

"You don't," Lowess said. "Now, you might begin with your first encounter with a dragon."

"It was when I was a kid," Kailas said slowly. "Back in this little mountain village I grew up in . . ."

Lowess stayed for two days, to Dewlish's mounting fury.

Then he left, and matters returned to normal, if the exaggerated awe his six friends paid him at every opportunity, calling him Horrible Hal the Hydra Hobbler, counted as normal.

At least they didn't do it in front of witnesses.

Two weeks later, the entire flight was assembled before evening meal.

Sir Fot Dewlish paced in front of the formation.

"This is an awards ceremony," he said, every word being pulled from his mouth by chains. "Serjeant Hal Kailas . . . post!"

Hal pivoted out of ranks, doubled to the end of the line, and then to the front of the formation, saluted Dewlish. Dewlish undid the ties on a scroll, began reading:

"'I, King Asir of Deraine, do in my wisdom grant this Royal Badge of Honor to my faithful servant, Serjeant Hal Kailas, and direct others to render him proper respect.

"'I grant this distinction because of Serjeant Kailas' bravery in combat on several instances, first destroying attempts by the Roche to infiltrate raiders with dragons, then, during battle, using ingenuity to devise a method of destroying the dragon scouts and their riders.

"'Serjeant Kailas is not only a brave man, a worthy soldier of the king, but clever to boot, and it is recommended that any officer who is privileged to have Serjeant Kailas in his command give full attention and implementation to the serjeant's ideas and opinions, knowing that Serjeant Kailas is worthy of my particular notice and favor.

"'Signed, this day, King Asir.'"

Dewlish's lips pursed, unpursed several times before he opened a small box and pinned a medal on Hal's chest.

"Congratulations, Serjeant," Dewlish said, in a voice suggesting he'd rather be reading the citation at graveside.

"Thank you, sir." Hal said.

"That is all. You may return to ranks."

Hal saluted, obeyed, ran back to his place, hoping Hachir the crossbowman had also been recognized. Saslic leaned over a bit, and speaking without moving her lips – a talent all of them had learned under Dewlish's tutelage – said, "And now you're for it, you know."

Hal nodded.

Three days later, he was called to Dewlish's office.

"Serjeant Kailas, I've a request for four fliers, volunteers, for special duty. I've detached you, Mariah, Dinapur and Sir Loren. You'll report to the First Army's headquarters in Paestum at once, with your gear, dragons and handlers, plus volunteers necessary to maintain an independent action, for further details about this special duty."

The way Dewlish's voice savored "special duty" made Hal think the mission would certainly be one that might be better described by the word "suicidal."

15

But there was no briefing at the First Army headquarters. Instead, there was a tall, solidly-muscled man with a barely healed sword-slash across his face, who considered them through yellowish eyes that reminded Hal of a tiger he'd seen in a menagerie once.

He was Sir Bab Cantabri, commanding officer of this special detail, and he took them to a secluded tower room in Paestum Castle.

"I assume the four of you are volunteers, as specified?"

"We're alla that, sir," Farren Mariah piped. "In the smashin' old army style of the first ranks rarin' to march out and die."

Even though it looked as if it hurt to give up a smile, Cantabri managed a rather wintry looking one.

"And the four from the other flight look to be that unit's cheese dongs," Cantabri said. "Figures. Nothing changes about the army, whether it's on land or air.

"At least you look smart enough. We can only hope for the rest. You, Serjeant Kailas. You're ranking warrant?"

"I am, sir."

"Do you happen to have the necessary sea-going experience that was requested?"

"Nossir," Hal said. "The only flier in our flight who does wasn't volunteered."

"And the gods wept," Cantabri murmured. "Do you suppose you can manage to land your dragon aboard a ship? We'll arrange to get your gear and crew out by lighter."

"I don't know, sir," Hal answered honestly. "I've never tried it."

"There's a first time for almost everything. All four of you, over to this window. Here, use this glass. See, far out there on the horizon, five ships?"

They could.

"Two are fast corvettes, three are transports. One transport is towing a barge. You'll land on it, then your dragons will be hoisted aboard and you can lead them to their cages. Aboard ship, you'll draw tropical kit."

"Can we ask what the special duties we've uh, volunteered for now?" Saslic asked.

"When you're aboard, and we've set sail, you'll be told all you need to know. I'll tell you just one thing, in case you fall off your dragon and drown, so you can die in a patriotic fashion, this will be as important a mission as you're likely to be given.

"I'll tell you the rest when we're aboard the *Galgorm Adventurer*." He snorted. "What an absurd name for a spitkit of a horse-hauler."

Hal expected the worst, and, for once in his military career, was disappointed.

The four dragons were unchained from their wagons, and took off, as ordered, away from Paestum, then turned to sea, and flew to the waiting ships.

The sea was a bit rough, tossing whitecaps, and Hal wondered if he came off his mount, if he could stay afloat until rescued.

As senior warrant, the man who should always go last, he waved Sir Loren in to land first.

"I'll let someone else take the honors," Loren shouted.

Hal pointed to Farren, who needed no further encouragement. He sent his dragon spiraling down, then pulled up on its reins. The monster flared its wings, and settled on to the barge with a screech of triumph.

The triumphant call changed to one of dismay and fear as sailors went down ladders to the barge, and a crane swung out. Wide leather bands went under the dragon's belly, and it was muzzled.

Then it was swayed neatly aboard, and Farren, keeping away from its lashing tail, led it to a large cage.

Saslic went next, but her dragon balked, and she had to make another pass before landing on the barge.

Sir Loren landed, was loaded without incident, and then Hal sent his creature diving down, pulling up at the last minute, and the monster's talons scraped on the wooden deck and he was safe.

It tried to bite a sailor, and Hal slapped it with his open hand on the neck in reproof.

Then, it, too, was hoisted aboard the ship.

Hal had a moment to consider the *Galgorm Adventurer*. Not being a sailor like Mynta Gart, Hal had little to judge the former merchantman by. It certainly wasn't the handsomest vessel he'd ever seen, having almost no curves to its construct above the waterline. It was almost 500 feet long, three-masted, square-rigged with a jib, and had one cargo deck, built with ramps to load horses, plus the main deck. These two decks had their stalls enlarged to accommodate small dragons, wooden bars extending to the overhead. Half of the lower deck had been closed off, for troop bunking. The upper and poop decks were large, fitted with cabins, no doubt for the horses' owners or trainers. These were now for the expedition's officers and the fliers.

Wide sliding gangplanks, jutting forward, had been added to either side of the hull, which didn't improve the ship's lines any.

Sailors escorted the four to their cabins, and they had a chance to meet the other fliers. Hal reserved judgement on them, since a gifted flier, contrary to what Cantabri and Dewlish thought, might not have the shiniest harness of all.

Already aboard were some 200 soldiers. Hal saw by the easy way they handled their weapons, the way their eyes constantly moved, and their air of superiority to everyone, especially the ship's crew, that they were experienced warriors.

Whatever this special duty was, it didn't appear to be one involving either maypole dancing or fishing.

"Tropical kit," Farren said with a smile. "It'd be nice to be flyin' somewheres warm. It's drawin' on toward winter."

But no one knew anything, everyone was waiting for Sir Bab Cantabri to show up.

Eventually his lighter, flanked by others with supplies and the dragon handlers, arrived, and goods and men were transferred aboard ship.

Hal was very glad to see Garadice, Rai's father, and twenty of his dragon specialists with Cantabri. The man asked of his son, seemed both unhappy and relieved that Rai hadn't been volunteered for this mission.

Within the hour, orders were given and the five ships set sail, due west from Paestum, into empty seas.

When all sight of land was gone, Cantabri summoned the infantry officers to the great cabin. An hour later, they were dismissed, and the fliers were called.

There was an elaborate plaster model of an island in the center of a table. Hal couldn't tell the scale, but the island was clearly large, covered with high mountains, interspersed with alpine valleys. There were two noticeable harbors, deep fjords knifing into the land, and a third inlet. The two harbors had tiny wooden houses near their mouth, and there were three other groups of houses further inland.

"This," Sir Bab said, "is Black Island. Our target."

Farren wailed. "I shoulda guessed he was lyin' t' us, an' a long farewell to the tropics. It'll be naught but ice, black dragons, cold, an' bum-freezin'."

Cantabri nodded.

"I did lie about the tropical gear. Just as I ordered a false course to be set west, to deceive any Roche spies in Paestum. We'll turn north within the day, and tomorrow issue cold weather gear to all.

"Being fliers, I suppose I don't need to tell you what Black Island's noted for. Dragons. We've heard from reliable sources that Roche is not only taking every dragon it can from the nests to train for their fliers, but their magicians have devised a way to make the dragons breed twins."

He went to a door, rapped. Three men entered. One was in his thirties, the others ten years younger. All wore dark garb, and had close-cropped hair and were clean-shaven. Were it not for the wands they carried, Hal would never have thought them to be magicians, but, perhaps, Cantabri's battle-hardened aides.

"This is Limingo, who's one of the King's Royal Magicians, and his assistants.

"They'll advise us of any Roche magic, hopefully cast counterspells and also keep us from being spotted on our journey north.

"We're at least three weeks or so away from Black Island, likely longer since we'll be hugging Deraine's west coast as we sail. During that time, I want you all to familiarize yourselves with this model, so that you can not only provide scouting as we approach Black Island, but can prevent any Roche fliers from seeing us and guiding their warships to attack us.

"I intend to seize this port, Balfe, here. Once we take the port, we'll attack this settlement here." He touched one of the fjords, then an upland cluster of houses.

"That's where one of our spies reported the Roche have their dragon breeder, from the time they're taken from their nests to be fattened and become familiar with man for a few months. Then they're taken to Roche to begin training.

"After we seize the island, those dragon babies – I understand you call them kits – will be taken to Deraine, trained and used to reinforce our own dragon flights.

"With any luck, we'll be able to sail in, take them by surprise, and be back out to sea within the day."

Hal and his friends looked at each other.

"With just three warships," Saslic murmured.

"Which impels the question," Sir Loren said. "If this raid's so important, why wasn't half the fleet sent north?"

"Because it's *most* doubtful we could devise a spell to keep a plan of that size a secret," the magician, Limingo said. "Given warning, we think the Roche would cold-bloodedly slaughter those kits we're after rather than let us take them."

Hal thought the Roche weren't that barbaric, but said nothing.

"Supposing," Saslic said, "we do encounter Roche dragons in the air. How are we supposed to deal with them?"

Cantabri hesitated.

"I heard rumors that a flier, down south, devised a way of dealing with them, but I wasn't able to find out his name or any details." He frowned as Farren began chortling. "What's so funny about what I just said?"

Farren looked at Hal, who shrugged a go-ahead.

"Th' flier you're after's standin' right there," Mariah gurgled. "A brave volunteer if I ever saw one."

"You, Kailas?"

"Yessir." Hal briefly explained his use of crossbowmen in the battle down south.

"Hells," Cantabri growled. "And I specifically brought no crossbowmen since we'll be moving fast, and on the offensive. I've never liked crossbowmen when I'm not on the defensive and they don't have a chance to prepare fighting positions.

"Could you do the same – I'll need you to give me details – for some of my archers? I guarantee you'd have no lack of volunteers."

"With longbows, sir?" Hal asked. "That's a problem."

Saslic nodded. "We'd be darting about, and they'd be wiggling their bows trying to get a firm aim . . . I don't think that'd work, sir."

"I know it wouldn't," Sir Loren said. "I've seen cavalry try to shoot a-horseback, and the results are miserable."

Cantabri stood, frowning in thought.

"Kailas, stay after. We need to discuss this matter."

"Yessir."

*

"I don't know," Cantabri mused, "whether having you aboard is a bit of luck or not. You had success in killing dragon fliers or dragons, which I heartily approve of.

"I maintain this war will only be won when the Roche get tired of being killed, and either defang or depose Queen Norcia. All else is wishful thinking.

"So you and I agree on purpose. The question is, can you come up with any scheme to match our present circumstance, without crossbowmen? Which is why I wondered about my real luck in having you aboard."

Hal thought of mentioning his crossbow a-building, still weeks from readiness, but determined to say nothing, since he had no idea whether his scheme would work. But perhaps his idea could be modified slightly, at least for this operation.

"Possibly, sir," Hal said. "Is there any way we can get our hands on some crossbows? There's eight of us fliers . . . maybe forty bows, and a thousand bolts?"

Cantabri considered.

"I can detach one of the corvettes, perhaps with one of Limingo's aides, to one of the west coast fishing ports. Maybe he can contact one of our armories and have the necessary tools waiting here . . . in Deraine's north."

"Not good enough, sir," Hal said. "We'll need time to practice."

"I do not like changing a plan," Cantabri said. "But there's no way around it, I suppose, if we wish to have weapons to face the Roche fliers. We'll have to send the corvette, then lay off that port until the crossbows appear.

"That is, if the matter can be arranged at all."

"Frigging dragons don't get seasick," Saslic moaned.

"Guess not," Hal agreed. The wind had freshened, and the waves crashed over the bows of the *Adventurer*.

"But I do, godsdammit," Saslic said, and bent over the railing once more.

Farren, who was distinctly greenish, looked away from her.

"This is the doom," he muttered. "To be sick, sicker, an' then freeze, an be et by black dragons.

"I don't like this even a bit. I've got plans for after the war, I do."

Saslic turned.

"Don't fall in love with them," she said, her voice harsh. "There won't *be* any after the war for a dragon flier."

The corvette was sent off to a medium-sized trading port, and the other ships sailed to and fro, well out of sight of land, away from the chart-marked trading routes and fishing grounds, waiting.

"Now, the question will be," Sir Bab mused to Hal, "how many crossbows will we get?"

"We asked for forty, correct, sir?"

"Kailas, you might have been in the army for a time, and fancy yourself an old soldier. But there are things still for you to learn."

"Not sure I want to learn them, sir."

"Don't think, Serjeant, you'll be able to keep that nice civilian core you had before the war started, and when peace breaks out, you'll be able to drop right back to doing whatever it was you were before being called to the colors."

"I wasn't called, sir, but taken. But you were teaching me about crossbows."

"No. I was teaching you about the army and numbers. If you want, say, forty of anything, ask for 120. They'll look at your requisition, and find reasons why of course you can't get what you thought you needed.

"So, if we're lucky, we get eighty.

"If we're lucky."

Three days later, the corvette returned with sixty crossbows, of which at least half were in sad shape. Fortunately Limingo's aide had looked at them, realized their condition, and bought skeins for bowstrings and wood to repair the prods. There were enough peacetime carpenters among the crew and soldiery to be put to repair work.

With the other crossbows, Hal, and a grizzled infantry serjeant set to, training the fliers how to shoot.

Sir Loren and Saslic became experts. Hal wasn't surprised – Loren was instantly good at anything he undertook, and Hal had learned years ago that women were, generally, better than men with arms, once they decided not to listen to the railings from males.

Farren was an acceptable marksman, which he said, with a shrug, didn't bother him, since "I don't much like the idea of killin' dragons, 'less they're tryin' to fang me, so I'll just have to fly closer an' shoot straighter at their riders." He nudged Hal. "Or get the Master Murderer here to get them for me."

Of the four fliers from the other flight, one was a decent shot, although he was hardly an eager warrior. Another was zealous enough, but was lucky to be able to hit the ship's side, let alone the target pinned to it. The other two were sullen, not caring about much of anything. Hal decided Sir Bab had been right – they'd been stuck with the other unit's cheese dongs.

They continued practicing while the ships sailed steadily north. Sir Bab didn't want any dragons flown, so the handlers and fliers were hard put to keep their mounts happy in their cages, eager as always to get away from the earth and into their natural element.

"It'll come, soon enough," Hal told his monster, while the beast grunted contentedly, munching on a piglet Kailas had tossed into its cage.

"There'll be one way to tell if we're lucky," Sir Bab told Hal. The two had gotten in the habit of exercising on the ship's low poop after evening meal then, when Hal had been worn out by Cantabri's grind, to lean on the stern rail, cooling off in the chill, near-arctic wind, and talk of most anything.

Cantabri was reluctant to talk of before the war, but Hal had learned he was married, had two children and had been a King's Advocate, specializing in land claims.

"A good way to get rich," he told Hal. "Or just make enemies if you're stupid enough, as I was, to stand against the rich when they try to grab some peasant's holdings."

Then, one night, he'd brought up luck.

"What's the way, sir?" Hal asked. "When we're sitting in some bar in Rozen with all our fingers and toes and kits swarming around us like we're their fathers?"

"That's one," Cantabri said. "Another one is if we don't encounter a Roche flier named Yasin. A nobleman, with a brother who's supposedly mounting Queen Norcia. He's—"

"I know him, sir," Hal said. "Ran into him before the war, when he had a flying show."

"I hope he was luckier for you than me," Cantabri said. He touched the livid scar on his face. "His damned dragons pointed me out to some heavy cavalrymen when I was wandering around behind their lines one time, just to see what I could see.

"Another time I was afoot, raiding a supply column, and his beasts caught me out and tore into my men. They weren't as tough as I'd thought, and broke.

"Dragons have no trouble taking men from behind, you know."

"I know," Hal said.

"The first time I noted the black bannerlet he had tied to his dragon's neck spikes. All of his fliers use that as a common emblem, I've been told, though only his has golden fringing. The second time, the same, and there was one more time when he, or at least some of his men, saw me on a diversion. Didn't lose anybody, I'm glad to say, but we had to abort and skit back to our own lines before we got trapped.

"So I'm no fan of this *Ky* Yasin.

"I heard he'd moved north, to Paestum, and hope to hell the bastard — or whatever magicians he's got working for him — hasn't scented us out.

"I was told by one of the First Army's intelligence sorts he — and his dragons — have become some sort of a fire brigade, sent wherever there's trouble along the front.

"He also told me this Yasin was the one trying to train black dragons — I was told they're supposedly untrainable, implacable enemies of man — and having some success, which would explain why the Roche are capturing the monsters up on Black Island.

"Kailas, there are some people who scare me, and he's one of them."

There was a long silence, then: "If I were superstitious, I'd fear the man carries my doom."

Again, stillness, then Cantabri laughed harshly, without humor.

"Talking like this is why soldiers should never be given time to themselves. They're liable to try to teach themselves how to think, and all they manage is brooding.

"Night, Kailas."

And he went to a companionway to his cabin.

Hal lingered on for a few minutes, thinking. How many million men under arms? And this damned Yasin kept cropping up.

At least, Kailas thought, he hadn't encountered Yasin in the air. So far.

And if he were truly learning to ride black dragons, from all that Hal had heard, he certainly didn't want to.

16

They'd been almost three weeks at sea, a few days to the fishing port, and a week waiting for the crossbows, then on north, when Hal went to Sir Bab, and told him the dragons had to be flown. If they were mewed up all the way to Black Island, they'd be lucky to be able to do more than flounder about in the air.

"You have your soldiers exercising," he pointed out. "Dragons are no different."

Cantabri didn't argue, just told Hal not to fly further north than the ships, for fear of being seen. And if they were sighted by any other dragon riders, they could assume they were Roche.

But Hal wasn't quite ready to put his monster into the air. For openers, he had no idea on how to navigate over water, and the constantly changing weather could easily confuse a flier, and lose him in the sea-mist.

He went to the *Adventurer*'s navigator, and asked for help.

The officer showed him astrolabe and chronometer, charts, and the rest of the apparatus he used to find their position. Hal had a bit of trouble envisioning himself standing on the back of his dragon, twiddling dials, a chart braced under one foot, and the chronometer hanging on a chain around his neck.

No.

Saslic said she was willing to take a chance, which made Hal think even harder.

He had an idea, then, and went to Limingo the magician.

"I need a spell that will let me find this ship, no matter what the weather," he said. "A spell that you could lay on all of us."

The magician thought, clucking his tongue against the roof of his mouth.

"An attraction," he said. "For what? Canvas? Ropes? Other dragons? No. Those, especially as we close on Black Island, might lead you into the heart of the enemy."

"What about an aversion spell?" Hal asked.

"To what?"

"Salt beef might do," Hal said, thinking with a shudder of the barrels of meat that'd been boiled, then kept in salty water. Farren had spoken for them all when he said, "This'd be enow to turn me vegetarian. No wonder the poor friggin' sailors spend so much time buggerin' each other. On'y pleasure life gives 'em at sea."

Limingo laughed, said that would certainly be an easy spell to build, and one that would surely take. He wanted an hour to prepare it, asked Hal to have all eight fliers in his cabin then.

The magician's spacious cabin had its furniture pushed back against the bulkheads. Eight small braziers were set in twin arrows, both pointing to a hunk of salt beef. Around it, semi-circles in various colored chalks were drawn, and in each a symbol or letter of a tongue known to none of the fliers.

Farren whispered that if "any of them letters require speakint, I'll never have a tongue snaky enough, despite what m'lady friends've said."

Saslic jabbed him in the ribs, told him to shut up.

Limingo, flanked by his acolytes, explained what Hal had wanted, and what they'd come up with.

"Then I bethought myself a bit," he went on. "An absolute aversion to salt beef, natural though it would be, might spell starvation while we're still aboard. So rather than impregnate you all with this counterspell, we'll give each of you an amulet.

"You can see them on the floor, next to that slab of what's laughingly called beef, which I've linked to the meat aboard this ship. I'll enchant them, and when you wish to know where this ship is, stroke your amulet, think of beef, and you'll immediately know which way to turn your dragon.

"Now, each of you come forward, and take an amulet."

"Strokin' m'amulet, eh?" Farren whispered. "I thought you got toss't out of the army for strokin' it too much."

This time, Hal was the one to kick him.

The amulets were tiny ovals of a variegated brown, each with a silver ring around it and mounting for chain or thong. Hal wondered how Limingo had been able to make these charms in such short order, decided he must have a pack somewhere, ready for various ensorcellments.

"My assistants are now putting various, efficacious herbs on the fire – adders tongue, hellebore, purslane, spurge. We ourselves are chewing bits of clove against the spell, since we don't wish to have it take root among us."

Evil-smelling smoke boiled that might have been pleasant if only one herb at a time was being burnt.

"Take your talisman in your right hand," Limingo went on. "Touch it to your heart, then hold it out toward me."

The fliers obeyed. Limingo began chanting:

> "*Beef of old*
> *Covered with mold*
> *We shun thee yet*
> *Your odor set*
> *We turn away*
> *Our stomachs at bay*
> *Protect us all*
> *From your horrid pall.*"

He then chanted, in a monotone, words in an unknown language, nodded at his assistants, who capped the braziers, just as Hal was about to break into uncontrollable coughing.

Another assistant opened a vast port on to the seething ocean at the ship's stern, and the chill wind quickly cleared the smoke out.

"I never thought," Sir Loren said, "having a strong stomach is a perquisite for wizardry."

Limingo heard him, grinned.

"It is an *absolute* necessity. I recall the first five years of my apprenticeship as being mostly nausea. I suppose that kept my master's expenses for his larder down, though.

"Now, all of you, try your amulets out."

Hal touched his, thought of salt beef, and instantly did not want to go in three directions. He asked Limingo about it, who had him indicate those directions.

"Very good," he said. "One aversion, of course, is to that bit of beef on the deck there. The other would be to the hold where the provisions are kept. And the third would be to the galley, which suggests what we're having for the evening meal.

"All of you? Did you feel the same?"

All did, but two had only a single response.

"Good enough," Limingo said. "Each of you has his – or her, pardon milady – personal compass.

"So you can go flying now . . . and be content you'll be back aboard before the cooks finish boiling our meal into submission."

They started for the dragon deck.

Saslic noticed Farren Mariah had a long face.

"'Smatter, small one? You don't want to eat some fog?"

"'Tisn't that," Mariah said. "Just realizin' what small beer I'd be as a wizard. Not only havin' to pack-sack all that gear, and learn all kind of tongues, none of which anyone without a split tongue could ever speak aloud, but havin' such pretty, pretty assistants.

"Not my cut of beef at all. Pardonin' the expression."

Hal and the others took their dragons high, circling in the sheer joy of flying after so long, swooping, making mock attacks on each other.

As the sun sank and it grew colder, the ship's warmth called, and, one by one, they circled back to the *Adventurer* and its salt beef.

"That incantation Limingo was saying," Saslic said to Farren as they groomed their dragons. "It was damned poor poetry."

"'Twas," Mariah agreed.

"Since you're supposed to have some talents as a witch, Farren," she asked, "does it matter how good your poems are? Do demons – or whoever helps magic work out – like good poetry, or crappy stuff, like soldiers go for?"

"Don't seem t' matter," Farren said. "M' gran'sire said it just focused the mind an' will on the spell."

"So a magician could be going doobly, doobly, doobly, and it'd have the same effect?"

"Nope," Farren said. "Best if you've got to slave some, writin' the chant, and then, sayin' it, keeps you payin' attention."

"And if you don't pay attention," Hal asked from his cage, "the spell won't work, right?"

"Mayhap," Farren said. "Or a demon eats you."

"There goes one of my choices for an after-war career," Hal said firmly.

Hal ordered all dragons to have their carapace scales pierced and smallish hooks installed that he'd had the ship's artificer make, patterned after the pelican hooks used in the rigging. The dragons seemed to have no feelings in their scales, save where they were attached to the beast's skin, and so did no more than growl when the handlers were at work with their bow-drills.

He assembled the dragon riders, gave instructions, and issued two crossbows and four bolts to each rider. The bolts were colored for each rider.

A small raft was tossed overboard from the *Adventurer*, with a block of wood covered with bright cloths in its center and a long towrope connecting it to the ship.

Each dragon rider flew off, then assembled, in a line, behind Hal.

In turn, each dragon swooped on the raft and its rider fired at the block, climbed away while the rider rehung his first crossbow and prepared the second. Four passes per dragon, which took almost three hours as riders aimed, lost their aim, pulled away to try again, and then dragons were landed, and the raft dragged aboard.

The results were fairly wretched – Hal had three hits, as did Saslic. Sir Loren had two, Farren one, and one of the other flight's fliers managed a strike.

Not good, Hal thought, pondered long, but couldn't think of any better way to train the fliers. He talked to Limingo, and asked if magic could help.

"Certainly," the magician said briskly. "If you could bring me a bit of a Roche dragon flier's tunic, preferably with a little of his blood on it, I could cast a similarity spell, and that would do the trick."

Hal grinned wryly, found Sir Bab, told him not to be expecting much if the Roche and Deraine fliers came in contact.

"I always expect nothing, or almost," Cantabri said. "That way, I'm almost never surprised.

"Look at it like this, Serjeant. If you buzz a bolt close to one of their fliers, something he can't be used to, that should scare him off.

"At least for awhile. And maybe, when he gathers his courage and tries again, the flier he goes against will have better aim."

Hal saluted, called the fliers together, told them they'd be flying twice a day against the evil raft until they got better.

They did. Slightly. But only slightly.

They spent almost as much time studying that model of Black Island as they did in the air. The soldiers' warrants and officers did the same.

Hal was impressed, seeing how many of the common warriors spent time in the room, lips moving silently as they walked around the model, then pointing to various places with their eyes closed, whispering the place names to their mates.

And there was always the thunder of soldiers running back

and forth on the decks, exercising, practicing swordplay with wooden swords against each other.

When they reached Black Island, they'd be as ready as soldiers could be.

"The problem with war," Sir Loren mused as the four fliers sat on the deck one morning too foggy to fly, "is it's no fun any more."

"Di'n't know it ever was," Farren said. "Killin' people ain't my snappy-poppy idea of pure joy."

"That's the bad side of it," Sir Loren admitted. "But when it's a clear morning, and you can hear the horses neighing across a camp that's bright with banners and knights' tents, or when you're riding out on a spring day on a country patrol, or even when you see a castle besieged in its splendor . . . You've got to admit there's a certain glory."

"No," Saslic said flatly. "I don't."

"Never mind, Sir Loren," Hal said. "You're in the minority here. But what made war no fun . . . in your eyes?"

"The damned quartermasters and victuallers," Sir Loren said. The other three blinked.

"An' a course, you've an explanation," Farren said.

"It used to be," Sir Loren said, "that soldiers would assemble, at the will of the king or whatever nobleman had their fealty or could offer gold or loot, in either spring or fall, after the harvest or after the roads thawed, most generally in the fall, after the harvest was in.

"We'd campaign for three months, then, when the army couldn't find any more peasants' farms to loot, and if there hadn't been a knockdown battle that settled the issue, everybody went home."

"Except the poor looted peasant, who didn't have a home to go to," Saslic said.

"He could enlist for the next campaign, hoping for loot to compensate," Sir Loren went on. "But now, we've got efficiency, with victuallers riding here and there, dealing with contract merchants for so many hogsheads of hogs' heads or corn or whatever, and all that goes to depots for issuance to the army.

"And so we can stay in the field forever, not like my father and father before him, who'd have a chance to return home, let his wounds heal, and rest for a time."

"And possibly procreate more killers for the next king to call on," Saslic said.

"Well . . ." Sir Loren let his voice trail off.

"Sorry, Sir Loren," Hal said. "No sale here. Although I'm sure Sir Bab'd agree with you."

"Not him," Sir Loren said. "He's of the new school of warrior. Fight until the enemy's down in the ditch, then stab him a few times to make sure, paying no attention to anything like a white flag."

"A bleedin' *monster*," Farren said, mock horror in his voice. "Bet he doesn't curry to ransomin' brave knights, either. Stick a bit of iron in their armpit, where the armor don't cover, an' march on, knowin' they're no more a threat. Right?"

"Aargh," Sir Loren said. "There's no chivalry in the lot of you."

"And thank the gods for that," Saslic said.

It grew colder, and a flier reported he could see the northernmost headland of Deraine, sinking into the ocean. The seas grew larger, sweeping across the vastnesses of open ocean, and Saslic was seasick again, moaning that she thought she'd gotten her sea legs, but somebody lied to her, and if she ever found them she'd either kill them or throw up on them.

But she staggered to Nont, and was airborne with the others. Hal thought the epitome of courage was seeing her tight, pinched face, ignoring nausea, fighting her way into the air.

One day, all fliers were in the air, and a sudden storm swept down from the north, bringing rain and fog with it, the seas rising.

The dragon fliers used their amulets to drive hard for the *Adventurer*, and the handlers rushed each from the landing barge on to the ship, another dragon already approaching, spray reaching up and soaking its belly.

Eight dragon fliers had taken off.

Seven came back.

The missing flier was Saslic Dinapur.

Hal tried to take off, to look for her, but Sir Bab forbade it.

Limingo was afraid to cast any spells this close to Black Island, for fear of being discovered by Roche wizards.

Kailas wanted to rage at him, rage at Cantabri, but fought himself under control.

All that long night, as the storm boomed, and the ships rolled, taking green water over the rails, Hal stood on the poop, out of the way of the watch and helmsmen, feeling no cold, no wind, none of the waves' drenching, eyes burning as he tried to peer into blackness.

His mind kept running the thought – I never told her I love her, over and over, never willing to change the word to loved.

Cantabri came on deck at dawn, saw Hal, and ordered him below for hot soup and a change of clothes.

Kailas obeyed, his loss overwhelming him, his mind numb.

Less than a turning of a glass later, the lookout reported a dragon, flying toward them.

Hal was on deck, lips murmuring prayers from his childhood, knowing uselessness, knowing that this was nothing but a Roche scout who'd sighted them.

But it wasn't.

It was Nont, and Saslic Dinapur, weaving in the saddle, almost falling, as she brought her dragon down on the barge. A wave almost took it, but there were handlers on the decking, heedless of the storm, fastening bellybands under Nont and bringing it aboard.

Saslic tried to stagger up the gangplank to the *Adventurer*, stumbled, almost went overboard, and Hal had her in his arms, carrying her to her cabin.

She was near-frozen, body unfeeling. Limingo and the ship's chiurgeon were there, stripping her clothes away, and putting her in a tub of heated salt water, constantly refreshed.

She stirred, came back to consciousness, saw Hal, and a smile quirked her lips.

"That," she managed, "was the longest damned night of my life."

Then she went out again. Limingo had herbal rubs, hot plasters and drinks, and she was put to bed with high-piled blankets, and slept for a full day and night.

She woke ravenously hungry, and all the delicacies the mess cooks could provide were hers.

Hal sat beside her while she ate. She burped delicately.

"I think I feel like getting screwed," she said. "Just to convince myself I'm not frozen in some wave."

Kailas was only too happy to comply, and moaned, in the height of passion, his love.

After they were finished, she looked at him strangely.

"You mean that?"

"Yes," Kailas said firmly.

"Me, too," Saslic said. She sounded a little embarrassed, and hid her face against his shoulder.

"Would you like to tell me how you came to live?" Hal said, a bit relieved to change the subject.

"It was all Nont," Saslic said. "Did you know dragons can swim?"

"No," Hal said, then caught himself. "Yes. We take them down to the river for washing. But that's just splashing about."

"They swim like godsdamned ducks," Saslic said. "That's what kept me alive. When the winds got too strong to stay in the air, Nont ignored what I was trying to get him to do, and dove for the water.

"I thought we were dead, but he spread his wings just yards above the waves, and flared us in with a great damned splash.

"Then he folded his wings over his back, over me, and we bobbed around. It was almost warm, like I was in a weird tent.

"It was dark and, well, smelly, and the water kept drizzling in. Then it got colder, and Nont put his head in the tent with me. He was breathing on me, and it was like being on a battlefield three days after the fighting, maybe worse. But it was warmer, and I could just concentrate on not throwing up.

"I wonder if dragons can cross oceans like that, just hunched up, letting the currents carry them? Maybe they don't come from the north, like everybody thinks.

"Anyway, I think I spent a lifetime under his wings, but it got gray out, and the waves didn't look as high. I didn't know what to do, but Nont did. He waited until we were on top of a wave, and then I could feel his feet paddling hard, and his wings spread, and we went up the next wave, before it could break over us.

"The wind caught us, and lifted him in the air, and we skipped across the water and he flew like he's never flown before, and then started listening to the reins and what I was shouting.

"I used the amulet, and it worked perfectly, and brought me back home."

She was silent for a moment, then smiled, in childlike happiness.

"I do love you, too.

"And I want to sleep again now."

*

Hal sought out Garadice, told him what Saslic had discovered about dragons.

"I'll be whipped," the trainer said. "This certainly shows that nobody knows anything about the beasts. I can picture this great flotilla, swimming, or being borne by the storms, from some far-distant land to the northern lands. I'd heard tales of dragons settling on water, but I thought just to drink, or rest for a moment.

"Nobody knows anything about dragons," he repeated. "Or, come to think about it, anything else, as far as I can tell, the older I get."

The next morning there were alarums. A lookout on one of the flanking corvettes reported something in the air at a distance.

Hal and Sir Loren hurried their dragons from their cages, went aloft, climbing in tight spirals.

But they saw nothing.

They circled the tiny convoy for an hour, came back in for a landing, chilled to the bone.

No one other than that single lookout had seen anything, and Sir Bab decided it was likely an illusion, for the dragon was reported flying almost due east, rather than north to Black Island or south to Deraine or the mainland.

There was nothing east for leagues, so the lookout had to have been mistaken, or perhaps had sighted a wild dragon.

But no one relaxed after that.

The following day, Hal was on high patrol, and saw something to the west of the convoy. He took his dragon lower, ready to flee, expecting to see ships, and there could be none but Roche in these waters.

But the tiny dots – Hal counted more than forty of them – stayed very small, and he chanced going still lower.

Then he made them out, and a chill went up his spine.

The dots were dragons, wings folded over their backs, heads tucked inside the tent, being carried along by the current and waves.

Dragons migrating . . . toward where? Black Island? The unknown wastelands to the north of the island?

Was this a regular process? Or were the dragons fleeing something?

Hal flew low over the dragons. One, near the lead, lifted its head, looked up at Hal, saw no evident menace, and put his head back under cover.

Hal had no answers, nor did Garadice, who added a further question that perhaps some ultima Thule to the west was the dragons' real homeland, and the northern wastelands a current-ordained temporary destination.

Hal puzzled over it, put the matter aside as one more intrigue about dragons, and returned his mind to the war.

Two mornings later, just at dawn, a high-flying dragon rider reported, just lifting from the northern horizon, gray land bulking out of the gray seas and mist.

Black Island.

17

Black Island, from about five thousand feet, looked exactly like that plaster model in one of the *Adventurer*'s cabins, barring the cloud-scatter below Hal and his three fliers.

Clouds, and the moving dots that were two of the transports, landing soldiers on the horns that enclosed Balfe's harbor.

There seemed to be no other sign of life below them, and then Hal felt a surge of sickness, knew the Roche magicians were casting what spells they could bring up in time.

He scanned the town, saw nothing worth reporting, looked to sea, which was gray, speckled with white.

He motioned to Saslic to stay high on patrol, and pointed to his other three fliers to dive.

They shot down, dragon wings furled, across the northern-most point of land, saw soldiers, in formation, trotting along a dirt road toward the settlement. Still lower, they saw two bodies sprawled outside a shack, couldn't tell if they were Roche or Deraine.

Hal led his flight in a sweep around the island, saw no sign of alarm. They flew past a huge seamount, and saw half a dozen full-grown black dragons crouching, watching. Hal shivered at their size – fifty or sixty feet – far larger than the beasts they rode.

He kept his hand near the two crossbows hooked to his dragon's carapace until the wild dragons were out of sight.

They flew over Balfe, saw no dragons with riders trying to get in the air, but smelt the strong reek of the beasts from long roofed pens below.

Running toward the settlement, from the other point, came other Deraine soldiers, as the *Adventurer* and the other two transports hove toward the settlement's single pier.

The escorting corvettes stayed clear of the bay, watchful for Roche ships.

A handful of Roche soldiers ran out of a guardhouse, and either died or surrendered to Cantabri's soldicry.

The second flight of dragons came off the *Adventurer*, landed near the barracks to wait their turn in the sky.

Hal saw Garadice and his specialists disembark from the *Adventurer*. The other transports unloaded bulky stretchers and small carts. Soldiers were detailed by Sir Bab's warrants to assist Garadice.

Then the craziness began, as dragons were taken out from their pens, and chivvied, coaxed or carried to the transports. Hal, swooping overhead, trying not to fall off in his laughter, counted more than fifty dragons of various ages, saw them snapping, trying to claw, and tail-lashing, heard shouts of pain, and squeals of rage from below. The soldiers trying to help Garadice may have been deadly warriors, but as dragon handlers they were bumblers.

Farren flew close.

"Glad to be out of that!" he called.

"Aye," Hal shouted, pointed up. "Relieve Saslic. It's cold up there."

"Bastard," Farren called amiably, and took his dragon upstairs.

The dragons went up the gangplanks on to the transports reluctantly, but they went.

Saslic's dragon flapped down alongside Hal.

"Nothing here?"

"Nothing," Hal shouted back. "No dragons anywhere but on the ground."

"Can't believe . . . Roche sloppy . . ." Saslic said, words torn by a gust of wind. But Hal understood.

He swept back and forth over Balfe, then it was his turn to freeze.

Bastards didn't want to get up there in the wind, where it's freezing. I'll have them sorted out, he thought, starting for his dragon.

Then he saw dots to the east. Five, flying close together.

He shouted a warning, and his three fliers saw the oncoming dragons, had perhaps a moment to hope they were a wild covey, then realized wild dragons never flew that closely together, and were in their saddles.

Hal jumped on to his mount, jerked the reins, and the dragon growled in protest, but turned away from the last of the salt beef, and sprang into the air.

The flight climbed, circling over Balfe as the last soldiers tumbled aboard, pulling up the transport gangplanks. Anchors had been dropped when the ships pulled up to the pier, and now the ships kedged back from shore, laboriously came about, and put on all sail. Hal saw signal flags going back and forth from corvettes to transports, had no time to watch others as five Roche dragons dove toward the second flight, about a mile away from Hal.

The on-rushing Roche dragons flew hard, wings driving, straight into the four.

The air was a swarm of dragons, beasts slashing at each other with their talons, fanged heads snaking.

A Deraine flier was struck by a tail-slash, sent spinning down toward the sea below. Another was fumbling at his crossbow when his dragon banked sharply, away from an attacker.

Hal could hear him scream as he lost his footgrip, above the screech and scream of the dragons and fell. Hal's flight was level with the free-for-all, and Saslic looked at him, for orders. He pointed up. Better to have altitude before they closed, he knew.

He glanced at the mêlée, saw it break apart, one dragon with a Roche pennant on its carapace spinning, wing torn away. Another Roche monster was far below, diving, wings folded, into the ground. The two surviving Deraine dragons howled, attacked the three survivors. The Deraine fliers may not have been the best, but they were certainly brave.

The Roche fliers wheeled their mounts and fled, just as a Deraine flier from the second flight slumped down over the neck of his mount, and slowly slipped out of the saddle, falling limply toward rocks.

Then the Deraine fliers, five of them, were alone in the sky over Black Island.

Hal was amazed how much time had passed, looking down, seeing the five Deraine ships well clear of land, at full sail toward the south-east.

He was about to signal his flight to make for the ships, then saw, against the gray haze on the horizon, the specks of ships. He counted twenty, and his eyes were tearing from the cold and wind, unable to make out more.

Hal's fliers were waiting for orders.

He knew what must be done, knew he was probably sending his fliers to their deaths. Hal waved his hand in a circle – keep patrolling. They must stop any oncoming dragons, to keep the Deraine convoy from being followed and destroyed.

The fliers obeyed, waiting.

Hal knew Limingo and his acolytes would be casting every possible spell to turn away Roche magic.

He thought about his warm bunk, about hot soup, about anything other than the cold creeping up his arms and legs.

Time passed.

The dragons honked unhappiness at the boredom.

The Deraine ships were over the horizon, and the Roche fleet, now counted at thirty-five ships, was closing on Black Island, when Hal saw another flight of dragons – once more, five – flying toward him.

He pointed, and his three, followed by the last survivor of the second flight, flapped toward the Roche.

His dragon whined protest, wing muscles tiring, but obeyed Hal's orders.

He had slight altitude on the Roche, motioned for his dragon flight to climb even higher.

The Roche dragons came up toward him, and Hal saw, with a chill, two of them were huge.

Huge and black.

Roche *had* learned how to train the feared black dragons.

He pushed fear away, picked up one of his crossbows, already cocked, bolt in its trough, steered toward the lead Roche.

They rushed together, and the fear vanished, for icy calm.

At the last instant, the Roche flier broke, afraid of collision, kicking his mount down, trying to dive under Hal. Hal aimed, pulled the trigger and it was an easy shot. The bolt took the Roche in the chest, knocked him back, bolt pinning him to his mount's back.

The dragon bucked, was gone, and Hal forgot him, pulling his dragon's reins as a black monster, almost twice the size of his mount, slashed with its dripping fangs at his dragon's throat.

Then they were past, and Hal pulled his dragon up into a climbing turn, saw a black dragon trying to turn inside him, wings shaking as he slowed into a stall, the sound like dull thunder.

He had his crossbow cocked, a bolt ready, and the black was almost on him, mouth gaping. He put his bolt fair between the beast's jaws, and it howled, bucked, and its flier almost fell, caught himself on the carapace, legs dangling, kicking for a foothold as his dragon rolled on its back, and dove toward the ground.

Again, the brawl was joined. Sir Loren's dragon tore at a Roche's wing, and Saslic took it from the front, talons ripping at its neck.

The last survivor of the second flight was flying in tight circles with a Roche dragon. The Roche broke the circle, was on the Deraine beast, ripping at its chest. Ichor spurted, and the Deraine beast convulsed, fell.

Hal had his second crossbow up, shot the Roche rider in the back, dove under the dragon, fumbling the crossbow string over the cocking fingers, stuffing a quarrel in, and there was a black Roche above him. He sent a bolt toward its gut, missed, hit neck armor, and the bolt skittered away.

The dragon was turning toward him, and Saslic dove on it, shot the dragon in the body as Farren put his bolt into its rider.

A dragon slammed into Hal's mount, almost knocking him free, the Roche monster's fangs ripping at Hal's mount behind the wing. Hal was trying to cock his crossbow as his dragon rolled, lost it, almost grabbed for it, and yanked the other bow from its nook.

Ichor sprayed across Hal's face, almost blinding him, then he saw the Roche dragon turning back to finish him.

But it was very slow, and he had all the time he needed to cock his crossbow, tuck a bolt into the notch, lift it, and fire. The bolt took the Roche rider in his guts, and he grabbed himself with both hands, fell back from his saddle, bounced once on his dragon's tail, and was gone.

His riderless mount dove away, and the sky was clear of Roche, just as Hal felt his dragon shudder and saw the terrible wound in his mount's side.

Then he was diving down toward the sea below, pulling

helplessly at his reins, his dragon trying to recover, trying to fly.

He almost made it, lifting himself on one wing and torn remnants of the other, bravely trying for land. But he ran out of sky, and Hal and dragon smashed into the ocean, Hal tossed away, to go deep, water green, turning black, while his thick fingers unfastened his sword-belt, let it fall away.

He kicked at his boots, slid out of his thick coat, and the water was lightening. He broke the surface, gasping.

Not a dozen yards away, his dragon thrashed at the water in death agonies, shrilled, then sank.

Hal Kailas was alone on the tossing gray ocean, the wind catching the tops of waves, turning them white.

Hal waited until a wave lifted him to its crest, rubbed salt-burning eyes clear, looked for land, thought he saw the peaks of Black Island.

A long ways away, but there was nothing else, and so he started the swim, arm over arm. A shadow came over him, and he flinched down before he realized, and looked up.

Saslic's dragon, Nont, banked above him, then, whining in protest, spread its wings as Saslic forced it to the water, splashing down on the back of a wave.

"Need a ride, sailor?" she shouted.

Hal, half drowned, didn't have strength enough for a reply, stroked toward Nont, caught hold of a wing, pulled himself along it and on to the monster's back.

"I guess we should think about going home, hmm?" Saslic called as she goaded Nont into a flapping run through the water, up the back of another wave, and then ponderously in the air, climbing, up to where Sir Loren and Farren flew.

"Before the rest of the party shows up."

18

The five ships docked in one of Deraine's western ports, and the stolen dragons were transferred to barges, and sent upriver to a secret training ground of Garadice's.

Hal and the other dragon fliers had expected to be put on a transport, with their three surviving dragons, and sent back to Paestum, the Eleventh Dragon Flight and the charming attentions of Sir Fot Dewlish.

Instead, the dragon fliers, Sir Bab Cantabri, half a dozen of his soldiers and Limingo were given special orders and transportation to Rozen, Deraine's capital.

"An' what do yer think that pertains to?" Mariah wondered. "We got away wi' it, so there'll not be a court martial."

"Medals, lad," a gray-bearded serjeant said. "We're heroes."

"Mmmh," Farren said, thought for a moment. "That's nice, an' such. But I'll wager it means the army acrost the seas has taken it up the wahiny of late, and the king's lookin' for someat to distract the masses."

"Prob'ly," the soldier agreed. "But haven't you learned to take yer medals where they fall?"

Hal suspected the serjeant was right, since the transportation north wasn't the usual oxcarts soldiers got used to, but carriages more suitable for officers or minor lordlings.

It was cold traveling in the beginnings of winter, but there were crowds down the main street of each village, cheering the soldiers, sometimes even by name, generally Sir Bab, and every night the twelve were put up at decent inns, not crouching over fires in their stables.

Again, Hal noted there were few men about, and the farmers' winter tasks were being done more and more by women.

Saslic and Hal slept in each other's arms each night, waking to make hungry love, evidence they'd lived through the icy seas.

Others took full advantage of the adulation they were getting, and Hal wondered how many village maidens would have children nine months gone.

Saslic commented acidly that she truly admired the patriotism of her fellows, "trying to personally compensate for any war losses. Heroes all."

The two surprises were Sir Bab, who smiled politely at the invitations to linger beyond dinner from the country noblemen's wives and daughters, but no more.

"He's married," Sir Loren announced.

"An' what of that?" Farren asked. "As if anyone'd peach on him."

"No," Sir Loren said. "He's *really* married. Which means all those saddened virgins, mourning widows and lonely wives are forced to make do with the second best." He smiled, stroked the pencil-line moustache he was cultivating.

The other surprise was two-fold: first that Limingo favored young men rather than women, and the second part was how many small villages had boys eager for his embraces.

Saslic was a little taken aback, thinking that such practices were mostly restricted to cities, but Hal just grinned. Between the road and the army, very little of what people did in bed surprised him any longer.

A day beyond Rozen, the soldiers stumbled into the rather casual formation Sir Bab required for a headcount before the carriages moved off.

"Thank some gods," Farren moaned, peering through red-rimmed eyes at Hal, "pick your lot t' pray to, that we'll be in the city tomorrow. I thought when we lit off, I'd as soon spend the rest of m'life ridin' along, eatin' only the best, and beddin' the lustiest. But I'm worn frazzled. An' walkin' bowlegged."

"Better to ride your dragon," Saslic suggested.

"Y'know," Farren said, changing the subject, "there's not been a maid I've met who objects t' the gamy smell of me. One said dragons make her randier."

"I don't even want to think about her dreams," Saslic said, with a shudder. "And if you'd bath more, like we've been doing, you wouldn't still stink of the beasts."

"Lass," Farren mourned, "you're not thinkin'. If th' ladies love it, who'm I to arguefy?"

If the villages and towns were gleeful, Rozen was hysterical.

"Isn't there anybody at work?" Sir Bab marveled as the carriages made their slow way toward the city's center. He smiled at a woman who tossed him a rose from an apartment window overhanging the street, ducked as someone threw half a winter melon through the carriage window.

"*Damn*, but I wish they'd stop thinking we're unbreakable," he muttered.

All of them had learned to wear pleased smiles, and wave slowly, to keep from wearing their arms out.

Again, there were far more women than men to be seen, and those men were generally boys, elders or in uniform.

The warrants were betting on which of the City Guard's barracks they'd be put up in, but nobody won the bet, as the carriages were guided into the great Tower complex, where the government of Deraine and King Asir's main castle were.

"An' aren't we shittin' in tall clover?" Farren marveled as they were given separate rooms built into the walls of the Tower itself. "M'mum'll never believe me. I'll have t' steal somethin' of real moment t' prove I was ever here."

The throne room was a dazzle of tapestries, gold, silk and noblemen and women. But Hal barely noticed. He and the other soldiers, save perhaps Sir Bab and Sir Loren, had only eyes for their king.

King Asir was a bit shorter than Hal's six feet, stocky, with very tired eyes. He wore scarlet velvet breeches and vest, over a white silk shirt, and a mere gold ringlet for his crown.

The soldiers had been issued new uniforms that were tailored to fit in a few hours, told to stand by, and the gods help anyone who had brandy on his or her breath when they were summoned.

They were marched into that throne room, surrounded by Deraine's nobility, and all knelt, bowed their heads, as instructed, when trumpets blared and the king entered.

He was flanked by an elderly lord with a beard and martial stance that challenged belief, and a pair of equerries carrying velvet boxes.

Asir went down the line, and Hal was most impressed at *his* training, for he knew the names of each man and woman, although a bit of Kailas snickered about what would happen should, say, he and Saslic change places.

He spoke briefly to each of them, a bit longer to Sir Bab, paused at Hal, looked him carefully up and down for a time. Hal tried to hide his apprehension.

"Serjeant Kailas," the king said. "This is the second medal I've given you in three months, the first in person."

"Yes, Your Highness."

Asir took a case from the equerry, opened it, and looped a medallion on a chain around Hal's neck.

"I'm delighted to honor your bravery, not just over Black Island, but in other places as well. You've served since the beginning," Asir went on. "Quite bravely, without proper recognition, both because of circumstance and evident jealousy.

"Fortunately for your building reputation, you're one of the favorites of the taletellers."

Hal, very nervous now, nodded, gulped.

"Yessir . . . I mean, Your Highness."

Asir smiled.

"Don't get goosey," he said. "Remember, I sit down to crap just like you do."

Hal had no idea whatsoever what the response to that should be.

The king nodded, went on down the line.

Farren, next to him, nudged him, subvocalized: "Whajer get for your medal?"

Hal ignored him.

The king returned to his throne, remained standing.

"I am mindful to make two further awards. Sir Bab Cantabri, come forward."

Cantabri obeyed.

"I now name you Lord Cantabri of Black Island, and declare this title shall be passed down to your heir and his heir, to keep the memory of your bravery fresh in men's minds until the ending of time. It is also in my mind to reward you with more earthly goods, estates, rights, which we shall discuss at a later time.

"Kneel, sir."

Cantabri obeyed, and King Asir took a small, ceremonial sword from the lord, tapped Cantabri on his shoulders and head.

"Rise, Lord Cantabri."

The king embraced him, and Sir Bab saluted, and returned to the ranks. Hal was surprised to see tears running down the hard man's face.

"There shall be one other honor this day," the king went on. "It was in my mind earlier today, but I wanted to meet the man first.

"This is an unusual honor, given not merely because this man is most brave, but is a pioneer member of our dragon fliers, what I have heard some call, before this lamentable war, dragonmasters.

"If any deserves this title more, I know it not.

"Through him, I am also recognizing all those who've struggled under the sometimes imbecilic traditions of the past, of a peacetime service that, at times, seems not to know times have changed, and that we are in the most bitter war of our existence.

"These men, and women, have fought, sometimes without success, to make the army, and I include myself as Supreme Commander, realize that just because something has been done in a certain manner for decades or centuries, that doesn't mean there isn't a better way.

"Frequently it is necessary, and I charge all of us to recognize this, to think hard on the way we fight, and consider other ways of doing things, instead of holding close the dead hand of the past.

"Serjeant Hal Kailas, come forward."

Hal gaped for half a lifetime, then Saslic, beside him, kicked him in the ankle.

"Move, you git!"

Hal obeyed, almost doubling up, as the army required, to the king, realized how unseemly that would be, almost stumbled, crimsoned, hearing a snicker from the rows of nobility.

But he kept his feet, and saluted the king.

"Kneel, sir."

Hal obeyed, and felt three taps on his shoulders and head, taps he felt with the crushing weight of the burden they brought.

"Rise, Sir Hal Kailas," the king said.

Hal did, saluted the broadly grinning king, and was never sure how he got back to his place in the file.

"Not just a friggin' medal," Farren Mariah marveled, "which means I'll not have t' plunder somethin' to show me mum, but a whole week's leave.

"Mayhap I'll not come back. And what'll you think of that, *Sir* Hal?"

"I'll hunt you down in that warren you live in," Hal said. "And drag you, kicking and screaming, back to the war."

"Now, that's not the way a proper knight knights," Farren complained. "Speakin' of which, how're you plannin' t' spend *your* next glorious week?"

Hal came back to a bit of reality, realizing he didn't have anywhere to go, had no family other than Caerly, and that held nothing at all for him.

"Be damned if I know," Hal said. "Thank the gods we got paid, and I can afford an inn."

"Paf to that," Sir Loren said. "You can always come home with me. I haven't a sister for you to lust after, so you'll not have to worry, Saslic. But even though the old manse is gloomy and stony, there's more than enough room for you."

"Or if you don't want to be fartin' around some frigid castle in th' bushes wi' strange beasties an' stranger bushcrawlers," Farren said, "there's an attic room one of m' uncles been wastin' away in too long."

Hal looked at Saslic.

"I'm to be back with my family," she said. "I don't know if you fancy being around dragons, or around suspicious fathers, even if they are Royal Keepers, but there's room."

"Sir Hal's living requirements are already provided for," a voice said, and the three turned, saw the taleteller Thom Lowess. "I'll be claiming my own reward on the man, though he's welcome to visit any of you.

"My townhouse is but ten minutes ride from the Menagerie, Serjeant Dinapur," Lowess said. "And I'm hardly suspicious around nightfall."

"Uh . . ." Hal managed.

"Sir Hal, you're not being consulted. You're being told," Lowess said firmly, taking him by the elbow. "Now, come with me."

The four hastily scribbled addresses and instructions to their respective places, and went their way.

"Now, young man, come pay the price," Lowess said.

"For what?"

"For your knighthood."

"Huh?"

"I would like a little respect, sir," Lowess said. "Who else has been slaving away, night and day, making sure your name is on everyone's lips, that the court itself buzzes with your bravery?"

"Oh. You mean . . ." Hal remembered what the king had said.

"I mean, I've been promoting you as if I were on your payroll."

"Why?" Hal was suddenly suspicious. Lowess spread his hands, smiled blandly.

"Why? How else does a taleteller advance himself, once he's become the voice of the nation, save by pushing causes and people who deserve it?"

Hal looked at him carefully.

"I'm not sure I understand."

"You're not supposed to," Lowess said cheerfully. "Chalk it up to a strange man's strange hobby. Now, come. We'll be late for dinner.

"There are certain ladies of the court who've made it very clear I'll no longer enjoy their favors unless they have an opportunity to meet you."

*

Thom Lowess' manor house was intended to show Lowess' vast travels in unknown lands, his notable friends, savage and civilized, in those lands, and the dignities that had been shown him.

It did that very well. Walls hung with paintings, weaponry, exotic objects. It was also very clear there was no wife or lady living there. The house oozed masculinity, all leather and dark wood, a bit too much so for Hal's tastes.

Lowess' table was also a marvel, with dishes Hal had never tasted, or heard of only from lords' braggadocio. There were cooks serving splendid items, servitors making sure no plate remained bare or glass empty for more than a few seconds.

And there was Lady Khiri Carstares, just seventeen, but with a glint in her eye suggesting experience beyond her years. She was slender, small breasted, almost as tall as Hal, and wore her dark hair curled and hanging down one side of her neck.

Hal couldn't decide whether her eyes were violet, green or some unknown shade of blue.

Lady Khiri was bright, quick with a laugh, or to be able to bring one. She appeared to follow news of the war closely, and was very aware of Hal's exploits.

Hal, before her eyes drew him in, had the sudden feeling of being a fat bustard, pursued by a relentless hawk. But he put that aside, thinking that he'd been too long in the company of mostly men, and was missing Saslic fiercely.

After the meal, there was dancing in a great ballroom, with a small orchestra. Hal tried to beg off, but Khiri insisted she was the finest teacher, and "surely a dragonmaster like you, Sir Hal, can learn anything as simple as the dance within a moment."

Kailas didn't know about that, but he managed not to step on her feet nor trip.

Hal felt guilty, remembering the men in the mud across the water, then laughed at himself. They surely wouldn't begrudge him, and if they were here in his place wouldn't think of a poor dragon flier's loneliness for even an instant.

There was punch, mild in taste, but strongly alcoholic, and magicians, really sleight of-hand artists, wandering through the crowd showing their tricks.

There was a break, and Hal found himself on a balcony, with a hidden fireplace, where they could look out over the city of Rozen.

"So whereabouts in this maze do you live?" he asked Khiri.

"For the moment, here, with Thom."

"Oh. He's your lover, then, or . . ." Hal let the sentence trail off.

"No, silly. He's just a friend of the family. But my family's holdings are largely on the west coast, or in the north. So, I have my own bedroom . . . a small suite, actually, like four or five other friends of Thom do. All we're required to do, he's said, is keep what he calls the loneliness wolves away, which in fact is no more than laughing at his jokes – which are very, very funny – and pretending not to have heard a story when sometimes you have." She shrugged. "That's a very cheap rent."

Khiri smiled up at Hal, came closer.

"Besides, it gave me an opportunity to meet a real hero, not one of these posers with their brass and polished leather."

The moment hung close, and Hal felt a sudden impulse to kiss her.

Fortunately, the orchestra started again, and he pulled back, took her hand.

"Come on. We're not through dancing, are we?"

Khiri looked disappointed, then smiled brightly.

"You're right. What's now is now . . . and what's later is . . ." She didn't finish.

Hal, feeling very confused, hoped there was a lock on his bedroom door. Or, perhaps, on hers.

But locks weren't needed.

That night he slept as he couldn't remember doing, since . . . since being on solid land in Paestum, with the rain beating down and no flight scheduled for the next dawn.

He woke, yawning, late the next morning, wondered if he could borrow a horse from Lowess and ride over to see Saslic.

As he was dressing, a courier came with a sealed message:

YOUR LEAVE IS CANCELLED. RETURN TO FLIGHT IMMEDIATELY WITH OTHERS. YOU ARE HEREBY ORDERED TO TAKE COMMAND OF ELEVENTH FLIGHT AND RETURN UNIT TO FIGHTING STANDARD. FULL SUPPORT AND REINFORCEMENTS ARE AVAILABLE.

The order was signed by the lord commanding the First Army. Somehow, somewhere, disaster had struck.

19

"It is most unfortunate," Lord Egibi rumbled, his snow-white mustaches ruffling in a most martial manner, "the Roche chose to test their new secret weapon, deploying infantrymen in baskets slung below their damned dragons, on your Eleventh Dragon Flight. Sir Fot Dewlish and his men fought hard, but they were sadly outnumbered.

"*Most* unfortunate," he repeated.

Hal tried to hold back his anger, wondering what stove his reports of the Roche tactic months earlier had served as kindling for. Lord Egibi noticed Hal's expression.

"Is something the matter, Sir Hal?"

"Nossir."

The Lord Commander of the First Army had a good reputation among the troops as a man who'd given his life to soldiering in the service of the king, first against bandits in the north of Deraine, then on loan to the barons of Sagene to advise their own campaigns against highwaymen, then, just before the war with Roche, on the east coasts, quelling an outbreak of piracy.

He was a very big man, with very big appetites that he never bothered to deny, and boasted that he had no enemies, other than the Roche, living, who were worth acknowledgement.

The Lord Commander of the First Army got up from his padded chair, moved his bulk to a large-scale map, tapped a point.

"First the Eleventh is hit," he went on. "With the success of their attack, I can only assume the Roche will be striking at other flights.

"Sir Hal, I need a tactic to combat this! That's why I ordered you recalled from your sorely earned leave. I desperately need my dragons to prepare for the summer offensive, and if the Roche continue decimating – hells, destroying – my flights, I'll be blind!"

Hal's anger vanished. Finally someone in high command was admitting the dragons were more than just parade toys, only two years and more since the war had started.

"I've read the citation at your knighting, and agree with the king. We must have new ideas, new thinkers, or this war will just keep grinding us down and down until one side or the other collapses from sheer exhaustion. Which will hardly be a famous victory."

"Yes, milord," Hal said, trying to sound like a man of intelligence and action. "Give me a few days with my squadron, getting a full picture of what happened, and I'll do my best to come up with something."

"Go ahead," Egibi said. "But do more than your best, lad. Deraine needs help, desperately."

Hal saluted, started to leave, turned back.

"I'll need one thing, sir. A magician. A very good one. If possible, I'd like the services of a man named Limingo, who's still in Deraine."

"This matter has the highest priority. I'll have a courier off on a picket boat within the hour, requesting this Limingo be assigned to First Army and to you. And anything else you need will be provided."

"There just might be some other things, sir," Hal said.

"Just ask," Egibi said. "And we'll try to provide. I correct myself. We *shall* provide. Oh, by the way. A serjeant is a poor rank to command a dragon flight. Effective immediately, you're promoted captain on a brevet basis.

"Do well, and I'll confirm the appointment as permanent."

The crossbow thudded, and a bolt whipped down the long room into a target. Hal worked the grip under the bow back, then slid it forward, and another bolt dropped down into the trough from a tray clipped above the bow's stock.

Hal fired, and the second bolt buried itself beside the first.

"Good," he approved.

"Perhaps, as I warned you, sir," Joh Kious said, "a little light on the pull, due to the cocking lever design. But it will kill you your man. And five more with the other bolts.

"Or, precisely aimed," Kious added, eyeing the dragon on Hal's breast, "even a dragon. I applaud your design of this weapon."

"Not mine," Hal said. "One of my men, remembering a sparrow shooter of his youth."

"Very well," Kious said. "Your spare bolt carriers and bolts are already wrapped. Will there be any other way I might be of service?"

"Yes," Hal said. "I'll need crossbows built for my three fliers upstairs, plus thirty more crossbows made to a general pattern, plus ninety bolt carriers. And a thousand bolts. For a beginning."

"Young man," Joh Kious said, sounding slightly shocked, "do I look like a factory?"

"No, but you are about to look very rich," Hal said. "I want you to set up a plant building these crossbows. Hire as many as you need, price the weapons reasonably, which doesn't mean what I'm paying for this one, and start work. Payment will be immediately made by First Army's quartermaster on acceptance by me, in gold."

"Of course you want these crossbows yesterday," Kious said.

"Certainly," Hal said. "As I said when I ordered the first one, if I'd wanted them tomorrow, I would have ordered them tomorrow."

Kious smiled.

"I've read about you in the broadsheets, Sir Hal. You certainly aren't a man unsure of himself."

Hal didn't reply.

"Very well," Kious said. "I should have known when I came across from Deraine something like this would happen and I'd be drawn into the maws of the military system once more.

"At least I'm providing for my old age," Kious said. "Which, remembering what it's like to deal with the army's quartermaster corps, looms close."

Hal and the three other fliers had expected the Eleventh's base to be thoroughly worked over. But the reality was worse – the farm estate was a shambles.

The main house appeared to have been set afire, and then some sort of explosion had scattered bricks across the grounds. Most of the other buildings had been fired as well, and the survivors of the flight occupied hastily pitched tents, scattered here and there.

Hal, riding behind Saslic on Nont, saw no sign of the flight's dragons as they lowered to land.

Around the flight's base was a garrison of infantry, also quartered in tents.

Very secure, Hal thought. Especially now that the barn's been burnt and the horse butchered for its meat.

Mynta Gart limped out to greet them, saw the captain's tabs Saslic had managed to find in Paestum, saluted.

Hal returned the salute, a bit embarrassed for some unknown

reason, looked around as a scattering of handlers, some still bandaged, came out to take charge of the dragons.

"I think," he said, "I want you to tell me what happened, exactly as it happened, before we do anything else."

"Yessir." Gart's use of the title came easily, and Hal knew she must have seen others promoted over her head as a sailor, and thought little of the matter. "I think it best to repair to my tent.

"It's not a particularly lovely tale."

It wasn't.

The Roche, estimated two or three flights, all with basket-mounted infantrymen, had struck just as the sun was coming up.

"The first target was the nine dragons still on the ground, the bastards. That was where I picked up an arrow in my thigh, doing nothing in the way of good, trying to save my beast. I never was much of an infantryman.

"They killed the dragons, and went after anyone wearing flying insignia, then started killing anyone who fought against them.

"I came to just as they were looting and firing the buildings. That was where our fearless leader got killed."

Gart seemed reluctant to go on. Hal nodded at her, and she continued.

"Dewlish was in his office . . . I guess he was hiding. They came in, and saw his rump sticking out from under his desk. Someone put a spear in it, and drove him into the open.

"They beat him to death with that godsdamned dragon statue of his. Broke Bion in about a dozen pieces, and shattered Sir Fot's skull.

"They finally ran out of things to break, got back in their baskets and flew off. I don't think they took more than a dozen casualties, all told. Bastards!"

There were only two good notes.

The attacking dragons had been normal, multi-colored beasts, so evidently the number of black dragons thus far trained was minimal.

And the second was that none of Hal's fellow students in dragon school had been killed. Rai Garadice had been off on a dawn flight, not returning until the carnage was complete.

"Our own Feccia seems to have seen the Roche approach, and vanished. He claims he was going to alert the closest fighting unit, tripped in the woods and knocked himself unconscious, not coming to until the fight was over."

Gart smiled cynically. Hal made a note that, sooner or later, the coward would have to be dealt with. But there were more important matters to deal with.

Hal thought for a moment.

"What's our strength?"

"Five dragons ... your three, and Garadice's and his partner. Nine fliers. Twenty-three survivors. Not much in the way of equipment. Morale is nonexistent."

"New gear is on its way, as are replacement dragons and fliers," Hal said briskly. "Now, I want you to take over as my adjutant, since Dewlish's crony got killed, simplifying matters.

"And I want the unit assembled in front of the main house in half a glass."

"Adjutant?" Gart said. "But I'm a flier."

"And so you'll remain. On this flight, there'll be only two sorts of people – fliers and those helping them "

Gart managed a smile.

"That'll be a surprise for some people."

"The first of many, I hope," Kailas said.

"Do you know what you're going to say?" Saslic asked.

"I think so," Hal said. "But for the love of the gods, don't you – or Farren – smirk at me, or I know I'll start laughing."

"What's it to be, then?" Saslic asked. "The old tyrant who bites nails in half routine?"

"Pretty much. Now get your ass out to formation, woman."

"Yessir, master sir."

The formation was as ragged as the tents the men and women fell out from. The fliers were at one end of the rank, curiously waiting.

Gart called them to attention, turned the formation over to Kailas.

"If you haven't heard by now, I'm the new flight commander," Hal said. "And I propose that we set about winning this war, instead of farting about the fringes as we've been doing."

There were mutters, some of agreement, others sounding surly.

"Here are the changes we'll start with," he continued.

"First, I want this damned camp straightened up. The tents will be rowed as they're supposed to be, and the grounds'll be cleaned. I don't want a flight that looks like a palace guard, but there's no particular reason you have to frowst about like vagabonds."

"Hard to wash, get clean, when all your gear's been burnt," someone in the ranks called, reluctantly added a "sir."

"Supplies, including rations, will be here by nightfall," Hal said. "For the moment, we'll keep that infantry contingent, in case our Roche friends decide to come back.

"Now, the second thing is from now on this flight is only going to concern itself with one thing – fighting the war. Anybody who thinks anything else is more important is welcome to apply for a transfer.

"I'll be in that tent over there after this assembly. Anyone who wants out will have all the help I can give.

"The same goes for anyone who doesn't want to soldier. The way out is wide open."

"The frigging Roche hit us once, now you're acting as if it's our fault," an unshaven man growled.

"No. It's nobody's fault," Hal said. "As long as it doesn't happen again."

"The hells with it," the man said. "I'll take you up on your transfer."

"Fine," Hal said. "The infantry always needs some more swordsmen."

The man looked alarmed, and there was a ripple of amusement.

"That ain't right," he grumped. "Almost die here, and then you'll put me where I'll get kilt for sure."

"Not my doing, friend," Hal said. "From your own mouth."

"But—"

"But nothing," Hal said. "You're gone as of tonight. And anyone else who's looking for the easy life can go with you.

"We got knocked down, but we're getting back up. And we're going to strike back. I promise you, the Roche who tried to destroy us will be destroyed in their turn.

"They'll be very damned sorry they ever heard of Eleventh Flight.

"We weren't much of a unit before, but all that's going to change, and change now.

"From now on, when anyone thinks of dragon fliers, they'll think of the Eleventh.

"That's all. All surviving section leaders report to me as soon as I dismiss you."

*

Hal had the beginnings of an idea, and ordered the clean-up crews to carefully set aside any Roche weapons or gear, and marked the spot where the few Roche casualties had been buried.

The wounded had been taken away when the Roche departed, so there weren't any prisoners to interrogate for what he needed, although he questioned the surviving members of the flight again and again.

At least, he noted with relief, none of them reported black dragons being used. But little else came – not the name of the attacking Roche units or anything else of value.

That, he hoped, Limingo the wizard would provide.

Egibi's promise was good. By late afternoon, wagons began rolling into the compound, filled with everything from foodstuffs to new uniforms to the necessary tools to squealing pigs for the still-to-materialize dragons.

Hal had been thinking of other things he needed, specifically one other man. Once more, a rider went off to First Army headquarters and again the request was granted, and another picket boat set out for Deraine.

"Yer might 'swell go for anywot and everywot," Farren said. "Soon enow the gleam'll be off the rose, and we'll be lookin' for the hind tit to suck like the rest of the army."

"I'll bet," Saslic said, "you haven't thought about us."

"Uh . . . what should I be thinking?" Hal wondered.

"Men!"

"I've had other things on my mind," Hal said, only half apologetically.

Saslic growled incoherently, found calm.

"Look, you. You're now the muckety of this flight, which means you've got to be a moral upright."

"Oh," Hal said in a small voice.

Saslic nodded. "Moral uprights don't go around screwing their underlings. At least, not directly, and not if they want to have their soldiery fawning and yawping at their feet."

Hal sat down heavily on his bunk.

"Hells," he said.

"Just so," Saslic said. "Here I have to go and fall in love with this bastard determined he's gonna be a Lord of Battles, a Dragonmaster above all, which means he better not show any human failings."

"I don't like this," Hal said. "I do love you and don't want things to change."

Saslic softened.

"I know. I don't either. But I don't see any way that can happen."

"What do you want to do?"

"I *have* thought about things," Saslic said. "If I were a tough warrior, which I'm not, I'd transfer to another flight. But I'm not that strong."

"Thank some kind of god for that," Hal said.

"But I can't see any way that we can keep fooling around. At least, not on the flight. Can you?"

"I suppose not," Hal said miserably.

"Maybe we can sneak around, like we're married to other people, when we're in Paestum or away from the Eleventh. But no more."

"Shit."

"Shit indeed," Saslic agreed.

"I guess I shouldn't be whining," Hal said. "Considering what it'd be if I'd never met you, or if I was back in the lines. But . . ."

Saslic shrugged, her face as downcast as Hal's.

"War's a crappy business, all the way around, isn't it?"

Hal very quickly became too busy to worry about his private life or, indeed, to have any.

Support replacements came in, and were fitted into their slots.

Morale stayed low, for there wasn't anything to do until the dragons and the new fliers arrived.

Then ten dragons arrived, chained in great wagons. They were only half-trained, and the handlers had to work very carefully to avoid being bitten or clawed.

Farren Mariah found one handler, a new man, lashing a dragon with a chain. The man went to the infantry that same day, after Hal had assembled the flight and, as scathingly as he knew how, said the handler was no better than a Roche, trying his damnedest to lose the war.

The new fliers arrived, even less trained than the dragons, and Garadice and Sir Loren were put in charge of their training.

Hal had his own worry – training his own dragon not only to obey his commands, but all of the nuances he'd laboriously taught the dragon he'd lost off Black Island.

Remembering Saslic's advice, he grudgingly gave the dragon a name, remembering the tales he'd heard as a child of his mountain people, when they were reivers instead of being miners. The name he picked was Storm, after the fierce hound a legendary warrior owned.

Limingo arrived, with a mountain of gear, his two acolytes, a little put out at having to give up the flesh pots of Deraine.

But he forgot his complaints when Hal told him what he needed.

"Hmm," he said. "An interesting idea, and one I'd never thought of before."

Hal showed him the piled Roche equipment, and he seemed unimpressed.

But when Hal took him to the graves of the Roche dead, he brightened.

"Now this," he said, "is matter we can work with."

His smile wasn't pleasant, and Hal's stomach roiled a little.

"I assume you'll want to be present at the ceremony, once I figure it out?"

Hal didn't but knew he must.

Next to arrive was Serjeant Ivo Te, the leathery warrant from flight school.

Hal's orders were simple – Te was to beat the flight into shape. Nothing mattered except flying. He'd report to Gart, to Hal in extraordinary circumstances.

"Any preferences on how I train 'em?" Te asked.

"None," Hal said. "As long as it's quick, and not too bloody."

"I never draw blood," the serjeant said. "Welts and bruises are generally more'n enough.

"The incorrigible'll go off to be Roche fodder."

Hal dreamed, and knew he was dreaming. He was not a man, but a dragon, soaring high, free, with nothing below but tossing waves and ahead a land of mountains, rocks, crags.

Here there were animals for food, animals to hunt.

There were no men in this world, and the dragon rejoiced.

He floated from current to current, diving sometimes through clouds, the harsh wind and rain a balm to him.

Somewhere in those crags was a cave, empty now, but in time, in season, a place for a mate and kits, a place to live from year to year, while the seasons rolled past, ever familiar, ever unknown.

A reveille bugle sounded, and Hal's eyes came open.

He sat up on his cot, looked out through the flaps of his tent at the flight's other tents, at a dragon grumbling as he was saddled, ready for the first patrol.

Hal remembered his dream, realized he was happy, feeling a great, quiet, sense of joy.

Kious' crossbows came in, and Hal had them issued. He ordered his fliers to begin practicing, first on the ground, then in the air, putting Serjeant Te in charge of the firing range as well. He made sure their confidence wasn't shattered by starting them on large targets, the size of cows, then working his way to man-size targets.

Thirty archers, real volunteers, from the infantry unit still guarding them were detailed off, and instructed in being dragon passengers.

Limingo sent one of his acolytes to Hal, saying he was ready for the ceremony, and would Hal please honor him by attending?

The acolyte said that he would be transcribing the results, assuming there were results, so Hal needn't worry about having to rely on memory.

The ceremony was scheduled at noon, rather than midnight, as Hal had expected, but Limingo had requested that all dragon flight personnel remain in their tents, for fear, the acolyte said, "of disrupting the ceremony." Then he added, a bit disquietingly, "or being disrupted."

The disciple, at the appointed hour, took Hal to the gravesites of the Roche raiders. The air was soft, late autumn, and a thin sun shone through the multi-colored leaves of the trees.

Buried in the gravemounds were spears, swords, arrows, all with their blunt ends pointed at a huge, round, bronze mirror or gong, hung about ten feet above the ground from a tripod.

Directly under it, an arrow had been mounted crosswise on a stake, set loosely in the ground so it could turn easily, like a wind indicator.

Limingo greeted Hal, noted his obvious nervousness.

"You don't have to worry . . . I'm not going to try to raise the dead. That isn't possible. At least I don't think it's possible . . . certainly not without some very potent, very dark magic.

"We're merely looking for some memories. Now, if you'll stand over there . . ."

Braziers were lit, and Hal wrinkled his nose. Maybe this spell wasn't dark magic, but some of its ingredients were certainly foul-smelling enough to qualify.

Limingo stood at one leg of the pyramid, motioned his disciples to the other two, then began chanting:

> *"Once you lived*
> *Saw, fought, lived*
> *Bring back that time*
> *When your eyes still saw*
> *Still saw."*

He reached up with a wand, barely touched the mirror, and it began humming, like a great, strangely tuned gong. Again, he took up his chant:

> *"But then you bled*
> *Then you died*
> *You could not*
> *Return.*
> *But were left*
> *Here on soil not your own*
> *Forever wanting to go back*
> *To the place you should*
> *Not have left*
> *The place with your friends*
> *Your officers*
> *A place of warmth*
> *A place of life*
> *Show us now*
> *The direction of your dead longing."*

The drone of the gong became louder, and the mirror came alive, showing huts, soldiers in Roche uniform, dragons, the dizzying view from one of the infantry baskets, dragons carrying soldiery, then, below, the farm the Eleventh Flight was quartered on. The scenes passed faster, faster, and there were men with swords, spears, soundlessly screaming Deraine soldiers, then the ground rushing up, and the gong's sound rose to a near-scream, then went black.

"Now, watch the arrow," Limingo ordered.

It swung back and forth, then steadied in a single direction.

"Mark!" Limingo ordered, then reached up and touched the gong, dulling it to silence.

"We should have enough power in the mirror to make this spell again," he told Hal. "Perhaps two or three leagues south of here.

"Draw those two lines until they come together, and—"

Hal's smile was wolfish.

"And we'll know just where the Roche came from."

Hal flew out before dawn, by himself. His dragon, Storm, was irritable, and the darkness let him remember a time when he was free, and he snapped experimentally at Hal, got a kick in his armored head for his pains, settled down.

Hal climbed high, then sent his dragon over the barren wasteland that was the front line, static now that winter was close.

His map was on his knees, a tiny dot that marked the intersection of the two magical lines his target, nothing more. In case he was brought down by the Roche, they would have no clue as to his mission.

There was heavy cloud for a time, and he flew by compass heading. Then it broke, and Hal checked his bearings, saw he was on track, and began scanning the ground far below.

He saw what he was looking for almost immediately.

It was well camouflaged, with huge nets over the two open areas the Roche dragons would fly from, and the roofs of the barracks and the fliers' huts were painted to look like farmland.

But not well enough.

"I must say, Sir Hal," Lord Egibi said, leaning back in his oversized chair, "you've taken long enough to return to me."

"Sorry, my lord. But I needed certain things, and then my magician took some time to prepare his spell."

"*Certain* things," Lord Egibi said with a snort. "You requisition materiel like you're . . . like you're a lord, dammit."

His attempt at looking angry failed, and a smile could be seen under his mustache. Then it vanished.

"I hope, for all this expenditure of time, supplies and the king's money, you have something for me."

"I do, sir," Hal said. "I now know where the three Roche flights that wiped out the Eleventh flew from."

Lord Egibi looked puzzled.

"And with that, you propose what?"

"I am going to obliterate those flights," Hal said quietly. "Every flier, every dragon, every soldier who attacked us will die.

"The Roche struck us with terror. Now I propose to give that back to them. To the last man."

20

The Eleventh Dragon Flight came over the wooded hillcrest just as the sky lightened. Ahead of them was the Roche dragon field.

Hal hadn't dared scout the base more than once, for fear the Roche would realize they were the target. But he assumed almost all armies were the same, and their leaders despised anyone wanting to sleep past a time when he could see his hand in front of his face.

Roche soldiers were, indeed, straggling out of their huts and barracks toward morning formation, and there were three dragons being saddled, prepared for flight.

The Eleventh was in a shallow vee, Hal in front.

Each dragon carried a flier and one archer, except for Vad Feccia's monster. Behind Feccia rode Serjeant Te, who not only had a bow like the others, but a ready dagger.

Hal had told Feccia that Te would be his passenger, and added, "He'll be most helpful to you, and make sure you don't stumble over any more tree roots."

Feccia had protested volubly about being misunderstood, and that he was as proud to be taking part in this revenge attack as anyone, smiling, but his eyes held pure hate for Hal Kailas.

Hal might have worried about being backshot, but not with Te around, and especially not since he'd learned, in his cavalry days, to turn his back on no one.

The dragons overflew the Roche formation, crossbow bolts raining down, and even a few of the archers managing aimed shots. They dove on the three dragons, who were barely awake. One reared, and Saslic's Nont ripped his throat open. The second took three bolts in his chest, thrashed, and died.

The last's wings flared, and he stumbled forward, trying to get aloft, as Sir Loren's dragon tore the rider away, and Garadice's beast's tail smashed its neck.

They banked back, and Hal motioned for a landing. They touched down, and, as ordered, the archers tumbled off, and, carefully picking targets, began their killing.

Hal motioned his dragons up, and they took off again, flying low across the field, shooting at anything that moved.

The Roche base was a howl of confusion and disarray, much, Hal thought, like the Eleventh must have been when the Roche came a-raiding.

He steered Storm over one of the camouflage nets, very low, and the beast seemed to know what he wanted, reaching out and grabbing the net, then, flapping hard, it went for the sky.

The net was far heavier than Hal had figured, and Storm was about to fall out of the sky when, to his considerable surprise, Feccia's dragon was on the net, just beyond Storm's wing-reach, lifting, and then Garadice's dragon was alongside, and the net was coming up and away.

It was like overturning a rock to see scorpions scatter. Under the net were the dragon pens, the monsters screaming in surprise at the sunlight, fliers running for their beasts, handlers trying to get them ready to take to the air.

Hal grabbed the bugle hanging from one of Storm's headspikes, tootled unmusically, but his flight heard, and responded.

The dragons swept down across the dragon pens, their riders firing at the beasts, banked back, and made another attack.

Hal motioned ahead, seeing his infantrymen beset by Roche. One was down, then the Roche saw the on-rushing dragons, broke and ran.

Hal brought the dragons down, and the archers scrambled aboard, one pulling the wounded man with him.

Then the dragons were stumbling forward, gracelessly leaving the ground, becoming instantly elegant as they climbed for the heights, back toward the Deraine lines.

But that was not enough. That evening, at dusk, Hal brought his dragons back, with a fresh group of archers.

There were two Roche dragons in the air, and they went down under a hail of crossbow bolts.

The dragons dove, landed their archers, and again, swept back and forth across the base, this time tearing away the second net.

Hal had brought a new weapon with him – thin glass wine bottles filled with lamp oil, and given a conjuration to burn.

The bottles were scattered by the fliers, flaring into life as they struck and smashed.

Flames grew, jumped to the camouflage, spread to huts and barracks.

Other dragons were shot down as they stumbled, screaming,

out of their burning pens, their masters shot down in cold blood, no mercy being given.

Then the raiders were gone.

Hal was not through with the Roche.

Again, he came back at dawn, and this time there was little to burn, few to kill. But the dragon fliers methodically combed the fields, shooting down any Roche they saw.

They made one more pass, each flier dropping a pennon of the Eleventh Flight so the Roche would know who had attacked them.

Two days later, word came from spies who'd crossed over the lines.

The Roche squadron had been all but obliterated, with no more than two or three fliers still able to fly, and all dragons killed.

The unit was broken up, its few survivors sent to other Roche dragon flights. This made Hal grin, for these broken men would surely tell the tale, and Roche morale would further dip.

Another report came – responsibility for the Roche dragons opposing the First Army had been taken over by *Ky* Bayle Yasin, and his newly established Black Dragon Squadron.

Some looked fearful, but Hal nodded in satisfaction.

Now he would get a chance, he hoped, to fight the man he illogically felt a grudge against, going all the way back to the death of Athelny of the Dragons.

21

The broadsheet fairly screamed:

The Dragonmaster Strikes!

Hal winced.

"The dragonmaster, eh?" Lord Bab Cantabri said, mock admiration heavy in his voice.

"The broadsheets have a vivid imagination," Hal said.

"Still, that might look good, tastefully embossed on some stationery," Cantabri said. "Here's another good one," and he read the screamer aloud:

Hero of Deraine Modest,
Worshipped by His Men

"Oorg," Hal managed, picking up another sheet from the impressive pile Cantabri had brought to the flight:

"His long, blond hair streaming, Sir Hal shouted his
dragon fliers in to the attack with his battlecry, 'The Gods
for Deraine and King Asir' . . ."

"Bastards can't even get my hair color right," Hal grumbled, rubbing his close-cropped brown hair.

"Heroes *always* should have long, blond hair," Lord Cantabri said. "Makes 'em much more followable.

"Here's another:

"An exclusive account of the dashing raid against the
Roche, as told directly by Sir Hal Kailas to Deraine's
favorite taleteller, Thom Lowess—"

"That great liar I haven't seen since getting my leave cut short back in Rozen," Hal interrupted.

"Now, now, Sir Hal," Cantabri said in a soothing voice, his wicked smile undercutting any attempt at comfort. "Never let the truth stand in the way of a good story."

Hal grunted, listened as, outside the window, Farren Mariah read from another broadsheet with suitable emendations:

"Teeth gritted against the bleedin' autumn gales, grindin' his tongue to powder, our own Sir Hal lashed his dragon with his crop, forcing the enormous beast to whirl in his tracks, and smash into two attacking Roche monskers.

"Whirl, whirl, like a friggin' top.

"An' then the dragon took one Roche horror by its neck, usin' two talons of one claw, and dandled it up and down, then hurlin' it away, whilst our own Sir Hal grabbed the second horror by the tail, swung him about his head, and then—"

Hal closed the window with a bang, as a patrol of six soldiers marched past.

"I suppose," Cantabri said, "those square-bashers are just in case *Ky* Yasin decides to come back on you."

"They are."

"Best you should think about changing bases entirely," Cantabri suggested. "But keep the base support at your new post. The Roche have spies as well who might winkle you out."

"I'm already scouting for something," Hal said. "Preferably closer to the lines, so we'll be able to get a little flying in when winter comes."

"Ah, but I have a better suggestion," Cantabri said, smiling blandly. "One guaranteed to keep you out of the winter weather, nice and active, and fighting for your country as proper heroes should.

"And not just you, but the whole flight, should you choose to volunteer them."

"I should've known you came here with more than delivering papers on your mind."

"If you have a map about – in a nice, secure place – I'll show you where the further opportunities to cover yourself with glory are."

"Or get dead."

"That," Cantabri sighed as he followed Hal into an inner room, "seems to go with the territory, does it not?"

He went to one of the maps in the briefing room, a fairly small-scale map of the entire front.

"Now, as we all know," he said, deliberately taking on a false tutorial manner, "the war is currently at something resembling a stalemate.

"What has been proposed by the king and his advisors, is a bold masterstroke, to quietly pull selected units from all four armies, move them to Paestum, together with new units currently training in Deraine, and Sagene allies.

"We'll go by sea, around Sagene's western border, then east, until we're beyond Sagene and the lines, and then make a bold assault on the Roche heartland.

"I'll not tell you just where yet, but it's along a river, that we can follow up to reach Roche's capital of Carcaor."

"How many men?"

"At least a hundred thousand."

"Which you'll be able to keep from talking about their coming glorious adventure?"

"If they don't know, they can't talk. We'll probably arrange some camouflage scheme, like issuing them arctic gear, reversing the promises we made for the Black Island expedition, or arranging for a map of Roche's northern seafront to be captured."

"What happens when we round Sagene's south-western cape? I assume the Roche have some sort of navy."

"Deraine's ships will be screening for the convoy."

"Mmmh. How many dragon flights?"

"Four have been selected."

"Not many for a hundred thousand men."

Cantabri lost, for a moment, his confidence.

"I know . . . but dragon fliers are scarce, and new formations won't be ready until spring, at the earliest."

"And you're in command of this operation?"

"No," Cantabri said, realized the note of his voice, and tried to put confidence back into it. "A close friend of the king's, a Lord Eyan Hamil, will command."

"I don't know the name."

"As I said, he and the king are very close. The story I've been given is that he's been in command of the approaches to Northern Deraine, and has begged the king for a more active command. He's an older man, quite charming."

"But he's never led an army in the field."

"No."

The two men stared at each other for a moment.

"Well," Hal said, "I'll put it to my fliers."

"You command most democratically."

"When it's convenient," Hal said. "Has there been any more of a plan developed beyond get ashore in this spot you won't name for me, and start marching upriver?"

"Not really," Cantabri said. "What deployments we'll make after the landing will depend on the Roche reactions."

Hal rubbed his chin.

"Is this the way you would have run this expedition?"

Cantabri stared at him.

"I don't think I'll answer that."

"You don't have to, sir."

Hal got up.

"I'll call the troops together, and have an answer to you – I assume you're at the First Army headquarters – by nightfall."

"You won't find me there," Cantabri said. "But I have a deputy there. As for myself, I have three other armies to canvass for brave men and heroes, so I've leagues still to ride this day."

"You really think we can pull this off?" Hal asked, watching Cantabri closely.

"Yes," Cantabri said, then, with growing confidence, "Yes, I do, and end this damned war for once and all."

22

The sea beyond Paestum was aswarm with ships, from transports converted from merchant ships to hopefully ocean worthy ferries and deep-water fishing boats without their nets to, Hal was glad to see, the *Galgorm Adventurer*. He was even more pleased to find that someone – he suspected Lord Cantabri – had arranged for it to be the Eleventh's transport.

This operation had been in the planning for some time – the *Adventurer*'s upper troopdeck had been hastily converted, with a raised and arched topdeck, to provide more dragon shelters.

As they were loading the beasts, trying to avoid being maimed by a dragon tail or drowned by being kicked off the quay by one of the fairly unhappy monsters, the rumor ran around that this was the beginnings of a great operation, to attack behind the northern Roche lines, and smash through to the capital.

"Which means codswallop," Farren said. "All we need now is to be gifted with winter gear, and I'll know for surely-certain we're goin' south.

"Friggin' military always thinks it can think, when by now it oughta know better. I could cast a little witchy pissyanty spell and find out where we're going, so you know damn-dast well the Roche wizards are already laying in wait."

Hal thought of telling him to button it, that his guess was far too close, but that would've only made the tale run faster.

"*Damned* fine thing," Saslic said dryly, looking out over the fleet, "that we're able to move in such secrecy. Thankin' the gods there aren't any Roche spies over there on the waterfront, spitting in the water and taking notes."

"Anybody else want to contribute?" Hal said.

"I think not," Sir Loren drawled. "I'm sure we're just off to the homeland for our holidays."

The ships, loosely gathered into lines, sailed north until they were out of sight of land, then swung west down the Chicor Straits, as had the *Adventurer* in its masking maneuvers before turning toward Black Island.

Hal didn't think it would do much good to conceal the operation from the Roche.

Mynta Gart spent a lot of time on deck, when she wasn't tending her new dragon, and Hal asked her if a seaman like her didn't like being below decks.

"Doesn't matter much to me," she said. "And I didn't notice I was above decks as much as you say. Perhaps I'm worried about the weather."

Hal lifted an eyebrow.

"This is damned late in the year to be sailing toward the open ocean," she said. "Winter storms're coming, and that bodes no good for the spit kits we've got around us.

"I can only hope we've got weather luck. Or some damned powerful wizards casting spells in the flagship."

Perhaps so, for no gales tore down on the fleet before it turned north again, and found a sheltered anchorage behind a long, narrow island, the Deraine port of Brouwer, where another great array lay waiting.

Some of these ships were brand new, others converted to merchantmen, and they were packed with troops, mostly new formations raised in Deraine.

Now, Hal thought, we should put out to sea as quickly as possible, before the tales have time to spread.

But they sat at anchor, waiting.

Hal's soldiers began grumbling, and so he put Serjeant Te to work on them, running them around and around the decks, up and down ropes, keeping them fit, with little time to get bored.

He flew off two three-dragon patrols each morning and night, and that kept his fliers from getting bored.

And they waited.

A royal messenger was rowed out to the *Adventurer*, with a request, from Lord Cantabri, to meet the expedition's commander, Lord Hamil, at a dinner to be held by Thom Lowess.

It seemed the taleteller had his fingers in everywhere.

*

It was a small, intimate gathering, at least by Lowess's standards. He'd rented a beach-front pavilion, and brought several of "his girls," including Lady Khiri Carstares.

A dozen men sipped wine in the antechamber. Hal was the lowest ranking of them all, and Lowess the only one not in uniform.

"Sir Hal," he smiled at Kailas. "At last I'll get a chance to see you in action."

"You mean you're going with us?"

"Lord Hamil has specially invited me, which pleases me no end." However, Lowess didn't look that thrilled. Hal wondered, and thought poorly of himself for the cattiness, whether Lowess preferred concocting his tales of derring-do a bit farther from the clash of battle.

Lady Khiri spotted him, and made for him as if he were magnetized. He tried to make polite conversation, but was all too aware of Saslic, back on the *Adventurer*, not to mention that the gown Khiri wore was scooped low enough in front so that he could've seen the color of her toenail polish without undue effort.

"And so you'll be one of the lucky ones," she said. "Not with us, freezing our poor little heinies off, here in the northland."

"How did you know?" was the best Hal could manage, hardly a way of dissimulating.

"Why, simply *everyone* knows," she said, in considerable astonishment. "It's been the talk of the court for weeks now."

"Wonderful," Hal muttered.

"If I didn't know better, and hadn't been aboard some of the terribly crowded ships you men will be sailing on," she went on, "I'd wish that you and I might be sharing a cabin, watching for the first flying fish, and feeling the wind grow warm around us."

Hal felt a bit warm at that moment, was relieved to see Lord Cantabri beckon him over. He excused himself, joined Cantabri and the other man he was with, medium height, white-haired, distinguished and looking most regal.

"Sir Hal, I'd like to introduce you to Lord Hamil," Cantabri said.

Hal guessed, at an event like this, it would be better to bow than salute. He evidently guessed correctly, for Hamil made a curt bow in return.

"So you're the young man on whom Lord Cantabri said we might well be depending?"

Hal fought for the proper words.

"I'd think, from what I've seen, we're more likely to be depending on him."

"A good, gentlemanly answer, sir," Lord Hamil approved, then turned to Cantabri.

"When this war first began, and the idea of men – and women – flying dragons, I was bothered by the idea, first that a measure of chivalry might be slashed from the nobility of war, and secondly, that these fliers might be less than gentlemanly warriors.

"But from what I've read of this young man, and the men and women he commands, I find that my suspicions were false.

"Indeed, to soar high over the muck and blood of the battleground might be creating a new nobility, a nobility of the air, and one which, were I beginning my military career, I might well envy and wish to join."

Neither Hal nor Cantabri found an answer to that one, although Hal tried feebly.

"I can only hope, Lord Hamil, to be worthy of your hopes."

"I'm sure you shall, lad," and Hamil smiled, and turned to another, passing lord.

"I say, Lord Devett, a word with you?"

Hal was about to say something to Cantabri, when Lowess approached them.

"Ah, the two sharpest arrows in my quiver. Are you enjoying yourselves, gentlemen?"

Hal took the moment.

"I'd be a deal happier, sir, were our expedition not on everyone's lips."

Lowess frowned.

"I know. I like it little myself. But the word has been going about for weeks. There's even been mention of a betting pool as to just what our destination is, and what I've heard mentioned is uncomfortably close to our plans.

"I suggested to Lord – to certain parties – that some replanning might be in order. He chose to disagree with me, so there appears little I can do.

"I wish there was more, since I will be sharing your fate this time."

Cantabri drained his wine glass.

"Might I ask you something, *sir*?" he said.

Hal noticed the slight emphasis on the sir.

"Anything within reason."

"You just said the two brightest arrows in your quiver. I'm not sure I understand."

"What I meant was quite simple. Just as I seem to have made certain people, and perhaps the nation of Deraine, aware of Sir Hal's propensity for valor, so I plan on doing the same for you as we progress to . . . to our eventual goal."

"I would rather not be so favored," Lord Cantabri said dryly.

"But Deraine needs heroes, sir. Don't pursue false modesty, sir," Lowess said, a bit sharply. "Heroism unnoticed, and unrewarded, does the nation little good.

"I'm afraid the burden is one you'll be forced to bear."

Cantabri sought for something to say, forced a smile and nodded.

Lowess fielded a glass from a passing servitor, and left them.

"It's nice to be in the company of a budding hero," Hal said.

"Damn, damn, damn," Cantabri growled.

"Now, what was it you were saying, Lord Cantabri," Hal mocked gently, "about not letting the truth stand in the way of a good story, just a few days ago?"

"Damme for dooming myself with my own mouth," Cantabri grumbled. "Now we'll both be laughing stocks, I fear."

Hal grinned, and a gong sounded. A door opened, and the guests began filtering toward the dining room.

The dinner began with a toast by Lowess:

"To our victory, and to the noblest of Deraine's warriors, gathered here tonight."

That, of course, was drunk to only by the women carefully positioned between each guest.

The next toast was by Lord Hamil:

"Confusion to our enemies."

That everyone drank to, Hal particularly, although he barely tasted the wine, since he'd been doing no drinking lately, and didn't think part of being a noble hero was throwing up on his host's linen.

The room was a marvel of old paintings and silk hangings. Four musicians, behind a screen, played softly, and a magician and two assistants worked interesting illusions that appeared, vanished, against a muslin curtain against one wall.

The illusions were of patriotic themes, great warriors, interspersed with sentimental scenes of life in Deraine. Hal wryly noticed that all these scenes were of the rich and their estates.

That made sense, he thought. No one in the room, with the exception of Hal, came from a poor family.

He was seated next to Lady Khiri Carstares, who, he thought, grew prettier each time he saw her.

"I want to apologize," she said.

"For what?"

"I saw you were upset that I know about . . . about certain matters."

"I am," Hal admitted.

"Do I look like a Roche spy?"

"I never saw one wearing a sign yet."

She smiled.

"Maybe not you," Hal went on. "But what about that waiter who just served us this fish pancake?"

"That, you barbaric soldier, is caviar . . . fish eggs. With sour cream."

"Oh." Hal chewed. "I guess I like it. But us barbaric soldiers like anything that isn't trying to eat us."

"Stop trying to be clever," she said. "Leave that for Thom Lowess."

They chatted on, about almost anything and everything except the war, and Hal found Khiri a delightful conversationalist.

Of course you do, a part of his mind said coldly. She's agreeing with almost everything you say.

The next course was perfectly cooked steak in a green peppercorn sauce, followed by herb-baked potato thins, puréed spiced vegetables, a watercress and endive salad with a lemony mustard dressing, and dessert was a meringue tort. Each course was accompanied by a different wine, which, as before, Hal barely tasted.

"You're quite the abstainer, sir," she said.

"Sometimes," Hal agreed. "When I don't want a thick head the next day."

"You needn't worry about that," she said, leaning close, and glancing around to make sure no one was listening. "You won't be sailing until the winter storm the wizards have forecast has passed, and that won't be for at least four days."

Hal was brought back to reality. Again, Khiri noticed.

"I'm sorry," she almost wailed. "Should I be a total ninny, and not talk about *anything*?"

Hal thought of explaining, decided if she didn't understand by now, she never would.

But Khiri realized her mistake, and began asking him about the habits of his dragons. Hal, eager for the change, talked on, then caught himself, realizing he was probably beginning to sound like Dinner Bore, Category Thirteen, the Dragon Expert.

He was about to apologize, when he realized Khiri had taken off her evening slipper, and, hidden by the long tablecloth, was rubbing her soft foot up and down his inner calf, above his dress half-boot.

He found himself gently sweating, looked at Khiri, saw her smiling, delighted with the effect she was working.

He made some inane comment about one of the illusions, a soldier and his lover walking arm in arm through a swirling garden.

"You are married?" Khiri asked.

"No," Hal said.

"But you have a lover."

"Uh . . . well, yes." Hal was ashamed of his hesitation. "How did you know?"

"The best men always have lovers," Khiri said mournfully. "Tell me about her."

To his surprise, Hal found himself yammering on about Saslic, and Khiri seemed most interested.

Then Hal's glass was empty, and Thom Lowess was standing again.

"I thank you all for attending my gathering," he said. "Boats are at the landing below, and I suggest it's time for those who're aboard ship to leave, since the weather appears likely to change within the hour.

"The promised storm is, indeed, upon us."

Khiri walked him down to the dock, shivered as a chill wind caught her.

"You'll forgive me, Sir Hal, for not staying, but this gale is freezing my poor little marrow."

Before he could respond, she leaned close, and kissed him, her tongue darting for an instant between his lips. He reached for her, reflexively, but she pulled away with a bell-like laugh, and ran up the steps into Lowess's mansion.

Hal tasted that kiss for a long time on the ride through the choppy waters back to the *Adventurer*.

The storm broke as predicted that night, and the ships put out double anchors but still heaved restlessly as the rain and wind beat at them.

Hal spent most of his time, as did the fliers and handlers, making sure the dragons were as happy as they could be, feeding them tidbits of offal the ship's cooks were only too glad to get rid of.

He tried to spend his time thinking about how his fire bottles might be improved, either magically or with better material, but Khiri's face kept intruding.

Saslic asked him why he was so pensive, and he was rude to her, and apologized hastily.

She looked at him strangely, but said nothing.

Four days later, the storm ended, and the sky was a wintry blue, the seas calm as a lake.

Signal flags went slatting up and down masts, and anchors were weighed, and slowly, laboriously, the great fleet made its way out into the open sea.

Hal was standing next to Sir Loren, Vad Feccia and Mynta Gart, awestruck at the vast number of ships, and Loren pointed.

"Look."

Half a dozen warships, sleek three-masters, bulwarks heavy with infantry, their rams, beaks, catapults menacing, boiled past under full sail, banners streaming.

Gart stared after them, eyes shining.

"Shows what a damned fool you were, coming to the dragons, when you could be mate of one of them now, coverin' yourself with glory," Vad Feccia said, with more than a bit of a senseless sneer.

Gart looked him up and down, but said nothing.

Hal determined that Feccia would be chosen to supervise some detail, preferably involving dragon shit.

Winds rose, and another storm threatened. Hal saw sailors praying in the small niche behind the *Adventurer*'s mainmast, guessed that seamen aboard the countless smaller ships would be praying even harder.

But the wind blew out before dawn, and once again the fleet sailed on.

Hal took his dragons up daily, staying close to the convoy, under orders not to fly south of the ships, toward land. The last headlands of Deraine fell away to their stern, and Sagene's coastline was, at most, a dim blur they never closed on.

Then the ships turned south, and even the thickest soldier realized they weren't about to campaign in the frozen north.

Morale and mood improved steadily.

They turned a bit closer to land, and twenty Sagene ships, plus escorts, joined the convoy. They were cheered by the Deraine soldiers and sailors, gave back huzzahs in return.

The fleet was at full strength.

Hal was on the foredeck at night, and one of the watch officers paced back and forth a few yards away.

Something to the landward caught his eye, and he asked to borrow the sailor's glass.

A darker bulk showed – Sagene. He stared at it, then saw a flare of light grow, start blinking.

"What's that?" he asked the officer. The man took the glass, scanned.

"Shit," he muttered.

"What is it?" Hal asked. The officer passed the glass back. The blinking light flashed again, then died.

"Two fingers to starboard," the sailor said, and Hal swung his gaze.

Another light came to life, blinked.

"Navigation beacons?" Hal guessed.

"The charts show none," the sailor said. "More likely signal beacons."

"Signaling what?" Hal asked, then caught it. "Oh."

"You have it," the sailor said grimly, and hurried to the captain's cabin to report they were being tracked.

Storm fairly leapt into the air, and honked in glee. None of the dragons liked being aboard ship. Hal wondered about that – how they could sail like boats, but despise these wooden creations, guessed it might be the stink of men, or perhaps the unnatural swaying as the ship rolled.

He sent Storm high, two other dragons climbing behind him, swooping in pure pleasure.

The wind was from the west-south-west, and almost warm, even here, a thousand feet above the water.

Hal scented a different wind – the wind of battle.

Sailors put out long trotlines, and pulled fish in, fish multi-colored and unknown to any of the men and women of Deraine.

The cooks set braziers on deck, and fried the fish, basting them in butter, and drenched them with hoarded lemons from Sagene. Hal thought he had eaten a record number of the crispy small delicacies, then saw Farren Mariah, still inhaling, two bites per fish, no more, not concerning himself with bones, crunching them like he was a beast.

"I'm catchin' up on a d'prived childhood," Mariah explained.

"You mean depraved," Saslic suggested.

"That too."

The dragons also liked the fish – fed to them raw, in bushel baskets.

Signal flags from the flagship went to the *Adventurer*, and Hal took half his flight aloft, flew east obeying the orders from Lord Hamil.

Great headlands rose from the sea, the ocean smashing high against them, empty bluffs that, according to his map, marked the farthest westering bit of Sagene.

Hal looked back, saw the fleet slowly turning west, following the coast toward Roche.

He saw something and, against orders, motioned Saslic to follow him down.

Storm's wings folded, and the dragon dove until Hal pulled the reins back.

The monster flared his wings, came level, and the headland's flat plateau was only a few hundred feet below.

Hal saw half a dozen tents, and something he couldn't quite make out. Then he saw it clear – a large mirror, gimbal mounted. There were half a dozen men around it, some looking out to sea.

Then smoke flared, and a small fire grew below the mirror.

It moved, beginning to flash rapidly, in some sort of code, pointed east. Hal squinted through the haze, thought he saw an answering blink.

He hoped this was an unmarked signal post of Sagene, but suspected far differently.

Hal waved to Saslic, and turned, at full speed, back toward the fleet.

A ship's boat took Hal to the fleet's flagship, a huge warship with holystoned decks and brightwork everywhere. Barefoot sailors in spotless uniform scurried here and there, as busy as housemaids, under the shouted orders of boatswains.

Hal saw Thom Lowess on the poop deck, nodded to him, ignored his obvious curiosity.

He was escorted to the enormous cabin of Lord Hamil. Hal thought it almost as large as a dragon pen.

They reported what they'd seen on the headlands to Hamil, Cantabri, two Sagene noblemen and staff officers.

Hamil said calmly, "I like this news but little."

Lord Cantabri nodded grimly, but said nothing.

Hamil got up, paced.

"So we must assume we've been seen . . . I'd guess those mirror-men could be Sagene traitors."

One of the Sagene nobles growled in anger, but made no comment.

"Or," Hamil went on, "more likely, long-range penetration agents from Roche.

"In either case, that means we've been seen by the enemy."

He looked worried. Hal couldn't understand – the fleet, and its design, had been known to everyone, including the gods on high, since before they sailed from Paestum.

Why should this latest be an astonishment?

But he held his tongue.

"Ships of the Roche fleet might be readying to sail against us," the other Sagene nobleman said worriedly.

Hamil nodded agreement.

"Very well, Sir Hal," Hamil said. "I'll notify the other three dragon flight commanders, and from now on you'll mount constant patrols to the east and north as we sail on toward Roche.

"You must be totally alert, watching especially for any unknown ships.

"From now on, as Lord Cantabri suggested to me back in Deraine, our fate could well be in your hands."

23

From aboard ship the Deraine fleet was most impressive. But from two thousand feet, the ships weren't nearly as awe-inspiring. Hal finally had a chance to count them, as Storm climbed for height. He made about seventy Deraine ships, thirty from Sagene and, in front and along the flanks, another twenty-five warships.

No one had any idea how many ships Roche might have in their navy, their size or deployment, since most of them were evidently berthed in southern waters.

It had possibly made sense to ignore the Roche navy as long as the war was fought on land, and the only sea-guard that needed keeping was over the Chicor Straits. But how no intelligence could have been gathered once Deraine decided on this amphibious invasion . . .

Hal turned that part of his mind off. He would never understand the thinking of generals and such.

Garadice and Sir Loren flew at Hal's flanks, and he set a compass course due west, eyes searching for any ships. Other than a scatter of fishing smacks, he saw nothing, and turned back after a three-hour flight, half of a dragon's comfortable range.

Hal and his team mates landed on the *Adventurer*'s barge, and another scouting flight took off from another transport.

He reported to Lord Hamil on the flagship by coded pennant, ate, waited for his next turn aloft.

Hal spent the time inventorying the fire bottles he'd had made up, with spells by one of Limingo's assistants, wondering just how he'd use them in the invasion. He dreamed of a new device, something that would really explode, something as big as a man, but had no idea how such a killing machine might be built, either by normal engineering or by magic.

His next shift began at midnight, and so he chose Saslic and Garadice to accompany him as the most capable fliers, and paid close attention to his compass on the way out, and on the way back.

Nothing was seen.

Saslic brought him an interesting sheet of paper.

"Look you," she said. "We're not doing all we could."

"Explain, if you would," Hal said.

"Easily. We fly out for three hours, then back for three. That gives us a known area, like I've drawn here, which is no more than the fleet takes to travel in two days."

"Two days is a long time."

"To plan a battle?" Saslic asked, glanced about. "Particularly with these dunderbrains in charge of us?"

"You have an idea?"

"Surely. If there's such a thing as a good chart . . ."

"Maybe," Hal said, "from the captain."

There was, a merchant seaman's map from before the war.

Saslic spread it across the navigator's table, ignored his scowl, and studied it closely.

"Just what are we supposed to be looking for?" Hal asked.

"For this," and her finger stabbed at the map. Hal bent closer, saw three tiny dots, just beyond the Sagene-Roche border.

"Islands. Uh . . . the Landanissas."

"Smart, smaaaart man," Saslic said. "A bit more than – what's the scale on this damned map? – eight hours flight time, assuming the fleet is about here. We wait until we're within six hours' range, then what we do is take, oh, two other fliers, and fly off to those islands. That'll give us a forward base to look for the Roche . . . Assuming they've got any ships out there."

"Supposing those islands, which look pretty damned small, don't happen to have anything like water or something we can feed the dragons with?"

"They will," Saslic said confidently. "Look. This little one's got a littler dot, with the name of the port – Jarraquintah. Damned barbarous names these Roche use. Any place with a name has got people. Any place with people's got pigs and water.

"Admire my strategic abilities, O Sir Hal."

"I'm admiring," Hal said. "Four fliers."

"You, me, Garadice and Sir Loren. The best we've got."

Hal took Saslic's plan to Lord Cantabri, figuring that anything irregular was more likely to be approved by him, or at least go to Lord Hamil with Cantabri's hero stamp on it.

Cantabri studied the map and a brief outline thoroughly.

"You'd need gold," he said. "Both for bribes, and for supplies, assuming Dinapur's right, and the island's inhabited.

"What happens if it's garrisoned?"

"We'll make a sweep first," Hal said. "If there's sign of soldiery, we'll shelter on one of the islands until our dragons are rested, then fly back."

"And if all three islands have soldiers?"

Hal had thought of that.

"The only thing we'll be able to do is fly due north, toward Roche, and land on the water if our beasts are winded. Wait for a time, then go on to the mainland.

"We'll try to find a source of supply there, either by force of arms or with the gold, then fly back to the fleet."

"Assume you can't," Cantabri said.

"Then we'll make our way north, as we can," Hal said. "North and west, toward the Sagene border and our lines."

"And if you're captured?" Cantabri said.

Hal shrugged.

"Try not to talk as long as we can. Then . . ."

"Anyone can be broken," Cantabri said grimly. "I'm glad you're not laboring under illusions of heroism."

"I stopped that the first time I got wiped out," Hal said. "Back with the cavalry."

"A hard lesson to learn," Cantabri sighed, looking about Lord Hamil's cabin and the swarm of brave-looking staff officers. "Sometimes I think . . ."

"What, sir?"

"Nothing," Cantabri said. "I'll have to take this to Lord Hamil, of course. But I see no reason he won't approve.

"Go ahead and make your preparations, and I'll signal the *Adventurer* with the decision.

"And if I don't get a chance to give you my blessings and prayers, for whatever they're worth, when you fly off, you have them now.

"Go, and find the damned Roche, if they're out there. *But come back!*"

The four dragons took off through a lowering rain and cloud cover. Hal orbited the *Adventurer* until all four were together, then pulled Storm's reins back, and prodded its flanks into a steep climb.

He vanished into the clouds, hoping that the other fliers weren't prone to vertigo. Or dragons, either . . . And he realized nobody knew if they could lose their mental balance.

He would've prayed, if there was anyone left to pray to, or cross his fingers, except that bold dragonmasters didn't do things like that.

Then they broke out into warm sunshine, still in the formation they'd gone into the clouds with.

Hal checked his compass, set a course, and then there was nothing to do but wait, occasionally checking the small clock that was the rest of his navigational tools.

Time dragged, for man, woman and dragon. The beasts were laden, carrying emergency rations and weapons.

Hal would have liked to dart through fingers of cloud stretching upward toward him, to relieve his boredom, but didn't dare alter his plot. What wind there was came from the rear, hopefully speeding them on their way, and he hoped there weren't any side-gusts that would drive them off course.

After five hours of monotony, broken only by the occasional fear that he'd gotten all four of them irretrievably lost, to vanish into the wastes of the Southern Sea, Hal blatted on his trumpet, and motioned down.

Again, they went down through the clouds, and a chill drizzle embraced them.

Hal was beginning to worry that the clouds went all the way down to the sea when they broke out, and heaving gray ocean was below them.

There was no sign of land, no sign of the islands.

The other three formed in a tight vee formation behind him. Saslic gave him a worried look, and Hal forced that traditional Leader's Grin, proving he was in full control, knew exactly where they were, and there was no reason to be concerned.

Half an hour dragged past, and Hal could feel Storm's muscles begin to tremble a little as the dragon tired.

Then Hal saw something gray, grayer than the sea or air, ahead. Land of some sort, and he didn't care all that much what it was.

The gray became an island, then three islands, directly ahead, between Storm's horns.

Hal looked left, right, preened visibly, and his heart slowed to something resembling a normal rate.

Since the chart showed no other islands in the area, let alone islands grouped in three, these had to be the Landanissas.

He took Storm high, just below the overcast and overflew the islands once, then again. He saw no signs of warships, no other craft except small fishing boats.

Emboldened, he dove down toward the small settlement on one, which he guessed would be Jarraquintah. There were a few men and women below, mending nets, working in small fields or in boats.

They gaped up at the four dragons, but didn't wave.

That might not be a good sign. But to balance that, he saw no one visibly armed, and no sign of uniforms.

Behind the village was a plateau, with a pond in its middle, and he motioned the flight to land.

They floated in, and were down. Hal slid out of the saddle, legs almost collapsing under him, and led Storm to the pond, the others behind him.

"Well, we're here," Saslic said.

"We are that," Garadice agreed.

"Are we ready to go into our song and dance?" Sir Loren said, pointing to a straggle of a dozen men and women coming up from the village.

The original plan was for them to pretend to be a Roche dragon flight that had gotten lost, and to beg the mercy of the fishermen.

However . . .

"They appear to be armed," Sir Loren said. "And their expressions aren't friendly."

"Do we have time enough to run, and get the dragons in the air?" Saslic asked. "Just being cautious, not cowardly, you know."

Hal shook his head, unbuckled and dropped his dagger-belt, and walked toward the fishers, arms out, hand extended.

One of the fishermen drew a fish spear back, ready to cast, and Hal, in turn, got ready to duck to one side.

But a woman in front of the dozen snapped something, and the man lowered his spear, but looked sullen, not shamefaced.

The woman advanced toward Hal, but didn't put aside the long flensing knife she carried.

"Who you?" she said, in Roche, in a barbaric Roche accent Hal could barely understand. Clearly the islanders spoke their own language, another good sign. "Roche bastards?"

"Not enemy," he said, discarding the original deception plan.

"Who?"

"From another country," Hal said.

"Name?"

"Hal."

"Not Roche name. Name country?"

"Deraine."

"Not hear of," she said, with finality, as if her knowledge should cover the known universe. "You demons?"

"No," Hal said. "Men. Women."

"Maybe."

"What your name?" Hal said.

"No," the man with the spear said. "Demon know name, have power."

"How we know *you* not demon?" Saslic said, walking up beside Hal.

"I real!" the man said indignantly, thumping his chest.

"I real too," Saslic said, doing the same.

Someone laughed.

"My name Zoan," the woman said. "I lead, after Roche take men."

"Why they take men?"

"To serve on ships," Zoan said. "Ships of war."

"Deraine at war with Roche," Hal chanced.

There were grunts, mutters of evident approval.

"You ride monsters?" Zoan said. "I hear men do that now."

"We ride dragons," Hal said. "We fight from dragons."

"How you fight ships?"

"We have ships . . . Back there . . ." Hal waved vaguely. "We look for Roche for them."

"What you want with us?" the spearman said.

"We want to buy pigs. Chickens. Fish. We want to sleep up here. For three, maybe four days. We look for Roche."

"How you pay?"

"We pay," Hal said, not about to show these people any gold until the situation settled down some. "Good money."

There was a buzz.

"What else you want? You want women? Boys?"

"No," Hal said. "We are soldiers, not . . ." He couldn't find the word.

Zoan said a word in Roche Hal didn't catch, explained by running her finger in and out of her fisted hand.

"That," Hal said. "Not that."

"Good," Zoan said. "You buy pigs for you?"

"No. For dragons. For us, chickens. Fish. Or we buy fish and chickens for dragons, too."

"Demons don't eat," the spearman announced positively, as if he were on first name terms with several. "They men, women, I think."

Zoan considered, nodded.

"You welcome in Jarraquintah, that Roche name. We call it Wivel."

And so Deraine came to the Landanissas Islands.

The pigs were scrawny little creatures, but there were many of them, and so Hal bought eight.

The sight of the gold coins made the islanders chatter excitedly.

Zoan took out a talisman from around her neck, touched it to the coins.

"These real," she announced. "Now we have feast for you."

The feast was fairly elaborate, several courses of fish, and chicken spiced so hot tears streamed down Hal's cheeks, while Saslic sneered at him for being a baby.

There was drink – home-fermented corn beer. Hal ordered no one to touch it, not sure the islanders wouldn't wait until they were in their cups, then decide to do further testing on whether or not demons bled.

The other three fliers shrugged unconcern, especially after Saslic sniffed one of the great pottery jugs that held the brew. Hal was grateful he hadn't brought Farren Mariah along – the diminutive flier would have found some way into the drink, or else would have had to be chained to a tree.

They'd brought waterproofed canvas sheets, and spread their blankets under them. The night was balmy, a bit misty.

Saslic and Hal had found themselves a place away from the others, and, disregarding their agreement, made love slowly, tenderly, before falling asleep.

The two had the first patrol, at dawn, and flew out for an hour and a half, on a west-north-west heading, then back to the island. They saw nothing except a scatter of boats. Hal, even though she wasn't his best flier, wished he'd taken Gart along, since the seaman might've told him what to look for to navigate: shoals, outcroppings, other clues. He did notice the direction the seabirds flew in, and, watching his compass carefully, discovered they were headed back to the islands.

Garadice and Sir Loren took the next patrol, while Hal and Saslic wandered down to the village, where a woman happily grilled small fish and fresh vegetables, gave them a fiery dipping sauce.

They sought details on the Roche kidnapping, found that it had happened six months or more ago, and so far none of the men pressganged had returned home. Hal hoped this bullying policy was commonplace among the Roche – that, in the long run, might make the war a bit more winnable.

But such thoughts were for another place and time.

Satiated, they went back to their campsite, groomed and fed their dragons, and found their blankets for a nap.

Hal kicked his dragon in the ribs, pulled on the reins. The beast's wings beat harder, and he went to altitude and relieved Farren.

He saw nothing, and Sir Loren replaced him.

The biggest of the Roche dragons from the hatchery – they were about twenty feet long, Hal guessed almost yearlings – were being loaded as his flight landed, and the second flight took off on patrol.

Handlers had already offloaded barrels of beef, and hacked their tops open, one for each dragon. The monsters gulped hungrily, eyes darting back and forth, daring any of the two-legs to bother them.

Soldiers were passing out buns stuffed with smoked fish, onions and pickles. The fliers got their noon meal, cups of tea, and watched the madness.

Hal noted Garadice, standing near one of the dragon pens, and went over. The dragon trainer had a worried expression on his face.

"What are you eating your fingers about, sir?" Hal asked.

"I have no idea what secret – if any, other than endless patience – the Roche trainers are using to train these black dragons."

"Whyn't you ask one?"

"The soldiers say all of the trainers fled into the hills while we were landing. Maybe they're telling the truth, or maybe the trainers had time to disguise themselves as common guards.

"I was hoping we'd take prisoners of either the trainers or magicians, and find out the Roche secrets. But no such luck, and we don't have the time to beat the bushes for them," he said, and as he spoke, a trumpet blared.

"Back aboard," Sir Bab was shouting, the command echoed by his warrants.

One of Limingo's assistants scurried by.

"What's the problem?" Hal called.

He shook his head.

"Not sure, not sure at all. But we've detected some sort of magic out there, just a wisp."

"From where?"

"From the east," and the man was gone.

Hal's back prickled. That unknown dragon that maybe didn't exist had flown away to the east, too.

He looked up at the second flight, saw with a grimace they were very low, no more than two thousand feet overhead.

The day was sunny, just warm enough to warrant stripping naked for a bit of sun.

Naturally, that led to lovemaking.

Finished, Saslic yawned, looking up at the sky.

"Now, would this be a life? Get up, go out on your boat, cast your net, come back with fish, and your pigs and fowl and garden would give you the rest.

"Would that be a life?"

Hal considered, was about to answer, when Saslic spoke first.

"Naah. I'm full of shit. I'd go nuts from boredom in a month."

"Not to mention," Hal put in, "if I lived here, I never would have met you."

"Why you romantic demon, you." She kissed him, rolled away. "Now go to sleep. We've got the night shift."

Hal tried to obey, but as he drifted off, a thought came.

Nor would I have ever ridden a dragon.

The sadness that brought convinced him he was following a true course, as Mynta Gart might've said.

Now, remembering what Saslic had said about there being no after the war for a dragon flier, all he had to do was figure a way to live until the killing stopped.

Sir Loren and Garadice flew back. They'd patrolled due north, to the Roche mainland, and had seen nothing.

Hal and Saslic flew out at dusk, keeping a course almost due east. The sky was spotted with clouds, and both moons were clear in the sky.

They were an hour and a half out, Hal trying to keep from yawning, and then, he saw what he thought to be stars, low on the horizon.

He shouted to Saslic, and they changed their dragon's course slightly.

The stars grew larger, were below the horizon, and became ships. Many ships. Hal counted at least twenty masthead lights.

The Roche fleet.

Then Hal saw something else:

Flying in lazy circles above the ships were two, no four, dragons.

24

Hal's orders to his flight had been very clear. He fancied he could see Saslic scowl at him, but she obeyed his instructions, and Nont broke away, back the way they'd come. She was to return to the island, report contact, and get the others ready to move. If Hal didn't return within two hours, they were to assume he was lost, and fly off to alert the fleet.

Hal himself, unobserved as far as he could tell, found a thickish cloud to hide above, ducking out momentarily now and again to correct Storm's direction until he was flying in the same direction as the convoy.

Hal checked that compass heading twice, frowning. The Roche ships weren't sailing west, to make contact as directly as possible with their enemies, but in a north-north-westerly direction.

That boded poorly for the invasion fleet, he suspected, but there were other matters to deal with before Hal could duck from his cloud and fly hard for the Landanissas.

He counted the ships below. Sixty, at least, in three waves, sailing close together. All appeared to be galleys, of a fairly uniform size, so Hal assumed they were all warships. Their oars were raised, and they were traveling, at about the same speed as the Deraine-Sagene fleet, under power of the two squaresails on each ship's masts.

He thought about going lower, remembered Cantabri's warning, and climbed, keeping that cloud between him and the Roche. Once or twice he saw dots that were the patrolling dragons, but they didn't see him.

Very high, he set his course back the way he'd come.

They'd found the enemy. Now to report his presence, and also his very obvious intents.

"Very good, Sir Hal," Lord Hamil said. "I have no doubt that you'll warrant another decoration from the king, since you've made it possible to obliterate the Roche."

"Uh, sir," Hal said. "There's something else. Something more important."

"What could be more important," Hamil said, with a bit of a scowl, "than being able to destroy the enemy?"

The cabin, thick with staff officers, was very quiet, waiting.

"The Roche direction of sail, sir."

"Explain, if you would?"

Hal went to the large map on the bulkhead behind Hamil.

"Sir, we're pretty sure our fleet's been tracked since we left Deraine."

"There's no certainty of that," Hamil said.

"No, sir," Hal said agreeably. "But consider that these Roche aren't not sailing toward us. Instead. . . ."

His fingers touched the map where the Roche galleys should be.

". . . instead, sir, they're on this course."

He traced the heading until it touched the Roche mainland. "They're making for this rivermouth port, sir, Kalabas."

Hamil jolted, and there were gasps from some of the staff officers.

Cantabri's eyes widened, as he got it.

"What of it?" Hamil tried to brazen it out.

Hal didn't know how to pursue the matter. Of course he wasn't supposed to know anything about the fleet's point of landing, but he'd remembered Cantabri saying the invasion would be at the mouth of a navigable river, leading north toward the Roche capital of Carcaor, and the great river at Kalabas, labeled the Ichili, met the description perfectly.

Finally Kailas said, rather lamely, "I thought that would be of import to you."

"Mayhap," Hamil said. "An interesting note, and one which I'll take into consideration, after we've destroyed the Roche."

Putting Hal out of his mind, he strode to the map.

"Gentlemen, I propose a simple plan. We'll change our course like so, and sail to catch the Roche on their flank. Our magicians will be casting all of the confusion spells they're capable of.

"We'll take those ships on their weakest point, and smash them. I know a bit about galleys, and how structurally weak they are compared to our ships, which is why we've built none in Deraine for any purpose other than harbor tugs.

"We'll hit them first, hit them hard, and leave them to their fate.

"This blow will ensure our landing will be successful.

"Now, I wish to see all ship division captains aboard here by midday, gentlemen. See to it."

Hal saluted, wasn't noticed in the bustle, and he and Cantabri edged out on to the flagship's main deck.

"Pardon me, sir," Hal said. "But . . . Son of a bitch!"

"Indeed," Cantabri said. "Went right over his head. Lord Hamil didn't live to be as ripe as he is by worrying about anything more than today's sorrows."

"So we're supposed to proceed with the landing," Hal said, "even though it's certain the damned Roche know exactly where we're going ashore, and, noting that river, exactly what our plans must be."

"As you said," Cantabri said grimly, "son of a bitch!"

Even if Lord Hamil couldn't see the morrow's dangers, he was good at dealing with today's.

The fleet changed course, curving south-south-east for half a day, then changed its course to north-north-east.

They would be in sight of the Roche in the late afternoon, the fleet navigator said, when the first dogwatch began. All four dragon flights were ordered to be in the air an hour before the meeting. Two were to observe, a third to attack the Roche dragons, and Hal's flight ordered to take its fire bottles against the galleys.

The Roche ships came into sight, and Roche dragons rose to meet the Deraine dragons.

The beginnings of the battle went like an infernal clockwork toy. The transports were ordered to drop sail until signaled to join the fray, and the warships put on full sail.

If Hal could forget about the probable disaster of the invasion, and he tried very hard, it was quite a spectacle, the sails of the Deraine and Sagene ships catching the falling sun, and, ahead of Storm, the vees of the Roche.

The dots of the four Roche dragons were met by the dragon flight, and the monsters swarmed together.

Someone reported the Deraine fleet, and suddenly the Roche sails came to the wind, and the oars dropped raggedly down into the water as men manned their fighting stations. Long waves creamed behind the galleys as they came up to full speed.

Hal had a glass, and saw pennants flap to the mastheads of the Roche ships.

The admiral in charge of the Roche ships evidently decided to split his vees, the left diagonal turning to meet the enemy, while the right formed a broad second line, probably intending to envelop the Deraine and Sagene ships.

But it didn't work that smoothly, or at all.

Ships crashed into ships, lost headway rather than risk collision, and it was a swirling maelstrom two thousand feet below.

Some of the madness may have come from the spells cast by Deraine and Sagene wizards, spells of fear, alarm, panic.

Hal glanced around, saw no sign of dragons, guessed they were fully involved with the Deraine monsters, signaled for his flight to dive on the Roche.

They dove hard and fast. Hal, who'd never done this kind of fighting before, estimated the right moment and hurled a fire bottle out and down. Other bottles cascaded with it.

He pulled Storm up, banked, and cursed, seeing all of the bottles smash harmlessly into the sea, twelve flashes of fire and smoke, hurting no one.

But the Roche must never have heard of such a weapon, because the echelon he attacked went crazy, trying to turn away from the threat. Ships smashed together, and Hal fancied he could hear shouts and screams from his position.

He readied another fire bottle, and sent Storm down, determined he'd hit this time, or by the gods dive straight through that damned Roche galley.

He was low, very low, low enough to see oarsmen screaming, pointing, jumping overside, and he lobbed his fire bottle.

It hit just abaft the foremast, burst into flames, and the sail above it caught.

Fire roared up, took the ship, and Storm was speeding just above the waves, then up, barely clearing another galley's mast, and Hal went for the heights.

He looked back, saw three other ships afire, approved, and went down again with his third and last fire bottle.

This one missed, like his first, but four other fliers had better luck, and fire raged on the waters.

Ships were out of control, some oarsmen pulling pointlessly on one bank, the other side abandoned.

Ships collided with burning galleys, and the fire took them as well.

Hal and his flight, all intact, climbed high, just as the last Roche dragon plummeted past, into the sea.

There was nothing to do but watch now, as the Deraine fleet crashed into the swirling mass of galleys, their rams smashing, tearing the fairly flimsy hulls of the Roche ships, the galleys trying to send their soldiery across to board.

At first the Deraine ships refused close battle, smashing galleys down, sailing through into the second line, and attacking them. They turned, and awkwardly sailing almost into the wind, struck the rear of the Roche fleet.

Signals went up, and certain Deraine transports sailed into the middle of the battle, closing alongside crippled galleys, and sending infantrymen across to finish the ruination.

Another sweep by the Deraine and Sagene warships, and that was all the Roche sailors could take.

More than twenty of their ships broke away, skittering like waterbugs west, away from the battle.

But ten or so ships had harder men aboard, and fought on, refusing to strike.

They killed . . . but were killed in turn.

By dark, there was nothing left of the Roche fleet but crippled, burning, sinking galleys. The Roche had been shattered, for the loss of half a dozen Deraine or Sagene warships.

The way to the beachhead was now open.

Hal dreaded what might well happen next.

25

Victorious, the armada proudly sailed up to the Kalabas Peninsula. The town of Kalabas appeared abandoned, and there were no Roche warships, save two tiny patrol boats, securing the enormous Ichili River.

The way was open into the heart of Roche.

But the fleet just sat there, for all of a very long day.

Hal took his flight far up the peninsula, saw no sign of soldiery, saw nothing on the river to block Deraine.

But nothing happened. The warships cruised about, the transports sat, boats launched, ready to board the impatient troops crowding the decks.

When Hal brought his dragons at midday, he asked, almost in a stammering rage, what the hells was going on.

The answer, somewhat unbelievably, was that Lord Hamil was holding commanders' conferences aboard the flagship, to make sure everyone understood his orders.

They'd had many weeks aboard ship to rehearse and memorize, but now Hamil appeared to be letting opportunity slip past him.

"Th' bastid's afeared," Farren Mariah said. "He's had nought all his life but little pissyanty soldiering, and now he's got all these frigging ships ready to sail widdershins if he commands, and he's got both thumbs up his arse, walking on his frigging elbows!"

That unfair summation seemed most accurate.

The flight grabbed hasty sandwiches, took off again, without orders. Hal decided to scout the peninsula as far as he could go.

The land was rocky, with high cliffs surrounding the small village. There were only two winding roads climbing to the top of the plateau. They ran north, on either side of the land, through narrow passes broken by open land, with only low brush for cover.

Come on, Hal found himself muttering. Get ashore, before the damned Roche show up, because if you don't take the peninsula now, you'll never be able to hold it.

He passed another dragon flight, and its commander held up his hands in equally helpless anger.

It wasn't until late afternoon that the landing commenced, troops getting into the boats in a leisurely manner, as if they were on a holiday outing.

The cavalry's horses were hoisted on to small lighters, and rowed ashore, to splash about in the low surf.

Hal saw no signs of any of the smaller ships the fleet had brought with them securing the river.

At dusk, on another flight up the peninsula, he saw dustclouds on the roads. He flew lower, saw endless columns of Roche infantry and cavalry pouring toward the peninsula's tip.

Saslic held up her crossbow, pointed down. Hal shook his head. Each bolt could kill one man, and that would hardly slow the horde. And where and when would replacement bolts be available?

Hal flew hard back to the flagship, chanced putting a protesting Storm down in the water almost alongside it. A boat was lowered, and he told the coxswain to keep the reins to the dragon close. He'd be back directly.

Aboard ship, he reported what he'd seen to Lord Hamil, who

seemed unworried, telling Hal that the troops were already forming up for an attack from the town to secure a foothold atop the
plateau. In fact, Lord Cantabri had just gone ashore, to get the
men moving.

There was nothing for Hal to do, except go back to Storm,
who was hissing unhappily at the poor sailor. Very grateful for
not being eaten, the man shouted for his oarsmen to row hard
back to the flagship, away from this damned monster and his
demon-bound master.

Hal's next problem was taking off. The sea was calm, and
there was almost no wind. Storm tried hard, but couldn't break
free of the water.

Hal had to swim his beast to the *Adventurer*, and have Storm
hoisted aboard the takeoff barge before he could get in the air. He
took a moment to toss his dragon a squawking hen. Storm swallowed it in a gulp, but didn't appear that mollified.

Saslic, leading his flight, swooped low as he took off.

"The bastards have the heights," she shouted.

The Roche infantry, moving at a run, now controlled both
roads going up to the plateau.

The Deraine infantry began plodding up the winding tracks.
Hal saw a cavalry formation push past them, and try to charge.
Arrows, crossbow bolts rained down, and men and horses
screamed, died, fell back.

Another dragon flight swooped on the Roche positions. Two
riders carried bows, and fired down at the enemy. A shower of
arrows came up to meet them. The dragons rolled in midair,
clawing at the shafts buried in their sides, stomachs, and smashed
into the ground, writhing, dying.

The infantry mounted their attack, and were cut down in
rows. None even closed with the Roche.

They tried again, going straight up the rocks, off the road, got
within sword-reach before they broke, stumbling, jumping back
the way they'd come, leaving men sprawled on bloody rocks.

The Roche seemed to have no interest in counterattacking,
content with their commanding positions.

And then the sun dropped into the sea, and the first day's disaster was complete.

Hal and the other dragon flight commanders were summoned to
the flagship, where Lord Cantabri awaited them. He was dirty,
haggard and worn.

"We're attacking again tomorrow," he said. "I'll lead the assault. Straight up and at them, which is the only way we've got left now." He put emphasis on the last word, which the fliers noticed.

"We must gain a foothold on the plateau . . . or else the whole invasion may be lost.

"I want all of you to put every effort into doing anything to make the attack succeed.

"Sir Hal, I want your flight to scout behind their lines, and give me warning if Roche reinforcements appear."

"Sir," Hal said, "I think I can do better service than that."

Hal told him his plan. Cantabri winced. "That'll burn up – pun not intended – a valuable reserve."

"But you said—"

"I know what I said." Cantabri sighed. "All right. Cabet, you'll do the scouting I assigned Sir Hal to. That's all, gentleman. Pray for Deraine . . . And for all of us.

"You're dismissed."

The attack began at dawn. Men who'd gotten little sleep after the ordeal of the day before took position, and started up toward the plateau.

They moved in line, guides shouting orders to keep the lines even, as they'd been trained. Hal winced, seeing the Roche cut them down like a peasant scythes wheat.

The entire front line went down, and then the second. But the third pressed on, suddenly forgetting their training, darting from rock to rock, archers and crossbowmen firing only when they were sure of a target, closing on the clifftop.

Hal sent Storm into a dive, the rest of his flight behind him, well spread out. Each flier had a fire bottle ready, and looked for a target as the ground rose up at them. Hal threw, didn't know if he hit the knot of crossbowmen he'd aimed at, dragged Storm around, and came in on the level, dropping one, then his last fire bottle.

Flame gouted along the cliff, but Hal wasn't finished. Crossbow ready, he looked for targets – officers, men who looked important. He fired, reloaded, fired, and sent Storm back along the line.

Sometime in this sweep, he lost his first flier – the dragon hit in the throat, screeching, diving down toward the town, smashing through infantrymen moving steadily upward.

But he sent his flight back again, sniping at anything worth shooting.

Then he was out of bolts, and pulled Storm up, looking back and seeing Deraine banners top the cliff, and smash into hand-to-hand fighting with the Roche.

By dark, Sagene and Deraine held a precarious toe-hold on the plateau.

Some infantry units had been completely wiped out, almost all in the attack lost most of their officers and experienced warrants.

Lord Cantabri took an arrow in the side, fortunately a wound that looked far worse than it was. Bandaged and in a stretcher, he swore he could still lead the fight from the village, at the very least.

Hal had expended all the fire bottles he'd brought, as well as 200 irreplaceable bolts.

Instead of being able to sleep, he found every bottle the *Adventurer* had, enough lamp oil to fill them, and had them rowed across to the flagship, for Limingo to cast a spell on them.

The next day, with Lord Hamil himself ashore, accompanied by his staff and a distinctly unhappy Thom Lowess, although sensibly not going as far forward as Cantabri had done, the attack went forward, and Hal's fliers rained fire on the Roche.

By day's end, Deraine held a perimeter half a mile deep, a mile long.

But no more.

The Roche dug trenches, and further attacks were driven back, with heavy losses.

Hal lost another dragon, but the flier managed to save himself.

There were now thirteen left in the flight.

The attack up the peninsula was a failure.

Hal had wondered, rather dully, having other matters on hand, why the damned fleet didn't attack up the Ichili River, since that was the intended invasion route.

Perhaps Lord Hamil had been waiting for the peninsula fight to be over.

But when even he had to recognize there'd be no victory on the plateau, he finally ordered an attack upriver.

Sages cast runes, decided in three days there'd be a favorable wind from the south.

There was, and so the smaller, shallower-draughted ships started up, tacking from bank to bank.

Overhead were the dragons, scouting for an ambush.

There were no surprises for about eight miles, then the river narrowed into a gut, barely a quarter mile wide, the current fast-rushing, more than some of the ships could manage.

Supposedly someone asked Lord Hamil's main wizard for a spell to reduce the water-rush, and was laughed at.

"Gods make those kind of spells," the magician said, "not men. But I'll give you some advice – wait until the tide is on the flow, and that'll make it easier to sail through."

Gart, who'd watched all this from above, sat at dinner in the messdeck of the *Adventurer*, shaking her head.

"It's not so much the stupidity of the godsdamned army that bothers me," she said. "It's that it's somewhat like a disease. There must be seamen, even rivermen somewhere in this expedition of idiots who could've figured that out. But no, they've got to be as thick-headed as Hamil the Dolt."

"Careful," Lord Loren said, grinning. "That's treasonous."

"No, treasonous is the fool who named Hamil as commander of—"

Gart broke off hastily, remembering it was King Asir himself who'd chosen Hamil.

"So what now?" Saslic asked Gart.

"We'll try to force a passage through," Gart suggested. "Unless other things happen first."

Other things happened first.

At dawn the next day, there were Roche soldiers on the heights above the gut, equipped with catapults.

But that gave Hal a target, and so he and his flight went out with fire bottles, and the catapults roared up into flames.

Before the narrow passage could be sailed through, though, patrol boats found the river below the gut blocked, trapping two dozen ships.

The blockage appeared, at first, like a huge net, somehow stretched, in the course of a single night, across a half-mile-wide stretch of the river. The ends of the net were guarded by Roche battalions, who drove off attempts at landing.

Other Roche units reinforced the heights above the gut, until that passage was secured.

Lord Hamil decided to take larger warships upriver, and ram the net. Once the net was holed, the trapped ships could escape.

He also decided to make the attack at night.

It was blowing hard, so none of the dragons could handily fly, which Hal was very grateful for, later.

Three ships drove under full sail at the "net," and it came alive, lifting out of the water like so many conjoined serpents, reaching out for the ships as they closed. Certainly it was magic of a high order as the net took the ships, and tore at them, climbing over their bulwarks and pulling the ships down, until water surged over their rails, pouring down into their holds.

The three rolled, back, forth, then capsized, men spilling into the water, swimming away from the nightmare.

There were creatures in the river, creatures no one could later quite describe, that tore at the men until the river turned muddy brown with blood.

Few of the sailors aboard the three ships made it to the banks, and those that did were killed by Roche soldiers.

The net appearing to be broken, the twenty-four trapped ships tried to push for freedom. But the net, or whatever it was, reformed, ripping at these small ships, tearing out masts, winding like corpse-sheets around the hulls, pulling them under.

Seven of these small boats, carrying as many men as they could pull aboard, until they were down to the gunwales, made it to the river mouth and safety.

Something no one had appeared to plan for, or at any rate hadn't planned well, was resupplying the expedition. The fleet itself had to land all supplies, then sail back toward Sagene for more men, more equipment, more of everything.

Only a few ships were left – picket boats, the flagship, hospital ships and the dragon ships, among others.

With them went Thom Lowess, who'd taken Hal aside the night before sailing.

"I think it's time I moved on."

Hal lifted an eyebrow, Lowess drew closer, making sure there was no one to overhear.

"I came out to write tales that would build morale back in Deraine. This disaster is hardly my cup of tea. And, to tell you my own personal feeling, things aren't likely to improve.

"But don't worry, Hal. I'll make sure your career stays on an even keel. Yours and Lord Cantabri's."

*

Lord Cantabri sourly watched, from shore, as the ships sailed away, leaving the soldiers marooned, and said, "A frigging whale. We're nothing but a damned stranded whale on this strand. Deraine forever. Hurrah, hurrah, hurrah."

26

Ninety days later, the beachhead was even worse. There was more debris along the shore, more broken, abandoned weaponry scattered on the heights and below. The village had been ransacked again and again for materials for shelter, firewood, or simply for the joy of having something to ruin that wouldn't ruin back.

The Roche archers and crossbowmen killed their share, waiting in concealment until someone had a careless moment, and ensured he'd never have another one. More died through Lord Hamil's insistence the Roche would only "respect" Deraine by aggressive patrolling. So every night patrols went out, and were ambushed.

But still more died from disease. The sere Kalabas peninsula hid strange sicknesses, some that killed quickly, others that tore until a man or woman screamed for death's relief.

The expedition had run out of room to bury its dead, and so priests and sorcerers burnt the bodies in tall pyres. Soldiers swore they'd never be able to eat mutton again, the smell being just like that of a burning corpse.

But that was just one of the stinks — decaying bodies of horses and men, spoiled supplies, burnt wood, decay and shit hung over the peninsula like an invisible fog.

No one had allowed for the winter storms, even in the more placid Southern Ocean, so the supply line was constantly overstrained, in danger of snapping, and the troops mostly lived on iron rations, almost never seeing fresh food. Officers and staff personnel seemed only too ready to "borrow" a cabbage or a ham for their own use, figuring one item would never be missed. Of course, by the time everyone took his little bit on the way up to the plateau, the fighting troops got damn all in the way of foodstuffs.

Reinforcements arrived, were assigned to different formations, plodded up to the top of the plateau, and came back down, wounded, dead or mad.

Hal was down to ten fliers, eleven dragons, and he couldn't tell which was in worse shape, the dragons with their lean sides and nervously flicking tails, or the fliers, with their twitching muscles, and remote stares.

He was, quite illegally, able to make it a little better for his fliers, ordering paired patrols "out to sea, to make sure Roche ships weren't returning."

Of course, the patrols went directly to the Landanissas Islands, one pocket of peace in a world tearing at itself. The fishermen welcomed the gold and strange, new foods, while the fliers were only too glad to trade hard biscuit and pickled beef, standard supplies, for fish or fowl.

Pig-raising had become a major industry on the islands, and so the Eleventh's dragons were a little less lean and weary than other flights'.

But not much.

Hal worried about everything, and had learned the worst of being in command. Sometimes he thought, when a flier died, he would almost have gone down in his place, rather than write the letter to whatever people he had, lying about how the flier had died instantly in an accident, rather than the probable truth that he'd been shot off his mount, and fell a hundred feet, screaming to his death, clawing at the air, trying to make it hold him up or, worse yet, killed by his own mount in its predawn irritation at being wakened for a patrol.

At least, there were no Roche dragons on the peninsula.

Not yet.

Hal worried about that, too, then found a possible explanation – the Roche knew very damned well where the Deraine forces were, and didn't need any scouts.

Hal wondered why the black killer dragons hadn't been dispatched to the Kalabas Peninsula, thought, forlornly, that Queen Norcia and Duke Yasin knew the beached whale was well contained by the forces at hand. But he wondered how soon the Roche would adopt his arming of dragon fliers as policy, rather than a scattered experimentation.

The invasion, to Kailas' eyes, was indeed a beached and dying whale.

But the broadsheets from Deraine swore the invasion was a roaring success.

"Damme," Sir Loren said. "Look at this broadside. You went and did it again."

He passed the sheet across, and Hal read the tale by, of course, Thom Lowess, of how the expedition had been attacked by barbaric Roche warriors, from the far east, barely human, and how they'd broken the lines at the north side of the foothold, and only Sir Hal Kailas and his Eleventh Dragon Flight, heroes of Deraine, envy of the nation, and so on and so forth, had stopped the attack, landing their dragons and fighting as infantry until Sir Hal's friend, Lord Bab Cantabri of Black Island, had arrived in the nick of time with reinforcing infantry, and driven the Roche back.

Of course, no such attack had happened, and Hal certainly wouldn't let his men and women be wasted fighting as simple infantry.

"Wonderful," Hal muttered, handing the broadsheet back. "Aren't the people at home fed up with such crap? Haven't they been able to figure out that if we're such godsdamned heroes, every one of us, why we're still stuck on this sandy-ass desert?"

"Of course not," Saslic said. "You don't think anybody who isn't actually fighting a war *ever* wants to know the truth, do you? Otherwise, there wouldn't be wars at all, let alone fools like us to fight 'em."

"Fine, I calls it *damn* fine," Mariah said, "to be allow't to serve with such friggin' heroes. Almost makes me not wisht I'd stayed at home and learnt more about castin' lovespells. Ain't that right, Feccia?"

The man nodded thinly, forced a smile, and went out on the deck of the *Adventurer*.

Hal wondered how, in such lean times, Feccia managed to keep up his bulk, decided he didn't want to know. The man held up his end, even if he never went beyond what duty required.

These days, that was more than enough.

Hal, scouting up the peninsula, saw more Roche soldiers coming toward the front.

Other flights, over the Ichili River, saw transports heading toward the river's mouth.

But the lines remained fairly quiet, with only the daily probe and nightly raid to make sure no one was likely to die of old age.

Soldiers who'd cheered when they were told they'd be coming

south for the winter couldn't find enough obscenities, especially
as they realized winter was ending, and they had nothing to look
forward to except the increasing heat of spring and the drought
of summer.

"I've decided something," Saslic said as they strolled one night,
clothes in hand, along one of the empty beaches beyond
Jarraquintah. "I think I want to get killed before you do."

"Gods rotating," Hal said in considerable astonishment.
"Here we had a nap, a bath, a nice dinner, some marinated raw
fish, green vegetables, some chicken that burnt the taste of all
that pickled monkey meat out of my mouth, a real salad, another
swim, a little hem-heming around, and you go and say something
like that!

"Yeesh, woman! You're a true romantic!"

"Nope, just a realist," Saslic said. "Which is one reason I'd
better get killed before the war's over, because no godsdamned
civilian would ever understand me."

"All right," Hal said. "You're obviously intent on pursuing the
subject. Why do you want to get killed first – remembering that
I've decided I'm immortal, which means you're safe?"

"Because you're big, strong, brave." She paused. "And dumb.
So you'll be able to handle the blow a lot better than I would
when you get ripped in half by some dragon."

"What a charming thought," Hal said. "I love you."

"I love you back," Saslic said. "But dumb, like I said."

The Roche hit them at dawn, the day after Hal and Saslic had
gotten back from their illicit leave. They struck cleverly, sending
the first and second waves across in a suicidal frontal assault,
which the Deraine and Sagene defenders cut down.

The Deraine and Sagene forces didn't notice other formations
slip through the gullies and ravines of the rutted peninsula, and
thought the first two waves were all there were. They relaxed,
some coming out of their trenches to exult, to loot the dead,
maybe even a few to try to help the writhing wounded.

Two more waves debouched from the Roche positions, and
this time there was confusion. Yet another wave smashed into the
mêlée of hand-to-hand fighting, and this one broke through to
the Deraine trenches for a moment.

They didn't deploy along the trenches as they'd done in the
past, trying to kill all the Sagene and Deraine in them, but

jumped over the trench's rear parados, going for the edge of the plateau.

The Deraine were about to cut them down from the rear when yet another line of Roche rose up and charged.

Then all was madness, and the Roche had split the position on the plateau in half.

Hal, awaiting orders on the flagship, saw signal flags go up. The flag officer deciphering them turned ashen.

"Lord . . . Lord Cantabri's down."

Hal's stomach shifted, even though he'd realized some time ago that no one could be as impossibly brave as Cantabri and expect to live forever.

"Dead?"

The officer glanced at him, then lifted his glass again to the flags fluttering up from the shore station.

"No. Wounded in the chest . . . Refused to give up command . . . He's being taken to one of the hospital ships now. There's a chiurgeon with him.

"Nobody knows if he'll live or not."

Lord Hamil was on deck, shouting for boats, strapping on his sword, telling all and sundry that he'd lead the counterattack himself.

Hal went for his own boat, back for the *Adventurer*.

And then black dragons, flying pennons Hal recognized as they swooped close as *Ky* Yasin's, smashed over the plateau top, circled the ships, and went back the way they'd come.

By the time Hal reached the *Adventurer*, they'd torn the patrolling flight from the skies.

Some of the Roche fliers had crossbows, crossbows of a new design depending on a wound-up coil spring, like a clock, for their energy.

But most of them needed no more than the brute ferocity of their mounts, who screeched in joy as they tore riders from their mounts, ripped into the dragons themselves.

Hal waved his flight up, trying to get above the dragons, to gain altitude, then shouts came. Rai Garadice was pointing down at the ruined village.

There was Lord Hamil's banner, atop a pile of rubble, and wave after wave of Roche infantry attacking. Hal hadn't seen them move down on the village, but now saw Roche cavalry cantering down from the plateau.

Death above, death below, and Hal Kailas knew his duty.

234   *Chris Bunch*

He blasted on the trumpet, and dove toward the embattled Lord Hamil. Out of the corner of his eye, he saw troops, Deraine or Sagene troops, going over the edge of the plateau, retreating back toward the beach.

But there was nothing ahead but the torn banner of his commander, and his dragons, all ten of them, flashed over the pocket battlefield, crossbow bolts raining down.

The surprise sent the Roche reeling back, time enough for the soldiery around Lord Hamil to regroup and begin falling back on their boats.

A shadow came over him, and Hal ducked as a black dragon tore over him, talons reaching, missing.

He fired a bolt straight up, without aiming, but heard the dragon howl as the bolt hit him somewhere.

Then there was another dragon coming at him, jaws gaping.

Saslic's Nont was there, between them, claws flailing, far outsized.

Hal's world stopped as he heard Saslic scream, saw Nont torn by the black monster, a wing coming off, then Nont was spinning, falling, Saslic screaming as she fell out of her saddle, down into death's madness below.

Hal kicked Storm into a turn, trying to get to Saslic, and then the world was night and he smelt death as an unseen dragon, coming up from below, tore at his shoulder, his side, and then there was nothing at all.

27

There was a dull keening in Hal's ears, and he dimly thought he must not be dead – demons of the other world would be rejoicing at having a man for their feast, for surely that was the afterlife he was intended for, not one of gentle lambs and flowers.

He was lying on sand, he realized. Wet sand.

The keening kept on.

Hal tried to force his eyes open, couldn't.

Oh. I'm blind, he thought, ran a hand across his head, felt stickiness. Blood.

The keening changed to a yip. Hal recognized it as a dragon sound. He pushed himself up on an elbow, felt down, found ragged cloth. Hal ducked his head, scrubbed across his face, winced at the stabbing pain, and wiped blood away.

He could see, dimly, through a red mist.

He sat up, used both hands to lift his tunic, ignored the pain and rubbed hard.

Now he could see.

Storm was lying next to him, and now he could smell the dragon's fetid breath. Blinking hard, he reached out, found a scale, and pulled himself to his feet. He staggered, almost fell, but had his balance.

He was on a beach somewhere. Then he heard the smashing sounds of battle to his right, looked up, saw cliffs, vaguely recognized them as being west of the beachhead at Kalabas.

The war was still going on.

He looked down at himself, winced. There was a long tear in his side, up across his ribs, that had missed gutting him by an inch. Another pain came from his shoulder, and there was a gouge there, probably from a dragon claw.

That black dragon had also gotten him across his forehead. Blood ran freely down into his eyes, and he wiped again and again.

He still had his belted dagger, at least.

Then he realized Saslic was down, was dead, and there was no more world for him.

He almost collapsed back on the sand, caught himself.

The hells.

All right. She'd died first, as she'd wanted, his mind said, refusing to allow pain.

But I'm not dead.

That means that I'm to seek revenge.

She wouldn't have wanted me to just collapse here on this damned beach, and give up.

Maybe it was her spirit that made Storm call him back from wherever he was.

All right, he thought again. If that's the way it's to be.

Storm made another noise, and Hal looked at him.

The dragon had a slash down one side, and several headspikes were torn away, green ichor clotting over the wounds.

There were other cuts down Storm's side. He'd fought hard as he fell.

Hal saw, lying in the low surf, the motionless body of a black dragon. There was no sign of its rider.

"Good on you," he whispered, and his voice sounded as if he was gargling glass.

He wanted to lie down, get his energy back, but knew, if he went back down on the sand, that called to him more loudly than the softest feather bed, he'd never get up again.

Storm made a low cry.

"I hear," Hal said, and pulled himself toward the monster's forelegs. He almost fell, but made it to Storm's neck.

All that he had to do was pull himself up, into the saddle, but that was a million leagues above him.

But somehow he was there, where his saddle should have been, ripped out of its mounting rings, gone. His map case and quiver of bolts still hung to their rings, but his crossbow had vanished.

The reins dangled just out of his reach. He stretched for them, and pain stabbed. Hal almost cried, wouldn't allow himself.

"All right," he said once more. "Up, Storm."

The dragon whined, but came to his feet. Hal tapped reins, and pain came again. Storm thudded forward, slowly, then faster, and each time one of his feet struck, agony rolled through Kailas.

He heard shouts, looked up, and saw, on the clifftop above, a handful of soldiers. His vision was too clouded to tell, but an arrow arced down, then others, and he knew the soldiers had to be Roche.

Storm leaped for the air, wasn't strong enough, came down again, then, just short of the water, was in the air, feet dragging through the waves, then the dragon was up, climbing for the sky.

"Up," Hal whispered. "High."

Storm obeyed, and Hal could look along the coast.

There was Kalabas, not many miles distant, a scattering of ships moving out to sea, ships on fire, men in small boats.

Deraine was beaten, was retreating, the last of its soldiery fighting clear of the peninsula.

If Hal chanced going there, where could he land? Would any of the ships stop for him? Sure as hells, none would take his dragon aboard. He bleared, saw no signs of the *Adventurer* or any of the other dragon flight ships.

"You and me," he said, tapping reins to the right. Storm obediently turned south, out to sea, wings lifting slowly, coming down faster.

Hal found his eyes closing, fought them back open. If he went to sleep, he'd fall, and they were a thousand feet, more, over the water.

His fingers groped to the map case, opened it, took out the compass. No, don't let it go, don't let it fall, and he looped its lanyard around his neck.

He knew the heading well, and turned Storm until he was headed a bit further to the east.

Toward the Landanissas Islands.

Blood clouded his eyes, and he wiped them clear, swayed on Storm's back, refused to allow pain. He considered his revenge, but that could lead to a dream, and in a dream lay death.

All that could keep him awake was his pain, and so he embraced the agony as his dragon flew slowly, limping, across the gray skies.

Below was the water, welcoming water, that would cool the fire raging across his body, and he and Storm would forever roll in the sea's currents, flesh picked by multi-colored fish, white bones being polished as their skeletons turned, turned, turned—

Hal jerked himself awake, started singing, every song he could remember, from the bawdy chants of the soldiers to schoolyard nonsense songs.

And the miles reeled past.

Then there was land, three small dots, ahead, and Storm needed no urging, dropping down.

Hal thought – hoped – the islanders would still be friendly, now that he was begging, not buying.

They were. Zoan summoned the village witch, who used herbs and spells on Hal's wounds, wanted to give him a sleeping potion.

He refused, fearful that he'd been followed by Roche dragons, or a Roche warship would come on the island while he was unconscious.

But he sagged down into unconsciousness anyway, waking, stiff and in pain a dozen hours later.

Zoan had assigned someone to sit with him, and the boy ran to get the village head.

She came within minutes, ordered the boy to get the witch, and bring broth.

"You must stay until you recover," she said.

"No," Hal said. "I can't."

"You talked in your sleep," Zoan said. "About Saslic. That was woman with you before?"

"Yes." Again, the crashing wave of her death bore him down. Zoan saw his face, patted his hand.

"We all die," she said. "Soldiers die first."

"That's what Saslic said."

"She was wise. Perhaps, when you die, you will meet again."

Hal didn't answer.

"I am sorry to do this," Zoan said. "But men ask questions I cannot answer for what comes next."

"I don't know if I can answer them."

"They are afraid," Zoan went on. "Will Roche come here again?"

"I don't know."

"Did they follow you?"

"I don't think so." Hal struggled up. "Where is dragon?"

"He is well," Zoan said, pushing him back. "We fed him four pigs, and he slept. Witch put herbs, she not know what heals dragons, but work for men, for our beasts.

"Herbs and sew leather . . . pigskin, tanned, on wound, strong bandage. When he woke, he did not tear off. Maybe good for him."

"I sleep," Hal said. "When dragon wakes, wake me."

"What then?"

"I leave."

"For where?"

"For home."

Hal set his course back toward the mainland, but westering. He was in constant pain, but that kept him from falling off Storm.

He'd expected the dragon to be angry, unwilling to fly. But Storm seemed to understand where they were heading, and screeched no complaint.

Below him, high waves swept the seas, a summer storm. From time to time, he saw small boats, tattered and holed, limping their way away from the disaster of Kalabas. Sometimes they waved up, in friendship or thinking Hal was a scout for a rescuing force.

But he had nothing, and could only hope to be able to rescue himself and his dragon.

They made landfall, and Hal flew west, along the Roche coastline, until he found a forested headland where they could land.

He and the dragon shared a meal of dried fish, but Storm snorted away from the cornmeal mush Hal offered.

Hal woke, with joints and his wounds screaming, and Storm seemed in no better shape. They watered at a creek, took off, continued their slow odyssey west.

The pain of Saslic's loss tore at him, more painful than his wounds sometimes.

Hal dared not fly Storm longer than a guessed-at three hours, then looked for shelter, a hiding place where no Roche cavalry or dragons could spot him.

If they did, and challenged him ... No. He would not surrender.

Once, he flew over a bluff, where sheep sheltered against the onshore winds. Storm honked longingly, and Hal obeyed, had the dragon turn back and land.

Storm had a half-grown sheep halfway down his throat before Hal could dismount, swallowed it whole, went for another, killed it, and was beginning to feed when Hal heard shouting.

He saw the shepherd, and his dogs, running toward them, the shepherd waving a club.

Hal admired the man's courage or foolhardiness, killed him with one pass of his dagger. The dogs snarled at him, tried to nip at his heels, and Storm ate one of them, and the other fled, yapping.

He killed a sheep, rough-butchered it, and dragged it on to Storm.

They flew on until they found an abandoned farmstead further west. Hal landed, used the remnants of a shed to build a fire, and ate roast mutton, while Storm slept at his side.

The dragon moaned once or twice, and Hal wondered again if dragons had dreams, and if so, of what?

That far land they appeared to have come from? The northern wastes? Black Island?

He didn't know, vaguely wished to find out some day.

Some day, after he'd revenged Saslic.

At dawn, he went on, west.

Again, he found a herd of cattle, and Storm and he ate. But this time, if there were herders, they were sensible enough to avoid the ragged, bearded, bandaged flier, and his torn dragon.

And west, and west.

Then one day, after he'd flown for a week, a month, a year, he never knew, he flew over a burnt-out village, then wasted farms.

The ruins brought what might have been a smile, and he drove Storm on, harder.

Then, spread out below him, was a soldiers' winter camp.

He swept low over it, saw banners he recognized.

Sagene pennons.

He'd made it, flying all the way across Roche, back to his own lines, and suddenly, the end a hundred feet below him, pain took him as a terrier shakes a rat.

He brought Storm into a clearing, an improvised drillfield, surrounded by log huts, canvas-roofed, slid out of the saddle.

Men ran toward him, buckling on their weapons, passed by a man in armor.

"You!" the knight barked, sword sliding out of his sheath. "Stand still!"

Hal obeyed. Storm hissed, and the knight's horse jumped sideways.

"Who are you? Are you Roche? And keep your monster under control!" the knight called, fear obvious in his voice.

"Don't worry," Hal said, about to let go. "He won't hurt you. We're on your side. I'm Sir Hal Kailas, Eleventh Dragon Flight. Come from Kalabas."

The knight jolted back.

"You're one of the—"

"I'm one of the," Hal agreed. "Now, if you'll have someone see my dragon's fed, watered, and his wound treated?"

"Why . . . yes . . . but . . ."

Hal smiled gently at him, let go, and slipped quietly to the ground.

He'd made it back. Now it was the turn of the others for awhile.

Then it would be time for red vengeance.

28

There came a blur of dressing stations, creaking ambulances, anxious attendants and, for some unknown reason, the peering curious.

Hal didn't bother with full awareness, except for making sure twice that Storm's wounds had been treated, and that he was safe.

He thought he must be in good hands, and if he wasn't, there wasn't anything he could do about it. So he drowsed, mind floating, trying not to return to that dreadful moment when the dragon tore at Saslic, and she fell away, and there was nothing he could do.

Then one day, he woke to a clear mind. He was in a room by himself, in a bed with clean sheets, warm and cozy. There was a window in front of him, with autumn sleet lashing against it.

He wriggled, realized he was clean. He lifted an experimental hand to his cheeks, realized he'd been shaved while unconscious.

There came a giggle.

He looked to one side, saw Lady Khiri Carstares, as lovely as ever, in a chair beside his bed. She wore what should have been a prim white uniform that buttoned down the front. Khiri had unbuttoned the top three buttons, so the effect wasn't quite what nursey efficiency intended.

"I've never shaved a man before," she said. "Let alone one who's snoring."

Hal blinked, lifted an arm to point out the window, felt his bandages and stiff body.

"Deraine?"

"Of course, silly. You've been here, in hospital, for almost a month. Which gave me time to learn about your whereabouts from Sir Thom – you know he's been knighted for his courage in battle – even though your travels are all over the broadsheets, and arrange things so that I'm your nurse."

Hal blinked again.

"My nurse."

"Until you're well enough to be discharged."

"From the hospital?"

"No, no. From the service."

"What?"

"You've been hurt, remember?"

"I know." Hal started to get angry, realized this was hardly the time, and let sleep wash up on him again. Before he went under, he managed a smile at Carstares.

"Thanks," he mumbled. "For the shave. And . . . for being my nurse, I suppose."

*

Days drifted by. Hal knew he was feeling better, because the simple broths Khiri spooned into him became boring. She told him he definitely was recovering, since he was being altogether too bad tempered.

Hal apologized.

But he *was* bad tempered, and brooding. The news that he was going to be invalided out did not sit easy.

What was he supposed to do then?

Beg in the streets?

Limp back to Caerly to go down the mines?

Logically, he doubted that anyone with a knighthood would end up swinging a pick, but since when have invalids been logical?

What about flying? Starting his own flying show? But that would almost certainly be impossible at the present. He could guess there wouldn't be any dragons on the civilian market, and those that might show up would be thoroughly spavined or rogues.

Lord Cantabri came to call one day. He'd lost a deal of weight, and his face had new lines. He walked with a cane, and talked with a wheeze, but nevertheless said he'd be back in the wars by the time winter ended.

Hal grumped at him, and Cantabri just laughed.

Kailas, feeling ashamed once more, asked for details on the invasion.

"You're sure you're up to it?"

"That bad?"

"Worse," Cantabri said. "Of the hundred and twenty thousand, more actually, when you include Sagene's replacements, we managed to evacuate about thirty thousand."

Hal grimaced.

"And many of those were wounded, too many unable to return to the army," Cantabri went on. "Lord Hamil was killed shortly after I was wounded."

"I assumed that, sir," Hal said. "I was overhead, trying to figure a way to come to his aid. But there were too many Roche down there."

"Too many Roche *everywhere*," Cantabri said, almost to himself.

"I'd ask a favor, sir," Hal said. "Would it be possible for you to look up the Eleventh Flight's casualties?"

"I figured you'd ask," Cantabri said, and took a sheet of paper from his belt pouch.

"You had about seventy-five when the invasion began. Of those, about fifty still live. The *Adventurer*, even though the black dragons tried to attack it, made it to safety. You had ten fliers when that final attack came, and eleven dragons. Six dragons, five fliers are still alive."

Hal asked about his fellow flying school graduates.

"Vad Feccia, unwounded," Cantabri went on, and Hal shook his head, thinking only the good die young.

"Rai Garadice, also unscathed. Sir Loren Damian, wounded. Farren Mariah, wounded. Mynta Gart, wounded. All of them swear they'll be able to return to combat, although I understand this Mariah character voiced his status rather colorfully."

"He would," Hal said.

"Other dragon flights took worse casualties, including one completely wiped out.

"They're training dragons pell-mell upcountry, and realize they've got to build the flights back up, and add more to boot," Cantabri said. "The appearance of those black dragons, and their aggressiveness, has shaken the army badly.

"The formation, by the way, is led by one *Ky* Yasin."

"I knew that," Hal said. "I recognized his pennant."

"As our spies had said, his force is a squadron, more than four flights strong. Word has it, Queen Norcia of Roche has ordered it further augmented. He'll be a force to contend with," Cantabri said.

Hal started to say something, kept his own thoughts for the moment. There would be other matters to clarify first.

Cantabri and Kailas chatted on a bit more about inconsequentials before the lord got up.

"I'll say this, Sir Hal. The army without you will be a far lesser place. Far, far lesser."

"I've the best news," Khiri said.

Hal, who was still brooding about his seemingly unavoidable retirement, grumped something, which Carstares took as interest.

"You'll be permitted to leave the hospital under my care any day now," she said.

"For where?"

"For wherever you want to go. I've got estates in the west, although I don't know if you'll want to go there, they're pooh-gloomy, a dairy farm south of Rozen, sheep holdings on the highlands north of here . . . Or we could even possibly impose on

Sir Thom. I'm sure he'd let us stay in that great house in the capital.

"You can decide . . . or I will."

"I might as well let you do that," Hal growled. "Since it appears I'm no better than a lady's handsome man these days."

Lady Khiri froze, her face went hard.

"And just what is *that* supposed to mean?"

Hal should have shut up, but his shoulder was hurting.

"Just what it meant. A nice, scar-faced popsy to flaunt about, eh?"

Khiri came to her feet.

"Has anyone ever suggested, Sir Hal Kailas, that you are more than a bit of a shit?"

Hal opened his mouth.

"No," Khiri went on. "You've said quite enough for the present. It's quite obvious that you have the manners of one of those damned dragons you love so well.

"You think that I've been attracted to you because of your reputation. No, Sir Hal. I despise killers, and you're one of the bloodiest-handed.

"I like – liked – your company because you could make me laugh, which comes hard enough these days.

"I know that you lost your lady in battle. Do you think you're the only one to suffer a loss?

"For your information, my father was killed at the war's beginning, and my only brother, who I loved most dearly, two months later, not to mention someone else I thought I was beginning to . . . to care about.

"That's why I left those damned gloomy stone halls on the ocean, why Sir Thom was kind enough to take me in. I thought I was doing my bit for the war, and it turns out that you thought I was no better than a back-alley whore.

"Sir Hal, you should be very ashamed of yourself. Very damned ashamed, and I hope you treat your new nurse better than you have me."

And she went out, the door crashing behind her.

Hal's anger had risen as she spoke, but vanished moments after Khiri had gone.

He thought hard, staring out at the snow, just beginning to fall, not seeing it.

Very good, you imbecilic moron. If you had brains, you'd take them out and play with them.

At least now, he thought, I've really got something to be glum about.

And try to figure out how to apologize.

If I can.

Hal was still figuring when Sir Thom Lowess bounced through the door.

"And what, my fine young lad, have you done this time? I saw my dear friend, Lady Khiri, crying bitterly in the nursing office, and she said that you'd ruined things.

"Might I inquire?"

Hal reluctantly told his story. Lowess listened, shaking his head.

"Dear me. Dear me. You do, as the soldiers say, know full well how to step on your cock, don't you?"

Hal nodded.

"Just for your information, not only did Lady Khiri tell the truth, but she's given great sums to various hospitals.

"She's also, I suspect, without knowing, still a virgin, or so near to it as to not matter, so your shame should be complete. She originally came to stay with me in the hopes that I could introduce her to suitable men, men who weren't just after tossing her into bed, or looking to marry her estates.

"Have you any ideas on how you're going to recover from this gaffe?"

Hal was about to shake his head, then had an idea.

"Sir Thom – and congratulations on your knighting – how is my credit with you? I haven't been paid since before we left Paestum, and I assume sooner or later the paymasters'll—"

"Don't try to offend your other friend," Lowess said. "Even if you were stony broke, you could still have my last piece of gold."

"Thank you, sir," Hal said, shamefaced. "I apologize if I insulted you, for I need not only some of your gold, but a bit of your help."

Hal explained.

"Well, that might do for a beginning," Lowess judged. "And it's a matter handled just down the street. Sit here and contemplate your sins, Sir Hal, and I'll take care of things."

He was gone for half an hour, came back smiling.

"The lady I dealt with shall be singing your praises until the day she dies, as will all of her friends. And you should be most grateful her shop is – was – very well supplied, particularly for an autumny time of year."

"How long will it take?" Sir Hal asked.

"An hour," Lowess said. "She's bringing in her neighbors to help. And there's a wizard down the street who can provide some spells to keep things fresh.

"Now, while we wait, would you care for any news?"

"What's this about them forcing me out of the army?"

Lowess lifted an eyebrow.

"Of course they're going to retire you, Sir Hal. You're cut all to shreds."

"No more so than Cantabri."

"He's different. He's too mean to let go."

"Some people had best think of me as mean," Hal muttered.

"*Some* people already do," Lowess said.

Hal winced.

"Besides, you're giving everyone a chance to wallow in your heroism, for which I take some measure of credit. You'll be told, in time, that the Eleventh Flight will now be known as the Sir Hal Kailas Flight.

"Great recognition. Plus I imagine there'll be some more medals, most likely a pension. You'll not starve."

"I wasn't quite starving when I got dragooned into the damned army," Hal said.

"So, then, what do you have to complain about? You'll be out, a civilian, not that badly impaired, and with your life, which is a deal more than many can say."

Hal remembered Saslic, kept from snarling at Sir Thom.

"Oh, one other thing, which I'll make much of in one of my tales. It seems there's a man in the flight who's from your own town, and has sworn to get revenge against the Roche in your name."

"From Caerly?"

"Yes, been a flier for some months, saw limited combat with the Fourth Army. You might know him, since he's knighted. A Sir Nanpean Tregony."

Hal, remembering the last time he'd seen Tregony, tormenting a dragon kit, suddenly found everything, from his situation to . . . to the world, hysterically funny.

He burst out laughing, so hard he thought he'd tear a wound open.

Sir Thom smiled with him at first, then looked concerned.

"Would you mind explaining?"

"Sir Thom," Hal said. "In time, I shall. But not right now."
And again he started laughing uncontrollably.

Lady Khiri Carstares, eyes still red, opened the door to her room,
and gasped.

It was full of flowers, so full she could barely make out her
small bed and tiny chest.

There were orchids, many varieties, dancing ladies, hibiscus,
roses, protea, night-blooming jasmine, other exotic flowers she
had no idea existed in Deraine's winter.

"And I am, truly, a shit," Hal said from behind her.

She recovered from her surprise, forced a hard face, and
turned. Hal sat in a padded wheelchair a few feet away. Down
the hall was Sir Thom Lowess.

"You are."

"I'm sorry," he said. "I can't say I'll never be a shit again . . .
But not in that way."

"Do you expect forgiveness?"

Hal shook his head. Khiri deliberately waited until the silence
was very uncomfortable.

"Then you have it."

She came close, leaned over, kissed him on the lips, mouth
closed.

"Now, since I somehow forgot to ask to be relieved of your
onerous care, shall we start thinking about where your convalescence should be best spent?"

29

Cayre a Carstares sat on a promontory overlooking the western
ocean. A high curtain wall enclosed a dozen acres and a small village. The castle itself was octagonal, with a round tower at each
corner, and could have comfortably held an army headquarters in
its stone magnificence amid the jagged crags.

"My forebears built this to keep off the raiders from the
north," Lady Carstares said.

"The people I came from," Hal said, finding a bit of amuse-ment.

"I'll add that it never fell to them."

"Never from without," Kailas murmured, surprised at what he was saying, not displeased that he wasn't entirely soul-dead. "But what of within?"

"What?" Khiri said.

"Nothing."

But it was evident from Carstares' lifted eyebrows and smile she'd heard what he said.

The castle was gray, as Khiri had promised, matching the gray seas beyond, and the wintry land. The dusting of snow made it look even more ominous.

Hal loved it, loved its gloom and dark menace.

It was the perfect place to mourn Saslic.

And to make himself back into a warrior.

The castle was fully staffed, many of the retainers having worked for Khiri's grandfather. They still tottered faithfully about their rounds.

"Don't be in much of a hurry around here," Lady Khiri advised.

Hal wasn't.

He found a round bedroom in the tower of the wing Khiri said was the castle's most inhabited, just below the roof, with shut-tered windows that looked out on the wild surf smashing against the rocky cliffs below. Khiri's bedroom, one she'd had as a girl, was one flight down, and she had the local witch cast a similar-ity spell on two tiny bells. If Hal needed something, all he needed do was tap his, and the one in Khiri's room would tinkle and summon her.

Hal's room was bigger than his parents' house, had its own washroom and dressing room, plus a fireplace, fresh wood brought daily by a man who could've been Hal's great-grandfather, but who refused, utterly shocked, Hal's offer to help.

"Never, Sir Hal," he said. "You're wounded, and to be recov-erin', and besides, you're *noble*."

"Only by the grace of the king."

The man's eyes rounded.

"You've *met* our gracious Majesty?"

"Yes," Hal said, realizing the conversation was going in the wrong direction and, from the man's expression, that now he'd *never* be allowed to do anything resembling manual labor.

Khiri found this funny, although she still wondered why Hal had chosen this place.

"Damp, and cold, and full of bad memories," she said.

"Maybe I picked it to exorcise them."

"Yours or mine?"

Hal didn't answer.

He started with slow, creaking walks, hardly better than the pace of the archaic retainers, around the keep. Then, feeling stronger, he went beyond, and walked along the curtain wall, through the orchards, unharvested since Khiri's father's death, and the grazing grounds for the small herd of sheep.

There were horses, and he took them sugar, or an apple he'd picked and thawed in his pocket.

Khiri went with him at first, then realized he wanted no company but his own thoughts, and the howl of the wind.

Hal wore a knee-length sheepskin coat, a matching hat, and thought he looked a perfect fool, a country bumpkin if ever one existed. But a warm perfect fool.

Once, when the storm broke, he went beyond the curtain wall, and found a hollow, out of the wind, warmed a little by the winter sun.

Full of a very good midday meal, he drifted away, then dreamed. All he remembered was Saslic's body falling, falling, and then she was on Nont's back, down below this very castle, the dragon's wings lifted to protect her from the waves.

She smiled up at him sadly, waved, and then Nont's wings closed about her, and the dragon turned out to sea, as Hal came to his feet, awake, pain tearing at him, but the pain hadn't brought the tears on his cheeks.

He began training, lifting small weights, gradually increasing them, forcing his body from a walk into a limping trot. Hal went beyond the curtain wall, found tracks down to the rocky beaches below, went down them. The first time he came back up, he thought he wouldn't make it, that he'd have to fall and wait for someone to rescue him.

But he forced himself on, lungs ripping, and made it, staggering, to the top, before he went to his knees.

Khiri ran up, knelt.

"Are you all right?"

"Just . . . just being stupid," he panted.

"Why do you want to do this to yourself?" Then she realized. "Oh. You want to go back to that damned war."

"It isn't . . . what I *want* . . ." Hal said.

"You're right! You are being stupid!"

She stamped away, back to the castle.

But by dinner that night, her sunny mood was restored.

He dreamed again that night of Saslic, again, on the back of Nont as his wings unfurled, and he beat hard, lifting, leaving a wake of spray.

Again, he saw Saslic waving, but this time, he heard her shouting, words dimly heard against the sea's roar:

"Another time . . . somewhere . . . somewhen . . . maybe . . ."

He strained for more, but couldn't make out what else she said. Then Nont was in the air, flying due west, in the directions dragons seemingly came from.

Hal Kailas woke, and there was melancholy in his heart, but he no longer felt dull, dead.

He was alive, he would live, until he was killed.

Once he might have felt mortal, but now he believed Saslic's words: "There'll be no after the war for a dragon flier."

Strangely, this made him feel better than he had since watching her die.

"I have an idea," Hal said. "I think we should have a party."

"A party?" Khiri said incredulously.

They were in her bedroom. Khiri disliked rising early, so Hal, after his morning run, generally took her a tray with the rusks she preferred unbuttered and some herbal tea.

For some unknown reason, neither one of them had tried romance, beyond an almost-brotherly hug and a brush of the lips at night and in morning's greeting.

"A midwinter party," Hal said.

"You're mad."

"Not at all. Or, at least, not noticeably at the moment."

"Sir Hal, love of my life, you have the brains of a sheep. It's winter. Everybody's huddling around his fire, dreaming of spring.

"And this castle – this whole district – isn't a happy one. The war's cost all of us too much."

"Exactly. That is why we need a party."

"You are not the kind of person who holds parties," Khiri said suspiciously.

"What kind of person does?"

"Sir Thom. Me."

"All right, then. You'll be the one throwing the party. You've got more money than I do, anyway."

"Uh-uh," Khiri said. "If you want to have a stupid party, with everybody glowering around at each other, and thinking about old feuds or . . . Or thinking about people who aren't here, you'd best have some kind of idea on what's going to make it work. Make it sing, as Sir Thom might put it."

Hal grinned.

"That was an evil smile if ever I saw one," she said cautiously.

He reached in his shirt pocket.

"Here's your invitation. You're to come as you were when you received this."

"Like *this*?" Khiri wasn't wearing much under a warm shoulder throw other than a thin nightgown.

"And here are two other invitations for you to give others. Pick the right moment," Hal said, "and we'll all be amazed at how people show up."

A smile ghosted across her lips.

"What about you?"

"When I," Hal said, "received my invitation from a dashing dragon flier, I just happened to be wearing full dress uniform. Hah-ha!"

"Perhaps you're not quite mad. Or maybe you are. I never thought you were the kind of person who would come up with an idea like this."

"I didn't used to be," Hal said, his smile flickering momentarily. Khiri saw it, looked away.

"So who are we to invite to this party? The local nobility, of course."

"Everyone."

"Everyone?"

"Servants, peasants, priests, popinjays, poopheads."

"The whole district?"

"Grandsires, grandmeres, babes, children, even a sheep if you fancy."

"Let's go back to your madness."

"Oh yes," Hal said. "Two other details. For every jewel you

somehow decide to wear, you bring a coin, copper, silver, gold, that'll go to the hospital fund."

"That'll keep some people from overdressing," Khiri said.

"And make others pile on the gems," Hal said.

"And the other detail is that everybody is to bring something to eat."

"Why?"

Hal picked his words carefully. "When you've shared another man or woman's meal, you're not quite as likely to be hating them. Anyway, not as hard."

He jumped to his feet, winced.

"Calloo, callay, it'll be a joyous occasion."

There was a broad smile on his lips, but none in his eyes.

Hal's workout grew more intense by the day.

Finally, it consisted, in the morning, of setting-up exercises, then a mile run, regardless of the weather. Sometimes he'd run down one of the half-wild, long-unridden horses, and go bareback with only a rope bridle for a ride out across the bleak landscape.

He made friends – or, if not friends, acceptable acquaintances, courtesy of sugar lumps – with the completely wild hill ponies, and sometimes he'd chase them over the rolling moors, through the scrub forests, or they'd chase him.

Other days, he'd hunt down the locals, and force an invitation to his party on them. He was quite pleased with the reactions he got, from petrified amazement to grumpiness to laughing joy.

After midday, and a brief nap, he'd begin his real workout.

First came setting-up exercises, then running up one of the ramps to the castle parapets. Another set of exercises, then running down the ramp. He repeated this five times.

Then the hard part, climbing up and down a knotted rope he'd hung from the parapets, forcing his wounded arm to recover.

Then repeating the ramp run and exercises five more times.

Khiri watched him once, shuddered, and went back to one of the great hall's roaring fireplaces.

The afternoon of the party was warmer than usual, an almost tropical wind from the south blowing in from the sea. For a moment, he was reminded of the Southern Sea, and death, but he forced those from his mind.

He wore the dress uniform Khiri had tucked into his trunk,

complete with half a chestful of medals. As he'd threatened, he made Khiri wear her nightgown, although Hal had allowed her to cheat, and wear a matching silk bathrobe over it.

The guests trailed in, sometimes singly, sometimes in village-size groups. Some of them were honest, and wore what they had on when invited, others blatantly cheated and wore their best.

From these, one of Lady Khiri's retainers extracted the penalty, dropping the coins into an ornately carved chest that had belonged to her great-grandfather.

Cooks took the viands from the guests, and whatever instructions needed to serve them.

Khiri suddenly gasped.

"But we have no band!"

"Oh yes we do," Hal said, pointed to three women and two men, holding the simple instruments of the peasantry. Their leader wore only a towel, and had been caught in the village sauna.

But they tootled, sawed and strummed mightily, and then there were dancers. Priests danced with beldames, merchants' wives with drovers, young boys with their mothers, young girls with their hopeful lovers.

Khiri had been right – the district had been decimated by the war. There were few young men at the dance, and most of those were clearly unsuitable for soldiering or else they'd served and come home, far worse wounded than Hal.

But they danced, they sang, and they ate.

Hal made a note of some of the dishes, served along two great tables. Perhaps they should have been organized and served in proper courses, but everyone was too hungry, and enjoying themselves too much.

There were small shrimp, boiled in beer and served in a tomato sauce from one of Khiri's hothouse gardens; crisp, fried young smelt, dipped in a seasoned mayonnaise; hearth cakes in butter; oysters, raw or grilled with bacon; grilled lamb sausage; marinated cucumbers; sea trout, poached in wine; potatoes cooked in a dozen different ways; smoked local ham; crab cakes; chicken livers baked with rice; lobster, fresh from the booming seas beyond the castle, served with drawn butter; puddings, from blood to fruit; tarts made from dried fruit; preserved orange cake; pies; filled cookies, and more.

They drank the strong local beer, or mulled cider, or wine from Khiri's, or the district's other minor nobility's, cellars.

There were those who drank or ate too much, and there were wagons outside to carry the casualties home. Or else those incapable of moving were carted off to another hall, where straw had been piled for the eventuality.

It was long after midnight when the last guest stumbled out, or was otherwise disposed of.

"And me for bed," Khiri yawned, waving at the tables. "We can clean up the rest in the morning."

"Good idea," Hal agreed. "I don't think I'm in any shape to be handling the family porcelain."

They went up the curving staircase into their tower. Hal stopped at Khiri's landing, looked out through a tiny-paned window at the sea. The sky was clear, with only one moon out, but that clearly showing the white lines of surf as they marched against the cliffs.

Khiri shivered, came closer.

"I'm glad I'm in here, and not out there."

"So am I."

It seemed appropriate for Hal to kiss her, and for her to kiss him back.

After a very long time, she pulled away.

"Well, I guess you're *not* that wounded."

He started to pull her close.

"Oh no," she said. "If you want to play those games, it won't be with that damned pincushion of a tunic on."

She took his hand, led him into her bedroom, closed the door.

"Now," she murmured, unfastening his uniform's loop and button fasteners, and lifting it off his shoulders. "That's a bit better."

"Sauce for the gander, and all that," Hal said.

"True enough, young sir," Khiri said, and let the bathrobe slip to the floor. "And my bare feet have been freezing all night, so perhaps you wouldn't mind dealing with the problem?"

He picked her up in his arms, carried her to the bed, and pulled back the feather comforter.

She lay looking up at him, half-smiling.

"And I don't want you dirtying my nice flannel sheets with those clompy boots of yours."

Hal sat, obediently pulled off the boots.

He heard a whisper of silk, turned, and saw Khiri, naked.

Hal suddenly felt thick-headed, and it wasn't from the wine. He undressed, fingers feeling like awkward balloons.

"Now, come to me," Khiri said, and her voice was a noble-woman's command.

Hal knelt over her, eased himself down, half across her body, kissed her, felt her nipples hardening against him.

Then it was if the seas outside took them, spinning them high into the night sky.

Near dawn, Khiri said, her face muffled by the pillow, "I guess . . . this means I'm not your nurse . . . anymore."

Hal gasped.

"Probably not."

"That's good," Khiri said, and then lost her words as they moved together.

From that night on, they shared a common bed, and no one in the castle seemed to disapprove.

Hal, in spite of Khiri's best efforts to decoy him into sloth, continued his exercising.

Then, one day, a bright day that hinted of spring, he knew.

He was fully recovered.

And it was time to go back to war.

30

Hal wrote his intentions to Lord Cantabri, but before he had a reply a royal messenger fought his way through the deep new year snows with a summons to King Asir's court.

"Which will be for what?" Hal wondered.

"Why, you dummy, your honors for being a good little hero about to go into retirement," Khiri said. "And then you'll get them all taken away for not being a good little hero who's going into retirement.

"You dummy."

The messenger was very glad to make his return to Rozen in one of Khiri's carriages, his horse tied behind. For an instant Hal had wondered why they were taking two carriages. Khiri had sighed in exasperation.

"Because, dummy, if there's another person in the nice warm carriage, I can't do this to you."

She slipped to her knees, and reached for him.

And so they set out, with three carriages, which included Lady Khiri's entourage and road supplies, slowly making their way east from country inn to country inn, until they reached the outskirts of the capital.

"I suppose we can find somewhere to put up," Hal said. "Still being unpaid, I can borrow money from you."

"You'll not borrow money from anyone," Khiri said. "We'll be staying at Sir Thom's."

"Oh. You wrote him?"

"Shut up, hero dummy. I don't need to."

And so it proved.

They were lavishly welcomed by Lowess, and given a separate suite.

"Now this shall be a tale," he said. "The bravest warrior, in love with Deraine's loveliest lady.

"I can hear the sound of whimperings from those not so fortunate already."

And he licked his lips.

Hal made himself visit the King's Own Menagerie to tell Saslic's father of her death.

"My only daughter," the man said sadly. "Bound and determined to fly, and to fight. My wife's gone, and now Saslic is with her.

"It's a cold, lonely world, Sir Hal. I'm glad to be old, and not long for it, for it holds little warmth for me, beyond my beasts."

The short, fat man was all business. He introduced himself as one of King Asir's equerries.

"Since you've already been presented at court," he said, "I shan't have to inform you as to protocol.

"The king proposes to make you a lord."

Hal blinked.

"In addition to other matters which he'll inform you of personally. One of the reasons I'm here is to ask what title you'd prefer to have.

"Lord Kailas of Caerly, perhaps?"

Hal smiled tightly. He found no need to mention the money he sent his parents every time he was paid.

"No," he said. "I don't think I'll be returning there, ever. Caerly's a good place to be from. A long ways from."

The equerry forced a smile in acknowledgement. "What, then?"

Hal had only to think for a minute.

"Lord Kailas . . . of Kalabas."

"Oh dear," the equerry said, sounding shaken. "The king will not be pleased with that, I know. Kalabas is something I doubt if he wants to be reminded of. Many of his most loyal subjects, including Lord Hamil, died there."

"I had . . . friends who died there, as well," Hal said.

The equerry saw the look in Hal's eyes, nodded tightly, didn't pursue the matter.

"Matters such as your pension, other benefits, can wait until later."

"As long as I'm ruining your master's, the king's, day, let me complete the job," Hal said, and went on.

"Oh dear, oh dear, the king will *definitely* be unhappy," was all the equerry had to say.

King Asir named Hal Lord Kailas of Kalabas with barely a flicker, said, as he had when he ennobled Lord Cantabri, there would be other honors as well, requested Lord Kailas' presence in his private chambers.

Another equerry escorted Kailas down a long corridor, into a surprisingly simply furnished room.

The king was pouring a drink from a decanter.

"You, sir?"

"With all pleasure, Your Majesty."

"I think I said something, back when I knighted you, that Deraine needed new thinkers."

"You did, sire."

"Why are new thinkers generally such pains in the ass?"

Hal sipped at his drink, realized he would probably never have as fine a brandy in his life, didn't respond.

"What I had proposed for you was giving you some estates, so you wouldn't starve, a proper pension so you could sire sons or bastards, depending on your feelings, who'd become warriors of Deraine as well fitted as you.

"Plus medals, of course. Umm . . . Member, King's Household; Defender of the Throne; and Hero of Deraine.

"I also proposed sending you on a grand tour of my kingdom,

with recruiting officers in your wake, scooping up all those starry-eyed sorts who'd want to be just like Lord Hal.

"Instead, I get . . . What? You don't want a nice, safe life. You want to go back to the damned front, where you'll be lucky to live a month.

"Do you have any idea of how long a dragon flier lives these days?"

Hal shook his head.

"Two, perhaps three months, at best."

Hal jolted, and King Asir nodded.

"It's not just those damned black dragons of theirs, but their tactics have changed. The Roche are now more interested in fighting than scouting, and when our fliers cross the lines, they're immediately attacked, generally outnumbered.

"At the moment, and I do not wish this repeated, we have less than no idea what Queen Norcia and her confidant, Duke Yasin, intend for the spring."

"And that's why I have to go back, sir," Hal said.

"What good will you do, other than becoming another martyr for Deraine?" Asir asked bitterly.

"I have an idea on how things might be changed, sire. *Ky* Yasin – that's the Duke's brother—"

"I know well who the bastard is," the king said.

"Yasin showed up over Kalabas not just with black dragons, but with them in strength. Instead of a flight, he had a full squadron, maybe four flights.

"Four against one, for that's how we were deployed . . . Well, those odds are deadly."

"They are," the king agreed.

"Some time ago, my old squadron was attacked on the ground by three flights, and nearly wiped out. I retaliated by striking back against those Roche, again and again, until we'd put the fear of the gods in them."

"I'm aware of the action," Asir said. "I do more than sit on my arse on this damned throne, you know."

"Yessir. I want command of my old flight . . . And can we get rid of the new name, and just call it the Eleventh?"

"We can." Asir had a bit of a smile on his lips.

"Build it up, until it's the size of Yasin's. Or bigger. And send us after those damned black dragons. If we hound them from pillar to post, never giving them a moment to strut about . . . Sir, I think we can start bending the odds back to where they should be."

Hal didn't speak his other thought – that if it was now fighting in the skies, perhaps one-on-one combat might be a momentary tactic, and other ways of fighting should be explored.

"Well," the king said. "You certainly don't go by halves, do you?

"You realize you're probably guaranteeing you'll get killed."

Hal thought of Saslic's words, shrugged.

"There's one thing I'm good at," Asir went on, "and that's judging men. So I know if I forbid this action of yours, all you'll do is slip away from your estates and somehow end up in Sagene as another dragon flier, probably named Anonymous.

"So I have no other options.

"Very well, Lord Kailas. We'll do as you 'suggest,'" the king said, now with a broader smile. "Now, get out of my sight, you blackmailing bastard."

Hal put his glass down, saluted.

"Oh. One more thing," Asir said. "I've heard a certain term used, and now declare it an official title, you to be the first to hold it.

"Dragonmaster."

"What a tale this will make," Sir Thom Lowess whispered, unable to speak through excitement. "What a tale!"

31

The remnants of the Eleventh Dragon Flight were waiting at their old base. They were a pretty sad relic.

They were tattered and torn, and most of their equipment had been dumped overside from the *Adventurer*, to make room for fleeing soldiers.

Some had been wounded – the black dragons had not only gone after dragons in the air, but had been able to identify the flights' mother ships, and attacked them, as had the Roche catapults as the beachhead was being cleared.

Worse, they knew how badly they'd been beaten. Now, without any real work, with only six dragons and five fliers, they could do little except make-work, and mope about, feeling sorry for themselves.

That would change, he knew, with replacements, new gear and, most importantly, more dragons and their fliers.

Hal noticed Nanpean Tregony, who was busily avoiding him, found Tregony was keeping company with Vad Feccia, which made perfect sense to Hal, the pair in his mind being equal villains.

At least Serjeant Te had survived the withdrawal, and had been doing what he could to take care of the Eleventh.

"But it's damned hard, sir, and I realize there's no excuses to be made but, without an officer in command, your requisitions tend to get ignored, and when you don't have any trading stock, any good souvenirs, it's very damned hard to go a-bartering for what you need."

"No officers?" Hal asked. "What about Sir Nanpean Tregony?"

"Do I have to say anything?"

Hal thought. "You do."

"He isn't worth a bucket of warm owl spit. Oh, he's a good dragon flier, and seems aggressive enough. But he surely doesn't give a damn about anything or anyone else in the flight, excepting maybe his personal dragon handler, and how many dragons he's killed.

"He's got plenty of money – guess his father's mines are really paying off in the war – but won't spend a copper of it on anything but himself."

Hal nodded. It was what he would have expected from a Tregony – except for being able to fly a dragon well.

Kailas set about putting matters in hand – first restoring the flight to its proper strength, then he'd worry about implementing his idea the king had approved.

The first item was calling in Feccia, and asking what had happened to him when the invasion collapsed.

He said that when the black dragons attacked, he'd gone for altitude, but been driven down and inland. Flying just above the brush, he'd managed to elude the two monstrosities on his tail, but his dragon had been exhausted.

He flew west, as Hal had done, found a resting place, with water. Then he'd tried to return to Kalabas, but every time had encountered the black flights, and was always outnumbered.

"I went back to my hiding place, and then, the next morning, my poor dragon was cramped from the attacks of the day previous. I found some wild hogs, and chased them into my dragon's clutches.

"But it was a day and a half later when I was able to fly back. The fleet was well at sea, only a few stragglers around the landing beaches.

"I followed the ships until I found the fleet, found the *Adventurer*, and was safe home."

That possibly wasn't the bravest story from the debacle Hal had heard, but then Feccia wasn't high on his list of candidates for hero medals. He seemed to scout with a degree of ability, and Hal wasn't sure it wasn't a sign of intelligence for a scout to avoid battle when he was outnumbered.

When the flight changed as Hal intended, Feccia might not fit in, in which case he could be transferred to a more conventional dragon flight, or possibly put in charge of the maintenance section.

Hal had an idea Feccia wouldn't be heartbroken to have an excuse to walk away from flying.

But that would be for another day. Hal was a little reluctant to harshly judge anyone from his flight training, particularly as the numbers dwindled.

Mynta Gart was the first to arrive from hospital. She'd been simply knocked from the sky by a particularly skilled three-dragon combination, not the blacks, Hal was surprised to find.

"Landed – not far from where Saslic crashed – and some bastard put an arrow in my other leg." She smiled wanly. "Now I limp on both sides, like I'm a lubber on her first day at sea."

"Did you see Saslic's body?"

"No," Gart said, looking away. "I saw her poor damned beast – what did she call him, Nont? – trying to get up, with his poor damned wing torn away. And then he fell back and some bastard put a spear in his throat. But I suppose, the way he was, that quick a death was best."

But her eyes gleamed a different story.

Hal didn't need to ask if she wanted revenge. He made a note to put her in charge of one of the new sections he planned.

Sir Loren and Farren Mariah arrived together, with their own stories.

Sir Loren's dragon had been struck by arrows from the ground. He landed, and was attacked by a Roche knight.

"I was fighting my best, which prob'ly isn't all that good,

killed the man after he wounded me sore with his blade, then his squire attacked me with a damned great axe. I killed him, too, saw my poor dragon had breathed his last, and, since they hadn't hurt me legs, I took off, running like a stripe-assed ape.

"Passed several dozen arrows, I did."

Farren Mariah had been forced to land by a pair of the black dragons.

"An' I was just standin' there, with me thumbs up, an' this horseshit great rock from one of their bleedin' catapoops slams down next to me, throwin' splinters and shit here, yon and everywhere. Got fragments in my eyes, thought I was blind, and if I lived they'd put me next to the Rozen city gates to beg, which ain't proper for a Mariah.

"But m'beast kept whistlin', and I could see blurry well enough to crawl aboard, and he trampled down some of their friggin' soldiers takin' off, and somehow found the *Adventurer*.

"I may marry the bugger."

Hal found himself missing Lady Khiri, but in a very different way than he'd missed Saslic, when she was still alive. It was a pleasant kind of melancholy, tempered with a selfish gladness that he had something, someone, far distant from these killing fields and, at night, could dream about her great gray castle by the sea.

He smiled wryly at that, remembering that he didn't have to be here in Sagene at all. He could be comfortably lazing about some estate somewhere, and he realized King Asir had been so surprised by his behavior he'd never gotten around to telling Hal just what estates he was being given.

With my luck, he thought, they'll probably be coal mines in some stony waste.

Hal decided he'd made Nanpean Tregony suffer enough, and summoned him into his tent.

Tregony was about two inches taller than Hal, and still good-looking, even if he was starting to get a bit heavy. Hal noted the livid scar along his neck he'd given the man years ago, rescuing the dragon kit, wasn't displeased.

"You may sit," Hal said, keeping his voice flat.

Tregony obeyed.

"So you're the one who was going to avenge me?"

"That was pap the taletellers came up with," Tregony said.

"Someone told them we came from the same village, took that, and ran hard with the information."

That could have been. Hal had certainly experienced the taletellers' willingness to brutalize the truth for their own ends.

"Very well," he said after a suitable pause. "Your records don't seem to have caught up with you. Perhaps you'd fill me in. Starting from when you entered the service."

"It was after the siege of Paestum was lifted," Tregony said. "I wanted to do something against the damned Roche, and there was a man – Garadice – who came through the district, looking for dragon fliers.

"I took the king's silver, and they trained me and sent me to Sagene.

"I went to a flight in the Second Army area. We got caught up in one of the Roche offensives, and did what we could – I credit myself with half a dozen or more dragons – then my dragon was taken down by one of their bastardly catapults, and I was captured."

Hal was interested.

"They have a special camp for dragon fliers," Tregony went on. "Far behind the lines, up north, on this island, well up an estuary."

"How many fliers are there?"

"There must have been thirty when I was captured. Probably there were fifty when I made my escape."

"Good for you," Hal approved, against his root feelings for the man. "And how did you make your escape?"

"I'm a bit of an athlete," Tregony said, looking down at his stomach. "Was, anyway. And being a prisoner helps you stay lean. I saw my chance, and kept it secret, since the Roche have spies in the camp.

"It's a terrible place, ruled by threats and cruelty and the lash, I can tell you.

"Anyway, I went out one night, when it was storming. Wore padded clothing. Pole-vaulted the first fence, and the padding kept the spikes from hurting me when I banged into it, landing. I used the pole to help me climb over the second fence, and then I was gone.

"I had some gold, some silver, and kept to the woods. The Roche peasants like their queen and their rulers no better than I do, and were willing to feed me, or sometimes put me up when it was raining. And so I worked my way east, always east.

"I stole a horse and, after that, it got easier. Then I reached the lines, turned the horse loose, and slipped across by night.

"When I got back from my leave, I said I wanted a chance to get back at the bastards for their cruelty, and the way I'd been treated . . . And so they sent me here, to the Eleventh."

Hal thought the story interesting.

"How many dragons have you brought down?" Tregony asked.

Hal shrugged.

"I don't keep track."

"I do," Tregony said. "More than I've killed?"

Hal thought of asking Tregony if he remembered a certain dragon kit, decided there wasn't any point.

"That's all," he said. "Go on about your duties."

Tregony, lips pursed, got up, saluted, went out. Outside the tent, he happened to look back in the tent, and Hal saw a look of utter, cold hatred on his face.

32

King Asir may have ordered the Eleventh Flight's augmentation, but even kings have limits.

There were few replacement fliers arriving in Paestum, and fewer dragons. At least Sagene was finally producing dragons and fliers, but those men and women were going to their own forces.

Hal had Rai Garadice write his father asking what was going on, and got an unhappy reply that the recruiters weren't able to bring in new men as fast as they should, and dragon training, what with many of the best trainers having gone off to the front and gotten killed, was even slower than it had been in peacetime.

"Besides, everyone," he wrote, "wants dragons, for everything from courier duty to parades, and all too many of these are great lords, well away from the fighting, with enough influence to get their way. I'm sorry, my son, but there's little I can do about it, at least for the present."

At least Hal, by pulling every string he could think of, and several Serjeant Te knew of, was able to bring the Eleventh up to a normal authorized strength of fifteen dragons and fliers.

Once or twice, Serjeant Te convinced a replacement depot officer to call for volunteers from the ranks of the unassigned enlisted men.

Since most of the new blood was headed for the front lines, and the spring offensive wasn't far distant, the idea of being able to stay alive a bit longer sang clearly, and so the Eleventh was actually a bit overstrength in its ground complement.

Te had an idea, which Hal found capital, and so a special, very secret section was set up, manufacturing authentic war relics. Men who could sew made up Roche battle flags, others scoured trash dumps for battered Roche weaponry. The flags were carefully bloodied – "aye, th' man who fell over this standard, defendin' it with his life's blood, as you can see, was a great Roche knight, bravest of the brave" as were most of the weapons. No one found it necessary to inform the souvenir's new owner the blood came from chickens, bought from local farmers, who were delighting in the flight's presence, since any beast, in any condition, was perfect dragon fodder.

Hal put his experienced fliers to training the new ones, so they might live beyond a single flight when the spring came, and, with the grudging concurrence of the First Army Commander, Lord Egibi, restricted his winter flights to reconnaissance along the lines.

While the storms raged, the soldiers along the front retreated into dugouts or, if they were lucky, huts. The enemy was not so much the Roche as King Winter, and the deathdealers were colds, fevers, the ague.

Magicians cast occasional spells, and fighting patrols went out, on foot or horseback.

But all three armies seemed content to wait for better weather.

On one flight, Hal found what he'd been looking for – a new base for his command. The old farm was not only too far behind the lines to suit him, but a constant reminder of defeat, the scars from the Roche raid still black and ruinous.

The new base was a small village at a crossroads, east of Paestum, a few miles behind the lines. It hadn't been looted too badly, and, best of all, had been a dairy commune, with huge barns ideal for dragon shelter.

The flight moved carefully to its new quarters, trying to ensure the ruined village still looked no better than a ruined village.

Hal's troops welcomed the change, one of the few objectors being Sir Nanpean. Hal puzzled at that – he would've thought any flier as intent on building his kills would have welcomed being closer to the fighting. But he quickly forgot about that, figuring Tregony probably had found a mistress at a farm around their previous station, and now was forced to be as celibate as the others.

Hal, rather gleefully considering his disgust with religion, set up his headquarters in the town church, an imposing high-ceilinged monument whose only flaw was that the tin ceiling leaked badly. But his artisans put that to rights, and Hal took over the gods-shouters' quarters for his own. Priests being priests, there were several excellent stoves, and so the building became an off-duty den for the men. Hal found something interesting – the small cubicle intended for the confession of sins to whatever god or gods this temple had been dedicated to had a small screen in its rear, low to the ground. The screen concealed a listening tube that went directly to the priests' quarters, no doubt for priestly entertainment and possible blackmail. He showed it to no one, except Serjeant Te.

The fliers found their own club/mess, one of the village's three taverns, and more top class relics were manufactured to fill the tavern's shelves as they should be. Hal found one of the replacements had worked in a tavern, and put him in charge of liquid victualing, under Te.

Te had the idea of bringing in whores from Paestum, which Hal quickly rejected. Dragon fliers already had a reputation for rowdiness, and having prostitutes in their quarters might be quite enough for him to be relieved. Hal couldn't quite understand the army's thinking on this, other than people talk to people in bed, and the powers were afraid of spies. But it was a commandment, and so he honored it. Soldiers with exceptionally strong lusts could get permission to visit Paestum and its authorized brothels.

Farren Mariah tried to cast a spell of invisibility around the base, failed completely, muttered about how he should have paid more attention to his grandfather.

Now, all he needed was better weather, and the promised addition of fliers, and he was ready to go after Yasin and his black dragons.

He spent hours in Paestum, at the First Army's intelligence

bureau, but nothing came from the spies who crossed the lines as to Yasin's location.

But he knew spring would bring the black dragons out of their dens.

"We have problems, sir," Serjeant Te announced.

"What now?" Hal asked.

"Lord Cantabri's come a-calling."

"Oh shit."

"You can't see the blood on his hands," Te announced. "But you know he's got to have some scheme afoot that'll be killing us."

Hal laughed, asked Te to escort him in, and bring some mulled wine. He didn't need to add that Te should have an ear at the confessional cell.

Hal trusted Te and knew that, if Cantabri's visit had nothing to do with the war or the flight, he'd go on about his business.

"Quite a little establishment you've worked here, Lord Hal," Cantabri said. He looked far better than when Hal had seen him last, ready for the campaign trail.

"So far our friends across the lines haven't spotted it . . . And when the fighting starts, we'll be a bit closer to the action."

"Ah. I thought you might have spied out our intent for the spring."

Hal tried to look sagacious and knowing, failed.

"Oh. You *haven't* spied out the land," Cantabri said, his yellowish eyes gleaming.

"No, sir."

"I think," Cantabri said, "after all this time and bloodshed, we can dispense with the sirs and lords unless we're in formal company."

"Yes, mil . . . I mean, Bab."

"I have two matters of personal business for you. Here's one," and he reached into his belt pouch, took out an elaborately sealed roll of parchment, gave it to Hal.

Hal saw the red seal, knew it was from King Asir. He broke the seal, read, whistled.

"I just happen to have a bit of a guess as to what it is," Cantabri said. "I, in fact, made a request of His Highness, when I heard you were to be lifted further into the nobility, and you'd be granted certain privileges, that if one of them included estates, you be given lands near the ones granted me.

"I do like to have neighbors I can turn my back on. So you're now the proud owner of some dairy land, quite a sufficient acreage, plus some villages, and I suspect fishing rights, along the east coast."

"You called it," Hal said. "Plus some islands off the coast, a rather embarrassing pension and a manor house in Rozen."

He lowered the parchment.

"A question just occurred to me. Where do these lands the king gives out come from? Didn't they have owners?"

"Certainly," Cantabri said. "But the owners perhaps aren't supporters of the king, or the war, or died without heirs."

"A hell of a system," Hal said. "And this business of owning villages. I suppose that means I could evict the villagers if I didn't like the color of their hair or such?"

"You could," Cantabri agreed. "And it *is* a hell of a system. But if the king heard of your tyranny, there just could be lands awaiting a grant to a newer hero.

"The whole matter comes to whether or not you happen to trust the king. I do."

"As do I," Hal said, glad he was telling the truth, and remembering Te's ear at the mousehole.

"I can add," Cantabri said, "that the king told me privately he was most sorry for not taking care of this matter at your audience.

"But you, and I am quoting directly, 'shook the shit right out of him.'"

Such language, given Te's near idolatry of King Asir, must've set the serjeant back slightly.

"The second bit of business from His Majesty is that he's most apologetic that your plans for the squadron haven't been implemented as yet, but that hopefully success in the spring and summer will make matters easier.

"He didn't explain, nor did I inquire."

Hal sipped at his mulled wine.

"Now," he said. "Might I inquire as to your business, Bab?"

"Why," Cantabri said, "if you've no better way to spend your afternoon, perhaps you might take me flying."

"Just to get a breath of nice, fresh air?" Hal asked skeptically.

"No more."

"There's enough fresh air about today to freeze your frigging nose right off," Hal said. "And, not meaning to call a greater lord than myself a liar, but you might wish to give me some hints as to which direction the best fresh air might come from."

"Oh, the hells with it," Cantabri said. "I told them you wouldn't be any help unless you knew what we would be going up after. North-east by east." He saw a map on the wall, went to it, and tapped. "Here."

Hal went to the map, studied it.

"I think," he said, now not so sure his clever-clever stationing of Te was that good an idea, "we'd best go on outside, see to the saddling of our mount."

They went out, putting on heavy coats, gloves, against the swirling winds. At least it wasn't snowing, Hal thought.

Cantabri grinned at him.

"You know, back when I commanded my first cavalry troop, I thought I was most clever, and had my most trusted senior warrant with his ear to the back of my tent when I met with superiors, so that if anything of interest to my command was heard, he could be dealing with the matter immediately.

"I won't bother you with details as to how I was caught in my own trap . . . But I was."

Hal didn't think he was capable of flushing any more, but he was, and Cantabri roared laughter.

"Now," he said, after he'd recovered, "let me give you the details of what's planned.

"I'll add that this plan comes directly from the king, after he had some most meaningful dreams his astrologer said must have been sent by the gods. The king, evidently, has felt his fate connected with a great river since a witch told him that, back when he was a boy."

"Oh dear," Hal said in a small voice.

"Perhaps so," Cantabri agreed. "First, you must remember His Majesty is not a man of war, and despises this horror Queen Norcia and, frankly, the prewar weakness of Sagene, forced him into.

"However, he feels he must rise to the occasion."

Cantabri and Hal looked at each other, and their faces were perfectly blank.

"He always felt that the invasion of Kalabas was an inspired idea, together with his plan to invade Roche up the Ichili River.

"It is a pity, in his view, that certain events, and possibly the hand of the gods – King Asir believes very firmly in the gods – intervened.

"Or perhaps he chose the wrong place."

"I see," Hal said, remembering the map. Cantabri had pointed to the fortified city of Aude, on the broad River Comtal. It was about fifty or more miles from the vaguely defined desolation of the lines, and some ten miles from Roche's northern coast. "Just like the last time?"

"Sort of," Cantabri said. "Except that, being closer to Deraine, our supply lines won't be as long.

"We've even now begun building craft for the invasion, but they'll be different, not a mish-mosh of cargo ships and such, but smaller, flat-bottomed river craft, able to cross the Chicor Straits in good weather."

"And of course, there are no Roche spies in Deraine reporting this construction and drawing the obvious conclusions," Hal said.

"The king's aware that there are," Cantabri said, a bit of frost in his voice. Hal reminded himself that Lord Cantabri wasn't near the cynic Kailas thought himself to be.

"Go ahead," Hal prodded.

"There'll be spells of confusion cast along the northern front," Cantabri went on. "Together with other spells I can't talk about right now.

"On a more physical level, we'll interdict all mail leaving Deraine for any foreign shore for the week before the attack."

"None of which will be noticed by Roche magicians or agents," Hal said cynically. "And no one will look to their defenses, remembering that good King Asir has a fondness for rivers."

"This time, there'll be a bit more subtlety," Cantabri said. "I hope. The First and Second Armies will mount an attack on Aude. All plans will suggest that is our only goal, that once we break through the lines, we'll regroup, and then move south and east on Carcaor.

"Instead, holding Aude, we'll have control of the upper hundred or more miles of the River Comtal. The invasion barges will carry the troops upriver, toward Carcaor.

"At the very least, holding Aude, we'll force the Roche lines back on themselves, and break this stalemate."

"If we take Aude," Hal said, but quietly, under his breath.

Hal told Sir Loren and Rai Garadice, his best pilots, although, if Sir Nanpean was telling the truth about his victories, he might well be a better choice.

But Kailas, having the safety of the man he considered

Deraine's most important soldier uppermost, wished to take no chances with the unknown.

Storm, recovered from the long flight and his injuries, was sleek, and roared pleasure at the thought of flying.

Hal and his two handlers got Storm ready to fly, with a double saddle. His new crossbow, and five ten-bolt magazines, a trumpet and glass finished Hal's equipage.

The other two fliers were outfitted similarly.

"All right," Hal said. "Now, if you'll just clamber up—"

He looked closely at Lord Cantabri, saw he was as pale as he'd been in the hospital, wondered if the man was concealing wounds worse than anyone knew.

Then he got it.

"Uh, Bab, meaning no offense, how many times have you flown before today?"

Bab said, in a curiously muffled voice, "This will be the first."

"Would you rather wait here? My fliers can scout the area around Aude without being caught."

"No," Cantabri said, iron in his voice. "I must see what we'll be facing."

"Very well, then. Let me give you a hand up."

Hal didn't think it would be wise to add the caution he normally gave first-time fliers, that if they got sick on him, there'd be several hells to pay.

He mounted up, made sure Lord Cantabri had a firm hold, and slapped Storm's neck with the reins.

The dragon plodded out of the huge barn, squishing through the winter muck, faster, wings swirling up, then thrashing hard down, and Storm was in the air.

Behind him, Sir Loren and Garadice's monsters lifted clear.

Hal glanced over his shoulder, saw Cantabri's eyes were tightly shut, but his hold on the dragon's scales could have bent them.

As briefed, they flew high across the front, keeping a sharp eye out for Roche patrols, then dove down, beyond the archers and crossbowmen.

They flew due east, until the land below was empty of soldiery, turned northerly toward Aude.

Hal flew behind the knoll, then darted up, and landed on the clear crest. Garadice and Sir Loren flew in circles, hidden by the knoll, watching for any Roche dragons.

Beyond, across the Comtal River Valley, lay Aude.

"And here we are," he said, sliding out of his saddle.

Sir Cantabri took his hand, staggered, then went to a patch of brush and threw up in a dignified way.

When he'd finished, Hal handed him his canteen.

"No," Cantabri said. "Get mine. It's got brandy in it."

Hal obeyed. Cantabri rinsed his mouth, then swallowed, sighed.

"I'd be most beholden, Lord Kailas," he said, curiously formal, "if you could find your way not to discuss my body's weaknesses unless you must.

"But I shall admit to you I have a desperate fear of heights."

Hal was surprised, not only that Cantabri was afraid of *anything*, but that he had the courage to admit to it.

He thought he still had a great deal to learn about bravery, took out his glass, and studied Aude. Cantabri did the same.

It was even worse than the map had suggested. The Comtal, deep, wide, unfordable, protected three sides of the city. And it was a city, almost as large as Paestum.

But where Paestum had grown beyond its walls, Aude still hid behind them. The city had been built on a high bluff. There were double turreted walls, machicolated and strongly held.

Inside the second of these ran the town, zigging, narrow alleys Hal knew would be deadly to fight through, easy to defend, to a final stronghold, with its own walls and round keep.

There was a broad ramp on the third side, but this was well protected with pairs of interlocking gatehouses.

Assaulting this castle would be an utter nightmare. Hal didn't think it could be taken by any human forces, not unless there were enough soldiers willing to have their bodies stacked to the tops of the walls for others to climb on, and then die, in their turn, within the city.

Hal remembered Serjeant Te's words, almost looked at Cantabri's hands, to see if there might really be blood dripping from them.

33

It was a brisk late spring morning when, to the roll of drums and the thunder of horses' hooves, the First and Second Armies went on the attack.

Hal and his flight were reconning for the First Army, and, from high above, it looked splendid – the Roche lines being broken by the heavy cavalry, light cavalry pouring through the gaps, and a steady stream of infantry securing the positions, then moving on.

This, Hal was glad to see, wasn't like the abortive invasion of Kalabas – Lord Egibi had given his commanders explicit instructions that they were to exploit any opportunity offered.

Hal saw two dragons, neither black, and he and his flight attacked, drove them down into the bloody hands of the soldiery below.

Kailas chanced flying south for almost an hour, and found the lead elements of the Second Army, half Deraine, half Sagene.

They, too, had been successful in the breakthrough, and were marching steadily north-north-east, toward Aude and the River Comtal.

They saw three dragons, killed two, and the third fled.

At base that night, most of the fliers were bubbling, sure an attack that began this successfully couldn't fail.

Hal tried to hold back their enthusiasm, but felt a warmth of hope in spite of himself.

The next few days they drove the Roche back again, and now, when Hal swooped low over the soldiers, he could hear singing, and see they were laden with loot the Roche had previously seized from the poor, vanished peasants of the area.

Hal took Garadice and Gart, flew over the Roche lines, such as they were, and on, deeper into the rear. Then an idea struck, and he blew his trumpet, waved for a course change, to east-south-east.

What he saw, or rather what he didn't see, sent him back at top speed, his bewildered wingmates trailing, until he spotted the pennons of the Armies' Combined Command.

He landed, told Garadice to watch Storm, and went looking for Cantabri.

"You're sure?" Lord Bab said.

"I'm positive," Hal said.

"Twice lucky," Cantabri said. "I remember what you didn't see on the day we invaded Kalabas."

"I hope the result is different," Hal said.

"It will if I have anything to do with it. Now for Lords Egibi and Desmoceras."

Bab's eyes were a-gleam.

"This, Hal, could win the war for us, in a week, or at most a month. Come on, man!"

"There appeared to be no Roche formations to the south?" Egibi said, trying to hold back incredulity.

"None, sir," Hal said. "I saw scattered light cavalry, and they were in full flight."

"This is somewhat astonishing," Lord Desmoceras, the Sagene commander of the Second Army said. He was a thin man, a bit shorter than average, but his face and body were seamed with the scars that proved him a fighting man to contend with.

"I have full confidence in Lord Kailas," Egibi said, but there was a slight question in his voice.

"As do I," Cantabri said, without ever a question mark.

"Thank you, sirs," Hal said. "Lord Desmoceras, I'm an experienced flier. I flew very carefully, saw no camouflaged camps or formations.

"The Roche have, from all I could see, been split in half. I'd guess some are fleeing toward Aude, the rest possibly to join up with other elements to our south.

"I'm ready to take out flights to find out just where they are."

Egibi nodded, didn't respond to Hal's volunteering.

"What do you think?" he asked Desmoceras.

The Sagene pulled at his nose.

"I think my Council of Barons would have my head for disobeying their orders, and turning away from Aude. Not to mention we have no spells ready, and it would take at least two days to change the army's orders."

Lord Egibi made a wry face.

"And here we've told our officers to take the initiative, not to be afraid to take chances.

"I myself wonder what King Asir would think if I changed the attack. First, we'll have a supply problem, turning away from the River Comtal, and—"

"Live off what the Roche have abandoned," Hal said, somewhat astonished at his effrontery.

Lord Egibi turned to him, face reddening. Then he controlled himself.

"Yes. Thank you, Lord Kailas," he said, voice cold. "If you'll wait beyond, to see if we have any further orders?"

Hal forced calm, saluted, and left.

An hour later, Cantabri came out, lips pursed, hand on his sword as if he wanted to draw and kill the first person he saw.

Hal didn't need to ask what the decision had been.

"Continue the attack?" he said.

Cantabri nodded, too angry to speak.

Hal stormed back to his dragon, took off for his flight base, barely noticing or caring that his wingmates were flanking him.

A drum kept pounding in his head – we could have won the war, we could have won the war, we could have won the war.

The next day, the advance continued toward Aude.

34

Two days later, Hal still not over his rage, the first scouts reached the River Comtal, facing light opposition from the Roche. Following them were the pioneers, who considered the deep, unfordable river, then began denuding the local forests for bridging material.

Then came the infantry, who looked across the river, and up at Aude's great walls, winced, then settled down to wait.

Logs were snaked to the river's edge, and small lumberyards put together, to begin planing and cutting the lumber for the bridges.

That night, fires flickered along the riverbank, and the cut lumber, green wood though it was, burst into flames. Aude's magicians were at work.

The next morning, Hal and his flight were told to lift a cadre of magicians to the knoll where Cantabri had first scouted the city.

The magicians conferred, then ordered their acolytes to begin laying out tapes in mystical patterns, and chanting preparatory spells.

Hal noticed Storm was making a low, pained noise, as if hurt. He examined the dragon carefully, saw no signs of harm, saw other dragons were also showing discomfort.

Magic, he realized, something the monsters liked no better than the layman.

He told the head magician of the dragons' problems, said he'd take them off, circle the knoll from a distance, and return when summoned.

Within minutes, he, too, felt uncomfortable, and knew a great spell was being sent against the sorcerers of Aude.

Then, suddenly, the discomfort vanished, and he saw a tiny, robed dot below, waving to him.

He brought the flight back, and took the magicians and their gear back to the rear area, just behind a ridgeline, where the high command had positioned itself.

The pioneers went back to work, and this time, their piled logs remained intact.

He heard, from a man who had a friend who'd been eavesdropping when a deserter was questioned that something horrible, invisible, had struck at the Roche wizards, killing at least a dozen or more.

He wondered, properly suspicious of the army's rumor machine, how much of that was true.

Replacements trickled in – none of them fliers – and they were a-babble of the new small ships, river barges, tied up in Paestum, or still building in the ports of Deraine, while two bridges inched across the River Comtal, the walls of Aude looming above.

If the Roche didn't know of King Asir's plan, Hal figured they'd gone blind and deaf.

The bridges reached the far side, and ranks of infantrymen trotted across, forming into attack echelons.

From the walls, catapults sent man-long arrows arcing down, and even a few crossbowmen, clearly inexperienced, chanced shots at this impossibly long range.

Hal, soaring above the city, saw a gate yawn open on Aude's landward side, and half a hundred knights debouch.

He scribbled a note, sent Storm diving toward the Deraine

infantry, tootling on his trumpet. Someone with rank got the note, and soldiers formed a wedge, ran to meet the cavalry.

Hal pointed at the open gate, dove on it, sent crossbow bolts into the scattering of soldiers atop the wall.

A Deraine light cavalry troop rode around their soldiers, into the Roche horsemen, as the infantry charged.

Then there were Roche dragons coming in, and he had no time to watch the ground. Two dragons dove at him, and he pinned the first's rider to his dragon with a bolt, pulled the charging handle back, forward, and shot the other rider in the stomach. He screamed, fell, and his dragon, unmanned, fled.

Then his flight was around him, and it was a swirl of screeching monsters and shouting men. A wingtip brushed Hal's chest, and he almost fell from Storm's back. He fired a bolt after his attacker, had no idea if he hit or not.

Sir Loren had a dragon on his tail, closing. The Roche rider wasn't watching his own rear, and Hal came down on him, shot him in the back. Sir Loren waved thanks as Hal banked away.

Hal looked around, realized he was very low over Aude. He flashed over the great roofed, turreted keep, big enough to land a dozen dragons on, near the main gate. Bowmen were shooting up at him. He gigged Storm, and the dragon shot away, low over the walls, over the river, and came back across Aude.

The last of the Roche cavalry was being cut to pieces, and the Deraine riders were breaking free, galloping hard for the still-open gate.

Hal thought he might be mumbling a prayer – if the cavalry made it inside, the battle could be a victory before it was even mounted.

Heavy cavalry, moving at a ponderous trot, came up from the river and around the walls toward the gate, supporting the light riders.

The air above the wall was a swoop of dragons, Hal's flight, and another formation. There were only two Roche dragons aloft, and one of those folded a wing, and spun down to smash across the outer wall's battlements. He looked for the second, but it had vanished.

The Deraine light cavalry was inside the city's outer walls, and there were spearmen running out, forming a wall before the inner gate. The Deraine horses reared, turned away – no horse will charge into a solid mass, romantic paintings aside, and Hal saw the outer gates slowly closing, brave Roche soldiers ignoring the cavalry at their back.

Hal heard the gates slam closed from 200 feet above, saw the last of the cavalry inside the wall shot down by bowman on the walls on either side. The accidental chance at a quick victory was gone.

Now, unless there was a miracle, the battle for Aude would be a long, bloody siege.

The hut was a blurt of excitement as the fliers unwound from the air battle.

"How many'd you get . . . sir?" Sir Nanpean called.

Hal shook his head. As always, he didn't think he was in the business of counting.

"He got four, four, the dirty whore," Farren Mariah chanted.

Tregony's face fell, and he turned away.

"Guess," Mynta Gart grinned, passing Hal a jack of ale, "who's been holding forth on his three victories."

The beer, chilled by sorcery, meant more to Kailas than whether or not Sir Nanpean Tregony was happy.

"I think we've got a problem, sir," Serjeant Te said.

"Of course we've got problems," Hal said. "We're sojers, ain't we?"

Te didn't smile.

"Very well," Hal said. "We do have a problem. A serious one."

"Someone's stealing supplies, sir."

Hal grimaced.

"What sort?"

"All sorts," Te said. "The fliers' club is missing brandy, the supply tent's missing clothing, boots, jackets."

"And I'm missing some maps."

Hal suddenly took things very seriously. The only people who might be interested in maps, outside the army, would be historians, collectors . . . and spies.

Hal doubted there were many collectors hiding in the forests around Aude.

"What sort of maps?"

Te nodded – Hal was beginning to understand.

"Marked ones, sir. Showing last week's deployments, some of the area around Paestum."

"Which naturally, we've been squirreling away, rather than destroying, against orders."

Te held out his hands.

"Tell me somebody who doesn't keep files. More files than he should."

Hal nodded reluctantly, thought.

"The clothing. Any particular size?"

"The first thing I thought of, sir," Te said. "No such luck. All sizes, which means the thief must be selling them."

"I'd haul everybody together," Hal said, "and read them the liturgy about thieving, and how we'll hang anybody we find stealing from the nearest dragon.

"But not with those damned maps gone. That suggests something else. Any ideas on who might be the guilty one?"

"Not a clue, sir," Te said. "So I've got to suspect everyone and no one."

"So it's up to us to play warder and investigate, then."

"Yessir," Te said. "And I'd rather no one be tipped the wink that we're alert. Maybe I can lay out and catch the bastard first."

"Maybe that's a good idea," Hal said. "And maybe, when I've got the time, I should do the same.

"It's pure hell when you don't know who you can – and can't – trust."

"It is that, sir."

Hal was summoned by Lord Egibi, informed the attack on the Comtal's mouth had been successful, and Deraine and Sagene were turning the port town into an impregnable fortress.

Now supply barges and small ships could sail or be warped upriver with supplies and reinforcements.

"However," Egibi said, "our scouts report the riverbanks are held by partisans – Roche irregulars. Our first convoy upriver was ambushed and forced back.

"Take your dragons, Lord Kailas, and scout for ambushes, and drive back those guerrillas. You have royal permission to land and burn any villages you deem to be supporting the enemy."

"Nossir," Hal said firmly. "I'll not be doing *that*."

There was an audible gasp from some staff officers, while Lord Cantabri hid a grin.

"And why are you disobeying orders?" Egibi said, in a voice that would have passed for summer thunder.

"Because," Hal said, "first, we're in Roche now. Any villages supporting these guerrillas, who I'll wager are no more than Roche soldiers who've lost their parent units, are no more than patriots.

"Just as you – or King Asir – would expect our Deraine villagers to stand and be counted should we ever be invaded."

Egibi glowered at him, but Hal refused to look away.

"I suppose," Egibi said, "you're right. Dammit, I know you are. Very well then. Go wage your damned moral war."

Hal took his entire flight down the River Comtal toward the sea. Taking off, he could see the pioneers, busy again, building siege engines.

Then he concentrated on ambush sites, flying low, just above the water.

He heard a whoop of glee, glanced back, saw Farren's dragon lifting its head from the water, holding an enormous pike in its jaws.

Hal noted several spots, saw horsemen gallop out of brush a few times, didn't pursue them.

After a two-hour flight, they saw boats in the river. Not trusting their own soldiery to hold fire, Hal draped a Deraine flag from Storm's neck, circled until he was waved in.

He landed on the bank, and one of the barges drew near.

"See any Roche?" the officer in the bows said.

"Probably," Hal said. "We ran them off, but I'm sure they'll scuttle right back. We'll orbit your forward ships, and give the alarm if they're still planning anything."

"Excellent," the man called, and someone on the ship shouted, "Good on the dragons!"

The journey back to Aude took two days. Three times the dragons sprang traps, coming down from above on the ambushers, showering crossbow bolts, and the escorting ships landed soldiers to finish the job.

Then, almost within sight of Aude, their escort duty was taken over by cavalry, and Hal signaled his flight back to their base.

He saw a storm front approaching, was glad it looked as if they'd be stuck on the ground for at least a day. His fliers and, more importantly, his dragons could do with a bit of a rest.

*

The storm lasted longer than expected, and by the third day, Hal couldn't find any more maintenance for his soldiery.

Serjeant Te reported no luck at all in finding the thief, but Hal told him to keep his watch out.

"I'll do that, sir," Te said, yawning. "But it's damned hard chasing the flight around by day and creeping through the bushes at night. Almost makes me think I'm back being an infantryman."

Hal was jerked awake by the duty officer.

"Sir. It's an emergency."

"It always is," Hal muttered, rolling out of bed and dragging pants and boots on.

"You'd best come armed, sir," the man said.

Hal belted his sword-belt on, went out into the rain.

There was a flare of torches back of the headquarters tent.

Women and men stood around a body in Deraine uniform, sprawled on its face.

"Must've surprised some damned Roche," someone muttered.

Hal knelt over the body, turned it on its back.

It was Serjeant Te, eyes wide, mouth gaping. A long knife was buried in his chest.

Hal knew the knife.

It was the dagger issued only to dragon fliers.

35

Hal ordered the flight to parade, in full uniform, as a gesture of honor to Serjeant Te. Of course, he really wanted to see which flier was missing his dagger.

There were enough shortages and uniform inadequacies for Hal to make quite a storm, and have his adjutant, Gart, make notes of what was missing.

But the dagger gave him nothing.

Some of the fliers swore they'd never been issued a dagger at all, which Hal had no way of knowing. Others, including Gart and Feccia, had lost theirs, somewhere. Sir Nanpean had the best reason – his, of course, had been taken from him when he was captured, and he'd never been able to get a replacement.

Nothing.

Hal, not having the slightest clue as to how to play warder, made what he thought were subtle inquiries, which also gave him nothing.

Worse, from the death of Te on, the thefts came to a halt.

Hal ground his teeth, got on with the war.

The pioneers had finished their siege engines, and they began thudding away, hurling huge stones against the landward wall, firing huge arrows at any target that presented itself, lobbing other stones into the center of Aude.

Hal, riding back of the lines for a meeting with Cantabri, saw men going forward. They were lightly armed, and carried the types of picks and shovels Hal recognized from Caerly. He also remembered them from the horror-drenched days in Paestum, waiting for the Roche mine to be fired.

He said nothing to anyone – the mine must be kept a secret.

Deraine controlled the air, although Roche dragons still fiercely contested the issue.

Hal took flights up in the morning and at dusk, and almost every day the Roche rose to meet him.

None were the feared black dragons. Hal began hoping that maybe Yasin had been eaten by the monstrosities, or they'd discovered they couldn't be depended on, or something.

Hal killed his share and more, as did Sir Nanpean, Garadice and Sir Loren. But the Eleventh Flight still took casualties, and the number of pilots gathered in their hut grew fewer and fewer, the revelry louder and louder, sometimes just short of hysteria.

Hal sent inquiry after inquiry back to the First Army Headquarters, some bordering on the insubordinate, raging, begging for replacements.

But none came.

The soldiers on line were put on alert, with no reason being given, and for all dragon flights to be in the air from dawn to dusk, prepared, as the order said "to take advantage of targets of opportunity."

Hal knew what it meant, but still kept silent. Perhaps the still-undiscovered thief/murderer in the flight was no more than that.

But most likely, not.

They were orbiting Aude in formations of three, other dragon flights soaring past them.

It was a summer day that promised heat, but in this morning was crisp and clear.

Hal saw wisps of smoke coming from the base of one wall, watched closely.

The smoke boiled out, and the timbers of the mine below cracked, and crumbled.

The outer wall cracked, tottered, and fell, crashing down, almost into the river below.

But no wave of Deraine soldiers rose to the attack. The space between the outer and inner city walls was too close for it to be anything other than a deathtrap.

Roche reinforcements were hurried to the inner wall, waiting for the assault that never came.

That was the first step.

Somewhere, not far distant, another mine would be dug under the inner wall.

In the meantime, the siege went on, daily patrols by cavalry and infantry to make sure Aude stayed invested.

The Roche developed a new tactic – bringing four or six dragons up just before dawn. These carried the great wicker baskets, but were filled with supplies. They flew out – when they could – with wounded soldiers.

Hal, still fighting his own war, told his fliers to attack the incoming dragons, but let the ones leaving pass.

His fliers, no more interested in slaughtering the sick and wounded than Kailas was, obeyed.

Except for Sir Nanpean, who argued that any dragon and its flier should be a target, and there was no place for mercy in war.

Hal, logically, knew he was right, and didn't ground him for disobedience.

But he liked Tregony no more than before.

. . . we lost two dragons today. The first was crippled in a fight with three other dragons, and we had to put her down. I frankly feel that the fault is that of the flier, who's less than experienced, and should have known better than to fly against such odds.

The other, Sir Nanpean Tregony's, fell sick of some unknown ailment. We isolated it in a barn, which made the poor beast even more forlorn. Tregony, of course, refused to spend any time with his dragon, saying he had no intention of catching whatever ailment the monster had.

We sent for a wizard, and asked around for an animal doctor. But no one had any experience with dragons, and the magician could do little but ease the beast's last hours.

I am starting to wonder if the poor damned dragons shouldn't have stayed in the west, without matter what enemies threatened them.

Certainly we haven't brought them anything but grief. Perhaps, when this war is over, if it ever is, we should free all the dragons, and let them fly to wherever they wish.

I write this, but I know it's foolish, for many of the dragons are now thoroughly domesticated, and prefer our company. Also, those captured young could hardly be released into the wild, for they'd live but a few days, certainly less if they encountered wild dragons.

And what of those who've been kept in zoos, thoroughly accustomed to having their sheep or whatever provided to them on a barrow?

Once again it seems whatever Man touches he turns first to his own purposes, then to ruination.

Sorry to end my letter on such a gloomy note, but that's how I'm feeling at this moment.

> *I do miss you*
> *Hal*

Hal hadn't known what would happen between him and Khiri when he returned to the war, and was quite surprised to find he thought of her often.

She wrote him daily, letters about the smallest, most normal things – what was going on with the sowing at Cayre a Carstares, the newest fripperies around the capital, what dinners she'd been invited to, and what she'd worn and eaten.

All of these, things Hal might've thought irritating, took him away from the war.

She was working at one of Rozen's hospitals, still living at Thom Lowess' city home, and missing him desperately.

Hal, in return, missed her, and wrote back as often as he could.

He was learning the loneliness of command, and, without

Saslic, had no one to confide in, especially about his feelings about war, and about dragons.

He wondered if he was falling in love with the beasts and also with Lady Khiri.

He snorted. He had no time for such weaknesses, especially not now.

But still, when he thought of her, at the strangest times, a smile came to him, and his mood lightened.

Again, the troops were brought to full alert and, this time, told to be ready for an all-out attack.

Hal, once again, overflew the city, looking for any signs of trouble.

This time, he found them.

He saw, not far from where the first mine had been dug, men suddenly explode out of carefully camouflaged tunnels, running as if there were demons at their heels.

He expected to see smoke, once again, as the pit props were fired.

But nothing came.

Heavy cavalry and infantry moved forward, guarding the tunnels.

Hal wondered what had happened. Something must have gone wrong.

The tale didn't take long to reach the squadron.

The miners had been within a day of undermining the second wall when suddenly – stories varied from nowhere or from a tiny, unnoticed crevice – monsters boiled on them. They were not men, all stories agreed, could not be men, being coal black, with a rigid carapace atop their head like a lizard's. They had sharp pinchers for hands, and tore at the miners as they panicked, tried to escape the trap.

The monsters, whatever they were, feared sunlight or possibly open air, for none of them came out of the tunnel, either by day or night.

Evidently the master spell of two months earlier hadn't gotten rid of *all* the Roche sorcerers.

There matters rested for two days.

Then magicians came up, staying well clear of the tunnel, and began chanting, dancing, weaving in steps as more magic was sent out.

There was no smoke, no fire, but somehow the wizards' thaumaturgy worked upon the tunnel props.

Cracking noises came, Hal was told later. Then, slowly, majestically, the inner wall began toppling, outward, just as the miners had intended.

It leaned out at an impossible angle, but its stones never shattered. And then it stopped leaning, and held at that impossible angle.

Hal shook his head. Wizardry confounded wizardry.

Then he heard a squeal from one of the dragons, looked away from Aude.

Hurtling toward the city, above Hal and the other dragon flight, came *Ky* Yasin's black dragons.

36

Hal had time for one warning trumpet blast, then had to concentrate on Storm, on trying to overcome Yasin's height advantage.

The other, experienced fliers of the Eleventh were doing the same, but the other flight over Aude, and some of Hal's less-seasoned fliers did little more than gawp at the black death coming down on them.

Yasin's fliers were experienced – they tried to avoid combat with their equals on the climb, and struck at the newer fliers.

They'd stolen a lesson from Hal and their own experimenters, and all their fliers were armed with short recurve bows, harder to fire accurately than Kailas' crossbows, but with a much heavier weight. The Roche fliers had become adept in clinging to their dragons' backs with their knees, reins looped around the flier's neck while he was shooting.

A Roche dragon veered away from Hal, but he launched a bolt, and hit the beast in its wing. It shrieked, and its rider fought the reins.

Hal slid another bolt into his crossbow trough, and was just under the Roche's wing. He fired, this time at the flier, hit him in the leg. The man reflexively grabbed at the wound, and Hal fired again, this bolt taking the man in his chest.

The black dragon, feeling no control at the reins, shrieked again, and flapped away to the west.

Hal banked Storm sharply, looked down at disaster.

Deraine dragons were falling, fleeing. He saw no more than half a dozen of his fliers still looking for a fight, dove down to support them.

He put a bolt in a black dragon's neck, another in a second beast's tail, enough to make it coil in surprise, hurling its rider down toward Aude.

A black dragon was flying at him from dead ahead, and Hal, dropping another bolt tray on to his crossbow, forced himself to hold his course.

At the last minute, the black dragon turned aside, and Hal swore the flier was Yasin himself. He fired at the man, and missed.

Then the blacks were gone, and it was time to limp home and count the losses.

They were severe. Hal didn't know how many fliers the other flight had lost, but he'd lost four himself.

One of them was Rai Garadice, who'd been seen trying to fight his crippled dragon across the river, into his lines.

Hal and Sir Loren went back into the air, flying low along the river front, hoping and looking.

It was just before dark when they saw the broken remains of a dragon, landed, and found Garadice's body a dozen yards away. It appeared as if he'd tried to jump for the leafy branches of a tree, hoping to cushion his fall. But he'd missed by feet.

Another of the old guard was gone.

It took Hal almost until midnight to find the right words for the letter to Garadice's father.

They buried Rai, full ceremony, the next day.

Then Hal found a horse, rode to command headquarters, and found Cantabri.

He was less than properly military, angry and demanding, that he had less than half his fliers left, and no more than one spare dragon.

As of this moment, he was standing down his flight, unable to accept any further assignments until his unit was properly rebuilt.

Cantabri listened, didn't show signs of anger at the insubordination, said the matter would be taken care of.

"When?" Hal half-snarled.

"Before the week is out," Cantabri said.

Hal stared at him, turned, remembered his courtesy, turned back, saluted the lord and stomped out.

"Isn't it a bitch," Hal said, staring at the half-empty bottle of wine, "that not only are you the only one I can feel sorry for myself around, including Khiri, but I can't even let myself get drunk."

Storm made what a serious dragon fanatic might have defined as a sympathetic noise, especially if no one considered his breath, palatable only to someone who likes the aroma of very dead sheep.

"Troubles," Hal went on, leaning back against the dragon, and considering the empty, dark barn. "Not enough fliers, and the ones I've got are fodder for that frigging Yasin. We're low on supplies, and nobody's answering Gart's requisitions for anything and everything from socks to crossbows.

"Plus I can't find that . . . that person I'm looking for," he said, cautious even when alone.

"I don't think we're fighting the Roche in the right way, but I'm just too damned tired keeping up with this minute's emergency to rethink matters.

"If I could have a month or so to myself . . ." His voice trailed off, and he wished he could uncork and finish the bottle.

"First, I'd go to Cayre a Carstares," he decided. "And I'd sleep for a week. Then I'd spend the next week in bed with Khiri. Then I'd eat for a week. Eat and drink.

"After I got over my hangover, I'd sit down, in that tower, and get the mud out of my brain on some of those ideas I had that looked so promising."

Storm made a noise.

"All right," Hal allowed. "You can come too. And we'd go out flying every day, or, anyway, every other day. Flying west, and looking at some of your relatives as they sail toward us."

Hal heard a flapping noise, looked out the open door of the barn, saw, not far distant, flying low, one of Yasin's black dragons.

Storm made a keening sound.

"You'd rather not go? You'd rather stay here and kill black dragons?"

Hal pulled himself to his feet.

"And me talking to dragons. There was more wine in that wine than I allowed for.

"I'm for bed."

At the far end of the barn, a canvas blocking a doorway moved, very slightly.

Hal Kailas didn't notice.

Cantabri's word was good. Three days after Hal had stormed his battlements, seven new dragon fliers appeared. They weren't nearly as trained as Hal's flight had been what seemed like a century ago. But they were present, didn't seem to have any significant flaws, and could be trained.

Or else they'd die.

"Now, yer see," Farren Mariah said to the seven replacements, "there's a gatillion an' three ways to fight a dragon.

"And all of 'em's right, as long as it's you that comes home all heroic and shit, and not the Roche."

"We don't need generalities," a dragon flier named Chincha said.

"Hold on, woman," Mariah said. "You'll get statistics and such, if you want."

Hal had happened by the open back door of the fliers' hut, heard Farren holding forth, listened, grinning.

"We'll start-a-tart by comparin' our two grayt hee-roes, Lord Kailas, who I can call Hal but you can't until you've gotten your paws thorough blooded. The other is Sir Nanpean Tregony, who'll, thank you, prefer you use his title. Or you can simply call him a god.

"He won't object t' that."

"Clearly a friend of yours," Chincha said.

Mariah turned serious.

"I'll tell you someat that'll stand you in great standings as you wobble through thisyere life.

"You don't got friends. Friends take yer heart with 'em when they die. Your friends are the people who can pull one of them friggin' black dragons off your arse, and who'll carry her, or his, end of a horrible dawn patrol wi'out snivelin' overmuch.

"Anyways, to turn serious. You takes Lord Kailas for starters. Now, he ain't the best shot in th' world. Good enow, but he'll win no country rumpkin-bumpkin fairs for shootin'. Which is why he gets as close to his target as he can.

"Ne'er shoot 'til you smells the reek of its breath, might be his motto in his grotto if he had a motto or a grotto.

"So he's friends – if friends you can ever be – wi' his horrid beastie. And he uses th' dragon's flyin' to get right up a Roche's butt. You'll note he steers wi' his foots an knees as much as the reins, which gives him a better chance t' take aim. Not to mention hangin' on, since it's not considered respectickle to fall off yer mount while chasin' some other sod.

"Also, he uses his wingmen, generally likes to have one t'either side, to keep th' Roche from tippytoein' up behint and arsassinatin' him, and in front to steer th' bad sorts into an intractabobble situation.

"A nice thing, if you're one of those wot counts bodies, he'll share or even give up a win to you.

"Now, *Sir* Nanpean, he's different. A dead shot. I mean that in earnest. He gets in 'til he's got a shot, and that's as he sees it, near or far, and then plonks 'em.

"He don't care what he hits . . . Which brings up another matter about our Hal. He rather goes for the rider, not the dragon.

"Got a soft spot for the beasties, he does.

"Back to *Sir* Nanpean."

Hal noted Farren's emphasis on the sir.

"He don't have much use for a dragon. If he weren't scared of Lord Kailas finding him out, he'd prob'ly pack a whip.

"I remember a flier, back in trainin', thought he was some kinda drover or shit, did that. Dragon went and killed him, it did.

"Another thing about Sir Nanpean. He don't have use for wingmen, neither. He figures it's your place to help him make kills. Never'll be the day come when he shares credit."

"What about you?" another replacement asked. "What's your secret, since you've been out for such a long time?"

Hal could imagine Farren's sweet smile.

"Why I gots none, other'n bein' a helladacious wizard on my mother's side, wit' charms and all *kinds* of shit. I just flies along, lookin' cute, and when somethin' moves, I shoot."

"How many dragons have you killed?" Chincha asked skeptically.

"Ours or theirs?"

Hal buried laughter.

"Dozens," Farren went on. "Hunnerds and hunnerds. Back of the Roche lines looks like a secret dragon graveyard."

"Then why aren't you the darling of the taletellers?" Chincha asked.

"That's a bit complicated," Farren went on. "Yer gots to start with me bein' the illygitymate daughter of King Asir, and—"

Hal, not having time for the rest of the tale, went on about his business, his dark mood of the night before gone.

Now the war became static once again. But more men, horses, dragons died, on both sides, than ever before.

There were more attacks against the walls of Aude, each time driven back. But each time, more of its defenders died.

The city walls were pockmarked from the huge stones hurled by trebuchets, and unshriven and unburied bodies lay scattered across the barren landscape, the bloated bodies of horses and oxen among them.

The soldiers were either entrenched or sheltered behind rocks, in gullies, folds in the ground. On the battlements of Aude were arrow-firing catapults, whose crews grew more and more deadly in their aim.

There were demons brought forth and sent into battle by both sides. Sometimes they fought men, and the carnage was terrible, and sometimes each other. And sometimes the other side's magicians were quick enough, and the demons vanished harmlessly into the air. But not often.

Neither Sagene's Council of Barons nor King Asir would give up their foothold in Roche terrain, and Queen Norcia was only too aware if Aude fell and the River Comtal became an open waterway, her country was very much at risk.

Hal took his dragons up over the city, against Yasin's black monsters day after day, trying to always choose the terms for combat: never less than three against one; never without the advantage of altitude; always with at least one other dragon flier in constant support.

There were other Roche dragons in the air – evidently training the blacks was as hard as Garadice's father had said it would be.

These other dragons Kailas wasn't as choosy about the fighting conditions for.

But still, he lost fliers.

Of the seven replacements, he lost four within two weeks. But the other three learned, and became as canny as the rest of the flight.

Hal was amused to see the tall, blonde Chincha become more than friendly with the short, dark, stocky Farren Mariah. He said nothing, however, after the night Sir Nanpean made some crack, unheard by Kailas, about the woman, and Farren beat him so badly he couldn't fly for three days.

Hal punished Mariah by making him fly Sir Nanpean's patrols in addition to his own.

Even though Hal refused to admit it, even to himself, a killing war began between him and Tregony. One day one would be up, the next the other.

Since Kailas frequently forgot to put in a claim, or gave the kill to one of his fellow fliers to make, there was no question within the flight as to who was the real dragonmaster.

It didn't matter to Hal. All he wanted to do was have more dead Roche dragon fliers than could be replaced.

Very secretly he hoped one day to meet, in the air, the bastard who'd killed Saslic.

That would be a victory he'd loudly claim.

In the meantime, he concentrated on the hard targets – Yasin's black dragons. But they flew in close support of each other, and took a deal of killing.

Then one day, Yasin's blacks vanished from the skies over Aude.

They reappeared, two days following, along the River Comtal. Flying very low, in pairs, they attacked the small supply ships bringing replacements and materiel to the besiegers, tearing rigging, raining arrows down on helmsmen and boat commanders and, when they got a chance, ripping apart any unwary soldier or sailor.

They also scouted for prepared ambushes, and forced Deraine to escort the boats with cavalry on the banks, which slowed progress.

"We have new orders," Hal told his assembled fliers. "You won't be surprised.

"We're to go after the black dragons, and at least make them stop harrying our ships."

"Shows what happens," Sir Loren said, "when your flight is the best. You get sent to do the impossible and, by the way, don't get killed until you've done it."

"Hell of a morale builder you are," Vad Feccia said.

"If you can't stand the heat," Sir Nanpean put in, silkily.

Feccia turned, glowered at Tregony. Hal lifted an eyebrow – he'd thought the two were the closest of – well, perhaps not friends, because he couldn't imagine either of them actually having a friend – but compatriots.

"We'll do it in flights of four," he said. "Two pairs, the second pair back of the first by, say, a hundred yards or so.

"If you spot a dragon, try to get height on him, and force him down into the water or riverbank. If you're seen by them first, and they've got height, get away from the river, and stay low. Maybe you can veer enough so the bastard that's diving on you'll eat rocks instead.

"Don't be too quick to fly around any of our barges," he said cynically. "Sailors have a great reputation for shooting at anything in the air, no matter whose pennons they're flying. Each dragon'll fly a banner with Deraine's colors on it, but don't depend on that being much of a shield.

"This time, everybody draws trumpets, and if you see anything – an ambush, a dragon – blast your little brains out.

"Gart, since you're the seaman among us, I want you to tell everybody how these river barges sail, so we can maybe anticipate what they'll do when they get hit.

"I'll lead the first flight out tomorrow. We'll fly north, where we'll link up with a river convoy. Chincha, on my wing. Mariah, you'll fly number two. Pick your own wingman."

The dragons lumbered into the still, summer sky at dawn. Hal led the four to the river, turned north. They flew slowly, Hal peering ahead to look for signs of the enemy.

Storm began snaking his head back and forth, sensing something.

Hal decided to trust him, waved for the other three to climb.

They rounded a bend, and saw two black dragons, sitting on a sandbank.

They waddled into the air, necks stretched like geese, but it was too late. The Deraine fliers were on them, bolts slamming into the fliers. One dragon squawked like a wounded goose, slammed into the water, a gout of spray around it.

The other ducked through river-edge brush, and flew hard east, deeper into Roche territory.

Hal let it go, signaling the others back toward the river, expecting the pair had been waiting for the Deraine boats to appear, which meant there should be an ambush laid nearby.

There was – twenty cavalrymen, some in uniform, some in ragged civilian attire.

They had only a moment before the four dragons were on them, talons ripping, tails lashing down, smashing horses and men.

The riders broke, and were harried by the flight away from the river.

Only a handful escaped.

Hal returned to base, sent an exuberant message to Lord Cantabri:

"Dragons love fishing. Took about eighteen bottom feeders this morn."

Another flight went out in the afternoon, and jumped soldiers setting up a block where the river narrowed, and attacked.

Hal heard, a day later, the Roche troops assigned to ambuscades along the river had started calling the dragons "Whispering Death," from the slight rush of air across their wings as they attacked.

"I would like," Limingo the wizard said precisely, "a flight around Aude."

"I have read the orders here from Lord Cantabri saying you're to get anything you want," Hal said, tapping the scroll the magician's extraordinarily handsome assistant handed him. "And I obey my orders."

"I know," Limingo said. "But it's always nicer to have some enthusiasm, rather than simple rote obedience."

"You can have that, and more," Hal said. "Provided you do me two small favors."

"Magical, I assume."

"Of course."

"No love philters until the war's over," Limingo cautioned and started laughing at Hal's annoyance until he caught on.

"I'd especially like," Limingo said, "you to fly me—"

Hal stopped him with an upraised hand.

"Tell me when we're in the air."

Limingo lifted eyebrows, but obeyed.

Unlike his master, Limingo was eager to clamber up behind Hal, and positively glowed as the dragon lumbered into the air, and changed from a waddling monster to a graceful creature of the heavens.

He leaned forward. "Are we a little suspicious of our fellows?"

"I'll explain later – when we're alone," Hal said. "Now, what do you want to look at?"

"The far side of Aude, particularly the main gate," Limingo said.

Hal did, swooping low, and getting a few arrows in his general direction for his bravado.

"They're getting better," he said over his shoulder.

"Let's hope," the wizard said, "this marks the limits of their expertise. If you could do what you just did, two or three more times?"

Hal obeyed. The magician seemed to have no idea of bodily harm.

"Very well," Limingo said. "I think I have enough."

Hal flew back to the base, landed Storm a ways from the barn, and explained his caution.

"My," Limingo said, "a possible spy. What happened to that dagger that was used to kill your serjeant?"

"I still have it. The matter hasn't been reported, by the way."

"Aren't you playing your cards a little close?"

"Maybe," Hal said. "If I let the provosts know, they'll be kicking through my whole flight, looking here and there and everywhere.

"We've got a war to fight, and it won't get any easier if my fliers are looking over their shoulders for spies or, for that matter, warders who'll suspect everyone."

"Why don't you give me that dagger," Limingo suggested. "A spell here and there might give some fascinating answers."

"That was one of the favors I was going to ask," Hal said. "I assume, the reason you wanted to fly where we did is there is a plan afoot?"

"I hope so," Limingo said. "This crap of sending men against solid stone is doing nothing but guaranteeing Deraine and Sagene are going to have some very empty counties for a couple of generations.

"But everyone, even our noble lords in command, know the Roche have paid close attention to their gates, so it's not a matter of just wandering up and knocking politely.

"I thought I might be able to devise something. And I think I was right, assuming the Roche thaumaturges don't pay attention to every detail.

"You mentioned you could use two favors. One we've discussed. What about the other?"

"I could do with some help looking for a dragon base," Hal said. "I took one of their flights out of the war once by attacking their base.

"Now we've got those black dragons, who're giving everyone a rough way to go. Maybe a good wizard could be of assistance?"

"I might," Limingo said. "Especially if you happen to have any scales, banners, whatever that belonged to the Roche or their dragons."

"I think we have a couple of souvenir keepers," Hal said.

He put Gart to rooting through the flight, and produced a pennon and an arrow that'd wounded one flier.

"Excellent," Limingo said. "My assistant and I'll set up this very night."

That night, at the far end of the field, there were strangely colored lights, flickering, and chants that seemed to come from more than two throats.

The soldiers of the flight shivered, and held close to their quarters.

In the morning, Limingo said, a bit angrily, that there were some heavy counterspells on what he'd been given.

"Perhaps," he suggested, "the leader of this black dragon unit is aware of the flight you obliterated, and is taking thorough precautions?"

"Perhaps," Hal said. "Yasin is no idiot."

"I'm sorry, Lord Kailas," Limingo said. "Perhaps, with my other incantation, I'll be more successful.

"In the meantime, stand by to be given special duties in the not distant future."

Three days later, Hal returned from a river sweep to find he had visitors.

Thom Lowess had arrived.

With him was Lady Khiri Carstares.

37

Hal followed his first instinct, and kissed Lady Khiri thoroughly. After awhile, she pulled back and whispered, "I'm certainly glad you're not one of those who believe in propriety."

Only then was Hal vaguely aware, through the roaring in his ears and his mind yammering for him to lug her into the nearest tent and work his lack of will on her, the cheering from the men on the dragon line.

He blushed a little, let her go.

"You know," she said, still in that wonderful whisper, "what they say about fliers is true. You all do smell like dragons."

"Uh," Hal managed. "I guess so. I suppose it's because—"

Khiri interrupted him. "I don't mind it at all. It makes you smell like sex."

A few feet away, Thom Lowess coughed discreetly.

"I'm also glad to see you, Lord Kailas."

Hal came back to himself, half-saluted Lowess.

"And I you, sir. What brings you here?"

"I, and my aide," Lowess said, indicating Khiri, "are in search of good tales. Tales to embolden the hearer, tales of victory and hope."

He made a face.

"And, right now, the dragon fliers are about the only good thing of notice around Aude. Although . . ." He let his voice trail off.

Hal looked at the taleteller questioningly, but got only a bland smile.

"Well," Khiri managed. "You certainly don't have to make any protestations of your virtue after that."

"Sorry," Hal said. "I didn't mean to lose control . . . at least not so quickly."

"So shut up," she said, lifting her legs around him, "and don't stop."

She moaned, then bit his ear.

"What would you say if I said I thought I was falling in love with you?"

Hal covered her mouth with his, didn't answer.

*

Hal vaguely expected some comments from his fliers about Lady Khiri, or at least some raised eyebrows. If there were any, they were very much behind his back, and it seemed that most soldiers in his flight thought it was perfectly all right for the "old man," as he'd come to be known, not yet twenty-five, to have a little joy in his life.

Both Khiri and Lowess busied themselves during the day interviewing everyone in the flight, including the dragons, or so it seemed.

"*Good* tales, m'boy," Lowess said. "Especially this duel you're having with Sir Nanpean Tregony for being the ultimate Dragonmaster. Especially especially with you both having come from the same town, and now being friendly rivals.

"It's the buzz of all Deraine, you know."

Hal thought of explaining, decided what he and Tregony felt about each other was no one's business, so long as it didn't get in the way of the war.

He did have one question of Lowess – how had this matter of their purported competition spread so widely?

"You certainly don't think you're the only young hero who's got a taleteller hanging to his coat tails, do you?" Lowess answered briskly. "You just happen to have gotten lucky and drawn the best."

Hal and his flight element, now down to ten fliers, nine dragons, went about their mission, escorting the convoys up and down the River Comtal. Sometimes they met the black dragons, and fought them if they had the advantage, but mostly were forced to flee, swearing at Hal's absolute orders, and sworn at by the sailors below, who had no reason to understand their abandonment.

Hal realized, after a day or two, that Lowess was just passing time, waiting for something.

Since he didn't get in the way much, and his presence kept Khiri around, that was well and good with Kailas.

He wanted her not to leave until he finished puzzling this matter of love over in his mind.

Now the rumor was everywhere – Deraine and Sagene were getting ready for a great offensive that would end the siege once and for all.

Hal cursed the inability of anyone in the army to keep his

mouth shut and his nose in his own business, but it didn't change matters.

Alarms were shouted, trumpets blared, and there was chaos in the village. Hal made it out of his sanctuary, no more than a towel wrapped around him, in time to see a huge black dragon climbing away from the village.

"What is it?" Khiri asked sleepily, coming out to the head of the steps. It was just dawn, and they'd been up later than they should, still delighting in each other's body.

Hal shook his head, saw a soldier running toward him, waving a tube.

"Sir!" the woman shouted. "It's for you."

Hal blinked, took the tube. Tied to it was a pennon Hal recognized – *Ky* Yasin's!

And his name was neatly written on the tube.

He twisted it open, forgetful of sorcery, and took out a note. It read:

Lord Kailas:

There appears to be a matter of honor between us, that you might find amusing to settle at your convenience.

I have heard that you are the ranking dragon killer of Deraine and Sagene, and have even had the temerity to dub yourself Dragonmaster.

I will meet you, just the two of us, over any place you name, at a time and date of your choosing, where we may discuss this matter at greater length.

If you have interest, and consider yourself an honorable man, return this container with your conditions across the walls of Aude. It will reach me.

> *Ky Bayle Yasin*
> *Commander*
> *First Guards*
> *Dragon Squadron*

Hal read it once, again. A smile came. He had an idea that might possibly solve two problems at the same time.

The dragon fliers listened closely as Hal outlined the challenge from Yasin. Lowess hovered in the background, beaming at yet another superb tale falling into his lap, pen scribbling frantically.

"First question I've got," Hal said, "is the bastard being honorable. Opinions?"

He pointed around. They ran from Mariah's "friggin' impossible. He's a Roche," to Gart's "maybe. Just maybe," to Sir Nanpean's "who gives a hang. What a chance to go down in history, win or lose."

Indeed, Hal thought. Especially if I lose, Tregony'll be the one going down in history. I'll just be going down.

"My own opinion," he said carefully, "is it's worth a shot. I personally don't believe Yasin'll be the only one to show up.

"But that doesn't mean we should play the utter fool."

He went to a large-scale map of the Aude region.

"Now, here's what I propose. I'll drop the message over Aude, agreeing to the meet. I'll set it for . . . oh, five days from now. At dawn. We'll meet here," and his finger stabbed at the map about ten miles downstream from Aude.

"Away from the front lines, and this is a huge damned meadow," he went on.

"I'll agree to fight him at, say, 500 feet."

"That'll give you some advantage," Sir Loren said judiciously. "The air's thicker down there, and his black will be a little harder to handle in tight turns."

"More than one advantage," Hal said. "Just in case he brings friends, I'll want the rest of you on the ground here," and he indicated an area about a mile from the meadow.

"Light trees, which'll give the dragons cover. If he fights fair, you can stay where you are. But if he shows up with his squadron, then you can get in the air fast, save my young ass, and maybe wipe out some of those blacks.

"Rumor has it we'll be needing all the help we can get in the not too distant future."

"You're a damned romantic fool," Khiri said.

"So it appears," Hal agreed. "But I happen to believe I can tear Yasin's nose off, and feed it to his damned black dragon."

"As if he'll be the only one there!"

"If that's the case, then I'll have the whole flight behind me. I don't think he'll bring his whole squadron to wipe out one dumb Deraine."

"You think!" Khiri said. "Men!"

"Shut up, and come here."

She came across the room, sank into his arms.

Hal nibbled on her ear, then whispered, "Even a romantic can be a sneaky bastard."

She lifted her head back, considered his smile.

"You have a plot."

"Maybe."

"Which you won't tell me about."

"Not now. Now, give me back that ear, if you will."

Hal rode to Command Headquarters, looked up Limingo.

"I'm sorry, Lord Kailas," he apologized. "But I've been running myself ragged, like every other magician with the army, with . . . with this plan we're developing. But I promise you, within the week, I'll let you know what clues that dagger gives."

Hal wasn't happy – he'd hoped sorcery could keep him from having to play out the game with Yasin.

But since it wouldn't, he found Lord Cantabri, asked him for a small favor, and explained.

"One company, only?" Cantabri looked at the map again. "I'll have two there, I promise. That might improve the quality of slaughter.

"You know, your duel with Yasin has shot around the army like an arrow-chase."

"What are the odds?"

Cantabri hesitated.

"Six to five," he admitted. "No one feels that the Roche will live up to their end of the bargain."

"Six to five," Hal mused. "That's the best life gives you, isn't it? Either way?"

Cantabri grinned.

"Perhaps, knowing what you told me, I might be convinced to have a bit of a go myself."

The days crawled past. Hal watched his fliers closely, but none of them behaved differently than before, and he wasn't able to narrow his search for the spy, if spy there was.

A courier came down to summon Sir Thom Lowess to the Armies' Command, the day before the duel. Hal knew that meant the offensive was drawing near.

Lowess sent the courier back, saying he'd be honored to join them, in a day's time, but he had another matter to take care of first.

"I don't know," Khiri said, "if I should be here, or not. If something happens . . ."

"If something happens," Hal said, "wouldn't you rather hear it directly?"

"I suppose so. Oh, dammit, I'm going to cry."

Hal slept badly that night. He was glad to be roused by the orderly warrant two hours before dawn.

He dressed quickly, went to the fliers' room. He'd ordered guards around the building, and the only people to be admitted were Sir Loren, Farren Mariah, Mynta Gart.

"I'm changing the orders," Hal said briskly. "I want each of you to take two other fliers out under your absolute orders.

"But don't, I repeat, do not, land where I ordered you to.

"Instead . . ." And Hal outlined his orders.

"A question, if I might?" Sir Loren asked. "Why the change?"

"You can ask, but you'll not get an answer. At least, not right now.

"You're dismissed. The other fliers and the dragons should be getting rousted out and fed by now."

Half an hour before dawn, the rest of the dragons in the flight took off. Hal had told each of them to obey any commands signaled by the three team leaders, no matter what they were.

He waited until they disappeared into the darkness, then went to Storm.

The dragon bubbled a greeting.

Khiri Carstares was waiting.

"I just wanted to say I love you."

Hal, mind already in the air, thinking about the meeting over a certain clearing, had to force himself to smile, give her a hug.

"I love you back," he said. He still wasn't sure if he did, but if he didn't come back . . .

He forgot that possibility, clambered into Storm's saddle, tapped the dragon's neck with his reins.

It snorted, ran forward, and leapt into the air, somehow sensing this day was different.

Hal let Storm climb until he was about 700 feet above the trees, the dark mass just beginning to lighten. He needed no compass or map to navigate to the Comtal, and up the river toward the clearing.

Just above him, about a thousand feet above the ground, was the usual scattered predawn cloud cover.

Very good.

Darkness became gray, and Hal knew, above the clouds, the sun could be clearly seen.

It was light enough to make out the clearing. Flying in lazy circles, about a hundred feet below him, a mile distant, was a single black dragon.

Hal checked his crossbow, eased a bolt into the trough.

"Let's go kill him," Hal said, snapping his reins.

Storm had already seen the dragon and, shrilling a challenge of his own, was flying toward it.

The dragon climbed to meet Hal, trying with its talons for Storm's head.

Hal jinked his dragon to one side, couldn't find a clear shot at its rider. But he saw Yasin's banner clearly.

He pulled Storm up as the black dipped a wing, turned hard, came back at him.

An arrow whispered past him, a foot or two distant.

Hal held his fire, still not happy with his shot. The two dragons sped past each other, talons reaching for a grip, finding none. Yasin's black flailed at Hal, missed him, and Hal fired a bolt into the monster's tail.

It thrashed, almost caught him, then the two were clear, climbing toward the clouds for an advantage.

The black shrieked three times, and, as Yasin turned back toward the attack, five black dragons dove down at their brother's signal.

Yasin *hadn't* played fair. Hal grinned tightly, did the unexpected, and instead of diving for the ground, came in again on Yasin. He fired at the man, cursed as his bolt missed.

Then he turned for the ground, diving toward the edges of the clearing, looking back as if he were panicked as the six blacks came after him.

None of the Roche saw the nine Deraine dragons plummet down toward them, from behind, from where they'd been flying, at Hal's orders, just above the clouds.

Hal had set a double trap, one for Yasin, one for the spy.

If there was a spy, Hal assumed Yasin had been told, somehow, about Hal's plans, which is why he'd changed them at the last minute, ordering his dragon flight to fly high above the meadow, and attack anything they saw below them.

Hal pulled Storm up, into a wingover, was rushing headlong at the Roche dragons. An arrow went above him, and he aimed carefully, shot one of the Roche fliers in the chest at point blank range. The Roche slumped, and the dragon banked, into Storm's talons. The beast howled, tried to dive away, but Storm's tail caught him, smashed his neck.

Then the Roche saw their pursuers, just as the Deraine monsters were on them. There was a swirl of fighting, and Hal heard shouts from men, screeches from dragons, and two black dragons went plummeting toward the meadow.

A trumpet blared, and the three surviving dragons dove toward the ground, intending to escape by flying at treetop level.

Well-trained, as Hal had assumed, they went low, very low.

Lord Cantabri's two companies of archers came out of their hiding along the fringes of the meadow, and arrows sheeted up toward the Roche.

They pincushioned the rear beast, and he squealed, lay over, and smashed into the ground, bouncing to stillness.

Two, Hal thought, and then, past him, came Sir Nanpean Tregony, having a bit of height, enough to close on the forward black. He was almost atop the beast, and Hal wondered if Tregony's dragon would tear the flier from his mount.

But Tregony was leaning out, aiming, and his crossbow bolt took the Roche in the back of the neck. He contorted, and fell away.

Hal was closing on the last dragon, Yasin's, but the black had speed on him, and slowly pulled away from him.

Hal broke off the fight, banking up and around, trumpet blasting the signal to return to base.

"An' you're a cagey, cagey bastard," Farren Mariah said admiringly. "Remind me to never wager with you, least not unless we're usin' my cards."

"And how did you know they'd be waiting for us in the clouds?" Gart asked.

"I pray regularly," Hal said piously, and Sir Loren snorted in laughter.

Hal, surrounded by congratulating members of his flight, leaning against Storm, who was almost purring in content, pulled Lady Khiri to him.

"I love you," he whispered, leaning back against Storm, and this time he meant it.

He smiled, as if well content with the day.

In some ways, he was. He'd lived.

More importantly, he'd confirmed the presence of a spy in the formation.

But he still didn't know who he was.

And *Ky* Bayle Yasin still lived.

38

Reinforcements started coming in thick and fast, as did supplies. Hal's flight came to full strength, and, wondrously, was given two extra dragons.

Kailas knew the attack was very near.

As did the enemy.

Ky Yasin's black dragons, also reinforced, were withdrawn from raiding along the River Comtal, and now flew close cover over the city of Aude.

Three other dragon flights, including Sir Lu Miletus', Hal's first combat unit, were stripped away from the Third and Fourth Armies. Hal was delighted to see that his former tentmate, Sir Aimard Quesney, was still alive, and, he discovered in the few minutes they had to chat, as wryly cynical as ever.

But there was little time for reminiscing. Hal spent almost as much time in conference at Command Headquarters as he did with the Eleventh.

He was pleased to see Lady Khiri, who he'd convinced to stay with Sir Thom, was the absolute darling of the staff officers. It kept her from worrying about him, he hoped, and, not being the jealous sort, he didn't worry about any of these popinjays being invited to share her bed.

He was not as pleased to see just how luxurious a life these back of the line slackers had carved for themselves, from the best rations, which should, by rights, have gone to the front lines, to uniforms and living equipment.

Cantabri told him to forget his anger. If these staff sorts spent their time trying to connive themselves a fine case of Sagene wine or whatever, instead of their job, perhaps the line units might not be as subject to their killing whims.

But Hal still wanted to put all of them in a long line, armed with their favorite pens and foolscap, and send them against the walls of Aude.

The Eleventh was chosen for special duties – to escort the army's magicians wherever they wanted to go to cast their spells on the day of battle.

Hal would rather have flown against Yasin, but Cantabri told him this was far more important.

"We'll not hit the Roche with one or two great spells," he said. "But little ones, here and there. If they pry open a crack, you'll be responsible for bringing in more wizards to reinforce the first spells.

"Also, since magicians don't seem to have much awareness of their own mortality, you'll be responsible for keeping them alive.

"Not that you can't take advantage of any targets of opportunity, once your two primary duties are in hand."

"Wonderful," Hal muttered.

His mood wasn't improved when Limingo told him he still hadn't had the time to pluck whatever secrets the dagger that murdered Serjeant Te held, but he would do it immediately. Or within the day . . . or perhaps tomorrow.

Hal took no chances that the spy within his flight might be able to give away their duties, and how much of the attack would be dependent on magic.

He grounded the flight, and had their base surrounded by troops, who were ordered to let no one except Kailas in or out.

His fliers seethed, not knowing why they were being held hostage, and, for most of them, that they were going to be nothing but a ferry service during the great battle.

Hal decided a little anger would be good for them when they were finally permitted to fly against the Roche.

Then, one day, the siege engines went into constant action day and night, smashing stone ball after stone ball into Aude's outer and inner walls, targets carefully chosen for structural weakness.

Troops moved out of their encampments, into attack positions.

The Roche were at full alert, but they didn't seem to know, any more than Hal or anyone outside the high command, just where the attack was going to be mounted.

For once, the flapping jaws of the army didn't have anything to chew on.

For the moment.

Limingo arrived at the base with four acolytes, a cheery face, and interesting news for Hal.

"I was going to put you off yet again," he said. "Then I realized if this was that important for you to consult me, it might have a great effect on the performance of your flight, which might mean on this battle.

"Which, incidentally, will begin tomorrow afternoon. Everyone fights at dawn, to give them the benefit of the day.

"Which is one reason Lord Egibi chose the time he did

"Also, this fight is expected to last over several days, and probably won't accomplish much on the first day, beyond, hopefully, putting our spells in place and clearing the walls of Roche archers.

"There'll be a courier arrive sometime today with your orders, but I thought you might like a bit of an advance warning.

"I can give you specifics on what I'll need. I want you, and four of your fliers, to take myself and my staff to that knoll we visited once before.

"At that time, I'll cast my own spell. You might have guessed it would have something to do with those gates on the main entrance.

"They're protected by Roche magic, but I'm betting they haven't thought of everything. Gates require hinges, and hinges, even huge ones such as we saw, corrode.

"Magic isn't all that great in building from nothing, but one of its great strengths is to destroy. To corrode.

"We shall see what my magic can do against them. If those hinges can be smashed, the gates can be toppled.

"And if the gates are toppled . . ."

Limingo smiled tightly.

"I do wish that there was a way we could get closer. The power of sorcery isn't improved by distance.

"But I'm hardly fool enough to try to thaumaturge from either the back of your dragon or, worse, from the front ranks amid an arrowstorm."

Hal let the man run on, realizing the magician was brave, but no one, except probably Lord Cantabri, could face the morrow's slaughter equably.

Limingo caught himself.

"Very well," he said. "Now for your business. Are we in a place where no one can overhear us?"

"We are," Hal said. He'd had the spy-ear in his quarters blocked after Te's murder.

Limingo nodded to his acolyte, who handed him a pouch. Inside was the flier's dagger that had killed Te.

"I can't give you everything," he said. "Magic doesn't generally work that way.

"However, I can suggest that the proper owner of this knife would be large and thick, a man, yes definitely a man, who'd look like a drover or a blacksmith. I don't think, though, that he was the one who committed the murder.

"There's a layer of blood and fog between him and that death. That's a very imprecise way of putting what my spells showed, but I can't find better words.

"This other person, and I cannot give you anything about him, would have been the killer.

"I'm sorry, but that's all I can divine. Possibly, with more time, and thought, coming up with greater spells, I might be able to divine a bit more for you.

"But not much."

"Thank you," Hal said. "I'll think on what you've said. It might be enough. Meantime, we'd best be preparing ourselves for battle."

All that day, and night, as the Eleventh readied itself for battle, making sure every bit of leather harness was oiled and soft, that the crossbow trays were fully loaded, that armorers had spare bowstrings and prods, Hal pondered the dagger, and Limingo's words.

He sat, staring at it, late, the sounds of dragons wailing in their sleep, aware of change and not happy with it, and the sounds of the smiths' wheels, sharpening already needle-like bolts, swords and knives.

He finally pulled himself away, checked his own gear and harness.

There were still lights about the former village, handlers making sure there was nothing amiss with the sleeping dragons, cooks preparing cold rations for the morrow, and, in the hut he'd assigned to Limingo, the muttering of voices and the occasional sharp reek of herbs being burnt.

His last visit was to Storm, who snored contentedly, head occasionally curling out, fangs yawning, as he destroyed another enemy in his sleep.

"When this is over," Hal said, "I promise you I'll find you the highest crag for your own, a herd of sheep and a cow worthy of your attentions."

Storm snorted, sighed.

Just after dawn, Hal was roused by Limingo, who wanted a flight close to Aude. "To get a feel for my castings," he explained.

The roads around Aude were alive with troops, making last minute moves. Heavy cavalry moved ponderously forward, pioneers bustled around the huge siege engines, which were never still, light cavalry trotted across the bridges toward the city, and infantrymen crept closer, keeping well under cover.

"Very good," Limingo shouted to Hal. "Now, all we have to do is wait."

Hal was making sure all was in order, yet without chivvying his fliers into despair, after the noon meal, on the dragon line as the monsters were being led out, saddled and ready, when it came to him.

He felt like a dunce for not being able to figure things out without magic.

He thought of letting matters wait until after the battle, decided he couldn't. He might have been able to keep the spy sequestered for a time, but once the fighting started, that would be impossible.

"I want to see Vad Feccia," he told Gart. "And Sir Nanpean Tregony.

"Have four men standing by, armed, for my orders."

Vad Feccia's eyes darted about the room as he entered. He visibly twitched when he saw the dagger, the only thing on Kailas' table.

Sir Nanpean Tregony looked appropriately bored and upper class.

"I hope this won't take too long, sir," he said, the usual subtle emphasis on his last word. "We're to be aloft in minutes."

"No," Hal said. "Not long at all. Vad Feccia, I formally accuse you, with Sir Nanpean Tregony as my witness, of the following crimes: Theft of war supplies; murder; spying for the enemy in time of war; and high treason.

"The last three are hanging offenses.

"You will be taken into custody by men I have waiting, and closely confined until you are brought before a court martial.

"I have used certain means to determine this dagger was originally issued to you, and falsely claimed to have been lost, after you murdered Serjeant Te for apprehending you in your crimes. There can be no doubt what the penalty—"

"No!" Feccia shouted. "Not me!"

"Be silent, you," Sir Nanpean said. "Stand up like a man for once in your monstrous life."

Feccia whirled.

"Stand up? And be hanged? No! Not ever! Mayhap I'm a thief . . . I'll admit to that, wanting my little delights, and never minding having a bit of cash about.

"But murder . . . Never. Nor treason.

"You're the spy, Tregony.

"And the damned traitor.

"You were the one who had me find out where Te kept his files, his maps. And you were the one who borrowed my dagger when you said there was a lock that needed prying.

"No, you son of a bitch! I'll not hang for your crimes!"

"Enough, Feccia," Hal said coldly. "Those words can wait for the trial.

"However, you, Sir Nanpean Tregony, now stand accused of most serious crimes."

"Lies by this thieving bastard," Tregony said loftily. But his eyes didn't meet Hal's.

"What was it?" Hal asked. "What did they buy you with? Was it gold? Or favors? Or just a chance to get out of that wretched prison camp? If you ever were in one at all, and rather turned traitor the instant you fell into their hands? Or maybe you were a Roche agent, right from the beginning. Certainly that'd hardly surprise me, knowing you for what you are, what you were as a boy.

"And how did you report, after we moved forward, and you weren't able to visit your contact?"

"I said lies, and lies they are!"

"Feccia surely can lie," Hal agreed. "But magic, especially magic of the highest order, cannot.

"And magic is what made me summon you and Feccia, in the hopes he'd behave as he did."

Tregony shook his head sadly, as if he felt sorry for Hal's foolishness, and then he moved.

His hand swept up the dagger on the table, buried it in Feccia's stomach. Feccia screamed, clutched himself, as Tregony dove into Hal, knocked him, breathless, to the floor.

Tregony rolled to his feet, and ran out the door.

Hal staggered up, gasping for breath. He took no notice of the dying Feccia, but went after Tregony.

The man was down the sanctuary steps, running for his dragon.

"Stop him! Shoot him down!" Hal gasped.

The four soldiers he'd ordered to stand by did no more than gape, utterly lost.

Hal swore, stumbled down the steps, his wind coming back, as Tregony reached his dragon, leapt up into its saddle, and shouted for it to move, move, dammit.

Hal thought of shouting for archers, but hadn't the breath, and ran toward Storm, pulling himself up, as his hands found the reins, and slapped the dragon into motion.

Tregony's dragon was at full gallop, and then in the air, as Storm, startled, began moving.

Then they were both airborne, climbing.

Tregony headed for Aude, kicking his dragon to full speed.

Hal called to Storm, words of encouragement, orders, and his dragon closed on Tregony.

Kailas was vaguely aware of the sound of the siege engines getting louder, more frequent, and, dimly, the shouting of soldiers from below.

The attack had begun, but he had no time for that.

The walls of Aude loomed up, and Tregony went over them, skimming the battlements.

Hal was just behind him, reaching for his crossbow.

Tregony glanced back, realized he was out of time, and steered his dragon toward the flat roof of the main keep.

He brought his beast in roughly, and jumped from the saddle, running toward one of the two closed doors that led down into the keep proper.

Hal reined Storm in hard, and the dragon's wings flailed.

Kailas fired, and the bolt took Tregony in the leg. He screamed, fell, came back up.

Hal, red rage dimming his vision, rolled out of his saddle, dropped ten feet to the roof of the keep, his dagger coming out.

Tregony turned, pulling his sword.

"Good," he said, "good. Come on, you damned peasant, with your hogsticker, and see what a *real* nobleman can do."

He lunged at Hal, and Hal barely parried with his long knife.

Again he struck, and this time his blade scored Kailas' ribs.

Hal spun, and whipped his dagger across Tregony's face, slicing it to the bone.

"Remember the last time, Tregony," he hissed. "Remember that piece of wood I scarred you with, back in Caerly."

Tregony screamed incoherent rage, dove at Hal in a long lunge. The man was very fast, but now time slowed for Kailas.

He brushed the lunge aside with his knife, smashed a fist into Tregony's face.

The man staggered back, sword clattering away, hands coming up in protest.

His mouth was opening to say something, but there was no time, as Hal's dagger drove up, under his ribs, thudding home in his heart.

Tregony mewed like that dragon kit he'd tortured long ago, fell.

Some measure of sanity came back to Kailas, and he realized where he was. There'd be Roche soldiers on the roof within moments, not likely seeking a prisoner, nor would Hal allow himself to be taken.

He had Tregony's sword in hand, and then Storm slid in, not a dozen feet away, and there was safety.

He was in the saddle, Storm needing no command to get away, and they were just clear of the roof when a shadow flashed overhead.

Hal had a moment to look up, saw *Ky* Yasin's pennon, his dragon, and the man glaring down at him.

The dragon's talons took Storm in the wing, tore it, and gashed his back, almost grabbing Kailas.

Storm howled in pain, turned, wing going out from under him, and they slammed down on the keep roof once more.

Hal rolled off, grabbing his crossbow, recharging it as one of the keep's doors came open, and two spear-carrying soldiers ran out.

Hal fired, worked the forehand, reloading, fired again, and both men were down, motionless.

There was a dragon flying toward him, and he took aim, saw Farren Mariah in its saddle.

He brought his mount down.

"Let's be gone! There're those about tryin' to kill us!"

Hal started toward him, heard Storm, keening in pain.

He stopped, stood still.

"Come on, man!" Mariah called.

Hal remembered Storm saving his life on that desolate beach, helping him time and again, and once more that red rage came.

"No!" he shouted back. "Both of us go, or none of us!"

"You're godsdamned daft!" Mariah called, and then there were three more soldiers at the stairs.

Hal spun, shot one, then the other was on him, and he dropped the crossbow, parried the man's pike, spitted him, looked for the third man.

He was stumbling toward Hal, a bolt sticking out of his guts, and then he toppled.

"You stupid bastard," Mariah growled, coming up beside him, reloading his crossbow. "Sir."

"Get your ass out of here," Hal said. "There's only room for one damned fool."

"Shut the hells up. Sir," Farren said. "Get another rack, and get over by that door, and don't make 'em come to us like we was ballroom dancers.

"I'll take the other one."

"Stupid!" Hal called, obeying.

He had a moment to pat Storm, say something meaningless, comforting, he hoped, then ran toward the open door.

Stairs led down, and there were men coming up. Hal shot three times, quickly, and the stair was blocked for a moment by bodies.

He saw Farren, at the other door, pressed by two swordsmen, and shot one out of the way, and Farren killed the other.

Hal heard screaming from above, looked up, saw two black dragons being swarmed by Deraine monsters, like owls in daylight being savaged by crows.

They dove, flapped away to the east, and the sky, at least for the moment, was Deraine's.

"Block the door," Kailas shouted, running back for his flier's dagger, pushing the door closed and ramming the blade into the jamb and kicking it home as a block.

Mariah was doing the same, using a Roche sword.

Then, for a moment, there was peace, except for the slam of the siege engines, the shouts of men attacking the walls, and the screaming of men hurt and dying.

Hal's panting slowed, and the world speeded up to reality.

Storm was looking at him, mouth opening, closing, like a stranded fish. But Hal could see his wounds, and knew, though ghastly, they wouldn't be fatal.

If he could get the dragon off this roof, and out of the enemy redoubt.

Which none of them would be able to do.

"Thanks," he shouted to Mariah.

"Fer what?" the small man asked. "Provin' there's more'n the one damned eejiot in the flight?"

Hammering sounds came from behind one door, then the other.

"Where's your dragon?"

"I slapped the silly git's butt," Mariah answered. "No need for everybody to die.

"And I damned well hope, when this is over, and they start handin' out the medals, there'll be a nice posthumerous one for Mrs Mariah's favorite boy."

"I'll be sure and write the citation myself," Hal said. "But it won't be posthumous."

Mariah stared at him.

"Yer actually thinks yer gonna live this one out?"

"Surely."

Mariah shook his head, and the hammering got louder.

Hal heard the sweep of wings, looked up, and saw Mynta Gart's dragon coming in. Behind Gart was Limingo and an assistant. Both of them carried bundles of gear.

Gart landed, and the two wizards slid out.

"Had I known you planned this," Limingo said, "I would've designed my spell differently."

He went to the edge of the keep, ducked back as arrows shot up.

The Roche soldiers had been cleared from the walls, and there were Deraine and Sagene soldiers between the outer and inner walls.

But they were still barred from entrance to the city, and there was a host of Roche milling around the keep's base, filing into it, toward the stairs.

"Unfriendly sorts," Limingo said. "I think we'll not need corrosion, this close. A nice melting will do fine."

His assistant nodded, began digging through their clutter.

"We'll need," Limingo went on, "a double triangle. Use the blue and the orange markers. Some flax—"

"No flax, sir."

"Hmmph. Well, then, fireweed of course, moonrot, and let me think now . . ."

Hal saw two more dragons coming in, Sir Loren and Chincha flying them, their backs loaded with an impossible number of soldiers. Both dragons sagged in for grateful landings.

"Grabbed all the spear-tossers we could," Sir Loren called. "Thought you might need them."

Hal felt for a moment as if he might actually live.

Then one door was smashed open, and Roche soldiers were on them.

There was a swirl of fighting, and a man stumbled toward Hal. Kailas was about to spit him, when the man's mouth opened, blood poured out, and he fell.

For a moment, the surge up the stairs stopped, and Hal heard the steady chant from Limingo:

> *Burn and build*
> *Grow, take strength*
> *Feed on what you have*
> *On what you are*
> *On the memory of the casting*
> *When all flowed, poured together.*"

A wave of nausea struck, and soldiers went to their knees. The Roche magicians were moving against them.

Overhead, three black dragons dove down at the roof. Hal saw Yasin's pennant in the fore.

He knelt, having all the time in the world, seeing nothing but that huge black dragon coming at him, then the pennant, then Yasin, grinning in anticipation.

He touched the trigger, and the bolt shot home, burying itself in Yasin's shoulder. The man jerked, almost coming off his mount, slumped forward.

Hal had a moment of triumph, hoping he'd killed Yasin, then the man sat up, shouting at his dragon, and it banked away from the roof, away from Aude, his two fellows guarding him.

Hal swore. It would have been perfect if he'd been able to kill the man responsible for the black dragons, and end the threat to Deraine . . . But the last bit of luck hadn't been given him.

Once more, there was a swirl of dragons overhead, and again the Roche attacked up the stairs.

This time, it was a steady stream, and Hal was attacked by two men. He wounded one in the arm, and felt pain tear down his leg.

He swore, lunged, and took the second soldier in the throat.

Hal looked across, saw Mariah down, clutching his arm, a Roche soldier about to spear him. One of the Deraine soldiers hurled a shield, taking the man in the head, and he jerked like a broken-necked chicken, fell on top of Farren.

"And there we have it," Limingo said in a calm, satisfied voice.

There was a great booming sound and Kailas, heedless of danger from the archers below, had to look over the keep's edge. One of the huge main gates was falling inward. Hal saw molten metal dripping down the stone wall.

It crashed down, and Kailas thought the sound filled the universe.

Then the other gate tottered, and creaked across to lie at an angle.

But the way was clear, and lines of soldiers came out of their hiding places in rubble, turns of the earth, and ran through the hole in the city wall.

Roche soldiers came to meet them, but they were no match, and Kailas heard cheering start.

The Roche on the keep roof realized what had happened, that they were now outnumbered, pelted back down the stairs.

Hal, ears sharpened, heard another sound, the sound of Whispering Death, and dragons plummeted down, sweeping the roofs clear of the enemy.

A dark wave beyond the wall grew, rolling toward the breach, and Deraine and Sagene cavalry crashed through their own troops, into the city streets, lances down, shouting their battle cries.

The last Roche lines broke and ran, into the heart of Aude, and the battle was won.

Hal Kailas, suddenly feeling the pain of his wounds, limped to Storm, stroked him, and the dragon's keening grew quiet.

39

It was dusk, a day later.

Hal Kailas uncomfortably sat a horse in the middle of a victory parade, through the shattered streets of Aude.

Now there would be an absurd ceremony, the keys to the destroyed city gates handed to the Sagene and Deraine Lord Commanders of the Armies.

Kailas had heard it took most of the night to bring the looters to bay, for few soldiers took kindly to a siege like this one had been, and had wreaked bloody revenge on the women and shops of Aude.

Windows were smashed, emptied wine casks were scattered here and there, and there were bodies, still unburied, sprawled and beginning to stink.

But that was the way of war, though Kailas despised it.

At least he'd gotten Storm off the keep's roof, and under an animal chiurgeon's care. He would heal, and fly again.

As would Hal Kailas.

Trumpets blared, drums thundered, and soldiers cheered.

But this was but one battle.

The might of Roche lay unbroken.

Kailas heard a faint noise, looked up, and saw, far above the city, a circling black dragon.

Perhaps it was *Ky* Bayle Yasin.

His, and Roche's, debt to Hal Kailas was still unpaid.

The Dragonmaster knew the war, and the killing, had only begun.

KNIGHTHOOD OF THE DRAGON

To Philip, a most decent sort of brother

1

The music crescendoed, then stopped abruptly; and the chatter was loud in the great hall, then swiftly muted.

Trumpets blared, and a leather-lunged herald shouted:

"Dragonmaster Lord Hal Kailas of Kalabas, Member, King's Household, Defender of the Throne, Hero of Deraine, accompanied by Lady Khiri Carstares."

The trumpets sounded again, and Hal bowed to Khiri, took her hand, and started down the long staircase to the dance floor.

"You barbarian," Khiri hissed.

"That's what the king pays me to be," Hal agreed amiably.

"You could have waited until after the ball," she whispered.

"Or . . . or else seduced me earlier, and given me time enough to straighten up."

Hal leered at her.

"My lusty impulses couldn't be restrained."

"If the king asks why my hair's mussed – and . . . and other things are awry – what would happen if I told him the truth?"

"That you're a horny devil who can't keep her hands off me?" Hal asked. "He'd probably chuckle in the beard he doesn't have."

"You!"

"I love you," Hal said.

"And I you," Khiri said. "Sex maniac. And at least we got you bathed enough times so you don't smell that much like a dragon any more."

They were halfway down the staircase, and Hal looked out over the bejeweled crowd, most of the men in dress uniform hung with medals and ribbons, the women, save for a scattering of ranking officers, magnificently gowned.

Kailas was six feet, brown-haired with green eyes. His face, when smiling, could be attractive. But he smiled seldom these days. War had hardened his features. Seeing, and bringing, too much death had made his face cold, watchful.

Hal wore black thigh boots, tight white breeches, a red tunic, almost hidden by decorations, with gold epaulettes and shoulder straps as befitted his rank, and a very practical-looking dagger at his belt. Against regulations, he was bareheaded.

Hal Kailas was just twenty-four.

Khiri Carstares was nineteen, as tall as Hal, dark-haired, with violet eyes. She wore a stylish gown, with less of a flare than common, ending a handspan above the floor, green with minimal white lace piping, elbow-length gloves, and white slippers. A jeweled necklace cascaded around her neck, matched by bracelets on wrist and ankle.

The trumpets blared again behind them, and the herald called:

"Lord Cantabri of Black Island," and a host of decorations, "accompanied by his wife, Lady Cantabri."

Hal looked over his shoulder, saw the tall warrior with the hard yellow eyes of a hunting tiger and scarred face coming down the stairs, in full dress uniform. His wife was small, a few years younger than Cantabri, and was dressed simply and expensively.

Hal continued on down to the floor, still limping from his leg wound at the battle of Aude, stopped Khiri until Cantabri joined them.

"You look wonderful, Lord Bab," Hal said, still not used to calling the man by his first name.

"Maybe," Cantabri snapped. "But what are we doing here, dancing to the king's command, when we ought to be across the water, killing Roche?"

"Bab!" his wife said sharply. "Behave."

Hal almost laughed.

"Why," he said, "we're doing just as you said, dancing to the king's command."

A baron came up, and Kailas and Khiri moved away, as other notables were announced.

"Does he think about anything other than slaughter, ever?" Khiri wondered.

Hal pretended to think.

"Yes, actually. I once caught him in a light moment, musing about maiming."

He fielded two cups of punch, gave one to Khiri.

But Cantabri had asked a good question.

Aude had fallen almost two months earlier, after a brutal siege. The Roche forces had fallen back from the ruined city in order, and taken fighting positions only ten miles from the battle-ground.

Hal knew why Deraine hadn't continued the attack – the siege had been most expensive, and the first line troops had been decimated.

Replacements had been rushed in, most barely trained, and with them came supplies, including new dragons for the dragon squadrons.

But the Deraine army still held in place.

Then came the surprise – more than thirty of the highest-ranking officers had been ordered to leave their formations in the charge of their second in commands, and journey, with all haste, to Deraine's capital of Rozen, "to await the king's pleasure."

That had sent Cantabri off. "What, for more medals, and leaving the damned Roche to keep rebuilding their damned army? That's plain foolishness!"

Hal agreed.

But King Asir's ways were set, and so the officers, with a scattering of enlisted men who'd distinguished themselves in the siege, obeyed.

Surprisingly, some of those summoned were Sagene, Deraine's not-always-wholehearted allies, with the written approval of the country's Council of Barons.

All of them, enlisted to generals, were cosseted in their journey north through Sagene to the Free City of Paestum, across the Chicor Straits, and upriver to Rozen.

They were ordered, to their great surprise, to take quarters in the king's castle, a high honor, and to stand by for further orders.

So far, that had consisted of being commanded to attend this ball.

Hal had thought wryly of his estates granted by the king somewhere north, next to Sir Bab's own holdings. They purportedly included several thousand acres, included dairy land, some islands, half a dozen villages, fishing rights, as well as a mansion here in Rozen. He'd seen none of them yet – the war was an all-encompassing beast. The closest he'd come was being notified of his monthly rentals and profits, paid into an account at a merchant bank recommended by Sir Bab.

Someday, before he was killed, he hoped to see his lands.

But those were thoughts for another day.

Now he and Khiri, who had been orphaned by the war and owned estates far vaster than anything of Hal's, were here, in the palace.

Allowances had been paid for new uniforms, and gowns for the ladies who might not be able to afford them. Tailors scuttled to the castle with orders to have their wares finished within two days.

Hal, who would have preferred to be back with his flight, training the new fliers and dragons, had learned to keep his mouth shut on occasion, and so put aside his impatience, and passed the time sleeping or dancing close attendance on Khiri.

Speaking of which, as the band started playing again, he took her by the hand and led her to the dance floor.

He was intercepted by Sir Thom Lowess, the taleteller who'd decided, some time ago, that part of his duties were to build Hal's reputation.

Sir Thom had also introduced Hal and Khiri, and so was very large in both their hearts.

He greeted them effusively, saying how glad he was that Hal had lived through the battle, and "covered yourself with even greater glory."

Kailas was embarrassed. Khiri tried to change the subject, saying perhaps they'd have a chance to have dinner with Lowess at his cluttered mansion.

"You might," Lowess said, holding back a grin. "You might, indeed, Lady Khiri."

"And what's wrong with me?" Hal asked.

"Nothing. Nothing at all," Lowess said, holding back a chortle. "Other than you'll notice the punch is remarkably weak, so even the hotheads won't have an excuse for their wits not being about them. Now, I must go."

He bustled away.

"That man and his trade are a perfect match," Khiri said. "He couldn't keep a secret if you threatened him with . . . with whatever you threaten a taleteller with."

"True," Hal agreed.

They both noticed something at the same time – equerries, in royal livery, were moving through the crowd, stopping here and there. Hal saw them pause at Cantabri, at Lord Egibi, Commander of the First Army, Lord Desmoceras, Sagene Commander of the Second Army, other high-rankers.

One stopped at Limingo, the king's most talented sorcerer, who was accompanied by a lithe young man both Hal and Khiri agreed could only be described as beautiful.

Something besides a formal dance was transpiring.

Hal wondered how long it would be before he was told.

Kailas was rather astonished when one of the equerries came

to him, bowed, and said, "His Royal Majesty summons you to an audience in the chamber beyond the green door."

He didn't wait for a response, but passed on.

"Interesting," Hal said.

"And there goes my dance ... and romance," Khiri murmured.

2

The room was large, a grandiose living room, with comfortable chairs in a large semi-circle, end tables next to them. Hal noted the tables had pitchers of iced water, nothing stronger.

Clearly the king had not summoned anyone for a celebration.

Around the room were the toughest fighters and most skilled commanders of Deraine's southern armies.

Something was very much in the offing.

Hal caught Limingo the magician's eye, raised an eyebrow. The wizard shook his head in equal ignorance as to what was going on.

The short, fat equerry Hal remembered from his ennoblement ceremony came into the room.

"All kneel for His Majesty," he ordered.

Everyone obeyed, except for the Sagenes, who, Hal was impressed to see, at least bent a knee as King Asir entered the room. It appeared the age-old enmity between Sagene and Deraine might be lessening.

Asir was short, stocky, and wore simple robes as was his style. Hal thought his eyes looked even more tired than the last time he'd seen him.

The war was grinding on everyone.

"Sit down," Asir said. "Thank you for attending me." Behind him, Sir Thom Lowess entered the room, waited by the door.

"What I'm going to tell you will, no doubt, displease some. As well as," and he pointedly looked at Hal and Sir Bab, "please others.

"This invitation was extended to all of you as part of a grand deception.

"I know that some of you have been loud in your unhappiness that I have not ordered our armies to follow up on their advantage at Aude." Again, he looked at Cantabri, smiled slightly.

"That was not accidental. First, it was necessary to rebuild the Deraine and Sagene units in the field, and give our soldiers a bit of a breather. Second, it took some ambassadorial conferring with the barons of Sagene until we were in full agreement as to the next stage.

"But now our forces are strong again, and our soldiers have had a rest.

"It is late summer, and the word is being spread that it is too late in the season to be mounting another campaign, and that we will be taking up winter quarters and securing the supply line from the ocean down the Comtal River to Aude.

"In fact, shovels, canvas and other pioneering tools have been loudly dispatched to Aude.

"Because of this planned inactivity, I decided to have a grand award ceremony for my victorious soldiers.

"There *shall* be medals awarded, but all of what I just said is a crock of shit."

There was a mutter around the room, a bit of laughter, a bit of shock. There were those who weren't familiar with the king's bluntness.

"My intentions are, in fact, to mount an attack on the Roche positions beyond Aude, striking in a great crescent with heavily guarded flanks. I intend to smash a hole in their lines, then turn left and right, turn loose my heavy cavalry and force their surrender.

"With that gaping hole, the way will be clear to the Roche capital of Carcaor, and the war's end."

There was a stir of excitement.

"Forgive me, Your Highness," a general said. "I applaud your audacity. But what does this attack have to do with us being here instead of with our troops?

"Did you want personal contact, to make sure we understand your orders?"

"Hardly," Asir said. "By this stage of the war, those who have trouble understanding are either serving in a rear echelon somewhere . . . or they're dead.

"You are the centerpiece of my deception.

"For those of you in this room, there'll be no comfortable rest here in the palace, although no one beyond these walls will know of it.

"The celebrating and feasts will go on, and those men still outside, and your ladies, will be my guests until the battle is mounted.

"Sir Thom, here, for those of you who aren't fortunate enough to be his friend, is probably the best, and most trusted, taleteller in either of our two kingdoms.

"I'm afraid that his credibility may be a bit shattered by what I'm requiring of him."

Lowess smiled, clearly not worried about that.

"He'll be putting out stories on a regular basis about the men and women he's interviewing, particularly our most steel-fanged heroes, some of whom are relaxing, more of whom are talking about their plans to wreak havoc on the Roche come spring.

"All – or as many as Sir Thom can connive – of your names will be taken in vain.

"Meantime, those of you here will be leaving before dawn tomorrow, back for Sagene and your soldiery. Since the weather is portending storms, which Limingo and his wizards shall be casting, you'll travel in covered omnibuses, as if you were just another convoy of replacements, if a bit more heavily escorted than normal.

"My equerries have already gone out to your units, and have provided them with written orders, which they are then instructed to return to the bearer, which shall give them an understanding on what is planned.

"I want the attack mounted within two days, no more, after your return to Aude."

A general whistled.

The king nodded. "Not long at all. And we shall attack without warning, without any probing attacks.

"This is the chanciest part, that the Roche may have prepared surprise defenses, although I'll have Limingo, and a small task force, journey south with you, with orders to magically search the Roche lines."

"But won't we be missed here?" an elderly general asked, a trifle plaintively.

"No," the king said. "There'll be soldiers wearing your uniforms, accompanying your wives or . . . or friends, that'll be seen from a distance."

The older man looked worried.

"I'll add," the king went on, "that all of them have been ensorcelled so there won't be any possibility of . . . problems."

Evidently the older man had, or thought he had, a wandering wife, for he visibly relaxed. Again, there was a bit of laughter from those who seemed to know.

"Obviously," the king said, "you can tell your wives, since we need their cooperation, although you must swear them to complete secrecy, for millions of lives, and perhaps even the fate of the kingdom, depend on this deception being carried off."

"I'll add," Sir Thom put in, "that there'll be no chance – or almost no chance – for any gossip to spread the tale. The king has officially told me that this gathering is intended to give his generals complete relaxation, and they are not to be burdened with any cares of the outside world."

"Easy to say, Sir Thom," a lord said. "But you don't have my wife, who'll kill anyone who tries to stop her from shopping, now that we're in the capital."

"Some of our most exclusive shops will be bringing their wares to the castle," Sir Thom said. "I doubt if anyone will be angered by the fact the tradesmen with them may not be as knowledgeable about silks and such as they should, because in reality they're disguised members of the royal household, since the items offered will be heavily discounted."

"Also," the king said, "the humbug will only last for five, perhaps six days, until you've returned to Aude, and battle is joined.

"I shall not keep you from the dance. Enjoy yourselves as best you can, but please don't tell anyone until you've returned to your quarters.

"You'll have enough time on the journey to study the plans that've been drawn up for you.

"Oh. One small thing. I know it won't alleviate your ladies' rage at me, but there'll be large amounts of leave after the battle. That's all."

He stood, and again the soldiers knelt or bowed.

"Lord Cantabri, Lord Kailas, if you'd remain for a moment?" The king waited until everyone had left.

"Your orders are a bit different from the others.

"Lord Cantabri, I require you to remain in readiness at the armies' headquarters. Your unit has already been turned over to your subordinate for the nonce.

"Your duties during the battle are to watch closely for any

hesitation, malfeasance or loss of command in any of the units, including the Sagene.

"You will have written authorization from me, and from the Council of Barons, to take over any faltering unit, Derainian or Sagene, and to relieve any officer you see fit.

"I am very damned tired of our plans being ruined by the hesitant or the timid."

Asir didn't wait for Cantabri to say anything, but turned to Hal.

"Your orders are somewhat simpler. I know your flight was badly stricken during the battle, and the new fliers I had sent to you are hardly combat-ready.

"I want you to take over three other flights – I've specified them in my orders to you – and provide aerial security all along the front. I don't want any Roche peepers overlooking our plans for the offensive.

"If they present themselves, make the new black dragon formations and their commander, Yasin, a particular target. We must have, and keep, command of the skies.

"When the attack is under way, you're to revert to normal duties, and provide reconnaissance for our advance, plus, with your added strength, defense for other, smaller flights.

"I know your formation won't be fully trained for what I require, but I have full confidence that you'll fulfill your duties.

"I promised you a great squadron of dragons that I simply haven't been able to provide.

"These four flights, once the battle is over, will be the formation of that squadron. At present, that is the best I can do."

The king smiled wryly.

"I hope that the war will not last long enough beyond this coming victory for you to accomplish that.

"Do either of you have any questions?"

Cantabri and Hal shook their heads.

"I'll give you a further order, but hardly in writing. Neither of you has my permission to get killed. I'll need both of you in the days to come. 'That is all."

"You swear," Khiri said fiercely, "you didn't know anything about this little game of the king's?"

"I swear."

"You swear you're not going to do anything dumb like get killed?"

"I swear. The king personally forbade it."

"You swear you'll be making love to me enough, for the rest of the night, to make me think you never left when you come back?"

"Uh . . . I swear."

"Then come here. And one more thing. You'd better be thinking, while you're off getting all dragon-stinky again, about doing something wonderful for me when you get back."

"Like what?" Hal asked.

"You just think about it."

3

Hal heard the eager honk of a dragon before he came in sight of his base. His horse reared at the sound, and he quieted it.

"If you're going to be dragon-shy," he said, "you'd best learn different . . . or think about becoming glue."

The dragon, a single rider aboard, passed about twenty feet overhead. It was green, with broad red streaks across its belly, and a male.

The monster was fully grown, almost fifty feet long, with twenty feet of that in its lethal tail. On the ground, it would stand around twelve feet tall. Its wings stretched wide, almost a hundred feet.

A dragon, in spite of its size and wingspread, could fly primarily because of its light bone structure, although it preferred, in its wild state, to spend as much time gliding as working its wings.

The warm-blooded creature had a heavily armored body, slightly less on its stomach.

Second only to man in its lethality, the dragon's weaponry was considerable: the head had twin horns, with impressive fangs, and spikes on either side of the snaky neck.

Its most deadly weapon was its tail, which the dragon cleverly used as a flail, a bludgeon, or a strangling cord.

At the neck's base rose a carapace, and behind it a flat area suitable for riders. "Tamed" dragons had holes drilled painlessly in the carapace for saddlery to be bolted into.

All four of its legs had three-taloned claws. There were also talons on the forward edge of the leathery wing.

No one quite knew how intelligent dragons were. In fact, no one had the slightest idea how to measure that intelligence. Everyone agreed they were smarter than dogs or apes, but as smart as a child? Some said they were, others said they were merely quick to learn.

Hal thought dragons were very smart at being dragons, and he didn't try to measure them against men.

Secretly, he thought that if he did, man might come up a bit short.

From here, Hal could smell the musky odor of the animal after it'd passed, and he grinned slightly, remembering Khiri's words about him getting dragon-stinky. Although there were other times she said she liked the faint smell that hung about him, times that made his body stir a little.

He put those thoughts aside as he turned off the "main road," just a rutted highway along the Comtal River, up a bluff to his landing field.

A few miles east, on the far side of the river, was the half-ruined city of Aude, and, beyond that, unseen, the front lines.

Hal hadn't recognized the dragon's rider, guessed he or she must be one of the three new flights he'd been given.

That might present a problem, he knew. He wouldn't have time to evaluate the other three flights, let alone put his stamp of command on them before this, hopefully war-winning, battle began.

Which brought up the idle thought – what would Hal propose doing when the war ended?

That begged the probability that he'd die before it was over. He remembered the words of his first, real love, Saslic, who believed "there won't be any after the war for a dragon flier." She'd died in the disastrous invasion of Kalabas, and taken a piece of Hal's soul with her.

Hal caught his mind's reel, lashed it back into line. There were many things to worry about first.

Such as the crowded near-chaos he saw as he topped the rise and looked down on his command.

Actually, it wasn't that bad, considering that the art of dragon riding had only been accomplished in his lifetime, and the idea of using dragons for anything other than aerial stunting hadn't begun until after the first year of the war, not half a dozen years before.

Especially since he'd planned the field to not only harbor, but conceal, a single flight of dragons.

At full strength, a flight numbered fifteen dragons and their fliers, and eighty men and women whose only duties were to keep the dragons healthy and flying. There were teamsters for the huge oxen-drawn wagons used to move the dragons about when they weren't being flown, cooks, clerks, blacksmiths, orderlies, leathersmiths, veterinarians and, Hal thought provided grudgingly, a doctor to keep the distinctly secondary humans functioning.

Hal had been most proud of finding this spot, heavily forested, ideal to hide the huge dragon barns. He'd had the brush and smaller trees selectively cut, concealing the other buildings of the base, and the paths were laid out to hide the movement of men.

He knew what happened when a field was discovered by the Roche dragon fliers, and had wreaked revenge for such a bloody attack.

Now, four flights had been jammed into this field. Trees were being cut down, tents for humans erected and canvas being pulled over skeletal iron hoops to shelter the dragons.

Men and women scurried here, there, intent on their tasks under shouting warrants, and dragons blared, some angry, some pleased, no doubt being fed, others just perplexed at being ripped from their homes to this new base.

A sentry blocked the road. Hal identified himself, and the sentry saluted smartly, and bade him welcome.

Very good, Hal thought. It appeared someone was in charge.

She was.

Mynta Gart came from under a dragon shelter. She was heavy set, an ex-seaman, the 11th Flight's adjutant, and a skilled combat flier. One of Hal's inflexible rules that he would be applying to the new flights, was no deadwood. Everyone, no matter what his assignment, was expected to turn to and keep the dragons, and their fliers, ready for combat, and do whatever service required when they came back.

"Welcome back, sir."

"It's nice to be back," Hal said truthfully.

Gart smiled slightly.

"I think we're all doomed, for there's no place that calls home to us except this damned war."

"That," Hal said, thinking of his estates, his villages, and such, "is an unfortunate truth."

"We were told you were on your way back," Gart said. "Or, rather, I was."

"And given other information to boot?"

"Yessir."

"Let's talk."

"Yessir."

Hal followed her not to the shabby tent he'd been inhabiting before he left for Deraine, but to a large, double-walled pyramid tent, with a wooden floor.

Hal dismounted, slung his saddlebags over his shoulder, and Gart shouted up a hostler, who took the animal away.

"Quite a mansion," he said.

"Anyone who leads four flights deserves a bit of comfort," Gart said. "You'll note the shelving, the chairs, all made of packing crates."

"How are the other fliers?"

"I assumed you'd ask that," Gart said. "Equally posh."

Both of them were talking around what was foremost in their minds – the coming offensive. Hal told Gart to sit down.

"How ready are we?" Hal asked.

Gart considered.

"Overall, we're at full strength, men and dragons.

"The eleventh is in fair shape. I've had all of the replacements in the air as much as possible, and had the experienced fliers working with the new dragons. All of the fliers and dragons have had flights over the lines, and are, hopefully, learning to spot a dragon in the air, and a catapult on the ground.

"I've put Sir Loren in charge of the training."

"Good," Hal said. "He's easy with the ignorant. And speaking of ignorant – and the old crew – have we heard from Farren? How is he healing?"

"I don't know how he's healing, but he's here," Gart said. "And troublesome as usual."

Sir Loren Damian, with Mynta and Farren Mariah, had graduated from flying school with Hal and two others, now dead. Farren Mariah had landed on the Aude rooftop with Hal, and saved his life before going down wounded.

Hal had no idea what had happened to the other nineteen graduates of the school and assumed the worst.

"If you agree," Gart said, "I'll have the trainees fly in pairs, new with old, when the attack starts."

"Fine," Hal approved. "At least, as long as it's a standard

recon. Don't put any of the virgins on anything shaky. And I'll give orders for any of them to break for the camp if they encounter black dragons. Speaking of which . . .?"

"We've sighted one or two," Gart said. "Well on their side of the lines, and damned skittish. I went after one, with three backups, and the bastard went for the ground and home. I turned back."

"Good," Hal said. "Maybe I got Yasin a bit twitchy when I shot him at Aude.

"Now, what about my new flights?"

Gart told him things were probably as good as could be expected.

"I can't really say, precisely, sir," she went on. "There's things I like, things I don't like, about all three of them."

"Details," Hal asked, then changed his mind. "No. I'll see for myself. First the dragons, then I'll meet with all four flights, then, this evening, with the fliers in – I assume it's still standing and you didn't put it off limits – their club."

"Off limits? Hah," Gart said. "Farren's decided he is the new officer in charge of the booze, so I think that shack is completely out of my – and probably your – hands."

"That's our Farren," Hal said. "Give me a moment to unpack my saddlebags, and then let's have a look at the shelters."

"Leave the baggage. I've appointed an orderly to take care of you."

"But—"

"But me no buts," Gart said firmly. "You've got over three hundred women and men to take care of. You don't need to be mending your own socks."

Hal didn't think that was very democratic, but conceded her point for the moment.

"I'll be back in a few minutes," Gart said, leaving the tent.

Hal got up, stretched, looking out at the bustle around him. He turned, trying to figure what he would do with an orderly, hoping Gart didn't mean for him – or her – to share the tent.

"Knock, knock," a voice said.

Hal knew without turning who it was.

"Enter, Farren."

"Arrh," the small, wiry man said, obeying. "Now that you're a full squadron commander, do I have to kowtow and genu-genu-genuflect?"

"I'll not hold my breath waiting for you to do that."

"That's wise, boss. Most wise," Mariah said. He looked

around the shelves. "Yer back an hour, and there's never a bottle about. Th' damned king's gone and reformed you."

"I doubt that," Hal said. "How're your wounds?"

"Still stiff, still bothersome."

"Why didn't you stay in hospital, or on leave?"

"The thought occurred," Farren said. "Howsomever, there were ladies who seemed to feel marriage'd set right with Mrs Mariah's favorite son. Two of 'em."

"And so you fled?"

"Aye, back to the safety of the front. I don't mind a deal of grief when I go, but I'm not of a mind to start makin' widows and orryphins. At least, not by the set."

Uninvited, he straddled a chair.

"So, we're off to war, eh?"

Hal tried to hide his reaction, evidently without success as Farren snickered.

"What in the hells makes you think that?" Kailas tried, somewhat feebly.

"Ah, when you're supposed to be gone, livin' on the viands of His Royal Hisself for a couple weeks, and then, just after you're gone, all these couriers start zippin' up and down the highways, and Gart's bustling about making sure the pikes are all sharpened and the talons burnished . . . what's a poor lad to think?

"Although, bein' as how there's a grand collection of numbnuts about, I've said nothing, feeling there's none worthy of my wizardy talents."

Mariah did have a bit of the Talent – he claimed his grandfather, back in the warrens of Rozen, had been a notorious witch. And every now and then his spell-casting did work, most spectacularly when he managed to dump a wagon of shit on the dragon-fliers' school's most hated warrant.

"And you're making no move to dig in your duffle and buy me a congratulatory drink," he said.

"I brought no alcohol with me."

"For certain there's a battle brewing . . . not to mention your brain's a bit askew."

"Perhaps." Hal looked at Mariah steadily. "So what's your call on the squadron?"

Farren held out his hand flat, wiggled it back and forth.

"That good?"

"I'm a real old soldier now, you know," he said, "and there's none to match the old ones who've gone past and under."

Mariah turned serious.

"You know, your dragon, Storm's finally on the mend."

Hal hadn't wanted to ask about the dragon who'd saved his life time and again, but that was, of course, the reason he'd wanted to visit the barns first.

"He took a bad turn, but as soon as I got back, and put him on a diet of farmer s stolen pigs and the odd sheepdog, he started back to health, instanter. And I'll not say whether I cast a spell or six to help."

There was a moment of silence.

"All right," Hal said. "You've wormed it out of me with your wiles. We are going to battle. The day after tomorrow."

Farren made a noise.

"All that traveling up to Deraine was a deception," Kailas went on. "Now, secretly, everyone's back, and we're to attack at once."

"Without running patrols, or aerial searches?"

"Exactly."

"That," Farren said, scratching the top of his head, "will give a bit of surprise, I suppose.

"And we should be hopin' the Roche haven't got their own surprises."

"We'll be taking dragon flights up along the lines, as close to crossing as we can get, tomorrow morning," Hal said. "And by the way, you and Gart are grounded until the battle."

"F'why?" Mariah's voice was an outraged shriek.

"If you go down, you might be made to talk."

"Me? Course, if captured, I always planned on singing like . . . like one of those birds out there on the tree, assuming the dragons haven't snapped 'em all up for snacks. But Gart'll never talk.

"And you need me up in the skies, fightin' ready for good ol' Deraine. So you might want to be rethinking that order, or I'll sic a dragon on you."

Hal considered. He'd wanted them on the field to keep order, but if it was to keep the secret from leaking, why was he himself proposing to fly? Not to mention the probability that somebody in the ground forces would let slip, and the Roche would find out the secret.

Hopefully it wouldn't be believed by Roche headquarters, which, when Hal had gone north, had been commanded by Duke Garcao Yasin, head of the Household Regiments and, it was rumored with a snicker, Queen Norcia's "confidant."

Or, if it was, there wouldn't be time enough for the Roche to prepare their positions against the onslaught.

No, keeping Gart and Mariah in the rear, just for the stupid reason of giving them one more day of life, made no sense.

"All right," Hal growled. "Order cancelled. You'll fly with me, as my backup."

Farren grinned.

"I deserve no less. Dragonmaster and Companion of the King."

Hal threw a dagger, fortunately sheathed, at him.

Storm was indeed mending, kept in a pen by himself.

He recognized Hal's voice, staggered to his feet, and yawned.

Hal's stomach curled at the dragon's breath.

"We fed 'im a passel of geese an hour or so ago," the stableman said. "T'at hits 'im like a padded hammer."

The veterinarian accompanying Gart and Kailas nodded. "We use poultices, and let the dragon sleep as much as possible, then feed him the best. Your man Mariah's been most helpful."

Storm, having given Kailas recognition, curled around himself, flapped his great wings with a noise like leathery thunder, curled back up, and put a paw over his nose.

"When will he be flying?"

"Oh . . . short flights, no strain, maybe two weeks," the vet, whose name was Tupilco, said. "No combat for a month."

Hal turned to Gart.

"I assume you've another dragon for me?"

"Already chosen," Gart said. "You can take her up any time you wish."

"After I talk to the flight commanders."

They went on through the cavernous, if drafty, shelters. The 11th's older dragons were a bit battered, but all were well-fed and were stirring about, as if expecting the action to come.

The 34th's were almost as spotless. The 18th's were worn-looking, but Cabet's flight had seen much action. The 20th's were acceptable, although the stablemen could have done with a bit of a cleanup.

Hal's dragon, Gart said, was named Sweetie.

Hal winced.

Gart shrugged.

"A little letter came with her. She was hand-raised by some

backcountry girl, then given to Garadice when he came through looking for remounts.

"You could always write a letter to the girl – we've got her address – telling her how fond you are of her dragon."

Gart snickered.

Hal gave her a hateful look.

"We'll leave that for Sir Thom, on his next pass through."

"And I'll make sure to tell him," Gart said, and burst into laughter.

"I'm delighted," Hal said, "to be taking charge of such a *cheerful* frigging squadron. I think I shall have all of you whipped."

Cabet was the first flight commander to arrive, which was just what Hal had expected. He was a small, precise man, with a small, precise moustache, and was known as a worrier. That may have hurt his digestion, but it kept his flight away from any foreseeable disasters, since Cabet managed everything very carefully.

Mariah had told Hal it was rumored that Cabet planned just when, and where, he would take his twice-daily shits, and was about to elaborate when Kailas told him to get out.

Pisidia, of the 20th, was the second. He was lean, with a hungry face and close-trimmed beard. He wore an eyepatch, from a wound early in the war, and Hal wondered how he was able to judge perspective with just the one eye. He, too, had a good reputation for taking care of his fliers and dragons, without much regard for the niceties of uniform and decorum the army preferred.

Last to arrive, announced by a booming laugh, was Richia of the 34th. He was heavy, with a jolly face, a booming voice, and ready laughter. It wasn't until you looked closely at him, and saw his eyes were hard, cold, those of a hunter, that you knew him to be a dangerous man.

"Sit down," Hal said. "You know who I am, and I know, at least by name, all of you."

He glanced out of his tent, made sure the posted sentry was just beyond earshot.

"I have no idea what you think of being put under my command, and don't, at least for the moment, give a damn.

"There is no time whatsoever for personalities."

He told them of the upcoming attack.

All reacted in their own ways: Cabet began scribbling notes on a slip of paper; Pisidia began stroking his beard, looking into nowhere, making plans; and Richia barked a surprised laugh.

"This could be a chancy thing," Cabet said, looking up.

"Very much so," Hal agreed. "Which is why I don't propose to make any changes in the way you gentlemen have run your flights, at least until this offensive is over.

"However, I will issue one standing order. I want your new fliers to be paired with experienced ones, as much as possible. I realize, Cabet, that you were badly struck during the siege, and won't be able to always follow that order, but do what you can.

"I'll also want a flight of four fliers on constant standby. We'll take one from each flight.

"This will be a reaction element. If any Roche dragons approach this field, this flight is to get in the air and climb for altitude, whether or not orders are issued, and engage the bastards.

"I don't fancy the thought of having any of *Ky* Yasin's black dragons springing a surprise on us.

"And, speaking of Yasin, any black dragons that are sighted on our side of the lines are to be attacked immediately, always in pairs or more, and hopefully will be outnumbered.

"I want any other Roche dragons to be treated roughly, and I have no interest in any fair fighting or dueling.

"Kill the Roche when we see them, don't let them escape, especially if they might have gathered any information."

"What about claims, Lord Kailas?" Richia asked.

"I don't understand."

"Say one flier attacks a dragon, wounds it. He loses the dragon for a moment, and another flier kills it. Who gets the victory?"

"It'll be split," Hal said, "and I'll let you figure out how you'll explain to your granddaughter that you killed half a dragon."

There were smiles.

"Whatever your policies are," Hal said, "you might know mine. The only dead dragon I care about counting is the last one of the war."

"So we've heard," Pisidia said. "I think getting numbers-happy does no good for a flight – or a squadron's – morale."

"And I quite disagree," Richia said. Cabet said nothing.

"Another thing," Kailas went on. "I don't much give a damn about titles, or even being sirred, except when things are formal or when there's outsiders about."

"Good," Pisidia said. "There's too much flumpf about this war already."

"Formality has its place," Cabet said.

"Agreed," Pisidia said. "In the king's court, not over here."

"Well," Cabet said, "my men and women will continue to show proper respect."

"Run your flights as you wish, as I've said," Hal said, standing.

"Now, before I talk to the squadron, I want to wring a few knots out, and make sure I still know how to fly."

"Well," Hal said, "let's see what we're made of." He shuddered a little. "Sweetie."

The dark red and brown dragon looked over her shoulder at him, blatted. Hal couldn't tell anything from that, but, since the beast seemed to know the name she'd been given, that meant he wouldn't be able to give her a better name.

He grabbed a scale, pulled himself up into the saddle, settled back and tested the reins. They were taut.

Kailas noted about half the squadron had drifted to the sides of the field, and were watching carefully, pretending to do other tasks.

This was part of the ritual of command.

If a dragon flier was worth a damn, he or she believed she was the absolute best. Around outsiders, a flier would swear that her flight commander was just a touch better, although that came from greater experience, not ability, of course.

So when a new commander appeared, it was expected that he would show his flying ability – unless he was one of those who led from the ground, which meant being held in complete, if unspoken, contempt.

It was stupid but Hal admitted to himself that he believed the same as any other flier.

"You're going to hate me before this is over," he said, and kicked the dragon in its slats.

It lumbered forward, lurching from side to side, its huge wings reaching out.

Then the awkwardness was gone as the dragon was in the air, wings striking down hard, lifting more slowly, and the ground shrank below Hal's boots.

He let Sweetie climb to about two thousand feet, then, using reins and feet at first, tapped her into a series of turns. She

responded well, and Hal went through another series, this time
just with the reins.

Again, the dragon obeyed.

Hal realized he shouldn't have been surprised – she supposedly
had been trained by Garadice, a dragonmaster before the war,
when the term meant a man who traveled about, giving rides, and
doing stunts. Garadice's son had trained and served with Hal,
and had been killed by Yasin's black dragons, during the siege.

He put the dragon into a gentle bank, first right, then left.

He was looking far out, beyond the torn city of Aude, beyond
the ribbons of trenches, where far mountains were lined in pink
and gold as the sun moved down the horizon.

He thought he would give almost everything to be over those
mountains, with nothing but this dragon under him, perhaps a
pack with necessities lashed behind him, Khiri clinging behind
him, or even on her own, and no one and nothing to worry
about, except where he might land, buy a sheep for his mount,
and cook a sparse meal before laying out his bedroll. At the next
dawn, he'd be flying on, into the unknown, day after day,
until . . . until he didn't know when.

He brought himself back to the present.

"Now, let's see how you can work," he said.

The field was just below him. He put Sweetie into a steep dive
with his reins, let the ground close a little, pulled her out at what
he guessed was a thousand feet.

He sent the dragon into another, more gentle dive, brought her
back, turning, almost flying inverted, leveled her on an opposite
course.

"Good," he said. "You can have a pullet or something with
your dinner. You didn't lose a foot of height."

Again, he sent Sweetie down and down, the ground rushing up
at him, the wind whipping at him. The dragon honked protest,
but didn't try to disobey.

At about three hundred feet he pulled back on the reins, and
the dragon's wings flared.

As it pulled out, a bit over a hundred feet above the field, he
tapped its left side, and, obediently, the monster banked, its great
wing almost brushing the ground. He brought it out, then turned,
and turned again, alternately left and right, then sent it down,
and pulled hard.

The dragon's wings snapped out, and its feet reached for the
ground, and they were on the ground.

Handlers ran up, and Hal slid from the saddle, tossing his reins across it.

He took a moment to pat the dragon's head as it snaked back, looking at him.

"Good," he approved.

His fliers were approaching, Farren Mariah at their head.

"Not bad . . . sir," he said. "I'd never trust a new one to be that well mannered."

"That's because you didn't pay close enough attention in dragon school," Hal said. "I don't have any trouble keeping my mounts in hand."

Farren sneered.

Hal had a wagon pulled into the middle of the field, and the flights surrounded him.

"Sit down if you want," he said, and did the same on the wagon's railing.

"Welcome to the First Dragon Squadron. We're trying something new, and I'll explain, later, just what I've got in mind. But I hope that my ideas are right, and this squadron is the signpost of the future.

"You know who I am . . . and I've yet to learn about you.

"Let's hope it's as pleasant an experience as it should be.

"We're going to be very busy for the next couple of weeks, which I can't tell you about yet.

"So the old bullshit about my tent's always open for anyone with problems can be set aside for awhile. I'm going to be busy, and you are as well.

"There won't be any time for lollygagging or farting around for awhile, so don't give me, my officers, and my warrants any grief.

"If you do, you'll reap the harvest you sowed.

"But I don't think there'll be any problems. You old soldiers know what's expected, and you new ones can study their ways and do the same.

"I don't expect anyone to have any questions this early in the game, and I'm not sure I've learned the answers yet.

"I'm not one who believes in speeches, and, as you've seen, am not worth much at making them.

"So fall out now for supper.

"That's all."

*

That night, Hal stood in a corner of the pilot's club, nursing half a pint of weak beer, and watching his pilots.

They were more than a little nervous. The braver tried to draw him out, into a drinking contest or a game. He smiled thanks at the offer, but refused.

The veterans he knew greeted him, and were bought a pint. In Sir Loren's case, that meant a mug of nonalcoholic cider. He was as abstemious before combat as always.

The replacements listened to Hal's easy banter with envy, and thought to themselves that they'd soon be considered worthy of equality as well.

Mariah was behind the bar with Chincha, and Hal was pleased they were still together and, frankly, still alive.

Hal and Gart talked briefly, and he knew the fliers were trying to figure out what they were discussing. If they'd known, they might've worried.

Hal was noting the fliers who were drinking heavily. It wasn't that he gave a damn how much someone drank – by this stage of the war alcohol was the only thing keeping some of the more worn fliers together.

But drink wasn't a good habit for a young flier to get into, unless he knew what he was doing.

The old hands could take care of themselves.

As a gentle guidance Kailas was scheduling all of the replacements who were guzzling heavily for a dawn patrol. They'd quickly learn that flying with a hangover wasn't the easiest way to spend a morning.

And he would be in the air with them.

Hal's orderly was a man old enough to be his father, named Uluch, who looked on anything and everything sourly. But he couldn't be faulted in his duties.

Kailas was quite grateful, especially in the mornings, he hadn't gotten some godsdamned chatterbox.

Hal desperately wanted to work his squadron to the bone, to make sure they were as sharp as possible before the battle.

But he knew better. An exhausted flier can be a dead one, very rapidly.

So he ran his patrols up and down the lines. There was only one fight, and he wasn't lucky enough to get in on it, and it was inconclusive, the two Roche dragons being chased back over Aude.

It seemed the Roche fliers were holding to their side of the lines as well.

Kailas wondered what orders they were under, but there were no clues.

"His" 11th Flight was armed with the repeating crossbows that Farren Mariah had designed. The other three had motley collections of conventional crossbows and short recurve bows. Hal hadn't the time to order the repeaters from Joh Kious's works far to the north in Paestum – yet another thing that would have to wait until after the battle.

So Hal stewed, and flew, and waited.

And then the day of battle came.

4

The Derainian and Sagene soldiers came out of their hides with a roar, just at dawn, running hard across the dead space between the lines, closing with the Roche.

From the Deraine lines, ballistae hurled boulders into the Roche, and catapults shot their great arrows at clumps of officers on horseback.

Hal's squadron had been in the air for an hour, and dawn had come first to them, while the ground below was still black, and shadowed.

He had the 11th, the best armed, at about three thousand feet, the 18th at the same level, the other two squadrons providing high cover two thousand feet overhead.

The replacements were gaping down at the battle, the first real fight they'd seen, in spite of orders to keep their eyes on the sky.

Sir Loren Damian was the first to spot the Roche dragons, half a dozen of them, scattered, climbing for height.

Communication on dragonback was done by trumpet. He blatted his horn twice – enemy in sight – and Hal replied with one long note – attack.

The dragons, wings partially folding, dropped on the Roche, talons working in and out, mouths open, hissing, screaming, at least as eager for a fight as any human.

Above and in front of the straggling Roche monsters were two black dragons, a third as big as the others, known for their ferocity.

Hal steered Sweetie down on the lead one.

He had his crossbow lifted, aimed, and there was nothing else in the universe but that black dragon, and its rider, who gaped up at him, then fumbled an arrow out, and nocked it on his bowstring.

But it was too late.

Hal's bolt took the rider low in the shoulder, almost in his heart. The rider screeched, dropped his bow, and lost his foothold in his stirrups. He swayed, feet flailing, grabbing for a handhold, forgetting the reins, and slid out of his saddle, and fell, twisting, toward the battleground below.

Then Hal was past and below the Roche. He fought Sweetie back up, toward the other black.

But Farren Mariah had sent a bolt into that beast's neck, and he lost interest in the battle, and dove for the ground and home.

The air was a swirl of color, red, green, yellow, brown, and then it was empty of the Roche.

There were three Roche dragons fleeing, and nothing in the air around but Hal's squadron. In the distance, near the flank of the attack, Hal saw other dragons swarming, other Derainian flights.

That was the first skirmish, and Hal did a fast count. He'd lost no one, and relaxed slightly.

He took Sweetie back to height, and then he could look down at the battle.

It was a swarming melee, already behind the Roche positions. Deraine and Sagene had driven the enemy back, and were pressing hard. Reinforcements were coming up from the Derainian rear, and, on the flanks, the heavy cavalry was being sent in.

They cut in and out of the struggle, and again the Roche fell back.

But they fell back without panic, holding their formations, and the cavalry could do no more than nip at their heels, since horses will never charge into anything solid, whether a hedge or a spear-wall.

Hal didn't see any strong point he might take the 11th, the most experienced in ground attack, down against, so didn't consider wasting his crossbow bolts.

The Roche fell back and back, all that long hot day. Hal sent his dragons to the base in sections for the men and animals to feed, for no more Roche fliers came up to challenge them.

Hal had a bit of hope that maybe, just maybe, this attack would do what it was intended to, break the Roche, and the way would be clear for the Deraine and Sagene armies to close on Roche's capital of Carcaor, and end the war.

But that evening the Roche took up new positions, and Hal, swooping over them, saw the positions had been prepared earlier.

He was no general, but didn't think that boded well for the offensive.

His fliers were a chatter of excitement, not wanting to sleep, ready to fight their first battle over and over again. But Hal ordered them to eat and then to their tents, refusing Mariah permission to open "his" club for more than one beer per flier.

The next morning, they were up and in the air in darkness.

Below, Deraine and Sagene pressed the attack.

Again, the Roche fell back, still orderly.

By nightfall, the new line of battle was five miles or more into the Roche rear. But Hal had seen no sign of mass surrender, no sign of panic.

The cavalry tried to flank the retreating Roche infantry, but the Roche cavalry blocked them, and there were savage, inconclusive skirmishes.

Hal's fliers spotted Roche cavalry lying in ambush three times, dove, dropping streamers with notes wrapped around pebbles to give a warning.

Hal wished there was some way he could drop more than a pebble. A huge damned boulder on a Roche's head. But dragons couldn't lift anything that heavy, and it would take much training, even if such a device existed, for a flier to be able to hit a target.

Hal, feeling frustrated, with Mariah just behind him, went flashing over the Roche positions not fifty feet in the air. Heavy bolts from catapults flashed up at him, and he came to his senses and broke off the attack.

When they landed for a meal, Farren gave Hal a bolt almost as tall as Mariah, said he'd plucked it from the air at the top of its flight, and added, "Hee-roes might skedaddle along first in line, flashin' their cocks about, but it's their poor damned wingmates trudging along behind that give the fine target.

"No more showin' off, boss, unless there's something to shoot at, orright? That big damned arrow damned near put paid to your favorite flier."

Hal, grateful that Mariah had said this out of earshot of the other fliers, nodded sheepishly.

The attack went on, and every day the Roche fell further and further back.

Hal, isolated in his camp and in the sky, had no idea what the high command and Sir Bab thought was going on, but one evening, as he was making the last high patrol, it came to him.

In the distance, to the east, mountains rose, now no more than five leagues distant.

Hal suddenly thought he knew what the Roche intended: to retreat on this open ground, which gave neither side the advantage, and take position on the mountains. They could hold the heights until doomsday, and let Deraine and Sagene waste their best trying to reach them.

He thought of darting back, and giving his illumination to Sir Bab, then caught himself. Cantabri was hardly a fool, and could read a map as well as anyone, even if he was deathly afraid of going aloft.

And even if Hal's surmise was a revelation, what could be done about it?

Deraine and Sagene were attacking as hard as they could, leaving a strew of bodies as they advanced.

What more could be done?

A week later, the dragon fliers were groggy with fatigue.

They still hadn't had any major engagements with the Roche fliers – their command seemed to be keeping them back, though for what end, Hal had no idea.

Kailas knew if the fliers were tired, even though they were able to land at a base every evening, eat hot food, and sleep in a bed, what shape could the poor damned infantry and cavalry be in?

He remembered his days as a light cavalryman, before he became a dragon flier, and how he and his horse would be staggering with fatigue after scouting for an advance and skirmishing around the battle.

The Roche couldn't be in any better shape. It was demoralizing to retreat, and retreat again, even though done in an orderly manner.

By now, it was indeed clear the Roche had a plan, and it was just as Hal had feared: pull back to the mountains, really not more than a low range of bluffs, and then bleed Deraine and Sagene.

So what if Deraine was occupying Roche territory?

Queen Norcia couldn't care much about this border land, sparsely settled and garrisoned by the occasional castle.

When Deraine came on one of these, rather than waste time with a siege, they bypassed the stronghold. They could come back later and reduce it.

The retreat went on. There were no surprises to be found from the sky, and, after each dawn's reconnaissance, Hal started taking his dragons low, as soon as the Roche moved back.

They shot down soldiers, got lucky from time to time and killed an officer or courier. Hal was doing this not only to do what little he could to help, but out of pure frustration.

Kailas was flying back to his base, the setting sun reddening his wind-battered face, when it came to him.

He realized, and felt like a dolt for his thickness, what Khiri might have meant, back in Rozen, when she told him that he would be expected to do something wonderful when he came back to Deraine.

He landed, turned Sweetie over to a handler, and hurried to his tent.

Dearest Khiri,
  First, I love you, and I'm glad that you love an idiot like me. When I return, would you grant me the greatest honor I could have, and agree to marry me?

And then the ground began to rise, and, day by day, the Roche retreated less, and the Deraine and Sagene forces fought uphill.

There was no estimate of casualties so far, but there were rumors that entire Deraine units had been so decimated they had to be pulled from the fight.

And things could only get worse.

Then Hal was summoned by Sir Bab Cantabri to a conference. It was short.

The attendees were commanders of units on the Deraine west flank. Hal noted no Sagene officers.

"This is a last ditch effort," Cantabri said, "that I'll take command of. We've got to stop the bastards short of the hill crests, or this war could become even more of a stalemate than it's been."

He pulled the cover off a large-scale map. The canvas, as it fell to the dirt floor of the tent, rattled loudly in the silence.

"Our scouts have found a break in their lines, over here." He tapped the map.

"Our attack will be simple," he said. "We're going to feint on the right with cavalry, then hit hard on the left, here, into this break, with units we've moved away from the center.

"If we can break them, or round their flank, we can roll up their lines like carpets.

"If they stop us . . . Well, that's the end of campaigning for this year, and we'll be fighting them from here. But if we can smash them before they reach the top, before they start digging in . . ."

He didn't finish the sentence, nor need to. His hard yellow eyes gleamed.

Once more, Hal and half his squadron were in the skies before sunrise, but the hope that this attack would be the breakthrough had torn away their fatigue.

Hal had offered to recon the target area, been refused by Cantabri, who was afraid any extra attention in the area might tip off the Roche.

"Just like we'll attack without any magic. But once we start moving," he said, "anything you can give me will be appreciated."

Even this high in the air, Hal heard the thin blare of the trumpets as the attack was mounted.

Tired soldiery heaved themselves out of the temporary shelters they'd found at the end of the previous day's fighting, started forward.

There was a first, then a second, then a third line of dirty, weary infantrymen who went in.

Hal heard a trumpet toot twice, looked over as Pisidia swung close.

"Down there," the man shouted. "Just in front of the point men."

Hal looked, couldn't see anything, cursed that a one-eyed man could see more sharply, dug his glass from a saddle boot, sent Sweetie around.

"There's a great cave down there," Pisidia shouted. "Or, rather, a whole bunch of 'em."

Then Hal saw the darkness of the entrances. Worse, he saw the flash of metal, and the flutter of banners as hidden Roche soldiers charged out into the midst of the Deraine formations.

"Son of a bitch!" Hal swore. "They've laid a trap. Pisidia, take the message back."

He blew four blasts – assemble on me – and his squadron, scattered across the front, flew toward him. It might be a waste, but it was the least he could do.

He blew two blasts, and, pulling back the cocking handle of his crossbow, let a bolt drop down into the track.

Hal snapped reins down on Sweetie's neck, sent her into a dive, aiming for the mouth of one cave.

Other fliers saw the targets, and followed him in.

Hal brought his dragon out of its dive low, almost at treetop level, spotted a man on horseback, shot at him, hit his horse. He let go the reins, and worked the slide of his crossbow, reloading it.

Maybe he should've listened to Farren's advice about trusting a new dragon too much, for as he looked for another target, holding on to Sweetie's sides with his legs, something startled the dragon, and she jinked sharply sideways.

Hal lost his balance, slid out of his saddle, dropping the crossbow, grabbing for a hold on Sweetie's wing, scrabbling at the leathery skin, losing his grip again, and falling.

He dropped only about twenty feet, smashed into the top of a tree, tumbled, grabbing for branches, had one, and was safe for a moment.

Then the branch snapped, and dropped him, bruised, bleeding, ten feet to a soft landing on moss.

He rolled to his feet, reaching for his sword.

But there were five, no a dozen, shouting Roche soldiers rushing at him, spears ready to be cast, arrows ready to be fired.

5

The two leading Roche soldiers skidded to a halt, seeing Hal's ready sword. But they were experienced soldiers. One nodded to his fellow, and they split up, coming in on each side of Kailas.

One chanced a lunge, and Hal's sword flashed out, cutting the spearhead off at the haft. The second struck at almost the same moment, and Hal barely jumped out of the way.

That man was muttering, "dirty buggerin' dragon bastard,

kilt my brother, kilt my brother, dragon bastard, cut your balls off an' feed 'em to you for supper."

Hal saved his breath.

The man drew back, then thrust with his spear, cutting an ugly gash in Hal's thigh.

His fellow had dropped his spear, had a sword out and was about to attack.

Kailas was surrounded by half a dozen soldiers, cheering for the two going in on Hal when a shout came.

"Stop!"

They pretended not to hear, and the one whose brother had supposedly been killed by dragons tried another thrust, which was parried, and then Hal counterthrust, and lopped the man's ear off.

"You heard me," the shout came again. "Stop and stand to attention!"

One soldier turned, reluctantly, reacted.

"Attention!" he shouted, and this time the knot of Roche froze as ordered.

A young officer – Hal didn't remember Roche ranks that well – pelted in. He carried no weapon, only a short stick.

"When I give an order, it's to be obeyed at once," the man snarled. "All of you are on bunker detail when we get to the top of this hill.

"Now, you, Teat, get your butt to the herbist, and tell him what you've got is only what you deserve, so he's not to worry about causing you a little pain.

"Move out!

"You, and you . . . You'll escort the prisoner – and I'll be with you to make sure you don't kill him 'attempting to escape' – to company central."

For the first time, he appeared to take notice of Hal.

"And you, drop that damned sword, and unbelt that dagger.

"For you the war's over, unless you keep trying to play hero."

Hal looked around, saw, high overhead, one of his dragons, swooping down, a hundred feet above, which might as well have been leagues.

He dropped his sword, unfastened his belt, and let it fall.

Hal Kailas, Dragonmaster, was a prisoner of the Roche.

But the officer was the only one who might actually believe Kailas's war was over.

*

The Roche company commander seemed not at all disturbed that his headquarters was no more than one guard, one warrant, two runners, and a tattered chunk of canvas tied between two trees.

"Your name?" he asked.

"Lord Kailas of Kalabas," Hal said.

One of the runners gulped, whispered "Th' Dragonmaster!" and got a cold look from the officer.

"Your rank?"

"Commander."

"Of what?"

"I'm sorry," Kailas said. "That's information I can't give you."

"No," the officer agreed. "But we read the stories your taletellers publish. I know you're the Lord Commander of the First Dragon Squadron, and far too rich a dish for peasants like us."

He looked at the officer who'd saved Kailas's life.

"You'll be commended for this. Now, take this man – and two more guards – and escort him back to regimental headquarters."

"Yessir. "

The commander turned back to Hal, and Kailas knew what he was going to say before he spoke.

"Congratulations. Your war is over. And you'll be alive, if you cooperate, to see our great victory."

Hal didn't reply.

The young officer noted that Hal was limping.

"Can you walk?"

"I can walk," Hal said.

"If you're having trouble, I can assemble a party of litterbearers."

"I can walk," Hal repeated.

Regimental headquarters was a collection of skillfully camouflaged tents in a wide ravine that had been covered with netting stuffed with branches that was just back of the military crest of the hill Hal had been attacking when he was brought down.

A beribboned officer whistled when he heard who Hal was, immediately relieved the young officer, and took charge.

Hal had wanted to get an address for the young man and, when the war was over, planned to write him a letter, thanking him for his life. But the man saluted, and was gone.

The ranking officer was about to ask Hal a question when he noticed the dark stain seeping through his trousers.

"You're wounded!"

Hal nodded.

"Then you're for hospital, at once. I'll have no one of your rank ever thinking we Roche are uncivilized."

He shouted for a serjeant, and bade him assemble stretcher-bearers.

"There," the man said. "There'll be an officer arrive in the hospital to interr . . . ask you certain questions.

"Man, you look pale. Sit down, here, on this stump."

"My leg *is* starting to bother me," Hal admitted.

"Our potions and spells are the best," the man said. "So, for you, the war is over."

Hal almost laughed at the stock chorus, but then noted the officer had spoken with an unconscious note of wistfulness.

Pain was starting to wash over Hal, but he forced alertness, trying to take note of everything as the stretcher-bearers carried him to the rear.

A great deal of the trip was done under cover staked poles, with camouflaged netting over them. Hal didn't know if the Roche did this because they thought Deraine and Sagene were barbarians who'd attack the wounded, or because they didn't want any aerial observers being able to make estimates of the casualty rate.

There'd been tales that the Roche were beaten, stumbling, on their last legs in this offensive.

Hal saw no evidence of that.

The troops were battered and their uniforms were worn . . . but no more than their enemies.

Kailas was able to verify his idea of the Roche plan – that they'd be holding, and fighting, from this hill range. He saw almost as many soldiers working hard with mattock and shovel, making entrenchments, as moving forward with weaponry into the dying battle.

There were no signs that the king's great offensive would end the war, or be more than another killing ground for both sides.

The hospital was a good ten miles from the front, exactly laid out rows of tents, with graveled walkways between them, and white-painted signboards. Orderlies came and went, and wizards, chiurgeons and what Hal heard called nursing sisters, women in a sort of uniform, a gray smock and cap.

He was being logged in, and questions asked, when, very suddenly, the world swam about his shoulders, and he sank into peaceful, pain-free unconsciousness.

Hal awoke to a throbbing pain. He must have moaned, for a voice said, "Ah. Good. If it hurts, it means your leg is yet alive."

He opened his eyes, saw a rather tubby man bending over him. He had a thin fringe of hair, a rather scruffy beard he was trying to grow long, without much success, and plain robes.

"I am Mage Nizva," he announced. "I am in charge of the healing spells in this and three other tents."

"And I'm—"

"Hush. Talk later," Nizva said. "Concentrate your attention on letting the spells I've cast, and the herbs I've poulticed your wounds with, take effect."

Hal lifted his head from the cot he was on. The light was dim in the long tent, seventy-five feet by about twenty feet. Every few feet was another cot, with another wounded man, and a scattering of women, on it.

Somewhere Kailas had lost his bloodied uniform, and wore only a gray ankle-length nightshirt.

Hal nodded understanding to Nizva, and sank back into a stupor.

Hal was awakened by the preposterous shout: "Lie at . . . attention!"

He lifted an eyelid, saw a host of medal-heavy officers stamp into the tent, dancing attendance on an even more beribboned man with a very impressive white beard.

"I am General Ottignies," he said. "And I greet you, honored warriors of the Roche nation, in the name of Her Most Blessed Highness, Queen Norcia, who this day has authorized me to provide you with rewards for your heroism."

He started down the row of wounded, two aides beside him. At each bed, he'd select a medal, say a few words, pin the medal to the soldier's blankets, salute, move on.

Hal couldn't believe what was evidently about to happen.

But it happened.

General Ottignies looked benevolently down at Hal.

"Healing nicely?"

Hal nodded.

"Good. Good. We need warriors like yourself back at the front, to ensure our great victory."

He took a medal, attached it to Hal's blanket, saluted.

Hal found strength, was able to feebly return the salute.

"Good man," Ottignies said, not understanding the uncontrollable grin on Hal's face, and moved on to the next hero.

Hal reached down, lifted the medal. It was a tasteful bronze medallion, with a ribbon of red and white. On it was scribed: HERO OF ROCHE: SECOND CLASS.

Kailas choked back laughter, wondered what he'd have to do to become a First Class Hero.

"Oh gods," Nizva breathed. "You're not one of us at all."

"No," Hal said.

"You're Derainian?"

"Yes."

"Named?"

"Kailas." Hal left the title off, thought of substituting Second Class Hero Kailas, decided that might not be the wisest.

"Kailas?" Nizva said. "The Dragonmaster? The one who seems to have disappeared here?"

"I haven't disappeared," Hal corrected. "I've been lying here quietly all the time, letting your potions heal me, as you ordered."

"Oh my gods," Nizva said again, and scuttled up the aisle.

So the easy days were over now, Hal thought. He'd been playing sickling for two weeks, and was far stronger than he admitted to the sisters or the mage.

Now it was time to plan his escape.

6

Hal knew little of the fine art of escaping. There were many classes required of the soldiers of Deraine, from saluting and recognizing your superiors to how to wash yourself.

But escaping wasn't on the list.

Hal growled at that, but realized the subject was fairly out of bounds, since no proper soldier even conceded the possibility of capture.

Nevertheless . . .

Hal had been told by someone, he disremembered who, that the best time to escape was the soonest after capture. The longer you were in captivity, the further you'd be taken from your own lines, and, as likely as not, the worse physical shape you were in, since no army has ever fed its prisoners better than its own soldiery.

His wound had kept him from making an immediate break, but now it was healing nicely.

Now that he'd been discovered, no doubt the next step would be moving him into a proper prison.

Best he try to get away from this hospital.

The problem was finding a set of clothes. He had an idea that wandering the roads of Roche wearing nothing but his damned gray nightshirt might make him noticeable.

Shortly before being unmasked, even though he'd not planned his hiding, he had noticed there were some civilian workers in the hospital, no doubt local farmers who were pleased to be getting paid while their fields were being plowed into wasteland by war.

The Roche being what they were, the civilians changed into gray coveralls, almost uniform-like, when they arrived for work.

Hal had realized this when he was up just at dawn, using the jakes, and saw the workers troop in to undertake their tasks.

The day after his uncovering, Hal slid out of bed before false dawn, and crept out of the ward. He was grateful that Nizva and the hospital authorities, whose strength was trying to heal, not play at war, hadn't gotten around to putting a guard on him.

The changing tent was next to the two cooking tents. Hal hid in the flies of a nearby tent as the sky brightened, and the day shift came in.

The night workers left a few minutes later, and Hal went into the changing tent, and looked for a costume.

It took only a few minutes to discover one that fit him quite well, and made him out to be a rural bumpkin, wearing a knee-length smock, short breeches, a hat that had seen better centuries, and a padded coat.

Unfortunately, its owner didn't seem to be that fond of bathing, but maybe that would be an advantage. If he was checked by a patrol, he would wave his armpits at them, and flee in the ensuing disgust.

Hal went out of the tent, and away from the hospital as quickly as he could.

He was pleased to see that his leg only troubled him for a short while, then the muscles loosened up, and he could travel easily.

He wanted to run, knew better, and so strolled along, a straw between his teeth, thinking farming thoughts, in the event some magician might be able to read his mind. That was an impossibility, he'd been told, but wizards were always coming up with new evils.

He spotted a pitchfork leaning against a fence and added that to his costume. In the event, it could also serve as a weapon. Kailas had no intention of returning to captivity without a fight.

He'd quickly oriented himself by the scattering of troops moving forward, and the sun. That gave him compass directions.

His plan, and he thought it idiot clever, was, rather than go directly for the front lines, to head east for half a day, then turn, depending on what presented itself, either north or south for a distance.

That wasn't the direction anyone would expect him to take, and, besides, it could be very chancy trying to creep through the battle zone, where both sides were keyed to kill any strangers.

Once he was wide of the battle area, then he'd turn back to the west, and make his way into Deraine/Sagene lines.

Or so he hoped.

Hal's stomach reminded him that he was escaping with his victuals a bit on the nonexistent side.

It was midday, and he'd only stopped twice for water at abandoned wells, and was feeling peckish. Some nice peasant bread and cheese would set right with him, or even some of that horrible broth the hospital had insisted was strengthening.

The lane he was following curved down into a village. Even though he didn't have any money, maybe there'd be a field with . . . with whatever was ripe. It was summer, so that should be almost everything.

He was halfway through the village, just short of a stone bridge over a small river, when he realized there was something strange about the hamlet. There was no one, not man, woman, child, about. Nor did he see any dogs or animals.

He was about to dart up a side lane, and skirt the rest of the village when a man came out of an alleyway, and shouted:

"Halt! Drop that damned pitchfork!"

Since he had a drawn bow, aimed steadily at Hal's side, Kailas obeyed.

"Who're you?" the soldier said, advancing on Hal.

Kailas had spent some time coming up with a story.

"No one," he said, putting on a panicked peasant's fear-babble that wasn't really that much of a put on. "Or, maybe, I'm just named Haifas. Haifas. I went out from my home yesterday, wanting to join up, but they wouldn't have me, saying something about my heart's got an echo to it or something, and I'd probably fall over dead on them, so I guess I'm going back to the farm, and—"

"Silence," the soldier snapped. "You should have seen the sign, back about a mile, saying this road and the village have been sequestered by the army for quartering, and no civvies are allowed."

"Oh," Hal said. There hadn't been a sign.

"I saw something," he said. "But I've got no schooling. Never learned to figure."

"Ain't no excuse," the soldier said, coming still closer. "And you talk real good for somebody that's not lettered."

He glowered at Hal, and Hal tried to look innocent and doltish.

"C'mon," he said. "We'll go to my warrant, and he'll decide what to do with you."

Hal didn't think that was a good idea.

He snapkicked the soldier under the breastbone, and bow and arrow dropped in the dust of the road.

Before the soldier could recover, Kailas kicked him very hard, twice, in the face. He heard the man's neck snap on the second kick.

Hal dragged the man to the bridge, hoisted him up on the parapet, then bethought himself.

He went through the man's pouch, found a few coppers, one silver piece. He thought about taking the soldier's dagger, or his bow and arrow, but knew that'd be grounds for instant execution if he was caught with them.

He tipped the body over, into the river, got the bow and arrow and tossed them over as well, then took off running.

He hoped that the soldier's warrant and officers would think the man had an accident.

But he didn't think that was very likely.

*

He chanced no more villages, even with his coins, trying to put as much distance between himself and his victim as possible.

Hal skirted villages, going through the fields.

Fortunately, the district had been pretty well cleaned out of civilians, with only a stubborn couple here and there holding to their farms.

Barking dogs alerted him to these.

At dusk, he was exhausted. He found a deserted farm, whose cornfields hadn't been totally stripped by foraging soldiers, got half a dozen ears.

He took those to a brook, stripped, washed, then thought about dinner.

He saw a few fish flicker, tried to grab them from beneath, the way he'd been told country boys did it. He had no success at all.

Which left him with the raw corn.

Hal wished he'd learned how to cobble fire up from a bow or sharp rock, but in his travels he'd always paid a few pence for a firespell.

The ears of corn sat there.

Hal realized that, for all his complaining, like all soldiers do, being in the army hadn't been the worst he'd had it.

Before the war, before he found a dragon flier to follow, and had been a wandering laborer, he'd eaten raw corn, stolen or begged from a farmer's field more than once.

And, he reminded himself, had the shits to go with it.

But there was nothing else, and so he ate, rather greedily, the six ears.

It was still light when he curled up. But there was a bit of a wind, and he wished he had a blanket or two to pull around him.

That, also, was missing.

Hal could've felt sorry for himself, but he took deep breaths of the air of freedom and forgot his complaints.

He closed his eyes, sure he'd be tossing on this bare ground for most of the night, but when he opened them, it was false dawn.

Kailas came to his feet, muscles skreeking at him, did some stretching exercises after washing and defecating, wincing at the leaves he used to clean himself.

Then he moved on.

At the next crossroads, he decided he'd turn north or south, whichever looked easiest.

*

The area he was moving through must've been a long-term bivouac for the Roche army. The huts had been stripped, their roofs and the fencing around the neat fields used for firewood.

It was a desolation, barren of animals and people.

Hal knew this sort of desolation well – all armies brought that in their wake, little caring how the people of the district would live after the soldiers moved on.

He was about halfway across one such blasted heath when he heard the calloo of hunters.

But there was nothing to hunt around here.

Nothing but Hal Kailases.

The hunters were a formation of light cavalry.

There was another call, and the formation, almost a company, Hal guessed, lowered its lances and came after him.

Kailas wanted to run, but there was nowhere to run to.

He couldn't even put his back to a wall and go down fighting.

Hal waited, hoping the bastards wouldn't just lance him and ride on.

That would be a particularly pointless way to die, forgotten in this forgotten land.

The lead rider, an officer, reined his horse in short feet of spitting Kailas.

"And what," he said, voice mockingly triumphant, "do we have here?"

The cavalrymen trussed Hal like a shot deer, threw him over the back of a horse. Kailas bounced along until the horsemen found a camp of infantry, rode into its center, shouting for the unit commander.

When he arrived, they kicked Kailas off the horse.

"Got somebody for you," their officer said. "Either a deserter or maybe that escaped dragon rider everybody's hot after."

The infantry took him to the nearest town, turned him over to the authorities.

Two beefy officers frog-marched him into the tiny prison, opened a cell, pushed him inside.

One of them stared at Kailas consideringly, then, without warning, hit Hal in the stomach, very hard.

Kailas caved in.

The man picked Kailas up by the hair, and smashed his face into the stone wall.

That, for some time, was all that Kailas knew.

7

Kailas came to, slumped on one of the jail's iron cots. He sat up, tasting the cold iron of blood in his mouth. He checked his teeth with a probing tongue. The front ones were just a little wobbly, but would tighten up.

His nose . . . he was sort of glad there wasn't a glass in the cell because it felt like it'd been well and truly mashed. Oh well. Supposedly something like that made people think a man was more rugged.

He heard a laugh, looked up, saw the guard who'd smashed him into the wall.

"Damn' Deraine!" the man snarled gleefully. "Ha'n't been for orders, we coulda done a lot worse."

Hal made no answer, just kept looking at him.

The man's grin twitched away, then he scurried off.

Hal dreamed of having five minutes alone with the bastard, knew it'd never happen, leaned back against the wall, began planning.

So he was caught again.

The next stage would be a transfer to a prison camp. Or, perhaps, execution, but Kailas thought that was unlikely.

The best time to make another escape would be when he was being transferred, since the warders at a camp would be more experienced at dealing with prisoners of war.

There was a basin of water on the table, and he washed the blood off his face, rinsed his mouth, and spat into the chamber pot.

From somewhere, something he'd read or been told, came to him: a prisoner of war is just a soldier in different dress, and it's still his duty to fight back, in any way he could.

Another, rather forlorn thought came, and he counted days. It would be just about today, or maybe the day before, when Khiri would be getting his proposal of marriage.

And then, no doubt, they'd announce he was missing in action. Hal didn't think any of his squadron had seen him once he'd landed in the treetops, and would most likely think him slain.

Poor Khiri.

Now, he thought wryly, what would happen to his estates, since he had neither kith nor kin, his only survivors his parents, far north in the bleak mining village?

Not that that mattered much to him. As tramps, wanderers and soldiers say, "I came into this world without a coin, and expect to leave it the same."

And he'd had nothing before the king's benisons, so what did it matter, anyway?

Now all that he could do was wait, and be ready to seize any advantage.

For two days, no one spoke to him, and he lived on the thin soup the jail served its prisoners.

He was the only prisoner of war, being fairly far behind the lines.

The guards regularly beat the other prisoners who came in, but they left Kailas alone. The other, civilian, prisoners were whipped jackals or, at best, snapping terriers. Kailas was a crouching panther, and he made the guards – and the other prisoners – nervous.

He forced himself to hide his impatience, never pacing back and forth as his restlessness wanted, not speaking to anyone, trying to get as much sleep as he could, knowing he'd need it when he was out in the wilds again.

He was slightly proud of himself for thinking "when," not "if."

On the third day, he had two visitors.

He knew both of them, but in vastly different ways.

The first was a haughty-looking knight, wearing several decorations, who announced himself as Sir Suiyan Tutuila, by the grace of Queen Norcia, Respecter of Prisoners. Hal avoided a snicker. It was clear, from his expression, that Sir Suiyan thought prisoners could best be protected in a sealed dungeon, or, a little better, at the end of a rope.

He was the archtypical jailer Kailas had encountered in his prewar wanderings.

He glared at Hal with pursed lips, said no more for the moment.

The other man Hal knew, first from a card game years before the war, when his gambling-besotted dragonmaster, Athelny of the Dragons, had been euchred out of his flying show, and then his life.

The second time he'd seen him was over the rooftops of Aude, when his black dragon had swooped low, trying to kill Hal. Hal had sent a crossbow bolt into the man's shoulder, cursed at his bad aim.

He was *Ky* Bayle Yasin, a superb flier, the first, as far as Hal knew, to fly the dreaded black dragons into battle, and, unless he'd been promoted recently, Commander of the First Guards Dragon Squadron.

He was slender, a bit older than Hal, and when, before, he'd had the fringe of a beard, now was clean-shaven. Hal noted he was starting to bald.

"Lord Kailas," he said. "It is pleasant finally meeting you."

He refrained from the obvious addition – "under these circumstances."

"And I feel the same," Hal said. "How is your wound?"

Yasin flickered slightly. "Quite healed, thank you."

"Pity," Hal said, in a way he'd heard the word used by a great lord.

" You will be silent," Sir Suiyan said. "It is not the place for a prisoner to jeer at his betters."

Hal didn't respond.

"*Ky* Yasin wishes to have a few words with you," Suiyan went on. "Privately.

"And of course, I'm pleased to grant a great *Ky*'s wish." He stood, his chair scraping on the stone floor, and went out.

"I wanted to see you for several reasons," Yasin said. "One is disbelief that you allowed yourself to be captured at all. Most of *my* fliers would prefer to die in battle instead of facing this humiliation."

Again, Hal held his tongue. If he hadn't learned some control at jibes after all this time in the army, he was a fool indeed.

"Another is to inform you that your secret weapon was captured as well, and is being duplicated by our craftsmen. I refer, of course, to that repeating crossbow.

"Still another is to warn you that you are potentially in desperate circumstances.

"There was a soldier killed the same day you made your escape from the hospital."

Hal pretended surprise.

"You were captured wearing civilian clothes. By any tribunal, a soldier so dressed is a spy, and qualifies for immediate execution. If he also has murdered a member of Her Royal Highness's Armed Forces . . . the penalty could be adjudged in quite a severe fashion.

"Sir Suiyan wanted to bring you up before a tribunal right now, but I convinced him you were far too valuable to die a villain's death. I hope you prove me right.

"Of course you don't know what I'm talking about."

"I truthfully don't," Hal said.

Yasin smiled for a brief instant.

"I came here to offer you the chance of safety and life after the war. If you provide certain information to us – nothing that would cause any of your men or women to come to harm – I can guarantee this murder will be forgotten, and you'll spend the rest of the war in safety, in a rather comfortable detention camp."

Hal started to respond, but Yasin cut him off.

"Of course, I don't expect you to agree at the moment, but I wanted to put the idea in your mind. You may take advantage of it at any time you wish."

"Thank you," Hal said. "But I don't think I'll be accepting."

"Of course not," Yasin agreed, standing. "But keep my offer in mind.

"Something else. I thought you might appreciate news of the war. It is not going well.

"For Deraine and Sagene. Your idiot generals are persisting in attacking in the salient they were lucky enough to create.

"But our positions are completely impregnable, and Deraine and Sagene soldiers are being wasted trying to climb the heights.

"They will, no doubt, continue with their niggling attacks through the winter, weakening themselves, and then, in the spring, we'll mount a great offensive, and recover not only the territory we've lost, including Aude and the Comtal River to the sea, but drive a stake into Sagene, and convince Deraine that she has no interest in Sagene's fate.

"I'm hardly confiding any military secrets by saying that."

He went to the door, opened it, and Sir Suiyan came back in.

"I assume *Ky* Yasin has told you of the danger you're in," Suiyan said. "I can promise you that if I can get any evidence of the crime you committed, I'll gladly see you face the ax . . . or other forms of punishment that are even uglier.

"For the moment, though, I can tell you that you will not continue to be lodged here."

"Just when I was starting to enjoy country life."

Tutuila's lip twitched.

"You might just be able to escape, and a man of your rank, holding information that Roche could well use, cannot be treated in such a casual fashion.

"Roche has several prison camps that are much harder to escape from.

"And one that is impossible."

Yasin broke in.

"It's far to the east and north, up an estuary. Its name is Castle Mulde. There we've sent prisoners who've successfully escaped other camps, high rankers such as yourself, and dragon fliers, whose value is incomparable."

Hal suddenly remembered the late traitor, Nanpean Tregony, who'd claimed to be in such a camp before making his escape from the Roche, and thought perhaps that part of the man's lies might just have been truth. Or maybe Tregony had only heard of Castle Mulde.

"I could be melodramatic," he went on, "and say that you'll rot there. But that's not the case. Nothing so exciting ever happens. There you can sit and wither, while life – and the war – goes on around you.

"I understand, from captured broadsheets, that you are the favorite of a certain noble popsy," Yasin went on. "I wonder how long it'll take her to find another bedmate.

"Or bedmates.

"I frankly, have learned never to trust a woman alone for more than a few weeks."

Without bracing, without any giveaway, Hal kicked Yasin in the balls.

Yasin howled, clutched at himself.

Tutuila shouted for guards.

Hal was going after him, rounding the table, when three men burst in.

The one in front was the guard who'd broken Hal's nose.

Hal forgot about Sir Suiyan, and rolled across the table, on his back.

He kicked out, very hard, his feet together, and caught that guard in his chest. Kailas heard ribs crack, was off the table, and stamped on the man's face as he fell.

Then the guards were on him, beating him down.

He went into a ball, dropped to the floor.

Eventually they got tired of kicking him, and dragged him back to his cell.

It had definitely been worth it.

8

They took no chances with Kailas.

When they were ready to move him to Castle Mulde, a wizard and a blacksmith appeared. Black bands were wrapped around his ankles and wrists, and the magician cast a spell that "soldered" them in place.

Kailas was told, cheerily, that none of his escort had any idea of what the counterspell was. Only the mage of Castle Mulde knew.

They chained him to the bed of a wagon, with four guards, plus the teamster and his assistant. Behind that wagon was another, with twelve more guards in it, changed every three hours. Then came a supply wagon.

Twenty light cavalrymen rode in front and behind the convoy.

They set out, from the village Hal had never learned the name of, east, then turned north.

It was still summer, but Hal felt a chill as they continued on. It might have been his imagination.

Twice he saw dragons overhead, and once they were blacks. He assumed Yasin was keeping track of him.

At night, the convoy either stopped in a Roche army camp, or in open country, never chancing an inn or a city.

The head of the escort was a Lieutenant Hoj Anders.

He was solid, big, and his face looked like he'd placed second in several rough-and-ready brawls.

But there was intelligence behind the scars.

And training and experience.

He rode, contentedly, casually, beside Hal's wagon.

Anders was quite talkative, although his eyes never stopped sweeping the countryside and the escort. The slightest mistake by a guard, and the soldier would be ordered off his mount or his wagon, his wrists tied with a long lead to the back of a wagon, and he spent the rest of the shift trying to keep up, stumbling, running, sometimes falling and being dragged.

Anders' conversation was about Castle Mulde, and how incredibly secure it was, Roche's inevitable victory, and how Hal would do himself good by cooperating with the Roche.

"There's half a dozen guards to every prisoner at Castle Mulde," he said. "And they're carefully chosen for intelligence, alertness and patriotism."

"Pity they're not on the front lines," was Hal's reply. "Helping to fight the war, instead of scrounging about the rear."

That got a quick wince from Anders. But he persisted.

The castle was guarded not only by the visible bars and chains, but by magic as well.

"It has a great magician, who's completely devoted to keeping the prisoners secured."

"Therefore one that's not casting spells against our army," Kailas came back.

He may have been chained, only allowed to walk about for an hour in the morning and evening, when he washed and did his ablutions, but Hal kept fighting.

A broken piece of harness, and Hal would loudly sympathize about the poor quality of the Roche leather, and whether the maker wasn't secretly in league with the forces of Deraine, as so many sensible Roche were.

The soldier who cooked for the formation couldn't, and so Hal would lovingly describe how well Deraine, and especially Sagene, soldiers ate, making up the most absurd menus from meals he'd had with Khiri or Sir Thom Lowess.

But it was hard to keep cheerful as the miles creaked past, and they moved deeper into Roche.

Hal kept himself alert not only by chivvying the guards, but by studying and memorizing the land they passed through, mostly farmland, with scattered forests.

Kailas had no idea who or what lived in those forests, but they appeared untouched by man, with never a forester or woodsman to be seen. The soldiers became nervous each time the road narrowed and great trees reached high overhead, a seemingly perpetual wind soughing.

Kailas inquired as to the horrid monsters living in these woodlands. Anders told him to shut up, would say nothing else.

In the open country, they passed many small villages, and, at regular intervals, strongly-built castles.

Sometimes someone would ride out from them, and be greeted by Anders, and warned to stand clear, that there was a dangerous man, the Dragonmaster, in the wagon, and they were entitled to cheer him on his way to a lonely doom.

Few did.

All of them were frantic for news of the war and, when told Roche was holding firm, cheered.

Kailas noted there were few noblemen coming out to greet them, mostly women and children.

Similarly, he saw only a scattering of men working the fields. Roche had combed the north well for soldiery.

Anders told him they were bypassing the area's cities, "although there are not that many in these northlands.

"The people are Roche now, but they still remember when they were but savage tribesmen, before we brought them the benefits of civilization."

"I don't doubt that," Hal said. "Most people value their freedom. That's why we're fighting you, you know. When the war is over, you'll learn about freedom, and that your ruler doesn't always have to keep her boot at your throat."

Anders grunted, kicked his horse to the head of the column.

That was one small victory for Kailas.

But it was hard keeping his morale up.

Hal dreamed, and it was a strange dream, for it was completely real.

He was flying, but he wasn't on the back of a dragon, nor was he suddenly able to fly on his own. He'd had those dreams before, and woke sadly, realizing the limitations of his body.

It took a few moments for him to realize he was no longer a man, but a dragon. A real dragon, for his wing was sore, from a healing injury, and he had other, almost-vanished wounds on his back. He remembered the black dragon that had given them to him, fighting over a collection of stones that man built.

But there were no men on his back now, and he was floating happily in a strong wind.

Below him was the sea, the beginnings of a storm building, the waves white and gray.

He banked, feeling the air, the free air, rush past.

Behind him was land, square fields almost to the edge of the cliffs.

Here and there were small cubbies that Hal, dreaming, recognized as the huts of peasants, huts he thought he'd seen before.

Then there was a huge collection of piled stones, just at the cliff's edge.

Hal recognized it, with a great start.

It was Cayre a Carstares, one of Lady Khiri's holdings on the west coast of Deraine.

It was here that Hal had come to let his wounds heal, where he'd been nursed by Khiri, and where they'd fallen in love.

Hal dove, rolled into a ball, and dropped toward the ocean.

A dim memory came, from the time he was a very young dragon, floating on the current, the storms wailing about him, toward a new land. There had been other dragons around him, young, old.

Now Hal flattened, spread his wings, and the wind coming hard from the sea lifted him almost as high as he'd been.

Again, he was looking out to sea, and he knew what was across a vast ocean, a land where there was death and pain, a land he'd fled when he was a kit.

Then his wing began throbbing, painfully.

Very suddenly, Hal knew who he "was."

He was Storm, his battle dragon, wounded at the siege of Aude. But Storm, the last Hal had seen him, had been recovering from his wounds in a tent across the river Comtal from Aude.

How had he reached Deraine?

But there were more important things, such as a live sheep and some hot mash he had been promised in his comfortable, solitary barn, within the castle walls.

Far below was a tiny dot.

He knew who it was, and dove, then pulled out of his dive, circling.

The dot was a man, a female man, waving at him, and calling.

Hal/Storm brought his legs out, flared his wings, coming in for a landing.

He recognized the female.

It was Khiri, somehow now his keeper and guardian.

Very suddenly, Hal jolted awake in his wagon, feeling silent tears on his cheeks.

He managed to wipe them away, so the bastard Roche wouldn't see them, and mock him.

Hal Kailas slept no more that night, for something in his mind was telling him an obvious lie.

That hadn't been a dream, but for a few moments he'd been Storm, been in his head.

That was quite impossible.

No man could share thoughts with a dragon, nor an animal, any more than a man could read another's thoughts or command his actions.

But those moments of freedom, when he was Storm the dragon, with no rider, no one his master, stayed with him as they traveled on.

For the first time, they entered a smallish city, but moved directly through it to the docks. Here, amid fishing boats, light transports and a scattering of pleasure boats, they boarded a single-masted, large wherry.

There were staples in the deck, an overhead for his shelter. There was a cuddy forward and another overhead at the stern, around the long tiller.

Hal was unchained from his wagon, and his manacles refastened to the wherry's deck.

There were ten sailors, and half of the escort, including Lieutenant Anders, on the boat, when the mooring lines were brought in and the wherry slid off into the sullen waters, letting the current carry it north.

They raised a sail in midriver, let that move them faster toward the sea.

The river, named the Zante, felt hostile to Kailas, brooding, angry, and the small villages they passed were filthy.

Hal noticed, the further north they traveled, that the villages had palisades around them, but were open to the river. Then the palisades had guard towers at them.

Kailas chanced asking Anders.

"I told you the people of this region were once Roche's enemies. Now, those who've become sensible are regarded as enemies by their once-brothers in the wilderness, particularly when these peaceful peasants are prospering under Roche rule, and are frequently attacked by the savages."

Hal didn't think the villages looked that prosperous, said so. Anders snorted.

"Perhaps not by your nobleness's standards ... but they're doing very well compared to the forest barbarians."

"Would you believe," Hal asked, "that before the war I was a destitute commoner, no more than a wandering farm worker?"

Anders gave him a look that said, very clearly, he certainly wouldn't.

Hal went back to studying the terrain around them as the boat rode downstream toward the sea.

There were marshes, or, once away from the river, heavy forests that seemed to stretch on forever.

The river grew wider, then wider still, almost half a mile from bank to bank.

Once an arrow arced out of the wilderness and splashed down close to the boat.

The soldiers pulled on their armor, and crouched behind the wherry's high bulwarks.

But nothing came out to attack them.

"We shall reach Castle Mulde tomorrow " Anders said.

"A pity," Hal said. "I could travel like this, an endless vacation, forever, in the charming company of you and your fellows."

Anders gave him an odd look.

"By the way," Hal asked innocently, "how far is the castle from the sea?"

"A day's sail," Anders said, then caught himself. "But you do not need to be knowing anything about the castle's surroundings, for you'll never see, until we are victorious, anything but its stone walls.

"Or unless," he added, "you decide to accept Ky Yasin's generous offer."

"How could I ever forget," Hal murmured.

They sailed all that night. Anders said the shores were most hazardous.

"Particularly since," he said with an unpleasant grin, "we pay fifty pieces of silver for any prisoner captured alive, a hundred for one dead."

"Silver, eh?" Hal said, seemingly undisturbed. "Too cheap to afford gold?"

*

At dawn, they rounded a bend. The Zante River divided into two channels. In the center, a stone island stood five hundred feet above the water.

From its cliffs rose Castle Mulde.

A high curtain wall, with a balustrade along the top, circled the inner wall.

Inside the keep, a central building, six stories high, with peaked roofs jutting here and there, stood.

Three towers rose from the keep, and there were guards posted atop them.

Hal saw warders pacing the wall, at close intervals.

All was gray, dripping, lifeless stone.

This was a place that could erode a man's soul, make him give up his courage, his allegiance, maybe his life.

Hal glanced at Anders, who was staring up at the ominous castle. For once, he didn't chide Kailas about the impossibility of escape.

He didn't need to.

The sailors manned the wherry's oars, and rowed it out of the current, to a small dock, where they tied up.

Two soldiers struck off Hal's chains, and helped him on to the dock.

Steps led upward, to the castle's heavy gate.

Hal took the first step, and a gong rang across the valley.

He started, looked at his guards.

They, too, had heard it.

Hal took another step, and another, more dissonant, gong came.

Then a third and a fourth.

The instruments, if that was what they were, sounded, booming across the river, at each step as he walked to the gates of Castle Mulde.

9

And then the spell broke.

Raucous laughter rang down, and grinning faces peered over the battlements. The men, and a scattering of women, wore motley, or the remains of Deraine/Sagene uniforms.

"A proper greetin' for the Dragonmaster," a shout came.

Then came a BRRAAACCCK as someone blew a typical flier's welcome through his lips.

Hal recognized the man, vaguely. He'd been one of the dragon fliers lost, feared killed, during the Aude siege.

There was another familiar face, and a third, and then fuming, sputtering, Roche guards were muscling the prisoners away from the walls.

There was the rattle of chains, and then a door was unbolted.

Half a dozen Roche soldiers rushed out, surrounded Hal, and bustled him into Castle Mulde.

His escort was taken in another direction, and he lost a chance to throw a final insult at Lieutenant Anders.

A rather large, white-bearded man, wearing the carefully-kept, if tattered, uniform of a Derainian general, stood there, flanking a stone-faced Roche officer.

"Take the prisoner into processing," the Roche ordered, and Hal was muscled off.

He ended up in a small cell, looked about, assuming this would be his new home.

Then a tall, cadaverous-looking man, wearing robes, came into the room. A small wormy sort, wearing Derainian uniform, came in behind him, carrying a case and a wand.

"I am Ungava," the tall man said. "I am the wizard for Castle Mulde. It is my duty to ensure you'll never be able to escape. You'll be moved from here to a proper cell as soon as I've taken care of a couple of matters."

Without looking back, he held out a hand, and the small prisoner smacked the wand into it.

Ungava bowed his head over Hal's chains, muttered a phrase, struck the manacles, and the chains fell away.

Hal felt a moment of hope.

Ungava reached inside his robes, took out a atomizer.

He sprayed Hal with its contents.

Hal held back a coughing fit. Whatever magical items the atomizer held, all of them stank.

Ungava motioned with the wand to the four points of the compass, then began chanting. Hal could only make out a few of the words:

"...
Bind, bind . . . hold fast
Swirl about . . . . there is no north
You cannot see . . .
. . .
. . .
. . .
. . ."

Hal lost the last four lines completely.

Ungava did all this with an air of boredom, as if this were a spell he cast every day.

He handed the wand back over his shoulder, looked at Hal expectantly.

Hal stared at him.

Ungava smiled tightly.

"Think of north, and then face in that direction," he ordered.

Hal took a moment, closed his eyes, thought. He'd come in, then a left, then a right into this cell. So north should be over . . .

Sickness caught him, almost like vertigo, which, as a flier, Hal had never felt.

He stumbled, almost fell.

The prisoner caught him.

Ungava's smile grew broader.

"This is what binds you to Castle Mulde, more than any guard, any stone wall, any chain. You, and the other prisoners, are held by confusion, so that even if you were able to physically escape the castle, which you'll learn is an impossibility, you'd still never be able to find your way to your own lines.

"Now you can join the others."

He nodded abruptly, wheeled, and stamped out. The small prisoner looked back at the door, smiled sadly, and winked.

Hal didn't know what that meant, if anything beyond a slight bit of encouragement.

Waiting outside the cell was an officer in Derainian uniform who wore the dragon emblem on his chest. He limped over, saluted Hal and introduced himself as Lieutenant Sir Alt Hofei, formerly executive officer of the 66th Dragon Flight, with Second Army.

"But now," Hofei said, "I'm like all the others in here, rattling my chains and watching the world go past. Can't even escape, thanks to my damned leg. Tell me, sir," he said eagerly, "how goes the war? We get no news here . . . which is quite deliberate on the part of our peerless warder, Baron Patiala."

"It's like that damned spell," he said. "I saw Ungava the wand-waver go past a few moments ago, so I assume you're ensorcelled like the rest of us."

"It works as he said it does?" Hal asked.

"It does," Hofei said.

"Do we have any magicians here?"

"None," Hofei said. "And if there's any with a bit of the Talent, they're very damned quiet about it.

"You see, sir, Castle Mulde is for special cases. High-rankers, generals, noblemen . . . and fliers.

"There's hundred and forty-four – now a hundred and forty-five, counting you – fliers here. As for wizards, all of us were asked if we knew anything about magic when we were first told off to go to this damned place. I surely don't, but there were some who claimed they did.

"They were separated from the rest of us, and supposedly taken to a 'special camp.'

"Nobody knows for sure, but there's a cheery minority who think they were taken behind the nearest barn and had their neck stretched.

"Nice war we're having."

Hal nodded. "It is that."

"I've orders to show you to your room, sir," Hofei said.

"Room?"

"High-rankers such as yourself, Lord Kailas, rate a room, with but one or two mates." Hofei leaned close. "Although let me give you the warning, small rooms make a good place to start an escape from."

For the first time, Hal smiled.

"Escape, eh?"

"There's none of us . . . at least none of us who're fliers, who aren't always thinking, planning, maybe even trying something."

"Good," Hal said. "By the way. Since I'm a flier, like you said, so we can eliminate the lord business."

"Yessir," Hofei said. "I assume you'll be taking over as senior officer."

"You may assume," Hal said, a bit astonished, "but I know nothing of that."

"A lord outranks a general, even if he is a sir, I'd guess," Hofei said. "So you'll most likely replace Sir Treffry, who'd like to see you as soon as it's convenient."

"Treffry? That heavy-set one with grandfather whiskers?"

"That's him, sir. But don't think he's an ass, though he seems determined to make you think so, sometimes. Poor bastard was captured right at the start of the war. Tried to escape twice, captured twice, one of the first to be purged to Castle Mulde.

"Since then, he's made four more attempts. The last made it beyond the walls, and had the beastly luck of running into a Roche cavalry patrol."

Hal was grateful for Hofei's warning.

He'd known men like Sir Sen Treffry before the war, when he was a wandering farm laborer. They were bluff, hearty sorts, seemingly more concerned for their prize bull or racing stables than anyone who worked for them, although they could show surprising interest in their workers. Certainly Hal had never been cheated of his wages by one of them, which hadn't been true of some other country gentry.

"So I s'pose you'll be the new 'un in charge, Lord Kailas?"

"Not a chance, sir," Hal said. "You know the ins and outs better than I do."

Treffry humphed, grunted.

"I s'pose that's a compliment," he said. "Although heard good things about you, from fliers that've come in, even though none of 'em have the slightest idea of discipline.

"I do wish you'd take command, though, to be selfish."

Hal waited.

"We've got a rule here," Treffry went on. "All escape plans have got to be registered with either myself, m' adj'tant or Lieutenant Hofei, whose main detail is head of the escape group. That keeps tunnels from running into each other and such.

"That means, course, that neither of the three of us can make a runaway of our own without steppin' down for a month or so. Keeps us honest, and from sneakin' others' ideas.

"Y'sure you wouldn't like the task?"

"You just made me even more so," Hal said.

Treffry huffed through his beard.

"Since there's times the walls appear to be listenin', I'll not draw the obvious conclusions from that.

"But I s'pose you'd like a briefing on what you're into."

"I would."

There were 309 prisoners in the castle, over half Derainian. There were three generals, "includin' m'self," twenty-one noble officers, nineteen noble civilians, "poor sots who got caught tourin' the Roche lands when the war started, and now they're mewed up like so many hawks, nobody quite knowin' what to do with them," seventy-one soldiers who'd made thorough pains of themselves by repeatedly attempting to escape, "fifty poor sorts of infantrymen, none escapers, who've been detailed off as batmen who also do scut work for the Roche, under protest," and 145 dragon fliers, all of whom had tried and failed to escape.

"Y'can, if you wish," Treffry said, "think of this damnable castle as a sort of academy, and the other prisoner of war camps as primary schools. If you escape, and make it home, you've graduated.

"Failures are sent here, where they can try and try until they go quite mad."

Hal remembered something the traitor Tregony had said about being in a camp full of fliers, asked about him.

Treffry shook his head.

"Never heard of the wight. Friend of yours?"

"No," Hal said, then chanced again: "What about a woman flier, named Saslic Dinapur? Maybe killed, maybe captured, wounded, down in Kalabas?"

Saslic had been his first great love, had fallen into a melee of Roche soldiers, was presumed killed with her dragon.

"Don't b'lieve I have," Treffry said. "Though there's other camps for fliers who're better behaved guests of the Roche."

A last feeble hope died in Hal. If Saslic had lived, she would undoubtedly have tried escape. So she was truly dead.

Then he felt senseless guilt, thinking of Khiri.

Treffry noted his expression, turned away.

"We've all lost someone," he said heavily. "Some of us more than one someone in these stupid damned times."

Hal asked about letters.

"None in, none out," Treffry said. "That's another burden Baron Patiala works on us.

"Speakin' of whom, I'm supposed to take you to him. Then young Hofei'll show you to your chambers.

"By the way. He' s a very good man, and the current head of the Escape Committee."

*

Baron Patiala considered Hal icily.

He was about Hal's height, in his sixties, and wore a dress uniform with only one decoration on it. Hal decided, remembering a phrase of Farren Mariah's, that Patiala wouldn't say shit if he had a mouthful.

The commandant's office was in one of the castle's towers, and overlooked an exercise yard, and beyond the walls, a small patchwork of fields.

"I have always believed that you Derainians should be considered as nothing more than criminals for starting this war in the first place."

Hal suppressed a start.

"Oh yes," Patiala said. "Were it not for your country's refusal to consider reasonable demands from Queen Norcia, we would all be at peace.

"Instead, you chose to company with the loathsome Sagene . . . and now you are paying the price.

"You should be aware, Kailas, that your escort brought full details of your murderous behavior in your escape attempt, and the only thing that would please me more than to turn you over to a military court would be being permitted to execute you myself for murdering that poor soldier."

Hal said nothing.

"Be advised, Castle Mulde is run firmly but fairly. We do not torment our prisoners, unlike what I have heard your warders do to our soldiery.

"You are advised to follow my rules precisely, and, even though I consider you a common criminal, you will be treated as an equal with the others.

"Break my laws, and, at the very least, you'll be moved into a solitary cell.

"Obviously, any attempt to escape will be met with harsh penalties, and if, impossibly, you make it beyond these walls, the loyal Roche in the countryside will ensure your recapture."

Baron Patiala allowed that to sink in.

"You're dismissed."

Hal nodded curtly.

"So I am. Patiala."

He omitted a salute and the man's title, but didn't wait for a reaction.

Kailas spun, and stamped out of the office, determined, more than ever, that he would escape, and do it very damned soon.

10

Hal's room – cell – was halfway up one of the towers, and over-looked the river. He had two knights, captains, for company. They were out at the moment, Hofei said, "farming."

"Beg pardon?"

"Did you see those little fields when you were in Poophead Patalia's den? We've been given permission to work them, and harvest what we will."

"Hasn't anyone made a break .

"We're on parole when we're out there."

"Which nobody breaks?"

Hofei shook his head.

"You people are a great deal more moral than I am," Hal said. "But I suppose I'll have to go by custom."

Hofei took him out into the corridor.

"Treffry told you who I am?"

"He did."

"That's another point of morality we have," Hofei said. "All escapes get registered."

"Mmmh," Hal said. "How many successful getaways have there been?"

"We're not sure," Hofei said. "Six prisoners have gone out that've never come back. Whether they were killed or died in the forest, or what, we've never heard.

"We like to think the best."

Hal was about to tell him that, when he was captured, there'd been nothing heard about Castle Mulde. He would've expected to have heard something, considering his rank and the number of fliers imprisoned here.

But he said nothing.

Nor did he ask how many failed escapes there'd been.

The dank stone, the cold rain, and the mere fact of being pris-oners was demoralizing enough.

"One caution I've given everyone, so there's no offense meant, sir," Hofei said. "Ignore anything that isn't your own business. It might be part of an escape.

"Treffry says that if anyone sees him walking around naked, with his buttocks painted purple and a broomstick stuffed up his arse, no one had better flicker, because he's on his way."

Hal managed a grin.

He went to the window.

"Don't, by the way, put any leverage on any of the bars around here," Hofei warned. "They've probably been chiseled loose by someone."

"Ah." Hal peered out, and Hofei limped to the window.

"Can you get ropes?"

"We have made them from thread, other materials," Hofei said, a bit proudly.

"Long enough to get out from here, then down to that rooftop, and from there . . ." Hal puzzled for a further route.

"That roof you want to get to is one of the guards' barracks," Hofei said. "That route hasn't been tried since last winter, when three went down a rope from a floor below, then made a snow tunnel, trying for the wall.

"They were doing fine, until someone slipped, and they avalanched down to the courtyard. Two broken legs, one broken arm, and three months in solitary.

"But there's no reason, come winter, someone who's a little defter might not make it."

Hal nodded. He had no intention of waiting until winter.

Hal's two roommates kept very much to themselves, showed Kailas formal courtesy, but seemed uninterested in making friends.

Hal had his feelings slightly hurt, then realized the two men were most likely up to their armpits in some sort of escape plan, and didn't need or want a third along.

The prisoners ate twice a day, generally a soup called stew, that once a day had some bits of pieces of meat in it. Bread was baked by the prisoners, and shared with the guards.

The rest of the meal came from the gardens beyond the walls.

There were six prized hens, bought from the locals, and there was a drawing for the eggs.

It wasn't much, but just enough to keep from starving.

Just.

The eleven women prisoners in Castle Mulde were assiduously courted by the others. But there were very damned few places to be alone, and it took some arrangement to find an empty cell.

The second problem was avoiding pregnancy, which, so far, hadn't happened.

Baron Patiala had sworn that any woman getting pregnant would never be freed, and she and her "spawn" could keep on rotting where they were.

There would be no mercy, he said, until the Roche standards flew over Sagene's capital of Fovant and Rozen.

While Hofei was showing Hal around the castle, they encountered a man on a landing, in deep conversation with himself, talking, laughing, seemingly content.

When they were out of hearing, Hofei said, "One of our madmen. He's harmless. There're three others we keep in cells who want to do damage to others . . . or themselves."

"Can't you get a magician in to try to straighten out their minds?"

Hofei snorted.

Late that night, Hal heard the screaming of one of the madmen, echoing up the stairs from the cellars.

Hal's first lesson as a prisoner was finding some way to pass the time.

His first attempt was to sleep, the customary pastime of any combat soldier. He knew Patiala and his guards were watching him closely, and thought it might be wise to appear docile until they grew bored waiting for him to do something.

But, impossible as it seems to serving soldiers, it *is* possible to catch up on all the hours missed on detail, night guard, or action.

Eventually, Hal could sleep no more, and sought another way of passing the time.

As yet, no brilliant ideas had come that shouted "this is the way out."

So he set about learning Castle Mulde from top to bottom.

Hofei eagerly showed him plans the prisoners had drawn up, and Kailas memorized them.

But still, nothing came.

Once again, witless, he noted the pastimes of the older prisoners – some taught anything they knew, from the art of fishing with a net to history to music to blacksmithing to embroidery, which was taught by one of the Derainian generals.

Others took every "course" they could, even though this schooling might be no more than one man talking to another man in a corner of the courtyard.

The cell doors were magically locked at nightfall, unlocked at dawn, and the guards didn't bother the prisoners much, other than making irregular sweeps, looking for anything.

The unconfirmed story was that the guards had been chosen for a bit of prescience.

No one knew if that was true, but when a Roche passed, prisoners made an effort to think and talk about things other than escape.

There was a morning and evening assembly, but no more.

The occasional working parties were quickly volunteered for, doing various tasks in and out of the castle. They, too, helped the time pass.

"Interesting thing you might not be aware of," Treffry said one morning. "This castle had another face, once."

Hal brushed raindrops away from his eyes. The two were walking up and down a chill battlement, which was better than the rather smelly confines of the castle, and, best yet, fairly lonely.

"Let me guess, sir. A civilian prison."

"Close," Treffry said. "But not quite. It used to be a madhouse."

"*Used* to be?" Hal asked.

Treffry chuckled.

Hal noted another solitary man, except that he was clearly not mad. His name was Goang, and he spent most of his daylight hours outside, regardless of the weather, studying the birds of the castle, swifts, swallows, ravens, others.

When he was asked, Goang said he would, one day, when the war was over, write a complete history of this building, seen through its birds.

In the evenings, Goang would drift to the fringes of one or another of the dragon fliers' groups, and listen quietly, once in awhile asking a technical question about the nature of flying.

The man seemed harmless, and was sort of accepted as an odd hanger-on, no more.

Summer was almost over and still Hal fretted for a plan, even an idea.

Hofei said there was a plan afoot that could use another man.

"Doing what?" Hal asked, knowing nothing is free.

"Well, digging."

Hal went with the lieutenant to the castle's former meeting hall.

There were prisoner guards at regular intervals on the way, each scanning his own sector for a sign of a Roche.

In the assembly hall, a huge table had been levered up, and stones pried out of the floor.

Hal looked down into the cramped space, felt his stomach clench, forbade it recognition.

A prisoner with a fat lamp on a perch beckoned him down.

He slid through the entrance, down a rope ladder a dozen feet, past the prisoner.

"Now," the prisoner told him, "go on your knees, and duck your head. You'll see the tunnel mouth. Go on up it to the face of the digging. The only problem you'll have is about ten feet in, where there's this great godsdamned boulder you have to weasel your way under.

"It took us three weeks to dig under that."

Hal crouched, peered into the tunnel, saw, far ahead, a flickering where diggers would be at work.

He started into the tunnel, and clammy sweat came.

Panic tried to take him over, but he fought it down.

He took half a dozen deep breaths, but he felt no calmer, remembering the deadly hours, back at the beginning of the war, when he and others stood watch, during the Roche siege of Paestum, far underground, listening to diggers undermine the wall, waiting for the boulders to groan and bury him alive.

And he remembered the mines of his native village, and how, every now and again, there would be a cracking roar, and there would be screams, and other men with picks and shovels tore at the smoking earth, hoping to save their brothers, buried in a cave-in.

Sometimes they succeeded, and white, trembling men were pulled to freedom.

But more often there was nothing but despair, and a burial ceremony with never a body, and the next day, another shaft would be driven.

Hal straightened, went up the ladder without looking in the prisoner's face, pushed his way through the entrance.

He was sweat-soaked.

Hofei helped him to his feet.

"Don't worry, sir," he said. "I can't stomach tight spaces, either. Maybe that's what made us fliers."

Hal nodded, unwilling to speak, and reluctant to admit what he felt was cowardice.

One thing that was guaranteed to stop a conversation among the dragon fliers was the sight of a dragon.

Sometimes it was a wild monster, banking and swooping in the late summer winds above the castle.

Sometimes there was a man aboard, and the watchers' expressions would grow hard, envious.

Twice black dragons dove low over Castle Mulde, and Hal wondered if they were from *Ky* Yasin's group, keeping track of their prized prisoner.

The only hobby almost every prisoner had was alcohol.

A bit of fruit, water, perhaps some grain, warmth, and the beginning of a tremendous hangover was underway. Some called the result beer, others wine, the more sensible just used the generic label of headsplitter.

Bottles of any size were at a premium, and Hal could never figure where they were coming from.

But every prisoner had one or two, and when the sun was warm, in this dying summer, the bottles would line the parapets.

Surprisingly, at least after first consideration, the Roche made no attempt to stop the various home brewers.

Then Hal realized that of course they wouldn't. A prisoner obsessing about his jug of hooch or sprawled in blissful unconsciousness or crawling around the floor in the throes of what was considered the worst hangover in the world was not as likely to be making trouble or trying to escape.

Hal had no idea how, but somehow, without ever a word being said, "everyone" knew there was an escape about to happen. Who, where, how, no one knew, or those who did weren't talking.

Then another rumor went out – three men were gone. Where, how, the details weren't there yet.

But the guards had been, were still, completely fooled.

Then, after a week, someone slipped, and Patiala and his guards called for assembly after assembly after roll call. Ungava stalked the corridors of the castle, flanked by his woebegone little prisoner, but found nothing.

Little by little, word came out.

The escaped prisoners had been on parole working their tiny fields. But parole did not apply when they were recalled, and roll was taken outside the castle's entrance.

Three men, two Sagene, one Derainian, had ducked away, after other prisoners staged a phony mass fight. They'd gone over the balustrade behind the gate, then down the rocks, across the river, and hopefully away.

It took another two days before their method of covering was revealed: plaster dummies had been cast of the three escapers' heads, and mounted on boards. The plaster was painted precisely, using charcoal from the stoves, paint base for faces, scraped from the mortar holding the stones together, pigmented with various spices or substances from the castle kitchen.

When the melee had ended, the casts were draped with overcoats, and the boards put on adjoining prisoners' shoulders.

The head count was just that, and so the guards came up with the appropriate number.

Hal wished he knew of some reliable gods to pray that the escapers would succeed.

There weren't any benevolent gods in this part of Roche, at least not this year.

Two weeks after the escape, grinning hunters came to the castle, with slung, stinking, burlap bags.

The prisoners were assembled, and the bags dumped.

Out rolled the heads of the three escapers, and the hunters collected their bounty.

One of the hunters chortled, "Like huntin' blind pigs. We watched 'em stumble in great circles, lost as bastards, for half a day afore we got tired an' went in an' kilt 'em."

Ungava preened.

His spell of confusion was, truly, the greatest guardian Castle Mulde had.

Hal could feel the souls of the men watching collapse.

But at that instant, very strangely, Kailas felt the plans for his own escape click together.

11

"So what will be your escape route?" Sir Alt asked.

"I won't tell you," Hal said, "because it's one that only I can use."

"Those tend to be the riskiest," Hofei said.

"I'll tell you . . . in time," Hal said. "I just wanted to tell you that I'm planning something. Right now, I need some things: pen, ink, paper."

"Easily done."

"Then I need to know who're the traitors in here."

"We have none," Hofei said, a bit snippily.

"Come now," Hal said. "Someone – most likely several some-ones – have got to be talking to Patiala, or one of his men, in exchange for better quarters, food, or whatever. Let's not call them traitors, but, maybe, people who aren't as strong as they should be, or maybe aren't aware they're being played like a fish."

After a moment, Hofei grudged, "we have two . . . perhaps three."

"Who're their best friends?"

"No one with any decency will associate with them."

"You're doing it wrong," Hal said mildly. "You should have your people start cultivating them. It's always good to have some kind of subtle line in that you can use to your own ends."

Hofei looked at Kailas carefully.

"You're not just a dragon flier, are you?"

"I'm somebody who plans on being alive when all this is over," Kailas said. "And I'll use any talent I can think of to make sure of it."

Hofei nodded slowly.

"I have some strong-stomached men – and a woman – in mind."

"Good," Hal said. "I'll want them to leak something scan-dalous in time."

"What?"

"In time," Hal said. "And the second thing I need is any pris-oner who knows anything about magic."

"We have no one," Hofei said. "All wizards – or anyone with any Talent – were purged before they got here."

"There's always somebody," Hal said stubbornly. "I have a man in my squadron who's a bit of a witch. His grandfather was a full-fledged one. Sometimes my man can cast a small spell, sometimes nothing happens. But he'd never claim to be a wizard. That's the sort of person I'm looking for."

"I honestly don't know of anyone," Hofei said. "If there is, he or she is bound to be keeping it secret. But I'll see what I can come up with."

"Good," Hal said. "Now, if you'll get me my writing materials, I'll set to work."

"Might I ask what you're going to be writing?"

"My confessions."

He smiled sweetly.

A day later, the writing materials were delivered, and then Hal set to work, spending hours sitting in his cell, writing away.

He told no one what he was writing, other than this was his after-the-war money machine.

Since diaries and such were forbidden, Hal hid the paper in a hollowed-out leg of his cot.

Some of the noble prisoners sniffed – a man who'd been so favored by the king with vast estates should hardly be worried about gold, as if he were no better than a tradesman.

But they kept their councils to themselves . . .

"I think I may have someone," Hofei said. "One of our civilian internees has an interesting background. You might be interested in talking to him."

"I am, indeed," Hal said, and the next day Sir Alt brought the man by. He was young, thin, quite tall, most shy, and looked as if he'd be happier as a priest, or perhaps an archivist, Hal thought.

The man was Mav Dessau, eldest son of Baron Dessau of Anhewei, a title even Kailas had heard of.

"I don't know if my father still lives," Dessau said. "He was doing poorly when I left on my travels. Have you . . .?"

Hal said, apologetically, that he knew little about the nobility, and hadn't kept up with their lives.

"So I suppose I'll continue on as the eldest," Dessau said, "no more. Which doesn't displease my father, since he considered me a bit of a disappointment."

"Ah?"

"I love to study, to learn," and enthusiasm glowed in Dessau's voice.

"At one time," and here he looked about Hal's cell, as if there were an eavesdropper crouched under the wooden cots, "I wanted to be a thaumaturge.

"They said I had a bit of the Talent, and I'd been accepted by a tutor. When my father heard of this, he raged, and cut off my allowance, and swore he'd disinherit me. I should have told him to make one of his prize bulls the next baron, for it mattered . . . matters . . . little to me.

"But I'm afraid I'm a coward. I suppose any of us who come from wealth are always terrified that we'll be cast loose on our own, and that our devices shall not be sufficient.

"So I dropped that field of study, and decided that I would become an architect, a master builder, and that there might be a future amalgamating the styles of Deraine, Sagene and Roche.

"I was studying in Carcaor when the war started. Since my father is one of King Asir's strongest supporters, Queen Norcia thought I would make a good hostage.

"And so here I am, with nothing more to study than a damned monolith like this swamp of a castle."

"I think I might have something more for you," Hal said. "Something in the way of wizardry."

"Magic? As I said, I know very little, although I've read much, but haven't the training. And . . ." again came the frightened look. "I do not wish to be sent to . . . to wherever the captive wizards were sent.

"To be eaten by dragons, I suppose. Or demons."

Dessau took a deep breath.

"But I suppose I have no choice. Patriotism, and all that.

"So I'll try to do whatever you wish, although you'll most likely be disappointed by my best.

"And I'll ask but one favor. If you make good your escape, would you mind visiting my father? Or my brothers, if the baron has passed on?"

"I'll do better than that," Hal said. "If I make it back to Deraine, I'll hunt the baron up and tell him that it was your magical abilities that made it possible to escape."

Dessau smiled.

"Thank you. I'd just like to be there to see his face when the Dragonmaster, Lord Kailas, tells him that."

*

Sir Suiyan Tutuila came to the castle, summoned Hal, asked if he wished to confess, saying if he did, Tutuila and *Ky* Yasin would intercede at Kailas's trial, assuming he was willing to cooperate.

Hal made no response, just stared at Tutuila until the exasperated inquisitor ordered him returned to his cell.

The next part of Hal's conspiracy was having the little prisoner of war who was Ungava the magician's reluctant servant visit his cell.

"Ah knows nofing, nofing, about magic, or magicking," the man, who had only the single name of Wolda, swore. He was very nervous, hardly used to being in the company of a noted nobleman.

But Kailas hadn't been a cavalry warrant and then a unit commander without learning a few ways to put men at their ease.

He drew Wolda out about the small island he'd grown up on, off the west coast of Deraine, where he'd fished before deciding to join up, to end up on a coastal patrol boat.

Hal told him about Khiri's estates, and her village fishermen, although, of course, without sounding like he'd ever lorded it over them. He told Wolda about seeing the flotillas of dragons, on the water with their wings folded over their heads like tents, coming from the west.

"Ah've seen them too," Wolda nodded. "We used to try to reckon what they were comin't frae, where they was goin't, with not a clue."

Hal told Wolda about the time he'd tried fishing for a living, and how it was too much for him, and after the small man recovered from his surprise that a mighty lord had ever baited a hook, let alone run one into his palm, and said, "Ay, they say'n you're t'be born t'it. An' Ah'm hopin't Ah lives, an' gets back t'it. Ah misses th' sea."

Wolda recovered a bit of his suspicion, and asked Hal why he'd summoned him.

"Because I'm hoping you'll help me get off this damned rock," Kailas said.

"Ah doubt there's aught Ah might do."

"You're Ungava's assistant."

"On'y 'cause Ah was told to it."

"I need to know a couple of spells," Hal said.

"Nah, nah. Ah'm no wizard."

"Do you remember what Ungava says, when he takes the irons off a new prisoner?"

"Cours't. Tha's simple. He rubs oil, which Ah've got in a vial, on his fingers, not lettin' anyone see it. Then he whisper't, 'Chain, bend, steel, work, uncoil, uncoil.'"

"That seems simple," Hal said. "Could I work it?"

"He told me once't Ah could, so Ah'd wager so," Wolda said. "Course, y'd need a bit of th' oil."

"Could you steal some of it for me?"

Wolda looked frightened.

"He tol't me once if Ah did him false, he'd change me int' a sea monsker." Wolda took a deep breath. "But Ah'll help. Th' oil, for your learnin', is made of some kind of rock serpent from th' east."

"That's one thing I need," Hal said. "The second is the spell he casts to keep us confused."

"Ah'm noo lyin't," Wolda said. "Ah dinna know it. He whispers it close."

Hal made a face, and his hopes sank. Then he had an idea.

"You know what hypnosis is?"

"Cours't," Wolda said. "Afore m'boat sank, and th' Roches caught me, went to a turn one night, an' they had a woman. Fair, she was, and she put spells, but said it was hypnotizing, on m'mate, and made him think he was a woman, and should be kissin't th' skipper.

"Fair laughed til Ah 'most pissed myself, Ah did."

"Would you be willing to be hypnotized," Hal said, "and have somebody ask about that spell? They say everything you hear, or see, gets tucked away in your mind, and needs only a little prodding to come out."

"Ah dunno," Wolda said. "I don't think—"

Hal cut him off before he could refuse.

"Go think about it. And remember, if I get out, you'll be one step closer to being home, and back on your boat, fishing."

Wolda licked his lips, looked piteously at Hal, but Kailas bustled him off.

"I don't suppose," Hal asked Dessau that evening, as they strolled along the battlements, "you happen to know anything about hypnosis?"

"I read a book about it once," Dessau said. "Seems fairly simple, assuming you've a subject who doesn't object to the idea.

"And you know, of course, that nobody will do anything they don't want to when they're hypnotized, so you can't get one of the guards to open the gates for you."

"I just want a simple bit of remembering," Hal said.

"I'll give it a try," Dessau said. "But no guarantees."

"I've been a soldier too long to expect anything like that," Kailas said.

"Ah've thought," Wolda said. "An' Ah'll let y' try wi' th' hyp-notizin't."

"Good," Hal said. "This evening, before lockup, after assembly."

"All right, Wolda," Dessau said in a soothing voice, tucking the bit of stolen oil into a pouch. "Just relax, lean back, and watch this medallion."

"Ah'll try."

There was no one in Hal's cell but the three of them. Hal had run his roommates out, thinking the less confusion, the more likely this might work.

"See how it turns," Dessau said. "See how it spins."

"Ah do."

"Now, don't talk," Dessau said. "Just watch the medallion, and listen to my voice."

Dessau kept talking, about soft, gentle things, and always, always, the gold medallion he'd gotten from somewhere kept turning.

Wolda looked quite alert.

Hal felt himself getting sleepy, wondered how long Dessau would keep trying, wondered if Wolda had a godsdamned mind to hypnotize, got sleepier, and suddenly realized Wolda might not be going under, but he surely was.

Kailas looked at the ceiling, afraid to move as the voice wove on, talking about home fires, with the rain and wind beating against the window panes, and a good meal warm inside, and the fire crackling, and then Hal got his shin kicked.

He looked back down, and Wolda had his eyes closed, and a happy smile on his face.

"Can you still hear me?" Dessau asked.

"Aye."

"Do you want to tell me some things?"

"P'raps."

"Do you want to tell me some things about Ungava?"

"Do Ah have to? He' s tryin' t t' take me away frae m'fire."

"I'll not let him, and soon I'll leave you alone to toast your bones. Ungava is a magician."

"Aye."

"An evil magician."

"Aye."

"He uses a spell to keep prisoners from being able to escape."

"Aye . A secret spell."

"But you've heard it."

"Aye."

"Would you like to tell it to me?"

"You'll not let Ungava turn me int' a sea monsker?"

"No."

"Th' spell goes, " and Wolda' s voice took on a sing-song, and deepened, to match the Roche magician's:

> *Spinning compass*
> *Bind, bind, hold, hold fast*
> *Swirl about with my wand*
> *There is no north*
> *You cannot see clear*
> *There is no south*
> *No east, no west*
> *All is fog*
> *All is lost.*"

"An' he tap't wi' his damned wand afore in all directions, sprays wi' that evil shit, an' as far as Ah know, that's all."

"Good," Dessau said. "Go sit by your fire."

Wolda fell back into unconsciousness.

Dessau motioned to Hal to follow him out of the cell.

"Well," he said, "I guess I'm a real hypnotist.

"I was hoping there'd be herbs, or something else," Dessau said, "that Ungava uses to lend the spell power. But there's nothing but that damned wand of his and whatever's in the atomizer.

"I don't think it's just the words."

"Try it," Hal said. Dessau handed him the tiny vial of oil, and Hal put a bit of it on his face. It stank as badly as he remembered.

Dessau, face most skeptical, chanted the spell.

Hal turned to the setting sun, knew that as west-north-west by knowledge, felt for north, found nothing.

"No," he said. "You're right. It needs the wand. I hope nothing more."

"So all we need to make the thing work is to steal Ungava's magic stick, we hope," Dessau said. "Something tells me that might be a bit of a challenge."

Hal nodded, gloomily. Then an idea came.

"Maybe not. You said that you can't make somebody do something he doesn't want to do."

"Right," Dessau said. "At least, that's what I've read."

"But what about something he might want to do, if he had the courage?"

Hal explained.

"Mmmh," Dessau said. "I'll give it a try. I just hope it works . . . and that our poor little fisherman in there doesn't get turned into a sea monster.

"Although I've never seen any magician with that kind of power."

The next day, Ungava the wizard was stalking through the prisoners' areas, peering about, looking for anything resembling an escape attempt.

As always, he was flanked by his small prisoner aide, Wolda, carrying a bag of sorcerous implements and, in his other hand, Ungava's wand.

They rounded a corner, and a prisoner cannoned into Ungava, sending him flying back into Wolda.

Wolda fell heavily, the wand under him.

Unexpectedly, it shattered like glass.

Ungava shrieked like an impaled baboon, knelt over the broken remains of the wand.

Wolda tried to help, chattering that it wasn't his fault, and please, please, don't transform him.

Ungava ignored him, came to his feet, and started screaming at the prisoner, who'd been supposed to grab the wand and run, flattened against the wall as if being beaten.

Ungava ran out of words, and stalked away, Wolda, carrying the bag and the bits of the wand, scuttling after him.

Later that afternoon, he gave the bit of the wand he'd hidden to Kailas.

"Let's see now," Dessau said. "You're properly oily.

"Now we point at the four compass points with this little

piece of whatever the hells it is . . . damned glad you drew the
headings on the floor, since I can't tell direction any more than
you can, and then . . ."

And then he muttered the spell.

It was if a fog had cleared.

Hal knew north, south, the other directions, had a vision of a
crude map, with the Zante River and the castle, and, a bit to the
north, the welcoming ocean that led to the Chicor Straits and
home.

His eyes were moist.

"It works," he managed.

"Good," Dessau said. "Now, what about the rest of that oil?"

"I'll give it to Hofei," Hal said. "There'll be other escapers
after me. I hope."

Hal saw the next escape in the making.

He was finishing up his "diary," and enjoying a rare, sunny
day, a nice breeze from off the river cooling the castle's hot
stones.

He heard a small crash, looked up.

A slate had fallen from one of the turrets. Then he saw a hand,
carefully taking other slates inside, until there was a sizeable hole
in the turret.

Other prisoners had seen the same thing, and Hal noted the
eeriness – no one shouted, or did anything more than find a van-
tage point where he could unobtrusively watch whatever was
happening.

The hole grew, and then a prisoner clambered awkwardly out
on to the roof.

Hal recognized him as Goang, and thought for a moment the
man was about to jump, suiciding down on to the flagstones of
the courtyard below.

Others must have had the same fear, for prisoners began
moving toward the steps into that turret, hoping to stop Goang
before he jumped.

But Goang wasn't suicidal – at least, not directly.

Two other prisoners handed something out to him, and he
fitted them together.

Hal saw that they were wings, made of paper, he guessed,
glued on to thin lathes.

The wings were curved back, like a swift's.

Goang attached them to a harness he'd made, and Hal

marveled at the amount of work the man must've gone through, first studying the birds until he understood their wings, then making his own.

Goang braced, then jumped, and now there was a sound from the watching prisoners, something between a hiss of surprise and a gasp of fear.

The wind caught Goang, and lifted him.

Now a guard saw the flier, and shouted an alarm.

Goang was pulling on lines that led to the front of his wings, forcing them down, and he dove at an angle.

Hal figured he would just clear the castle walls, and then have a fair shot at being able to fly over the river.

What Goang would do then, Hal couldn't think, since he saw no sign of the weapons, food or clothing Goang would need to evade the hunters and make his escape.

The wind eddied, and Goang's left wing dipped.

He was just over the wall when his wingtip caught a battlement.

Instantly what had been a birdlike thing of grace and beauty, collapsed, and Goang was falling.

But he was able to reach out at the last minute, and grab that same battlement.

He slipped, almost fell, then had a firm hold, and pulled himself up, on to the parapet, just as half a dozen guards had him.

The bits of his bird machine were ripped apart, and Goang hauled off to the baron, and from there to a solitary cell.

But his failure gave the prisoners a bit of hope, and something to talk about.

Hal wondered why it had taken a non-flier to come up with this idea, decided he would think more about this device.

But that was for the future.

Now, he was finally ready to go.

Within a few days, the story of what the Dragonmaster had been writing so laboriously was all over the castle.

It was the story of his capture, and imprisonment, supposedly complete with details of Castle Mulde.

Some said that Kailas was keeping this diary to stay sane, others for it to be used as evidence in the trial of Baron Patiala, after the war, "for surely the bastard has to be tried before we can hang him."

*

Hofei whistled.

"Now I understand why you refused to tell me your escape plan."

Hal shrugged. "It was the only idea I could come up with."

"But what happens if it fails, anywhere along the path?"

"Then," Hal said, trying to sound nonchalant, "they'll hang me. Tell mother I died game."

The guards burst into Hal's cell just before dawn.

Very efficiently, they bundled him out of bed, and put him against the wall while they searched his meager possessions.

Kailas noted that they deliberately behaved as if this were a blind search, and they "just happened" to come on the hollowed-out cot leg.

Obviously Patiala had no intention of exposing the big mouth or traitor who'd passed the story about Kailas's manuscript along.

The guards dragged out the manuscript and, whooping with glee, hauled Kailas off to one of the solitary cells.

"One thing that has always pleasured me about life," Baron Patiala said, "is that villains will out."

He reached out and tapped Hal's manuscript, lying on his desk.

Hal tried to look like a not particularly bright villain, caught red-handed.

"Not only did you have the cold-blooded ruthlessness to murder one of the queen's soldiers, but you were stupid enough to brag about it, even after you'd been warned both by *Ky* Yasin, Sir Suiyan Tutuila and myself that you were being watched, and would face prosecution for this capital offense as soon as adequate proof was amassed.

"Truly, you played into our hands, and now you shall pay.

"I have sent word of your idiotic behavior to Sir Suiyan and *Ky* Yasin, and that you will be escorted, on the morrow, from Castle Mulde to Carcaor, where you shall be court martialed, as common law admits, and then punished, I hope to the fullest extent of the law.

"I knew it was just a matter of time."

Hal didn't know any of the guards detailed off for the escort.

All he was permitted to take were the clothes he'd arrived in, now somewhat more worn in the months he'd been prisoner at Castle Mulde.

The prisoners turned out to watch him leave.

No one spoke, and few could meet his face.

Most of them had heard the tale of Hal's stupidity, writing about what he'd done after escaping from the hospital, and thought while Kailas was most certainly brave, they agreed with Patiala, and considered Hal a fool.

Ungava put the spell of the chains on, after the limber metal strips had been wound about his ankles and wrists. Hal felt them clasp him tightly.

He was half-carried, hardly able to stagger, back down the hill, to where a boat waited.

The warrant in charge of the escort laughed harshly as the boat was pushed away from the dock, and the guards started working the sweeps, driving the small craft back upriver.

Hal looked once at Castle Mulde, and spat into the water.

He waited until near dusk, just before the boat's commander would be looking for a place to beach the craft before dark.

The boat had passed three fishing villages since leaving Castle Mulde.

Then he knelt, and whispered the counterspell over his leg irons, hoping that Ungava hadn't been lying to Wolda when he said that spell could be worked by anyone.

He hadn't been lying. The metal uncoiled like a snake, and clattered to the deck.

Hal quickly whispered the spell again, near his manacles, and they, too, fell away.

The clank was heard by a guard, some yards away.

He spun, saw Hal, standing free, and his mouth fell open.

Before he could shout, Hal kicked off his boots, dove off the boat, disappearing in a swirl.

Then there were shouts, orders, and the boat spun in the current, coming to a halt as guards dropped their oars, strung bows, nocked arrows, and had spears ready for the cast.

But there was nothing but the eddying, muddy waters of the Zante River to be seen.

12

Hal swam underwater as deeply and as far as he could, then came to the surface slowly, turning on his back, and letting only his mouth appear long enough to gulp air.

Then he dove again, and kicked for the river bank.

He had to surface for air twice more, the second time staying up long enough to look at the bank, and pick his landing place – where thick brush grew into the water.

He surfaced in this thicket, and finally let himself look back at the boat.

They were rowing in circles, still watching the water, waiting for either Hal or his body to surface.

Hal slid out of the river, and crawled into the bush. On its far side, he came to his feet.

Sooner rather than later, the Roche would be checking the shoreline, and he thought he'd rather not be there.

Hal started downriver as fast as he could travel on bare feet. He'd deliberately left his boots off as much as possible over the last month, trying to harden his soles.

But it hadn't done much good.

By the time he'd walked a third of a league, he was starting to limp.

And, as it grew darker, it was getting cold.

Fall was definitely either here, or about to arrive.

But he was free!

That thought, and the sight of the first village, drove his aches away.

He wanted to enter the village and beg a handout, but rather appreciated his head being attached to his neck.

Also, this village, even if they didn't kill him for the reward, would be the first the Roche soldiers would go to, looking for additional searchers.

Besides, the next village held his dream.

He skirted the village, and went on.

There was a rough cart track behind the village.

Kailas knew he shouldn't use it, that he should be deep in the bush.

But he figured that, with no alarm out yet, he'd most likely hear any oncomers before they saw him. As for the hunters that were his real fear – they'd be working the brush, since game animals quickly learned to avoid anything of man.

It was well after dark, and both moons had risen when Hal came on the second village.

He crept down to the water, and slid into it. It was very cold, and he tried not to shiver.

Hal swam out, let the current take him for a bit, washing him past the outer palisade into the village's heart.

He'd spotted, going upriver, several skiffs pulled up on shore.

Hal swam hard for the bank, keeping his hands and feet below the surface.

He came up on the bank in the middle of four boats.

The village was still alive, with two fires in the squares, and most of the huts still lamp-lit.

Hal wanted to grab the first boat, and pull away.

But he made himself take a bit of time, and found one with an unstepped mast with a sail furled around it. None of the boats had oars in them, which he hadn't expected, and "his" boat had, at least, a long pole.

There was a locker in the bow, but he wasn't calm enough to see what it held.

Instead, he crawled onshore to that boat's painter.

Hal grinned. For the first time, he had a bit of luck.

The painter was a bit frayed.

Hal saw a jagged rock at water's edge, used it to saw the painter away.

That was good. With luck, the boat's owner would find the end of his moorings unraveled, and curse his carelessness, never thinking of a thief.

Especially not a dragon-riding thief.

Hal went back into the water, and slowly eased the boat off the bank.

It floated free.

Hal looked around for any guards, sentries, afoot or on the walls, saw none.

Perhaps they had magic wards set.

He shuddered, preferring the thought that they were just careless.

The current was pulling at the boat, and Hal let it take the craft, staying in the water and holding on to the stern.

There were no shouts, outcries, but he waited until the village was round a bend before he clambered aboard.

The boat rocked, and Hal almost went overboard. It would be just his luck to lose the boat and drown now.

But he didn't.

The boat was traveling smoothly downstream.

Hal could relax for a moment, and in that moment he realized there was a chill wind coming upriver.

He had no time to be cold.

He went to the forward locker, opened it.

There were some net floats, some bits of wood, rope, oakum for leaks, fishing lines, and the great discovery – a long, sharp, fish knife.

Hal, armed, felt quite cheerful.

Now, for that sail.

He stepped the mast, and unfurled the sail.

At that point, his luck ran out. The sail hadn't been raised in too long a time, and was mildewed, rotting. It tore apart at the first gust of wind.

Probably just as well, at least for the moment, since Hal hadn't the slightest idea of how to tack back and forth in a river.

He found and mounted the rudder, and let the river take him.

Hal passed the third village at midnight, and there were no lights or other signs of life.

Something loomed, rushing up at him. Hal thought he was being attacked by some kind of river monster, readied his knife.

The something was a huge tree trunk, its branches reaching, menacing. But as long as he stayed clear, the log seemed to offer no harm, and went past him.

After it was gone Hal realized, that if he were a true riverman, he would've tied up to that log, and let it carry him down to the sea.

But he wasn't, and so forgot about it.

Just at dawn, Hal passed Castle Mulde. He tried not to look at it, tried to think like an innocent fisherman, out early to check his nets or whatever sort of fishing they did on the Zante River, in case Ungava was mounting his own form of guard.

He was hardpressed, as Mulde fell behind him, to not cock a snook, or even show them his bare arse.

But he didn't, and then the castle was swallowed up by the dawn mist.

Hal, yawning mightily, feeling like he was almost truly free, was swallowed by deep fatigue.

He had to sleep, had to be alert when he reached the river mouth.

He saw a small islet, managed to use his pole as a crude oar to close on it. The boat was pulled under an overhanging branch, and Hal had the branch, almost lost his boat, then hand-over-handed it to the shore.

He pulled it up on to the bank a few feet, thought he was adequately hidden, curled up in the stern sheets and was instantly asleep.

He wasn't sure what woke him, but something said to lie very still.

Hal peeled an eyelid back, saw it was midday at least.

He waited.

Then he heard a whisper, and the squish of river mud.

From his right.

He braced his left leg, and his right hand found the fish knife.

Dark hair lifted over the boat's gunwale, and he saw a pair of eyes.

No more, for Hal was up, rolling, his knife in his left hand, and lunging.

He caught the man just below his chin line, driving the blade into his neck almost to the hilt.

The man gargled, fell back.

Hal came over the gunwale, into the mud, ignored the man bleeding to death at his feet, saw the man's companion, frozen in horror.

Then he came alive, lifting the crossbow he carried.

But it was too late.

Hal dove across the five feet between them, blade first. The knife took the man just below his rib cage, and he screamed in agony.

Hal whipped the knife free, had the man by his greasy hair, and drove him face first into the muck, and held his thrashing body until the convulsions stopped.

Then he was awake, throwing up, and his body shook.

After awhile, he recovered.

The two men were dressed in heavily-patched and mended hunting garb. Both of them had crossbows, skinning knives at their waists.

Hal ignored the bodies for a moment, went around the small island. He found the men's boat, not much more than a skiff, on the other side.

Maybe the hunters were good fellows, and had come to see if the occupant of the boat was in distress.

Or maybe they thought they could steal an abandoned craft.

Or maybe word was out, and they were looking for an escaped prisoner.

It didn't matter.

He went through the boat, found, to his great pleasure, blankets tied in sleeping rolls.

And there were oars.

There was also food, loaves of bread with meat stuffed in them, and flasks with beer.

Very good.

He went back to his boat with the blankets and food, and carried the bodies to their boat.

Hal was winded by the time he finished. Not only was he out of shape, but he'd lost a lot of weight as a prisoner.

No mind. He'd gain it back once he reached Deraine.

One of the hunters was about his size, and so Hal stripped off his outer gear, took the other man's coat. He found two very heavy rocks, stuffed one in each of the hunter's clothes.

The current was pulling at that boat. Hal stabbed its hull four or five times with his fishing knife, kicked it off into the current.

Then he went back to his own boat, pushed it into the river-flow.

It caught him, and was swept away.

He looked back at the sinking skiff near the islet.

With any luck, it'd go down quickly, and the bodies would sink, and all there'd be was another mystery.

If they were found, what of it?

Hal was already a self-confessed murderer, he told his uneasy conscience.

Hal used one set of blankets to make a crude sail.

He used fishing line to make awkward locks for the oars.

Now he was very close to the ocean, tasting salt when he dabbed a finger into the water.

He heard the ocean's roar growing louder as he neared the ocean.

Hal desperately wished he had Mynta Gart with him, or even that he'd listened more to her sea stories.

But what he had, he had.

It was late afternoon, and he dreaded going out into the ocean at dark.

But the tide was at full ebb.

There was a tiny settlement at the river's mouth, and there was a speck of bright color on its beach.

The figure waved, and Hal waved back, having no idea if the person was being friendly, or trying to warn him.

The river grew choppier, tossing him about.

Hal lashed himself to a thwart with a bit of rope, began rowing hard.

Ahead was the bar, a line of white solidly across the river's mouth.

Hal's mouth was very dry, but the river had him firm, and pulled him hard toward the waves.

One caught him as it broke, and white water drenched him.

Hal ignored the water, pulled even harder.

Another wave lifted him, and his boat almost capsized.

He was caught in a current-swirl, spun, spun again, and then another wave took him high, and he could see all the way back to that tiny settlement.

He teetered at the crest, then slid down its back, and was rowing even harder.

Now the ocean had him, trying to overturn him, but the river current was still strong.

Hal, gasping for air, pulled hard at the oars, caught a crab, almost lost an oar, then recovered his stroke.

He rowed endlessly, afraid to stop, not sure whether he was safe or not.

Then exhaustion caught him, and he could do no more, collapsing over his oars.

His wind came back to him, and he looked around.

He was well clear of the river and the shore, and the swells around him were those he remembered from being at sea.

He'd made it.

Now the worst that could happen to him was drowning.

No, he thought. The damned Roche must have patrol boats out.

But the hells with it. He had two crossbows, and three knives.

He'd not be taken again.

Hal restepped the mast, watched his blanket sail as the stiff wind tried to tear it free.

But it held, and bellied out.

West, there, into the setting sun, and steer a bit north.

North for Deraine.

North for home.

13

Hal, hardly a seaman, didn't know if the weather was supposed to get worse the further he drew away from the Roche shore, but it did.

He'd been on ferries, and on dragon transports, but seldom this close to the heaving ocean.

He didn't understand it, didn't like it.

With full dark, the world closed in about his tiny boat. The night was as black as any he'd experienced. But maybe that was just as well, he thought. He didn't have to see the waves that rushed on him.

They lifted and dropped his boat, and the wind screeched like a fishwife. His mast was bending, creaking, and he thought he'd better take in some of his blanket/sail. With the sail down, the boat pitched worse than it ever had.

He remembered one of Gart's stories, about having been caught away from her coaster in a small boat when a storm hit, and she set something called a sea anchor.

Hal grudgingly tied the other set of blankets into a bundle, and lashed rope around them. He'd freeze, but he'd rather be cold than drown.

He couldn't remember whether the sea anchor was supposed to be tied to the stern or the bow, decided the stern had to be more logical.

That seemed to help a little, holding the little boat's prow into the oncoming waves.

There wasn't anything he could do, and so he secured the oars, and crept up into the bow, trying to cram as much of his body into the tiny cuddy.

It started raining, but it took awhile for him to notice it, since there seemed to be as much spray as air for him to breathe.

He felt miserable, but not that miserable.

Then he remembered the sandwiches, and dug one out, keeping it under his coat.

The meat was unfamiliar, but that didn't bother him. He inhaled the sandwich and half of one flask of beer.

The beer also tasted strange, and he wondered if it was some kind of bark beer, that he'd heard peasants made.

He hadn't had alcohol in some time, not being much at stomaching the home brew the prisoners made, and found himself a little tipsy, and singing.

Maybe it was as much being free and feeling defiant as the brew.

At least he wasn't getting sick from the boat's motion, and as soon as that thought had come, he regretted it, swallowing mightily.

But the meal stayed down.

Hal was afraid to go to sleep, but his body would have none of that, and his eyelids sank, opened, sank, and then it was gray twilight out, and he discovered he'd been right not to want to see the storm around him.

Everything was gray, except the white froth atop the monstrous waves that the wind took and whipped along the water's surface.

But at least it wasn't raining any more.

And he thought the wind was dying.

No doubt it was his damnable optimism.

But, some time later, he realized the wind *was* lowering, and the storm was passing.

He chanced putting the sail up, and caught enough of the sun glow through the clouds to get a rough idea of which way he should be sailing, again, into the choppy seas.

The wind held strong, but the waves died, and he was cutting through a gray, calm sea.

He remembered the sea anchor, and brought in the sodden blankets, spreading them across the thwarts to dry out a bit. But they were wool, and still would hold warmth, even wet.

He treated himself to half a sandwich and the rest of the first flask of beer.

Finally, Hal Kailas had a chance to take stock.

He wondered how many days' sail it would take to reach

Deraine, hadn't a clue. He knew small boats didn't sail as fast as big ones, but didn't know much more.

He also realized he itched.

Kailas felt a deal less sympathy for one of the men he'd murdered, whose coat he'd taken. The bastard had fleas.

Oh well.

It wouldn't be the first time he'd had armor-clad dandruff in this war.

Three days later, Hal had long-finished the soggily-stale sandwiches. He'd been able to nurse the beer along, since it rained daily, for which he tried to feel grateful.

It had cleared on one day enough for him to improvise a sun compass, and get an accurate reading for north.

To his considerable relief, his instinct had been true, and he had been sailing in the direction he wanted, not, as he'd feared, either in circles or back toward Roche.

Deraine was out there.

Somewhere.

Hal was awakened from his drowse by a mournful honk that brought him fully alert.

The honk could only have come from a dragon.

He sat up, and saw, about twenty yards distant, a dragon, dark and light red, bobbing in the mild seas like a cork, its wings folded.

It had been tamed – its breastplate was drilled for a saddle, and the remnants of harness dangled down across its side. Reins had also been torn away, maybe by the dragon itself?

Itself?

Herself, Hal realized.

The dragon saw Hal was alive, honked again.

Hal saw the monster had scars along one side, and the rear of one wing had been torn.

A dragon flier's mount.

The flier must have been killed, and the dragon fled the battleground.

Hal made a tentative noise, comforting.

The dragon replied equally tentatively.

Its huge tail lashed back and forth on the water's surface.

Hal reached slowly for an oar, and began to canoe-paddle toward the beast.

Froth appeared at the dragon's chest, hindquarters, as its talons back-paddled away from this unknown man.

Hal tried more soothing noises.

The dragon waited.

Hal paddled closer, and again the dragon swam away from him.

Hal cursed.

He paddled closer, very slowly.

The dragon bellowed, and its wings unfurled.

"No, dammit," Hal said. "Don't . . ."

But the dragon's wings were flailing at the air, and its talons digging into the water. It skated away from him, bounced off a wave crest, crashed through the crest of another, and was in the air, climbing toward the clouds.

Hal slumped back.

The dragon circled him once, curiously, then set a course.

Hal didn't need the compass he didn't have to tell its course.

North. Due north.

Toward Black Island and the far northern tundra.

Hal dangled one of the lines over the side, wishing he'd saved something for bait.

But it didn't seem necessary.

A fish, a large fish, Hal didn't know what sort, but it looked edible, took the hook as if it was the only edible thing in this ocean.

Hal grinned, started hauling in, hand over hand.

Then a bigger fish, almost as big as the boat, came from nowhere, and took fish, hook and line away with it.

"Son of a bitch," Hal said sincerely, and found another line.

Another fish took the hook, and Hal jerked the fish out of the water into the boat, just as that monster predator came back for seconds.

Hal sneered at the beast, then regretted it, as the huge fish, with far more teeth than any creature not a demon had a right to have, kept circling him, eyeing him as he cut the fish open, gutted it and then devoured the rest.

It appeared as if this great fish thought Hal now qualified, having kept the fish, for the monster's dinner.

Hal thought of potting it with one of his crossbows. He found it mildly funny that he knew exactly where to hit a man or dragon for a killing shot, but no idea whatsoever for a damned fish.

It was a day and a half before it gave up, having chased all other fishes away.

There was nothing Hal could do but keep on his course, and try to keep his mind busy.

He started thinking about Khiri, and his base intentions, but that didn't go very far, considering his rather malnourished condition.

Meals were better dreams, and, even though he'd never been much of an epicure, he planned enormous menus that he and Khiri would inhale, and then he would work his wiles on her, given more energy.

Then an idea came, pushing food and sex out of his mind.

He became very busy making a plan, and deciding how he would broach it to the king, and perhaps Sir Bab Cantabri might be willing to involve himself.

Hal was so busy plotting it took him almost an hour to recognize the thin dark line on the horizon as land.

He closed with the land, dropped his sail a half a mile from shore, when he realized what he was looking at was great cliffs, with never an inlet to be seen.

Hal guessed that he was somewhere on the south-eastern coast of Deraine.

Or, rather, he hoped, since that was the only part of Deraine that had steep cliffs.

That he knew about, anyway.

Otherwise, he might have been cast far into the seas, and might be about to wreck on some unknown land.

Hal guessed what he should do was bear south or north, looking for some sort of port, or, even better, encountering a friendly ship.

Then he saw a bobbing dot, about a mile away.

Very awkwardly, he managed to steer the boat in its direction.

It was another boat, smaller than his, with two men in it.

Fishermen in oilskins, working what looked like crab pots, very close to the surf line.

They saw him, waited.

Hal didn't really know what he should say.

"Ahoy," was what he settled for.

"Eee-yup," was the response.

"I need help," Hal said.

"Looks like," the other fisherman said. "You one of them Roche spies?"

"No," Hal said. "I'm an escaped prisoner."

"Eee-yup," came back. "Who's the boat belong to?"

"Nobody," Hal said. "I mean, nobody now."

The two fishermen looked at each other.

"What sort of rewards they give for prisoners?" the first asked.

"Damned if I know," the other one said.

"Bet they're not as good as for spies," the first said.

"Look," Hal tried. "Help me ashore, and I'll give you this boat. Free. And gold, when I'm able."

Both fishermen looked interested.

"Don't know about gold," the first said. "Everybody's always been promising me some of that, and nobody ever came through."

"You think we could use something like that boat?" the other asked.

"Dunno," the first said. "But spies don't give things away. They need all kinds of things for their deep, dark doings."

"Guess he might be telling the truth, then."

"Maybe so. Welcome to Deraine, mister. We'll take a claim on the boat before we take you ashore. People forget, sometimes."

14

The fishermen searched Hal, took away his weaponry. Then they pulled their nets, keeping a careful eye on Kailas, put him in their smaller boat, took it in tow, and rowed south, rounding a promontory after an hour, and entering a cove with a tiny village nestled in it.

The village had one warder, who also ran the general store and tavern.

Hal introduced himself, and the warder gaped.

"But . . . you're dead!"

"If I am," Hal said dryly, "then I'm a damned solid ghost."

"But . . . what . . . If you're the Dragonmaster, what do you want me to do?"

"Nothing," Hal said. "Especially not let anyone else know who I am."

He was about to give instructions, when one of the fishermen ostentatiously cleared his throat.

"Oh," Hal said. "First, bring me pen and paper. I've a deed to write."

The warder, still in shock, obeyed.

Hal wrote out a bill of sale, signed it, gave it to the fishermen.

"Now you've got the start of a fleet."

One of the fishermen thought things were amusing.

"If you're some kind of muckety," he told Hal in a low voice, "then you're the most important person who's come here since . . . " He had to think.

"Since that duke who got lost, whatever his name was," his partner put in. "Back when we were toddling."

"That was the man."

Hal asked them not to say anything to anyone, hoped they'd keep their word, since he'd promised to send them gold. But it didn't matter that much. If important people didn't come to this nameless village, it was unlikely to have a cell of Roche agents, either.

He asked the warder to ride to the nearest duty station and arrange for a coach to pick him up.

"Make it a prison coach," he said, thinking he was used to that. "There'll be no wonderment about a mere prisoner being transported."

The warder nodded jerkily, bustled off, utterly perplexed about the situation, and forgetting about whether Hal was who he said he was, and if he wasn't he should be secured somehow.

In fact, he left Hal with the keys to the tavern.

Kailas made himself at home. The warder was single, so there was no family to explain himself to.

He sorted through the man's wardrobe, found pants and a jerkin that weren't too impossibly large.

Behind the house was a large vat. Hal lit the stove in the kitchen, heated buckets of water from the well, and stripped naked.

He ceremoniously burned the clothes he'd worn in the warder's backyard, not much caring if there were holes in the fence around it and peepers behind every hole.

Then he bathed.

He'd been happily torturing himself staring at the man's larder, but at last could hold back no longer.

There was smoked fish, and a large ham.

There was half a loaf of bread, country butter, and Hal carved slices off the ham, sipping at a flagon of the warder's strong beer, real beer, made from grain and hops, not the Roche bark – or whatever-it-was brew.

He fried some of the ham in butter, seasoning it with herbs from the cupboard, then sat down at the table. He just stared at the meal for awhile, not remembering when he'd been able to eat so well.

Then, like a worried cat, glancing around him, as if afraid someone would take this feast from him, he set to.

Fatigue took him after that, and he found blankets, and spread them on the floor.

It took him only seconds to fall asleep.

When he awoke, many hours later, it took him some minutes to remember where he was, that he wasn't still in Castle Mulde, waking from a most elaborate dream.

He ate, slept, ate, and then the carriage came back.

With it was the warder's commander, and four guards, none of them at all sure Hal was who he said he was.

It didn't matter.

Now he was bound for Rozen and the king, and it didn't matter what anyone thought of him.

One thing was solved at their first stop: a warder who'd been discharged, wounded, remembered Hal from the Kalabas campaign, so there was no longer any question as to his identity.

The man was sworn to secrecy.

Hal asked the warder's commander to continue the pretense.

The man was puzzled.

"Why, Lord Kailas? You deserve, and you would undoubtedly get, an escort to the capital more in keeping with your fame. I know that any of the nobility still living in Deraine, who aren't abroad with our fighting forces, would give their left arm to so honor you."

"Thank you," Hal said. "But there are reasons."

The warder waited, but no explanation was forthcoming.

Hal gave him further orders: once they reached Rozen, they were to take him to the town house of Sir Thom Lowess.

"The taleteller?"

Hal nodded.

"But ... if you wish your presence to be secret, then

why . . .?" The warder broke off, realizing this question would
most likely go unanswered as well.

"Great gods in heaven," Sir Thom said. "So you weren't killed at
all."

"I was not," Hal said, his mouth full of roast. He'd been
lucky, and Sir Thom was in-country, and it was just dinner time.

"Oh, what a story, what a story," Lowess said, rubbing his
hands together. The last time he'd said it was when Lady Khiri
and Hal declared their love affair.

"My fellows will give half their pay for this, but it's mine,
mine, all mine."

"No," Hal said. "It's not all yours. At least, not yet."

Sir Thom goggled.

"I want no one – and I mean no one – to realize I've escaped
and come back to Deraine. Except for the king. And . . . where's
Lord Cantabri?"

"He's afield. Still with First Army, still battering their heads
against the heights beyond Aude."

"I want an audience with the king, as soon, and as secretively,
as possible."

"There should be no problem with that. What else?"

"Nothing. Except nobody can talk about me. This is very
important, Sir Thom."

"What about Khiri? Lady Carstares?"

Hal hesitated. He wanted to see her in the worst way.

"I can't chance it," he said. "She'll have to remain a widow for
the moment."

But Sir Thom noticed the hesitation.

"Let me see about the king," he said. "In the meantime, you
should concentrate on putting some weight on those bones of
yours."

"I can do that," Hal said. He smiled, but it wasn't much of
one. He damned his dutiful soul to several perditions, thinking
about Khiri.

Two days later, Hal was sitting in Sir Thom's library, sipping
mulled wine, finishing a letter to his land-steward, sending a
fairly astonishing amount of gold to the two fishermen. It would
be taken to the steward after Hal's plans were either denied by
the king, or granted and set in motion.

But his mind kept drifting to the map on a nearby table. He

finished the letter, sanded and sealed it, and his mind forgot about it, and leapt to his plan.

He went to the map, going over, not for the first nor the tenth time, a map.

His plan, his scheme, did have a chance, he thought, then bent over the map again, looking to see if there was anything that could go wrong.

Everything could go wrong.

But maybe, for a change, it wouldn't.

He didn't notice the soft click of the door behind him closing.

"I assume," Lady Khiri said, "there's some good reason for you avoiding me."

Hal spun, tried to say something, saw tears in her eyes, and was in her arms. He was quite amazed at the feelings – very well, use the word love – that swept him.

"I'm really glad you're still alive," Khiri said.

"So am I," Hal managed, picking her up in his arms and carrying her to a window seat. "So am I."

"I think," Hal said, "you're more beautiful naked than with clothes on."

"I will not allow you to talk to my dressmaker," Khiri said.

Hal had explained his plan, why he was staying hidden.

"And you don't think I can keep a secret."

"No," Hal said. "It's not that. It's just that—"

"That somebody might see me walking about with a great happy smile, instead of the gloom I've been broadcasting for the last several months."

"Well . . . yes."

"Hmmph. Well, for your information, I brought suitcases. Sir Thom said I'm not permitted to leave this house without your permission."

"Which you won't have," Hal said. "Not when I think about how much I love you, how much I've missed you."

"Well then," Khiri said, rolling on to her stomach, "start making up for your absence."

Hal moved over her, nuzzled her shoulder.

"A day at a time?"

"An hour," Khiri said throatily. "Perhaps even a minute."

"I guess," Khiri said, "you really do love me."

"Of course," Hal said.

"You haven't asked about your damned dragon that I so carefully stole from the army and moved to Cayre a Carstares, where he's getting fatter and stinkier by the day."

Hal thought of telling her about his dream of being Storm, which had just proved itself truer than he thought, but for some reason didn't.

It was after dinner that night, and Khiri, wearing a dressing gown, was wrapped around Hal. Rain was tapping at the window.

Sir Thom beamed at them, and poured himself another snifter of brandy.

"I suppose one should ask," he said, "when you plan on uniting your holdings, to put it as coldly as possible."

"He hasn't asked me," Khiri said.

"I've been afraid you'd turn me down," Hal said.

"Coward."

"I am that."

"Screw your courage to the sticking point, young man," Sir Thom said. "What, after all—"

His butler entered.

"A visitor, sir. Three of them, in fact." His voice was a little shaken.

Sir Thom got up.

"All right. You two upstairs, and I'll make sure there's no suspicion . . ."

His voice trailed off.

In the doorway stood King Asir.

"I dislike being out on a night like this," he growled. "But it's easier than trying to slither you into the palace without notice."

Hal, Khiri, and Sir Thom were on their knees.

"Get up, all of you," he said irritably. "Someone pour me a drink, old brandy by preference, and make sure my equerries have one, too."

The butler scampered out to obey.

The king shed his cloak, unbuckled a sword belt and slung it over a chair.

"I shall be damned glad when this war is over, and I can stop carrying real weapons about. Too damned heavy. No wonder they say that soldiers are more than thick, wanting to lug all that iron about."

He took Sir Thom's snifter and drained it. The butler came

back in with a decanter, and King Asir refilled the snifter, made no motion to return it to Lowess.

"Now," he said. "You wanted to see me?"

"I'll be upstairs," Khiri said, and was gone.

"And I'll find some business of my own," Lowess said.

"Good people," King Asir said. "They know when to vanish.

"First, my congratulations on being alive, and escaping from whatever hells the damned Roche had you mewed up in.

"Now, I assume you're ready for a good long leave before we figure out what job you'll be suited for next."

"I know what job I want, Your Highness," Hal said. "The same one I had before, and maybe now there'll be enough men for me to build the full squadron that we talked about.

"But I don't want any leave.

"That's why I made sure I came back to Rozen as secretly as I could.

"I want to put together a raiding force – maybe with Lord Cantabri as its commander – and go back to Castle Mulde.

"There's more than three hundred men and women I want to set free."

The king reacted, started to down his drink, thought better, and set it down.

"I assume you have a plan?"

"I do, sire," Hal said. "And I think it will work . . . if it's mounted quickly enough."

"Ah," the king said. "And that explains why you're being so secretive."

"Yes, sire. If the Roche find out I escaped . . . they might start taking precautions."

"Over three hundred men and women, you said," the king said thoughtfully.

"Yes, sire. And many of them are fliers. Or noblemen."

"At this point in the war," King Asir said, "I can do without nobility. But dragon fliers are another story.

"I think we'd better send for Bab Cantabri at once."

It was suddenly obvious that all of Hal's careful arguments he'd prepared on his sail for home wouldn't be needed.

He was going back to Castle Mulde.

This time with sword in hand.

15

A grim Lord Bab Cantabri arrived within the week. His bleakness lifted a bit when told of the upcoming raid, and he and Hal set to, looking for men and units.

Hal asked him how badly the battle was going.

"Worse than you can imagine," he said. "Lord Egibi doesn't seem to have any better ideas than to keep hurling his forces up those damned mountains."

Lord Egibi was Commander of the First Army.

"The problem is," Cantabri went on, "neither does anyone else.

"Those mountains we're hitting," he went on, seemingly irrelevantly, "nobody knew their names when we first attacked them, although I suppose the Roche maps called them something.

"They've got names now: Desperation Rise. Bloody Nose Hill. Slaughter Vale. Massacre Mountain."

Hal winced.

Cantabri shook his head.

"Ah me, ah me. One of these centuries the war'll be over, and we can sit on our estates, phoomphing at each other and talking about the good old days when we weren't bored orry-eyed."

"What a future you predict," Lady Khiri said, coming in with a tray of sandwiches. "It's time to feed the inner warrior."

After some debate, it'd been decided by the king that the planning headquarters for the raid would be at Sir Thom's mansion. His staff had been handpicked for their discretion, and would not talk.

Lowess and Carstares had both been told the secret. They were used as couriers to the palace, which lessened the number of uniformed messengers going back and forth.

Hal picked up a sandwich, pointed at the map.

"If we could take the—"

"Stop that," Khiri said firmly. "Meals are important. Both of you get away from that damned map, and concentrate on eating. Otherwise you'll get ulcers the size of your heads, and be worthless to anyone."

"She's right, you know," Cantabri said.

The two men went to a table, and sat down.

But Hal found his eyes creeping to the map, and he was eating faster than he should.

He caught himself, shook his head.

"I wonder if we'll ever be worthwhile as people, once the war's over?"

Cantabri glanced to make sure Khiri had left the room.

"Don't worry about it," he said. "Neither of us are likely to make it that far."

Hal shivered a bit, remembering Saslic's words, "There won't *be* any after the war for a dragon flier."

"The most important thing," Hal said, "is speed. If we fart around, and piecemeal our troops together, and then they're inspected, and every hinkty little lord and lady gets to visit our camp, we might as well let the prisoners in Camp Mulde rot, because we'll be on a suicide mission.

"Not to mention the godsdamned Roche could well do something nasty, like massacre everyone in the castle before we take it, if they hear about the raid."

There were only two men in the room – Cantabri and the king.

"I must say," King Asir said, "I'm not used to being preached at."

"I'm sorry, Your Majesty," Hal said.

"No, no," Asir said, and his voice was tired. "I said once, a long time ago, that people like you are sometimes uncomfortable to be around.

"You're living up to your reputation."

Hal desperately wanted to bring his own First Squadron back from the front for the raid, but knew that could well be a red flag to the enemy.

Instead, a rather battered pair of flights from Second Army, due for a rest, were rotated back to Paestum, and two freshly-trained green flights went back in their place.

Cantabri pulled a battalion here and there until there were three waiting in a camp west of Paestum for orders.

That should have made 1500 men. But that would've been in peacetime. There were only a few more than 700 infantry for the raid.

"Wouldn't it be nice," Hal said, "to have a special unit, a Raiding Squadron call it, on standby for things like this?"

"Maybe," Cantabri snorted. "If they had a good commander, who had enough clout to keep them from being thrown into the line any time some lord wanted reinforcements or line troops. And if . . . higher-ranks . . . realized what they had, and kept them from being wasted."

Hal knew Lord Bab meant the king.

"And there'll still be the drawback . . . these elite men might have gotten higher rank, and medals, and accomplished more, staying in their base formations.

"Not to mention things like morale," he went on. "What do you think the average infantryman, or cavalryman, is going to think of himself and his own unit when he keeps hearing of the King's Own Specially Dangerous Guards, or whatever they'd be called?"

"Still," Hal said, and let the conversation drop.

Maybe Cantabri was right. And maybe all that Hal wanted was first line, rested troops, instead of the tired warriors he was getting.

And on the other hand, he also might want solid gold toenails, and they weren't forthcoming either.

"You know, Lord Hal," Limingo the wizard said, "there are other magicians in the king's service who can be volunteered for your dirty deeds, many of whom are no doubt better than I am."

Hal grinned. At least in the field of magic he was getting the best.

"It's just that you're like an old shoe," he said. "You get more comfortable the more I'm around you."

"Oh, thanks ever so for the compliment," Limingo said. "I wish I knew a spell that would give warts."

"No you don't," Khiri said. "For I'd put sand in your lubricant."

Limingo looked shocked.

"Well, I never. Well, hardly ever, anyway.

"And so to business," he went on. "I assume you want the usual spells of confusion, multiplication of forces, and such."

"I do," Hal said. "And I'll want a big spell . . . It's not just the folks in the castle who should be confused, but the people in the area around aren't exactly well-disposed."

"Let me consider," Limingo said. "Perhaps there's something better I can come up with for them."

*

"Do you remember," Khiri asked, "back a couple of weeks or so, when the king came in on us, to our great surprise?"

They were lying in bed, spooned together.

"I do well."

"Do you remember what we were discussing when he did?"

"Uh . . . yes. Marriage."

"Sir Thom probably thinks it's very romantic that – what I hope, at least – a marriage proposal was interrupted by royalty. Or was I mistaken about your intent?"

"Well . . . I've never been married," Hal said.

"Neither have I, dummy."

"Well, then, would you like to try it?"

"Gods," Khiri said. "How romantic."

"I'm new at this," Hal tried to explain.

"You're supposed to be on your knees, looking deep in my eyes, clasping my hands in yours and vowing eternal devotion," Khiri said.

"Oh," Hal said. "But that floor's cold."

Khiri didn't say anything.

"All right," Hal said, and got out from under the covers. "I'll do it the way I'm supposed to."

"That's far enough," Khiri said. "I just wanted to see if you'd do me right sooner or later."

Hal gratefully dropped back down into bed, and pulled the heavy comforter over them.

There was silence for a bit, then:

"Well?" Hal asked.

"Well what?"

"Godsdammit, do you want to marry me?"

"Of course," Khiri said, her voice sounding a bit choked. "I thought you'd know."

"I don't know anything."

"You'll make a wonderful husband, then," she said. "Easy to train."

"So when do you want to do it?"

"If it's marriage, then after you get back from playing hero. And then you'll take some leave, and we'll finally do the Grand Tour of your estates.

"But if you're thinking of some other sort of it . . ." She rolled over on to her back.

"Seize the moment, as they say."

*

Ships were assembled, including the ex-horse transport *Galgorm Adventurer*, the wallowing tub that had been converted to a dragon carrier.

The story around Paestum was that the two dragon flights were being taken back to Deraine, for rebuilding and further training.

Certainly no one thought they'd be thrown back into combat.

Much the same story was passed around about the three battalions of battered infantry, who were loaded on common ferries, and transported across the Chicor Straits.

But they didn't land in any of the normal ports, but were taken north to a patch of bare ground, near an abandoned village, where nothing waited but rows of tents, fresh uniforms and supplies.

The wiser ones moaned when they saw the twenty new warships anchored, waiting for them.

The dragons were fed, but not offloaded from the *Adventurer*. Their fliers went ashore, and waited.

The soldiers were landed, escorted to their assigned tents. Enormous vats of hot water and soap waited for them, and, once they were bathed, shaved, and clean, they were formed up in a large open area.

It was an overcast day, almost winter, and a chill wind was blowing off the sea.

Most of the troops knew the two men waiting for them on a crude stand, and now all of them knew they were not coming home for a rest.

They were called to attention, then given "at ease."

Cantabri walked forward. He needed no magical implements for his voice to carry to the rear ranks.

"Good afternoon. I assume you know who I am.

"I'm the one – and this other man, here, the Dragonmaster – who's been lying to you.

"Not to your faces, but it might as well have been."

There was a ripple, half astonishment, half amusement, from the troops. Generals didn't usually talk to common swordsmen like this.

"We pulled you out of the lines, and let you think you were due home leave.

"You'll get it . . . after one job."

There was an incoherent shout from the ranks. Outraged warrants moved to find the man, and have him skinned. Cantabri held up his hand.

"No. He's right to be doubtful.

"Lord knows people like me've been lying to him, either directly or otherwise, since the war started.

"So I won't add to the bullshit.

"Here's what we're going to do:

"There's a Roche prison somewhere behind their lines.

"Lord Kailas was a prisoner there until six weeks ago. Then he made his escape, swearing to go back and rescue the other prisoners.

"There's at least three hundred of them, some who've been caged up since the war started.

"We're going to set them free.

"Then you'll get your leave . . . and have a story to tell your children's children."

He stopped. There was silence, except for a forlorn dragon bleat from the *Adventurer*, and the whisper of the wind.

A soldier stepped out of ranks.

"What are our chances?"

Cantabri nodded to Hal, who came forward.

"If the Roche haven't magicked this secret out, fairly good," Hal said. "Your warrants and officers will be given everything we know, when you board ship again, and you can judge for yourselves."

"I've been in too many fights where everything was a secret," the soldier shouted. "And then the godsdamned Roche were there, waiting for us."

Hal nodded.

"I have, too.

"But think about this. If everything does go wrong," and his voice dropped, so that the soldiers had to lean forward to hear his words, "is there a better reason to die than rescuing your brothers?"

16

Eighteen dragons dove out of a thick fogbank on Castle Mulde. Each was heavy-burdened with three passengers, two unarmored infantrymen and a flier, sometimes a woman.

Hal Kailas was at the head of the ragged vee formation.

It was false dawn, and the Roche guards on the walls goggled at this attack from nowhere.

They goggled, and then died as the fliers pincushioned them with crossbow bolts.

Hal wished he'd had some of Joh Kious's repeating crossbows, but there was no time to have them made, and so the fliers were armed with everything from standard crossbows to short bows.

Hal forced his dragon down, toward an outer battlement. The dragon shied, and he cursed, and kicked it.

It grudgingly grabbed an allure, and the two soldiers behind Kailas leapt on to the wall walk.

Around Castle Mulde, other dragons were being forced to land long enough for their passengers to jump off, or even balk with their wings flared and give the archers time to slide off.

Then the dragons, like gigantic, multi-colored crows, dropped down toward the river, and vanished into the fog.

The thirty-six volunteers held to the heights as the alarm was shouted, and half-awake guards stumbled out, buckling on armor.

One of the volunteers was one of Limingo's assistants, who paid no attention to the battle, but busied himself casting a spell.

Most of the Roche warders died before they could fight back.

The prisoners were coming awake, banging at their cell doors.

Then the wizard's spell worked, just as Limingo had guaranteed it to, and doors banged open, and the prisoners streamed out.

In his turret, Ungava screeched disbelief, and tried to cast a counterspell to lock the cells up again.

Then, below, on the river, twenty warships appeared, backing sail, and dropping anchor.

Two were bold enough to close on the tiny jetty, and Derainian soldiers poured off.

It was just a week since the small armada had set sail from Deraine.

The soldiers had been transferred from the secret landing to the warships, and the ships set sail north by north-east, arcing up into the northern sea before turning south for the Zante River.

No one had been allowed to lollygag about.

Hal spent the time taking his two under-manned and -dragoned flights off from the *Adventurer*, teaching them to fly formation with each other, trying to get the two flights to fly a common track, and then, hardest, making the dragons land within a small space, the barge the *Adventurer* towed alongside, touching their talons to the wood, then scrabbling back into the sky.

He also sent them off in foul weather, getting them used to the idea of flying when it was somewhat blind out, using homing spells devised by Limingo, and careful compass reading.

Volunteers were called for, with only a handful standing forth until Cantabri, in some disgust, promised gold and decorations.

"Damned sure wouldn't have had to beg for men back when the war started," he snarled to Hal.

"No," Hal said. "But all those eager young bodies are dead now. Dead, crippled or maybe a few learned better."

Cantabri gave Hal a dirty look.

"Are you sure you're a soldier?"

"I'm damned sure I'm not one," Hal said. "At least, if that means marking time and saying yessir, nossir to every idiot idea that comes along. *Lord* Bab."

Cantabri had the grace to grin ruefully.

These "volunteers" became dragon riders, such as Hal had used years ago in the battles around Bedarisi, armed with bows or crossbows.

The *Adventurer*'s barge became a target range on clear days, at least until one particularly inept bowman put an arrow in the *Adventurer*'s helmsman's leg. After that, empty wine barrels were cast loose for targets.

The assault troops were also trained as thoroughly as it was possible to do aboard ship – being rousted around the decks by their warrants, singing, exercising to exhaustion.

They'd found a map of the Zante River mouth in the royal archives, used that to make models of the area.

Hal had sketched, growling at his inability as an artist, Castle Mulde. From that, Limingo and three assistants had made five scale models of the castle, which Hal critiqued over and over, and new models were spellcast. Then they were taken from ship to ship, and every soldier had to memorize his individual and group's mission.

"This," Hal said, "is the way soldiers should fight, not charging blindly ahead at some hilltop or other."

"Here's your Special Raiding Squadron again," Cantabri said. "Which is starting to sound like a good idea. I assume you'd like to be put in charge of it."

"Not a chance," Kailas said. "I leave it for one of nature's noblemen – you, for instance – while I flit about above the clouds without a care."

Cantabri growled, and went looking for an erring junior officer to savage.

Certain soldiers, considered by their officers to be more intelligent than the common spear-carriers, were given special training in the handling of prisoners, and then, one wintry day, the coastline of Roche was in sight.

It was too rough for fishermen, which was a blessing for Deraine.

A small pinnace was sent into the river's mouth, to track the changes of the tide.

Three days later, just as the tide began to flood, the ships sailed into the mouth of the Zante.

As they did, Limingo's fog bank roiled up from the surface of the sea, and moved inland.

Limingo had considered his other spells, including the standard fear and confusion incantations. But he decided not to use these, since any combat soldier might recognize the castings, and assume there was an attack in the offing, no matter how far behind the lines the Zante River was.

Instead, he cast a spell of general malaise: the weather was foul, so of course animals wouldn't be out, and, for some unknown reason, the fish probably wouldn't be biting.

It would be exhausting, he told Hal, because it was a piece of "soft" magic, relying on the magicians' forced moods to "color" the spell, and repetitive chanting rather than herbs or forbidden tongues to give it strength.

Hal, remembering his own travails in a tiny boat, admired the skills of the warships' captains and master's mates, especially in the fog, as the ships went upriver in short tacks.

They didn't anchor that night, but pressed on, and, just when the sky began to lighten in a gray sort of way, Hal took his dragons and riders aloft.

He wished he was riding Storm, instead of the rather battered, sour monster he was aboard, whose name he kept forgetting, but that, like bringing the First Squadron up, was a chance he couldn't have taken.

The two dragon flights followed the river to the heights that marked Castle Mulde, struck hard, dropped off the troops, then flew back to the *Adventurer*, landing and taking off in rapid succession. When a dragon landed, a bundle of swords was slung over his carapace, and the monster was back in the air.

There was a collision, dragons crashing into each other just above the barge, spitting, striking with their snaky necks, and rolling into the river.

But they recovered, splashing about angrily, and neither rider drowned. After the rest of the flights were gone, they were derricked aboard the *Adventurer*, and sent off again.

Again, the dragons came on the castle, and dove low, letting the bundled weapons thud down into the courtyard.

Even a hundred feet in the air, Hal could hear the shouts of glee as the prisoners armed themselves.

An arrow screeked off his dragon's carapace, barely missing him, and he quit mooning about, and climbed for altitude.

A handful of dragon volunteers fought their way down to the courtyard, armed prisoners joining the fray, and they made the main gate.

Half of them were down, and there was a hacking melee around the gate tower, then, with a great crash, the gate slammed open.

There were Roche guards on the wall walks, firing down at the Derainian soldiers making their way up the winding track to the main gate.

Hal blasted a command on his trumpet, and his dragon fliers sent their mounts spiraling down, shooting as they went.

They weren't very accurate, but the very idea of being shot at from the skies sent many of the guards pelting for the stairs and cover.

There were Derainian troops running hard, through the gate, into the castle, and boats were landing reinforcements.

That was enough for Hal.

He sent his dragon skittering down toward a wall walk, sliding out of his saddle as the beast closed on the castle.

It was against his orders, but Hal cared not a whit.

He jumped, landed hard, rolled, and his dragon flapped upward, to go wherever he wished.

Hal had a crossbow in hand, and a man was running toward him, waving a spear.

Hal sent the bolt into the man's abdomen. He screamed, clutched himself, fell. Hal tossed the crossbow away, drew sword and dagger, found a stairway, went down into the battle.

He saw the diminutive Wolda, screaming joyfully at the top of his lungs as he hammered Ungava's corpse with a balk of wood, ran on.

He went up other stairs, into the heart of the castle. Here was a knot of guards, holding the doorway to the central keep.

Then arrows whistled, and the way was clear as the Roche fell.

Hal was the first through the door, went down a familiar corridor, and smashed into a closing door.

There were two men in the room – one of the guard warrants, and Baron Patiala.

The warrant had a halberd, swung it at Hal.

Kailas had no time for such nonsense, lopped the halberd's head off, and smashed the warrant's face in with the butt of his dagger.

Patiala had an old-fashioned broadsword out, and, recognizing Kailas with a start, jumped toward him, swinging the blade.

Hal parried, struck back, missed.

Neither man spoke, intent on the other' s death.

Patiala lunged, and Hal kicked him in the forearm.

The Roche shouted in pain, and the sword spun away.

Hal slashed the man' s throat open with his dagger, let him fall.

That was one payment made.

He heard shouting, went back into the corridor, saw a man in an ornate uniform running.

An archer slammed Hal out of the way, and sent a long shaft into the running man's back.

He screamed, contorted, went down, and rolled over.

Hal went to him, and saw, with near infinite glee, it was Sir Suiyan Tutuila, the "Respecter of Prisoners," and Hal's would-be hangman. He must've chosen to visit Mulde at precisely the wrong time.

Now the screaming and shouting was dying away. Guards were either surrendering, the surrender sometimes accepted, lying in their blood, or scrambling down the rocky sides of the island and diving into the water.

Hal doubted if the local hunters would have any objection to them as prey, even if there wasn't a bounty.

Hal saw a jovial Treffry, a bloodstained sword in hand. Flanking him was Sir Alt Hofei, beaming as if it were his birthday.

Warrants and officers were shouting for order, and slowly the blood rage died.

Some of the prisoners were ecstatic, others were in complete shock.

This had been allowed for.

The trained men escorted them out of the castle, not listening to their pleas to go back to their cells for anything, not letting them retreat into numbness.

Within two hours, the castle was empty. Even the madmen were taken, with infinite care and pity, to boats, secured against themselves and taken to the warships.

The raiders returned to their ships.

They'd lost only thirty men killed, twice that wounded, a more than acceptable price.

Castle Mulde's gates hung open, ripe for the looting.

Carrion kites were already circling overhead, under the dragons' constantly circling umbrella.

One of the riders swooped low, where Hal had been signalling from the boat landing.

Hal pulled himself up behind the rider, and the dragon's wings beat, beat, and they were climbing as the sorcerous fog lifted.

"What happened, sir? Did your dragon get hit?"

"I had some business to take care of," Hal said.

He looked back at the gray stone nightmare that had been his prison, wishing that stone could be burnt.

Then he forgot about Castle Mulde, and started considering what would be the most spectacular wedding in the history of Deraine.

17

It had begun snowing gently just after dawn. But the weather was warm, and so the snow melted as it struck the ground.

The king had proclaimed the wedding day a royal holiday, and cheery crowds packed the streets along the route the broadsheets had announced.

They were held back from the great square the great temple stood in by dress-uniformed cavalry.

Bands and street performers entertained the throng as they waited.

A keen-eyed little girl saw it first – a dot, high in the sky, spiraling down toward the square.

She squealed, and everyone looked up.

Hal Kailas brought his dragon, Storm, down in a glide. Its claws skittered on the cobblestones, and it was down. Before Hal had returned from the raid, it had been arranged by Khiri to bring Storm from her castle to Rozen.

He was most unhappy until he saw Hal, then tried to larrup him with his great tongue.

Storm's breath hadn't improved in his convalescence, but Hal was quite used to the various odors dragons emitted by now, and hoped that Storm felt the same about human smells.

Kailas slid down from Storm, and a man ran out and took the dragon's reins.

Hal wore a white tunic, with his decorations on a dark blue sash. Blue breeches, bloused in black thigh boots, complemented the sash, as did his gloves. He wore the red forage cap of the dragon fliers.

Kailas was armed, not with a ceremonial sword, but with the long, single-edged, most functional dragon-fliers knife at his waist.

He was cheered by the crowds as he waited, standing not quite at ease, not quite at attention.

There was more cheering, coming toward the square like a wave, and a carriage, drawn by eight matching white horses, appeared.

Hal had been warned by Sir Thom to expect surprises, but not this.

The carriage was the royal carriage, an old-fashioned box on iron springing, all red and gold leaf.

It drew up in front of the temple, and King Asir got out.

The crowd gasped, and went on its knees, as did Hal.

Asir was a rather remote king, especially since the war had started, and so most of the throng had never seen him.

He looked around in approval, and motioned the crowd back to its feet.

They slowly got up as he handed Lady Khiri Carstares out of the carriage.

She was utterly gorgeous.

Her close-fitting wedding gown was pewter satin, with a

lace bodice. Tiny gems, given a spell, flashed in many colors on the bodice and in her long, dark hair. She wore a short lace jacket over the gown.

Hal thought he'd never loved her more.

She grinned at him, and the king took her arm, and led her up the steps. The train of her gown had evidently been ensorcelled, for it waved as she walked, a bit like a dragon tail.

Hal thought this was a bit much, but didn't say anything.

The square was a boil of cheering as he followed Khiri and the king up the broad flight of stairs into the temple.

Music swelled out of the huge doors.

The crowd tried to push forward, but was held back.

The temple was quite packed. Every nobleman and woman not off fighting had been wrangling for an invitation for weeks to this, certainly *the* social event of the year.

Khiri and the king, flanked by a gaggle of bridesmaids, were moving slowly up the aisle toward the altar.

Hal was met by Lord Bab and Sir Thom.

"Since your lady is an orphan, the king thought it might be appropriate for him to present the bride," Sir Thom whispered.

Hal bobbed his head.

It wasn't as if anyone would gainsay the monarch.

Lord Bab nudged Hal with his elbow, and the three of them started up the aisle, as the music soared around them.

In the third aisle from the front were Hal's parents, Faadi and Lees.

Hal hadn't planned on inviting them, and Khiri had torn into him like a drill field serjeant, asking if he didn't love them . . . Well, yes, of course he did, but he really hadn't gone to see them in the hated tiny northern village of Caerly, even after the army had given him enough rank so he had the freedom to consider it. And why not? Hal wasn't sure. He'd always sent them money, and, after the king had ennobled him, and given him estates, he'd written them, asking if they would accept a house on his property. He'd wondered why he felt a bit relieved when they wrote back, saying they'd prefer to stay in Caerly minding the tavern they'd always had. Hal had immediately bought the building the tavern was in, and deeded it to them.

Why he felt a bit uncomfortable thinking about them, he could not figure. Perhaps, the thought came once, he felt he'd failed them somehow in getting involved in the brawl that had forced him to run away. Or . . . or perhaps something else.

He didn't know.

But he did feel that he'd done right in obeying Khiri, and sending them the invitation to the wedding, as well as dispatching a carriage and outriders to bring them to Rozen.

He shut off that line of thought, concentrating on Khiri, waiting for him.

The king nodded to Hal, then, quite against protocol, left Khiri and went up to the altar. The high priest behind it raised an eyebrow, but it was, again, certainly the king's right to do this.

"Please stand," the king said, and all obeyed.

"I wish to invoke the blessings of the gods on the man and woman about to be joined in matrimony, and that their union be long and fruitful.

"But beyond this, I request the blessings of the gods on our war efforts. Some think that it is not right to call to the gods when the cause is bloody.

"But I deny this, for our cause is for freedom, and against tyranny.

"Our people, and the men and women of Sagene, have bled too long in this nightmare, and I require the gods to see the justice of our fight, and to give us their aid.

"I ask this in the name of the people of Deraine."

Hal noticed that the king, unlike the others in the temple, didn't bow his head when he prayed, but stared up, as if demanding what was rightfully his from equals.

He wondered, wryly, not only if there were any gods, which wasn't the first time he'd had the thought, but if the priests of Roche made similar prayers, and if Queen Norcia also laid her demands on the heavens.

He decided that if he were a god, he'd have done with humanity, at least until the slaughter ended.

Then he wondered why his mind was coming up with such cynicisms on a day like this.

The king stood aside, and the priest began the ceremony.

Hal's mind went blank, and he lost track of the words.

Khiri kicked him in the shins, and he realized he'd been asked the question.

"Yes," he said, as memorized, "I, Hal Kailas, Lord Kailas of Kalabas, welcome pairing in holy wedlock with this woman, Lady Khiri Carstares."

The question was asked of Khiri, who suppressed a giggle, and agreed.

Hal wondered why women always seemed to be able to handle things like this better then men.

Then, hearing snuffling, he wondered why women also seemed impelled to cry at weddings.

He withdrew the thought, realizing it was Sir Thom Lowess leaking the tears.

"You are as one," the priest said, and Hal kissed Khiri.

She was very chaste, and kept her lips closed.

They bowed to the priest, to the king, then turned and bowed to the congregation.

Hal's mother was crying . . . as was his father.

Local lad makes good, he thought, keeping a pleasant smile on his face as Khiri had told him to.

He realized, very suddenly, why he was bearing such cynical thoughts. He was scared silly at the idea of getting married and, more immediately, at being in the middle of all this ceremony which he felt so very insecure in.

He would never make a courtier.

But the pair made it back down the aisle, and then outside, where a real surprise waited.

Since this was sort of a military ceremony, he'd half expected something like crossed sabers to walk under, or something.

Something turned out to be six dragons drawn up, three on either side of the temple steps. Hal had no idea how the hells they'd been maneuvered into position without him hearing it from inside.

But there they were, heads snaking back and forth, fangs occasionally bared. They clearly didn't like being in the middle of this city, and surrounded by people.

Then Hal recognized the riders:

Farren Mariah, Myna Gart, and Sir Loren Damien sat the closest three. Behind them were Cabet, Richia, Pisidia, his flight commanders.

Hal had a moment's wonder at who was running the squadron, realized that was belittling.

Khiri was goggling at the huge beasts as they walked under the moving necks.

It was that moment that caught Hal, and made him start crying. He fought the tears back, tried to look properly martial.

On the other side of the dragon-row waited the royal carriage, and, nearby, Storm.

Hal and Khiri got in the carriage.

Storm blatted disappointment. Evidently he thought he should be the honeymoon transport.

The carriage horses, restive at being around dragons, were held in control by footmen, then led away until the driver could take firm control.

As the carriage moved out of the square, there was a commotion behind him.

Hal craned to see what it was, but Khiri jabbed him in the ribs.

"Try to look noble, milord," she said.

Hal obeyed, putting that pleasant smile back on, and moving his hand back and forth, as they moved down the packed streets toward the royal palace, where the wedding celebration would be.

He thought it was snowing harder, realized there were flower petals falling from the sky, coming from nowhere.

That would be Limingo's wedding present.

The crowd's roar washed over them.

Hal leaned over for a kiss, got a return peck.

"That's the best you can manage?" he said.

"Behave yourself," Khiri said.

Hal's grin changed to an evil one.

"I am thinking of you, lying on a bed," he whispered. "You're naked, and your hands are tied with a silk scarf to the bedstead, and your legs are apart—"

"Stop that," Khiri hissed.

Hal didn't.

By the time they reached the gates of the palace, there was a fine bead of sweat on Khiri's brow.

"And you said you had no talent as a taleteller," she whispered.

"At the clean stuff, none," Hal agreed, then leaned close and put his tongue in her ear.

"I said behave yourself," Khiri said. "And if you go and get yourself drunk like my father did at his wedding, after making all these cheap promises, I swear you'll be a capon before dawn."

"I promise to be good," Hal said.

The king made the opening toast, to the couple.

Hal, making the royal toast in return, barely sipped the wine.

Others were not so decorous.

The members of Hal's squadron in attendance had evidently

sworn an oath that Kailas was not to be permitted to walk to the marriage bed, but would have to be carried.

But Hal evaded their efforts.

He'd slipped a gold coin to one servitor, and told him to pour him nothing but charged water, no matter what he or others asked for.

Before things got too drunk, he made a point of introducing his parents to the king, who chatted with Faadi and Lees until they lost a bit of their awe.

"I'll never forget this," Lees said to Hal.

"I hope not," Hal said. "I only plan on doing this once."

"Good," Faadi said. "I made the same promise."

Lees glowed, and hugged her husband.

Then they were swept away in the throng.

Farren Mariah was there, holding out a glass.

Hal took it, pretended to sip it, put it behind him on a table.

"What," he asked, to disguise his duplicity, "was all the excitement about when we were leaving the Square?"

"Aarh, it was your dragon," Farren said.

"Is he all right?"

"*He's* fine," Farren said. "He saw some old fat sort with too many jewels on her dress, and didn't like her on sight, I guess. She had some little white dog in her arms who kept yapping at Storm."

"What happened?" Hal asked.

"Nothing to worry about," Farren said. "The woman's healthy. Storm just ate her dog, was all."

Hal let himself be dragged away by Lord Bab, who wanted to drink his health.

Kailas circulated around the huge room, only sipping at his glass.

After an hour or so, he found Khiri, and jerked his head toward the stairs.

She looked momentarily disappointed, then started making her apologies.

"Were you a good boy?" Khiri said, then hiccuped.

They were in the apartment the king had given them for the night.

"I was . . . and am," Hal said.

"I wasn't," she said, looking not a bit ashamed. "I thought you might be interested in a bad girl tonight.

"Not that it matters," she went on. "All I have to do is lie here . . . if you'll give me a hand with this dress.

"And you'll find a scarf in the top drawer of my trunk . . . the biggest one.

"This bedpost looks strong enough.

"Just take off that damned uniform first. I've got enough creases from dancing with enough generals with their damned medals."

The first half of their honeymoon was spent touring Hal's estates, the first chance he had to travel their vastness. The people in the villages greeted him with a bit of caution to their exuberance.

But Hal made no mistakes, no missteps.

By the time the pair left for Khiri's own holdings, the people had decided Hal was worthy of their fealty.

They were especially taken that the Dragonmaster had brought Storm.

Hal had asked Farren Mariah about Sweetie, the dragon who'd dumped him into captivity, had been told the dragon never came back to the base. Hal knew better than to think dragons could have guilty consciences, hoped mildly that Sweetie had gone back to the little girl who'd supposedly raised her.

He rode Storm daily, and even enticed Khiri aloft once or twice, when the winter winds died, and it was calm.

She swore she enjoyed it, but Kailas wasn't sure she wasn't just being in love.

In the west, on Khiri's lands, Hal had already made his name, and the time there was unrestrained joy.

One thing that happened, Kailas would always remember.

Dressed warmly, they were on the winter beach below Cayre a Carstares, Khiri's great castle on a promontory. Chunks of ice were being washed ashore by the tide, and it was a bleak day, the sort of day Hal loved.

Hal saw, not more than half a league to sea, four tented shapes – dragons, their wings over their heads.

They were being carried north-north-east by the currents.

"One of these days," Hal said, "I'd like to travel west, and see what the dragons are fleeing."

Khiri shivered.

"I suppose I'll have to go with you," she said. "And keep you from the clutches of the princesses of those lands."

Hal watched them, until they were out of sight, dimly aware that he'd made a promise to someone . . . himself, perhaps?

Their time together ended, and now Hal had to make his squadron into the mailed fist he'd dreamed of.

18

Khiri had wanted to come back to Rozen with Hal, but he'd asked her forgiveness, and said that he would be too busy to give her any attention, let alone the amount she deserved.

She sniffed, complimented him on getting a bit more politic, stayed at the castle.

Hal returned to Sir Thom's, and was immediately just as busy as he thought he'd be.

He'd requested Farren Mariah and Mynta Gart to stay on when the other dragon fliers returned to the squadron, which the king had ordered withdrawn from the lines until Hal returned to duty.

His dream of a fully-manned unit, made up of the best fliers, had been approved by the king more than two years earlier. But shortages in both men and dragons, plus the devouring offensive east of Paestum, had prevented him bringing the dream alive.

Now Hal had enough of equivocating, and used every bit of clout he had with the king to obtain one weapon.

It was a parchment scroll, in Asir's own hand, ordering that the bearer, Lord Kailas, be given anything he requested, or face royal displeasure or worse.

That was a start.

Hal, sadly familiar with the ways of the army, knew there would still be many who'd find a way around the order, never quite refusing cooperation, but never giving it, either.

The second weapon was a tale for the broadsheets, carefully crafted by Sir Thom.

It announced that Lord Kailas of Kalabas, the Dragonmaster, was building a super squadron, intended to take on anything the Roche could put in the air, and that this would be the spearhead for the inevitable spring offensive.

Volunteers were being accepted immediately.

The trick, Hal told Sir Thom, was that he wanted to attract the best, but without slighting other fliers who weren't good enough, or, Hal said grimly, "without enough of the killer in them."

Also, other flights couldn't be made to feel inferior. Morale was low enough as the endless war dragged on.

Hal's plan was simple – he would fly south, calling on every Deraine dragon flight. He knew commanders would try to shuffle their worst and slackest fliers on him, in the manner of every army formation in history. But he knew enough names, and fancied himself a good enough judge of fliers, if not necessarily men and women, to bring only the best back with him.

One thing he had to take care of in Rozen was tracking down Goang, the prisoner who'd built a glider and tried to escape Castle Mulde.

He found him after some effort – he was a civilian, Lord Callo Goang. He'd been studying the chants of certain Roche hill tribes when the war caught him up. The Goangs were a famous family in Deraine, so naturally he became a hostage in Castle Mulde, where he made four unsuccessful escapes.

He was the darling of his family, who tried their best to keep him safe from the batterings of the world.

"I don't understand, Lord Kailas, just why you want me to join your squadron, although of course I'm more than flattered."

"You don't think like the rest of us," Hal said.

"Beg pardon?"

"A castle full of fliers, yet you're the only one who studied birds and tried to fly out."

"It seemed quite obvious to me."

"Exactly."

"I certainly had no interest in the war, but I must say I have developed a certain dislike, even before the fighting started, for the bullying ways of the Roche. I do not think the world would miss the absence of their form of government at all.

"Besides, until I'm able to travel the hills of Roche freely, my studies are at a halt."

"Good. I'll give you the rank of lieutenant, at first," Hal said. "And the minute the war ends, you'll return to civilian status."

His family was horrified that Kailas was putting their jewel in harm's way, and Hal swore he had no intention of letting anyone harm him.

Goang settled the matter by saying he was joining, and that was that.

Hal felt a bit like a kidnapper, taking Goang from the heart of his family. The man left burdened with packages, warm clothes, advice and money.

It was very different, calling on Mav Dessau's father, Baron Dessau. The student of architecture and magic had survived the raid, but just after returning to Deraine had fallen ill, and died within a week.

Hal, as he'd promised Mav, called on his father, a bluff, boisterous country man. He didn't seem much interested in Hal's account of his son's help, nor of how he clearly looked up to his father.

The man offered Hal a drink, then said, "Well, I suppose I'm glad you came to call, Dragonmaster. But I'm sure you'll have to admit that Mav's help was purely accidental. You could hardly call him worthy of soldiering, now could you?"

Hal set the untouched drink down, looked coldly at Dessau, and said, "Baron, you may be a big supporter of the king, but I'm sure you will have to admit you're more than a bit of a shithead, and damned unworthy of having a son like Mav."

Dessau goggled. Clearly no one had ever, or not within memory, had the temerity to call him that.

He glared at Hal, considerably smaller than he was, and reached for a coach whip hanging on the wall.

Then he noted Hal's hand was on his dagger, the catch of the sheath unsnapped, thought better of doing anything, and stamped off.

Hal let himself out, rode away, trying to think that he'd somehow revenged Mav, but knew the dead could never be avenged.

Hal was summoned for a final audience with the king, who gave him only one instruction: that he was to visit all Sagene dragon flights as well as those of Deraine.

Asir had already gotten permission from Sagene's Council of Barons for such an irregularity.

"And," he added, "be sure to pick more than a token number of Sagene. You, by the way, will be flying a dual banner of both countries' standards when you take the field."

Hal was starting to realize there was a great deal more to high command than merely bashing the enemy.

He picked up his cap, clapped a hand to his chest, was about to back out of the royal presence, when the king held up a hand.

"One other thing," Asir said. "I know Baron Dessau is a shithead. In fact, I'd most likely call him worse names. But to myself.

"That's all."

Hal found a frizzy-bearded man with a sad face waiting at Sir Thom's.

It was Garadice, chief dragon trainer, who'd withdrawn to a secret base with some fifty black dragons, gathered in the raid on Black Island. His son, Rai, had trained and flown with Hal and had been killed in the siege of Aude.

"I have a small present for you," Garadice said. He attempted a smile, failed. Hal wondered if he'd ever smile again. "The rest of the army will think me a villain, and you a conniver who only succeeds because you're the king's favorite."

"A small present can do that much damage?"

"Well, perhaps it isn't that small."

Hall waited.

"I have some forty-six trained black dragons, which I have been instructed to provide for your new squadron."

Hal whistled, then asked, "How trained are they?"

Garadice chose his words carefully.

"I don't think I'd walk up to one on a dark night and shout Boh, and I'd make sure they're well fed at all times . . . but other than that, as trained as any dragon by a show-flier before the war."

"Good," Hal said. "Very good. Now we might have something to really shake *Ky* Yasin in his boots."

"There will be more in the offing," Garadice said. "We've had some luck setting out trapping ships like the *Adventurer*, keeping well south of Black Island, putting out lures, and have snared some twenty or so kits, almost yearlings.

"Some, interestingly enough, come from the west, and are a bit war-torn, even though, as far as I can tell, they've never seen man or his wars.

"It makes me wonder what the dragons coming west are fleeing. But that's for another time, when there's peace.

"With several wizards, I'm working with them and hope to have them in shape by the time they're a year older, perhaps less."

Another man sought Hal out, just as he was completing final packing for his trip across the Straits to Paestum, to start his quest.

The man limped up to Sir Thom's mansion, knocked on the door, announced himself, and was taken immediately to Hal.

"I don't suppose you might have room for a crippled flier," Sir Alt Hofei asked, a bit tentatively.

"Great gods, yes," Hal said. "I've never heard of a dragon flier who needed to run footraces.

"Welcome to the First Squadron, my friend," he said, pouring Hofei a brandy. "I was wondering if you were going to decide to serve on."

"Why not?" Hofei said. "There's little joy to be had here in Rozen these days. The time's past, and I missed it fair, when a man in a uniform would never lack for a damsel."

"I don't think it was around very long at all," Hal said.

"That's what the old soldiers say," Hofei said. "A war sucks away all the best things, and leaves nothing."

Hal looked at him closely.

"Are you sure you want to go out again? I'm sure you could find some nice soft posting training new fliers or something."

Hofei shuddered.

"I think being around half-trained glory-boys and -girls, not to mention quarter-trained dragons, might be even more dangerous than finding some Roche fliers to bother.

"No, Lord Kailas. I'm in it for the duration . . . or until they succeed at killing me."

"Then be welcome."

Hal had assigned Farren and Mynta two of the black dragons, in spite of their protests.

"It's simple," he explained. "We want to make as good a show as possible."

"You think a good show's one of those nasty bastards chewing my leg off.

Hal considered.

"It could be."

"What about you?" Farren said. "I notice you're still on that old beast you had before."

"He's the Dragonmaster," Mynta explained. "He can do as he likes."

"Damned great monster we went and created," Mariah whined.

Two days later, they flew across the Chicor Straits to Paestum, and started looking for fliers.

*

Cabet was running the squadron and, Hal grudged, doing a good job, even if his attention to the smallest detail was driving everyone slightly insane.

There'd been orders issued by King Asir other than the all-encompassing one Hal had in his belt pouch: the First Squadron was almost overwhelmed with supplies, from new tentage to farriers and wine and beer.

Mariah licked his lips at the thought of all that alcohol going down the throats of the undeserving, and wondered again if he was really necessary on this recruiting trip.

Hal said he was. Farren grimaced, but didn't object, and went to spend some time with Chincha, the dragon flier he was sweet on.

Two days later, the Grand Tour commenced.

It was fairly grim.

They started in First Army's area, which was the hardest fought through, so Hal comforted himself that this was as bad as it would get.

It didn't make him feel better.

He encountered two sets of dragon fliers at the first three bases. The old, experienced fliers were worn out, exhausted. The newer fliers were eager, inexperienced, and fell fairly easy prey to *Ky* Yasin and his black dragons across the lines, or the other Roche flights.

Of the names he had for prospective volunteers, the response, all too often, was: "Sorry, sir. But he was killed a month or two months or three months ago."

Or: "Wounded. Sent home. Won't be back. Hope he makes it."

Or: "Gone missing on a dawn flight. We think we saw his dragon heading north that day, with nobody in the saddle."

Or just a slow shake of the head.

Hal had twenty-seven fliers in all four flights of the First, and needed at least another thirty-three.

He'd thought that wouldn't be an impossible goal, but was starting to wonder.

He had many volunteers – at one base, the entire flight turned out, drawn by the magic of the name Dragonmaster.

Hal put them through two tests in the air – one against either Farren or Mynta, and, if they appeared competent, then against himself.

In neither case did he insist on a mock victory. He wanted to see if the fliers had a feel for the air and, more importantly, for their mounts.

A mediocre flier with a good dragon, and some empathy for the beast, could destroy a superior flier who had no feelings at all for his dragon.

After these tests, he interviewed the prospective volunteers.

He rejected those who were flying out of revenge, or anger, just as he refused those who seemed intent on building a score.

The new fad with the broadsheets was to keep track of the top-scoring dragon flier.

Hal considered it absurd, since he had less than no idea of how many men – or dragons – he'd killed, and wasn't interested in trying to keep track.

The days were bloody enough as it was.

He also rejected those who spouted patriotism. These were invariably either the inexperienced or the fools. Flag-waving didn't last long on the front lines, and, when it vanished, the flier was most likely to be killed in a short while. What gave true tenacity were things like inner strength, in a very few cases, religion, or, the most common of all, fighting for the others in your flight.

They found ten acceptable volunteers in all of First Army, and moved on south.

The situation was a little better in Second Army – they hadn't been as heavily engaged for as long a time as the First, and the fliers weren't quite as shattered.

Twelve more volunteers were picked.

They, like the first, were told to secure their gear, given chits for meals and fodder, and told to make their way to Paestum and report to the squadron.

Mynta muttered that, as adjutant, she should have been left behind at the base to make sure the replacements were slotted in properly.

Hal didn't tell her there would be another change made when they returned – he still wanted an adjutant who'd been trained as a flier, someone who'd have a degree of sympathy for the poor bastards aloft. But this time, he would look for one who couldn't fly any more. A flier as able as Gart was too good to waste on the ground for even the few hours allotted.

It was desolate winter, the ground gray and muddy below the dragons' wings, the skies dark and foreboding when they weren't storming.

Hal's thoughts were equally bleak, wondering how much longer the war would go on, and what would, what might, happen when it ended. He wondered if he'd be content with his estates, and Khiri, but suspected not. But he had no idea of what might interest him, if he lived.

He also wondered why both sides couldn't just quit, and say this whole nightmare had been a mistake. He didn't say anything, of course. The Dragonmaster's face could only be turned to war.

Besides, there'd been too much blood shed for a painful, inconsequential peace to be declared. There would have to be a winner and a loser . . . and so the war would drag on to a dark and unknown conclusion.

The lines they flew over appeared deserted, although now and again there'd be the moving dots of horsemen as light cavalry foraged or patrolled, and were driven back by infantry or heavy cavalry.

Hal knew there were infantry down there, huddled in their winter shelters or, if they were lucky, in some castle that hadn't been razed or in the ruins of a village or town.

Occasionally they saw other dragons in the air, sometimes on their side of the line, sometimes on the other. Generally the Roche fliers had the odds, and so Hal and his two companions would dive for cover.

Hal had the idea that the Roche had the edge in the air at present, and determined that would be changed as quickly as he could manage.

Yes, there was still a war to be fought, no matter how tired the soldiers were, and so he continued his search.

19

Bedarisi, to a less jaundiced eye than Hal's might have been charming at one time. It was an ancient city, close on the Roche border.

It had winding streets, old buildings that leaned toward each other, and was known for having the best food in Sagene, better even than Fovant, its capital.

But it was here that the second great Roche offensive had been bloodily repelled, where Hal had seen his first combat as a dragon flier, so he had considerable prejudice against the place.

The city had been smashed by magic and by the soldiers of Deraine and Sagene – the Roche had been driven back on the city's outskirts. There'd been unfought fires that burned whole districts to the ground, and Hal could still smell the acrid reek of the ruins.

The people in the streets were pinch-faced, dressed raggedly, looked hungry, and scurried away from anyone in uniform. There were almost no young women, only a few young men. But everyone on the streets moved like they were aged, even the youngest children.

Another reason for Hal's dislike of the city was personal – there'd been a terrible episode before the war, back when Hal had been apprenticed to a dragonmaster, Athelny of the Dragons, who had great talent and skill with the monsters, but was also a driven and inept gambler. He'd wagered everything, including his show, in a card game with a Sagene nobleman and *Ky* Yasin, who at the time had his own flying show and was pretending to be a civilian.

And he'd lost to the Sagene – a Lord Scaer.

Trying to flee north to Paestum on his one remaining dragon, Scaer's guards had wounded the dragon flier. Athelny had vanished without a trace.

That was another mark against Bedarisi.

But it was the Third Army's headquarters, and it was here that Kailas chose to take a break from the road, and let the prospective volunteers come to him.

He set up shop about a third of a league distant from Army Headquarters, which was in a large manor house just beyond the city. Third Army officials found an abandoned farmhouse for the trio that hadn't been too ravaged by the battles.

It was Kailas's intent to screen prospective fliers, rest a bit, then move east, and, following King Asir's orders, comb out the Sagene dragon flights.

The volunteers trickled in, and Hal was very sure that someone in Third Army was sabotaging his – and the king's – efforts.

He couldn't figure out who, although he'd narrowed it to someone in army headquarters, who probably resented Kailas's taking "his" reconnaissance elements.

Or, conceivably, the person could have been a traitor for the Roche.

But Hal had expected something like this, and was vaguely surprised there hadn't been more obstructors.

He still managed to get six good fliers, four of them women.

Another volunteer showed up.

"I don't know about this one," Gart said. "He's very new, fresh out of flying school."

"Wring him out, and we'll see," was Hal's response. He was a bit irritated, fingering an invitation from the "Noblemen of Bedarisi," asking him to a banquet before he left the area.

He didn't want to go, but remembered King Asir's caution about being diplomatic, and grudgingly sent a message back that he'd be most pleased.

He'd just finished giving the response to the messenger who'd brought the invitation when Gart came back.

"He can fly, sir," she said. "He's still got a lot of the school ideas . . . but he's fairly good."

Hal, wanting to get a bit of the paper bumf out of his system, took Storm up against the man, and was surprised when the man was able to force him into what was called a winding contest – two fliers trying to turn inside the other until either one of them succeeded and was able to make a direct attack on his enemy, or when the dragon's wing folded under the pressures and the beast spun out of the skies.

The volunteer was very much at home on his dragon, and forcibly made the animal bank, its wings almost vertical to the ground.

Kailas heard the dragon squawk in protest and grinned.

He tapped Storm with his left rein, and kicked it with his left foot. Storm obediently ducked, folding a wing, about to turn into a dive.

Hal pulled back sharply on both reins, and Storm squealed, but obediently flared his wings, and the dive was broken off, and Storm climbed.

Just in front of Hal was the volunteer, who'd anticipated wrongly that Hal would continue in his dive.

Hal sent Storm over the man's head, blasted once on his trumpet that he'd killed him, and signaled for him to return to Hal's farmhouse.

Hal brought Storm down just behind the other's dragon, who was whipping its long neck back and forth, clearly unhappy at being bested.

Kailas slid out of his saddle, went to meet the other flier.

He was vaguely familiar.

The man noted Hal's puzzlement, grinned.

"You don't remember me, do you, sir?"

"No."

"I was your crossbowman, back when the Roche were trying to take Bedarisi."

Hal remembered.

"Right. Your name's . . . Hachir. Married. Used to be a teacher."

"That's me. Also used to be married."

Hal waited.

"After I flew with you, going back to shooting knights off horses got a little tame. Someone said they were looking for fliers, and so I volunteered."

He smiled, a bit twistedly.

"I got a surprise home leave before I went to the school . . . and found out my wife had made . . . other arrangements."

"I'm sorry," Hal said, a bit awkwardly.

"These things happen, I guess," Hachir said, but there was still pain in his voice.

"So I went to the school, graduated second, came back here, and got in some flying time, and a bit of fighting, before the weather closed in. Now the Roche are only accepting a fight on their terms, which means about three or four to one, and over their lines if possible.

"I'm not suicidal."

Hal remembered that Hachir had appeared quite nerveless behind him on a dragon, even though he'd never been in the air before.

"I'll be cold about this," he said. "I can tell you haven't gotten over what happened yet from your voice. I don't need any volunteers who're looking for me to help end their problems."

"As I said," Hachir said. "I'm not that suicidal."

"I hope you're telling me the truth," Kailas said. "Dragons are expensive."

He stuck out his hand, and Hachir took it, grinning.

Now all he needed was another five to be full up.

But he wanted ten or more, if he could get away with it.

Unsurprisingly, the lords and ladies of Bedarisi did not look as if they were dying of hunger. The tables were piled high with the finest foods, and a different bottle of wine accompanied each course.

Hal could have gotten angry, could have stamped out. But what good would that have done?

But the food was tasteless in his mouth.

He pretended hunger, pretended interest in the lord to his left, the lady to his right, who'd made it most clear that her husband was off with the Fourth Army, and she would dearly love someone to see her home after the meal, "considering just how dangerous the streets are these days."

Hal made polite noises, had as much interest in going home with her as he would slithering into a snake's den, and then he saw someone, a small, thin, expensively-dressed man, sitting halfway down the right table.

"Who's that?" he asked the woman.

She brightened – that was the first interest she'd gotten out of Kailas the whole meal.

"Why, that's one of our noblest. Lord Scaer. From a very old family."

Hal's smile was tight.

"I think I want an introduction to him."

After the interminable meal ended, the woman obliged.

"I'm surely pleased to meet the Dragonmaster," Scaer said.

"And I you," Hal lied. "Actually, I've heard of you in Rozen."

"Oh," Scaer said. "It's delightful that my reputation has gone before. In what area?"

"I've heard that you're a sporting man," Hal said.

"Well, yes," Scaer admitted. "I do like to hear the rattle of dice and the whisper of the cards."

"Since I plan another day here in Bedarisi," Hal said, "perhaps we might have time for a friendly game or two."

"Certainly," Scaer said, looking at Hal's expensive uniform. "Certainly. I'd be delighted to share a table with Lord Kailas . . . at any stakes you prefer."

Hal was starting to accept the possibility that there might really be a live god or two.

"Innaresting," Farren Mariah said. "But I've a wee bit of a problem with this."

"Which is?"

"I'm not thinking, shrinking, that this business necessarilably has a great deal to do with winning the war. And as we all know, I'm a deep-down patriotical sort, who'd shrink, nay vanish, at the thought of doing anything not dedicated to movin' the end of the war one day, nay, one minute, closer."

"What he means," Gart said, pouring another round of wine, "is that his curiosity's eating his weather leg off, and he won't help you with any magic until you fill him in on the details."

Hal ground his teeth. He didn't much like indiscriminately telling his secrets.

But Mariah seemed firm, and so he told him the story of Athelny of the Dragons.

"Y'see," Farren said at the tale's end, "you don't give yourself near enow credit for being a duty soldier. I think this Scaer is definitely a villain, and don't it say somewhere in the King's Regularations that we should trample villains?"

"Probably," Hal said.

"Is Scaer a cheat?"

"I don't know," Hal said. "It wouldn't surprise me, although Athelny didn't need a sharp to clean him out."

"Now, let's us to practical thought. We want to punish this bastardly bastard, in his own style. Now, it'd be easy to stack a deck, or even use a little wizardry to make certain cards come up in that deck at a certain time.

"But assuming this Scaer-face shit is a confirmed gambler, he'd be the first to call for a new deck if he even suspicioned the one he was using happened to be rigged. Hmm, hmm, hmm."

He sat in silence for a moment.

"I have it, I have it fine.

"I think," Mariah continued. "This is one I've not cast nor seen, and all I've done is heard my grandsire prattle about it, and how proud he was for having come up with it.

"It's a bit tricky, but I think, maybe, with different matters . . ."

Again, he lapsed into silence.

"Yes indeedy, I do think," he said. "But what we'll need is a few little herbies here and there. Lord Kailas, do you have any idea where we might find a little vervain?"

"Maybe one of the chirurgeons?" Hal said.

"Of course, of course. Now, you toddle off and get some, since you're the rankest person around, in more ways than one.

"Mynta, dost thou happen to have any beeswax in your traveling gear?"

"I do, for my saddlery."

"If you'll go and procure . . . I'm for whittling a bit of oak off one of those trees out there in the downpour."

It took almost an hour, but the necessaries were procured.

"Now, the spell," Farren said, "assuming it'll work, which is a great assuming right there, is to be keyed to something. Like . . . like . . . ah-hah. Lord Kailas, if you'd beg me the borrow of your little dragon-fliers emblem?"

It'd been given to Hal when he graduated from flying school by Garadice, and become an emblem for all dragon fliers since.

"You'll not hurt it?"

"Sounds like a little weenie girl," Farren said, "wavin' her butt around the street fair. No, I'll not hurt it."

Hal unpinned the emblem, passed it across.

Farren opened a fresh deck of cards, separated the high markers from the rest, laid them flat, face up, on the table.

He consulted a scrap of paper he'd been scribbling on, while he rubbed the emblem in the wax, in the juice of the vervain, and against the oak.

"Now, you think of a word that'll set this off," he told Hal. "And I'll want you to say it, proper loud, but not shouting, when I point, which shall be after I mutter twice."

Rubbing the emblem against the cards, Mariah began chanting:

> *"Your enemy*
> *Turn away*
> *Find another*
> *For this day*
>
> *Scaer' s luck*
> *Is gone*
> *Long in disarray*
> *And his goods in pawn.*
>
> *Shun the man*
> *Fortune's foe*
> *Give your best*
> *To the one who sowed."*

He repeated it again, pointed at Kailas, who snapped: "Athelny."

"There," Farren said. "That's that.

"And some damned rotten poetry to boot. I think I'm losing my touch. Mrs Mariah's favorite son used to be the bard of the boulevards . . . but now, just another mangy, ragtail soldier."

He passed the emblem across.

"Rub it on the deal when you want to change somebody else's luck . . . and your own.

"So that's that. Lord Kailas, if you'd to bed . . . you've work to do on the morrow evening."

For the first time in his life, Hal Kailas wished he had the unctuous smoothness of one of the sharpsters he'd seen working the fringes of a dragon show.

He had to force himself to be polite to Lord Scaer, but couldn't manage the cloying friendship he knew to be required.

But he made it through a dinner that was even more painful than the one the previous night, and accepted the fine brandy Scaer poured.

Scaer's townhouse, which he made sure to tell Kailas, was very small, modest, compared to his country holdings which "if it weren't for the damned war, I'd be preparing for the racing season," was, in fact, most palatial.

There were two other men invited to dinner. One of them wore some very flashy uniform of a unit Hal had never heard of.

He asked, found it was a cavalry reserve squadron, kept on standby in case "those damnation Roche dare come back across the border. Plus it lets me get paid for spending time in the saddle."

The other man, Bagseg, was no more than a sycophant of Scaer's, always ready to laugh at Scaer's quips, or prod him into another reminiscence of the "old days."

Hal thought that a bit odd, since Scaer was no more than in his mid-forties.

The idea of a round of cards came up.

The idea met with approval, and they moved into the library, with leather-bound books and scrolls that looked unread, and riding and hunting gear that looked very well used.

Hal waited for almost an hour into the game, making sure to lose a couple of hands, then suggested maybe the stakes were a little low.

Scaer licked his lips.

Hal wondered if Bagseg was feeding Scaer cards or information, wasn't enough of a card player to tell.

He made sure he lost another hand, then, when Scaer was shuffling, touched his dragon amulet, and whispered "Athelny."

Scaer's eyes widened, seeing his hand, then he hastily covered his reaction.

Hal didn't think he was bluffing.

Kailas let his own eyes go wide.

"I think," he said carefully, as if the brandy was beginning to work, "something this good needs to be treated right."

"Like a lusty trollop," Bagseg said.

Hal made himself laugh with the others.

Scaer raised the bet, Hal re-raised.

The toady and the horseman tossed their hands in.

Scaer matched Hal's bet.

"Beat this," and laid down a high hand.

The two Bedarisans whistled in awe.

Hal set his hand down.

"Damn!" Scaer said. "I've but seen a hand that precious half a dozen times in my life."

"Just lucky," Hal said, raking in the pot.

"I don't suppose you'd be interested in raising the stakes again," Scaer said.

"Well," Hal said, pretending to think. "I'd be less than a proper guest if I didn't, though it's getting steep for a mere soldier."

Scaer won the next hand, Hal the next two.

Again, the stakes went up, and again Hal massaged the little dragon.

After three more rounds, the cavalry sort pushed back.

"I'm skint," he said. "Spent more'n my wife allows per night, anyway."

He pulled on his cloak, made noisy farewells, left.

Bagseg stayed in for one more round, then folded out, but stayed, watching.

"Shall we make this a final round, Lord Kailas? Hardly any fun with only the two of us," Scaer said. His thumbs were working rapidly against the base of his index fingers.

Hal nodded, unobtrusively stroking the dragon emblem.

Scaer didn't ask Hal if he wanted to deal, and Kailas suspected the fix was in, however Scaer could rig it.

There was no sound but the whisper of the cards sliding across the felt.

Hal picked up his hand. His face showed nothing.

Scaer bet, very heavily.

Hal matched the bet. Almost half of his stake was in the pot. But Scaer had even fewer coins left.

"This is getting expensive," Kailas complained.

"You could always use some of the king's gold you're carrying," Bagseg suggested.

Hal looked at him, and the man shriveled.

"Sorry. Didn't mean anything."

Kailas turned back to the game.

"I'll take one card," he said.

"I'll play these," Scaer said.

Hal shoved the rest of his stakes into the center of the table. Scaer counted them.

"I'm shy," he said.

Hal shook his head

"So I'm winner."

"No!" Scaer said, almost shouting.

"We agreed, table stakes, didn't we?"

"Will you take something else to make up the difference?" Scaer said.

Hal pretended to think, looked about the room.

"I rather fancy this mansion," he said. "And Bedarisi might be a good place to live . . . after the war."

"That's absurd!" Scaer stormed. "This place is worth a million, maybe more."

"Play fair, Lord Kailas," Bagseg whined.

Hal said nothing.

Scaer looked again at his hand, stared hard at Hal, then at the huge pot.

"If I didn't believe in what I hold . . . very well then."

"I'll take a bill of sale first," Kailas said.

"Don't you trust me?" Scaer said, his voice ugly.

Hal, again, didn't respond.

Scaer went to a sideboard, found paper and a pen, scribbled, tossed the paper scornfully on to the pile of silver and gold.

Hal picked it up, read it, while Scaer fumed.

"It seems in order," he said.

Slowly, having full faith in Farren Mariah's spell, he laid his six cards out, one at a time, snapping them against the felt.

At each click, Scaer's eyes got wider. He wasn't aware that his mouth hung open.

"And yours?" Hal said.

Scaer looked at Kailas, then hurled the cards against the wall, and stamped out of the room.

Hal picked them up.

"Tsk. Tsk," he told Bagseg. "I'm afraid Lord Scaer is going to need a new place to live."

"Won't you give Lord Scaer a chance to come up with the money to redeem the deed?" Bagseg asked.

"No more than he gave a man named Athelny a chance," Hal said.

Bagseg looked perplexed. Hal didn't explain.

He folded the deed, put it inside his uniform. He saw a pair of saddlebags on the wall, pulled them down, and started filling them with the gold on the table.

"Tell Lord Scaer I'd appreciate his vacating *my* mansion within the week," he said, putting on his cloak.

The charity hospital was very crowded, very busy, and it took Hal almost an hour before the hospital's director was free.

She looked at him, and her expression made it very clear she had little use for soldiers, evidently considering them, and the war, as the cause of all her patients' troubles.

"I want to make a donation," Hal said. "You seem crowded here."

She softened. Just slightly. "We are," she said. "All the wards are full, and we've patients on mattresses in the halls, and my chirurgeons are working themselves to exhaustion."

"First, I wish to donate this mansion to your order," Hal said. He handed the deed across, waited while the woman read it, then took it back and countersigned it. "Sell it, use it, do what you will with it."

"Gods," the woman whispered. "That's Lord Scaer's. Isn't it?"

"It *was*," Hal said. "And you might need some gold to refurbish it into a proper hospice."

The saddlebags went across. The woman almost dropped them from their weight.

"Why . . . why are you . . . who are you?"

Hal thought about it. No, titles weren't right.

"The name's Kailas," he said. "Hal Kailas."

"Why are you . . . I mean, if you don't mind my asking?"

"Taking care of an old debt," Kailas said. "And, by the way, I'd like you to name the place after someone I knew.

"A man named Athelny of the Dragons."

Hal hoped that the bones of the old reprobate stirred a bit in amusement, wherever they lay scattered in some unknown forest.

20

Hal gladly left Bedarisi behind, and moved on into Sagene flying territory. Their fliers did things a little differently than Deraine's. In fact, from what Hal saw, they did everything their own way.

Discipline was a bit more relaxed, but when it was applied, it was far more severe, and with less appeals than Deraine.

When fliers weren't required for duty, they could go and do as they pleased.

The flight roster was taken most casually, but there was always the required number of fliers on their dragons at the appointed time.

The fliers wore pretty much whatever they wanted, frequently civilian clothes when they were off-duty.

The dragons were well-kept, if a little dirtier than Hal would've allowed, just as the enlisted men and their billets weren't always of the cleanest.

But the flights were very aggressive, and would attack any Roche dragons they could.

Tactically, they could do with some lessons, but that would be a simple matter to teach.

One thing Hal thoroughly approved of was the diet. Working with pretty much the same issue rations Deraine had, a Sagene mess cook would improvise them into a masterpiece, using local herbs, garlic, wine, and careful attention.

Naturally, Farren Mariah despised the diet. "Foreign muck," he'd growl. Gart, too, didn't seem that impressed with the cooking, but was more politic about her comments.

At one flight, she was utterly charmed by a slim, well-spoken young flier, and disappeared with him for the night. The next day, she was a bit sheepish, but both Hal and Farren behaved as if nothing had happened.

Hal figured a flier's life, as long as it didn't get in the way of flying, was his – or her – own business. It would be short enough as it was.

Hal had four more volunteers when he came to the Sagene 83rd Flight. He'd been told about the 83rd's best flier, stories both good and bad, and was very unsure about the man.

Once again, the man came to him, lounging into the farmhouse room Hal and his fliers had been given.

The man wore a thin moustache, carried himself like royalty, and somehow managed to have a sneer on every inch of his slender, small body.

"Good morning, Lord Kailas," he said, ignoring Farren Mariah and Mynta Gart. "I'm Rer Alcmaen. I assume you want to talk to me."

"First," Hal said, "you can stand at attention, and salute as you've been taught."

Alcmaen unfastened himself from the doorway, and managed a salute. Somehow that sneered, too.

"Now, why do I want to talk to you?" Hal said.

"Because I'm easily the best flier in all Sagene," Alcmaen said. "Not to mention I'm the high-scorer. Or would be, if those shitheels at army headquarters weren't hells-bent on denying my victories."

"Why do you want to join me?"

"Because I think you'll give me a chance for some action, more than I'll see here with a solitary flight. And you also seem to be close with the taletellers. A little fame never comes amiss," Alcmaen said.

"You certainly know how to win your way into a commander's heart," Hal said sharply.

Alcmaen shrugged.

"I know what I am, what I can do, and expect others to do the same."

Hal stood, picked up his flying jacket and gauntleted gloves.

"Some of us don't," he said, not knowing whether to laugh or snarl at the arrogant little bastard.

It was just as he'd been told. There were other tales he'd heard that Alcmaen was very close to a born liar, claiming everything from being of noble, if illegitimate, birth to having been a spy for Sagene in Roche before the war to the vast estates he'd lost gambling to the beautiful women in Fovant whose hearts he'd broken.

"Why not?" Alcmaen said. "It's always good to have matters in the open."

Hal nodded him out, and slammed the door behind him.

Mariah and Gart looked at each other.

"Hoboy," Mariah said. "He'd better be better than I think he is."

"It'll be interesting to see," Gart said, grinning, "if our fearless leader doesn't decide to go for real blood."

"Five to four he doesn't."

"No bet."

Half a glass-turning later, Hal came back alone.

He slammed the door more loudly than he had on the way out, threw gloves and coat across a chair, thudded back behind his desk and used three words even Gart hadn't heard in her sea-faring days.

"Well?" she asked.

"The son of a bitch is almost as great as he thinks he is in the air," Kailas growled. "He beat me three out of three, and didn't seem like he was working that hard."

"So you took him?" she asked.

"I don't see how I have any choice," Hal said.

"How's he going to fit in a nichy little niche in the squadron?" Mariah asked. "Can't see him being the coziest of tent mates."

Hal shook his head.

"He won't be. I'll give him to Richia, let him drive the 34th insane."

He leaned back in his chair, sighed.

"The bastard's killed almost as many Roche as he claims . . . and that's all that counts these days."

"I'll wager a badger," Mariah said, "back when you was a tiddly little cavalryman, you loved to put burrs under your saddle, too."

"I am sorry, Lord Kailas," the Sagene captain, Sir Rhaetia, said, "but I cannot allow you, and your recruiters, on this flight."

"I beg your pardon," Hal said. "But I have the explicit permission of your Council of Barons."

"There are times that a patriot must oppose the commands of his superiors when they've lost sight of the important things."

"Obviously," Hal said, "you're aware that I want to talk to Danikel, Baron Trochu."

"Of course," Rhaetia said. "But it is important to the people of Sagene, to the soul of Sagene itself, that this man, our greatest flier, remains to fly and fight with a Sagene squadron."

Hal thought only a Sagene could say – and mean – something like that without sounding ridiculous.

He thought of arguing, then shrugged.

"Can I at least have the hospitality of your mess? It's getting late."

Rhaetia frowned. Clearly he wanted to say no, but his innate gentility forbade that.

"Very well," he said. "For the night only. In the morning, after the first meal, you must be on your way."

Hal inclined his head.

"Your dragons can be groomed in that tent there, and, at the far end, there's a trio of vacant tents for you and your team. I shall arrange to have a meal served there. But I shall put on guards to ensure you do not try to subvert my orders."

Rhaetia was a man of his word. There were a pair of sentries walking a post around the tents, and none of the Sagene fliers approached Hal.

But at least the food was superb.

"What are we doing to do?" Gart asked. "How good is this man, anyway?"

"The best," Hal said. "At least, unless the taletellers and medal-givers are complete liars."

"You're doubtin' that, ever?" Mariah said. "You should reassure yourself that all they tell is the truthiest truth of all."

"I suppose we'll have to try to get some kind of direct order from the Council," Hal said. "Or let the man stay where he is.

"Hells, come to think about it, we don't even know if he wants to volunteer."

"Yes we do," Gart said. "If he didn't, why would that captain all but lock us up here on the far side of nothing?"

It was an hour later when there was a tap on Hal's tent pole. Hal was still awake, updating his report.

"Come in," he said.

A slender, young flier slid in. He was very good-looking, in a feminine way.

"Lord Kailas," he said. "I'm Danikel."

Hal grinned.

"You're welcome, Baron Trochu. How'd you subvert the sentries?"

"It is Danikel, sir. The baron is for other places, other times.

As for the sentries, neither of them would deny a request from me. May I sit down?"

Hal shoved over a tack box.

"The amenities didn't go far enough for a suite of furniture."

Danikel smiled slightly.

"My captain is a good man, but there is no holding him back when he makes up his mind.

"I share the same trait, I hope. Which is why I am here. Would you consider allowing me to join your squadron?"

"I would indeed," Hal said. "And I've read enough about your performance that I don't need to put you through the tests I've devised for the others.

"Not to mention doing so might be a little difficult."

"It could indeed."

"Might I ask why you want to fly with me, instead of staying here? Especially when Captain Rhaetia thinks you're the soul of Sagene, and must fly with a Sagene squadron."

"That is a pretty thought," Danikel said. "And I am honored most deeply.

"I wish to join your unit because I think you will give me greater opportunity to kill Roche fliers. And that is all that matters.

"The more I kill – the more I am able to help others kill – the more quickly the war shall be finished, and Roche shattered so they'll never again set foot on my country."

Hal realized he was looking at the exception to his rules about patriotism – this man had seen enough fighting to have become cynical, but most clearly had not. Again, the Sagene thought differently.

"I see," Hal said. "Might I ask a question? You're a baron. Where are your lands?"

"Far west of here, west of Fovant," Danikel said. "May I ask why?"

Hal had been grasping at the last materialistic explanation for Danikel's bloodthirstiness – that his lands might have been ruined in the Roche invasion that started the war. But that was clearly not the case.

"Just curious," he said.

"One request, though," Danikel said. "Might I have two dragons?"

Hal lifted an eyebrow.

"I find I can fly more than any dragon I've yet ridden,"

Danikel said. "That's one reason for my wanting to move on. Our flight seems to be far down on the list for resupply, and I've been asking for such a favor from Captain Rhaetia for some months. He's tried his best, but without avail."

"Two dragons," Hal said. "I've got quite a few black dragons, and will be giving them to the best of my riders, which certainly will include you. But we're hardly oversupplied. Can you think of a way you can leave this base with the dragon you have now?" Hal asked. "Assuming you want to keep him."

"I do," Danikel said. "Hoko isn't the strongest, but she's used to my ways, and would make my transition easier. Yes, I'll take her."

"This is not going to improve my relations with your good captain, you realize."

"Naturally," Danikel said. "So I expect you should leave tomorrow, as the captain has told us you will. I'll be out on a dawn patrol, and join you somewhere along your route with what little baggage I need. Perhaps you can fly along the eastern highway, and we can link up sometime tomorrow?"

"How, exactly, are you going to handle Captain Rhaetia?"

"I'll leave him a note."

"That will drive him mad," Hal said. "And I'm sure he'll do something such as issuing a warrant for you as a deserter."

Danikel held out his hands.

"I care little about that." He grinned slightly. "What will he do? Make me fight in a war?"

Hal laughed.

"We'll do it that way . . . and travel, very quickly, back into the areas Deraine controls. You might be forgiven, being a hero sort of person. But I'm liable to end up in a Sagene jail charged with . . . hells, I don't know. Dragon-stealing. Flier-stealing. Whatever."

"There shall be no problems," Danikel said confidently.

There were none. Danikel, astride a fairly small, quite young blue-black dragon, swooped down on them an hour's distance from the Sagene flight, and they made it back to Bedarisi within two days.

Hal was now overstrength by nine fliers.

But he wasn't worried about that.

The Roche would reduce the roster in short order, and he would likely find some volunteers who wouldn't work out for one reason or another.

Now, there was only one more army to cover, and he could afford to be very choosy in his fliers.

"You know," Captain Sir Lu Miletus said, "there's a part of me wishes that you came to recruit me for your flying carnival, sir."

He looked marginally less exhausted than he had during the battle for Bedarisi.

"I'm sure," and it took effort for Hal to hold back sirring the man who'd first commanded him in aerial combat, "if you want to go, there'd be a way."

"No," Miletus said. "And don't tempt me further. I've got people to take care of right here. Although I could do with a few more to worry about . . . we're down to nine fliers."

Hal, remembering the lives that had tied him to the cavalry until they had all been killed, nodded, then asked the question he wasn't sure he wanted an answer to:

"Is Aimard Quesney still . . . "

"He is very much still," Miletus said. "Even if he does have trouble keeping roommates."

"And Chook?"

Chook was the enormous cook who'd once driven off a Roche attack, single-handed, with his cleaver.

"Hah. He's immortal."

Miletus's flight was quartered in a former dairy. The big milk barn served perfectly to house the dragons, and there were enough outbuildings for everyone.

Miletus, after making Hal promise to stay for the evening meal and drinks afterward, directed him to a small byre.

He found Aimard Quesney, who was even thinner than he'd been before, and with even more preposterous mustaches, lying on his bunk and reading a book of poetry.

He lowered his book when Hal entered.

"Good gods. It's young Hal . . . sorry. Lord, uh . . ."

"Stick with the Hal," Kailas said. "But you can leave off the young. I don't think I've been that for a couple-three years or more."

"So I've read."

Quesney swung his feet to the floor, sat up.

"And you're forming some sort of a super flight."

"I am. Do you want to join?"

Quesney's eyebrows crawled up his forehead, and he twirled a mustache.

"I guess that's a compliment of sorts.

"I don't suppose you remember the last time we had any words of significance, I cursed you for being a born killer. That's hardly the best relationship to have with one's commander.

"And I've not changed my mind about you.

"In fact, if half of what I read is true, you've gotten much more efficient at slaughter."

Hal, instead of being angry, was slightly amused. "Perhaps I have. And I certainly see why Sir Lu said you were having trouble keeping shedmates.

"Do you, by the way, know of any other way to end the war than by killing?"

"I'd like to try telling everyone to just frig off and go home," Quesney said. "Or maybe some of us . . . enough of us . . . on both sides . . . frigging off and saying we won't fight on, we're tired of dying and killing . . . maybe that'd have some effect."

"You dream."

"I dream," Quesney agreed. "And until I have the guts to refuse to get on that damned dragon one day, or the bastards succeed in killing me, I'll keep on doing my share of the death-dealing.

"But no, Kailas. I won't join your squadron, nor will I thank you for inviting me to.

"Now, leave me alone, dammit. I was very happy, reading poetry about a world that isn't eyeball deep in blood, and maybe dreaming I was in it, when you appeared and made me think.

"I'm tired of thinking in a world that appears to have abandoned any kind of thought.

"The hells with it all, Kailas. And the hells with you as well. Go on back to your war, and see if killing everything in sight works."

21

Hal could feel it in the wind – winter was drawing to a close.

The war would begin again in earnest.

Other signs were the constant stream of couriers coming in

and out of First Army headquarters in Paestum, fast dispatch boats coming across the Chicor Straits from Deraine and mud-spattered coaches from Fovant to the Sagene commander.

Less welcome were the streams of paperwork from headquarters and, worse yet, the Most Important Visitors from anywhere and everywhere, eager to "inspect" the famous – without anything yet on which to base it – First Dragon Squadron, and, even better, a meeting with their commander, the fabled Dragonmaster.

One visitor who was very welcome was Lord Bab, who showed up, and announced that the next time Hal had a Great Idea, he might keep it to himself. Cantabri admitted that he'd mentioned Hal's Special Raiding Squadron in Important Circles, which meant to King Asir. He'd immediately been given orders to form such a unit, at least battalion size, and have it ready for special tasks during the spring offensive.

Hal had offered very mock sympathy.

He had enough troubles of his own.

Somehow, when he'd envisioned this squadron, some years earlier, of dragon fliers who were trained, experienced, and the most dangerous Deraine and Sagene could offer, he didn't think that many of them might well be a shade on the arrogant side.

But so it was.

Rer Alcmaen had no sooner been checked out on a black dragon, requiring almost as short a time as he'd bragged about, when he cozened a fellow Sagene flier into going out across the lines pre-dawn, against Hal's standing orders.

Kailas ripped into him, but half-heartedly, since Alcmaen came back with two victories. Of course, he claimed four, but unfortunately only two were witnessed, and sulked magnificently when Hal refused to send the claim forward to army headquarters.

Alcmaen's boasts had, in turn, fired Danikel, Baron Trochu, who also went out, without bothering to select a fellow flier, and came back with three claims. All of his dragons had gone down within sight of the lines, and were confirmed.

Naturally, the Sagene broadsheets went wild with these five victories, and trumpeted loudly about the true superiority of the Sagene fliers.

These brags meant the world to Alcmaen, nothing at all, it seemed, to Danikel.

But it meant, to Hal, that he couldn't discipline the two without incurring the wrath of the broadsheets and, most likely, King Asir.

Hal damned his new diplomatic nature, went back to work.

The overall problem with his experienced fliers was that few of them thought they had anything to learn.

Hal knew better, but had to pose his lessons very carefully, for fear of throwing pouts into his killers.

He had figured out six rules for living while flying dragons about:

1. Always get the upper hand before you go into a fight. That meant use altitude, surprise, blind angles, clouds. If you don't have the advantage going in, don't fight. Always beware the dragon in the sun, coming at you from your blind spot, and always try to be the dragon in the sun.

2. Your dragon probably knows better than you do. In any event, it can't hurt to pay attention to his or her squeals, honks, and moods.

3. Always have a back door out of a fight. Never get cornered. If you are, try to climb out of it. Never get into a diving or a turning contest with a Roche if you can avoid it – he and his dragon are liable to be better at it than you are, and if you learn that fifty feet above the ground, you are pretty well out of options.

4. Always have numbers before you attack. Never one to one, seldom two to one, and don't get cocky and assume you've got a kill with three to one.

5. War isn't a sport. It's a killing time, so don't think about chivalry, or about "being fair."

6. Finally, the situation makes the rules. All of the first five can be made meaningless in a second, and then you'd best be able to figure, and fly, your way to safety.

All most logical. But Hal had to be very wary of just how he got his fliers to learn them.

"I think," he grumbled one evening to Gart, "I'd just as rather use a godsdamned bungstarter to get things into some of these peoples' minds."

"Howsabout," Mariah suggested, "I winkle up a wee spell. It'll either make 'em smart . . . or perhaps change the lot into dormice."

"You aren't that good a wizard," Gart said.

"Want to bet?"

Gart considered, then shook her head.

"I'd play hell losing ... especially as a dormouse. I understand they don't take being beaten with any sort of composure."

Hal was making the armorer Joh Kious a rich man, if not necessarily a happy one, since Kious despised working with a bureaucracy. Even with Hal walking point for him, there was still too much paperwork for the independent-minded craftsman.

He had to hire several men to built the multiple-bolt crossbows for Hal's squadron, and was also busy making modified firebottles. These had originally been thin glass bottles, with a fire-making spell and flammable liquid inside.

Hal had come up with the second generation, working with Lieutenant Lord Callo Goang. This was a long dart, the length of a man's arm. It was cast of cheap lead alloy, both to save money and for ease of breaking. It was made in two parts that screwed together, In the hollow center was more of the flammable liquid, sealed with a spell.

These firedarts were vastly more accurate and handy than the old firebottles, although a good supply of the latter was kept in the armory, in the event of shortages.

Hal had the niggling of another idea for another weapon, couldn't quite get it to appear.

Maybe it'd come to him during the battle.

"Here, then, is my plan," Lord Egibi, Commander of the First Army said, his white mustaches ruffling slightly in the breeze blowing into the room of the manor house serving as First Army headquarters.

Hal tried to keep his expression neutral, studied the map on the easel.

"It appears to be the same as other offensives we've tried which have failed," Egibi went on. "A frontal assault, all along the Roche lines, intended to finally drive them from the heights they've held for over a year.

"But it isn't ... quite.

"First, we won't have the usual build-up from our siege machines, which seems only to give the Roche warning. Instead, chosen units will attack, and the Roche will think it's only a raid in force.

"Then, as they move forward, there'll be a great spell mounted against the Roche, and the entire front will attack in unison, as part of the second wave.

"A third element, over here, will be making a flank attack.

"Your opinion, Lord Kailas?"

Hal decided to be politic.

"I'm just a flier, sir. I have no opinion, and wonder only what you intend for my squadron to do."

"I want no special efforts before the day of attack that might give the Roche warning," Egibi said. "Then, on that day, I want you, in force, over their lines. I want you to have complete control of the air, so the Roche have no warning."

Hal nodded, thought.

"I have a better idea, sir."

Egibi waited.

"I would like to make reconnaissances, starting today, of all Roche landing fields behind their lines.

"None of the fliers will have any idea of your grand strategy," Hal continued, thankful that he hadn't used the lesser word tactics. "So, if they're brought down, they'll have nothing to tell their inquisitors.

"Then, on Attack Day, instead of being over the lines, I'll have my squadron over the Roche fields. With any luck, their fliers won't able to get airborne at all."

"Hmm. Interesting," Egibi said. "And certainly it's easier to shoot down a duck frowsting about in a marsh than when it gets into the air.

"Yes. Yes, I like your idea a lot."

Lord Bab Cantabri stormed into Hal's tent.

"What do you have to drink?"

Hal gauged Bab's anger, decided to pour a very strong brandy instead of wine.

Cantabri shot it down, held out the glass for more.

"And what put you into such a charming mood?" Hal asked.

"Have you been briefed by our good lord and master about the upcoming offensive?"

"I have," Hal said. "The day before yesterday."

"Did he happen to point out a certain diversionary attack aimed at the Roche right flank?"

"He did."

"Did you happen to notice what unit is to make that attack?"

"Uh-oh," Hal said.

"Uh-oh is right," Cantabri stormed. "I've spent the last two months carefully building up my stock of killers to be good at everything from creeping through the bushes to swimming across a river and leaving nary a splash.

"And so, for my sweat and their blood, what do we get? The chance to stand shoulder to shoulder, just like we were basic line animals, and march forward until some numbwit with a spear kills us.

"What a godsdamned waste."

"At least you're not part of the frontal assault," Hal said.

"Big godsdamned deal," Cantabri said. "Don't you think the Roche might just happen to have built up their flanks? And that if they see a bunch of warriors pelting uphill toward them they might be able to fight back?

"Or, worse, since my men are lightly armed, putting a few companies of heavy cavalry downslope to wipe 'em out?"

Hal nodded reluctant agreement.

"The only damned chance that I can think of to help is to get some light cavalry elements on *my* left flank," Cantabri growled, "and scare the bastards.

"Not that I think anybody on either side gets scared very easily these days."

It was nice, this high above the earth, Hal thought, as Storm arced around a towering cumulus cloud, and dove through a tunnel in the next one.

Behind him, to the west, bigger clouds promising a storm were onrushing.

But Hal would be finished with his mission before they arrived, although he might get a little wet and blown about going home.

The dragon seemed just as happy to be up here sporting about, no one else in the sky, instead of snarling after enemies as Hal was.

But as soon as Kailas looked down, he was torn back to reality, seeing the bare bluffs of the Roche front lines below him, so fought over that nothing could grow, and there was nothing but man's dugouts and shattered, torn things that had been trees.

He was too high to see the rotting bodies underneath them, didn't want to think about how many more the forthcoming offensive would bring.

Hal prodded Storm on east, and took a map from the pouch clipped to Storm's carapace.

Little by little his fliers had filled in where the Roche dragon fields were.

There was only one "hole," a blank spot some three leagues back of the Roche forward positions.

Two fliers had reported black dragons orbiting that area, and so Hal had decided to take the last and possibly most dangerous reconnaissance himself.

He was grateful for the spotty cloud cover that let him duck in and out, hopefully not seen by anyone on the ground who might give the alarm about a lone flier, and set a trap for his return.

By now Kailas was a good judge of distance traveled, and as he came up on three leagues, he began scanning the ground below very carefully.

His eye was caught by a bit of a blur, as if he'd gotten something in his eye.

Instead of rubbing it, or looking away, he stared harder into the blur.

Very suddenly, two black dragons came out of that blur, out of nowhere, taking off.

The blur was a fairly high level spell, cast over what must be a dragon field.

Hal decided he should go lower and make a swift pass over the blur, to see if he could make out any details, hopefully surprising the two Roche dragons below.

This, he thought, would be a decent way to get killed. He ought to be scooting for home.

But duty – or maybe his own pride – called.

He lifted the reins to put Storm into a dive, and two more blacks came out of a cloud at him, less than half a mile away.

Hal swore.

Caught, mooning about as if he were on his first combat flight.

They had a slight height advantage, and were coming in fast, keeping close on each other.

Experienced fliers.

Was that *Ky* Yasin's squadron below, under that spell?

Later for ponderings.

Hal yanked Storm's reins, but the dragon needed no guidance. He'd seen the blacks, and was already banking into them, shrilling a challenge.

Dragon pride was almost as suicidal as man's.

Hal cursed again, realizing he hadn't readied his crossbow when he crossed the lines into Roche territory, a violation of one of his standing orders.

He was thinking, as he cocked his crossbow, and made sure the ammunition carrier was locked firmly atop the weapon, that he wasn't fit to fly with his squadron, let alone command it. He'd been too long away from combat, and had let himself get sloppy.

Hal steered Storm toward the dragon on the right, flying head-on at the monster, fully half again as big as Storm.

There'd either be a collision, or someone would veer away.

The Roche flier's wingmate could do nothing except fire his conventional bow at Hal at a distance when they closed. If he tried to do more, there'd be a good likelihood of collision.

Hal had his crossbow up, aiming.

The Roche flier saw it, flinched, broke at less than twenty yards, pulled his reins to bank away.

Hal fired, as the black's wing almost brushed Storm, and his bolt caught the flier in the side.

He heard the scream as the man contorted, fell from his saddle, spun down toward the ground far below.

Hal forgot him, working his cocking handle and reloading.

He pushed his left knee against Storm, and the dragon veered to the side in a flat turn as the dead flier's wingmate brought his dragon around after Hal.

Now, just ahead, was one of those clouds.

Hal headed straight for it, the back of his mind wishing that the cloud would be as soft as it looked, a fleecy pillow.

It wasn't. Suddenly the world was gray, spattering rain, and Hal couldn't see Storm's head. But at least the wind around him wasn't a gale.

The dragon didn't like clouds any better than any flier did, and blatted a complaint.

Hal kept his mental image of where he was, where the other Roche flier was, counted four, then pulled Storm into a hard bank to the right and up.

He held the climbing turn until Storm was almost headed back the way they'd come, then snapped his reins hard.

He could hear, even if he couldn't see, Storm's wings crack harder, and then they were out of the cloud.

Just below, and to one side, as he'd hoped, was the other flier, pulling his own dragon into a bank, unwilling to follow Hal into the cloud.

He heard the sound of Storm's wings, looked up and saw the dragon, just as Hal fired. The bolt took him in the neck, and he flopped forward on his mount.

Hal turned Storm again.

Somewhere, coming up fast, would be the other two dragons, who surely would have seen Hal.

He gigged Storm again, and they went back, fast, the way they'd come.

Behind him, still below, were the other two Roche dragons.

There was a solid bank of clouds ahead.

Hal thought about turning back, and attacking the other two black dragons, held back his blood lust.

He'd been lucky once.

He knew too many soldiers who had counted on their luck one too many times.

Storm dove into the cloud, and this one was the other's big brother.

The dragon was caught, lifted a thousand feet, then driven back down by the wind, while rain spattered Hal's face, feeling like rocks.

They were on their side, Storm frantically trying to control himself, and then they were out of the cloud, under it, the world around them gray with rain.

The ground was less than a hundred feet below them, and there was no sign of life as the storm hammered the earth.

Hal went for the lines, climbing to about three hundred feet as he crossed them.

To his right, a catapult spat a long bolt up, missed him by yards, and Hal was safe, on his own side of the lines.

He had seen enough to fill in that last blank on his map.

Now to plan the squadron's doings on Attack Day.

He saw Sir Thom Lowess at Egibi's headquarters, looking innocent, and knew the day for the offensive would be very soon.

22

Hal blew one note on his trumpet, kicked Storm, and dove for the still-nighted earth below, out of the glow of the rising sun's arc.

Four dragons were veed behind him, all armed with the firedarts, and extra magazines for their crossbows.

Below them was that blur that marked a hidden airfield, that Hal hoped was *Ky* Yasin's base.

Out of sight, other elements of his squadron were attacking other dragon bases.

Hal pulled up into a more gentle dive. He wasn't sure whether he had enough height to dive through the blur and still be off the ground but looking at the trees on either side, he thought he had fighting room.

He felt a strange quiver in his mind as they "struck" the blur, and he felt Storm shake.

Then they were in the open, about a hundred feet over a large patch of cleared forest. Below were the huge canvas domes that were dragon shelters, and, along one side of the field, tents of various sizes that marked the fliers' quarters and ground sections.

"First the dragons," Hal had ordered, feeling his stomach coil within him in self-disgust. "Get fires going in their shelters, and that'll slow them down a bit."

His fliers obeyed, and the firedarts spun downward, punching through the thick canvas and padding. White smoke curled up.

Hal brought Storm up and around, barely twenty-five feet over the ground.

He saw running men, headed for catapults at each corner of the field, paid them no mind. They wouldn't have time to load their weapons, let alone shoot them.

Hal went down the neat line of tents, dropping firedarts as he flew. He deliberately chose the smaller ones, thinking those were the most likely to be fliers' quarters. He realized he'd always rather kill a man than a dragon.

Again, he pulled Storm up, looked back, seeing his four fliers seeding the field with more fire.

One, then two, of the dragon shelters gouted flames, and Hal heard the dying screams of dragons inside.

He wanted to vomit, fought control, blew a signal on his

trumpet, and his four flight mates climbed away from the sea of flame below.

Hal still didn't know if this was *Ky* Yasin's squadron. He reluctantly decided it probably wasn't, since the base wasn't big enough for a full squadron. But perhaps it held a flight or two of Yasin's since, after all, the dragons were black, and, as far as he knew, hoped, Yasin was the only Roche with the blacks.

There was another base about four leagues distant, and Hal steered his dragon toward it, to give that attacking flight support.

It was two hours before Hal was able to signal his formations to return to their base for a new assignment. They'd done an excellent job of bashing the Roche fliers before they could get in the air.

Hal could only see a half dozen or so dragons in the air as they closed on the front lines, promptly forgot about them.

Below him, the battle raged.

He had no idea how many waves Egibi had sent up the bluffs from the Deraine positions below it.

There was a thin line of soldiery, fighting about halfway up the bluff.

Behind them was a thick spray of wounded and dead.

It looked to be even worse than Hal had worried it would be.

He looked to the flank, to see if he could see how Cantabri and his Raiding Squadron was doing, saw nothing, didn't know what to make of it.

He had his own task.

They closed on their base, landed. Fliers piled off their mounts, all a-chatter about how they'd leveled the Roche before they knew what was happening.

Hal had accomplished his mission without casualties.

There were men feeding, watering the dragons, rearming them with more crossbow trays, more firedarts.

Other victuallers tried to get the fliers to slow down, drink a glass of wine or beer, eat a high-piled beef sandwich.

But most of them had no appetite, the blood-rush of battle humming in their veins.

Hal called them together.

"We did well," he said. "Now, we're going to do better." He pointed to three fliers, including Danikel and Alcmaen, then at Cabet, a man he knew wouldn't get excited or lose track of his orders.

"You four, go high. If any of the Roche fliers get over being hammered, and attack any one of us, take them out."

Danikel nodded dreamily, and Alcmaen grinned, and the four sprinted for their dragons.

"The rest of you, split into pairs. I want you combing the battlefield. You see any Roche banners, anything that looks like commanders or even officers – kill them. Use darts when you can, and try to stay out of range of their catapults.

"When you run out of firedarts, use your crossbows.

"I don't know how we're doing, but maybe we can give the men on the ground some help.

"Get gone."

Minutes later, Hal was back over the bluffs. He was wondering a bit about this squadron of his. Here he'd put together, with a lot of grief and pain, this great formation, and so far he hadn't fought it as a whole, dribbling it away in sections and pairs.

He'd have to consider that, after the battle.

Assuming he survived.

He came in low, against his own orders, toward the bluffs. It was warm enough for an updraft, and he let Storm ride it toward the top.

He glanced over at the flank, and finally saw movement.

Hal guessed Lord Bab had waited until everyone was fully engaged, then sent his Raiding Squadron into battle.

The Deraine infantry was creeping forward slowly, using ravines, ditches, tree stumps for cover. On this steep ground, there was no way they could bring mantlets or carry shields.

Hal saw a cluster of banners ahead, and pulled firedarts from their canvas bags on either side of Storm's neck, cast them down, didn't look to see what happened.

Ahead was a knot of riders, and they, too, got darts.

Then he crested the bluff, saw a catapult aimed at him, and pulled Storm away, as the gunner lifted the firing lever. The weapon had evidently seen hard usage, for the right prod snapped, and the bow rope whipped back, and cut the gunner almost in half.

Hal saw a man on a horse who looked noble, dropped him with a crossbow bolt, then was over the Roche right flank.

Cantabri's raiders were moving forward not in line, as infantry was trained to attack as if they were on the parade ground, but moving in bounds or slow crawls toward the enemy above them, one soldier covering his mate, one section covering another, one company giving fire support to another.

Hal turned Storm, scattered firedarts over the Roche line, heard screams and saw Roche soldiers start falling back.

Horns blasted below him as Cantabri sent his reserves in, and Hal flew along the line. He reached for more darts, but his bags were empty.

He felt pain, saw an arrow stub buried in his lower arm, the bloody head sticking out. He hadn't noticed when he'd been hit.

Hal took Storm up to a thousand feet, braced himself, and snapped the arrowhead off, and yanked the shaft free.

He was bleeding, used his dagger to cut off a bit of his breeches, and tied off the wound, still not feeling much pain.

He looked over the field, saw his dragons, and other Deraine flights, rising and falling, like carrion crows, diving down for prey.

The field of war justified the comparison. Bodies were piled, stacked, up the rise, a darkening crimson carpet.

But the carpet climbed steadily upward.

Hal was about to turn back for more darts, when a cacophony of trumpets came.

He saw, on the Roche right flank, Cantabri's raiders sweeping over the top of the bluff, and lines of Roche falling back and back.

A roar of pain, rage, he didn't know which, came from below him, and the Deraine and Sagene infantry that had fought their slow way up the bluff came to their feet and charged.

The Roche line broke in two, three, a dozen places, and then they were running over the crest, back and away.

Egibi had won his great victory.

But all that came to Hal, as he looked down at the carnage, was a dull wonderment at how men could stand such pain and, worse, bring it on others.

Storm's honk seemed just as dismal as Hal's thoughts.

23

The butcher's bill for the Battle of the Bluffs was high.
  Very high.

84,000 Deraine and Sagene soldiers had died in just the final battle, and an estimated 75,000 Roche. Counting the earlier engagements, a million soldiers were killed, wounded, missing.

The armies of Sagene and Deraine had lost numberless experienced warrants and officers, men who it would take a year or more to train and replace.

Among them was Lord Egibi.

He'd gone forward, to watch his siege engines fire boulders up the slope.

A catapult's beam had snapped, scattering boulders from its net every which way. One took Egibi in the back, and killed him instantly.

Lord Bab Cantabri was named to take over the First Army.

Some of his staff officers tried to throw a celebration, but Cantabri refused to allow it.

"Too many are dead for any of us to feel any mirth," he said. "There'll be time enough for parties when we take Carcaor and end the war."

He took the Raiding Squadron with him to headquarters, to ensure it would never again be misused as it had during the battle.

Cantabri sent for replacements from Sagene and Deraine, and, as they trickled in, moved on, deeper into Roche territory.

The Roche would take a position, hold it, and fight fiercely, sometimes to the death.

They, too, were bringing up replacements.

Hal thought that if the war continued at this rate, he'd best be having children with Lady Khiri, getting them ready to fight on in this war that promised to last forever.

But at least they were moving, instead of crouched below those damned hills they'd been holding on so long.

It took awhile for the squadron to adjust to the change – many of the fliers, and, more importantly, the ground crew, had known nothing but static warfare, having joined after the lines firmed.

They generally moved every fourth or fifth day. The fliers would scout for a new base, looking for a clear field, hopefully on a height, since it was easier for a dragon to take to the air with a bit of an advantage. Then the tents would be struck, and the wagons loaded, and the squadron would lurch forward, in the wake of the front line soldiers.

At the new location, everyone worked, first pitching the dragon shelters, then putting up the work tents for the support elements, finally the fliers and ground staff pitching their own tents.

Hal, in spite of his still-healing wound and rank, worked with the rest.

An advantage of the change that quickly came clear was the increase in looting opportunities. The dragons would fly just in front of the advancing troops, and when they spotted a farm-house or, better, a village being abandoned, a flier or two would land and ransack the huts, even before the infantry could claim its proper share.

Twice they were a bit too quick, and men were wounded by Roche soldiers, who hadn't retreated as far as it appeared.

But the diet of fresh meat and vegetables instead of the spell-preserved issue rations were more than enough for the danger to be ignored.

There wasn't much fighting in the air. Hal kept his forma-tions strong, and the few Roche dragons they saw generally fled to safety. But there were those who stood and fought. Hal lost three dragons in the rolling advance.

He downed one Roche, as did Farren Mariah and Sir Loren. One-eyed Pisidia had caught two, just at dawn, and slashed them out of the skies. Danikel scored once, but Alcmaen was unlucky, to his increasing fury and the rest of the squadron's increasing amusement.

There was, as yet, no sign of *Ky* Yasin and his dreaded banner. Some of the fliers suggested he'd been promoted to a staff pos-ition, out of the field, under his brother, Duke Garcao Yasin, one of Queen Norcia's favorites.

Kailas knew better – not only hadn't they encountered Yasin, but had seen nothing of his Guards Squadron, either, since the Battle of the Bluffs, and then only in limited com-mitment.

He kept after his men never to relax, reminding them that the war was not over, or even half over, and sooner or later the Roche would come back in strength and there would be blood in the skies.

Hal woke one night with the idea for a new weapon very clear in his mind. Kailas knew that most darkling ideas are worthless and forgotten by the time the dreamer's fully awake, but he'd trained himself, on the off chance that one might prove fruitful, to bring himself awake very slowly, concentrating on the thought.

When he was fully alert he examined what he'd come up with, and decided, with mounting excitement, that it was still good.

The next morning he turned the squadron over to Gart, told her to follow standing orders, and keep patrolling, and he flew back to Paestum.

He met with Joh Kious, made sure his crossbows were being produced without problems, then went to army headquarters, which functioned as the overseas command for all four Derainian armies.

He wanted a magician, and was pleased that one of Limingo's assistants was available. The man's name was Bodrugan, and, like all of Limingo's people that Hal had met, was slender, good-looking and, in Hal's mind, a bit effete.

"I'm hardly a wizard," Hal said. "But I understand one of the primary rules of wizardry is that the part remains potentially the whole."

"That is so."

"What is wrong with the idea that if we took a boulder, smashed it into fragments about the size of my hand, and put a spell on it so that anyone, magician or not, could recite to make those chunks suddenly as big as the boulder was?"

Bodrugan thought.

"Why . . . nothing at all. A fairly simple incantation."

"Would you be interested in preparing such a spell?"

Hal told him what he intended to use those fragments for. Bodrugan grinned. "I like that. I'm just surprised that nobody else, such as a catapult hurler, came up with it."

"I am, as well," Hal agreed. He set Bodrugan to work, told him to bring the spell, when he had it, to the First Army's headquarters, where they'd know where to find the First Squadron, and thanked him.

Then he went to the provost's office, and arranged for a work crew of Roche prisoners to start reducing a granite boulder Hal had found to rubble. He arranged for the broken-up rock to be brought forward, assigned the highest, most secret priority, to First Army headquarters in the field.

Then the war changed.

Ky Yasin's First Guards Squadron, at full strength, returned to the war.

They hit a dragon flight, not, thankfully, one of Hal's, on noon patrol, smashed all six of the fliers out of the air.

Panic-stricken riders had alerted Hal's squadron, and Gart ordered the flight commanders to split their flights in half, and put them aloft.

When anyone encountered Yasin's blacks, they were to return to the squadron base, and other fliers would go out to alert the other flights.

There'd been a swirling fight in mid-afternoon that had cost Kailas's squadron three fliers, with three victories.

The flights were just now coming back to feed and rest the dragons.

Hal considered the weather, a bit windy with scattered clouds but fair, and made a hasty plan.

Hal ordered the commanders up, issued fresh orders.

He told Cabet to take his 18th Flight out, in two waves, scattered and not within easy support range of each other, with orders to patrol north-south just over the Roche lines.

"If you're hit," Hal said, "go high, and we'll be coming down to help."

"I'm *quite* entranced with being bait," Cabet said.

"You understand perfectly," Hal said. "And I may need you to do it again, so don't do anything rash like getting killed."

Cabet smiled, without much humor, ran back to his flight.

Within a few minutes, hastily watered and fed, Cabet's dragons were in the air again.

Hal called for Richia and Pisidia, gave them orders, and the rest of the First Squadron was airborne.

Kailas took his three flights up, made the dragons climb steeply, up into and through the clouds, east, into the setting sun, then turned back.

Below and west of him, he saw Cabet's flight, flying slowly, as ordered, to the east.

Hal was as high as was safe. The air was thin, and Storm hissed unhappiness.

Then he saw the Roche.

They came around a great cloud, rising like a mountain, in a formation of threes, each wingman supporting the lead dragon.

A nice, tight formation, Hal approved. The fliers would be paying more attention to not colliding with another dragon than anything else, except that nice, fat collection of Derainian idiots about a thousand feet below

Hal blasted once on his trumpet, gigged Storm into a dive, out of the sun toward the Roche.

He had not needed to issue the command.

His three flights were already nosing down, spreading out in a loose formation, each flier picking a target below.

Hal ratcheted the loading lever on his crossbow back, chose a target, the leader in the third in the string of vees.

The flier looked up when Hal was about fifty feet above, as Storm screamed a challenge.

Then Hal was on him, fired once, and killed the man, Storm ripping at the other dragon's neck as they closed.

He let Storm dive through the Roche formation, then brought him back up, toward the underside of the Roche dragons. He slammed the loading lever back, forward, shot at another dragon's stomach, didn't see a hit, was up above the flight.

The sky was a swirling mass of dragons, trying to get close enough to rip a wing, or tear a flier out of his saddle.

Hal almost collided with one of his dragons, who didn't seem to see him, banked over, and saw, turning, a flier on a huge black, a pennant flying from the dragon's carapace.

It had to be Yasin.

Hal kicked Storm into a bank, was closing on Yasin, the smaller dragon turning inside him, when another black, a Derainian, cut past him, its rider shouting something.

It was Alcmaen, grinning broadly.

Hal's attack was broken.

Yasin rolled his dragon on one wing, dove away before Alcmaen could fire at him.

Hal recovered, saw a Derainian dragon with two Roche dragons on its tail, thought the rider was Hachir.

He had a slight height advantage, used it to close on the rearmost Roche, shot the rider in his thigh

The man screeched, almost fell, and his dragon pinwheeled away.

Hal forgot about him, came in on the foremost dragon flier, who had forgotten to always watch your rear until the last minute.

The Roche looked over his shoulder, saw the onrushing Storm, and pulled up sharply, almost colliding with Hal.

As he went past, almost within reach, Hal put a crossbow bolt into the man's side.

The man fell, just as Storm's head snaked out, and tore the dragon's throat out.

Blood sprayed, and Hal was blinded for a second, then rubbed his eyes clear.

Just below him a blue-black dragon, Danikel's, was diving behind a wounded Roche monster. Danikel was methodically snapping bolts into the beast's stomach as he fell.

There was another dragon, about five hundred feet below, trying to flee.

Hal sent Storm down on him, pulled out just before they collided.

Storm's talons tore the other rider out of his saddle, and Hal turned his dragon into a bank, climbing up and away.

Storm wanted to go back and finish the Roche beast, but Hal wouldn't let him.

The sky, so tumultuous with killing a moment before, was empty.

Hal climbed for height, made for his own lines.

He landed, counted the others as they came in.

There were a few wounded men, more wounded dragons. The black dragons were deadly.

There were four missing, including Sir Loren Damian.

But they'd brought down at least seven Roche.

Sir Loren was reported safe in hospital with a broken leg by nightfall.

No word ever came about the other three.

Hal allowed himself one brandy, was leaving the mess tent to write letters to relatives of the missing men as Rer Alcmaen approached.

He saw Hal, grinned most unpleasantly, said, "Sorry, sir. But I thought I had a better chance than you did at that man."

Hal took a deep breath, then stripped off his coat.

"Here now," Alcmaen said. "You can't go and—"

Hal hit him, quite hard, in the gut. Alcmaen whoofed, caved in.

Hal let him drop, bent to pick up his coat, and Farren Mariah was there, holding it.

"Damn shame," he said guilelessly. "Poor bastid went and trippy-tripped over his own flattie footies.

"You best be on your way, sir. I'll help the poor ox to his tent and tuck him in cuddly and put a little kiss on his forehead."

The next morning, Hal waited for repercussions from Alcmaen. It was, indeed, seriously against regulations for a commander to strike any of his men or women.

Not that Hal regretted punching the man for an instant.

But Alcmaen said nothing, then or later.

Hal did notice that the man had quite a few additional bruises on his face, and walked very carefully.

He must have fallen down several more times on his way back to his tent.

24

Evidently, *Ky* Yasin had expected to knock Hal's squadron out of the war immediately for, after the first battle, his black dragons were far more circumspect about looking for a fight.

They patrolled their side of the lines vigorously, and occasionally ventured over the Deraine lines, but only when they had clear superiority and skies.

Cantabri wanted constant reconnaissance flights, preferring Hal's squadron, since he could trust what the First reported.

Hal managed to convince Cantabri he was pounding a square peg into a round hole, that there were other flights not intended for pure combat as his was.

Put up the recon dragons, he suggested, preferably in pairs, and put half a flight from the First with them on the same level. The other half would fly high above, waiting for Yasin or the other Roche units to go after the other dragons. The recon flights were slower, since they generally carried a second man, the expert at deciphering what was going on below them on the ground.

The slow advance continued.

The general battle plan was that the infantry would be sent forward, against the Roche, who wouldn't have had time after their previous retreat to do more than dig scrapes.

The light cavalry would try to drive in the Roche flanks, and the heavy cavalry would wait to exploit the advantage.

Once in awhile, there'd be a break, and the Deraine and Sagene forces would make as much as a mile.

But the Roche became experts at counterattack, and all too often the big breakthroughs would be driven back, sometimes almost to their start line.

All very traditional, very expected.

The real battles were going on far behind the lines, as Hal learned when Cantabri called him back for a very private briefing.

"And how goes the war?" Hal asked.

"The war," Cantabri said carefully, "goes as well as it should. But there are problems which you should be aware of, not just because you're my friend.

"The biggest problem is we're having trouble getting recruits. People are feeling, not without reason, that we're pouring men and women down a rathole, and the war is unwinnable.

"Our spies on the other side report the same feeling. At least the Roche have got the big advantage of having heavy-handed goons with truncheons to chivvy people into the ranks, although I suppose I'm not supposed to think that way.

"Also, just to dispose of our enemies, Queen Norcia is supposedly carrying on like a harridan, saying that she never dreamed there'd be a day with Sagene soldiers on her soil, let alone the accursed Deraine.

"There's word that she's relieved half a dozen generals, with more promised, if someone can't come up with a way to reverse what's going on."

"That's not too bad," Hal offered. "Maybe there'll be a revolution, and she'll be overthrown for somebody who wants to put a flower in their teeth and dance around the maypole instead of killing folks."

"Right," Cantabri said. "Those sorts are ever so common these days.

"Anyway, back to our side.

"There's talk, and of course you must not mention any of this to anyone, that King Asir may institute some sort of draft."

Hal whistled. "That'll not go well with anyone."

"But if that's the only way to feed bodies into the army . . . I don't know," Cantabri said, shaking his head. "Oh yes. Another piece of wonderful news is that the Sagene Council of Barons is restive."

"That's the sort of thing I'd expect," Hal said. "I wasn't very impressed with the way anyone in Sagene ruled, when I was over here before the war. Of course, I was just a kid."

Cantabri made a face.

"I had the misfortune of falling madly in love back then . . . mind you, this was before I met my wife. The woman was Sagene and noble. So in my mad pursuit, which never went much of anywhere, I spent a fair amount of time over here, traveling around and meeting the nobility.

"Like you, I wasn't much taken," Cantabri said. "Of course," he went on quietly, "I've never been much impressed by a lot of people with titles.

"Not the king, of course," he added hastily. "And now I'm one of them . . . as are you."

"What sort of restive is the Council?" Hal asked.

"There's talk of forming a peace coalition, and maybe trying to open negotiations with Norcia," Cantabri said.

"And what's the matter with that?" Hal asked. "Sooner or later, *somebody* has to sue for peace."

Cantabri started to fume, caught himself.

"True. True enough, I suppose. But I'd rather it be under conditions that are as demeaning as possible to the Roche. I'd rather they couldn't come up with some lies about how they were betrayed into peace, and want another godsdamned war in a generation or two.

"I really don't want my grandsons or their sons to go through this."

Hal nodded agreement, even though children were a long ways from his serious plans, at least at the moment.

"It's a pity that someone like Limingo, or some wizard like him, couldn't come up with a spell that'd make everybody as patriotic as they were back when the war started," Hal said.

"Sometimes," Cantabri said heavily, "magic doesn't appear to have much of an effect, here in the real world, at least not for a whole cluster of people.

"At any rate, that's as much as I've got. I suppose the reason I called you back," Cantabri said, "isn't just to have a shoulder, to cry on.

"What I'd really like – what the army, and Deraine really need – is something spectacular. Something that'll make people realize we're winning, even though it's taking a bit longer than the flag wavers put on, in the beginning.

"You've generally been able to come up with something dramatic in the past.

"This time, young Kailas, there might be a great deal more than an engagement or even a battle riding on it."

25

Hal was busy in the operations section tent the next day when a rather plaintive Mynta Gart came in.

"Uh, sir . . . there's a delivery for you."

"Which is?"

"It appears to be, well, two wagon loads of pebbles."

"Just what I've been expecting," Hal said, putting eagerness into his voice.

Gart looked at him plaintively, wanting an explanation.

Hal, for pure meanness, didn't give her one, but carefully inspected the loads of broken-up granite, ordered them moved to a secure location, and, just because he didn't have any latrines to dig, ordered Gart to put the unit's sinners on guard over the rocks.

Mentally cackling, he went back to his maps, laying out arcs east and south of their location. The arcs roughly represented the range a dragon could fly at one time – six hours, a distance of about forty leagues, depending on weather, load, winds and such.

He found it a bit hard to concentrate. Where the hells was that damned Bodrugan?

The wizard showed up two days later, accompanied by Limingo, his superior.

"We had a bit of a problem," Limingo said, "figuring out a way to make the spell universal, but not so complicated that somebody with his mind on other things – say, not having his head eaten by a Roche dragon – couldn't still remember it.

"But we're now adept at turning stones into crags, as soon as I cast an enchantment over your pebbles that's guaranteed to make them ambitious little rocks. Do you have a wizard on the squadron?"

"Barely," Hal said, and sent for Farren Mariah, and, after thought, Lieutenant Goang, who he'd been rather ignoring of late.

Mariah came, was informed he was now Official First Squadron Thaumaturge, protested loudly, was told to be silent and obey his orders by Kailas.

A bit sullenly, he went with Limingo, Bodrugan and Goang to the still-guarded rock heap.

Hal lagged behind, found reasons to go back to the map

tent. In spite of everything, he was still a little nervous around magicians.

In about an hour, Limingo and the other two came back to him.

"There," the wizard said. "Your man here can now do the resupply, when you run out of the present pile of pebbles, although the quartermaster corps may raise an eyebrow when he requisitions oil, hemlock, dried yew.

"And, by the way, after the war I've suggested he could do much worse than study wizardry."

"The question remains," Mariah said, ignoring Limingo's words, "just who's about to be playing rocksmasher first before I workies workies workies my wizardry?"

"You," Hal said. "If you don't watch yourself."

"Aarh," Farren said cheerily. "I'll be watchin' myself when the army issues me a mirror." His expression turned dreamy. "Now, there's a thought. A nice, full length glass, made of polished silver, that I can hang over my bunk for when I have visitors."

"Shut up, " Hal advised. "Now, Limingo, if you'll show us the next stage?"

Bodrugan handed Hal a pebble.

"Now, " the young magician said, "you're going to repeat after me, the following—"

"Uh . . . shouldn't we hide our little heinies outside the tent first?" Mariah said.

"Good point," Limingo said.

They went out.

"Repeat after me," and Hal obeyed:

> *"Antal, Hant, Wivel*
> *Grow*
> *You were*
> *Now be again*
> *You must*
> *You shall*
> *Antel, Hant, Wivel."*

The tiny rock was writhing in Hal's hand. He hastily let it drop. The rock grew, hurting Hal's eyes to watch. It got bigger and bigger, and Hal had to jump out of the way. It caved in the side of the map tent, then stopped growing .

"Good gods," Hal managed. "I didn't remember that rock being that frigging big."

Goang was looking at the boulder in considerable amazement.

"I thought I'd had some ideas," he said, mostly to himself. "But I never thought about using magic."

Fliers were running toward them.

Hal, trying to recover his calm, looked at Limingo.

"Those words at the beginning and end . . . do they mean anything?"

"They do . . . sort of," the wizard said. "I'm not sure just what, though. Maybe they send out vibrations to other worlds, other forces. Maybe they even call demons. Or maybe they're some sort of a prayer.

"Mmmh," Hal said. He turned to Mariah.

"Get Mynta here. I want her to know that anybody who even breathes about what just happened can count on becoming a spear carrier within the day.

"And bring Storm out. I'm going to headquarters."

"Ye gods," Cantabri said. "This will work all the time?"

"Limingo said it would."

"And your intent?"

"I'm going to go throw rocks at Queen Norcia in her capital."

"That will drive her even further into raving," Cantabri said. "And certainly won't make her underlings any happier.

"But . . . Carcaor is a long, a very long flight from here."

"More than two hundred leagues," Hal agreed.

"How will you be able to reach it?"

"I'm working on that right now," Hal said confidently. "But I'm sure it can be done. There's wild country between, and all I need is feed for my dragons. I think it'll take about three or four weeks before I'm ready to mount an attack."

"And if your raid succeeds?"

"Then," Hal said, voice hard, "we can train other flights to do the same, not just to Carcaor but to Roche's other cities. Take the war home to Norcia, and all the noblemen who think the war is something at a great distance."

Cantabri considered.

"I'm going to messenger the king, requesting permission for the First Army to refuse its left flank against the Roche, and turn south. For Carcaor. I think it's time to go for the throat.

"Now, perhaps, the end of this damned war is in sight."

*

Now there were many things to accomplish.

Hal's study of the maps of Roche, even though they were frequently sketchy, suggested way stations for his dragons.

His plan, most risky, was to take a flight of dragons toward the capital, Carcaor. Each night they'd fly to the dragons' limits, then land at previously-chosen fields, rest and eat, then continue on.

The problem, of course, was that they must not be spotted by any Roche en route.

It was complicated, but not overly so, Hal thought.

The first stage was to seal off the First Squadron's base. No one was permitted out, and anyone arriving with supplies or replacements would not be permitted to contact more than a handful of people.

He thought he was perhaps worrying too much – all that his fliers could know was that Hal had suddenly developed the ability to create large rocks – the map tent was still half-crushed.

What he intended to do with that was known only to Hal and Cantabri.

But still . . .

Naturally, the word quickly spread that something was in the works as First Army headquarters again swarmed with dispatch riders.

Someone told the taletellers that the Dragonmaster's First Squadron was closed to all visitors, which of course made them swarm around.

Hal was forced to borrow two platoons of Cantabri's Raiding Squadron to walk guard around the field, which they considered most humiliating and beneath them.

Hal agreed . . . but he knew these men wouldn't talk, no matter what they heard.

Besides, he'd need, he was fairly sure, at least three of them for his plan to work.

A couple of taletellers tried creeping through the woods into the camp, were caught by the raiders, and escorted out. One had a thick ear, and kept peering about as he went, expecting, Hal supposed, to see some sort of secret weapon a-building.

Certainly he saw nothing in a stupid boulder that must've rolled into the map tent, almost wrecking it.

Three days after he'd told Cantabri what he intended, a sentry reported there was a man on the main road who refused to leave without seeing Hal.

"Have you tried chousting him with a halberd?"

"Thought of it, sir," the sentry said. "But he's a sir, and I don't know shit about the military, but I'll bet if you start whacking sirs and dukes and earls and barons about, you're going to get yourself in trouble."

"Very well," Hal said. "I'll take care of him."

The visitor was Sir Thom Lowess, who sat comfortably in an expensive-looking surrey, laden with boxes.

"Good day, Lord Kailas," he said.

"Good day to you, Sir Thom," Hal said. "And I'm afraid I'm busy, and can't spare the time you deserve."

"I need no time from you," Sir Thom said. "I desire entrance to your camp."

"It's closed."

Sir Thom just looked at him. Hal thought.

"If you come in, you won't be able to come out for at least three weeks," Hal grudged.

"Let me ask you this," Sir Thom said, looking about to ensure there was no one within earshot except the pair of sentries. "If I come in, will my tale be worth my being mewed up for that long?"

Hal hesitated. "Yes," he said grudgingly.

"Then I'm fortunate that I brought sufficient luxuries, aren't I?"

"Let him enter," Hal said to the sentries. "And welcome, I suppose."

The most dangerous part of the mission was at the start. That would involve scouting for the layover points, and must be completely hidden.

Hal decided he'd take four other dragons. He'd be happier with less, but he'd need them for the passengers they'd carry.

Since he'd be leading the formation, he didn't want to overburden Storm, in the event he had to do some rapid maneuvering.

He first chose Farren Mariah, not because he was the strongest flier in the squadron, but because he trusted him absolutely. Mariah had already saved his life once, and Hal hoped he'd never have the chance to do it again.

Second was Danikel, Baron Trochu, since he was not only Sagene, but the best flier Hal had.

Third was one-eyed Pisidia. Hal was learning he was one of the most dangerous killers in the squadron.

Fourth was Sir Alt Hofei, from the prison camp.

Sir Thom was frantic for the full story of what was up, which Hal refused him.

"If I don't come back," he explained, "then I don't have to look like a damned fool as a corpse."

"But what will I say then?"

"Start a story," Hal suggested, "that I vanished into the unknown, in a raging battle with sixteen black Roche dragons."

Lowess looked at him dubiously.

"You wouldn't have made *that* bad a taleteller, you know. Sixteen . . . let's go for ten."

Hal shrugged, and told his orderly, Uluch, what he'd be taking. In spite of it being summer, flying at height would be chill.

Carcaor lay at the conjunction of three fertile valleys, on the Ichili River that bisected Roche.

To keep things secret, Hal planned for the reconnaissance flight to keep to the mountains, where they'd be less likely to be seen . . . and where flying might be a little chill.

So high-top boots, sheepskin coats, gauntlets and lined tied-down caps were in order.

"One of these days," Farren predicted gloomily, "my gods-damned dragon's going to be peckish, see me in this damned coat, and think I'm dinner. Or breakfast."

Chincha, his flying- and bed-partner, giggled.

"You are, you know."

Farren actually blushed.

Kailas set all four flights to practicing what appeared to be utterly nonsensical flying, half expecting to return to a mutiny.

Hal had asked Limingo for a weather spell to give him some cover. Limingo had said that would be easy, since the Roche magicians would also like a break in the spring balminess that might slow the slow Sagene-Deraine wheel to the right.

It wasn't quite raining, but what Farren called spitting near dawn.

Hal's troops were assembled and fed.

The dragons seemed to realize something unusual was coming, and stamped in eagerness to be away.

They loaded, each dragon with two men, the flier and one man from the Raiding Squadron with a heavy pack, plus, slung under their bellies, a butchered sheep wrapped in canvas.

Then they lumbered down the long field, and were in the air, flying almost due east.

Hal had ordered them to keep close to the ground, and give the alarm if they spotted any Roche dragons.

They saw none, and whisked over the Roche lines before any bolts came up, although Hal saw a couple of hastily-fired arrows lifting through the mist.

Then they were over the Roche rear lines, and Hal saw confusion and tumult spread as they passed.

He waited until he'd reached open country, then turned his course, by compass, to south-south-east, and went high.

The first leg of his scout would be the longest, which he liked because it would get him further from the Roche lines, and the possibility of prying cavalrymen, but he disliked because, on the return, if there were casualties or wounded, that could be the killer.

He was fairly certain that first day's destination would not be a problem, since his target had been scouted by a daring cavalry patrol a few weeks earlier.

It was an open, supposedly uninhabited meadow in the middle of a cluster of low hills.

The land below wound past. Most of the farms had been abandoned, a few looted by the Roche, as the armies approached them.

The ground climbed, and now there were trees, growing thicker. Here and there was the smoke from a cottage's cookstore, or bigger plumes from charcoal-makers.

Then there was nothing but trees and, here and there, ponds and small lakes.

The sun was moving down the sky when they found the meadow. They circled it once, made sure it was uninhabited, and landed.

They fed the dragons half a sheep each, ate their own iron rations, and the fliers slept, while the raiders kept watch.

Hal woke well before dawn, and turned the men out.

One raider would stay here, keeping guard, until the raid.

Again, they took off, headed almost due south.

Toward Carcaor.

The first step had gone so smoothly Kailas had to beat back a bit of hope.

He'd learned that elaborate plans never work in war, and wondered why he'd allowed himself to come up with this cockamamie idea.

Probably getting his ear blown into by Lord Cantabri as being the War's Solution had a lot to do with it.

Or maybe he was turning into a glory hound like Alcmaen.

He gloomed on, while Storm's wings beat steadily.

The land below flattened, and large, rich farms and ranches reached on either side. The farmhouses were manor houses, and cattle grazed quietly.

One of the dragons behind saw all this meat on the hoof, and moaned plaintively.

A pair of bulls looked up, saw the dragons, and went back to grazing.

A good sign, Hal thought. They'd never seen the questing beasts before.

Or else, being bulls, not steers, they simply didn't give a damn, and welcomed those aerial monsters to come down and try their battle skills.

But the war had come here, too, Hal noted. There were few herdsmen in the fields, and the few people about looked up curiously. Hal hoped they thought the dragon flight was Roche, since this was a distance behind the lines.

The maps he'd consulted had gotten more and more slender the deeper they went into Roche.

Hal's goal for the second night had been marked as a hunting camp, a summering place for the nobility of the valley they'd left behind.

But as they circled it, it was evident the camp had been turned into some kind of farm. The open meadows, where stags might have grazed, waiting to become targets, had been plowed and worked, growing what, Hal had not the slightest.

The other fliers had seen this as well, and looked to Hal for guidance. He waved them onward.

His second choice was another hour's flight on, but that put them closer to Carcaor.

Hal hadn't thought it nearly as satisfactory, since all the map showed was a small lake. Where there were lakes, there could well be people.

He found the lake, signaled twice with his trumpet, waved for the others to orbit the lake.

Hal took Storm low, until the dragon's wings sent wavelets across the lake. Some kind of fish jumped, and a few birds took off from the trees that almost overhung the water.

But there was no sign of people, now or in the past.

Hal blasted once, and the trumpet rang across the hills rimming the lake.

He brought Storm down on water.

It had been awhile since Storm had made a water landing, and didn't much like the idea.

But he splashed down, and then realized this was a great deal softer than landing on turf.

The dragon blatted in pleasure, as the other dragons came down.

Hal prodded Storm to swim toward a shelving beach, and the dragon waddled up on it, wings whipping, water spraying.

This would do very well for a second base.

The rest of the sheep were eaten by the dragons, and watch was posted again.

But it was very hard to feel any particular threat in this lonely place.

Hal called the raider who'd been detailed as guard/signaler for this spot.

"What do you think?"

The man grinned.

"I like it."

"You won't get lonely?"

"Sir . . . I was a poacher, back before the war. And I've seen animal tracks about. No. I won't get lonely. And I'll stay busy."

Hal doffed and dove into the lake. The others followed.

Farren swam up to him, cavorting like an eel.

"You notice one thing, O my fearless leader?"

"Many things," Kailas said. "Such as you're leaving a disgusting wake. You need to bathe more often."

Farren snorted.

"I'm as clean as any animal that walks, stalks, staggers or wanders the earth, so there'll be an end of insults to the lower ranks, if you please."

Hal suddenly realized something, almost blurted it, caught himself.

"So what am I supposed to notice?" he asked instead.

"All this godsdamned open land, furrow and burrow, here and there."

"So?"

"So why'd these slimy bastards start this war, anyway?"

"I didn't know you needed a reason for a war," Hal answered, turning serious.

"Surely you do. For land, for freedom, for naked women . . . some kind of purplous purpose," Mariah said. "When we win, I think we ought to take a good chunk of it away from these eejiots, since they don't know what to do with it.

"Enough for a decent province, and give it to some deserving lad."

"Named Mariah, by chance?"

"Ah, that'd do for a starter, wouldn't it? Land for all . . . now there's a motto worth fighting for."

"Or," Danikel said, having swum up beside them, "give it to the dragons."

"Now that's an idea," Hal said.

"But it'll never happen," Danikel said. "They're our partners . . . as long as the blood keeps flowing. When that's over, we'll forget 'em. Or put them back in flying shows."

"Why not?" a suddenly bitter Mariah said. "You don't think they'll remember us sojers the turning of one glass after the last bowshot, do you?"

Hal decided this was depressing, decided to follow the lead of Pisidia, who was floating, quite motionless, on his back in lake's middle.

The third day's stop was at the same time the least laid out and the one Hal was least concerned about.

Again, it led along a winding valley, with a navigable river at its bottom.

They saw the outskirts of two small cities, avoided them, and flew on, up into foothills.

There'd been little on the maps about this area, but Hal had quizzed Goang about his studies with the hill tribes. This part of Roche he knew, after a fashion, and apologetically, saying he wished he knew more, told Kailas what information he had.

One bit of data had been vital, and Hal hoped the war hadn't changed this, as it had so many other things.

It hadn't.

It was, again, late on a hot and wearisome afternoon when the fliers saw what Hal had hoped they would: rolling hills, with vast herds of sheep grazing on them.

The region was a dragon commissary on four legs.

All they needed to do was find a landing ground near one of the flocks, which were grazed unattended, and close to a stream.

The dragons were in heaven, and got two sheep each.

Then the fliers drove them back, to keep them from surfeiting themselves into a happy coma.

This time, they posted close watch, in the event of seeing a shepherd, but no one disturbed them.

The third guard was let off, with orders to stay well out of sight, but if he was sighted, to make sure he killed both shepherd and dogs.

Then the dragons flew on.

The final day's flight was fairly short, ending not long after noon.

The maps had improved, and Hal had chanced selecting one peak that was marked as having RUINS on its flat summit.

Nothing more.

They saw the ruins as they closed on the jutting peak. Someone had built a castle a long time before atop the crest, and Hal wondered how they'd brought the great stones up the steep slopes.

They landed in an open, once-paved area.

Far below, the Ichili River curved, the river that led south to where Deraine and Sagene had seen a great defeat at Kalabas, and Hal's love Saslic had died. There was a steady stream of trading ships and barges, and so Hal kept below the horizon, even though he'd be no more than a dot to the ships below.

Two bends of the river, and they would reach Carcaor.

Hal said they could expect Roche surveillance in the air, and so took their dragons downslope a bit, to where trees curled.

They were strange-leafed and -shaped. No one could remember having seen ones like them.

The dragons were nervous, without cause, and Hal felt his skin crawling a bit.

He decided it was nerves, being this close to the Roche capital.

The others were just as ill at ease, and no one could offer an explanation.

They fed the dragons and ate.

Hal chanced walking up to the castle, to see if he could determine anything of its purpose or origin.

The walls were smashed in, as if a giant's hand had battered them down. It had to have been winter storms after the place was abandoned, Hal thought.

There were a few open passageways remaining, oddly constructed, very wide and very tall.

Hal went through one, into the keep.

It stretched roofless above him, made of huge monolithic stones, notched for wooden floors here and there.

Whoever built it had fancied high ceilings, Hal thought. Even with thick beam floors, the ceilings would still have been twenty feet high.

He couldn't tell how tall the keep had been – its roof had been torn away, and the keep's stump was jagged, like a skull's teeth.

Hal wondered why he'd thought of that image, decided it was getting on toward dark, and he didn't want to chance slipping in the night.

He went back to the others, who had, in spite of the heat atop the mountain, built a low fire concealed by a pile of rubble.

At full dark, they reluctantly put the fire out, and settled in for the night.

Now, with three of the raiders gone, it was the fliers who stood watch along with the last raider, who was to be left here.

Hal drowsed, had ugly dreams he couldn't remember when he jerked awake.

He fully expected something – he didn't know what – to happen atop this mountain.

But nothing did.

The next morning, they prepared to leave.

Hal wanted to chance flying around those bends, to make sure Carcaor was really there.

But he knew better.

For some reason, he told the raider to stay clear of the castle, and make his watch somewhere below it.

The man glanced up at the ruin, shivered.

"There's no worry about me going near that, sir. No worry at all."

Hal told him they'd be back within a week, and for him to stand firm.

"After all," he said, trying to embolden the man, "you're the furthest forward soldier in this war. Something to tell your children in another time and place."

The man nodded, didn't smile back.

The five dragons took off, and wended their way back toward the front lines without incident.

Stage One was complete.

Now for the battle.

26

Surprisingly, none of the fliers had mutinied, not even Alcmaen, in spite of the seemingly absurd training Hal had ordered before he left.

This had included flying over a secluded field behind the lines, and dropping, from about fifty feet, pebbles at circular rope targets, time after time, with the accuracy logged by squadron members on the ground.

Another task was flying very low over a ruined village nearby.

Very, very low, which meant having to zigzag between a ruined church and a battered grain silo.

Naturally, the fliers turned it into a competition, and Sir Loren Damien, who'd returned to the squadron and insisted on flying with his leg in a splint, was the winner.

He crashed through the remnants of a thatched roof, and rebroke his leg, effectively grounding him for the mission.

Hal thought of saying something to him but realized he couldn't come up with anything worse than Sir Loren was already muttering to himself.

More logical training had included each flight flying in open formation, which made the fliers think there was some sort of aerial parade scheduled, perhaps a celebration of Lord Cantabri taking over First Army.

But that didn't answer the question of why First Squadron had been forced into isolation.

Nor why the formation flying was done at night and through cloud cover.

So the rumors spread, further irking Sir Thom, who was beginning to wonder if he'd out-cagied himself by volunteering to be held in seclusion with the fliers.

Hal gave no answers for three days.

He continued the training, but added something – having the entire squadron fly formation.

Now it had to be a parade, the other fliers agreed.

They didn't see the preparations Hal was working out of sight: army victuallers had been combing the area for sheep, hogs and calves. These were taken in herds to other flights on other fields, and butchers assigned.

Everyone knew something was up with the fliers.

But no one except Hal, the magicians, and Lord Cantabri knew just what.

Or so Kailas hoped.

Limingo and Bodrugan were quite busy with a small project Hal had given them. They took two days to complete it.

On the fourth day after his flight into Roche, Hal assembled his squadron, plus Sir Thom.

"My congratulations," he said. "You've been surrounded by what looks like a pack of foolishness for some weeks, with never an explanation.

"Now, you'll get one."

He told them what the magicked rocks were, and that they were intended for use against the heart of the Roche. He said the mission would take eight days, and the people on the ground didn't need to know the details of the flight, nor the target. In time, they'd be told.

Now that boulder still against the map tent got admiring looks, and comments were made about just how much damage that would do against Queen Norcia.

Hal broke the fliers, and Sir Thom, away from the non-flying members of the squadron, and took them into one of the dragon tents.

The dragons had been moved out, and all that was in the tent was a magical, very precise, model of Carcaor, from the river to the surrounding hills.

"Here's our target," Hal said, and stepped into the model. He went to its center.

"This is Queen Norcia's palace, and here is the Hall of the Barons. Those are our prime targets, as well as anything else that looks impressive or military.

"This model was made by our magic men," he indicated Limingo and Bodrugan, "from paintings and sketches of Carcaor, and the memories of half a dozen men and women who were familiar with the city before the war.

"Probably it'll have changed somewhat.

"But I doubt if the palace will have moved.

"We will leave the day after tomorrow. I want you to study this model all this afternoon. Our wizards will be giving you a memory spell, so you won't be able to forget what you're learning.

"Tomorrow morning, we'll practice the squadron formation

one last time. You'll have the afternoon to rest and think about our target.

"We'll leave an hour after sundown tomorrow night."

There was one further bit of business to take care of, that Hal had been reminded of during the recon flight.

He'd gone to Lord Cantabri for permission.

"Why not?" the scar-faced man had asked. "I should have thought of it myself. Your fliers don't seem to have a long life, and they might as well live what they've got with all the advantages we can give them.

"But I can't knight them. Only the king can do that."

"I don't think," Hal said, "that I've got many fliers that give a rat's nostril about being a sir.

"Unless, of course, there's money or a particularly gaudy medal that goes with it."

Mynta Gart was promoted captain, as were all three of the flight commanders. Farren Mariah was commissioned lieutenant, as were Sir Loren and the Sagenes, Danikel and Rer Alcmaen.

It should have made for a raucous celebration. But not with the mission on the morrow. And not under Hal's controlling eye.

A glass of sparkling wine with the evening meal, then a brandy, and that was enough.

Cabet came up to Hal, looking a bit worried.

"Yes, young Captain?" Hal asked jovially, even though Cabet had to be five years older than Hal.

Cabet wondered what these promotions were going to do to discipline.

"Nothing," Hal said. "Or there'll be a sudden increase in ex-officers."

"If this goes on," Cabet said, "we'll have the whole damned squadron commissioned."

"And what would be the matter with that?" Hal asked.

Cabet started to say something, stopped, frowned, then shook his head and left Hal alone.

Farren Mariah, of course, said he was outraged, that he didn't want to be an officer, that none of his family had ever been officers, whose only real job was kissing the ass of noblemen, but they were proud, independent.

However, when Hal left the mess, he saw Farren, sitting on a wagon with Chincha, and saw his hand continually stroking his new rank tab.

The butchers at the other fields had set to their task, killing the animals intended for dragon fodder, and canvas-wrapping the carcasses, as had been done for Hal's reconnaissance.

"I should ask to fly with you," Sir Thom said. "For this will be a tale worth the seeing. The eyewitness account of how the Dragonmaster singed the Queen's . . . uh, she doesn't have a beard, now does she?"

"No, you shouldn't ask," Hal said flatly. "First, if we run into any Roche dragon flights, you'd weigh me down.

"Second, somebody's got to cover the First Squadron with glory.

"And if you go and do something dumb like fall off, who can we bring in to sing our praises?"

Sir Thom was palpably relieved. Hal hid a grin. He still remembered Lowess's discomfort at being close to the sharp end during the battle of Kalabas.

The greater moon was on the wane, the smaller already set as they took off that night.

Hal was the first away, and he brought Storm, who was carrying the carcasses of a pig and a calf strapped under his belly, around over the field in a slow orbit as the others cleared the ground and formed on him.

There were fifty-nine dragons in the air. Hal thought that was perhaps the most that had ever been flown at once, certainly the most that had ever taken off on a single mission.

They circled the field one final time, climbing for height, and far below Sir Loren's dragon sent up a lonely honk.

Still climbing, they flew toward the lines.

A single Deraine lookout, on a rocky, bare outcropping, saw the dragons, and began waving.

It was a sign for Hal, he decided, but he didn't know of what. He took it as good luck.

They crossed the lines at five hundred feet, flying above the scattered clouds.

Hal flew at the point, followed by Cabet and his 18th flight. On either side flew Richia's 34th Flight and Pisidia's 20th. Above the formation flew Hal's own 11th flight, Gart at its head, guarding against the slight possibility there might be a Roche patrol aloft and above them.

But the air was empty, and if they were seen by the Roche below, Hal saw no sign of an alarm.

Hal led the formation on, flying by the moon and by compass, all that night, and into the next dawn.

It was early morning when their first stop came clear, and Hal brought the dragons down toward the meadow.

In its middle was a long yellow cloth panel.

That was the arranged signal the stay-behind raider was to use if there were no intruders. He'd been spell-sealed by Limingo not to reveal that information, even under torture.

The great formation landed, and each flier unloaded and fed his dragon.

Richia came to him, said one flier from his flight had to turn back. His dragon was flying oddly, as if a wing had been sprained.

Fifty-eight fliers.

Hal decided to press his luck, and not wait for nightfall, but get farther away from the front lines.

This second stage would be a long day, for as soon as the dragons were fed and watered, and given two hours' rest, their gear was loaded on, and, protesting, tired, the flight moved on to the next stop.

Again, they crossed the rich valley, and this time were seen by some riders, and a group of farm workers, who shouted and waved.

Hal had given orders if something like this happened, and so his fliers waved back, and shouted enthusiastically. Hal had a Roche banner rolled and tied against his carapace, and he let it fly free, and heard cheering from below.

They flew on, and saw, once, far in the distance, a pair of dragons. Hal couldn't tell if they were wild or not. But they saw the formation, and hastily dove out of sight.

It was late afternoon when they came down on the lake, after having seen the yellow banner waiting.

Hal had worried about the dragons wanting to sport about in the water, but they were too tired, and, after being fed, curled under the trees and went promptly to sleep.

The raider they'd left as guard had taken game, set up racks, and had smoked meat for the fliers, an unexpected change from the rations they carried.

As he'd said, he was quite happy in this lonely valley, and said he wouldn't mind staying on until the war ended, if Hal wanted.

Hal tried to sleep, but found it hard, his mind bringing up visions of Carcaor from many angles and their attack, and which would be the best way to approach.

But eventually sleep rolled over him.

He was brought awake by the raider, standing sentry. It was growing dark, and, around the lake, the dragons were coming awake, walking into the lake and thrashing about.

Most of the fliers followed suit, and again they strapped their gear on, and climbed into the skies.

Hal was beginning to have a bit of hope that his overly-elaborate plan might be carried off.

His mood was heightened by the flight along the empty winding forest valley. They stayed low, for the area around Carcaor might be patrolled by dragons, although Hal couldn't think of a reason why, since there'd been no threat to the capital.

Yet.

They saw only one person that evening – a young boy, fishing in a bright green rowboat, just at dusk, in the middle of a winding creek. Hal waved, and the boy waved back, and then the formation was gone.

Hal wondered what the boy had thought, and if he'd ever learn that the dragons were his enemies, or if he'd think they were fellow Roche, and maybe be drawn to flying himself.

He grunted at himself for being a damned romantic, concentrated on his flying.

It was, thankfully, a dull flight, and so Hal was glad to see the rolling meadows marking their third stop appear, just before false dawn.

They landed, and it was a rather bloody paradise for the dragons as they steered panicked sheep this way and that, always ending in a dragon's satisfied gullet.

Some of the fliers got a bit greenish at the sight, and even Hal had to admit a touch of queasiness.

One flier who paid fascinated attention, though, was Danikel. Hal asked him about it, and the man said, very seriously, that the more he knew about dragons the better he'd be at killing Roche.

There was no argument about that.

Hal was glad to see there were no outraged shepherds to deal with.

He decided to press their luck once more, and so ordered the fliers to be roused late the next morning and flew on to their final stop, the crag just beyond Carcaor.

Each dragon carried two carcasses tied in canvas – one for this night's meal, the next for the day after the raid. Hal wasn't sure how that would work out – if there were dragons patrolling Carcaor, or if they'd be able to get out as smoothly as he hoped they'd go in.

But that was for the morrow.

It was hazy that day, which gave decent cover for the squadron. Once again, Hal saw no dragons in the air, wondered if every one the Roche had captured was serving at the front. But that was impossible: they would have to have some way of training dragons – and their fliers – and they'd hardly do that in combat.

The Ichili River was below them, winding toward the capital, and the crag that would be their final layover loomed.

Hal felt another inexplicable chill seeing it.

He took Storm in over the ruined castle, looking for the yellow banner.

There was none.

Hal thought about finding another base, but it was late in the day. He certainly couldn't raid Carcaor with the supplies still on the dragons, and his boulders and the firedarts he'd brought unready to deploy.

He blew a blast on his trumpet, but there was no sign of his raider.

But there were no signs of Roche, either.

Hal took a deep breath, brought Storm in below the castle, on that open parade area.

Storm didn't seem to like landing there any better than Hal did.

He dismounted, crossbow ready.

But the crag was deserted.

There was a soft wind across the crag, and leaves moved on the weird trees below the crest.

No more.

Hal blew an alerting note on his trumpet, not wanting to, somehow reluctant to disturb the silence.

The dragons came in, and none seemed glad to be on this mountaintop, although Hal thought he might be putting his own feelings on the obviously tired beasts.

He told the flight commanders what had happened, and, even

though the fliers needed rest, put a third of the squadron on alert.

Farren Mariah came to him as he was going over the last details of the attack.

"I like your home very little, sir, even though it has a great view."

Hal hesitated, then told Mariah of his own feelings.

"I'd guess the raider got spooked and ran off," Farren said. "I surely would've considered it. But from what I've seen of Cantabri's killers, there's nothing on the earth or beyond it that would scare them.

"And I'm starting to scare me," he went on. "I think I'll shut my hole and get my head down.

"Although I won't be pissing and whining about having to take a turn on guard.

"I always feel better with a sword – or anyways a good solid tree branch – in my hand."

Hal nodded agreement, found his flight commanders, and made sure they were ready for the morrow, which would come early.

He took the first watch, and would take the last as well.

All was quiet, except for the occasional snore of a dragon, or the rattle of a wing as they moved in their sleep.

The last of the dying moons were setting as Hal came off guard, and curled up near Storm to get an hour or so's rest.

He slept . . . and he dreamed.

Hal was in the minds of several men as he tossed and turned.

A crude savage who traded for furs with the bearded men who came up the river with strange gifts.

One of the traders, craftier than his fellows, for he had a post on the river, and was clearing land beyond it for farming.

A still cleverer man who ended up with his post, and the land.

Then it was as if he were standing at a distance, watching a moving tableau.

There was a town a-building on the land, after the farmers who'd thought they'd owned it had been run off or killed.

But the river rose, and took the town.

The men rebuilt it on higher ground, and it became a city.

Then something came on them from the heavens above.

Hal couldn't tell, in his dream, if it was a demon, or some sort of earth spirit. But it was so fearsome that men died of fright just seeing it loom down on them.

It ravaged the city in a night, smashing and killing and, when dawn came, there were but few survivors.

They were stubborn, and there were wizards among them.

They cast spells, and determined that spirit or demon had come from the highest crag in the range that ran alongside the river.

Some peoples would have fled, or tried to placate whatever it was.

These men were different.

Using the labor of many slaves, the last of the native peoples of the region, and magic, they built a great castle, and assigned their strongest wizards to stand guard against the spirit, giving them power and the best of food, drink, men and women as payment.

Time passed, and the demon didn't appear again, nor did the guardians sense any sign of its presence.

They thought it might have died, if something beyond life could die, or perhaps had left this universe for another.

No one knew.

But there seemed little purpose in keeping the watch, and so the castle was abandoned.

Three storms within a year of its abandonment tore at the castle, and smashed it down.

Some people in the city on the river, growing larger and more powerful by the day, said this was a warning, or a sign the spirit still was present.

They were laughed at.

There were more important things to think of for the men and women of the city now named Carcaor – power, and wielding that power to form a great nation.

The magicians had lost their authority, so now barons, and then kings and queens ruled Carcaor and the lands around that were named Roche.

No one cared about the ruins far above the city, and no one visited them.

Perhaps there was still something there, something sleeping under the crumbling walls.

No one knew.

Hal woke, sweating, feeling like he'd not slept at all.

It was almost time for the last guard, and so he relieved the post he'd assigned himself to, not fancying returning to that dream, and what else it might show.

It took the entire watch for him to come fully awake and rid himself of the dread that pulled at him.

But eventually it was gone, and there were other things to concern himself with as the dragons were saddled and readied for battle.

The firedarts were unpacked from their straw covers, and put in baskets on either side of the saddles. A pouch was hung on each dragon's carapace, holding the ensorcelled bits of that great boulder.

The dragons were fed, and the men flew them off the crag to the river below, to water them.

Then it was time, and they took off again, and circled up and up, out of the canyon, above the crag, and then on up the Ichili River in the dark.

It was bare minutes before false dawn when they rounded the last bend.

Carcaor, still sleeping, with only a few lights gleaming, was before them.

If Limingo and Bodrugan's model was at fault, Hal couldn't tell. The waterfront and warehouses sprawled to his left, along the river, and the suburbs stretched ahead of him, on Carcaor's far side.

The city's center was very obvious, all tall buildings, elaborate parks and palaces.

In the center was Queen Norcia's palace, two golden domes on either side of the huge entrance.

Hal tooted his trumpet once, and the four flight commanders echoed his command.

The dragons spread out on line, as trained.

Hal steered Storm at the palace.

Dragons had been called "whispering death" by the Roche front line troops. Now their capital was about to experience this death.

He fumbled open the pouch in front of him, took out a small fragment.

For an instant he panicked, not being able to remember the activating spell. But then his battle nerves steadied, and the spell came back.

He chanted the words as the palace closed, finished, felt the fragment squirm unpleasantly in his fingers, as if it were jelly instead of stone.

He tossed it away, and, as it arced downward, past Storm's wings, it grew and grew. Then it was a monstrous boulder.

It hit one of the palace's rooftops, bounced high, and smashed through one of the domes.

Two other great boulders tumbled down from other dragons. One crashed on the palace steps, rolled through four columns, breaking them like toothpicks.

The portico sagged, as another boulder missed the palace, striking short of the palace. But it bounced like Hal's had, and shattered a wall.

Then Hal was past, bringing Storm back around.

Not far distant was the Hall of Barons. Hal saw a pair of boulders destroy its flat roof, then he was leaning forward, a pebble in his hand, and, as he said the spell, he pitched the pebble at the back wall of the palace.

It tore through it, and stones cascaded down.

To one side was a great stable, and a mis-aimed boulder tore its wall away.

He heard the scream of terrified horses as he came around once more, and his boulder struck the palace square in the center.

I would hope, he thought savagely, that it landed on Queen Norcia's bed. With her and her favorite in it.

He heard dragons scream, saw, in the streets below, a unit of heavy cavalry in formation.

Hal, remembering his hatred and fear of the heavies when he'd been a cavalryman himself, took Storm low, and tossed a pebble at them.

It grew, and tumbled horses and riders aside like bowling pins.

There was a great building, perhaps an office, perhaps luxury apartments, and Storm barely turned aside in time.

Hal glanced back, saw Farren Mariah as he hurled his pebble at the building.

It grew, smashed into its center, and stone crumbled, and fell.

Again and again Hal struck at the palace.

Other fliers were crisscrossing the city center, and Hal almost rammed one, a blue female, recognized Danikel, and saw the fierce look of glee on his face, staring down at Carcaor, not seeing Kailas at all.

The palace was tumble-down, and Hal, with only a few pebbles left, went after large buildings behind it, not knowing what they were, offices or, this close to the palace, apartments for the powerful.

Then the last pebble was gone.

Below, the Roche were streaming out of their homes in wakening panic.

You've not good reason yet for a frenzy, Hal thought, and took a pair of fire darts from their baskets, clung to Storm with his knees, and cold-bloodedly pitched them down into the middle of a mass of men.

The darts exploded, and Hal could hear the screams.

Now have your riot, and that'll teach you to go and play at war, he thought and took Storm over the ruined Hall of the Barons.

Two firedarts went down into the shatter, and flames bellowed up.

Other buildings were afire as well, and fire was licking at the heart of Norcia's palace.

There was no one else in the skies except Hal's dragons, and he went down a broad boulevard, almost below the rooftops of the buildings around him, dropping firedarts as if he was a peasant, sowing a furrow.

Behind him, the inferno gouted.

Then he was dry, with nothing left to kill with, and took Storm high.

Other fliers had spent their weaponry, and were climbing as well.

Hal saw a single Roche dragon, boring in from the east.

A brave man, he thought.

And a fool, as he sent Storm diving down.

The Roche flier looked up, just as Hal triggered his crossbow.

The bolt took him in the chest, and he dropped off his dragon.

There were trumpet blasts from the flight leaders, and the squadron had finished its raid.

Hal took Storm high once more, then back to the west, toward the crag, his squadron in a ragged echelon behind him.

He came around the first bend, and saw the crag, now with ominous clouds rolling around it.

There'd been no sign of weather when they'd taken off, but over mountains things can change rapidly.

Hal was trying to decide if he'd chance staying on the crag through the day, or just feed the dragons and fly on, back toward that meadow, when the ruined castle ahead of him lifted, as if there was some creature digging out from underneath it.

There was.

The creature, brown like graveyard earth, reared, the castle stone cascading off its body.

He was, Hal thought, trying to suppress panic, more than two hundred feet tall.

But it was no bear, for its body, if that's what it was, moved, shifting, as if seen through rippling water.

There was no head, but just fangs, and a mouth, screeching like no animal or legend Hal had ever known of.

It had long talons, and thick arms, reaching for the fliers.

Hal forced his shock away, blasted a command to turn right, away from the monster, the demon, the spirit, into the clouds boiling around the summit.

The dragons were flying as hard as they could, at least as afraid of the spirit as any of the men.

Hal realized he was moaning in fear.

Then they were in the cloud, and the winds caught Storm, and tossed them, then they were in calm for an instant, then winds from another direction took them, and hurled them about.

Hal reached for his compass, but it was under his tunic, and it was all he could do to hang on to Storm's reins.

At least they were headed away from the nightmare, flying north.

He broke out of the clouds, and almost screamed, for somehow the clouds had turned them about, and they were flying straight at the mountain peak and the waiting demon.

Hal had an instant to realize the clouds had been summoned by the monster, wondered if it was a creature of the earth or air, realized it didn't matter.

Behind Hal came the rest of the squadron, drawn by this death dream as if it were a lodestone.

Hal managed to reach for his crossbow, knowing that it was like hurling spitballs at a lion.

From his right Pisidia plummeted past, followed by his flight, diving straight into the monster.

Pisidia was screaming something that Hal couldn't make out, and firing bolts from his crossbow into what might have been the demon's face.

Kailas had his trumpet up, and was blowing a retreat. But the 20th Flight seemed deaf, determined to join Pisidia in death.

The monster reached out, almost casually, took Pisidia's dragon in its grasp, and smashed it down, spinning, spinning, into the canyon and the river below.

The spell, if spell it was, broke, and Hal was able to kick Storm into a tight turn, away from the horror.

Behind him came the others in the squadron.

He saw the creature swatting the air, hitting two of the 20th dragons, and knocking them out of the sky. Then the spell broke for the others in the flight, and they, too, tried to break away after Hal.

Then Kailas was back in the cloud, this time finding his compass, and leaning close over it as the winds tore at him.

The winds, accomplices of the nightmare, tried to turn him, send him back into its maw, but he managed to hold his course.

The clouds were intermittent, rushing past, and he saw, now and again, beside and behind him, other dragons, battling the storm, all following his lead.

Again they were in the clear and this time the crag was gone, hidden behind them. Mountains were below them, clean, honest peaks with no eldritch horrors hidden under ruined battlements.

Hal realized Storm was flying as fast as he could, and would soon wear himself out.

He bent forward, stroking the beast's neck, saying meaningless words in as soothing a tone as he knew.

Storm's wingbeats slowed.

Again, he looked back, and saw the ragged formation of dragons behind him.

Hal forced Storm up into a climb, then a turn, heading back on his unit.

There were trumpet blasts, and shouts, and slowly the panic broke, and the dragon fliers began sorting out their formation.

Assembled, it made two complete orbits while Hal counted his beasts.

Fifty-two were still flying, not including Storm.

He'd lost five dragons in that nightmare over the crag, or possibly one or more in the attack on Carcaor.

Hal turned the squadron again, holding a return course, back for the sheep-meadow.

It was no more than midday when they reached it, and landed.

None of the dragons were hungry, nor were their fliers.

Everyone was pale, shaken, jabbering about what they'd seen, whether it'd been real or not.

Hal shouted for a formation, and, reluctantly, the fliers obeyed.

"You will stay silent," he ordered. "We did well today. What that . . . that thing was, I have no idea.

"Right now, you're to eat.

"Then we're going to punish ourselves, and push on. We haven't been pursued or hit by the Roche yet, and I'm hoping we can make our lines before their wizards have time to alert the Roche squadrons there to be prepared.

"Now, to your dragons, and make sure they eat something, even though they're still winded and wound up. We'll be taking off again in an hour. Move out."

He quite deliberately said nothing about Pisidia's death, nor the others of his squadron. A little anger at Kailas's heartlessness might do a deal to break the shock the fliers all felt over the monstrous demon, or whatever it was.

As the fliers finished, he had them shoot down and hasty-dress sheep, then tie them under the dragons.

An hour later, by the sun, he had Storm watered and fed, although the dragon ate little, compared to his usual voraciousness.

They took off, and assembled in formation, then flew on, north and a bit east.

One flier carried the raider who'd been assigned to the meadow with them.

Hal kept careful account of his compass heading, and his estimated flying time as the shadows walked long on the land below.

There was just enough moonlight for him to see the lake below, and bring the dragons down.

None were hungry, but all were thirsty and exhausted.

He ordered the fliers to force the dragons into the lake, and splash them about.

It seemed to help – they came out of the water hungry, and devoured the sheep, while the fliers made do with the smoked game.

Then everyone slept as if stunned.

Hal should have posted a guard, but didn't think anyone, outside of maybe an airborne magician, would find this cleft in the hills.

The caretaking raider was enough of a guardian.

They got up at dawn, and flew hard to the first night's base, the peaceful meadow, arriving in the afternoon.

"An hour's rest," Hal ordered. "And food. Then we're off again, as soon as the sun dips down. I'm hoping we can muscle through the lines by dark. Once we're across, I'll worry about where we land."

There were mutters, but quiet ones. Most of the fliers still had some energy from the excitement of the rage, and none of them, not even Danikel, wanted to face Yasin's black dragons with exhausted mounts.

The dragons were complaining when they were resaddled, snapping at the riders and honking complaint.

But they stumbled into the air, and Hal took them high, feeling for a wind. He found one, blowing due west, and let the dragons glide on it.

Again, he was counting time, and by the early morning, guessed he was closing on the front.

He blew a warning note on his trumpet, and took his fliers in a long dive to less than a hundred feet above the ground.

Hal looked up into the skies as they came across the rearmost Roche positions and saw half a dozen dragons, dots in the sky, waiting for him.

The magicians had alerted Yasin, or other Roche dragon flights.

But they'd guessed he would be high, and Hal had fooled them.

They dove hard for him, but turned away as they closed, realizing the squadron wasn't breaking formation, and that they were vastly outnumbered.

Then the pits and tents of the infantry were below, and they were across the dead ground between the lines.

Hal was trying to see just where they'd crossed, to get an estimated direction toward their base, if possible.

But he was having little luck, as fatigue crawled over his body, fogging his mind.

Storm snorted in surprise, and Hal saw, to his left, a spatter of whirling, magical lights in the sky.

There was someone alive, and awake, over there, and he steered the squadron toward the lights.

Landmarks below became recognizable, even in this dark, and he realized the lights were coming from somewhere close to the First Squadron's home base.

They weren't close, they were in the middle of it.

Hal, believing in miracles, brought Storm in. A handler ran up to him, caught him as he slipped out of the saddle, almost falling.

"Limingo the magician cast a spell," the man said, unbidden. "Said you were approaching, and would need a guide. I dunno how he knew it."

Dragons were thudding down on the field around Hal.

"We've got food – and fodder – ready," the man went on. "And drink."

Hal nodded dumbly.

But all he could think of was that wonderful cot in the quiet little tent that was waiting.

He stumbled off the field, as two men led Storm away, toward his shelter.

Sir Thom Lowess was there.

"Well, did you do it?"

Hal nodded.

"Do you want to tell me . . . " Lowess caught himself. "Sorry for being a damned fool. Maybe, when you wake."

Hal nodded, pushed past Lowess, and then there was the cot in front of him.

He slumped down on it, managed to pull one boot off.

His orderly, Uluch, was there, trying to help. He pushed him away, reached for his other boot. Then the world swirled, and was gone as sleep took him for its own.

27

Hal woke, undressed, in his cot. It was just a bit after dawn. He hoped he hadn't slept more than the clock around.

Peering cautiously out of his tent, he saw the dragon handlers currying and feeding the still-disheveled monsters, and realized he'd only slept a few hours, although he felt as full of energy as he had before the raid.

He suspected he would run out of energy later that day, but determined to ride the spurt as long as it lasted.

Hal swung out of bed, realized he had a bursting bladder, and walked carefully to the small circular canvas pisser behind his tent.

Vastly relieved, he came back to see a steaming mug of tea, and a plate of crisp bacon and eggs scrambled with chives on a small table.

"Thank you, Uluch," he said into thin air, didn't wait for a reply, but ate, famished.

He went to the bathing tent, came back clean and shaved. A fresh uniform was laid out for him, and he was very grateful he'd been talked into having an orderly.

He came out, and Gart, looking a bit bleary, was waiting.

"I want Storm ready to fly in . . ." And he stopped himself. "Sorry. Dragons need rest, too."

He thought.

"Ask Sir Thom if he'd lend me his carriage. And say that he'd be welcome to ride along with me to army headquarters."

"Yes, sir," Gart said.

"And have the goods of the men who died wrapped up," Kailas said. "Have someone sort through them to make sure there'll be nothing embarrassing go to the family."

Such as love letters to another woman or man, fish skins, and the like. What military goods were in the casualty's locker would be auctioned off on the squadron, generally for ridiculous amounts, and the moneys sent on to the dead man – or woman's – family.

Supposedly there were now pensions for those maimed or killed in battle, but the old habit begun at the start of the war still hung on.

Everyone may have respected King Asir, but almost no one had full confidence in his, or anybody else's, government.

Sir Thom clattered up in his surrey, quite unable to hide his eagerness.

Hal assumed he'd already heard bits and pieces from squadron chatter, but told the story from the beginning on the ride to First Army headquarters. He first swore Sir Thom to secrecy, and knew the man's word was good.

He left out the spirit or demon, not sure if that should become common knowledge.

At headquarters, he told Cantabri everything that had happened, and told him he'd be handing in a written report later in the day.

He also said he'd told Sir Thom the essentials of the raid, leaving out the demon.

Hal asked Cantabri if that should be included.

"No," Cantabri said, then stopped, and thought for long moments.

"Actually, there was a request from the king for you to proceed to Rozen and report directly to him."

Hal thought of civilization, a chance to be under a real roof instead of canvas, a meal not cooked by the numbers, but most of all of Khiri.

"No," he said, then made a quick revision, seeing Cantabri's frown. "Sorry, sir. Of course I'll go ... if you order me to. But I've been on leave more recently than anyone else in my squadron, and I don't think it would be fair. Plus there's work to be done with the squadron, and I can't forever be running off to ... to do whatever I do."

Hal had reconsidered what he was about to say at the very last instant.

Cantabri gnawed a lip.

"No," he said reluctantly. "No, it wouldn't. The king won't be pleased, but he'll understand. I hope. He'll damned well have to. But you'll have to get a report ready ... a good one, with details and color, not just a facts-blurt."

"Yessir," Hal said.

"Now, back to this matter of that demon or whatever it was," Lord Cantabri went on, frowning. "I wish I could keep it a secret, for it surely is a noisome matter. Especially as you don't seem to know whether this monster can be summoned by the Roche ... or if it appears spontaneously.

"But I doubt if we can gag everyone on your squadron and make them keep silent for long."

"No," Hal agreed, thinking of Alcmaen, Farren Mariah, the dragon handlers. "No, I can't keep it that quiet. They'll be talking on the squadron, and it'll get out sooner or later."

"So I guess you'd best tell Sir Thom. But tell him to keep it silent until someone – you or myself – gives him permission to write about it. That might keep the rumor from exploding completely out of control. Maybe." Cantabri nodded. "That's all."

"One more thing," Hal said. "When do you want the squadron to return to normal duties? I want to start cycling my men out on leave. Some of them haven't been home for a year or more."

"I'm thinking at present that the First Squadron may never be on normal duties," Cantabri said. "Whatever they are. I'm thinking that I want them as a special duty squadron, like the raiders."

"Thank you, sir," Hal said. "I'll be glad of that."

"You, and the other killers only," Cantabri said. "Because anyone who's sane, and I don't think there's a dragon flier around who is, would realize special duties will increase the chances of their getting killed."

"They're all volunteers," Hal said, a bit of harshness in his voice. "That's part of the bargain."

"So it is, so it is," Cantabri sighed. "As for this leave, go ahead. Say, five at a time. I can't see anything on the horizon in the next couple of weeks, not until we know how Norcia and the rest of the Roche hierarchy took their capital being attacked."

Hal stood, saluted.

"Thank you, sir. But I'll also want to have my men making patrols over the front, just for training." He made a face. "And if you'll excuse me, I've got letters to write after the raid."

Cantabri nodded grimly.

Hal had been too intent on his squadron and reporting to Cantabri to notice the small pile of letters waiting for him, weighed down by a gauntlet.

All, except a plaintive bill from his tailor, were from Khiri.

He should have written those letters to Pisidia and the other casualties of the 20th Flight's next of kin.

But he allowed himself a moment of selfishness, and read the letters from Khiri.

Written almost daily, they were precisely what he needed: a chronicle of her daily life, and the life at Cayre a Carstares, her castle on Deraine's west coast. Nothing to do with the war, but the trivia of summer, and the approaching harvest, and who was reportedly doing what to whom in Rozen.

Except for one:

Dear Hal

I probably shouldn't be writing this to you, since I don't want to worry you ever, but two nights running I've had a most disturbing dream. It only lasted for a moment, but I woke, crying, both times. If you were here, I'd wake you up, and let you tell me what a silly I am. But you aren't, so please indulge me for a moment, and let me tell you about it. Then, if you wish, you can write me, and tell me I'm a silly.

I dreamed I was on this great plain, and the ground was torn up, as if there'd been a battle. There were ruined catapults, and torn tents, and broken swords and lances. But there were no bodies, no soldiers. This landscape stretched on and on, almost to the horizon. But just before it, was a city I didn't recognize.

The only thing moving, coming toward me, was a dot that became a dragon. I think it might have been Storm, for it wasn't black like the dangerous dragons you've told me about. But you weren't riding it, even though it was saddled.

That was all there was to the dream. I didn't feel threatened, by the dragon or anything else, but as I said, I woke up crying.

You told me once that dreams have no meaning, that they aren't prophecies or anything. But I worry. Are you all right? Write me soon, please.

Your Khiri

Hal made a face. Certainly he didn't write her as much as he should, as much as he wanted. He didn't have the gift of putting words on paper. But now he found paper and a pen, and decided he would write her a long, cheerful letter, before he turned to the grim matter of the other letters.

Pisidia, as it turned out, had not only a wife, but three children as well. That letter was hard, but the hardest was to a Sagene widow, whose only son had been killed by that great monster.

It was with true relief that Hal finished the letters, and turned to the king's report.

"You wish?" Hal asked Lieutenant Goang. He was sitting in a corner of the mess, watching his pilots cavort drunkenly. He was watching them carefully, for a favorite flier game, when drinking, was to somehow suck their commanding officer into their stupid games, such as rubbing ashes on their boots, and having other fliers turn them upside down, so they could "walk" on the ceiling, or riding a horse into the mess or swotting at each other with rolled up broadsheets, blindfolded.

Often enough, Hal, and other flying officers, felt like playing the fool themselves and let themselves get drawn into the idiocy.

But, for some reason, this night Hal didn't feel like drinking and carrying on. Maybe it was the letters, or maybe he was finally letting down after the raid.

"A word with you, sir," Goang said. "An idea."

"Good," Hal said. "That's what I pay you for. Or, rather, the king does."

"I've been thinking of various ideas," Goang said. "But none of them have been worth bringing to you. I think I wasn't thinking right."

"And you're sober, saying that?"

"Yessir. I wasn't considering magic, until we were told about those pebbles."

"So consider magic." Hal decided Goang didn't have much of a sense of humor.

"That's what I've been doing, while you sorts were off being heroes. You're from the north of Deraine, aren't you?"

"I was," Hal said. "But that was a long time ago."

"Was your home around any mines?"

"To put it mildly."

"Did you ever have any disasters? Any mining explosions?"

The memory came to Hal instantly, from when he was no more than six or seven. There'd been screams, and running men, and then the big bellows alarm at one of the mines had started screaming.

There were twenty men trapped, far down.

The village miners started trying to dig them out.

Everyone else did what they could to help. Hal's mother and father set up a kitchen near the mine, and someone else put up a tent for the rescue workers to sleep in, out of the omnipresent drizzle.

But they hadn't dug more than half a day when the ground rocked, and flames spurted out of the pit head. They'd gone up maybe a hundred feet, then died as the blast wave shot out after them.

The twenty trapped men were dead, and another ten rescuers after them.

"Once, twice," Hal said shortly, not comfortable with the memory. "Firedamp, it was."

"Just so, sir," Goang said eagerly. "Gas that explodes when flames hit it."

Hal nodded.

"What would happen if we somehow got some of that, and confined it in a bottle, then set fire to the bottleneck, maybe with a rag?"

"It would explode, I'd imagine," Hal said.

"Suppose we wrapped the bottle with a bandage, with nails, bits of glass, things like that inside it?"

Hal considered.

"A nice, light weapon," Goang went on. "Ideal against troops or cavalry."

"If it worked," Hal said.

"Maybe it would, if there was a spell igniting it," Goang said.

"Another idea I've had . . . When you were coming back, even though you were a day early, Limingo sensed it. Or, rather, he told me he'd cast a spell on your saddle, so when it drew near, he could feel it, and have those signs in the air to guide you."

"Damned helpful it was, too," Hal said, realizing he was starting to sound like a curmudgeonly old fart, typical of a unit commander. "Sorry. What would Limingo's magic do elsewhere, since I assume that's what you're driving at?"

"Suppose – I don't know how – but suppose we could get a bit of, say, what *Ky* Yasin feeds his black dragons. Suppose Limingo put a spell on it, and that spell could be passed along to all the fliers, so when Yasin's dragons are in the air, somehow we'd know about it, and be able to get airborne ourselves and maybe above his squadron?"

Hal thought.

"I'm damned if I see how we could do that. But it is a hell of an idea. I'm not sure about the firedamp, either." Hal shuddered. "Most likely it's my own memories stopping me.

"What I think you seem to need now is to talk to a magician. Limingo?"

"Not yet, sir," Goang said. "He's too important and busy to take much time with the likes of me. But I could use his acolyte Bodrugan."

Hal nodded slowly.

"There might be something to either or both of your ideas. I'll see that Bodrugan is sent for, and – YOWP!"

Hal, intent on his thoughts, wasn't watching his pilots. Three of them, led by Mariah, had crept up and jumped on him, knocking him to the floor.

Hal noticed none of them were wearing trousers, and fought futily as Mariah and Chincha started clawing at his breeches.

"This is damned undignified," he yelped.

But no one was listening.

Someone on the squadron wrote home about the fabulous monster his fliers had overcome, and the person who received that letter wrote about it to someone in the army.

The story spread, getting more evil and dangerous by the telling.

Lord Cantabri reluctantly gave Sir Thom permission to write the whole story of the raid.

*

Hal heard nothing from King Asir about his report, or about anything in it.

He wondered if he'd finally overstepped the bounds, by refusing to hurry to the king's side.

But it didn't matter.

What could Asir do?

Send him to Sagene to fight a war?

Hal thought about it long, then called Danikel to his tent, and
told him he wanted the baron to take over the 20th Flight. He'd
been pleased with the idea, since that would put a Sagene in
charge of a quarter of the squadron, and he never forgot the
king's orders to use diplomacy.

Danikel didn't need any time to think.

"Nossir, I can't do that."

"And why not? You'll get your captain's sash, and have more
of a say about fighting the war."

"Nossir. I joined the service to kill Roche. Anything else will
get in my way."

Hal growled, but sent Danikel away.

He pondered more, and, as much as it would complicate his
life, and increase his paperwork, he made Mynta Gart the 20th
Flight commander.

Sir Loren, in spite of his objections, became adjutant, and,
surprisingly, did well.

The first fliers went off on leave. Hal began training the
others. There were howls of protest when he brought in hand-to-
hand instructors from the raiders, but Hal kept remembering his
own captivity, or the fight on the rooftops of Aude, and paid no
attention.

Since these were already combat-experienced fliers, he made
sure at least one patrol a day went out over the lines. That kept
everyone honest, even though he lost a flier on the second day.

But replacements were streaming in, after Sir Thom's tale of the
next daring stroke by the Dragonmaster struck the broadsheets.

Everyone wanted away from the drudge killing of the front
lines, and somehow thought a death, high above the mud, would
be cleaner and more honorable.

Hal doubled the watch on the skies, assuming *Ky* Yasin would
be instructed by his brother to take revenge on the First and
attack the squadron.

But Yasin's black dragons weren't in the skies as the summer drew to a close.

Hal had his own idea of what training he himself needed. He didn't know whether his squadron would be used with the sorcerous pebbles again, hoped they'd train other flights, since he frankly didn't consider ruining the lives of civilians, and improving the lot of builders, doing that much to end the war.

He admitted arrogance, wanted special duties.

Or else going after Yasin, once the bastard and his damned black dragons made their appearance.

Hal trained one on one with each of the other fliers, made them fly company on him through tight maneuvers, reversed their roles, until he had a decent idea of each of his fliers' capabilities.

He also flew the entire squadron as one great formation, teaching each flight how to cover another, led them in darting sweeps across the lines, putting down all Roche fliers.

He had an idea of a change he wanted to make in the way dragons were fought, particularly when the offensive picked up and they hopefully closed on Carcaor.

But what he wanted to do was fly, by himself, on Storm, out over the gray seas, fly west, thinking about where the dragons came from, what their enemies could be.

But the army was too far south, too far inland, to permit that.

He was starting to understand war. In its simplest form – beyond that of simply killing your enemy – it was denying things to people. The army denied him being able to fly when and where he wanted, he denied the Roche the same thing. Ultimately the army denied its enemy land, freedom and, in the end, its life if there was no surrender.

It was a much cleaner way to think than dwelling on the gore.

Or thinking about the poor bastards below, infantry, cavalry, pioneers, dots who killed and died, without changing the course of the world or the war one degree.

Cantabri summoned Hal, and greeted him with a truly evil smile.

That cheered Kailas immensely – the only thing that seemed to please Cantabri was some reverse to the Roche.

"We finally have word from Carcaor," Cantabri said. "One of our agents crossed the lines last night.

"According to him, Queen Norcia had said, back at the start

of the war, that there would be no way Roche, nor any of its people, would be harmed, but that full revenge would be taken on the evil folk of Sagene and Deraine, if they were so stupid as to side with the corrupt Sagenes, and so on and so forth.

"So when your dragons started throwing rocks, it upset the Roche.

"Especially their rulers, after there were protests in the streets.

"I guess Norcia isn't used to peasants and such displaying their feelings, unlike Deraine.

"She – and her barons – overreacted, sending cavalry out to smash these protests.

"There have been more and more of them, and, even better, a few scofflaws who've taken to pegging rocks at anyone seen abroad who looks rich, or wears royal livery."

Cantabri rubbed his hands briskly.

"Nothing better than stirring up a wasps' nest, now is there?

"So now we'll think about how to make matters worse."

Whatever Cantabri had in mind, he didn't say.

Hal considered rocking another Roche city, but realized their dragon fliers would be alerted now, and tried to come up with something new, as well as nasty.

Replacements came in, and Hal wasn't pleased to see they weren't the first flower of youth. There were older men and women now, and some of them didn't look much like the athletic soldiery so beloved of the taletellers.

The war was grinding down everyone.

But that, thankfully, wasn't his concern. The dragon flights were still getting the best, many of them former front line soldiers.

Hal's squadron was ready to fight, at its peak, and almost all of the fliers had gone on leave.

Hal was cursing a mound of paperwork in his tent, when a sentry came running down from his post on the road, shouting incoherently.

Hal came out, buckling his sword on, wondering what the alarm was. He saw, coming into the squadron base, more than a hundred men and women.

They were richly dressed, and the armor of their cavalry escorts gleamed.

There were banners galore, and all of the horses were groomed as if for a parade.

Riding just in front was King Asir.

But Hal wasn't staring at him, unlike the rest of the squadron as they streamed out on to the field.

Four riders behind the king was Lady Khiri Kailas.

28

A cloak was dropped on the ground by two equerries, and the king dismounted on to it. He looked about, at the kneeling fliers and the other men and women of the squadron.

"You may rise," Asir said, and, as Hal got up, he wondered if there was voice training for kings-to-be, so their orders carried as far as they wished.

"I came to visit this squadron," the king said, "for it has pleased me most well. I have authorized, from this time forward, it shall be known as the King's Own First Dragon Squadron, and appropriate emblems shall be made for your uniforms and guidons."

"Thank you, Your Highness," Hal managed.

The king nodded.

"There shall also be medals and promotions given out within the hour, if your commander is pleased to assist me.

"I now wish to converse with him on the matter, in private."

Hal wondered wildly where he could take the king that was not only away from the squadron's ears, but properly dignified.

There simply wasn't anywhere.

Hal must have showed his worry on his face, for the king grinned at him.

"Perhaps, Lord Kailas, we might wish to walk in those woods beyond? Such an pastime might prove relaxing after my long journey."

"Yes . . . of course, Your Majesty."

Hal followed the king, but his eyes kept straying to Khiri, still not sure he really had seen her.

Behind the king and Kailas came six hard-faced men-at-arms, all with the rank sashes of officers, but with the ready, well-worn weaponry of front line soldiers. They kept discreetly out of hearing, discreetly within range of being able to rescue their sovereign if any hostile chipmunks attacked him on his walk.

"Of course," the king said amiably, "you realize I didn't come all this long dreary way through the ruins of war, the first time I've been out of Deraine since the damned Roche attacked us, just to hand out some medals."

"Uh . . ." Hal managed, who'd had no such suspicion, figuring that kings did things like that. "Yessir. Of course, sir."

The king looked at him, lifting a single eyebrow, but said nothing.

"The purpose of my visit to the lines is two-fold. Hopefully to build the morale of my soldiers, but also, after I finish waving the flag, to attend a conference with Sagene's ruling Council of Barons, in Fovant. This, by the way, will be the first time any Derainian monarch has been to their capital.

"Briefly, I'll propose that the barons join me in a grand attack, all along the front, with all four armies."

Hal didn't say anything.

"You think that's stupid?"

Again, Hal held his tongue.

"On the truism that he who attacks everywhere attacks nowhere?"

Hal had heard the phrase.

"It's not my place to have an opinion, sir."

"It may be in time," Asir said. "But there is a bit of method to my madness. I see the Roche as being almost to the stage of tottering. If we hit them hard, we might make the front collapse, and end the war much more rapidly than just hammering away here, as Lord Cantabri and the Sagene are doing.

"In any event, this is the course I propose.

"I will want, naturally, to make my visit to Fovant as splendorous as possible. Which means I want to attach one flight of your squadron to my visit. I'll also be taking representatives of my best cavalry and infantry along.

"Your presence will not only give glamour, but give me security from the air.

"I have great respect for the Roche dragons, their fliers, and their spies, and have enough on my mind to not want to worry about what may be coming out of the skies at me.

"Will you join me, and bring your best?"

It was just like Asir, Hal decided, to put the matter as a request, when he could have made it a simple order.

"Of course, sire. And we're deeply honored."

"Damned well better be," the king said. "Now, if you'll give me some names – I propose to hand out Royal Badges of Honor and Heroes of Deraine medals most promiscuously, following dinner – I'll let you go to your lady.

"Since you were such a snitty little duty-minded commander, and did not return with a report on your raid on Carcaor, I figured you might appreciate it if I brought the Lady Khiri on my visit.

"I also, for your information, plan on using her in Fovant, officially at least, since no one, especially the Sagene, believes that a beautiful woman might have a bit of brains, to listen to any idle gossip that might pertain to the war."

"Uh . . . thank you, sire," Hal managed. He named the survivors of the 11th Flight, other noted fliers, his flight commanders, and several Sagene, including Danikel, and through slightly gritted teeth, Rer Alcmaen.

"Good," the king said. "I realize you've listened to what I told you back in Deraine about coddling the Sagene fliers, and heartily agree with your making sure they're on my honors' list.

"That way of thought is one reason that I agreed to come to the barons, rather than invite them to Deraine.

"Now, shall we return to the others?"

Hal barely remembered returning to the formation, calling the men and women to attention, and dismissing them, with orders to reassemble before the evening meal.

Half-dazed, he led Khiri to his tent, later hoping he showed a bit of dignity in not picking her up in his arms and racing toward the nearest cot or, still worse, tossing her over his shoulder and bolting back into the woods, booming like a bittern.

When he came back to himself, they were both naked, his small field desk was overturned, with papers scattered everywhere.

"You're certainly . . . abrupt in your romancing, Lord Kailas," Khiri managed, still breathing heavily. "In certain circles, it would be regarded that I was raped. Or, maybe, that I raped you."

Hal murmured something inconsequential.

"Now, I suppose we should find a way of cleaning ourselves, and investigating all those crashings and thuddings that came from outside."

"Not yet," Hal said.

"Then what are you planning to . . . " Khiri's voice broke off into a moan.

When they eventually were satiated, it was late afternoon. Uluch had managed to fill and heat a half-barrel, and pitch canvas around it, just outside their tent. Also inside the canvas were Lady Khiri's trunks.

The water was tepid by now, but that didn't matter. They washed, dressed, and Hal put on dress uniform.

Hal still felt dazed, but another kind of dazed, as they came out into the approaching twilight.

He barely recognized his squadron's base.

Certainly it was most romantic for the king to appear on horseback, with his nobles, caparisoned for battle, the very picture of a lean fighting monarch.

Asir may have been romantic, but he was hardly a fool, Hal realized, seeing the panoply that spread around him.

There were large tents, small tents, wagons, covered and open, hostlers with spare horses, cooktents, changing tents, dining tents, and everywhere bustling servants in royal livery, very much a tiny city under canvas.

Khiri saw Hal's expression, started laughing.

"How far behind our liege does all this travel?" Hal asked.

"At least an hour, sometimes half a day."

"So you've been sleeping rough – I suppose this must be called rough for a king – since, what, Paestum?"

"Only twice," Khiri said. "And that was when we were caught out. Normally outriders find a place for us to stay – most generally a Sagene nobleman's castle – in the afternoon."

"It must be nice," Hal said.

"It is," Khiri said. "And I say that smugly."

Hal looked about, saw no one was watching them, slapped her buttocks. She laughed more loudly.

Medals were, indeed, given out liberally, which Hal was glad to see, remembering the early days of the war, when no one except senior officers or the suicidally brave got awards.

As Cantabri had said once, "If a bit of tin and ribbon makes a man fight harder, and stand taller in the eyes of his fellows, why begrudge it?"

Hal sometimes wondered if a liberal policy might cheapen the value of an earlier medal, given under stricter circumstances, but caught himself. It was most unlikely, just for openers, that someone who'd won a medal in the early days was even alive to gripe.

That, in turn, made him think of his own mortality, and, once again, of Saslic's words.

The king invited all in the squadron to be his guests at dinner, which made even Mariah gape a little.

Before the squadron trooped into the great tent, Limingo and Sir Thom Lowess had shown up, Sir Thom muttering his usual incantation at good times about "what a story, what a story."

The meal was interesting – the meats were all roasts, and had been cooked in advance, then preserved by magic until needed, requiring only a few minutes of heating before being ready. There were vegetables, gathered along the way or bought in small villages. The only thing prepared from scratch were the desserts.

"Hard as hell," the king said quietly to Kailas, "being a king, sometimes, particularly when you're traveling. You descend on someone, who's honor-bound to give you the best he can manage, eat the whole damned district out of victuals, then move on, like those damned insects down in the south . . . you know, the squiggly ones with wings."

"Locusts, your Majesty."

The tables were lined with various bottles of wine, but Hal noticed no one had more than a glass or two.

He also noticed that the king barely touched the plates of meat covered with rich sauces, and his main course seemed to be no more than bread soaked in milk.

Asir noted his attention.

"Damned stomach hasn't been worth a damn since this war started," he said a trifle sheepishly. "Acts like a Roche traitor. Another good reason to want peace . . . maybe I'll be able to go back to gourmandizing."

That was a price of sovereignty Hal had never considered.

Hal announced, after everyone had eaten, their new mission, protecting the king while he toured the front.

He didn't mention the upcoming trip to Fovant.

The longer that remained a secret, the safer things would be. He, too, respected Roche dragon fliers, and he guessed their agents, although he'd had only one serious encounter with a spy thus far.

Kailas took his leave early, after eating sanely and, with Khiri, went back to his tent.

They made love deep in the night.

When Khiri finally slept, Hal remained awake, thinking about the conference.

He hoped it would produce results, but, selfishly, the thought kept coming to him that he would be with Khiri and also be away from the front.

His life, and those fliers he chose to take with him, would be extended for at least another month.

And that was a royal favor greater than any medal.

29

A day later, Hal and his dragon fliers moved off with the king's entourage, to Lord Cantabri's headquarters and the front.

Hal, paring detachment requirements to the bone, took a full fifteen fliers – a dragon flight – plus each dragon's pair of handlers, Tupilco the veterinarian, and a handful of orderlies and clerks. He would mess on the king, and the cavalry's smith, armorer, and such could handle the other needs.

The fliers chosen were the 11th's original survivors, Gart as second-in-command and Chincha. The rest were Sagene, including Alcmaen and Danikel. He left Cabet in charge of the squadron.

Those fifty he'd chosen barely counted among the king's company – Asir had at least six hundred retainers with him.

Khiri told Hal that the king was, in fact, traveling very light.

After the king and his retainers reached Cantabri and his generals, Hal made sure he stayed in the air and in the background, wanting as little as possible to do with the high-rankers.

That night, there was an alarum as the guard was turned out. Four men, armored and armed, had tried to break through the cordon around the king. They got as far as the king's tent stables before being seen. One was killed, the others fled, seemingly without doing any damage other than murdering a sentry while getting into the perimeter.

Cantabri, outraged, put his entire Raiding Squadron around the royal household as guards.

The second day was spent resting, and then, for the third, King Asir said he wanted to go forward, into the front lines.

Hal swore the collective gasp from the staffers could have sucked a black dragon down from a thousand feet.

Everyone protested that it wasn't safe, and darted about, gurgling about what would result if something happened.

The worriers were already half apoplectic about the king's habit of riding out just after dawn, with no more than two escorts accompanying him.

Asir didn't listen to either set of objections, and so, early the next morning, Asir, Cantabri, four aides and six escorts crept out toward the lines.

All of them wore drab garments, and were heavily armed. However, the king couldn't let go of being a king, and so a golden, gem-crusted circlet was on his head.

Hal thought that was amusing, hoped that nothing would happen.

He had all his dragons in the air to make sure, at least from his side, nothing would.

Five dragons went high, including Hal. The others orbited the royal group below, in circles as wide as possible not to pinpoint the greatest target the war had seen.

The second line of defense was the rest of Hal's squadron, since they were still within its operating area, and four other flights were on standby.

Hal was watching the lines closely, figuring that the most likely threat would be from a cavalry patrol who happened to see what was clearly an officers' group – all of the men mounted, not riding in any sort of formation or dispersement – and attack.

There would be enough infantry below to drive back any sort of footsoldiery mischief.

Instead, Farren Mariah, below on the close security, blew an alarm on his trumpet.

Hal saw a great wedge of black dragons driving toward the lines.

He counted thirty of them.

The sky was alive with trumpeted warnings, and the Derainian and Sagene fliers climbed for altitude.

The low element was level with the onrushing Roche, and Hal thought he could see *Ky* Yasin's banner on the leading monster. He wasn't close enough to tell if there was gold trim on the banner, which would denote he had a chance at Yasin himself.

He pointed at the oncoming Roche, blew the attack, and his five dove for the point of the wedge.

Hal hoped it would be Yasin, then decided it didn't matter so long as the attack was broken up.

Rather than hit the lead, dive through and climb back up for another target, Hal brought Storm out of his dive just feet above the Roche formation.

The lead monster was rushing toward him.

Hal loosed a crossbow bolt, missed, reloaded, sent Storm into a skidding half-turn with his knees as the lead Roche dove away.

In the back of his mind, Hal decided that Roche couldn't be Yasin, who'd never been known to avoid a fight.

He came in on the wing of the second dragon, fired. His bolt hit that dragon in the neck, and it scrawked, rolled away, as Hal shot the third through the wing, doing little damage, but annoying the big black.

He reared in the sky, and Storm's neck darted, got that dragon just above the breastbone, and ichor gouted.

Storm let go before the Roche dragon could get him in its death flurry, rolled away and down.

Hal let Storm go inverted through a loop, then climbed back up toward the belly of the Roche flight pattern.

Two fliers, flying close together, smashed into the scattering formation, Alcmaen and another Sagene.

A Roche dragon flopped limply, fell, and his mate went after him.

Alcmaen let that one go, hit another one, and a third.

His aim was very true, hitting one dragon in the guts, the second in its eye. Both went down, screaming.

The bastard may have been a bastard, but he was also a most competent killer.

Hal looked for another Roche.

The formation was scattered, diving away.

He started down after a fleeing dragon, recollected his duty, blew the recall.

Slowly his flight regrouped, assembled, as two other Deraine flights hurtled in, just a little late, to support.

Below, over the king's group, Alcmaen was doing slow rolls, to celebrate his triple victory.

*

"Congratulations," King Asir. "You made quite a show today."

"Thank you, sire," Hal said. "I would just like to know what made you such a target."

"So would I," Asir said. "I can't believe anyone has eyes keen enough to have noted my crown. They must have just been lucky."

"I suppose so," Hal said, unconvinced. The king didn't realize how hard it was to launch any kind of dragon strike without notice, let alone one the size of that day's attack.

"I particularly noted one flier," Asir said. "I thought I saw him down three dragons by himself. He was the one flying close attendance on me after the battle."

"Yessir," Hal said, trying to sound neutral. "That would be the Sagene flier, Alcmaen."

"Sagene, eh?" Asir said. "I think I might have heard of him."

"He's a favorite of the Sagene taletellers," Hal said.

"I think it might be politic – in the true sense of the word – to make much of him," Asir said. "I'll make him a Defender of the Throne, which he certainly was."

"Thank you, your Highness," Hal said. "He'll be quite pleased with your having noticed him."

He hoped his voice wasn't as sour as his thoughts.

The king spent three more days visiting the lines. Each day, there were black dragons in the air, but they didn't attempt the attack, since Hal had the First Squadron in close attendance.

Asir announced Alcmaen's award, said it would be formally given in time, which meant when they reached Fovant.

Medals given to the ground troops, weighty nods of approval made, the flag correctly waved, the royal column packed, and began its slow journey west, toward Fovant.

Four black dragons flew toward the formation, and were chased away by Hal's fliers. He decided the four had just been reconnoitering a large formation, not knowing what it was.

For the next three days, Roche dragons scouted the formation but never chanced an attack.

Days later, they reached the Bluffs, where the great breakthrough had been made, and continued on.

Still later, they crossed the border into Sagene, and kept on to the west.

As time passed, the countryside grew less barren, not having been fought over since the first days of the war, then they moved deeper into Sagene, where there'd been no battles at all.

The land on either side of them, though, was still picked bare, villages looted, farmland stripped, forests denuded, just by the passage of the Sagene forces toward the front.

Hal barely noticed, being used to the desolation, but the countryside depressed Khiri and other civilians who'd never seen such ruination.

She importuned the king, and he agreed to turn aside, to take smaller, country windings untouched by soldiery, and within a few miles they entered a dreaming land unknown to the sword.

Hal couldn't decide which was the greater pleasure – to fly the high station, drifting through the late summer day, hot and still, baking, the last of the fogs of the Roche northland out of him; or to swerve about down low, Storm chasing birds, not very sure what he'd do with one if he caught the mouthful of feathers.

In either event, he was reminded of the days before the war, when he was advance man for poor damned Athelny of the Dragons, with posters and a small bag of copper and silver, and no one to look over his shoulder.

A long, long time ago, he thought, a bit wistfully, and wondered if, when peace came and if he still lived, he could find such a peaceful life.

He shook his head at the idea: even if he lived through the damned war, he was now Lord Kailas, with estates and tenant farmers and fishermen to worry about and care for.

Hal thought he'd almost like to go back to those days when his stomach couldn't keep his spine and navel from being the closest of friends.

Kailas sighed, put the past out of his mind.

He wished he could ask Khiri to get on behind him, and share this lazy pleasure, a moment of peace in the midst of ruination.

But there was still the army, and its rules, below him, with jealous courtiers watching him closely, wishing him to do something that might usurp his standing with the king, so they might move a bit closer to the throne.

At least he and Khiri had each night together, in Hal's small tent.

And that made up for much as they made love fiercely, as if trying to affirm life and deny the death behind them.

*

Fovant had been built in a valley, with steep, defensible hills around it, and a river running through its middle, where the great farming region spread out to the west and north.

Rozen, too, had a river. But that was wide, and unfriendly, better for ship and boat passage than for the scenery. Fovant's river had also been navigable, but steep-banked, narrow and deep. The city's builders had concreted its banks and later its bottom, so their river was most civilized, save every century or so when it rose over the banks and the boulevards that wound along it.

The city had been walled for defense from hill to hill, and, for a change, the city builders had allowed for growth, so it was only now that growth had spilled beyond the wide walls.

The city had grown up more than out, and its streets were either broad, suitable for many horsemen, or narrow, twisting, close enough to give a pony pause.

There were many parks dotted through Fovant, from the great one beside the river to tiny vest-pocket patches of green, with no more than a dozen trees.

The houses were mostly stone to the first floor, half-timbered and plaster above that for the most part. Businesses and government buildings were stone, but not hard, cold gray, but in cheerful shades of red.

Hal and Khiri saw it first at sunset, Hal from a greater height, and it gleamed like a city of dreams.

Both of them fell in love with Fovant on sight.

It was not just that Fovant's people thought themselves more beautiful, more handsome, wittier and more cultured than anyone, including their fellow Sagene. It was that, in many areas, Hal and Khiri thought they might be right.

Their opinion wasn't hurt by the Fovant priding themselves on their skills at cookery. Hal and Khiri couldn't remember having a bad meal, from the most expensive banquets to meat and vegetable sticks grabbed on the run from a street vendor.

Sagene's Council of Barons had arranged for King Asir and his party to be housed in a disused palace, just short of the outer walls.

The palace was big enough to hold all of the Derainians, plus the considerable staff the barons had given Asir for his stay.

There was even enough room for the dragons, although dragon-tents from the Sagene fliers had to be set up inside the grounds.

A peculiarity of this palace, and one which gave it its name, was that the rulers of Sagene had stocked the grounds with deer. The animals were most tame, and it was common for a soldier to be working at a task and realize three or four deer were peering, as curious as cats, over his shoulder, about to offer advice.

The barons invited the Derainians to hunt the deer as they pleased.

Asir put the word around that killing one of them would be like killing a pet, and he would prefer anyone in his retinue not do that.

Most of the Derainians agreed with him, or felt it improper to go against the king's wishes.

Others didn't.

Hal wasn't surprised to see that Alcmaen was one of the dissenters, and, every couple of days, would lug in a carcass across his horse's withers, as proud as if he'd hunted down a forest bear with a spear.

He'd wanted to hunt the tame animals from the air, from dragonback, which Hal was able to forbid, since it didn't contribute anything to the war effort.

None of this did anything to increase Alcmaen's popularity on the squadron.

Khiri, Hal decided, had put it well, when she said, "That man reminds me of a boy I knew, growing up, the son of one of my father's headservants. He wasn't that ugly or stupid, but no one much liked him. He desperately wanted to be popular, but everything he tried seemed to produce the exact opposite."

"What happened to him?" Hal asked.

"He left a letter, saying he was running away to sea." Khiri shook her head. "We all expected to get boastful letters, lies about how he was becoming a famous ship's captain. But no one, including his parents, heard anything ever.

"I suppose, if he actually did become a sailor, he must have been drowned."

"Or," Hal said, "just as likely tossed overboard by a shipmate whose tolerance he'd pushed beyond the limit." He thought about it a minute. "I guess children can do things like that, not realizing they're making the absolutely wrong impression. But why an adult?"

"Did you ever think," Khiri said quietly, "that there's many of us who never grow up?"

"Like dragon fliers?"

Khiri smiled.

"Some of you."

"Me?"

"I'll never tell."

The first two days were spent in banquets and mutual celebration of the everlasting bond between Sagene and Deraine.

The Deer Park's gates were open to the public, and any suggestion that better security might be in order was met with raised eyebrows and, sometimes, the hint that Fovant was five hundred leagues or more behind the lines.

Hal thought of the distance Carcaor was behind the lines, and how that hadn't kept the city safe, but didn't say anything.

The best he could do was have the attached raiders outfitted in mufti, and wander about the palace grounds, trying to look innocent and civilian. It didn't work – if hidden dagger bulges didn't give them away, their close-cropped hair and military boots did. But it was better than nothing, he supposed.

The king insisted on going out for his morning rides, and everyone worried.

The king snorted at them, and, probably to show his independence, went further beyond Fovant each day.

Kailas overheard the officer in charge of the raiders muttering, "It isn't enough that our royal shithead has got to dress himself up in king gear, but he sits his damned horse so well that he really doesn't need the bangles and fripperies. Hell, if I were a Roche sympathizer I'd try to pot the bastard merely for looking noble. But that damned horse blanket of his is better than a godsdamned herald riding in front with a godsdamned trumpet."

The blanket in question was imperial red, with yellow fringes and yellow embroidery with the king's initials.

But Asir was Asir, and most set in his ways.

Hal got used to hordes of children following him around, in awe at being in the presence of the Dragonmaster.

Other hordes, Sagene taletellers, followed Alcmaen and especially Danikel about.

The slender, withdrawn, almost-beautiful young man was becoming a legend in his country, to the barely hidden fury of Alcmaen.

Danikel was credited with a dozen, no, two dozen, no, a brace of dozens of kills. He smiled when asked the precise number, and would only say, "not nearly enough, since the war still continues."

He got letters by the bale, proposals, indecent and decent, by the cartload.

The fliers were wondering if, perhaps, Danikel preferred men, or perhaps had no sex at all.

He began keeping company with a most beautiful baroness, five years older than he was, with a regal bearing and hair that appeared to have been silver from birth.

But Danikel's life seemed completely focused on his dragons and the war.

The conference began, sealed to all.

But even kings and barons have to talk to somebody.

In Asir's case, it was to Sir Thom Lowess, who, in turn, let little bits drop to Hal.

Everything was going most wonderfully, amicability oozing on both sides.

The only stumbling block was the city of Paestum, long a sore point, being Derainian, on Sagene land. Battles had been fought and lost centuries earlier, but Sagene still thought Paestum rightfully theirs.

Too much Derainian blood had been shed in its defense to ever consider handing it back to Sagene, though.

Asir broke that stumbling block by suggesting that Paestum become, after the war, an open city, belonging to no one and everyone.

There were grumbles from the Sagene, but then cheerfulness came back.

Lowess suggested cynically that the barons took the open city proposal as a prybar in the door that could be used, in the years to come, to make Paestum Sagene once more.

Hal didn't give a damn either way, remembering the coldness he'd encountered as a broke, stranded wanderer before the war.

Besides, as he kept reminding himself, politics wasn't a soldier's business.

"And what is this?" Hal asked suspiciously, peering about the room.

It was the great room of an apartment that was larger than most merchants' houses. It was on the top floor of a four-story building that overlooked Fovant's river, with four bedrooms, a jakes for each room, the great room, a banquet hall that could've served a dragon flight, and servants' quarters a half-floor below. Outside glass doors was a roof garden that Hal thought he could land Storm in without hurting either the dragon or the plants.

"It's ours," Khiri said. "I bought it as a birthday present."

"But it's hardly my birthday."

"Then it's for last birthday ... or next." Khiri looked carefully at him. "You don't like it."

"I didn't say that," Kailas protested.

"I've been looking for something like this ever since we got here," Khiri said. "Since we both love Fovant so much, after the war, we'll have a place to stay."

Hal started to say something, stopped himself. It would have been bitchy at best, probably something about he didn't like not being consulted.

It wasn't as if Khiri didn't have more than enough money of her own, which Hal had never an intent of controlling.

He forced a smile.

"And now we do," he said.

"Are you really sure you like it?"

"I'm really sure," he half-lied. "I just never thought about after the war."

He walked to the doors, went out into the garden, looked down at the afternoon strollers below.

Khiri came up behind him, put her arms around him, nuzzled his neck.

"I'm just sorry there's no furnishings yet. Like a bed."

Hal turned, kissed her, cupped her buttocks in his hands.

"And Lady Carstares is suddenly too humpty-hoo to even consider having her little lights screwed out on the floor?"

Khiri looked down.

"At least it's polished wood," she said. "Better than some old castle stone."

"So 'tis," Hal said, unbuttoning her dress.

She stepped out of it.

Khiri wore only a shift under it, her breasts not needing support.

She kicked her shoes off. One arced high in the air, disappeared over the garden wall.

"Oh dear," she said. "I hope it doesn't skull some good and proper Fovanian."

"If it does," Hal said, his voice getting throaty, "they can look for another apartment. This one's vacant."

Khiri giggled, came into his arms.

Later, he wondered why he'd almost behaved like a total shit. Was it worrying about living through the war? Or wasn't he sure he loved Khiri as completely as, say, Saslic? He'd gotten almost as cranky when she'd brought up having children a month or so ago.

The train of thought was making him most uncomfortable, and so he turned away from that, and began nipping, gently, at her nipples.

In a few seconds, they both had something else to think about.

The talks were going very well, and there was distinct optimism in the Deer Park.

An attack all along the front – how could that not break Roche for good and all?

Hal remembered what the king had said about the man who fights everywhere fights nowhere, but that couldn't break his mood.

The endless war, having an end . . .

The other fliers seemed to feel the same, and Hal was reminded that their normal easy cynicism was as much a façade as anything else, little more than a pose youths have always found attractive.

After all, the fliers were all young – even the oldest, Mynta Gart, was just a bit over thirty. Hal suspected Alcmaen was probably older than that, but he was adamantly twenty-five by his claims, and Hal suspected he'd be so long after the rest of his thinning hair vanished.

If there was real pessimism, and Hal suspected there was, it would be among the older men, the infantrymen who were hurled forward, day after day, never being told their place in things, never allowed to see any more of the war and the world than the muddy patches around them.

Hal came into one of the common rooms of the Deer Park's mansion to see a group of his fliers, including all of the 11th Flight's survivors, and Danikel in the background, standing around a great wall map that had the front lines scribed on it.

He'd intended to get a nightcap from the attendant, and nurse it for a few minutes, leaving his fliers alone. No organization is better for having its leader try to be one of the boys, hanging about constantly.

But Farren Mariah saw him, and waved him over.

He got his drink, and obeyed.

"Sir," Mariah said, careful as always to maintain military formality with outsiders close, "we're having a proper go-diddle about after the war, and what our plans are.

"Everybody's bein' most closed-mouth about everything, so perhaps, you being the man in front and such, you'll enlighten us with what a proper flier does when peace breaks out."

Hal took a sip of his brandy.

"First," he said slowly, "I'd guess he'd kiss his dragon, then the ground, then his own sorry ass for doing something as surprising as living. That's what I'll do."

There was laughter.

"You're as bad as the rest of us," Mariah said. "C'mon now. Serious as it lays."

Hal thought.

"I'll be honest. Damned if I know. Maybe start a carnival or something. Gods know I can't see sitting around some castle diddling myself until I die of boredom."

"Perhaps you might stay in the army," Sir Loren suggested.

"Perhaps I might find someone with the last name of Damian to be orderly officer for the next two weeks for even *thinking* that," Kailas said. "One war's enough for anybody.

"And why am I in the barrel, anyway? You, Gart. You're far more upstanding than the rest of us."

"I'll buy myself a coaster," she said. "And start carrying cargoes every which way. Maybe even up some of these damned rivers we've flown over. Gods know the Roche'll be needing everything after we whip them."

"I can see it now . . . ten years gone," Mariah said. "There'll be this great warehouse, right on the waterfront of Rozen. GART SHIPPING. WE TAKE ANYTHING ANYWHERE AND MAKE A DAMNED GREAT PROFIT DOING IT."

"Is there anything wrong with that?" Gart asked.

"Of course not," Mariah said. "It's my purest of the pure jealousies that's speaking."

"I know very well what I'm going to do," Sir Loren said, sounding very mystical. "There's a spot on my land, not far from my manor house that, long ago, before there were dragons, when men lived like gods and the gods drank with them, was most sacred, and, to this day, is very beautiful. It's a tiny vale, and the gardeners have it planted in roses.

"What I'll do is build a bower, and train roses to climb up

through it. In the bower, I'll have a marble stand made. On the stand, I'll put my crossbow, which I'll have silver-plated, with gold trim."

The fliers were goggling. Sir Loren was known as one of the most anti-military of the fliers, although he kept his opinion generally to himself.

"And every morning," Loren went on, "just at sunrise, I'll go out, just as the sun's rays strike my crossbow . . . and piss all over the son of a bitch!"

When the laughter died, Hal looked at Farren Mariah.

"What about you? I know you're a city rat and all. Are you going to take Limingo's advice, and study magic?"

Mariah's face was serious for an instant.

"P'raps," he said. "More likely, I'll go into government. Real government, you know, the kind that lets pretty fellers like the Dragonmaster and all those lords and ladies speak to the king for their regions, and meantime these other fellers stay in the background, with good red gold handed out here and there, to make sure things happen the way they're supposed to happen.

"It'll be all over Rozen, if you want to have something done, legal or no, go see Farren. I'll have the urchins write ballads about me, and I'll be surrounded with the wittiest of balladeers and the prettiest of girls.

"P'raps it might not be bad for me to stand for all veterans. Nobody else is going to, once the killing stops."

His voice had become a little bitter, and the fliers were quiet, knowing the truth of his words, not meeting each other's eyes.

"And what about me?" Chincha asked. "When you're out cavortin' with the ladies?"

"Aaarh," Mariah said. "I'll buy you a fancyman from Sagene, who knows tricks with massages and like that. You'll not want."

That broke the mood.

"If any of us had any decency," Danikel, Baron Trochu, said from the fringes of the group, "we'd try to pay back what we owe to the dragons."

"What?" Mariah said, pretending outrage, "those smelly bastards out there, honking and slobbering? What do we owe them?"

"Our lives," Danikel said quietly. "Our chances of winning the war. The best tool to beat the Roche back and keep them in hand. And if you think we'll be forgotten about after the war, what the hells do you think'll happen to our dragons?

"Stuck in a cage in an exhibit somewhere. Or part of one of those damned flying carnivals. Giving fat merchants and their squealing daughters rides, up, down, three gold coins if you please, sir?

"Or maybe just taken out and killed, since they're pretty much of an annoyance. Doesn't anybody think they deserve better than that?

"Mariah, if you're really looking for a cause, you could do better than help the dragons."

"And what would that get me?" Mariah said. "Right now, I stink like dragons, true. And that brings the maidens out . . . did before I met Chincha, at any rate. But do you think that stink's going to be so popular when we're at peace?

"No, young Baron. You've got your lands and your peasants to keep you in clover. The rest of us will have to find something else."

Danikel seemingly hadn't been listening to Mariah, but looking at Hal.

"You know what I'm talking about, don't you, sir? Don't we have a debt?"

Hal took a deep breath.

"Yes. I know what you're talking about. And yes, we do owe them."

He drained his snifter.

"And I'm for bed. All this is getting far too serious for me."

Again, there was laughter, and that marked the end of the evening.

But Hal lay awake, listening to Khiri's bubbling snore for a long time that night.

Outside, in one of the barns, a dragon shrilled in his sleep.

30

The cheering started just before noon, and rolled, like a wave, from the gates of the Deer Park to the mansion.

No one needed to know what it meant.

An agreement had been reached between the ruling barons of Sagene and King Asir.

Hal felt his heart leap, went looking for the details.

As matters turned out, there were three levels of agreements. The first, since there had to be something to tell the masses and leak to the Roche, was that Sagene and Deraine had reached a general treaty of goodwill and close cooperation from now until forever, to ensure there would be no stab in the back by the Roche or anyone else.

Paestum, as rumored, would become an open city once the war was over.

Both countries formally agreed there could be but one end to this war: complete and unconditional surrender by the Roche, and occupation, at least for a time, of their lands while a less bellicose regime was installed.

Most civilians thought this an obvious requirement.

Many soldiers did not, arguing that would make the Roche fight even harder if they knew Queen Norcia and her court would be replaced by something, someone, unknown.

Others snorted, saying they didn't see how the bastards could fight any harder than they already were, and wanted to make sure their children or children's children, wouldn't be attacked by the Roche, or at least not this version of them.

Hal didn't know, seeing good argument on both sides.

The second level of the treaty agreed there would be a massive attack in the far south, in the Fourth Army's area. All other armies would go to full alert to disguise the build-up.

This level was intended for discovery by Roche spies, and was false.

The real treaty included not only the first articles, but the agreement for the general offensive, from all armies, against the Roche, intended to smash their lines from north to south and seize Carcaor.

There were banquets, parades, and general goodwill from all.

King Asir couldn't go beyond the Deer Park without being buried by hurrahing crowds.

Before the goodwill was inevitably worn down, the Derainians packed for their return to the front.

On that last night, Hal jerked awake in the small hours.

A thought, a dream, had come, and he managed to keep from losing it.

He was sitting on the bed, feet on the floor, sweating.

"Whassamatta, love?" Khiri murmured.

"Nothing. Something I forgot to check," he said. "Go back to sleep."

"Ummuck," she said, and obeyed.

Hal dressed hurriedly, went to the planning room, consulted maps. They suggested he wasn't even slightly about to cry wolf.

He went to the stables, and further confirmed his suspicions.

Then he found the officer of the guard, and got directions to Limingo's rooms.

"But my master has given orders not to be disturbed," the servant-acolyte said, pulling himself up from the cot across the entrance.

"King's orders," Hal lied. "Now, go get whatever Limingo needs to wake up."

"But—"

"Move!" Hal said, in a voice that would carry across a parade ground.

The man obeyed.

Hal shoved the cot out of the way, opened the door.

Limingo was not alone – a handsome, tousled, naked young man was getting up, fumbling for a sword.

Hal ignored him.

"Limingo, I think we might have problems."

The wizard started to say something, stopped, then told the young man to get dressed and go back to his quarters.

He pulled clothes on, looking at Hal cautiously, as if expecting Kailas to be shocked or enraged.

Hal felt neither and, in any event, hadn't time for emotions.

By the time Limingo had washed and dressed, his servant was back with a tray with a steaming tea-kettle on it, and cups.

He poured.

"Now, what's the great alarm?" Limingo said. "I hear no sounds of tumult or disaster."

"If I'm right, you won't, not for three days," Hal said. "Listen to my thread of logic, and please tell me I'm full of shit, so we can go back to bed," he said. "Back on the front lines, we were jumped when the king visited Lord Cantabri, straight out of nowhere by a battle formation of dragons.

"We drove them off, but for the rest of the time we were on the lines, there'd be a dragon or six hovering just out of range.

"When we pulled out, coming east to Fovant, we had a pair or more of Roche dragons – always black, and I'd suspect from *Ky* Yasin's elite squadron – tailing us.

"I was wondering then if there was a spy with us, or if the Roche had some very skilled recon soldiers in the bushes, reporting to a wizard who passed the word along to their dragon fliers.

"But I never saw any sign of their scouts, either afoot or on horseback, lurking about, when I was airborne. I asked the raider captain if he'd seen anything, but he hadn't.

"Isn't it possible that, if you have, say, a bit of the cloth of someone's pants, assuming he's a filthy sod and never changes, you could use magic to track him?"

"Certainly," Limingo said. "It's not that hard a spell, either.'

"Well, let's say somebody breaks into the king's stable-tent, and cuts a few strands off that damned royal red blanket he's so fond of?"

"That would work very well indeed, as long as the tracker was only concerned with when the king was a-horseback," Limingo said. He was starting to look a bit worried.

"Remember those four Roche who tried to attack the king the first night after he left my squadron? We killed one, ran the other three off, with no gains. Or so we thought.

"However, I just went out to the stablery, and looked at the king's riding gear. And that blanket has about four or five of its long fringes cut off.

"Do you think maybe that's what those infiltrators were after?"

Limingo nodded slowly.

"Now, let's put another bit into the equation," Hal went on. "Remember how desolate our way was, even after we crossed the border into Sagene, and now some of the king's favorites asked if we could turn away from the main road to Fovant, which we did?"

"Yes." One of the many things Hal liked about Limingo was that he actually listened when you were speaking, and saved his comments until you were through.

"I just looked at the map, and traced the route we were supposed to follow – and the one we'll take back to the areas we already hold.

"Two days after we turned off the main highway on to the byways, we would've passed through a rocky place. Chasms, draws, small but steep peaks. It's called the Pinnacles. Looking at the map, and remembering my days as a cavalryman," Hal said, "I would've loved to have ambushed somebody right in the middle of that, particularly somebody who doesn't have a heavy escort, not needing one that far from the front.

"What do you think about that, my sorcerous friend?" Hal said, with a bit of triumph.

"I think we'd best wake up the king," Limingo said. "And I don't think anybody's going to get a lot of sleep for the rest of the night."

"You're wrong there," Hal said. "I think the only one who won't be getting any sleep is me."

The king looked at the maps Hal had laid out once more.

"I don't normally like guesses about what the enemy is going to do, Lord Kailas. But your suppositions make entirely too much sense for me not to allow for them.

"I suppose now we roust out a baron or two, borrow whatever guard regiment or regiments we can, and have them march east to the Pinnacles and winkle the Roche out. We can use that damned blanket of mine – and I should have known, remembering my father's warning against fripperies – as bait."

"That is one option, your Highness," Hal said carefully. He didn't like any of it, particularly exposing to the Roche they'd caught on to the blanket trick, having a vague idea about putting the principle to use himself against the Roche.

"But not the one you clearly prefer," Asir said.

Hal made a noncommittal noise.

"What would be your plan, then?" Asir said. "I just realized one thing: there is no way in the world I'll sit on my ass here in Fovant and let the Sagene clean up the mess I've been responsible for."

Limingo looked alarmed.

"An excellent idea, sire," Hal said. "Might I ask which of your sons is the most qualified to be regent?"

The king frowned, then jolted as he got it.

"Kailas, when I suggested you learn a few tricks of the diplomatic trade, I didn't mean for you to get this sneaky."

Everyone knew Asir was not only unmarried, but didn't even have any royal bastards hanging about the palace.

"Very well," Asir grudged. "Perhaps – especially after reaching this covenant with the Council of Barons – I'd best not be out there playing soldier."

Limingo relaxed.

"As for sending the Sagene out," Hal went on, "suppose that I'm wrong, and there's nobody and nothing in the Pinnacles but wild boar and rocks? We'll look more than a bit stupid."

"True. But what can we do?" Asir asked. "And, by the way, do you have any idea how the Roche will mount this ambush? Just with dragons, as they tried the last time?"

"No," Hal said. "I'd guess they might have infiltrated light cavalry through the lines, and had them hole up. They'll have been horrid disappointed that we didn't waltz into their talons, but most likely figure we're going to come back the shorter route, since we've got important matters for the army to implement.

"Another possibility is they've brought infantry across in dragon baskets, like they used back around Bedarisi."

"You and your fliers took care of that rather handily," Asir said. "I'd think they'd be reluctant to try it again."

"Why?" Hal asked. "If everybody thinks that tactic's elderly, doesn't that make it fresh again?"

Asir nodded.

"But you still haven't offered a plan," he said.

"Very simple," Hal said. "I take off right now for the First Army, with orders from you to Lord Cantabri to take, say, two companies of light cavalry, two companies of heavy cavalry, plus as many dragon flights as I can get, and march west to the Pinnacles. The Roche, if they're in there, shouldn't be watching their back as they should.

"Meantime you . . . " Hal caught himself, and saw the king's grin. "Sorry, sir. I meant that as a suggestion, sir. Maybe you could get a couple of companies of heavy cavalry to ride west with you as escort, to keep you from getting any surprises."

That was Hal's intent – to get *Ky* Yasin and his First Guards Squadron between a rock – the Pinnacles – and a very hard place. Which would be them on the ground with Hal's dragons overhead and Derainian soldiers on the ground. With any luck, and assuming Yasin was involved with this elaborate scheme to murder or capture the king, Hal might be able to strike a great blow against the Roche.

The king pondered for a few minutes.

"Very well. Get you airborne and headed west. I'll move east as slowly as possible until I get word you're on the march."

"A better idea, sire," Hal said. "Wait here until I've reached Cantabri, and send a messenger back that we're on the move. *Then* take the road.

"And you could have someone, maybe Sir Thom, write a story about the route you'll be taking, making sure you mention the

Pinnacles as maybe being some kind of natural wonder that you're sorry you've missed.

"There's got to be spies here in Fovant that'll report that."

"I'll do it," the king said. "But I feel like I'm being ordered about, instead of kinging the way I'm supposed to." He sighed. "Back and forth, back and forth. It's a great damned pity that our magicians haven't come up with any way to communicate over distances. But I suppose that's an impossibility."

He sighed once more.

Hal got up, saluted.

"Thank you, Kailas," the king said. "If you're right, and there are murderers waiting, I shall truly be in your debt."

"So you're going to fly off, all by yourself, and play hero again?" Khiri said. "Oh well. At least it isn't that dangerous . . . at least not until you start coming back toward us.

"Then you'd best be very careful."

"I'm always careful," Hal said piously.

Khiri just snorted.

Hal took Storm into the air a little before dawn. He wanted to fly east, back to the armies, as quickly as he could, but without exhausting the dragon or himself.

There would be other tasks for him once they reached the First Army and Lord Cantabri.

Flying in a straight line, it would take five days for Hal to reach Bedarisi, where there would be dragon units to leave Storm, but he'd take an extra day avoiding the Pinnacles.

He probably should have taken a wing mate, but there were few enough dragons with the king already, and so he decided to fly solo, and feed both Storm and himself on emergency rations.

Khiri, Limingo and Hal's orderly, Uluch, were the only ones to bid him farewell. Hal turned the detachment over to Gart, and she was the only one to know that Hal was on some other mission than flying north-east, to see what the Sagene dragon training camps were like.

Hal went high, where the air was thinner, and it was easier flying for Storm, who could glide vast distances with his wings at full stretch.

He landed after dark at a recommended Sagene inn, and was able to husband the emergency rations for a night, feeding Storm on a pair of lambs, and himself on chops with mint.

He was grateful for the warm bed they put him up in, since the late summer was a bit snappish. Storm was curled up behind the inn's stables.

Once again, before dawn, he was roused, and gulped some tea and cold meat. He fed Storm on ten pounds of raw, ground meat, since the dragon didn't seem terribly hungry, then pushed on.

That night, he slept away from the road, in a grassy nook next to a creek. Storm sneered at what he was offered, went fishing in the creek, his long, snaky head hovering like a heron over the water, then darting down.

He caught enough fish for himself, and for Hal to grill a couple over an open fire.

The third day covered the shortest distance – to the immediate north was the main east-west road, and the Pinnacles.

Hal desperately wanted to overfly the crags, to see if he could spot any sign of the Roche ambush, not knowing if it was still set . . . or if, in fact, it ever had been.

He hoped he hadn't made the classic intelligence officer's mistake of seeing an enemy behind every bush, when there wasn't one there, and, sometimes, there wasn't even a bush.

But he held back, and flew low that day, arcing around the Pinnacles. Storm growling at not being allowed to go high.

There was an inn, at a crossroads, and Hal chanced landing beside it.

He ate a gigantic omelet, and Storm munched on a heifer.

Hal allowed himself two glasses of wine, and was nursing the second as his plate was cleared away, when he overheard a pair of teamsters grumbling about the godsdamned bandits in the godsdamned Pinnacles, and how the godsdamned army wouldn't send in some godsdamned troops to clean the godsdamned bastards out.

"They're scar't," one wagoneer said. "Those godsdamned bastids are too strong for a rooty little company. Hells, they've got dragons to scout for 'em. Bet they're not godsdamned bandits at all, but more like, godsdamned deserters."

"Typical gummint," the first said. "Allus too eager for your taxes, but never gonna give anything back."

He snorted, went back to his beer, and Hal drank up his wine and went to bed, feeling a little better that perhaps he wasn't dreaming about the Roche.

The rest of the flight was smooth, if tiresome.

He left a rather plaintive, but exhausted, Storm in Bedarisi, promising to come back for him within days, when he'd rested. Hal wondered if the dragon understood him, decided he was getting a little strange, what they were beginning to call dragon-happy.

He got a brown-orange male dragon that was promised to "be fast, but, sir, I'll warn you, he can be skittish."

Another hand broke in: "He's the Dragonmaster. Not to worry about him."

Hal thought he should have said bushwa, that the Dragonmaster was feeling more than a little delicate, and whoever had said he was a master rider, but stupid pride kept him from it.

The brown was a bit on the high-strung side, but when he realized Hal was proposing to let him fly as hard and fast as he could, settled down and went like the wind.

Now they were over familiar ground, the area fought over by both armies.

Hal realized he'd grown used to the ruin and spoliation. But after having spent a few weeks in something resembling civilization, the shambles came afresh.

He wondered, briefly, what it would be like for him when and if the war was over. Certainly he wouldn't be able to fit into a civilian niche easily, nor could he see remaining a soldier.

Kailas turned off his thoughts, concentrated on flying fast.

A pair of dragons came in on him as he was closing on the First Army headquarters. He didn't recognize them, nor the flight banner on both dragons' carapaces, but they knew him, and asked a shouted question about needing an escort.

Hal called back that things were fine, but the riders must have recognized his rather harried appearance, and dropped in on his flanks.

They waved farewell as he brought the brown in, just short of Cantabri's command tent.

Sentries ran up, challenged him, saluted, and obeyed when he asked to be taken to Lord Bab at once.

Cantabri listened, took a few notes, consulted three maps, and asked for his top aides to be sent in, plus the liaison officer with the Sagene forces.

Hal listened, a bit enthralled, having forgotten what it was to be with quiet competence.

Within an hour, two battalions of heavy cavalry had been told off, with orders to draw two weeks' supplies and march east toward Bedarisi. One of them was a crack Sagene unit.

They would be the slowest to move, next to the infantry, and therefore had been the first to be put on the march.

The footsoldiers came next, a full regiment of conventional infantry. Supporting them were four reserve transport companies, to carry the infantry and its supplies in wagons.

Next were three battalions of light cavalry, with the same orders.

With them went Cantabri's raiders. "They'll march at the stirrup, and their rations'll go with the cavalry."

Hal nodded. That meant the footsoldiers would hang on to a horseman's stirrup, and keep pace with him, half trotting, half being carried. It was hard on horses and men, but it doubled the pace the raiders would be able to travel. They well earned their jaunty uniforms and tough reputations.

"I'll depend on them to at least pin the Roche until the heavies can arrive," Cantabri went on. "Then we'll wipe them out.

"Now for you, Lord Kailas," Cantabri said. "I would like your squadron to move east as my long range scouts. Do you have any additions?"

"Yessir," Hal said. "We'll need to send a flier – two of them – east, looping around the Pinnacles, to alert the king that he should begin moving slowly in four or five days say, when we're on the other side of Bedarisi.

"I'd also like to draw from the other flights on the front," Hal said, "and bring my squadron at least up to full strength.

"I'm assuming Yasin is in command of those dragons, since he seems to be fond of anything smacking of dirty deeds, and I'd like a chance to wipe him – and his unit – out for once and for all.

"That would be a desirable end," Cantabri said. He nodded to an aide. "Has there been significant air fighting lately?"

"Nossir," the aide said. "And I've been wondering why."

"I'd guess the explanation might be that their best is behind our lines, looking for a chance to take out King Asir," Cantabri said.

He thought, tapping fingernails against a map.

"That should do it, for a starter," Cantabri said. "Now, all of you – except Lord Kailas – out. I assume he's got things for my eyes only."

Hal waited until the tent was empty, reflexively checked to make sure the posted sentries were the only ones close to the tent's canvas.

"I do, indeed, sir," Hal said. "The treaty has been agreed on with

Sagene. We'll have full cooperation with the barons. And both parties agreed the only peace will be unconditional surrender."

Cantabri looked wolfish.

"Good," he said. "Now, with an offensive to plan, I should remain here with my maps. But I'll allow myself a bit of privilege first."

It was a forced march to Bedarisi, where Hal reclaimed the rested Storm.

The formation went on east, moving as fast as it could. Stragglers were simply abandoned, told to catch up or return to the First Army, it didn't matter which to Cantabri.

Hal, his First Squadron, and the augmentation kept airborne. Hal hadn't briefed anyone on what the mission was, any more than Cantabri had told anyone but unit commanders.

The weary messengers sent to Fovant returned, reported that the king's party was moving out of the city.

"Deceptions," Cantabri told Kailas, "are underway by the king's party."

Hal, while Storm drifted above the formation, considered what those deceptions might be.

He had the idea that Limingo, with a couple or three of his bedmates, plus a small cavalry escort and two dragons, was marching west to meet them, toward the Pinnacles. The wizard not only had the king's blanket on his mount, but had cast a deceiving spell around the group so no Roche spies could see what they were about to attack.

For some unknown reason, Hal pictured the blanket, and Limingo, on a rather contrary and braying gray mule, an image that amused him, and one he never bothered to correct.

Two days short of the Pinnacles, Cantabri gathered his men in a great natural arena.

His speech was short, and pointed:

"Derainians! Our king is being stalked by a Roche enemy. We are marching to the rescue.

"Sagene! Your barons have agreed to a great plan that will end this war.

"We must not let anyone stand in that plan's way.

"Two days from now, we shall encounter the Roche, and ambush them where they would have waylaid His Royal Highness.

"There are moments in history where one man – or one company of men – can make a difference.

"This is one of them.

"Years gone, you will tell your grandchildren you were here, and no one will be able to say he did greater fealty to his country.

"For Sagene!

"For Deraine!"

The men cheered until the hills gave back the echo.

Hal insisted on flying the first reconnaissance over the Pinnacles.

The Roche camp, fairly well concealed, was hidden just where Hal would've put it himself, assuming that no one would be looking for Roche this far behind the lines.

It looked as if there was a small flight of dragons, about ten monsters, and about two companies of infantry, around 150 or more men.

They were quartered under trees, and the transport baskets the dragons had brought them in were hidden in a draw nearby.

Hal wondered how the Roche were going to lift out their infantrymen after the ambush, or if they were proposing a suicide operation.

That didn't make sense – the Roche weren't known for their stupidity.

But that wasn't his problem, nor that of any other Derainian. Better if every Roche died in place as far as Kailas was concerned.

Before they had left the front, Cantabri had a large-scale map of the Pinnacles cast by a wizard, and used that for the final briefing. Some officers were worried that their camp was less than a league away from the Roche, but Cantabri was confident of surprise. The Roche wouldn't be looking to their rear.

Hal hoped he was right.

That night, the raiders went out on foot, and came back with a clear scout of the terrain.

A dragon was stationed on a peak, in a shallow cave. A raider officer, with a glass, and the flier waited with it.

They reported that Roche dragon scouts went out that dawn, flew west, looking for the king.

They came back, landed. There was no particular excitement around the camp, so the raider officer flag-signaled to another raider to the east, who sent the word to Cantabri's camp.

They waited another night, and then most of a day as the Roche dragons went out once more.

The Roche hurtled back at speed, late in the day, and it was clear to the watchers the king's column had been sighted.

There would be two choices for the Roche – either ambush the king at dawn, when the column was rousing, or immediately, near dusk.

From the bustle that was signaled back, it was evident the Roche commander had decided to attack what he thought was Asir's column immediately, not taking a chance and betting on fatigue and hunger to fight on his side.

They definitely wouldn't be watching their rear.

Cantabri ordered his forces into attack.

The heavy cavalry went straight up the main highway, planning to divert up a wide draw that wound into the Roche camp.

The light cavalry and the infantry took a winding herdsman's path the raider scouts had found, moving at the trot.

A league – an hour before the fight would begin.

One turning of the glass.

Hal would begin the attack.

He took his dragons off after half an hour, swept once back over the camp, forming an arrow formation and drove for the Roche.

They came in over the Roche camp, a fairly defensible nest in the rocks, just as the Roche were getting ready to move to the main highway and their ambush positions.

Hal took Storm in low, and a black dragon fairly leapt into the air at him.

Kailas had an instant to recognize the dragon's banner on its carapace as being, in fact, Yasin's First Guards Squadron. Then he put a bolt in its rider's chest, another shot into the dragon's throat, and it scrawked, pinwheeled, and thrashed down to the ground, knocking another two dragons sprawling.

The Roche infantry froze for an instant, then rigid discipline returned. They formed extended lines, knelt, and brought up their bows, ready to destroy the dragons.

The Roche dragons were trying to get into the air, but Hal's formation swept across the field, dragon riders spattering down crossbow bolts.

Hal suddenly remembered when he'd used bowman mounted behind the fliers, cursed that he'd not had time to use the tactic again.

A dragon in front of him was hit, tucked its head down as if entering a rainstorm, and crashed, rolling, bouncing across the field, killing half a score of Roche as it and its rider died.

Then the light cavalry and the raiders came into the nest, still on line, not pausing to reform into a battle line, but spreading out as they came.

They hit the Roche hard, smashing them back, into knots. But the Roche held firm, trying to reform as the cavalry came back on them.

The Roche dragons were all in the air, and banked hard away from the field.

Hal sent his dragons after them, and there was a low-level melee that sent four Roche and one Derainian dragon down.

Trumpets blared, and Hal chanced a quick look back at the Roche base.

The heavy cavalry had come on the field, its ponderous chargers moving from the walk into the trot, long lances coming down.

The Roche men held for an instant, then broke, running, scattered.

As they broke, the light cavalry and infantry swarmed after them, swords slashing.

The Roche dragons clawed for altitude, but Hal's squadron denied it to them.

The black monsters fled low, across country, heading east, back for their own lines, abandoning the men on the ground.

Hal sent his dragons after them, and there was a long pursuit in the dusk, dropping a dragon here, and there.

None of them carried the fringed banner of *Ky* Yasin.

No more than a handful of Roche were able to escape their harriers.

Finally, Hal blew the recall, and they turned back to the Pinnacles.

Hal wondered if the Roche dragon fliers had also panicked and fled, or if they'd been under orders to abandon the footsoldiers, fliers being vastly more valuable than any ground troops.

Ordered or not, that tasted very nasty to him, and he wondered if the flight also rang sour in the mind of Yasin. Hopefully it had, and would eat at him, possibly clouding his judgement in the future.

It was near dark when they came in on the battlefield, the dragons' wings cracking as they braked for a landing.

It was strewn with bodies, and there were only a few wounded. The Roche hadn't asked for quarter, and, generally, none had been given.

Hal landed, reported to Cantabri.

Lord Bab was a bit angry. There'd been no ranking prisoners

taken, and so no one to tell Lord Bab – or the king – just what had been intended by the ambush, whether capturing Asir . . . or just killing him.

The formation's support units came up the road, and the Sagene and Deraine forces moved down to the highway, to rest, and wait for the king.

Skirmishers were still busy on the battlefield, stripping arms and armor from the dead, and, supposedly, succoring the Roche wounded.

Hal doubted if there would be much of that.

"So that's that," King Asir said, after full reports had been made. "If we had time, I would have liked to have visited that field myself.

"But we've wasted enough time as is.

"Now, let's get back to the lines, and get this damned war over with."

31

It took almost three weeks for the Grand Offensive to be mounted. By the time the banners waved and the bugles blew, Hal had revised his opinion of the plan's validity.

With almost a month of rumors and whispers, it was inevitable that the Roche would realize *something* was going on.

Their spies went to work up and down the line, and Derainian and Sagene counterspies went after them.

Roche dragons overflew the lines, trying to see what was happening below.

Hal and the other dragon flight commanders had patrols out from dawn until nightfall.

There were snarling fights in the skies as a Deraine or Sagene formation would attack a Roche scout. Roche reinforcements would hurtle to the rescue and Derainian support would be airborne within minutes.

The sky would be a great melee of death, dragons pinwheeling about, men and monsters falling, screaming, into death, and then, as if on a signal, there would be nothing but clear, blue, peaceful summer heavens.

Hal killed his share, probably more, but didn't bother keeping a count. He was too busy trying to keep his own men and women alive and fighting.

Alcmaen and Danikel did keep score, or rather Alcmaen did. He claimed seventy-five kills, although only forty were allowed.

Hal had decided that if people were going to make numbers important, the only way he'd allow them was with a witness. Naturally, Alcmaen always came back from a flight claiming a victory, although too many of them were accomplished with no other allied flier in sight.

Danikel didn't bother with numbers, but his chief handler did, and gleefully reported that Baron Trochu somehow always remained in the lead.

The supposed rivalry got out to the taletellers, and the First Squadron's base had at least one or two of them, generally Sagene, fawning over Danikel and Alcmaen on a daily basis.

At least they weren't bothering Hal.

Khiri had gone back to Deraine with King Asir and his company, so he didn't have her on his mind, as much as he would've liked to.

Then the orders came by courier, and, from the Chicor Straits to the Southern Ocean, Deraine and Sagene went on the attack. There was no subtlety here, no room for it, as the allied divisions stolidly marched forward against the Roche.

The Roche fought hard, but slowly fell back.

But they never broke.

A formation would be hit hard, and retreat. But the Roche would leave ambush teams in any cover that presented itself, who, as often as not, fought to the death.

The Roche, fighting on their own soil, poisoned the wells and used magic to blanch the soil when they could.

Their sorcerers sent spells against Deraine and Sagene, which were sometimes caught and stopped in time. Other times, demons would ravage and tear until Derainian wizards could cast a counterspell, then another spell aimed at the Roche magicians.

No one envied the wizards – a magician could be in mid-spell, all calm about him, and then fire would raven him, and anyone within range.

To Hal and the other dragon fliers, the world below was

almost meaningless. Their war was in the skies. But it was still fascinating, if distressful, to see a green land slowly being turned muddy brown as the armies fought and marched across it.

The days were a blur of flying, fighting, killing, and the nights blank unconsciousness, with not a flier wanting to remember if he dreamed or not, and, if he did, what his dreams were.

The days were bad enough.

Hal remembered a new flier who reported in one morning with a dragon he'd been trained on. He was sent aloft on a noon patrol, in a supposedly safe sector. But a flight of Yasin's black dragons was waiting, and neither flier nor his mount came back.

What bothered Hal was that he couldn't remember the flier's name, and had to look it up in the records.

That first time was troublesome. But after the sixth time the same thing happened, Kailas almost got used to it.

Brandy might have helped somewhat.

But Hal couldn't allow himself that luxury.

Bodrugan and Goang returned from Deraine. They'd managed to procure large glass carboys, journeyed to a mine, and somehow managed to trap the deadly firedamp gas in the carboys.

Now all that remained, Goang told Hal, was to put the gas in smaller containers, put the containers in some sort of sack with nails and broken glass, come up with a bursting spell, and Hal would have his anti-cavalry weapon.

A week later, the pair asked for Hal and a dragon to try the thing out.

Bodrugan said, apologetically, that the spell was still a little complicated, so he'd prefer to ride behind Hal, and cast it himself.

"Of course," he assured Kailas, "when it works, we'll have a much simpler incantation."

It was a misty day, and there were no more than two or three pairs of dragons assigned missions, so Hal summoned the squadron to witness the great event.

Bodrugan had a wicker basket with half a dozen small bottles inside canvas sacks.

They put a target in the center of the landing field, and Hal took Storm off.

He took the dragon up to about a hundred feet, then turned back toward the field.

"Now," he said over his shoulder, "I'll bring it down to about fifty feet, and then come in over the target. Are we safe that low?"

"Yessir," Bodrugan said. "I mean, I'm almost certain, sir."

"Wonderful," Hal muttered, and only dropped to seventy-five feet.

"Start incanting," Hal said, and he heard Bodrugan muttering behind him.

The target was below, then directly underneath, then past.

"I'll take Storm round again," Hal said, "and give you a longer approach. Do you want me to give you a release point?"

"Thank you, sir," Bodrugan called back. "I'd appreciate it."

This time, the muttering started earlier.

"And five and four and three and two and . . . drop!" Hal shouted, and the bag dropped down toward the target.

It struck the ground about ten feet short of the marker.

And nothing happened, at least as far as Hal could tell.

They tried again, and again, until there were no more sacks.

Hal brought Storm in for landing, trying to decide if he should be angry or amused.

He settled for amusement, especially when Farren Mariah reported, "the bottles smashing, crashing, sounded just like geese farts on a muggy day when they struck . . . sir."

Hal kept back laughter until Bodrugan and Goang had shame-facedly picked up their sacks and gone back to Goang's tent to figure out what went wrong.

Mariah watched them go.

"Ah," he said. "That's what 'tis to be a knight of the dragon, privy to all kinds of secrets and magics.

"You should've asked me to do the spell, sir.

"Give a *real* wizard from the depths of the city a chance."

Hal told him he was welcome – in his off hours – to work with the pair.

Mariah made a face.

"Nawp, nawp, nawp, as my grandfather used to say. Once a spell's been spellt and spillt, there's no place for somebody to come in behind the goat."

The firedamp never did work.

Hal was called to Cantabri's headquarters for consultation.

The king had decided there should be dragon flights devoted solely to casting the sorcerous pebbles, and had named a pair of non-flying but high-ranking lords – Gurara and Hakea, one Derainian, one Sagene – to command these flights.

They weren't nearly as dunderbrained as might have been expected. By this stage of the war, there was little room for fools.

The pair had already gotten flying volunteers, had Limingo on standby and wanted Hal to help them develop a training curriculum. This Hal did, starting with the idea that perhaps these casting flights should have two fliers aboard – one solely to fly the dragon and watch for intercepting enemy, the other to do the casting.

They also wanted a couple of fliers who'd been on the Carcaor raid, and Hal grudgingly loaned them a couple of Derainians.

Then Cantabri proposed a flanking attack on a fortified Sagene position, and needed Hal's entire squadron to give his plan a bit of surprise, and Kailas put the matter in the back of his mind.

Hal called Chincha in, told her she was being commissioned and would take over the 11th Flight. Hal had been trying to run both the flight and the squadron long, and had forced himself to let go.

"But . . . but there's fliers better suited," Chincha stammered.

"Such as?" Hal asked.

"Farren, for one."

"You think he'd take the promotion?"

Chincha considered, slowly shook her head.

"But he's going to cast a kitten when he hears about this."

"Tell him, from me, that he should consider adopting a more mature attitude toward life and such."

Farren Mariah, as Hal had known he would, found the whole matter hysterically funny, and it didn't affect his relationship with Chincha at all.

Chincha took the whole matter very seriously, and tried to spend all day and night at her duties.

That was something else Hal had known.

Moving was always painful. The fliers would establish a base, and fly from it as long as they could. But eventually the armies plodded on east, and it was time to move.

Hal or one of the flight commanders would find a new location, near to the front lines, and then the tents would be struck, the wagons loaded, and the squadron would creak into motion.

At the new base the tents were repitched, various holes dug, and paths made.

Then it would take days for a new routine to be established – just where the mess, the farrier's, the jakes, and such, were. Generally two or three mistakes, usually involving garbage or worse pits, were made in the learning.

The replacements complained bitterly about the discomfort, but there was generally a veteran around who'd remind them that it might be a little uncomfortable, particularly when it rained, but it wasn't even close to being as bad as it was for the infantry.

Nothing was that bad.

Some of the replacements never bitched, and Hal knew that they'd come from one of the line formations, and were most grateful that they could get out of a warm, dry bed before going out to be killed.

Someone in the commissary department made a mistake on one move, and didn't check the fresh meat that was bought.

Everyone, dragons and men, got embarrassing cases of the runs, promptly dubbed the "Roche gallop," and Hal was forced to take the squadron off the duty roster for three days, although Mariah insisted they should still be flying: "Just sit farther back in the saddle, and you and your beastie can come in on our foes and both poop 'em to death."

Then he grimaced and set out at a rapid trot for the nearest jakes.

Sir Loren called the hoary old army joke after him to be sure and cover his flanks.

One good thing that came out of the enforced idleness for Kailas was figuring out how he might use the locating spell the Roche had used against the king for his own ends.

But he still wasn't precisely sure how to do it.

There were four fliers in the room, part of a shattered manor house, listening to Lord Hakea and staring at the map he kept touching. His companion, Lord Gurara, sat behind the fliers.

The fliers were Hal and his four flight commanders: Chincha, Gart, Richia and Cabet.

"Yarkand is the key," he said once more. "It's one of Roche's most important trading cities. There's the major highway from Carcaor to the front, plus this north-south highway, and these two coming in from the north-east and east.

"The city is mostly stone, very ancient, so knocking down as much as we can will stop passage, not to mention ruining Yarkand as a warehousing center and replacement depot.

"It's packed with refugees and soldiers trying to get forward, so the attack should be a serious shock to Queen Norcia and her barons.

"We'll hit them with almost a hundred dragons, the biggest raid of the war so far."

"It's a long flight," Hal said.

"It is," Hakea said. "My casting flights will lift out of here not long after midnight, and I calculate, if the winds are right, that we'll reach Yarkand about midday.

"We'll want you to join us when we get over the Roche lines."

"Then we – or rather you – cast our rocks," Richia said, a bit doubtfully, "and then we fly back, getting back over our own lines about . . .?"

"Midnight."

Richia whistled, shook his head, eased his bulk to a more comfortable position. "A long damned flight," he said, almost to himself.

At least, Hal thought, the two commanders were going on the mission, even though they weren't fliers, but flying as casters.

"We've been training for this mission for two weeks," Hakea said. "And if everything goes well – and your squadron, Lord Kailas, keeps any attacking dragons away – this could be a major step toward ending the war."

The flight commanders looked at Hal

"We would have appreciated a chance to rehearse this attack with you," Kailas said.

"There wasn't the time," Hakea said. "Besides, you have enough duties on your plate already."

"I mean no offense," Hal said. "But this scheme is more than a bit chancy."

"It has been approved by the king himself," Gurara said stiffly.

"Then," Hal said, getting up, feeling weary, "there's nothing left to discuss except the details, is there?"

32

Things went wrong from the beginning.

Hal, and the rest of the First Squadron, were to take off three hours before dawn, since their dragons would fly faster than the casting monsters, and fly east on a compass heading until they reached Yarkand.

No one had allowed for a heavy summer fog.

Hal was roused a little after midnight by the watch, reporting the fog rolling in.

He ordered his squadron commanders wakened, then washed his face, and walked out on the field. The fog was dank, thick, and he could barely make out the dragon tents half a hundred feet away.

Now Hal was forced to make one of those decisions never seen in romances – one man, alone, staring up at the night sky and trying to decide what the weather would be at dawn and, more importantly, later, over Yarkand.

Not to mention, of course, whether the casting dragon flight commanders would abort or continue the mission.

For once, Kailas chose the safe option.

No one argued with him, when he announced it, but he could feel a swell of disapproval from the other flight commanders and pilots.

There was one way to check his decision to proceed, and so he took his squadron up, as scheduled, but with a slightly different compass heading.

The squadron took up a series of vees behind him, flying very close, but still barely able to see Kailas through the roiling fog.

The new dogleg took the squadron over one of the casting dragon bases. He blasted instructions, and the dragons climbed, hoping to get above the fog. Hal dove down, counting as he went. His palms were quite sweaty when he broke out at less than a hundred feet, almost over the base.

It was pitch black, but he could see the dragon tents were open, and empty.

So at least one flight had obeyed orders, and was in the air, heading for the target.

Hal went back upstairs, climbing and climbing, and then broke into a starry sky, and saw the circling bulk of dragons not a third of a league distant.

Hal flew to them, and blasted the follow me signal.

He took a slightly adjusted compass course east.

Toward Yarkand.

He couldn't see anything below, and couldn't tell when the squadron crossed the lines into Roche territory.

Hal was navigating by compass, and by his time in the air.

There were no other dragons visible, at least, none flying above the fog.

At dawn, they were deep inside Roche.

Hal thought they were well ahead of schedule, and chanced diving down on a deserted lake, and watering his monsters.

They wanted to eat, rest, were denied, and blatted their unhappiness.

Hal paid no attention, and the squadron flew on, very high, to ease the strain on the beasts.

Then the sun burnt the fog away, and they could see clearly, league after league below of yet-unravaged Roche countryside.

Every now and then, Hal saw, far below, someone spot the dragons, and panic.

Their interest wasn't in killing farmers or burning villages, though.

Two hours before midday, he saw his first dragon. It was a Sagene beast, and was flying slowly toward him, to the west. The dragon was favoring one wing, and there was only the flier on its back.

Hal flew close enough to see rips in its side, and the flier was swaying in the saddle.

He straightened, seeing Hal and recognizing the uniforms, waved, shouted something Hal couldn't make out.

They flew on.

Now the navigation was easy – they found the main east-west highway leading to Yarkand, and followed it, curving through low foothills.

Then a wide valley opened, and there was Yarkand.

It was a city under siege, not uncommon, but the first time this had happened only from the air.

Sagene and Derainian dragons swooped and dove around Yarkand, and Hal could just see buildings struck by the magicked boulders crash into ruins.

But the battle was not going to the casting dragons.

Someone had talked, or sorcery or spying had found the plan out, for, tearing at the Deraine and Sagene forces were half a hundred black dragons.

As Hal watched, two of them attacked a single Derainian, one ripping at its wing, the second, coming from above, locking a deathgrip on the dragon's neck.

The three monsters slammed together, then apart.

But the two blacks recovered, spinning, and climbed for the heights. The Derainian dragon, its neck flopping limply, rolled over on one wing, and fell toward the earth.

The Sagene and Derainian casting dragons were trying to fight back, but without training or experience.

A line of casting dragons was coming up on the center of the city. From above, black dragons dove down, shattering the formation. The already cast pebbles became boulders, smashed here and there in the city's heart.

Other casting dragons were trying to flee to the west, skimming the rooftops.

That was enough for Hal.

He blew the attack, and the First Squadron's sixty dragons dove into battle.

The Roche fliers had been intent on the battle, and were hit by surprise.

Black dragons screeched, flopped in the sky like fledglings, and died, or their fliers were torn from their perches by dragon claws or shot out of the saddle by the Derainians.

Hal looked for a Roche who looked like a leader to take out, saw a dragon, just above him, and the gold-fringed banner on its carapace, kicked Storm into a climb, toward the monster's stomach.

He hesitated, still reluctant to kill a dragon, then aimed his crossbow at the dragon's side, and pulled the trigger.

The bolt shot home, just as Hal recognized the dragon's rider.

Ky Yasin.

Hal grimaced, angry that he hadn't held his fire until the better target presented itself

Yasin's dragon keened, rolled, and Storm was on him, ripping with his fangs at the other monster's neck, horns stabbing upward as his talons dug on.

The black dragon recovered, stabbed with his horns at Storm, almost took him in the throat.

Hal had another bolt in the trough, aimed carefully, fired at Yasin, just as Yasin's arrow whipped past him.

Kailas missed, and Yasin jerked his reins to the side, and the black tucked and dove.

Storm, eager for the kill, ducked, almost tossing Hal, and dove after Yasin.

Ahead of them was a great square, and Roche soldiers were setting up catapults.

Yasin pulled out bare feet above the stones, and catapults sent long bolts aloft.

Hal, shouting at Storm, pulled the reins, again, and, reluctantly, Storm banked, flying down a boulevard, below building roofs.

Hal brought his dragon back up and back in a climbing bank, looked for Yasin, didn't see him.

He swore – he'd missed another chance at the bastard.

His mind reminded him that Yasin had also missed, but that didn't matter that much, with the blood dinning in his ears.

He climbed up to a thousand feet, saw the black dragons still attacking the Sagene and Derainian beasts who'd given up the attack and were trying to escape east, back toward the front.

Hal let Storm climb higher, blowing commands on his trumpet – break off . . . assemble on me . . . cover the other dragons.

Reluctantly, his squadron obeyed, going for height, then, as they saw targets, going in, sometimes from below, sometimes at the same height, against the Roche blacks.

It was grim, as the casting dragons fled, and Yasin's beasts, faster, less weight-burdened, savaged them.

The day wore on, dragons attacking, being attacked.

Hal saw, all too often, one of the casting dragons torn out of the skies and, worse, one of his own fighters.

He saw no sign of Yasin, guessed that his dragon had been wounded seriously enough to break off action.

Hal took Storm into a patch of cloud, brought him back and around, and surprised a black harrying a wounded casting dragon.

He aimed carefully, shot the Roche flier out of his saddle, and the black broke off, flying back toward his base. Hal nodded in satisfaction – a dragon he didn't have to kill.

He heard a high scream that had become too familiar that day, saw two dragons clawing at each other, stabbing with their horns.

The Derainian black was a bit smaller than its enemy, and the Roche monster pulled away, and its long tail whipped the other.

Again the scream came from the Derainian beast, and now Hal recognized its flier was Farren Mariah.

Hard hit, Mariah's dragon dove for the ground, open farmland, with workers in the field.

Mariah tried to pull it up, but the dragon was too badly wounded.

Its wings flared, and it slammed in, hard, went limp.

Mariah sagged in his saddle, then bleared up.

The workers had recognized the Derainian uniform of the flier, and, waving scythes, hoes, were running toward Farren, shouting rage.

Farren pulled himself out of the saddle, drawing his sword. He stumbled, nearly fell, in shock.

There were at least a dozen farm workers running toward him, too many for even a warrior to deal with.

Hal's standing orders were to avoid suicidal acts and sentimental bosh.

What he was going to do was clearly in those categories.

He sent Storm spiraling down toward Mariah, and his motionless dragon.

Hal came in behind the running workers, and Storm's talons slashed at them, and his tail whipped back, forth.

Then Storm was on the ground, and the graceful killing beast became a waddling behemoth.

"Get on!" Hal shouted.

Farren hesitated. A worker hurled a rock, hit Mariah in the chest.

Hal shot the man down, recocked his crossbow as Farren came back to himself a little, and stumbled toward the dragon.

Another farmer threw a spade, which narrowly missed Mariah, then the small man was beside Storm, weakly pulling himself up behind Kailas.

Hal shot down the nearest farmer, gigged Storm into motion. He ran ponderously forward, and there was a farmer in front of him, waving a scythe.

Storm trampled him, and his wings thrust down, and he was in the air.

A rock thumped Hal's leg, but he paid it no mind, bent over Storm, talking to him, getting him to climb.

Then there was a flashing shadow overhead, and a Roche black dragon dove on them, jaws widen.

Hal sent a bolt fairly blindly at the beast, and made one of the luckiest shots of his life.

The bolt thudded directly between the dragon's fangs, into his throat.

The Roche dragon screamed, its talons clawing at its mouth, then it rolled on its back and dove straight into the ground.

"I suppose we're even-out for my saving your ass back in Aude, then," Mariah said. "Sir."

"Damned right," Hal growled. "Now here, take this damned crossbow and keep the Roche off my ass."

The Derainian and Sagene dragons flew on, limping, exhausted, wounded.

Then, ahead, was the brown, mucky, bare ribbon that marked the front.

Derainian dragon flights were waiting, and Yasin's squadron, almost as weary as the Derainians, broke off, flying back into their own territory.

The casting dragons were escorted back to their fields and, eventually, the remnants of Hal's squadron found its base, and succor.

Someone helped Farren Mariah down.

"Are you all right?" Hal asked.

Mariah nodded.

Then Hal noticed tears in the man's eyes.

"There's no godsdamned reason I ought to feel this way about a godsdamned smelly beast," he said fiercely, and stamped away toward his tent.

Hal had no idea how much damage had been done to Yarkand, and didn't much care.

The day was an unmitigated disaster.

Forty casting dragons were lost, including both commanders of the flights. Three or four fliers managed to work their way to the lines afoot and across the lines.

Of the sixty dragons in Hal's squadron, twenty had been either smashed from the skies or were gravely wounded enough to be retired.

As usual, most of the casualties were the newest replacements, although three experienced fliers had gone down.

Hal tried not to think about the magnitude of the catastrophe, and busied himself with letters to the next of kin, pleas to

Garadice, back in Deraine, for replacement dragons, requests for more fliers.

He was interrupted by a courier, with new orders.

Hal, and the survivors of the squadron, were to withdraw from combat and proceed, with all expediency, to Deraine and Rozen for further orders.

The command was signed by King Asir.

33

Hal went to Cantabri while the squadron packed, and asked him if he had any idea what was going on.

Lord Bab shook his head.

"Nary the slightest, and I'm not pleased to be losing you in the middle of this offensive, especially after we got our head handed us trying to level Yarkand.

"We need to come up with a counterstroke that'll destroy whatever triumph they're feeling, and you're generally a good source for that.

"All I've gotten about your recall to Deraine was a formal notification from the king, with no explanation, and I've learned when his Highness does something this abruptly you're wasting your time protesting his decision."

"True enough," Hal said. He thought of the disastrous invasion of Kalabas, which had been the king's great idea, and hid his wince.

"The only thing I can tell you is that King Asir has had some secret plan a-bubbling ever since the conference with the Sagene barons, something that's got little to do with this offensive," Cantabri said. "And he's not talking about it with anyone."

"Well," Hal said. "I guess I'm off. Try to have a nice war without me."

"I suppose it's a measure of how things have improved," King Asir said, "that I am able to greet you openly, instead of having you snuck in through the back gate."

Hal made a wry face. "Possibly, sire. But I don't know about improvements, since everyone who hears of my summoning no doubt thinks it's because you want to tear an enormous strip off me for Yarkand."

"Oh dear," the King said in what appeared to be honest bewilderment. "That's not the case at all. The notion was entirely mine, and it was catastrophic enough that I certainly don't want anyone dwelling on it.

"I must start learning that repeating something generally leads to a debacle. Not to mention that your raid on Carcaor was mounted secretly and swiftly, and I'm afraid the commanders of my casting unit were rather lumberous, if there's such a word.

"Pour us both a drink, and I'll explain what my scheme is.

"I think it's good, but I've not exactly been the best strategist in this war, so I would honestly appreciate it if you tell me I'm once again playing the fool."

Hal hid his surprise at the king's honesty, went to a nearby sideboard, while the king walked to a large map, covered with a sheet of cloth.

Kailas hesitated. All of the spirits were in crystal containers, without labels.

"Oh," Asir said. "It's confusing when there's no markings on the chart, isn't it. The brandy is the second from left, the old brandy is third from left, and all the way on the right corner is the *really* old brandy, twenty years in the cask. Which I'll have, and so will you, for it's unlikely even a lord with elaborate properties and wealth will ever be able to find something that rare.

"Yet another thing the damned war has ruined.

"You might want to fill another glass with charged water to chase the alcohol with. There is a bit of a bite in the aftertaste."

Asir waited until Hal handed him a pair of glasses, then pulled the cover off the map.

There was no legend, but it was clearly part of Roche's north coast. There was a broad river delta, a city at its mouth.

Asir noted Hal's change of expression.

"No," he said. "I'm not proposing another river invasion. I learned my lesson at Kalabas.

"That is the River Pettau. It's a distance from the Zante, where you were a prisoner. It's in fact around the peninsula to the east of the Zante.

"The Pettau, we've discovered, is one of the main trading passages for Roche, to the eastern lands, which appear most unsettled.

"I'll make a confession here. It is one of the failings of my family that we have little interest in matters that don't concern Deraine, which is why we've never had much of a navy, and have made few explorations beyond the lands we have always dealt with.

"I might also add, speaking personally, that I have never had the slightest interest in war, thinking it a matter for men who are bloodyminded and like to dress strangely.

"That was utter stupidity on my part, and may account for the mistakes I've made. But I'd prefer not to dwell on that, but on the subject at hand: my, and Deraine's, ignorance about our world.

"That ignorance, once the war is over, will not be allowed to continue," Asir said grimly.

"Now, stare at that river, because, unless you think my plan is idiotic, you and your squadron will be committed to the area.

"Good brandy, is it not?"

Hal came back, realized he hadn't touched his snifter, and tasted the brandy. It was mellow fire, that went down easily, then warmed the throat with a gentle flame.

"Yes, sire," Hal said. "It's very good."

"Back to the subject at hand. I desperately want peace, as quickly as possible, for three reasons. The first, of course, is that I'm losing the finest Derainians, and we'll be paying for these deaths for the rest of this century. Second is the same concern for Sagene. And the third might surprise you.

"That's my worry about Roche. I proposed the General Offensive because I hoped Queen Norcia and her damned barons would see the light, and sue for peace.

"Thus far, there's been no such light on the horizon.

"Roche is our enemy, but if the war continues, and we reduce the country to a wasteland, we'll have done ourselves a great disservice.

"If Roche falls into complete anarchy, then who knows what can happen to our own land?

"And what about invaders from the east, from beyond?

"Roche as a desert, or if it falls back into a web of feuding petty baronies, such as it was three hundred years ago, would be a catastrophe for everyone."

Hal had never thought of that. His mind growled at the concept – it would suit him fair well for Roche to be reduced to barrens. But he grudged the king might well be right, yet another reason he was glad soldiers stayed out of politics, if they had any brains.

"In the middle of the conference in Fovant," Asir continued, "it came to me that I had no other position in mind if the General Offensive failed . . . or succeeded too well.

"Quite suddenly I came up with one, and, in the final days of the conference, discussed it with Sagene's Council of Barons.

"They thought it a good idea, one which might accelerate victory and, best of all, one that wouldn't significantly increase the slaughter. At least, not for our side.

"When I returned here to Rozen, I very quietly began building small, light ships, almost boats, that can hold a platoon or so of infantrymen, and reconditioning and converting fishing boats. I also set about finding the men and women to man them, preferably people with knowledge of the Eastern Sea, which the Roche call the Wolda.

"Briefly, I propose to mount a blockade on Roche. Sagene's fleet will cover the Southern Sea, Deraine the north."

"What about land caravans from the east?" Hal said.

"I don't know, " Asir said. "I can theorize that they're not that important, since, before the war, Roche had few large trading cities along its eastern border.

"The Roche main trading routes are from the south, up the Ichili River, and, in the north, down the Pettau.

"Roche is fairly independent, but Sagene raiders have seized baled cotton, and rice. From the north come furs, dried fish, and, most important, dragons from Black Island.

"The southern blockade is the easiest to deal with, geographically. The problem is the Pettau. I've had small craft scouting its mouth, or mouths, which come off this huge delta. The river's mouth is constantly changing, and most sea traffic is shallow-draft barges or hulks.

"They travel through the Wolda hugging the coast, sheltering behind barrier islands, enter the delta from the east, in any of several passages, move to the head of the delta, then upriver to the city of Lanzi, where cargoes are either broken up or continue on upriver to smaller cities.

"At first, I thought I might be able to blockade the north with the vessels I'm building for deployment close onshore, sailing, when they see a target, within the barrier islands.

"Roche ships will be seized when it's possible, burnt when it's unhandy to try to capture them intact.

"Then I had a better idea, thinking of you."

Hal waited.

"As I recall, your flight did an outstanding job of interdicting traffic on the Ichili, during the siege of Aude, correct? I even remember your dragons were known as 'whispering death.'"

"So I heard, sir."

"I propose your entire squadron, once it's built back up to full strength, as a reconnaissance unit for my small ships, and as a raiding, a casting, unit by itself.

"The rest of the northern blockade will be handled by the fleet, big ships out at sea, smaller ones hugging the coastline.

"If we can't fight the damned Roche into submission, then we'll starve them!"

Asir tossed back his brandy, set the glass down, and looked ferociously at Hal.

"Well? What do you think of the idea?"

Hal had been dreading the moment.

"Sir," he said, "does my answer have to be final right now?"

"No," Asir said, a bit grumpily. "You can have a few days."

"Thank you," Hal said. "I can give you my first reaction, which is that I like the idea. I don't mean I like the idea of starving women and children, but anything that ends the war soon can only be good.

"I don't see any holes, any problems, but I'd like to withhold my final answer until I've gone over the maps, particularly the one of the River Pettau."

Asir's mood had changed again. "I'm sorry I growled," he said. "I should have known you'd at least tell me your first thoughts. Not like some of my damned courtiers, who wouldn't say shit if they had a mouthful.

"Go on. Your squadron won't get here for another week, and I give you leave to join your wife.

"Oh. One other thing that might help. If you think the blockade is feasible, you'll be rebased here, in Deraine, somewhere on the east coast, although I think you and your dragons will be spending time at sea, which you've done before.

"Now, get gone, and I'll talk to you in a week."

Khiri met Hal at the castle, and their lovemaking was a roil of ecstasy.

They talked about what they should do for the promised week, decided they'd stay at Sir Thom's city mansion, where Khiri had been living when she first met Hal.

She was clearly most curious about what had brought him

back to Deraine. Hal refused to tell her, not having been given permission by the king, for two days.

Then he noted the taletellers were filling the broadsheets with stories of the brave Sagene navy, and the even braver Derainian mariners, and of the recently-discovered evils of the Roche traders in the primitive lands to the east.

Hal figured the hells with it. If the king's campaign to ready the civilians for the war to be continued on a pair of new fronts was already underway, what was the problem with telling his wife, who'd certainly proven herself not to be a babbling gossip?

She listened carefully, sat silently for a time, then asked, in a small voice, "That'll mean civilians – women and children – will starve as well as the lords and soldiers."

"It does, I'm afraid," Hal said uncomfortably.

"That doesn't seem right, since they didn't start the war," Khiri said.

"No," Hal agreed. "But I can't think of a way the king could do this without hurting some innocents. What of the Derainian women and children who've lost brothers, fathers, sons?"

Hal thought of Khiri's father, dead at the war's beginning, her brother, and someone who might have become her lover, killed in battle.

Khiri shook her head. "That doesn't make what King Asir is going to do right, does it?" Before Hal could reply, she went on: "and I know very well that the queen and the Roche barons and soldiers will be fed first. Won't they?"

"I suppose so," Hal said.

"Oh," Khiri said, and rather ostentatiously changed the subject.

The next day, she said she had some business to attend to, regarding one of her estates, and didn't invite Hal, which was most unusual.

He started to get angry, since he wasn't exactly the originator of the blockade, decided that wasn't right, and called for a horse to be brought around.

Something had been pulling at him for a time, and so he sought out Garadice, head of what was, archaically, still called the King's Remounts. Garadice's son had trained with Hal earlier in the war, and was killed during the siege of Aude, and Garadice, still mourning his only child, busied himself with replacement dragons and the dragon training schools for both beasts and men.

Garadice was headquartered at what had been the King's Own Menagerie, but now was turned over to the reeking dragons.

Dinapur, father of his dead love, Saslic, had been head of the menagerie, but, to Hal's relief, wasn't in sight.

Garadice took him into his common room, and ordered tea brewed.

Hal hadn't seen Garadice since the dragon-stealing raid on Black Island. His beard and hair had whitened, and there were new lines of determination and fatigue on his face. He'd aged but Hal supposed he had as well.

"I assume you have business," Garadice said. None of us seem to have any interest except the war these days . . . although, if you've come just to socialize, that'd be a blessing, uncommon as it is."

"No, I have business. Of a sort," Hal said. He told Garadice about what Danikel had said, during the Fovant conferences, that once the war was over the dragons would be discarded or even killed, and no one would give a damn, any more than they would for ex-soldiers.

"I've read of that young man," Garadice said. "Quite the hero . . . and now I see someone who's got more than a bit of brain."

He sat down heavily, staring down at his teacup.

"I'm afraid he's dead right. There's no provision for a crippled dragon, any more than there is for a broken-legged horse. Dragons either heal – and the gods be blessed dragons are tough, almost as tough as a man – or they're gotten rid of.

"If they're so seriously injured they can't recover . . . well, the unit vets are issued poison."

"I know that, sir," Hal said. "But what about the others that're not that seriously injured. Say they can't fly. I know they're taken off the station . . . I've seen enough of that. But I've never wondered what happens to them."

"They're put out to pasture behind the lines," Garadice said. "At one time, they were just killed, but I put a stop to that. Now, we have rations continuing for them, and they're cared for by wounded soldiery who volunteer. I'm glad to say I had a hand in setting that up.

"But once the war is over, all military funding will be sliced to the bone and further . . ."

He broke off, and shook his head sadly.

"Man is a long ways from being an ideal master. If he can't eat it, or make use of it, there's no use for it and it, whatever it is, beast or whatever, is put away."

The two sat looking at each other, then Hal thanked Garadice for his time, got up and left.

He went to the king's castle, sought out an equerry he knew, and asked who would be a reliable sort to draw up a will, or such. He got a name, an address, and rode into the heart of the city, thinking how truly inept he was at handling personal business that the army didn't take care of, let alone the rather more complicated affairs of a lord owning villages and great expanses of land.

The legal counselor was awed at meeting the Dragonmaster, and offered any help he could provide.

Business complete, and feeling a great deal of satisfaction, he rode back to Sir Thom's estate, and sought out Khiri.

He explained that he was having papers drawn up to take care of crippled and maimed dragons, to be paid for with a small deduction from his estate's profits. Since Khiri was his heir, he hoped she didn't mind, and, if he, well, failed to make it through the war, he wanted her to know what was in his mind.

"I certainly don't care for myself," she said. Then she looked at him a bit oddly. "But wouldn't your money be better spent, say, founding an orphanage? Or even a poorhouse for widows?"

"Why?" Hal asked, honestly bewildered.

"Because," Khiri said, in the voice of an adult speaking to a small child, "they're people. Dragons aren't."

"But nobody's taking care of the dragons," Hal said. "And there're lots of orphanages and poorhouses."

Khiri looked at him for a time.

"It's your money," she said. "You can do with it what you like."

Hal was not that unhappy to be told three days later that his squadron had arrived in Deraine, and he was to return to duty.

34

"Now this, young Lieutenant, is an example of what is called irony," Sir Loren Damian said to Farren Mariah. "Since you have ambitions beyond getting yourself eviscerated in this war, ambitions that I've heard include public leadership, learn to use irony whenever possible.

"It'll make the masses think you to be educated, and hence fall into line and obediently do your every wish."

"Aarh," Farren Mariah said, then considered what lay before them again. "But 'tis a bit of all around turn around. To think this is where we all began, and where we end up now."

Where, was the old monastery named Seabreak, where Hal and the other founding members of the 11th Dragon Flight had begun their training.

Gray stone against a gray sea and foggy skies, it looked no more inviting than it had almost ten years before.

Perhaps someone in the army had sensed the gloom, because Seabreak was no longer used as a dragon fliers school either.

Hal thought *that* was not frigging likely. Armies aren't known for being mood-sensitive.

But this would be the new base for the First Dragon Squadron in the blockade.

It might have sounded odd for Hal's unit to be based in Deraine, rather than in Paestum or the conquered fringe of Roche. But Roche, east of the Zante River, curved out, and the farthest reaches of the country that would be Hal's operational area were a closer flight from Deraine.

Not that anyone would have objected if it had been longer – what little comforts war can provide are easier to get hold of closer to the mother country.

"At least one thing," Mynta Gart said. "We know where the back door to the mess is."

She looked down, toward the heaving sea. Three frigates were moored there, plus two light corvettes, and the familiar *Galgorm Adventurer* dragon transport and a newer sister ship, the *Bohol Adventurer*. Her expression was unreadable.

"Are you sorry you didn't stay in the navy?" Hal asked quietly. She hesitated.

"No, sir. I don't think so, anyway." She forced her mood to change. "I wouldn't have met fine, upstanding gentle souls like Farren."

Mariah looked offended.

"O Captain Fearless Leader Lord Kailas, sir, I gotta lodge a complaint on being picked on by my superiors."

"Not nearly enough," Hal said. "But since you've problems with the present company, I'll put you in charge of divvying out the buildings."

"The student huts are for fliers, right?"

They were the best thing about Seabreak – four-person cottages scattered around the estate.

"Right," Hal said. "But first we make sure the dragons have enough. I don't think we'll have to pitch the tents."

They didn't. The dragons fit comfortably into the large horse-barns the religious order had built before the war. The explanation Hal and the other students had made up was the order, which seemed to have vanished, worshipped some sort of horse god. Or else their acolytes were most wealthy.

There was also more than enough room for the humans in the squadron.

It took about two weeks for replacement dragons and men to trickle in, and then Hal sent a courier to Supreme Army Command in Rozen to say that he was ready to go to back to battle.

There were five men on the single-masted sloop, in peacetime a patrol boat for the Roche fisheries, now a guard ship on the inner passage that led from the Roche border west to the Pettau River.

Their duty was to keep watch for any Derainian intrusion and summon reinforcements from their nearby headquarters, garrisoned with a half-company of marines and a very small hooker.

One man was at the helm, another in the prow, keeping watch, although the Roche were local sailors and utterly familiar with the passage, with its tidal vagaries and shifting sands.

The other three were forward, arguing about what the proclaimed blockade might mean to them.

They'd pretty well decided that the Derainians would try some sort of big raid, end up going ashore and finding little in the way of loot or enemies, and henceforth keep an almost-useless patrol far offshore.

None could see getting worried about anything. War may have been boring, but they were sitting quite comfortably on the trade route from the east, and anything they couldn't catch or their wives make could be traded or purloined from the small coasters headed for the delta and Lanzi.

One of them heard a sound, like the rasping of silk, looked up, and shouted an alarm.

Three black dragons dove out of the lowering cover toward them.

The sailors had just time to see the fliers wore Derainian

uniforms when a crossbow bolt whipped through the helmsman's leg. He groaned, let go the wheel, and stumbled back, just as a second bolt took him in the chest.

He fell on his back, lay still, just as the lookout was hit in the body by another bolt.

One of the arguing men ran for the wheel as the sloop yawed out of the dredged, marked channel.

He, too, went down.

The two survivors dove for shelter, one behind the upturned ship's boat, the other behind a bulwark. The bulwark wasn't heavy enough to stop the next round of bolts, and two took him. He stood, screaming, stumbled forward and went over the side.

The survivor stayed where he was, even as the sloop ran into the shallows, hard aground, then lurched sideways, its mast cracking overside.

The dragon riders didn't wait for the tide to take and wreck the sloop, but flew on, down the waterway, looking for another target.

Hal looked down at the ocean, and thought of the few hours it took to fly from Deraine to beyond the Zante River, as opposed to the days he spent as an escaped prisoner in that damned boat he'd killed for, tossed by the seas and hoping he was headed somewhere friendly.

From up here, the water looked friendly, bobbing whitecaps in the still-warm sunlight.

He knew if he was down there, conditions would be a deal less inviting.

Ahead of them, the barrier islands rose out of the sea.

Hal blatted an alert to the other three dragons in his flight, not that there should be any need to bring them to the alert.

Two of the dragons carried passengers – earnest young women with drawing boards firmly lashed to their saddle rings.

Hal touched Storm's neck with a boot, and the dragon obediently turned east by north-east, flying, at about three hundred feet, above the sandy islands that were covered with brush and scattered trees bent by the near-constant offshore wind.

The dragons flew as slowly as they could, and the artists busied themselves drawing.

Hal considered how much of war never appeared in the romances, tasks such as this, making maps for the ships that would keep the inshore blockade.

At least there weren't – yet – any Roche catapults or dragons to worry about, and he relaxed in the sun.

As much as he could ever allow himself, which was not much.

Too many dragon fliers had eased off, when they absolutely knew it was safe . . . and gone down to a very surprised death.

Hal thought about after the war, then grinned, remembering a story of Farren Mariah's.

"Ah, it'll be a grand, grand homecoming when somebody flinches and we're struck with peace.

"I'll land my dragon in the street outside my house, where my mother, the always-delightful Lady Mariah and my sisters, those she hasn't succeeded in marrying off to some dunderbrain with money, are waiting, having made all my favorite dishes.

"I'll whip out my sword in one hand, dagger in the other, then run, zigging and zaggetying through the gate and the yard, ducking any archers lurking about, kick open the door, flash up against the wall inside, and then bellow, 'Ma! I'm home!'"

It was raining, a dull soaking rain that had started before dawn, and looked to last for days.

Below Hal and his three dragons, eight coasters, under full sail, scattered among tiny islets.

The wolf was in the fold.

Four of the new shallow-draft raiding ships and three corvettes had been guided into the inland passage by Hal, and then led into the convoy.

Some of the Roche coasters gave up, and ran aground, their crews leaping into the shallows and running ashore for shelter. Others, stouter, more foolhardy, or, most likely, with captain-owners aboard, packed on sail, and tried to flee upchannel.

But there was no safety this day.

The sleek corvettes and raiding ships ran at their heels, and sorcerous firebottles were hurled from the Derainian ships.

Perhaps the Roche knew about pirates, who would dare everything before ruining their chances at loot.

The Derainians cared nothing about grain or furs, and so the ships roared up in pitch-fed flames.

There were three Roche warships based in Lanzi, and now they were coming out, after a Derainian corvette who'd chanced pursuing his merchantmen almost into the harbor itself.

They were fast, almost as fast as the corvette, and knew their waters far better.

The Roche sailors sensed a victory, something to savor after the weeks of their convoys being savaged by ships that struck and ran.

But the sailors weren't anticipating the full flight of dragons that dropped out of the clouds, casting pebbles that sent water-spouts climbing into the sky.

Two pebbles, now boulders, smashed into one ship, and the rest of Hal's flight came in low, with firedarts.

That warship took flame, and the others fled.

But they had bowmen aboard, and one Derainian dragon was hit three times in the chest.

Screaming pain, it climbed for the heights as the rest of the flight closed in about it.

Somehow the dragon kept in the air in the long flight back across the Eastern Sea toward Seabreak.

They were in sight of land when the dragon's indomitable will broke, and it spun down, into the waters.

Hal took Storm low, saw his flier swimming hard away from the dying dragon, went around again, shouting to Storm to go down, down to land in the waters, trying to rescue the flier.

But there was nothing to see but heaving gray waves, and the sinking body of the dragon.

"All right," Hal said. His fliers were drawn up in front of him, some still in the throes of their hangovers after the fliers' traditional wake for the dead flier.

"We're going to make things easier . . . and harder.

"All of you who've no experience landing dragons aboard ship are going to learn. Half of the squadron – the half that isn't on patrol – will practice.

"Here's the change. From now on, one flight will be assigned to each of the *Adventurers*. They'll be offshore, with the navy's great ships.

"The other two flights will be here, resting. Every three days, a flight at sea will interchange with one on land.

"You won't like it and the dragons will hate it.

"But if you're hit – like poor Patric was – you stand a chance of living, if you can get away from Roche to one of the dragon ships."

*

If the water hadn't been so cold, and the wind so gusty, and the seas so sloppy, it might have been funny watching the newer fliers learn how to bring their dragon down to the barge tied alongside the *Adventurer*, stall the reluctant beast until it thudded down, then was led up a heavy ramp on to the ship itself.

But it was, it was, and they were, and, on a regular basis dragons and men went overboard.

For the dragons it wasn't that upsetting. They honked displeasure, and either tented their wings over their head, as dragons had done for no one knew how long making the great passage east from unknown lands, or the more intelligent ones clambered aboard the barge or took off from the water.

Two of them actually swam to their unseated riders and waited until they hauled themselves back into their saddles before unfurling their great wings and thumped across the ocean into the sky.

Those beasts instantly became priceless.

Hal chanced a passage over Lanzi, seeing if a convoy was in port, wondering if he dared go after the small boats that would bring the cargoes upriver, as he'd done during the siege of Aude.

He was half looking for Roche dragons, half watching to see if the Roche had brought in any catapult units.

Lanzi was a wonderful city, he decided. Very ancient, very rich, with twisting cobbled lanes, houses and businesses that climbed for three or more stories, leaning crazily toward each other, gay banners flapping in the wind from the sea.

The gray world about the city may have inspired the Lanzians to paint their buildings in the rawest of bright colors.

Even the wooden parapets were painted, many with vivid murals.

Hal decided it would be a city he'd like to show to Khiri, when the war was over.

Below Hal, a fishing village was afire. It was true that a handful of Roche marines had been quartered on the village, which made it technically a justified target. But Hal doubted if the fishermen had been given much choice by the Roche soldiers when they arrived.

The village had a clear view of one of the deepest passages into the delta, and the watchmen would have ample time to see the

Derainians, and take a small boat, or even use signal flags, to warn any merchant shipping approaching.

And so one of the raiding ships, guided by the dragons, ran up on the beach, and armed sailors poured out, with orders to seize the marines and tell the fishermen they'd best become neutral if they didn't want to be treated as soldiers.

Hal had no idea what had happened, but suddenly flame had poured out from one hut, then another, then a third.

He sent Storm low, saw women and children being pushed into a group, some scattered bodies, and then the boats onshore burst into flames as well.

By the time the raiding ship was kedged out into deeper water, the oil-soaked boats and buildings were burning down into ruins.

He saw no sign of the civilians, wondered if they'd fled, or been taken somewhere as captives. Or . . .

Hal didn't think he wanted to know for sure.

In theory, having a personal life makes a warrior more vulnerable.

Hal decided there might be merit to the idea in the abstract, but he'd take the chance.

Besides, it didn't seem anyone was going to make it out of this war alive anyway.

It was very nice having Khiri show up from time to time. She was never obtrusive, taking rooms at the tiny inn in the closest village, as did some of the other wives, and gave Hal someone to talk to about things other than soldiering.

Fliers and groundsmen found lovers in the surrounding villages, or else visited Rozen and brought back friends. Every now and again someone – Hal studiedly kept from finding out who – imported a bevy of whores from the capital, and so most everyone had someone to cuddle as the nights grew colder.

Some of the dragons came into season, and Hal arranged for them to be mated with dragons from Garadice's host, which also gave the dragon fliers some time off in the capital.

Hal had worried there'd be problems with Khiri as the blockade tightened, but she never brought up the subject again.

He noticed she wasn't quite as much of a flagwaver as at the start of the war, but then, who was?

The squadron still suffered losses. But only one, the flier shot out of the sky over Lanzi, was the result of direct action. There still were no Roche dragons to worry about.

The casualties came from poor judgement but mostly from fliers getting lost, and not being able to find the *Adventurers*, or even Deraine.

Hal remembered what he'd come up with, years ago, before the raid on Black Island, and sent to Rozen for a magician. Bodrugan showed up, and cast a spell on the ever-loathed salt meat served aboard ship, so that a flier thinking of it would be drawn toward the fleet.

Another spell was cast for fliers trying to return to Seabreak.

An instantly-beloved dish on the squadron was tarts, made from the small apples of the district.

Those apples were used as the base for the second spell.

Losses dropped, and fliers used the second spell as an excuse to visit the area's farms, ostensibly to refresh the spell with new apples, actually to court the farmers' and workers' daughters and, naturally, wives in some instances.

It was still dangerous up there, but a deal less so than if the squadron had still been down south, back with Cantabri's slowly-grinding offensive.

The squadron was grounded by an early storm. The two *Adventurers*, unhandy pigs at sea as they were, had been brought back from the blockading squadron, and the dragons and their fliers had nothing at all to do for a few days.

The more experienced fliers spent their time drinking, maintaining their gear and sleeping. The newer ones still had energy enough for gaming, gambling and wenching.

The storm faded, but day-long, low-level fogs still clung to the sea and the shores of Roche.

Hal was fuming about the war's hiatus one day, watching some very bored fliers play a game of quoits, when the idea came.

Just after dawn the next day, he had two flights in the air. Seabreak vanished into the fog, and he set a course by compass for Roche.

Every now and again the wind scudded the fogbank open, but there was nothing but roiling ocean below.

He kept track of the time, and on the mark started looking down and around.

There was a long clear patch below, and Hal spotted a small-ish, uniquely-shaped island below.

That gave him a location from his map, and he took the flights north, following the invisible inland passage below.

Ahead, he saw things sticking through the fog, thin spikes that were masts, with yards vanishing in the mist and topsails here and there.

Hidden in the mist below were Roche coasters, happily believing they were invisible to any enemies.

But their masts gave them away, so many quoit pegs sticking up through the mist.

Hal, flying as slowly as he could, flew along the convoy's course, back and forth, casting pebbles and then firedarts as he went. Other fliers behind and on either side did the same.

Mostly he heard nothing but splashes as the pebbles grew into boulders and slammed into the sound.

But there were also crashes as a boulder smashed into a ship, and screams to be heard.

He cast until he'd run out of pebbles and darts, then brought the flights up, and set a return course for Deraine.

Whispering death had struck once more.

Kailas was brooding quietly in his hut about the blockade. It was very effective, but not a complete closure.

When he flew over Lanzi, he could still see coasters coming in and leaving, and river boats taking cargo inland.

Winter was almost here, and the weather would keep the dragons grounded, and probably drive the Derainian ships to seek shelter, while the Roche coasters could still bring in their goods behind the barrier islands.

He'd been scheming for several days, without product. His fliers knew he wasn't that happy, and why.

There was a knock.

"Enter," he said.

Danikel, Baron Trochu entered.

Hal offered him some tea from the pot on a trivet.

"You've got a problem?" he asked.

"No, sir," Danikel said. "An idea."

"I could use several."

"I think I've got a way to seal off the blockade. The only thing is," Danikel said, "it'll most likely kill off some thousand Roche children and women."

He smiled wryly, his face boyishly innocent.

Hal's plan of attack was sent off, by courier, to the palace, with a note that it would be implemented within the week unless it was countermanded by the king.

No response came.

That had been somewhat expected – the king, after all, ruled in the end by popularity, and Danikel's idea was one guaranteed to cause civilian deaths, not just in the course of the attack, but in the winter to come.

Danikel's plan was simple: burn the city of Lanzi to the ground, warehouses, docks, shipping, businesses, inns and houses. With no receiving and distributing point, either for incoming or outgoing trade goods, it would be difficult to move goods promptly into the heart of Roche.

Especially with many clerks, warehousemen, longshoremen and other trade experts hopefully being dead.

It was a simple plan . . . and an ugly one.

Roche had already lost access to some of its richest farming land, first with the assault that took the Bluffs, then with the General Offensive. Now the screws would tighten further.

Hal had no response from Rozen, and so, as he'd promised, the plan was set in motion.

Two flights were issued large amounts of firedarts – there should be no need of the casting pebbles on this attack.

They were dispatched to the two *Adventurers*, once again at sea off the River Pettau.

The other two flights were similarly armed, and put on standby.

The flights aboard ship flew out in the late afternoon of the set day, and the other two, at Seabreak, were airborne an hour after the first two.

Hal flew with the first element from the *Galgorm Adventurer*.

They took off, orbited the blockade fleet once, forming up, then made for land.

It was chill but clear as they flew up the delta. Fishermen and boaters saw the thirty dragons overhead, and went for any shelter they could find.

None of the Derainian or Sagene fliers paid them the slightest mind.

The waterway grew wider, and then they saw Lanzi ahead, ancient buildings along the city's canals and estuaries.

Hal heard trumpets blast ahead of them, and men running for catapults.

He blew a single blast on his own trumpet, and the two flights formed parallel lines, the dragons flying close.

Then he was over the wharves, and aiming as best he could while hurling the fire darts.

Again and again he made his throws, then the swamps of the city's outskirts were below him.

He blew two more blasts, and slowly the lines wheeled back over the city.

Here and there, he saw fire start to spurt, taking easily on the ancient lumber, especially along the waterfront where, for generations, fish oil had soaked the warehouses.

Again, he sent firedarts cascading, and then they were over water, and he was out of ammunition.

Hal set course back down the main shipping channel, into the delta and the open sea.

They were still in sight of land when the other two flights of his squadron from Seabreak flew past, toward Lanzi.

Then the blockading ships were ahead, and the flights broke apart, and, in line, dropped down for landings on the pair of *Adventurers*. There was beer waiting, and steaming roast meat on buns, but Hal had no appetite.

The dragons ate greedily from barrels of salt beef, then fresh firedarts in netting were loaded aboard the dragons, and they were airborne again, flying back toward Lanzi.

Once more, they passed the rest of the squadron, coming back empty.

Hal took his flights upriver. Now there was no need to check his compass – a pillar of smoke curled above the doomed city.

He circled wide to attack Lanzi from a different quadrant.

Once more they flew their course, seeding death and flame.

One of the newer fliers was gawping down at the boiling fires, didn't notice a catapult tracking her. Her dragon was hit near his hindquarters, screamed, snapping at the bolt, pitching his flier off, down into the roaring blaze, then followed her into a fiery death.

Hal brought the dragons back over Lanzi, dropping the last of the firedarts, then set a course back to sea.

Once more, they saw the other two flights, shuttling back to feed the fires in the dusk.

Hal kept his dragons in the air, and didn't land on the ships.

The other two flights would, and replenish and spend the night.

Hal and his dragons at least had the comfort of Seabreak.

The fliers were very quiet that night. No one seemed interested in drinking. Perhaps it was because they'd been told they'd be returning to Lanzi the next morning.

Or perhaps there were other reasons.

They took off in midmorning, laden with the old-fashioned firebottles. The two flights on the *Adventurers* should have been well on their way.

It was a still fall day as they sighted land, and then the two flights coming away from the city.

This time, there wasn't a smoke cloud to follow, but a writhing great flame that rose higher than his dragons. For an instant, he was reminded of the great demon that still waited outside Carcaor.

He signaled, and his dragons climbed to a safer altitude, above the flames.

Today, no one was interested in shooting at dragons.

All that existed below was fire and agony.

Hal steeled himself, went in over Lanzi, scattering firebottles as he went.

He saw, below, a fire wagon hurtling up a street. A gout of flame reached out from an alley, almost casually, and licked up wagon, horses, men.

Below him, as he swung back, still adding to the fire, was a small lake. There were bodies floating in it, and he saw, his stomach churning, that the water was boiling.

He had to bank sharply as fire came up at him.

Hal saw a wizard, easy to define in his robes, acolytes flanking, evidently casting a spell.

But the fire was stronger than magic this day, and the flames took him and his assistants.

Hal realized he could hear nothing – the fire was roaring like a great beast as it ravaged the city. The center of Lanzi was a mass of flames, and Hal blinked, seeing a stone building melt and pour across a street.

It was as hot as a still summer day over the city. Hal was sweating, not just from the heat.

They were over the docks then, and the fire had taken the warehouses and ships. There was a handful of boats on the river, and the flames were reaching them as well.

Out of ammunition, they went back downriver, seeing people fleeing the city below them.

They landed on the *Adventurer*, and Sir Loren came up to him.

"Sir, there's three fliers who came back with their firebottles. They've refused to go back over Lanzi."

Hal wanted to sympathize with them, but couldn't.

"Tell them to make their own way back to Seabreak," he said, his voice sounding like it was coming out of a metallic throat, "turn in their dragon emblem, and tell them to stand by. They'll be off the squadron as soon as I return."

Hal and his two flights spent that night on the ships. Kailas was totally exhausted, but couldn't sleep.

At first light, he took his two flights, freshly rearmed, back over Lanzi.

There were still flames, but there was little left to burn.

He saw a scatter of river boats up from the city, sent Storm down on them.

The sailors dove overboard when they saw him coming.

He coldly fired their ships, then led his dragons back out to sea, and to Seabreak.

Lanzi had been completely destroyed.

True to his word, forcing callousness, he ordered the fliers who'd broken – his three, and four from other flights – off the base, and back to the replacement companies.

What happened to them when they got there, whether they were grounded, or given another chance, mattered not at all to him.

He gave his fliers one night to drink themselves into sodden forgetfulness, if they could. The next morning, he put them into hard physical training and flying.

No one would be permitted time to brood about what had happened, even though he knew Lanzi would always be at the back of their minds.

There were no celebrations of this victory, no boasting, not even from Alcmaen.

*

What had happened to Lanzi quickly spread across Deraine, but in a very muted manner, without celebration.

Even the normally jingoistic broadsheets dealt with the horror with circumspection.

Possibly even the most rabid taleteller realized that something different had come to war, something even more terrible than the traditional sacking of a city. If men could ruin a metropolis from afar, without bloodying their hands, would common decency, already mostly a fiction on the battlefield, completely vanish?

It was a question never asked, never answered.

Now the feats, mostly made up by the taletellers, of the Dragonmaster and his squadron were muted, and the stream of love letters to Hal from strangers dropped away.

But there were exceptions. The adulation the Sagene had for Danikel seemed to redouble. Hal wondered if they had known the idea for leveling Lanzi had come from him would have lessened their adulation. On consideration, he thought not. Sagene, he'd noted, hated hard, and, after all, it was their country that had been invaded to start the war.

Kailas got a new group of supporters, members of groups with strange names like Deraine First, Derainians Supporting Our Men and Women in Uniform, Sorrowing Mothers For The War, Derainians for Decisive Action, and so forth. Those letters he threw away unanswered and unopened. There were also single letters, almost all from men, most of which began with: "Dear Lord Kailas . . . I never had the privilege of serving the colors, but what you've done strikes a chord . . ." Those too, after the first handful, went into the trash bin.

Hal supposed everyone thought there were two merciless monsters in Deraine's ranks – himself and Lord Cantabri.

He tried to push it away, but it bothered him, like it bothered the others who'd been in the attack.

Strangely enough, Khiri, who he expected would have been most upset by what had happened, with her husband as the cause, seemed to know nothing of the matter. She never brought it up on her periodic visits to Hal, and seemed more passionate, more caring than before.

Perhaps Hal should have brought it up with her, and exposed his heart, but he didn't, grateful for what appeared acceptance of the realities of the day, and feeling far too tired to look behind the surface.

*

The blockade continued, and Hal and the King's First Squadron returned to the normal duties of scouting for the inshore blockade, and chivvying any ships they found.

Lanzi remained a ruin, with only a scattering of people who returned to its desolation, evidently having nowhere else to go.

Now Kailas took his whispering death further upriver, where small boats met coasters in camouflaged inlets, hastily breaking down cargo into deck loads, and scurrying south, away from the dragons.

It was still dangerous – Hal lost two dragons to the weather, two more who just disappeared – but now it was becoming routine.

Hal considered, decided that it was time for him, and his fliers, to return to the real war. Any collection of dragon flights could handle the blockade. Enough people had told him the First Squadron was to be used for special duties and the most hazardous tasks for him to believe it.

Besides, he now had a target worth pursuing, one that was very capable of striking back.

Not sure of who he should importune, Kailas sent a request directly to the king.

He was owed a favor.

36

The streets of Rozen were a-tilt with cheering crowds, dancing trollops, blaring bands, amateur and professional, and happy drunkards.

It must be a famous victory, Hal thought, reined in his horse and tossed a vender a copper for a broadsheet. It was only a single sheet, which meant whatever had happened occurred just recently.

It was, indeed, a famous victory.

> Queen Norcia Overthrown!
> Barons Take Charge
> Of Roche, War

"Holy shit," Hal said in astonishment, then read on.

According to the broadsheet, the barons had been most unhappy with her conduct of the war for some time. That was news to Hal. Not that he doubted it, but he wondered how some hack had gotten intelligence that no one, up to King Asir, seemed to possess.

The head of the conspiracy was the queen's one-time confidant, Duke Garcao Yasin. After Norcia had been deposed, a caretaker government had been formed by the dukes and barons of Roche, under Yasin's direction.

There was nothing in the story about whether Norcia had survived the overthrow, who the caretaker government was caretaking for, nor even whether Norcia had any offspring, legitimate or not.

In any event, Yasin had issued a proclamation saying the war would be pursued more vigorously, with victory over the invaders, Sagene and Deraine, being the absolute and only acceptable goal.

So they wouldn't be suing for peace . . . at least if the broadsheet was correct.

Hal smiled, thinking his own thoughts.

This sudden change boded well for his mission.

"I suppose I do not stand particularly high in your esteem at the moment, Lord Kalabas," King Asir said formally, not turning away from the window he was staring out of.

Hal decided not to answer the question.

"King's aren't supposed to be cowards," Asir said. "But all too often, we are. That was why I didn't endorse your plan to destroy Lanzi, and have distanced myself from the results.

"But now . . . now, with Norcia toppled from her throne, which was directly caused by your action . . . now I not only look the coward, but the fool as well."

Hal managed some meaningless noises.

"So, before we go on any further, might I ask why you asked this meeting?"

"Yes, sire," Hal said, deciding to keep it brief. "The blockade is running very smoothly. I think a conventional group of dragon flights will suffice to continue the pressure.

"I wish to have my squadron deployed, back to the First Army.

"If you allow this, I intend to devote the squadron's full efforts to the destruction of *Ky* Bayle Yasin and his First Guards Dragon

Squadron. He's the best they've got, and now, if the broadsheet I read is correct about his brother, he will be even more in the public's eye. His destruction—"

The king held up his hand, and Hal shut up instantly. Asir turned, and Hal was puzzled to see relief on his face.

"Thank the gods for one thing," the king said. "I was afraid you'd come here to tender your resignation."

"Why would I do something like that?" Hal was honestly puzzled. Maybe it was growing up mean and poor in a corrupt mining district, but Kailas had never expected much from his bosses, whether they were kings or no.

The king blinked.

"If I had the time, which I do not, with this latest confusion from Roche going on, I would pour us both a drink. But I don't, and won't.

"I'll figure a way to reward you for the action that led to the change, which can only be good for us, since no group rules as efficiently – or sometimes inefficiently – as a single person, king or queen. We could have hoped this would be a regency for peace. It is not.

"So the war will go on, and we can anticipate it shall be with growing savagery. So be it.

"The Roche have had at least two chances. We can afford no more generosity.

"Now it will continue to the bitter end, until Carcaor lies in ruins, like Lanzi.

"I assume you have a plan to hound Yasin and his dragons to their deaths. Good. Go to it, sir. And I'll see you when the war is over."

37

Hal turned the task of packing and moving the squadron back to Cantabri's positions over to Sir Loren, and went back to Rozen. He sought out Limingo the wizard.

He thought he knew how to finally trap *Ky* Yasin, but needed a magician's help.

To his disappointment, Limingo turned him down.

"Your theory sounds perfectly valid," the magician said. "So your plan should work excellent well. But the casting of the spell won't take a great deal of ability. I'll lend you Bodrugan, who should be quite competent, and is clawing for a chance to get back to the front."

Limingo noted Hal's expression.

"I'm not turning arrogant on you . . . I'm up to my eyebrows in another task, one that might be a bit more important in the long run."

Hal made understanding sounds.

"Have a seat," Limingo said. "I was going to send for you in the next couple of weeks anyway, since the matter pertains to you.

"One thing that has troubled me is that damned great demon – if that's what it is – you and your dragon fliers aroused when you raided Carcaor. Assuming that apparition wasn't something spontaneous, which I certainly don't think, that means that the armies will almost certainly have to confront – and destroy – whatever it is when they close on that city, even though we have no idea whether it can leave its mountaintop and that damned castle it inhabits."

"I know," Hal agreed. "And I've been trying to think of what we might do."

"Well," Limingo said, "I happen to have a bit more information than you do. You remember that raider you set atop that mountain to stand guard until you returned with your dragons?"

"I do," Hal said. "Poor bastard must've gotten eaten by the demon . . . or been done away with however demons kill people."

"Not quite," Limingo said. "Three weeks ago, he wandered across our lines in the south. Somehow he managed to travel all those leagues without getting killed or captured.

"The problem is that he's quite, raving mad.

"They returned him to his unit, which thankfully is under Lord Bab's direct control. He remembered the man, and what had happened to him, and sent him, with a pair of minders, on to me."

"Mad, you say?"

"Babblingly so," Limingo said. "I've set a team of secretaries on him, so that everything he says, no matter how nonsensical, is recorded and transcribed."

"What does that give us?"

"So far, nothing," Limingo said. "But I'd like to send on a copy of his ravings, to see if you can find anything in it."

"So the man lived," Hal mused. "I wonder what he did – if anything – to escape being killed by the demon."

"I don't know yet," Limingo said.

"Have your writers try to draw him out about what happened," Kailas suggested.

"That might make him worse," Limingo said.

"Or it might give us something to work from," Hal said. "We'll have to take our chances that the man lives."

Limingo looked at him thoughtfully.

"The war is getting to us all, isn't it?"

Hal didn't respond.

Bodrugan was more than delighted to get out of Rozen. He listened to Hal's plan, and nodded.

"Of course," he said. "the spell will essentially be the same as the one Roche cast against the king to ambush him in the Pinnacles. That won't be the hard part at all. What will be a bit . . . difficult, shall we say, is actually belling the cat."

"Don't remind me," Hal said.

Hal reported to Cantabri, who said he was more than delighted to have Kailas – and the First Squadron – back.

"And it's good to be back," Hal said. "Lanzi left a pretty sour taste in my mouth."

He realized he wouldn't have admitted that to anyone except another butcher like Cantabri.

Lord Bab snorted. "If you figure a way to have a war without killing people – and that includes civilians – be sure and let me know."

That was the unanswerable.

"How long until your squadron arrives?"

"I figure about a week, with Sir Loren chivvying them along," Hal said. "When I left Rozen, he was still beating up assorted quartermasters to replace lost, worn and stolen."

"That's time enough for you to take charge of a delicate matter for me," Cantabri said. "I want you to head a court martial."

"Very well," Hal said, not liking the idea much. "But why me?"

"It's a fairly simple case of refusing to obey orders," Cantabri said. "But the culprit just happens to be a dragon flier."

Hal grunted.

"He's not the first," Cantabri said. "But he managed to make his refusal to fight a public issue. A couple of those damned taletellers reported the matter, so we can't handle it quietly as we have in the past by breaking him to the ranks and putting him in the front lines to get killed when the next battle rolls around."

"Do you happen to know his name?" Hal asked, hoping he wouldn't know the miscreant. But, considering the size of the dragon corps, he assumed he'd know.

"I do. And what's worse, he's a long-time flier, decorated, and has led flights. He's a rotten apple named Aimard Quesney."

Cantabri noticed Hal's expression.

"You do know him."

"Very well, sir." Hal told him about Quesney, how he'd been one of the first to fly with Hal in combat, been his tent-mate and someone who'd prized war flying as somehow cleaner than dying in a mucky infantry charge.

Cantabri hmphed loudly.

"A godsdamned romantic! How in the hells can somebody be a flier, a fighter, from almost the beginning and still have blinders on?"

"I don't know, sir," Hal said. "But he cursed me roundly back when for figuring a way to kill Roche fliers – as if I hadn't, no one else would've – and then, more recently, when I tried to recruit him for First Squadron. He's an exceptional flier."

"I don't give a damn about that very much," Cantabri said. "Very well. You're to take care of him. Give him a nice, fair trial, try to keep his lip buttoned and the trial over with in no more than a day, then convict and hang him before other fools start thinking of him as an example."

Hal stood, and saluted.

As he went out of Cantabri's tent, something came crashing in on him.

He, too, was a godsdamned romantic.

There was no way he was going to officiate at the murder of Aimard Quesney.

The question was, what could he do to change what looked like an immutable decision?

38

"The court will come to order," the bailiff said.

There was silence in the conference tent.

"The court martial of Aimard Quesney is now in session," the man went on. The words came easily to him – he, Quesney's counsel and the prosecutor were the only ones with any trial experience.

Hal, hastily briefed in military legal procedure, sat at the center of a table. On either side of him were his fellow judges – Lord Myricil, a beribboned if elderly infantry officer, and Tzimsces, an eager-appearing, young quartermaster captain.

In front of him, at another, smaller table, was Aimard Quesney, and the officer assigned to defend him.

Behind them were the assembled witnesses, including Captain Sir Lu Miletus, Quesney's commanding officer.

On the table in front of Hal and the other judges was an unsheathed sword. At trial's end, if the point were aimed at Quesney, he was guilty, if away, innocent.

No one in the tent thought there was any possibility of an acquittal.

"Lieutenant Aimard Quesney is charged with failure to obey a lawful order in the face of the enemy, to wit fly in combat against His Majesty's enemy, the Roche."

There were other charges – insubordination, improper behavior, and such that courts have always used to make sure the net they'd casting is sufficiently broad and fine-meshed.

"This case is a capital one," the bailiff said, "so it is emphasized the matter is an extremely grave one."

Everyone in the court looked appropriately grim, except for Quesney, who grinned wryly.

"The head of the court is Lord Kailas of Kalabas," the bailiff finished, "and all matters of procedure and evidence will be subject to his ruling."

The prosecutor stood.

"May it please the honorable members of this court, the king's representative, myself, will attempt to prove that—"

"You can stop there," Quesney said.

Wide eyes and shock spread through the tent.

For some reason, Hal wasn't surprised, nor bothered.

"The defendant will be silent until permitted to speak at the proper time," the bailiff said.

Hal held up his hand.

"A man on trial for his life might be permitted a few liberties," he said. "I'm sure the King's Justice can allow for that."

Now the shock grew larger.

"Lieutenant Quesney," Kailas said, "I assume you have something to say?"

Quesney looked perplexed, then took a deep breath.

"I do. I assume that the court is bound and determined to find me guilty of refusing to fly into combat.

"I say this considering who the head judge is, a man who brought death to the skies, and then to the innocent people on the ground.

"If this were a proper court, that is, one determined to decide whether or not I was right in refusing to kill any more men and women, it would exclude Lord Kailas as being prejudiced on the matter, since he is, with all due respect, sir, the bloodiest-handed flier in any of the three armies."

"Sir!" the bailiff snarled. "Sit down, or I shall be forced to have you gagged!"

"Gag me if you will, " Quesney said. "But this court should be prepared to delve into the matter of uniformed homicide before judging me."

"You are hardly helping your case, " Myricil said calmly.

"If you want to be hanged," Tzimsces added, "we're more than prepared to help you in your quest."

Hal rapped sharply with his knuckles.

"I gave Lieutenant Quesney permission to speak," he said, "and have not withdrawn that permission. I would request the members of this court to honor my authority."

Again, Quesney gave Hal a surprised look. Evidently Kailas wasn't behaving like the hanging judge the flier had expected.

"To simplify matters, and allow others to go back to their licensed murder," he said, "I concede freely that I disobeyed orders several times to fly, and will refuse any future orders given me, so all these assembled witnesses can be permitted to go their own ways.'

Quesney's defender looked hopeless.

"Treasonous bastard!" hissed Tzimsces.

Quesney looked defiant.

*

"*Perhaps I've gone loony,*" Hal wrote. "*Or perhaps ...*" He stopped writing, considered what he was going to say next, went on:

... this is to compensate for some other things that I've done.

But there is no way I'm going to hang Quesney, in spite of Cantabri's near-order. I don't think it has anything to do with the fact we shared a tent and he gave me advice when I was a new flier. There's been several who've done that. So I don't feel particularly indebted to him.

Nor do I feel that he's any particular example of virtue – he's at least as obnoxious in his self-righteousness as any street-corner priest.

Maybe – and I think I'm guessing – maybe he stands for something beyond this damned war and killing, something that should be protected.

Or, more likely, I'm just getting soft-headed in my old age.

Gods, but I miss you, and wish that I was with you, and all was quiet.

"So you decided, all on your very own," the prosecutor asked Quesney, "to declare peace with the Roche."

"No," Quesney said. "Not peace. But I was tired of killing."

"All of us are tired of killing," the prosecutor almost snarled. "But we are still patriots who know our duty."

Quesney shrugged, made no response.

"You're not on trial," Hal reprimanded. "Stick to the point." The prosecutor nodded.

"Sorry, your lordship." Then, to Quesney:

"Perhaps I might ask why you enlisted in the service of the king in the first place?"

"Because I wanted to fly," Quesney said. "And, frankly, because I wanted to do my part in the war, to drive the Roche back to their own lands."

"Your own part," the prosecutor asked. "As long as it didn't involve killing? Perhaps you're a bit unsure of what war is all about."

"Your lordship," Quesney's counsel said. "Lieutenant Quesney is being unfairly chivvied."

Hal thought.

"No," he decided. "I'll allow the question. I'd like an answer to that."

"I'm not a fool," Quesney said. "Of course I knew – know – war is no more than killing. But – I'll be honest – I hoped to be able to do my duty to my country without . . . without . . ." Quesney's voice trailed off.

"Without having to bloody your own hands?" the prosecutor sneered.

Quesney was staring at the wooden duckboards of the tent.

"I guess I wasn't being very smart," he admitted. "But I went along with things as long as I could . . . and then something broke."

"So you made out your own peace treaty," the prosecutor said. "Wouldn't it be convenient if all of us could do the same when we've decided we've fought enough.

"If we did, what do you think would happen?

"Do you imagine the barons who now rule Roche, and their soldiers would just smile happily, and go back to their farms and jobs?"

"No," Quesney said. "But . . . but someone's got to do *something* to end this war before it destroys all three countries."

Hal remembered what King Asir had told him.

"Doesn't it seem to you that *something* is in the hands of the barons who quite illegitimately now rule Roche?"

"No," Quesney said. "They're part of the whole killing machine – as much as Lord Kailas is, as much as I was."

"I see," the prosecutor said. "But you aren't now. That seems most arrogant of you."

"I don't mean it to be," Quesney said, and Hal could hear the honesty in his voice. "But I had to do something . . . and this was all I could figure out."

"Let me ask you, Lieutenant. What effect do you think your refusal, as an officer, to obey lawful orders will have on other soldiers?"

"I would hope that it would make them refuse to keep on with the killing . . . on both sides."

"You therefore advocate disobedience to the king's orders?"

Quesney hesitated, then nodded.

"That, sir," the prosecutor hissed, "is the highest of high treason!"

"He surely seems determined to hang," Myricil said to Hal. The three judges had decided to eat together, and discuss what testimony there'd been in the two days of trial.

"And I think we should oblige him," Tzimsces said. "If we didn't have a firm hold on what the taletellers say, his nonsense could be all over the armies in a day! Gods know what effect that would have on the average trooper, who, as we all know, isn't guilty of thought when he can avoid it."

"I have a bit more faith in our soldiery than you seem to," Hal said. "But you do have a point."

"You certainly can't say Quesney's a coward," Myricil said. "You and I, Lord Kailas, know there's a point where any of us can break. Quesney has just reached that . . . and gone beyond. Or perhaps, if we accept his viewpoint, he's suddenly become the most moral of men."

"As the prosecutor said," Tzimsces said, "if we allow Quesney to spout his drivel, then we create the precedent for any of us to decide we've had enough war, and just go home.

"We have a duty to the king – and to Deraine – to deal with the man most harshly." Tzimsces sipped at his wine. "Although I'll grudge that the man is clearly mad."

"A pity, for a man with his record."

Myricil nodded, smiling grimly.

"A warrior gone wrong, without doubt. And I agree about his mind having left him. We live in a terrible world, gentlemen. I do not wish to be the one who orders Quesney' s death as a reward for his services to Deraine.

"Aimard Quesney no long wishes to chance death, which certainly is an indication of being able to reason logically, particularly considering how deadly this war is to dragon fliers. Therefore, he cannot be insane, for an insane man would wish to continue on, until he is killed. What a predicament."

It came then to Hal.

"I think, Lord Myricil, that you have the solution to our problem."

Hal ordered the court martial recessed for the day, and set to on Myricil and Tzimsces.

It was dusk before they wearily agreed with Hal's suggestion.

"Thank heavens I'm not a career army man," Tzimsces said. "For I fear there'll be no promotion this side of the ocean for the three of us after King Asir hears of this."

"Don't worry about it," Hal said. "The king seldom remembers things like this for long."

"I'm glad to hear you say that," Myricil said. "For when,

when the war's over, I come begging on your doorstep asking
for a crust of bread, we can debate whether you were right or
not."

"Actually," Hal said, "it's not the king I'm afraid of, but Lord
Cantabri."

"We have unanimously decided," Hal announced the next morning, "that this court no longer needs to sit. We have reached a
verdict."

Both defense counsel and prosecutor started to yammer.

Hal thudded the butt of his flier's dagger on the table, and
only then did the men in the tent notice the sword that should
have been set between the judges and Quesney was gone.

"Our decision, justified by military code and precedent, is that
the defendant, Lieutenant Aimard Quesney, cannot be held
responsible for his actions, due to his clear impairment of mind."

Quesney was on his feet. "I never thought you'd be capable
of—"

"If you do not sit down," Hal said coldly, "I shall order you to
be removed, to be tied and gagged, and then returned to this
court."

Quesney's mouth was open, but he saw the look on Hal's face,
and slumped back down in his chair.

"We further order him, since he is evidently a threat both to
himself and to the public order, to be removed to a proper place
of detention in Deraine, for an attempt to restore his sanity and
then determine, at that time, whether he wishes to obey orders or
to continue to disobey, in which case this court shall be recon-
vened and the trial shall continue."

Two guards brought Quesney into the deserted tent.

Hal eyed him coldly.

"You wished to speak to me?"

"Yes, you bastard," Quesney growled. "You silenced me, and
you made my stand into a joke! How dare—'

Hal was on his feet.

"Silence!"

Quesney shut up.

"You two," Hal told the guards. "Outside."

"But sir, what if the prisoner attempts to escape?" one said.

"Then I shall cut his frigging weasand out myself."

The two saluted, left the tent.

"Now, I have less than no interest in hearing what you have to say," Hal went on. "Except for answering one question.

"Are you such a fool that you really want to have a rope strangle you? Remembering that your last letter will be held until the war's end, and there will be no one permitted to transcribe your last speech, no matter how noble.

"All you'll be is one poor damned fool in some unmarked grave somewhere within the borders of Roche.

"You have a family.

"What a memory to leave them. Now, answer my gods-damned question."

"No," Quesney said. "I'm not a madman, contrary to what you decided. Of course I want to live, and—"

"That's enough." Hal came close. "I put the guards out because I don't want any witnesses to what I'm going to say.

"You're going back to Deraine. They'll find somewhere to mew you up with women who think they're the king, men who scratch all the day and night, children who're in some private world of their own.

"That's a horrible damned thing to do to a man who's at least as sane as I am. Maybe saner. But it'll keep you alive. You'll live to see the war out. Stay mad until the war's over, when no one will care about a peace-spouting idiot, and you'll be quietly released from the asylum. Nobody'll be reconvening any damned trial, and no one will care about punishing you. Then you can, if you want, start prancing back and forth in front of the king's palace, shouting about what a murdering bastard he is. Or you can come to my estate, and do the same.

"If I'm still alive then.

"Or you can go around from town to town, preaching about the evils of war, and maybe enough people will listen to keep this kind of shit from happening ever again.

"I don't think you can succeed – people seem to like cutting each other up and down too much. But you can try.

"Because," and Hal spoke with great emphasis on each word, "you . . . will . . . be . . . alive!"

Without waiting for a response, Hal turned.

"Guards!"

He looked at Quesney.

"Now, get your sorry ass out of my sight . . . And when this is over, drink a dram to my memory. I've wasted enough time on you. I've still got a war to fight."

39

Lord Bab Cantabri considered Hal coldly.

"You know," he said, "I was not a terribly bright child. Some say nothing has changed from that day to this."

Hal tactfully kept silent.

"One of the dumber things I used to do, when I'd done something bad, was not to stay out of my father's way, like any sensible lad should have done, but seek his presence out. Maybe I thought he wouldn't have noticed whatever sin I'd committed, or maybe I wanted to be punished.

"In any event, not the brightest thing I've ever done, since the beatings I incurred were no gentler than if I'd kept myself hidden in the stables for a day or so.

"Now, let us consider your case.

"You and your fellow idiots commit a travesty of justice with Lieutenant Quesney, in spite of my rather clearly expressed wishes for him to be found very damned guilty. Which were also the king's wishes.

"Very well. If it had just been three idiots, I could have sent all of them off to, say, the tip of Deraine to watch for icebergs or such.

"But not with the Dragonmaster one of the crew.

"So I decided, until I cooled off a bit, I would do without your presence, to keep me from saying, or worse yet doing, something meritorious, such as hanging you by your balls for a week or so.

"I was quite pleased with my insight and my forbearance.

"Then you seek me out with this – no, I won't insult it – this plan.

"Are you trying to attract my lightnings?"

"No, sir," Hal said. For some unknown reason, he was having a hard time not laughing.

"I fully agree with you that *Ky* Yasin has been an unutterable pain in the ass for far too long, and he and his Guards Squadron should be dealt with harshly.

"Especially since his brother now seems to be atop the Roche group of barons that insist on keeping this damned war going.

"Clearly your plan – assuming this sorcerer of yours develops a spell – is promising.

"If I were a vindictive man . . . What is the matter, Kailas? Are you choking on something?"

"No, sir," Hal said. "A raspy throat from dawn flights."

Cantabri snorted.

"To go on. If I were vindictive, the thought might have crossed my mind that one of the virtues of your plan is – I assume you're planning on implementing this yourself – that you'll be behind Roche lines, with an excellent chance on getting yourself killed."

"I don't plan on that."

"But it could – notice I said could – have been a sidelight that might – notice I said might – have cheered me.

"But it didn't. We do need you, even if you seem to have the sappiest of ideas from time to time, which I assume comes from the thin air you breathe when you're atop your dragon.

"All you need from me is approval for your plan – which I grant – and two men from my Raiding Squadron. This I also grant. I'll send them along to your squadron at once.

"You'll also need an order from me commanding every gods-damned dragon leader in the armies to become your scouts to find Yasin's base, without asking any questions.

"This, too, I'll give, although I'm a bit surprised you didn't think of just how good a flier can be at disobeying orders if he doesn't want to follow them.

"Now, get your ass back to being invisible. I haven't forgiven you totally yet."

"Yes, sir."

Even though winter was coming in strong, Cantabri kept the army pushing forward, very slowly driving the Roche back and back, east and south, toward Carcaor.

Hal guessed there'd be no winter quarters this year, at least not unless the Roche forced a stalemate.

Now that we're prepared to bell the cat . . . at least when Bodrugan finally finishes his spell, Hal thought, and we actually have our foolish mice who'll attempt the feat, all we need to do is find the bugger.

Once Yasin's landing field was located, he planned to take in himself and the two raiders for the operation. That would require three dragons.

He pondered the reality of war, where the tail kept getting bigger and bigger. In this case, not a tail, but a head, someone to carry the warriors. Hal had considered the dragon baskets, that were about as dangerous to monster and master as they were to the passengers, thought wistfully of a *really* large dragon, able to carry, perhaps, a dozen men on its back, then wondered where in hell they'd find men – or women – with muscles and guts enough to tame it and pushed the whole matter away.

He would take Sir Loren, Farren Mariah and Chincha.

Hal put the three fliers off the duty roster, told them to stand by "for Special Duties."

"So I'm for it again, and again, and again," Mariah said.

"What makes you think that?" Hal asked innocently. "I could have asked for the three of you to, say, fly three of the king's popsies around."

"Narh," Mariah said. "First, you didn't ask us to volunteer, which is the biggest clue right there. Second, I didn't know the king had – popsies – at least out in the open – let alone three of 'em.

"And, come to think, if we were toot-toot-tootling tarts about, the king would've specified all women fliers, instead of virile young sorts like myself," he finished.

"And," he added reluctantly, "Sir Loren, I suppose, although nobody I know's measured the length of his thingiewhacker."

"All you're going to have to do is fly somewhere," Hal said, "escorting me with a passenger on your back, land on a nice, quiet hill, then wait for me, and the passengers, to take care of a nice, simple job."

"Nice, quiet hill," Mariah said. "I'm on to your shame-game, Lord Kailas. How far back of the lines is this nice, quiet hill?"

Hal looked at him, didn't reply. Mariah nodded.

"Just what I thought. I'll go help Chincha make out her will."

The two raiders arrived, and Hal wondered if Cantabri wasn't trying to arrange his death, after all.

One was a baby-faced sort named Gamo, who looked far too young to be in any army, let alone be a purportedly deadly warrior in the raiders. The only thing that might be a giveaway was his calmness, and the easy way he carried his sword and dagger.

The other, Hakea, was a chubby, sleepy-eyed peasant, who Hal thought should have been trudging the fields behind an oxen.

But if they were what Cantabri had given him, they were the ones he'd go in with.

*

Bodrugan still hadn't come back with the spell. Waiting, Hal set out, alone, on Storm, visiting other dragon flights on the front.

He took flight leaders aside, and gave them one simple instruction: if you're attacked by Yasin's black dragons, try to find out where their base is.

No one needed to know why the Dragonmaster wanted the information, and any clever sorts who figured out the obvious could damned well keep their mouths shut.

Don't advertise the knowledge, don't attack the base, don't fly over it more than once.

He continued the analogy of the cat in his own mind – the last thing to do is wake it up from its nap, when it might be hungry or cranky.

Contrary to Cantabri's cynicism, he didn't have to use the lord's direct order. There was a reason almost all the fliers on the front, Sagene and Derainian, had either faced Yasin's killing machine, or had heard of it.

All of them wanted the huge Roche black dragons destroyed, but none of them particularly wanted the honor of taking them on.

Again, the analogy of the cat came to mind . . .

Hal had thought, with almost every flier with the First and Second Armies looking, they'd find where Yasin and his dragons lived in a few days.

But it took two full weeks, and showed, yet again, Yasin's cleverness.

As well as the cleverness, and luck, of the Sagene fliers.

A pair of Yasin's dragons, on patrol, had been tracked by a Sagene flier back of the lines, and then the dragons dove hard toward a narrow draw – and vanished.

No one – yet – had been able to move dragons around by magic, so the tale made no sense.

Against orders, the Sagene flight leader sent two of his fliers to make a sweep over the area, just at dusk, when all sensible dragons were returning to their roosts.

Again, a flight of three blacks carrying Yasin's guidon were seen in the same area, and once more they dove for shelter, impossibly, up a narrow draw.

And were gone.

The two Sagene dragons chanced a lower pass, and at first saw nothing.

Then luck intervened.

One of the Sagene fliers happened to be color blind. He'd managed to join up and make it through flying school without his minor disability being discovered.

Then the disability became a prize, when his flight commander discovered that a color-blind man was almost impossible to fool with camouflage.

So it was here.

The draw was in fact a fairly broad valley. A base had been prepared on the valley floor and then heavy wires had been strung across the valley.

Treetops were hung on the wires, their greenery kept alive by magic, then, once more with sorcery, were being artfully faded through fall coloring.

But the magic either hadn't been renewed often enough or wasn't quite artistic enough, for the color-blind flier looked down, saw something very false, looked harder and saw a long, huge dragon shelter to one side of a leveled, rolled field, and, he was almost certain, tents, huts and sheds on its other side.

That was enough for Hal, when it was reported to him.

The entire area was proclaimed a no-fly zone at army level.

Now it was Kailas's turn.

"It wasn't the spell that took so long," Bodrugan said. "It was where it was to be applied."

"I'd suggested that it be attached to Yasin's guidon," Hal said. "If you'll recall."

"I recall quite well," Bodrugan said with a bit of asperity. "But I didn't think it was a particularly good idea. Suppose Yasin decided to change his banner if his brother renamed the squadron? Suppose the bits we'd somehow managed to ensorcel got blown away?

"So I bethought myself of other places to apply the spell. None of them were particularly good – I thought we could spray the dragons themselves, but that sounded most shuddersome in the execution, not to mention risky.

"Then, a week ago, a Roche dragon flight was overrun by a cavalry strike. I got myself forward as quickly as I could.

"Of course the dragons and their fliers were long gone, and those of the ground workers who hadn't been slain had fled as well.

"But most of their apparatus remained, and so I was able to

spend two hours wandering about before the cavalry was forced
to fall back and abandon their conquest.

"Makes you wonder what good all these fools farting about
on their horses do, in the long run.

"But I found a possible place for the spell. The most expensive
piece of a dragon's gear is the saddle, correct?"

"Of course," Hal said. "Just like it's that of a horse."

"I propose that we work our way into *Ky* Yasin's base, find the
tack room, and use the spell on the dragons' saddlery. Also, I'll
make up enough so that we can cover the bridles and such as well."

"What happens," Hal asked skeptically, "when all the saddles
that you've treated get lost in action or just get torn up with
wear and tear?"

"That is the second part of my scheme," Bodrugan said. He
held out a small can.

"This is the standard issue oil for the Roche leathers, it seems.
I've cast the spell on half a dozen tins I found in that dragon base.

"We'll leave them lying about, and every time an earnest
worker rubs his flier's tack, well, the spell will be renewed."

"Ingenious," Hal said. "Remembering how long our oil lasts,
if the war lasts beyond the supply you've worked on, we'll all be
dead."

"That, too, doesn't matter," Bodrugan said. "For Yasin and
his men will have gone before, which is all that matters, isn't it?"

Hal ignored that for the moment.

"So the way the spell will work," Bodrugan said, "and work
it shall, for I've tested it, is each flier, or each flight commander,
or however you decide, will have a small wooden plate. On the
plate, mounted so it can spin freely, will be a pointer. That
pointer will always indicate two places. The first is Yasin's base.
Since that's stationary, the flier can ignore that. The second will
be any of Yasin's dragons with gear that's been ensorcelled
who're in the air. Isn't that perfect?"

"I guess so," Hal said. Then something came back to him.

"Uh . . . a question. You said, a bit ago, that 'we' will work
our way into Yasin's camp.

"Of course I'm going," Bodrugan said. "You don't think I
trust a mere dragon driver to make sure my spell is properly in
place, do you?

"Besides, that young raider – the one with a face like a
depraved child – is quite striking, don't you think?"

*

"You have a plan afoot," Danikel said.

"Perhaps," Hal said cautiously.

"Without a Sagene flier to accompany it."

"As a matter of fact," Hal lied, "I'd just realized that, and, needing another dragon, was about to ask for volunteers."

"Which I am," Danikel said. "And it's a good thing I came to you. Would you rather have had Alcmaen?"

Hal briefed his fliers and the two raiders.

He'd had two men make up a sand model of the area from a hasty map, that showed not only the hidden valley, but the hilltop Hal proposed landing on, and leaving the dragons, about half a mile from Yasin's base.

They sat digesting their orders for a time.

"I suppose," Farren Mariah said, "that you've come up with some alibi."

"I don't understand," Hal said.

"Let us suppose that we slip into Yasin's camp, and get discovered. If we just take to our heels, toes following promptly along, Yasin might figure our intent. Shouldn't we be there for some other purpose?"

"That's taken care of," Kailas said. "We'll carry firebottles, and if we're surprised, we'll use them to fire that dragon shed. Or try to, anyway."

"You think Yasin'll believe you went along just because you love the bright flicker, flicker of the flames?"

"I won't be carrying any identification," Hal said grimly. "Nor will anyone else. And I have no plans on being captured again."

There was silence for a moment, then Gamo stood.

"If I may say something, Lord Kailas?"

"Go ahead," Hal said.

"I want to make one thing clear," Gamo said. "Once we're on the ground, until we get back to the dragons, I am in charge. You others know flying and magic, but raiding is Hakea's and my specialty. I want that very certain. If not, my partner and I will be forced to return to our unit."

Hal saw his expression, and suddenly there was something quite chillingly lethal about the man's baby face.

"Well, hickety-doo," Mariah said. "A mere warrant dictating to a bunch of ossifers. I love it."

"I'm sorry," Hal said to Gamo. "I should have made that very clear in my orders. You, of course, are in charge on the ground."

Gamo nodded, sat back down, studying the table.

"We'll leave tomorrow," Hal said. "At full dark."

The dragons glided in out of the cold night, wings spread, and thudded down on to the hilltop.

Hal, Bodrugan and the two raiders slipped off their dragons, and readied their gear.

Storm was looking about, nostrils flared, scenting the enemy dragons not far away. He opened his mouth to shrill a warning perhaps, and Hal tapped him on the snout.

Storm snapped his jaws shut, looked unhappy, or so Hal defined his expression in the dimness, and curled up.

The raiders shouldered their packs, and moved down the hill. All of them wore black, with darkened faces. Bodrugan had cast a nonreflective spell on their daggers and swords.

Hal had chosen the night carefully, when both moons were out.

Both Gamo and Hakea hadn't liked that at all, preferring to wait until the dark of the moons.

"That may be fine for you raiders, with eyes like bats," Hal had said. "But not for us fliers, who need all the help we can get."

"Whyn't you think of stayin' back, sir," Hakea rumbled, "and let us just go in and piddle that magic about?"

Hal had just looked at him, and Hakea shrugged and said no more.

The four went down the hill to its base, and crouched, moved across rolling brushland toward the draw.

Hal, from his cavalry days, thought he knew a bit about sneaking around.

But the raiders put him to shame.

Hakea, that hulking peasant, suddenly became an eel, slipping from shadow to shadow.

Gamo simply became one of the shadows.

Bodrugan must have done some hunting, or perhaps was just a moonlight wanderer, for he, too, moved without stumbling or crashing through brush and into stumps.

They went across the meadow, to the opening of the draw. They crouched, while Gamo watched, for long moments. Finally he nodded in satisfaction, and motioned the others to the far side of the draw. He moved like an ape Hal had seen once in a menagerie, bent over, keeping below the brush, creeping very slowly.

There was a nest of boulders outside the draw, and Gamo led them behind its shelter. He pointed out, and Hal saw, on the other side of the narrow canyon, slight movement.

A sentry.

Then he spotted two of them, and heard the murmur of conversation.

This far behind the lines security could get a little sloppy.

They went into the canyon, staying on the slope, away from the floor, where no patrols would likely travel.

Then they were under the cover of the false trees. The landing field reached out in front of them, and the huge shed was to their left.

Gamo looked at Hal, waiting for orders.

Hal thought.

If Yasin were logical, he most likely would have built the most essential supply sheds closest to the dragons.

He saw three such.

He pointed to them. Gamo nodded, and they crept off.

It was cold, getting colder, and frost was forming.

They'd have to be out of here by dawn, for their passage through the dying brush around the field would leave streaks in the frost.

There were still lights on, here and there, mostly across the field in the squadron's quarters.

No one seemed to be about.

Hal smelt the acrid musk of the dragons in the long bay, heard a long, bubbling monstrous snore from inside.

Gamo stopped outside the first shed.

Hal sniffed, wrinkled his nostrils. Blood and offal. That would be the dragons' butcher shop.

He pointed to the next shed, and then went on.

Hal smelt nothing, but Gamo must've, for Hal saw a grin flash in the moonlight.

The door of the canvas and wood shed wasn't locked, and they slipped inside, closing it behind them.

Gamo reached into Hakea's pack, took out a small bull's-eye lantern and lit it. He opened one panel, and Hal saw hanging saddles, bridles, other leather workings.

Bodrugan had seen as well and needed no orders.

He unslung his pack, and took out four small sprayers, such as women used for perfume.

Each man took one, and sprayed the hanging gear, and the saddles on their stands.

Hal's went empty, and he went to Bodrugan's pack, and took out half a dozen tins of leather oil.

He stacked them on a shelf, and their mission was successful.

All they had to do was slip away without wakening the cat.

Hal was beginning to have hopeful feelings as they left the shed that they'd get away with it clean, and then there was a surprised snort as a skinny man came out of a door in the long dragon shed, saw armed men in the moonlight, guessed they weren't there with good intents, and opened his mouth to shout an alarm.

Gamo snaked out, and his hand rose, fell.

The thin Roche grunted, went down, began making snoring noises.

Gamo motioned to Hakea, who came up, and knelt, his knee on the Roche's throat. The snoring stopped.

Hal had the idea this wasn't the first time they'd dealt with a surpriser in such a manner.

Hakea rose, lifted the body over his shoulder, and they went back out of the valley.

The sentries were quiet now, hopefully sleeping.

None of the Derainians made a sound as they crept out of the draw, and across the rolling ground to their hillock.

Farren Mariah rose from behind a rock, crossbow in hand.

"Any problems?"

"None," Hal said.

"Who's that?" he indicated the body across Hakea's shoulder.

"Someone who was where he shouldn't have been," Hal said.

"What I suggest, sir," Gamo said, and Hal noted the way authority had reverted to where it should be, "is we take the body out with us, and dump it in some lake. They'll think he deserted or, as like, not even notice. I've seen the Roche don't seem to give much of a hang about their help," he said.

They remounted the dragons, and took off along the far side of the hill.

Hal had the body across his knees and noted, with disgust, the man had voided his bowels in dying.

They saw silver in the moonlight, dropped down over a chill-looking pond, and Hal pushed the corpse over.

He felt a moment of pity. If the man had a family, they'd never learn what happened to him and be forever wondering.

Then he remembered the sentry he'd dumped in a river when he was an escaping prisoner, and forgot about the dragon handler.

There were bigger things to consider.

Such as the morrow, and the surprise he hoped to bring Ky Yasin and his fliers.

40

The dragons were trundling out of their sheds in the gray chill, when one of the field sentries announced a courier to Hal. He bore a rather sizable package, coming from Limingo the wizard.

Hal puzzled, then remembered he'd promised to look over the poor mad raider's ramblings that'd been transcribed.

But not right now.

Storm squealed at him, and, obediently, Hal clambered up into the saddle.

He popped his reins on the dragon's back, and Storm staggered forward, great wings spreading. He hopped, then leaped, and was in the air.

Behind Hal, the rest of his squadron lifted up, and began circling the field, reaching for altitude.

As Storm climbed, Kailas looked down at the tiny needle and board secured to Storm's carapace.

It pointed steadily in one direction, the direction of Yasin's base.

Kailas tapped the rear of the needle with a fingernail, but it stayed in one place. That meant Yasin's dragons hadn't taken off yet.

Hal blasted on his trumpet, and, still climbing, the squadron followed him east and slightly south.

Hal's course would, hopefully, intersect Yasin's flight on its way to patrolling the fighting ground.

He took the dragons as high as he could, until he was struggling to fill his lungs.

Storm's wings moved slowly, sluggishly, at this height.

Hal saw one dragon fall off on a wing, and pinwheel downward to thicker, safer air. But only one.

He forced on east. His course, if he'd set it correctly, should intersect with Yasin's, no more than a league beyond his field.

Now there was nothing to do but wait, and listen to the leathern creak of Storm's wings, and the faint sound of the other monsters behind him.

It was cold up here, even colder than the late fall weather below on the ground.

For some reason, Hal's mind turned to Aimard Quesney, who he hoped was now safely tucked away out of harm's way in Deraine.

He wondered what Quesney would think of this latest devise, almost certainly knew the flier would rage about Hal finding yet another way to bloody the skies.

The sky had lightened as they climbed, although the ground below was still nighthung.

They'd crossed the lines without Hal realizing it.

His target lay on east.

Now there was the peep of the sun, glaring at him.

Yasin's advantage.

Hal squinted, looked ahead and down.

He thought at first it was his eyes, then picked out small black dots ahead and below.

Dragons.

Storm had seen them as well, and snorted.

No Roche saw them, which Kailas had counted on. It would have been insane for any Derainian or Sagene formation to be east of the front this early in the day.

Hal chanced a blat of warning, looked back, and saw answering waves from his flight leaders.

He forced calm, counted, watching the blots get larger and larger below.

Then he could wait no longer. He didn't need his trumpet. The lift of an arm was enough to take the squadron diving down, in four vee-flights, on Yasin's black dragons.

Hal found it momentarily amusing that he, and everyone else, still thought of Yasin as being a black dragon unit, strange because there were now almost as many blacks with Kailas's squadron.

But the menacing label remained.

Hal swore at his mind for fripperies, coming up with nonsense to avoid thinking about the death they were plummeting toward.

Hal steered Storm toward the dragon at the head of the formation, hoping it was Yasin. He had a moment to realize it wasn't, its guidon unfringed.

Storm had that dragon by the throat, tore it down, bones snapping loudly.

Hal snap-fired at that flier's wing man, hit him in the chest, then was below the formation as the rest of his squadron tore into them.

Hal pulled Storm up, letting the speed of his dive convert into energy, lifting him back up through the formation.

He had his crossbow reloaded, aimed at another flier, missed.

Storm lay over on a wing, turning, skidding as a Roche dragon came in on him. Hal tried to aim at the flier, couldn't get a clear shot, sent his bolt into the dragon's throat. It tore at itself, trying to rip the bolt out, spinning, falling, and was gone.

The two squadrons were a spinning, swirling melee. Storm went after another dragon, rolling almost on his back, Hal swearing, clinging desperately with his knees to the saddle, and there was a Roche dragon almost touching him. Storm's talons ripped at the Roche, and ichor gouted, and the beast fell away.

Hal had control, was forcing Storm into a climb, and a Roche flier fell past him, silently, mouth opening and closing like a beached fish, and he was gone.

A Roche dragon, wing torn, was trying to escape. Hal closed on it from behind, shot the flier out of his saddle, forgot about the beast.

Another dragon, this time one of his, tumbled past him, dying, falling to the ground far below, and then the sky was almost empty.

Hal blew the recall, and obedient to his own order, turned back toward their own lines.

As he flew, other fliers assembled on him.

Hal could hear them shouting, cheering as they flew.

Hal realized he had a grin as broad and stupid as any other flier.

They went back before dusk, this time circling around Yasin's base and coming in from the east. Also, Hal forbade the flying of any squadron symbol. He wanted Yasin to think that he was being hit not just by one squadron, but by all the dragon fliers of Sagene and Deraine.

Hal's fliers had claimed five dragons down in the morning, and six more at dusk, for a loss of three dragons.

That night, his fliers wanted to celebrate, which Hal allowed, within reason. That meant beer only. No one should fly in the morning with a thick head.

Hal went back to his tent, tried to sleep, couldn't.

Muttering to himself, he lit a lantern and decided to leaf through the madman's ravings.

He wasn't sure what he was looking for, so started near the end:

Down, away, stumbling, not fall, come after me, abandoned, alone, silent like mousie like they taught me like they left me no squeaking, crying . . .

That was enough for that night. Hal decided he'd try again tomorrow or the next day.

The squadron was stumblingly weary. Not only was the drive against Yasin's squadron nearly constant, but they were constantly called for other duties, in spite of their supposed special status.

Exhaustion killed.

Hal now was used to writing letters to Sagene and Deraine, bemoaning the death of a flier, when, in truth, they'd been nothing more than names on the status report.

With an exception.

Danikel seemed beyond exhaustion, beyond fear.

He flew not only his detailed tasks, but whenever he could.

He and his blue dragon, Hoko, were in the air all the time, always across the lines, in spite of Hal's admonitions.

Kailas thought of grounding him, didn't know how he could, short of chaining him to his tent post.

Danikel never seemed to change, never seemed sleepy or tired.

He was buried under fan letters from Sagene, which he smiled at, but seldom read and never answered.

With one exception.

A letter came every day – or when the mails were on time – in a woman's hand, in gray ink, the addressing quite calligraphic.

He never told anyone who the letters came from, burned them after reading them twice and answering them.

Hal couldn't decide if they came from the baroness he'd been keeping company with in Fovant.

Danikel was beyond being the darling of the Sagene taletellers. Now they were referring to him as the very spirit of Sagene, the warrior soul of the country.

And day by day, his death-toll mounted, although Hal never heard him claim a specific number of kills.

Alcmaen was nearly beside himself, left far behind in the

count, but Danikel paid him little attention, treating him kindly, as a not particularly bright younger cousin, which further increased Alcmaen's rage.

Then, one morning, a clear day, Danikel didn't come back from his predawn patrol.

He'd told his dragon handler that he thought he'd "nip back of the lines, and see if any of Yasin's people were out this early," nothing more specific.

Hal checked the hospitals, sent orderlies to see if any of the front line units had reported a falling dragon.

None did.

Nor was any body recovered.

There were no claims from the Roche for a time.

Little by little it crept out: the soul of Sagene was missing, lost in battle.

The taletellers wailed like peasants at a village chief's funeral.

After a few days, word came from the Roche.

Danikel had been downed, in mortal combat, by one of *Ky* Yasin's fliers.

Hal didn't believe it – the claim was made very weakly, with no confirmation or interviews with the black-dragon flier who claimed to have killed him.

Hal thought it was the Roche taletellers' invention.

Alcmaen said, three days later, that he'd seen the Roche flier across the lines, and, in a terrible battle witnessed by no one, had killed the man and his dragon.

Even the Sagene taletellers had trouble with that one.

The gray-inked letters stopped coming, with never a query from their writer to Hal about the flier's death.

It was, other than the periodic wails in the broadsheets, as if Danikel, Baron Trochu, had never been.

The half-ring around Carcaor was slowly closing.

The Sagene blockade of the Ichili River was closed, and almost nothing was coming upriver to Carcaor. Deraine had sealed off the River Pettau and the Zante, and its navy was slowly making its way south toward Carcaor, capturing or isolating each Roche riverine city as they came. Each league they captured meant less foodstuffs and war materials for the beleaguered barons in the capital.

Yet still the Roche fought on, as if determined to destroy their country if they couldn't win.

*

Once again, Hal varied the squadron's tactics. This time, all the fliers had tiny magicked compasses, and flew out by themselves. Again, they held the heights, and waited over Cantabri's battle-field.

As they waited, Hal saw Roche formations break and fall back. The Sagene and Derainian troops, probably as exhausted as their enemy, stolidly moved forward.

When Yasin's black dragons flew into sight, the squadron hit them from all directions at once, as if the Roche were magnetized.

They took out four dragons that morning, Hal having killed three of them. Yasin's squadron fragmented on the first attack and fled.

Little by little . . .

Hal had the squadron stand down for a day. The fliers might have been up for more slaughter, but the dragons were wearying.

He started to catch up on the always-present paperwork, then stopped.

If he'd told Limingo he'd go through the madman's ravings, it was to find something that might suggest a way to defeat that demon.

And the time for confronting that spirit was drawing closer.

He sighed, pulled the manuscript over, and started reading, this time from the beginning.

Kailas forced attention, and then, abruptly, the babblings seized him:

Ruined, ruined, all is ruins, ruined stones, moving, lifting, coming toward me . . . brown . . . a bear . . . jelly . . . jelly bear . . . reaching . . . duck away, duck away, do not take death . . . spear . . . thrown . . . hit . . . through it . . . jelly, jelly, jelly, run, trying to run . . . screaming . . . crying . . . mother . . . a boy not wept . . . clawing at me . . . nor dashed a thousand kim . . . attacked . . . trapped . . . mother, this place stinks . . . death . . . the dagger, dagger, my grandfather's . . . sharp . . . a bit of rust on the blade, blade, iron, old iron . . . tunic flaming . . . embers . . . crumbling, reaching bear . . . and I threw it hard into jellyness . . . screaming . . . stupid so slight a hurt . . . jelly bear screaming at so slight a hurt . . . in back and away and chance to run, run from jelly, run from death—

Hal had it.
Maybe.

But it was worth a try.

Maybe.

If he could just figure out how to make his idea work.

41

Limingo rubbed his eyes wearily.

"All right," he told Hal. "I concede that your more careful reading – and thinking – seems to have given us a clue. I surely wouldn't have noted that your raider carried an irregular weapon, least of all what it was made of. And certainly cold iron is legendary proof against demons. So we have a bit of knowledge now, thanks to our poor mad friend."

"But not much more," Hal said, staring out of the ruined building Limingo had taken over for what Kailas thought of as Magic Headquarters. "If iron hurts that whatever it is, well and good. What we need is a big piece of iron to kill it, I guess, but I don't have the foggiest idea of how to deliver it, point first, into our demon. Maybe cast a big godsdamned spear out of iron, land some raiders who're a lot braver than I am on the rock, and, when and if the demon appears, they charge him and we give medals to the suicidal."

"Not good," Limingo agreed. "Not to mention the things we don't know, such as whether that demon was brought up by the destruction you wrought in Carcaor, or by your presence the night before in that castle.

"Plus, we don't know if the barons know about this demon, and if that's why they're being so foolhardy in refusing to surrender. Or if they're just pig-headed Roche like everyone believes."

"You know," Hal said carefully, "perhaps there is a way to hit that demon – if he appears – with my big spear. Maybe if we cast just the spearhead, and then fletch a wooden shaft like an arrow – maybe fletching that goes all the way up to the head – and then somehow rig it under a dragon, and come in against him – or it or whatever it is – very godsdamned fast, and use the dragon's speed to launch the spear, and . . . and there's too many godsdamned maybes in this."

He slumped back, looked out at the icy rain coming down.

"It's nice to have a roof over my head for the moment," he said. "My squadron and I are still out there with tents."

"It could be worse," Limingo said.

"It could," Hal said. "At least we've got tents. I saw a couple of foot soldiers trying to use a tree to rig a pretty small piece of canvas."

Limingo shook his head.

"This war's gone on too long."

"It has," Hal agreed, getting to his feet. "I used to be able to spring up like a goosed lamb. Now I'm a creaky old man."

He pulled a long waxed coat on, and shivered.

"But I suppose I'd better get back to my blacksmiths and start figuring out just how damned dumb I am."

The war had ground almost to a halt as the weather got worse. It took the hardest of officers to get the men out of whatever shelter they'd figured out, into the freezing muck, and stumbling toward the Roche positions. Horses stamped, and refused to come out of their stables, and lashed out at their grooms.

The dragons, accustomed to cold weather, were a little more cooperative, but not much more.

The Roche held as best they could, but they couldn't stand firm for long.

They were out of almost everything – fresh food, dry clothing replacements, and even their fighting supplies were now rationed.

Out of everything – except raw courage.

"That's about as cockermaymie a contrapatrapashun as I've ever seen," Farren Mariah said. "And I'm not even mentioning the dropping mechanism. I've seen amateur hangmen come up with better."

"Thanks for the compliment," Hal said. "Now, go get your dragon out. There's a spear and contrapashun for you, too. And the other squadron commanders."

"Why me all the time?" Mariah wailed.

"We all need to have an example set for us," Sir Loren said. "Whether good or bad is immaterial."

Storm didn't like the setup any more than Mariah did. The spear's head was about a yard wide, and the shaft twelve feet long.

Hal had come to the measurements by experimentation – dropping models off a nearby rise, and making note of which fell point first most readily. But then he cut the weight out of the head, since the spear would have to be cast from a flying dragon.

One of Hal's ropemakers came up with a cradle front and rear that was tied to the unhappy dragon. When a rope was pulled by the flier, the cradles came unhooked, and the spear fell free.

All that remained was to see if the contrivance worked in the air.

For awhile, it appeared as if it didn't at all, generally falling from the dragon and dropping straight down.

Spears were recovered, and weight was drilled off the head, added to the shaft, and that helped matters.

But it still required a flier to have his dragon at full speed when he released the spear. Then, if everything went well, the spear would wobble through the air, and hit the earthen bank it was aimed at.

After two days, everyone in the squadron had taken at least three shots.

The best shot was Hachir, the former crossbowman, and the second was Farren Mariah.

But no one knew if the weapon would work against the demon.

"Since we know somewhat less than nothing about our demon," Limingo said, "and since the time for his appearance looms near, I've set my young man, Bodrugan, to watch the mountain. With Lord Cantabri's approval, he, and half a dozen raiders and equipment, have been flown to another mountaintop to watch.

"I have dragons from another flight – sorry, Hal, but you appeared busy with other things – making unobtrusive fly-pasts morning and night to receive their flag signals.

"So far, everything on the mountain appears quiet. One strange thing – the ruins of that castle you reported the demon came from, further destroying the ruins, now appear undisturbed."

"I like that but little," Hal said.

"I imagine," Limingo said dryly, "our Bodrugan likes it even less."

Hal continued harrying Yasin when his squadron came out. But the war in the air was almost at a standstill as winter's first storms raged.

*

In spite of the weather, Cantabri lashed the armies back into motion.

Hal's squadron was detailed for another special duty – they landed teams of raiders to the east and south of Carcaor, with orders to hold their positions and stop any movement past them.

Other, stronger teams were told off to support these teams if they were attacked. Dragon flights were moved in to fly in these backup teams, and supplies for the teams.

Then, one gloomy day, Hal landed a team on a plateau, happened to look south-west, and saw the flurry of a cavalry patrol moving through the freshly-fallen snow.

He glassed the patrol, and saw they were Sagene.

Carcaor was surrounded.

42

The armies of Sagene and Deraine occupied Carcaor's suburbs on the west bank of the Ichili River. Reinforcements were rushed forward, and troops were fed and resupplied, getting ready for the final assault.

Perhaps Cantabri shouldn't have allowed the pause, for it gave time for old soldiers to talk about the horrors of the Comtal River crossing years earlier that led to the siege of Aude. And somehow there were stories – no one knew how they got out – about some horrid wizardly weapon the Roche had.

Everyone who knew of the demon swore they'd said nothing, but someone had.

Balancing those stories were the terrible ones of what it was like in the encircled capital. There were whispers that bodies had been found with steaks carved from their buttocks or thighs. The soldiers were on the scantiest of rations, no more than half-ground grain baked into flat breads. Civilians were simply starving while the barons continued to dine on their hidden luxuries.

Then flat-bottomed boats started arriving from the north and south, and were readied for the assault on Carcaor.

Roche wizards sent firespells and storms against the boats, but the spells were largely quashed by the Sagene and Derainian magicians.

Hal moved his squadron up to the river, made himself ready to support the crossing.

Cantabri summoned him one day.

"We'll be forcing the river in two days," he said without preamble. "And I want my soldiers to keep crossing and not get stranded on the other side without any backup. That means your task is first to cover the river against any dragon attacks. Your second task will be to take on the demon . . . If he appears, which I assume he will.

"Any questions?"

"No, sir," Hal said.

"Then I'll see you in the victory parade."

Hal was making last minute adjustments to Storm's harness, and making sure he had enough bolts and firedarts ready when Farren Mariah came up, looking carefully from side to side.

"What now, Lieutenant?" Hal asked.

"We don't have to worry our little nogs about what happens today," Farren said. "At least, not you and me."

"Oh?"

"I set a small spell up at dawn," he said. "And it said for sure and certain you and I and Chincha would live through the day. Barring certain things."

"How damnably reassuring. What sort of certain things?"

"Well, it got confused, but we're safe as long as we fight well, and stay clear of magic."

"Gods," Hal said, dripping sarcasm. "Now I can truly relax. You're sure of your magic."

"Sure as cert," Mariah said. "I cast that spell three times."

"What happened the other two?"

"Aaarh, you don't want to know, boss."

The soldiers had been formed up by boatloads, hidden from view across the river.

Hal, flying overhead with his squadron, diving in and out of the intermittent cloud cover, heard the shout of orders and the blast of trumpets, and lines of soldiers debouched from shelter to the boats waiting at the river's edge.

They pushed out into the current, and rowers heaved mightily.

The line grew ragged against the Ichili's swift current, and then the boats were in midstream, then into the shallows safely.

The soldiers leapt out, and Roche fighters came to meet them.

There was a flurry of fighting, then the Roche were pushed back, as the boats shuttled back for another load.

This time, they'd barely loaded and left the west bank when many of them began to twist and roil in the water. A few overturned, and there came up screams.

Hal took Storm low, to see what was going on, and saw strange creatures pulling at the boats. Some of them were driven away by alert archers or spearmen, but more came up from the depths to take their places.

It came to Hal – these were like the monsters of wizardry created back during the attack on Kalabao.

Some boat coxswains panicked, and turned back. Others tried to follow their orders, and the creatures tore at them.

On the far shore the Roche soldiers had gained heart, and were coming back on the invaders.

Step by step, the Sagene and Deraianian infantry were being pushed back toward the river.

Hal caught himself, reached behind him, into a case strapped to the back of his saddle. He came out with a firedart, sent Storm diving down.

He waited until the dragon was no more than fifty feet above the river, reflexively pulling out of its dive, then leaned over and pitched the fire dart close to a beleaguered boat.

It hit the water not five feet from the boat's gunwales, exploded, and the fire spread over the water, smoking greasily.

The creatures attacking the boat, who might have been blood-red seals with fangs and arms, rolled away from the boat and disappeared.

Hal took out another firedart, found another target, and then his squadron was down with him, and the Ichili was spattered with flames.

The boats straightened out, continued on their course, and Hal heard a warning blast from somewhere.

Above him, out of the clouds, dove Yasin's decimated but still deadly squadron. Now it was their turn to have the advantage of height.

A dragon was hurtling down toward Storm, and Hal sent Storm back toward the water.

He watched, waited, as the dragon closed, till he could see the tight grin of its flier, anticipating a victory.

Then he sent Storm rolling out of the way.

The Roche dragon tried to recover, had too much speed, and slammed into the Ichili.

Hal sent Storm climbing, into the heart of Yasin's squadron. At its head, and he absolutely knew without knowing how, was *Ky* Yasin.

He went for him, fired, and put a bolt in Yasin's dragon's foreleg. Then Yasin was gone, and it was a mad swirl over Carcaor.

Hal managed a quick glance down, saw the boats coming back across with another load, untroubled.

The magicians of Sagene and Deraine must've produced their counterspell.

Then there was a dragon just above him, and he put a bolt in its belly just as the dragon's tail flailed at him.

Storm had the tail in his jaws, tore sideways, and the Roche dragon screeched, was gone.

There was another, wounded dragon converging on him, and Hal aimed closely, hit the flier in the head, knocked him out of his saddle.

They had the heights then, the snarling fight about to begin, and Hal heard repeated blasts from a trumpet.

He looked, saw an unknown dragon, its flier blowing a horn frantically, and waving his free hand.

Hal knew that prearranged signal.

The flier had seen Bodrugan's flags from his mountain top. Either the demon had appeared or Bodrugan's magic said he was about to.

Just as Yasin's fliers dove away upriver to reform, Hal was blowing the recall, and going for the squadron base.

The dragon handlers heard his signal, and had the spear cradles ready.

Hal put Storm down almost next to one, and, in seconds, the cradle was tied around the dragon.

It seemed as if every nonflier in the squadron was helping, but Hal had no time for thanks, taking Storm up ahead of the others.

Storm didn't like the cradle or the heavy spear suspended under his belly, but confined his protests to a high whine, then concentrated on reaching for the sky.

At full speed, Kailas drove Storm downriver, toward the grim mountaintop and its ruins.

Then he rounded the last bend in the river, and saw the ruins, just as they shook as if taken by an earthquake, and then cascaded off the sides of that great brown demon, rearing from his underground or otherworldly lair.

This time he was taller than two hundred feet, and this time he didn't stay on the mountain top, but strode forward, impossibly walking down its near-vertical side, toward Hal and the river.

Maybe he had been called by Roche wizards, or maybe the bloodshed in Carcaor was his summons.

A dragon hurtled past Hal toward the demon. It was Alcmaen. Hal grudged him courage, when he should have been screaming in terror.

Alcmaen's spear came undone, and wobbled toward the demon. But he was too far away, and the spear dove toward the river.

Alcmaen tried to bank away, but was too close, and the demon swatted both the Sagene and his dragon down, crumpling them as if they were paper.

Hal banked around the demon, toward his side, and was coming in for an attack when a black dragon was in front of him, and a crossbow spat a bolt at him.

Yasin's fliers had taken advantage of the break in action, and were coming back on them.

Mariah was just above the demon, coming straight down, and released his spear. It took the demon somewhere in the chest, and the whole world rang with the monster's scream.

Two other dragons dropped their spears, both missing, as Hal turned Storm, into the face of a surprised Roche flier.

Storm tore at the beast's side with his double horns, and it fell.

The demon was swaying, expanding, very unsolid.

Its chest was pointed to Hal's side, and Hal hoped, as he sent Storm in again, that its attention was elsewhere.

He was close, very close, and Storm was whining in fear.

Hal pulled at the cord, and the spear arced away, and took the dragon in its chest.

It stumbled back, fell against the rock wall it had just descended, and Hachir came in and dropped his spear. It caught the demon in the belly, and it collapsed, fell forward into the Ichili, and then, very suddenly, there was nothing there as another flier's spear went through nothingness to clang against a boulder.

Nothing but onrushing Roche dragons.

Hachir was banking back toward Hal, and a dragon carrying Yasin's guidon dove on him.

Hachir rolled out of the way as Yasin recovered, climbing.

Hachir went after him, and the two vanished into a cloud.

Hal was bent over Storm's neck, calling for everything the dragon had, and they were climbing after the two.

Then one dragon came out of the cloud, Yasin's.

Hal saw no sign of Hachir or his dragon.

Yasin brought his dragon around, and dove on Hal. He was aiming his crossbow. Hal ducked, barely in time, and shot back, missing.

Both dragons circled, bare yards above the cliffs, as their fliers reloaded. Yasin aimed quickly, fired, missed, as Hal aimed his crossbow.

He was suddenly the crossbow, the bolt, and moved his aim a little left. Yasin saw his death approaching, sat frozen as Hal pulled back on the trigger.

The bolt shot forward, and *Ky* Yasin flew into it

He screamed as it hit him in the chest, and his dragon dove straight down, toward the Ichili.

It struck hard, a gout of brown water lifting.

Hal took Storm very low.

But there was nothing but ripples.

Then a dragon's foreleg rose above the water, sunk again.

Ky Bayle Yasin was gone.

Athelny of the Dragons was avenged, as was Saslic and all the other dragon fliers who'd been killed in this war.

Hal Kailas wondered why he was crying.

But it didn't matter. No one could see.

He took Storm back upriver, his squadron forming on him, to Carcaor.

The city was in flames.

Heavy lighters were on the east river's edge, and were loading cavalry.

The palace in Carcaor's center was a firestorm, like Hal had brought to Lanzi.

Soldiers were streaming across the river and through the city's streets.

Charging horsemen rode past them, shattering the few Roche formations that stood fast.

Then there was nothing but running men, and other men after them, killing as they ran.

White flags exploded through Carcaor.

The war was finally over and done.

43

It was stormy, and the winds from the nearby, whitecap-tossed, Western Ocean promised a gale this night.

But it didn't matter.

Hal – and Storm – would sleep warm this night, warm in Cayre a Carstares, Lady Khiri's castle.

The war was truly over.

Lord Bab Cantabri found it very difficult to make peace, since Roche's ruling barons had either been killed, took their own lives, or fled.

Not that it mattered.

Once the Roche realized their leaders were gone, it was if a solid bar of steel was suddenly revealed as rusted through.

Carcaor was the last holdings of the Roche, and now it was gone, as well.

There was some looting, some murders by the conquering Sagene and Derainian soldiers, but not that much.

They were almost as weary as the Roche.

There would be some kind of victory parade sometime in the next few weeks. Actually, there would be two of them, one in Rozen, one in Fovant.

Hal didn't give a diddly-damn if he was in either.

The war was over, and he was no longer a soldier. He supposed they'd send him some papers one day or another.

Many of the soldiers had felt the same, and had gone home on their own ticket, not waiting for any discharge or bonus, content with their lives.

That had been the case with Hal's squadron.

He'd been surprised so many of the old fighters had survived – Farren Mariah, Mynta Gart, Sir Loren Damian. Even some of the newer ones had made it – Chincha and Cabet. Richia had been killed in the final struggle with Yasin's black dragons.

Hal wondered what the death count was for the ten years and more of war. Two million a side? Three? More?

He also wondered what would happen to Roche, now completely shattered.

But not that much.

That would be for others, for diplomats and such, to worry about.

All that Hal wanted was to sleep, and then, maybe, go looking for the boy who wanted to be a dragon flier, who'd been dragged into the army so long ago.

He wondered, if he found him, he'd recognize him.

Hal shook his head, took himself away from the dark mood coming on.

Below him was Cayre a Carstares.

Storm gave a happy honk, swung around, and lowered toward the ground.

A dot came out of a building, ran to the center of the keep.

Khiri.

And that was all Lord Hal Kailas of Kalabas, the Dragonmaster, needed or wanted.

For a time.

THE LAST BATTLE

For Monsieur Jack-Attaque Demong
(d.o.b. 23-12-02)

1

Dragonmaster Hal Kailas, Lord Kailas of Kalabas, Member, King's Household, Defender of the Throne, Hero of Deraine, and so on and so forth, banked his great dragon Storm out over the Eastern Sea, and looked back at the land.

Spring was about to arrive. Here fishing boats ran out their nets. There, just inland, along the cliffs, farmers were beginning to plow.

The trees of the orchards were budding, putting forth green shoots.

Villages and farms dotted the landscape, the chimneys of their houses curling smoke up into the sharp air.

All was prosperous, all was peaceful, all belonged to the Dragonmaster.

Big frigging deal, Hal thought.

It was as if there was a gray gauze veil between him, his mind, his thoughts, and this world of peace.

It was two years since the great victory, when Roche had been driven down to defeat and ruin.

Kailas at times almost wished for the fighting to come back.

He wasn't bored – at least he didn't think so – but nothing much mattered to him these days.

The armies had been paid off, and the men and women had made their way back to their homes, if they admitted to them any longer.

Others went to the cities, found jobs, and tried to settle down. Still others just wandered.

They called themselves tramps, or beggars, but Hal, who'd been a tramp himself before the war, saw no sign of their wanting work beyond the moment, or even a full begging bowl.

They did not seem to want anything that was offered them, no matter what it was.

Whatever anyone had expected peace to bring, it seemingly hadn't brought anything for great numbers of soldiers – and civilians as well – too many of whom unconsciously missed the excitement of battles and victories.

Of the three great nations who'd battled, Deraine was in the best shape, having nothing worse than economic decline to worry about.

Sagene, once Deraine's ally, had had its eastern provinces torn and laid waste, the land lying fallow, unworked, too many farms abandoned.

Roche, as King Asir of Deraine had worried so long ago, was in chaos, barely a nation now, with barons fighting other barons for a meaningless throne, and little law on the land save what a warrior could carve out for him- or herself.

Hal Kailas, at least, didn't want for anything. The war had not only brought him fame, but land, honor and riches.

But happiness? Contentment?

Even his marriage to Lady Khiri Carstares now lay behind that gray veil.

Perhaps if they'd had children, it might have been different.

He wondered why his marriage seemed to have almost vanished, like one of the cloud wisps that drifted past Storm's soaring wings.

Maybe he and Khiri had wanted too much, expected too much, used their marriage to block off the war, to give them what comfort they'd been able to seize.

Perhaps there'd been too much blood shed. Blood of her family, blood of the enemy.

But now he went little to her estates on the west coast, nor she to his, here across the country on Deraine's eastern coast. Mostly, she spent her time in the capital, Rozen.

The little they were together, they still slept in the same bed, still made love. But Hal felt the coupling was almost mechanical.

He didn't know, was afraid to ask, what Khiri felt.

He banked Storm again, back toward land. Just on the edge of the horizon now was his great estate. He'd flown away from it just before noon, feeling its gray, its stone, its brooding.

Not that taking Storm up had improved matters any.

Realizing his mood was growing darker, he decided, since there was still time in the day, to travel north-north-east, to visit Bab, Lord Cantabri of Black Island.

He was certainly warmly clad, with a riding cloak covering him from stirrups to waist, and a hooded sheepskin coat. Hal could have flown for a week, loving the sharpness of the spring air against his face.

He felt the irony of his destination.

Cantabri, a yellow-eyed, scarred warrior, really had little in common with Kailas.

But he and Hal had soldiered long and well in the service of the king.

They had little else to unite them, though. Cantabri was frank about missing war's seductions of brotherhood, excitement, authority.

Hal missed none of that.

But he missed . . . something.

Like the wanderers, he didn't know what it was.

And, he realized, he and Bab seemed to be quickly turning into dotards, with not much to talk about besides their experiences in the war.

Storm honked a lazy challenge, seeing another dragon in the distance.

Hal hoped to see someone on its back, but the monster was wild.

He might have been a war dragon once.

But when the armies were cut back, the dragons were mostly set loose, abandoned, as the now-dead Danikel, Lord Trochu, Sagene's greatest killer, had gloomily predicted.

There'd been much discussion during the war of using dragons for quick transport.

But the beasts were deceptive – they might have been enormous, but their carrying capacity was slight. The Roche and, occasionally, the Derainians had used paired dragons to carry baskets full of infantry. But this was for very short distances, and was hardly a successful way of fighting.

There'd been some excitement about using them to carry people about, people who were in a hurry to get somewhere. But weather and the natural intemperateness of dragons brought that to a quick halt, as did the loss of half a dozen or so adventurous rich men.

A few dragons became polished popinjays, their owners offering flights for the citizenry for a few silver coins. But the monsters' eyes seemed as dull as the fliers who took the villagers aloft.

At least Storm was fat, happy, and lazy, although when he saw another dragon he still bristled, his huge tail whipping behind him, challenging combat.

He was in the very prime of life, perhaps seven or eight years old, gray and black. He was about fifty feet long, twenty feet of that in his huge whip of a tail, and about twelve feet tall, on all four legs. His natural weapons were many: his head with cruel fangs and dual horns, and spikes on either side of his neck. All four legs had taloned "hands," and there were talons on the leading edges of his wings. They stretched more than a hundred feet from tip to tip.

Fat and happy . . . but there were too many dragons, once feared weapons of the king's forces, now cast aside as unneeded.

There'd been enclaves set up by the King's Master of Remounts, to take care of wounded, crippled dragons. But Kailas had heard that these hospitals had gone unfunded. He had visited a handful of them, finding them all empty, and desolate but for the lingering reek of the monsters.

He'd heard rumors that these dragons had been killed, or taken to a desolate island and just abandoned, but they were only rumors.

In any event, to see a dragon with a rider these days was a surprise, the handful Hal had encountered being wild.

He'd sent letters to Garadice, at the king's palace, about the hospitals, offering to pay for their costs as best he could, but never received an answer. He'd heard that Garadice had quit his post in disgust over the maltreatment of his monsters, gone off on an expedition to Black Island and on into the north, but was never able to confirm the story.

Hal's King's Own First Dragon Squadron still existed, as a ceremonial unit only the size of a flight. There were two other such "squadrons" in the Royal Army.

They'd regularly written Hal, requesting the pleasure of the Dragonmaster's presence at one or another ceremony.

Hal had declined them all, somehow realizing that witnessing these hollow shells would further depress him.

As for the handful of men and women who'd flown with him, and somehow lived, he'd been able to find out what had happened after the war to only a few.

Mynta Gart had, as she'd vowed, put together a shipping firm that grew and grew. She was now very rich, with more than twenty-five bottoms under her command, and, seemingly, very content.

Sir Loren Damian had retreated to his estates in the west, and busied himself in stock breeding. Hal got an occasional letter from him, always swearing that he didn't miss dragons or flying.

He wasn't the only ex-flier to firmly remain ground-borne. Hal had wondered why people could walk away from the soaring joys of seeing dawn from the heights, long before the land-tied, or chasing a rainbow or just what lay on the other side of a mountain. Then he realized many ex-fliers remembered only the terror of being attacked by one of the Roche black dragons, or seeing a friend or lover torn from his or her saddle to fall screaming into death, and needed and wanted no reminders of those days.

Hal could understand what those fliers felt – the squadrons had taken a terrible toll during the war.

Farren Mariah, the city rogue, sometimes self-taught wizard, had simply vanished, and no one seemed to know of his whereabouts, although a few guessed prison or worse.

A flier he barely remembered from the squadron, a Calt Beoyard, who'd joined just before the war's end, still tried to keep some sort of squadron association alive, and circulated a round robin periodically. Hal read it, but without the interest he thought he should have felt.

Kailas, unlike his wife, went seldom to Deraine's capital, Rozen, or to the lavish apartment he and Khiri had across the Chicor Straits, in Sagene's city of Fovant.

Khiri, however, throve on travel.

Which made Hal's life on his estates more empty, but somehow the emptiness wasn't unwelcome.

Within an hour, Hal was overflying Lord Cantabri's land. When King Asir had decided to reward Hal with property, it had been Cantabri who'd pressured the king into making Hal his neighbor in the east, telling Kailas that he always felt more comfortable living near a man who'd been tested, and Cantabri felt the only real test of a man or woman was war.

Cantabri might have been a friend as well as a war leader, but Hal always had a bit of trouble using his first name, in spite of Cantabri's insistence.

The demarcation between the two lords' lands was clear – the farmhouses on one side were a little shabby, the lands not as well tended, the villages a bit on the rundown side.

Cantabri had been a fierce soldier, but he was, in Hal's eyes, far too indulgent to his farmers and workers, always ready to grant a boon, or an exemption from estate taxes.

But that was Bab.

Ahead was Cantabri's great castle, sitting solitary on an easily defensible promontory.

That showed another difference between the two – the manor

that Hal used the most was nestled in a valley that stretched to the sea, all rich farmlands with small villages nearby, with sere moorlands above it, on the fells.

Hal sent Storm slanting downward, already half smiling in expectation of his welcome.

Cantabri would growl him out of his foul mood, as would Cantabri's wife.

He was only half a hundred feet from the ground, just level with the castle walls, when he saw that the great banner that normally flew from the battlements was gone, replaced by a somber black pennon.

Other black flags hung from the ramparts.

Hal felt a sudden clench in his guts.

He brought Storm in for a landing in the huge forecourt, and an equerry ran out to take his reins.

The man's face was flushed, and his eyes red.

"The Lord . . . the Lord Cantabri is dead," he managed, and burst into tears.

2

Hal slid from his saddle, grabbed the man by the shoulders.

"How? When?"

"It must've been his heart . . . or something," the man said, fighting for control. "He . . . it was just after the morning meal, and he was going to ride out to see the new piggery . . . and then . . . then . . . he didn't even say anything . . . just fell on his way to the stables . . . no one knows . . ."

That was about all he could get from the retainer.

Grimly, Hal went looking for Lord Bab's wife. No, widow, he corrected himself.

Two days later, he was airborne, headed back for his own home.

House, he corrected himself. Home is supposed to be welcoming, and those cleverly piled reddish rocks offered him no seductions.

The last two days had been just as painful as he could have expected.

Lady Cantabri was very brave, and very firm, except periodically, when the reality of the loss made her dissolve in sobs.

Part of Hal was unshocked. He'd had too many friends die around him in the war to not have an armored shell around his heart.

Part of him found it a bitter irony that Cantabri, having lived through a nightmare, should drop dead before looking at a collection of pigs.

And a very selfish, unacknowledged part led him to the realization of just how alone he now was.

He wished Khiri would be waiting for him.

Then he corrected his thought. He wanted the Khiri that was.

His mind made another wry correction.

Maybe the Khiri that was . . . waiting for the Hal that the war had killed . . . the Hal Kailas had never been? The Hal that had been part of a flying circus, in the days when dragons were creatures to marvel at, and cosset?

The sprawling castle, built when Deraine was still torn by civil war, was even emptier than he'd thought it would be.

But Hal didn't notice it for a time.

Waiting for him were two letters:

The longest was, finally, from Garadice. It ran:

Dear Lord Kailas,

My humblest apologies for not returning your posted inquiries, but I have just recently returned to Deraine, after a protracted expedition to the north countries.

I took the assignment, which came directly from His Royal Highness, feeling the bitter frustration after my attempt to provide shelter for our dragons, which I trained, and which fought for us so well, and wanted little to do with my country for a time.

I will be preparing a paper before the Royal Society of the Sciences, but that will be months in the offing, and you might be curious about what we found, since you were always the dragon-flier most interested in the beasts we tamed and rode.

There were almost 200 of us who sailed from the north of Deraine, aboard the venerable Bohol Adventurer, which I assume you remember full well from the war.

It has not improved any in its lack of seaworthiness nor victualing.

There was also a frigate with the Adventurer, since no one knew what to expect once we sailed beyond Black Island.

Twenty of us were scientists in one specialty or another, three diplomats, one magician, a certain Bodrugan that you'll remember, who sends his greetings. All of the rest sailors or soldiers, already in the king's service. His Majesty mounted the expedition to satisfy his curiosity about unknown lands, and chose these men, and I quote him, "because they're already eating me out of house and home."

At any rate, to continue.

We sailed north and east, seeing no other ships in our passage, not even fishermen.

Black Island was exactly as we left it in our raid — Roche did not bother to rebuild its dragon-breeding station after we destroyed it.

But there was a cheerful note — there was more than a plethora of black dragons, soaring, dipping around the island heights. Evidently they needed little encouragement to breed, and those we studied from a respectful distance were very healthy, and had little interest in man other than barely suppressed hostility.

We sailed on, this time due north, and wearisome were the days for me, since I had no interest in labeling the various fishes that we brought up.

There were dragons a-plenty, some flying overhead, others on the water, being blown along with their wings furled over their heads, in the peculiar rafting position you, I believe, were the first to describe.

These last were sometimes healing from wounds suffered some time ago, and were being driven east.

They behaved toward us like wild dragons who'd never let Man on their backs. Some of the ones in the air seemed to recognize Man, but did not care to come close.

After a week's sail, while storms howled around us, we came upon a solid wall of ice, with bergs breaking off at intervals.

It was impassable, and so we turned east, keeping the wall within sight, hoping to find either a breakdown in it so we could continue our northern quest, or something other that would be of interest to the king.

We were almost on the land before we saw it. The day before landing, we sighted sharp rises, which we thought were skerries in the middle of the ocean. They were not.

They were sharp pinnacles that rose from an almost flat land, what is called tundra, no more than slowly drying peat, from long-vanished forests.

And here we found dragons galore.

They flocked to every pinnacle as if they were rookeries, living off fish they brought up like great cormorants or, more plentifully, the shaggy wild oxen that grazed in the tundra.

And here, too, we found Man.

There are fairly primitive tribes occupying these lands. They were not particularly friendly.

Bodrugan devised a language spell, so we could communicate with them. But mostly they seemed interested in procuring, either by trade or theft, our nets and fishhooks.

We found they were the remnants of other, more "civilized" tribes, which meant, as far as I could tell, tribes that had more sophisticated methods of killing.

These tribes had migrated south, and I'm told have been providing great pain to the poor damned Roche and other nations to the east.

The reason for the migration was simple – the coming of the dragons.

There were food supplies enough for only one race, these people thought, and fearing the dragons, sought other lands to vanquish. The dragons, we were told, had but recently come to these lands, within the memory of a grandfather's grandfather's grandfather.

Once again, the question becomes, what has made the dragons migratory, since it appears their real home lies to the far west?

I do not know, and have not a clue even as to what line of questioning I should pursue.

I do wish that someone would commission an expedition west, to discover the nature of dragons in what might be termed its raw state.

One thing of extraordinary interest came about when we studied the dragons.

Each of the rookeries was crudely organized, so there would be dragon leaders, and herdsmen, who would chouse the shaggy bison into death traps. Other dragons . . . not parents . . . would guard the nurseries, changing shifts on a regular basis.

I do not mean to compare intelligence, but these dragons behaved like particularly well-trained packs of dogs, except being far, far brighter, of course.

This alone, to me, justified the expedition, although I'm afraid the diplomats and soldiers were bored silly.

I wish I could write more about this society of dragons, but I'd barely begun my studies when we were attacked by a coalition of savages, and driven back out to sea.

I shall, however, go back, to learn more.

I shall write more when I deduce more from my notes, and, of course, will invite you to be present when I present my paper.

Your Obedient Servant,

Garadice

Pondering what this might mean lessened Hal's mourning.

Again, the mystery of the dragons' flight from the west was evident.

The second letter contained shocking information. It was a clipping from a Sagene broadsheet:

Roche Dragon-
Criminal To Hang

Arch-criminal Bayle Yasin, once one of the evil Roche hierarchy, and commander of an infamous black dragon formation guilty of the most heinous war crimes, including murder, arson, and rapine, has finally been brought to the bar of justice in Frechin, accused of controlling a smuggling ring, bribing public officials and personally flying many loads of contraband, including arms, from Sagene back into his native land.

Yasin sneered at the courtroom proceedings, arguing that it was no crime to attempt to feed starving people, nor give them weapons to defend their lands and lives, and refusing to recognize the obvious right of Sagene to try him.

It took less than half a glass for the court judges, two of whom had served nobly under the colors, to find him guilty, and sentence him to suffer the maximum penalty.

The sentence will be carried out immediately after the new year, and after Yasin, in Sagene's infinite mercy, has exhausted all appeals.

"Son of a bitch!" Kailas swore in shock.

His wartime nemesis still lived.

Yasin had been, before the war, head of a dragon circus that had almost certainly hidden espionage as it traveled Sagene.

Hal had hated him from the first time he saw him, helping euchre Athelny of the Dragons out of his circus.

Later, he and Hal had jousted in the skies when Yasin led a black dragon formation, and, when Kailas became a prisoner of the Roche, Yasin tried to have him killed as a criminal.

But, in the end, in the final battle over the Roche capital of Carcaor, fighting the obscene sorcerous monster beyond the city, Hal had killed Yasin, sending a crossbow bolt into his chest, watching Yasin's dragon crash and vanish into a river.

Or, at any rate, he thought he had.

The bastard still lived.

At least he would, until the Sagene fitted him with a manila neck cloth.

But to hang a man for smuggling?

Smuggling food?

That was no way for a dragon-flier, no matter how big a shit he might be, to die.

The weapons might be another matter, but that was to be determined.

Hal packed carefully, as if he were intending to go to the field.

The next dawn, he flew south on Storm, toward the Deraine capital of Rozen, not sure, or at any rate unwilling to admit, just what he planned to do next.

3

Hal took his time flying south, considering what might be either a noble gesture or climactic stupidity. He laid over just outside Rozen at a country inn he remembered fondly from his days wooing Khiri.

He shouldn't have stopped. The chef he'd admired had run off with a scullery maid, and there were new owners, determined to extract the maximum amount of gold from their guests.

They recognized Hal, about the time he saw a plaque behind the front desk showing a dragon landing outside the inn, with a rider wearing full antique armor.

Of course they wanted him to sign the plaque, somehow endorse the inn and its now pedestrian fare.

Equally, of course, they charged him full rates.

It was almost funny.

Hal flew Storm into Rozen early the next morning, scratching at what he was fairly sure was a bedbug bite on his ankle.

It had been some months since he'd been in the capital.

Then, he'd found it depressing. Gray, wintry streets filled with gray, wintry people, jostling, wearing shabbiness.

There were old men and women, children, and a scattering of young women.

He didn't remember seeing any young men, and realized they were either working, or casualties of war.

This time, in spite of spring sunshine, Rozen was even less attractive.

He flew low over streets whose businesses were boarded up, or whose shops clamored liquidation sales.

There were more beggars out than before, even this early in the morning. Many of them were clustered around the still-occupied palaces of the wealthy.

He passed over Sir Thom Lowess's palace. It was darkened, with no sign of occupancy. Sir Thom was most likely off finding someone or something else to glorify.

Lowess was Deraine's most famous taleteller, who'd figured out, early on, that the path to fame and fortune was less being a superb writer than a Presence, particularly a Presence Who Discovered and Heralded Heroes.

Hal was one of his first, and he never forgot that, were it not for Lowess's mythmaking, which sometimes in his case was the truth, he'd likely have gone to an early grave as an unknown dragon-flier.

Lowess also was the one who'd introduced Hal and Khiri.

Beyond Lowess's house was a large stable that had seen profit in housing dragons belonging to transient fliers.

Hal landed there, and Storm was the only dragon about.

The owners were eager to house and feed Storm, especially seeing Kailas's red gold, and they rented Kailas a carriage.

He smiled wryly at that. At one time, he wouldn't have been happy with anything other than a spirited charger. But time wears, and the spring weather was showery and brisk.

He rode to the apartment he and Khiri had bought, located in an immaculate sector not far from the king's palace.

He'd only been there half a dozen times, but Khiri loved it, close to her city friends, shopping, and exclusive restaurants.

He left the carriage in front, and stood, taking deep breaths, determined not to spoil Khiri's mood with his current dark thoughts.

Forcing a smile, and making himself think it was real, he put his saddlebags over his shoulder and went up the steps to the apartment.

Hal realized he'd left the damned keys back at his castle, and knocked hard.

A thousand thousand times he would relive the next few moments.

Khiri's voice came from inside, wondering who that could be.

Then came a man's voice, clear, much closer to the door.

"Prob'ly the post, lover. I'll get it."

The door came open, and a handsome young man, about Khiri's age, stood there. He was barefoot, wore expensive dress trousers, and was stripped to the waist. His face was half-lathered, and he held a razor in one hand.

Hal's razor.

The world stopped.

Hal's first impulse was to grab the man by the throat and throw him to the ground. Or draw the old dragon-flier's dagger he still foolishly wore.

But he fought for, and found, control.

The man stared at him. Over his shoulder, Hal saw Khiri, quite lovely in a wispy green silk dressing gown, and nothing else.

He'd bought her that gown on her last birthday, and somehow that made it worse.

Hal tried to find something to say that wouldn't be utterly foolish:

How long has this been going on . . . How could you . . . Who is this man . . . and various obscenities.

All were stupid.

Khiri's mouth hung open, and there was a great roaring in Hal Kailas's ears.

But all he managed was:

"I'll have my representative contact you."

There came a blur, then he found himself untying the reins of the carriage, and he was moving through the city streets, trying to keep the horse from galloping, and sucking in great lungsful of air, as if he'd been in battle.

Hal probably should have gone back north until his head cleared.

But he didn't.

He thought of various friends he could stay with in Rozen, didn't call on any of them. They, no doubt, would provide a place for him to stay.

But he thought of how many people found a cuckold's plight humorous, and didn't feel like making himself into a laughing stock.

Or rather, more of a laughing stock than he already felt himself to be.

That might well push him over the edge, and make him bring out the dagger.

He found an anonymous suite in one of the large inns that had sprung up during the war, advised the stables he wished to keep the carriage for an indeterminate time, and asked them to continue caring for Storm.

He had no thirst, which was good. Kailas had never sought the bottle when times were hard. He also had no appetite, which was not good, and so he found a comfortable tavern where no one knew who he was, nor would they have cared if they did.

He was chewing a ham steak, which he found tasteless, when his ear was caught by a man at the table next to him, talking about a certain advocate he'd come against in his business. According to the man, the bastard had three rows of teeth, all facing inward like a shark.

The man didn't sound like he meant disparagement.

Hal took note of the advocate's name. He slept little that night, and the next day got directions to that advocate's office.

The man was Sir Jabish Attecoti. Hal thought the knighthood a good sign. He'd obviously helped, in one way or another, someone with influence, enough to have him named to the peerage.

Attecoti was of medium height, and rather rotund. His face fairly beamed goodwill, and was framed in carefully trimmed muttonchops.

Hal might have thought Sir Jabish an amiable philanthropist, until he noted the man's eyes. Steel blue, they were as hard and cold as any warrior Kailas had known.

Attecoti listened intently to Hal's story, and Hal realized that while very few people actually heard every word, Attecoti could probably recite their conversation word by word a year later.

He finally finished, a little proud of himself that he hadn't burst into tears or raised his voice.

"Nasty," Attecoti murmured. "Very nasty indeed, Lord Kailas. There are many actions I might take in this matter. What is your preferment?"

"Why . . . to end my marriage, as I said."

"Since both you and Lady Khiri are known public figures, you might realize this will be a matter for the broadsheets. How do you wish it played?"

Hal thought of dragging Khiri's name through the mire. But what would that give? And his own would be equally tarred, no doubt.

"Just end it," he said. "She has great properties in her own right. Let her keep what was hers, and I mine. And I wish no mention, if possible, of the cause of the divorcements. Call it irreconcilable matters."

The words tore at his heart, but they were the truth.

"I shall open on that front," Attecoti said. "If it worsens, though . . ."

"Do what you must," Hal said.

"I have some instructions for you," Attecoti said. "First, stay away from the broadsheets. Do not go to any taletellers, even if you now think them friends."

Hal nodded, thinking of Sir Thom Lowess.

"It would be wise for you to absent yourself from the capital until the hearing is set," Attecoti continued. "Go back to your estates.

"If you have . . . shall we say lady friends . . . it would be wise to avoid their company for a time."

"I have none such," Hal said.

Attecoti nodded, didn't comment.

"This case could well be the biggest I have yet handled," he said.

"Name your price," Kailas said indifferently. "I can meet it."

"In time," Attecoti said. "Oh yes. One other thing. Try to avoid having contact with Lady Khiri. That will not make things easier for me."

"I have nothing to say to her," Hal said, and, surprisingly, found it to be the truth. He wondered how long it *had* been that.

"Be advised I shall be retaining a seeker," Attecoti said. "Less because I'm curious about either of your private lives, but because I like to know everything to do with a case I handle.

"Might I ask where you will be staying?"

Hal told him the name of the inn.

"But that will be for only a few days," he said. "I shall be abroad for a time."

This came, unbidden, from him, as he remembered the vague thoughts he had had while flying south.

"Have your seeker call on me," he said, "if you would. And retain a good one. I have another matter – matters – I would like his help with."

"I shall do that. Do keep me current as to your location," Attecoti said. "And . . . my sympathies, Lord Kailas."

He sounded as if he meant it.

Hal tried to force coherence on his jumbled brain, and looked up Calt Beoyard, who had a farm half a day's flight from Rozen.

Beoyard was delighted to see him, tried to insist on Kailas staying with him, "even though I know this place is far too simple for a lord."

Hal politely thanked him, said he had business in the capital. He wanted the addresses for Mynta Gart and Sir Loren Damian, and the last known place Farren Mariah had been seen at.

Tay Manus was slim, very calm, and very obviously an ex-warder specializing in crime investigation.

Hal told him he really wanted to find Farren Mariah . . . or, at least, if something had happened to him, what it was.

Then, cursing himself for being a romantic, he asked him to hunt up Aimard Quesney. Quesney had shared a tent with Hal when he'd been attached to another squadron, in the war's early days. He'd asked Quesney to join the First Dragon Squadron when it was being formed. Quesney, not for the first time, had called Hal a born killer and declined. Later, he had refused to kill any more, and been court-martialed.

Hal had sat on the board, and, realizing Quesney was facing execution for refusing battle, forced a verdict of insanity from the other board members, in spite of Lord Bab's rather explicit instructions that he wanted Quesney at least hanged as a traitor, if not tortured for being anti-war, whether or not the King's Regulations permitted such treatment.

The verdict may have been shameful and false, but it saved Quesney's life.

Now Hal wanted to see the man, and ask a few questions.

Manus said he didn't think either assignment would be difficult, and left.

Hal went to the shipping district, found Mynta Gart's rather imposing warehouses.

Gart was overwhelmed at Hal's emergence from the "northern bracken," as she called it.

She poured him a brandy, which he liberally watered, stared closely at him, and asked what the matter was.

Hal hesitated, then told her, without going into specifics, that his marriage had just crashed into the rocks.

"No hope of putting it back together?" Gart asked.

Hal shook his head.

Gart wryly poured herself a drink as well, closed the door to her glassed office, stuffed with ship models.

"Things like that happen," she said. "Remember Chincha? The flier Farren was sweet on?"

"I do," Hal said.

"Something like happened to them," Gart said. "I guess, when the fighting stopped, he and Chincha found out they didn't have much in common."

"So where is Farren?"

"I haven't a clue, sir," Gart said. "Which asks the question – what are you doing around here? Other than to renew old friendships, and all of that."

Hal told her, and she whistled.

"This nice suicidal idea didn't come to you after you and Lady Carstares came to a parting?"

"No," Hal said. "I was on my way down here, about half sure of what I was going to do ... and then what happened, happened."

"I'll put the word out in Farren's district," Gart said. "But I don't know. Oh. One person I know of who might be interested in your idiocy is Cabet. He's doing nothing but running a dragon patrol for the king, chasing smugglers around the straits.

"He might be up to doing something stupid with you."

Cabet was the thin, detail-minded flier who'd commanded the 18th Flight of the First.

"Thanks for the compliments," Hal said.

Gart smiled a little.

"The war's over. I don't have to watch my words now.

"And, speaking personally, I've too much sense to involve myself in your scheme ... outside of its launching, I mean."

"I didn't expect a stable young businesswoman like yourself to do something insane such as I propose," Hal said, letting just a bit of a sarcastic drawl into his voice. "And, since you said you'll help get things under way, pun not intended, I'd like to have you charter a transport for me, capable of carrying dragons around the capes to the Southern Ocean."

"I can do better than that," Gart said. "The old *Galgorm Adventurer*, which no one in his right mind would go near who doesn't want to lug dragons about, is set for the breakers' yard.

"I figure it ought to cost no more than a hundred pieces of silver, as she sits, just for the scrap metal in her hull. No one's ferrying dragons about these days, even for gold on the spot.

"I can have her in the shipyard tomorrow, being refitted."

"I may as well be hanged for a bull as a kit," Hal said. "Go ahead."

Cabet was the first to arrive, loudly proclaiming how little he liked peacetime bureaucracy, and that he spent more time filling out reports than he did chasing smugglers.

Hal hid a smile – Cabet was not only a good leader, but gloried in the fine details, never admitting that, somewhere inside, he had the soul of a bureaucrat.

Cabet had only one request – that if he was killed in this adventure, there would be an award for his widow.

He had been married less than a year.

Hal thought that a good idea, and had Attecoti find a bank willing to write such policies for anyone who would journey with him. He didn't tell anyone except Attecoti that it was in exchange for him agreeing to do part of his banking business with them.

Hal asked Cabet if he had a particular dragon he would like purchased for his mount.

Cabet said not – if he had time, he'd train any beast that came to hand.

Calt Beoyard also was an eager volunteer, having, to his surprise, found his excuses quite empty. Hal had him take a dragon up, and jousted with him in the skies over Rozen on Storm, refreshing his memory of how good Beoyard was.

Acceptable. Not a Danikel, not a Richia.

But, unlike the other two, still alive, which said something about his fighting ability.

The next recruit lounged into Gart's office, where Kailas was headquartering his expedition from.

"I heard," Bodrugan said, "you're planning something troublesome."

"Who's talking?" Hal asked sharply even before greeting the magician. If there was gossip about, his plan was probably doomed.

"No one," Bodrugan said. "But it's known that you've purchased a ship that happens to carry dragons. And I've heard you're not at your usual residence, nor staying with Sir Thom.

"I know nothing from nothing, but since the next expedition north won't set forth until next year at the soonest, I thought maybe you could use a wizard perhaps as demented as you are. I'm bored with civilization, I fear."

Hal grinned.

"Welcome aboard, you loon."

Hal didn't need to turn from his lists to see who'd come in.

The voice was enough.

"I heard, bird, you're seeking me."

Hal turned.

It was Farren Mariah.

"Could I ask your mean scheme, o my fearless leader?"

"You could," Hal said. "I'm proposing a jail break."

4

Hal took Farren to a waterfront dive, and, for the first time since discovering Khiri with her lover, allowed himself to have an unwatered brandy.

He hesitatingly told Mariah what had happened, still not wanting anybody's sympathy.

Mariah sat, silently for a time, thinking, then drained his glass and signaled for another.

"Your first lady, Saslic," he said, without a trace of his usual singsong cant, "may have been right when she said there wouldn't be any after-the-war for a dragon-flier.

"Like there hasn't been for you and your wife.

"And there didn't seem to be one for Chincha and myself, at any rate.

"She wanted to travel, I wanted to stay in Rozen. She thought we should start some kind of business, I wanted to try politicking."

"I remember you talked about becoming the gray father of

your district," Hal said, grateful to be able to think of others' tribulations instead of his own. "What happened?"

"Aaarh," Farren said, slipping back into his street tongue, "I said truth and they thought I was lisping. Nobody wants what is straight from the bosom, cousin, and maybe it's not the truth anyway, and you ought to be doing a fancy dance in grays.

"That didn't go anywhere, especially when I realized I was being used as a front man for the district's business as usual.

"I fell in on their scheming, and things came to this and that and someone pulled a knife, and I got six months in the bokey-pokey and some people had scars, and Chincha had gone by the time I got out, leaving me with just a note saying 'Dear Farren. Screw it.'

"So I took up mopery around the streets. Did some spells, sometimes they worked, sometimes they didn't.

"And you know, Lord Hal, I found myself looking up every time a dragon flew overhead.

"I thought I was just being strange on the range, and actually found a flying club, for the love of somebody or other. I went to a meeting, listened to all their crapetydoodah about the glory of the clouds and the wind whistling through their ears, and decided what they thought was flying wasn't what I thought it was.

"And so back to diddling my doodling, and then your seeker found me, and you owes me, I thought he was a warder and I near had heart seizure for thinking I was going back inside for doing something I didn't remember."

"Sorry about that," Kailas said, not sure if he was apologizing for Manus the seeker or what had happened to Mariah since peace struck.

"So we're to be busting somebody out of the old dinga-donga-dungeon, eh? Who, if I can ask."

Hal told him.

Mariah laughed immoderately.

"I love this. We spend a whole frigging war trying to kill this Yasin bastard, think we've succeeded, and now that the Sagene are going to top the evil son of a bitch, we're going to try to stop them.

"Aaah, life, I loves, loves, loves you."

They would need eight dragons, plus two handlers per dragon.

Work on refitting the cavernous *Galgorm Adventurer* was proceeding apace.

It was a hideous ship, like most that are intended for one purpose only, and then made worse by changing the purpose.

The *Galgorm* had originally been intended to haul horses and, secondarily, men. It was a square-rigged threemaster, with main and cargo decks. Both decks had stalls that had been later enlarged to accommodate dragons. Wide gangplanks had been installed on either side of the hull. Dragon "launching" and "landing" was done with a barge tied alongside, to the looward side. Dragons were led down one or another of these gangplanks to the open barge, and encouraged by their rider to take to the air. Since dragons never minded getting wet, a launch day could be fairly soggy for the fliers.

Since the *Galgorm* was now Hal's, he made certain changes, such as a proper-sized kitchen, and enlarging the cabins to be more than just man containers. He might be playing the fool, but he wasn't going to be an uncomfortable one.

He and Farren then went shopping for monsters.

There were more than enough on the market.

Kailas preferred black ones, even though Storm was a conventional reddish with gold streaks.

He took only the best.

The dragons were at least sixty feet long, twenty feet of that spiked tail. He never ceased admiring their talent for death-dealing, from the dual-horned head with its lethal fangs and cruel neck-horn to the whip-spiked tail.

All of the beasts he chose had some domestication, if dragons could ever really be tamed, and so their carapaces had been painlessly drilled for rings to hold the rider's saddle and bags, just as the armored head had been fitted for reins.

It was great fun for Hal, until he noticed the expression, if expression it was, on one unchosen beast.

He swore it looked as forlorn as an unasked maiden at a village dance.

Thereafter, the pleasure was considerably diminished.

He wished he could free all these captive dragons.

But then what?

Many of them had been captured as kits, and had little if any ability to live in the wild.

Once again, he thought, man befouled what he did not destroy.

That put him a thoroughly bad mood, quite ready to deal with his next caller, Sir Thom Lowess.

He came into the office quietly, and sat down, without greeting Kailas.

Hal turned and looked at him, hard, for a moment.

"How long have you known?"

"Maybe . . . maybe a month."

"And you didn't tell me."

"No," Lowess said. "And it pained me. But I was friends with Khiri, and you, and finding out about her . . . behavior put me in the middle."

"It did," Kailas agreed. His voice was harsh, flat.

"I came to apologize . . . but I realized that wouldn't be right."

Hal thought for a moment.

"No. No, it wouldn't."

"Lady Khiri desperately wants to talk to you."

"I've been instructed by my advocate to have no contact with her."

Lowess's jaw bulged. He was getting angry.

"Aren't you being a little sanctimonious, Lord Kailas?"

"Yes, I suppose I am."

Lowess nodded once, stood, started for the door.

"Wait a minute, Sir Thom."

Lowess stopped.

"Very well. I'll talk to Khiri. But in the presence of my advocate."

"That," Lowess said after a moment, "hardly sounds like you're interested in any sort of reconciliation."

"No, it doesn't, does it," Hal said. "But that's the way it will be."

Again, Sir Thom nodded.

"One thing," Hal said. "You've been a more than good friend to me. I do not want to lose that."

Lowess smiled tightly.

"Thank you for saying that. I feel the same. And I shall tell Lady Khiri what you have agreed to do."

They met at the office of Sir Jabish Attecoti. Lady Khiri looked very beautiful, Hal supposed. And he was a bit surprised that she came without her own advocate.

Khiri tried a smile, saw Hal's grim face, let it slip away. She looked at Sir Jabish.

"This hardly makes for an easy conversation, does it?"

Hal didn't answer.

"Would it help to say I'm sorry . . . that he was just a momentary impulse, and we'd been . . . well, together, for only a few days."

"Don't lie, Khiri," Hal said. "I know otherwise."

Khiri bobbed her head, shed a few tears.

"It was just . . . just that you've been so cold lately. I thought maybe there was someone else, and lost my temper, and oh hells!"

"There was never anyone else," Kailas said.

Khiri looked up at him, her face flushed.

"You sound like you're my commander, or something like that! Isn't there any room for forgiving me? Please?"

Hal just looked at her.

She took a handkerchief from her sleeve, wiped her eyes.

"I suppose . . . no. Never mind."

She snuffled once, got up and swept out.

Hal and Sir Jabish exchanged looks. Neither of them said anything.

It was a bright summer day, and the sunlight dappled the waves as two harbor boats warped the *Galgorm Explorer* out of Gart's dock, and swung its prow south, toward the open sea.

Sailors swarmed the yards, and a dragon honked in surprise as the first wave lifted the ship.

Hal looked back at the land, saw Gart waving, managed a smile, then looked ahead at the Straits of Carcaor.

There was nothing behind him any more to hold his mind.

5

Once, Frechin had sat on Sagene's coast. But ocean currents silted up the coastline, and, fifty years later, it was two leagues inland.

But the citizens of Frechin were canny, and built a winding, deep-water canal from the ocean to the city, and dug out a huge harbor.

The canal was guarded by twin fortified moles at its mouth,

and the city itself by the great fortress-prison above the city, making it a safer harbor than before.

In midsummer, wherries brought the *Galgorm Adventurer* to a berth near the canal entrance.

Sagene citizens flocked to see the wallowing tub, and its load of dragons. Speculation ran rife as to what the Dragonmaster, famous even in a foreign country, was planning.

A few well-trained sailors, apparently in their cups, let on that Lord Kailas saw adventure and profit far to the south, on the almost unknown coast across the Southern Sea.

In the meantime, he was waiting for additional crew members and soldiers, since the coast was reputedly rife with pirates and hostile tribes.

The *Adventurer*'s master said they expected to be tied up in Frechin for at least a month, and opened negotiations for food and drink to be brought to the ship.

Hal and the other dragon-fliers had spent every clear, calm day on the voyage south, down the Chicor Straits into the open sea, around Sagene's capes into the Southern Sea, flying and practising landing on the small barge that the *Adventurer* towed alongside as a landing stage.

It was good to make sure none of them had lost these skills, Hal said.

It might be very good. He hadn't seen Frechin's prison, but Hal had had an idea or two on how he might attempt to liberate Yasin even before they'd left Deraine.

With their story adequately established, he decided to visit Yasin in his death cell.

He was pleasantly surprised at the prison's warder.

Sir Mal Rospen was a long-mustached soldier, most dignified in his manner.

"I bid you welcome, Lord Kailas," he rumbled. "But I must advise you of something. *Ky* Yasin may be a convicted felon, and doomed to be hanged, unless his last appeal is successful, which, frankly, no one expects.

"But he did what he did in the conviction of rectitude, illegally purchasing supplies on the black market and flying them into Roche.

"In another time, in another country, he might be judged a hero.

"But the war savaged us all, and so he will hang.

"But he will hang as a gentleman, and I will tolerate no man mocking him."

"That," Hal said honestly, "is hardly my intention."

Rospen had a warder show him to a bare stone room, and Yasin was brought in.

At least they let him wear civilian clothes, rather than whatever monkey-garb Sagene prisons legislated.

He started, seeing Kailas, and then burst out laughing.

"This is proof that the gods have an evil sense of humor," he said. "The last time I saw you – other than when you shot me – I was the visitor and you were the prisoner.

"As I recall, I was full of pride, and just beginning to realize the war was turning against us, and I said some most intemperate things."

"You did," Hal said amiably.

"For which I was repaid by your first escaping, then returning and laying waste to Castle Mulde and liberating all of the prisoners we held.

"A fitting repayment for arrogance. I think . . . I hope . . . I have learned, if not to curb my haughtiness, to at least conceal it."

Hal indicated the other, rickety chair.

Yasin sat.

"So what brings you out of Deraine?"

"I have a question of my own first," Hal said. "I could have sworn I killed you, back over the realm of the demon outside Carcaor."

"You damned near did," Yasin said frankly. "I felt your crossbow bolt hit me, and a wave of pain, and then I was in the water.

"My dragon had crashed beside me, and was thrashing in its death agonies. All I wanted to do was join it.

"But I didn't.

"I think I swam away from the beast, and then I was on the surface, trying to breathe. Without much success.

"But somehow I managed to float downstream, flailing at the water. I guess I was afraid to die.

"Anyway, the current took me a mile or more away, where I washed up on a little beach.

"There was a scattering of huts. The people who lived there wanted nothing to do with cities or demons or fliers or war. But one of them was a passingly good witch and herbalist.

"She crouched by me, and I could feel I was fading, and she snarled, 'Breathe or die,' and that shocked me into wanting to live.

"I breathed, and then she lit a taper, and I was in a coma. Then came great pain, and I couldn't waken. The pain stopped, and I found out later they were pushing your crossbow bolt through me, until it came out between my ribs.

"They cut off the broadhead, pulled the shaft out, and packed the wound with herbs."

He made a wry face.

"And so I healed, while my country fell apart.

"But talking about wounds is like listening to old women natter about their ills, interesting only to them.

"I ask again, if I may, what brings you here?"

Hal tapped an ear, raised an eyebrow, and pointed around the room.

Yasin smiled. "You remember the skills of being a prisoner well. No. This cell is not listened to, unlike some. At least, I don't think so."

Hal had been lightly searched, but they hadn't found the tightly rolled linen in his boot. He pulled it out, unrolled it, revealing the letters of the alphabet.

"We have interests to the south," he said, his fingers touching letters.

W . . . E . . . W . . . I . . . L . . . L . . . T . . . R . . . Y . . . T . . . O . . . R . . . E . . . S . . . C . . . U . . . E . . . Y . . . O . . . U.

Yasin's eyes widened.

"Well," he managed, "That sounds . . . interesting. I wish that I could accompany your expedition, but I seem to have other commitments."

"And you have let yourself fall out of shape," Hal said. "You're hardly fit enough for an adventurer."

"This is true," Yasin said. "I fear that our exercise time, which is only two hours a day, just at noon, has been uninteresting to me, since I don't know of any calisthenics that prepare you for walking on air."

"Still," Hal said. "You should get outside as much as you can. Your appeal hasn't been denied yet, and walking, *in the open air*, is good for you."

He wondered, if there were eavesdroppers, whether his words sounded as stilted as they did to him.

"You're right," Yasin said. "I should start immediately."

"In the meantime," Hal said, "while we're still anchored here, is there anything we could bring you?"

"A new trial," Yasin said. "Other than that, the warders here have been most gentle, and my mother has sent money, so I'm not living on prisoners' fare."

"Good," Hal said, and led the conversation into dragon-flying and the war for an hour or so, then took his leave.

Hal's dragons became a familiar sight over Frechin, soaring close to the heights, and waving at warders on the prison's walls.

Again, Kailas visited Yasin, with his linen roll.

T . . . W . . . O . . . D . . . A . . . Y . . . S . . . B . . . E . . . R . . . E . . . A . . . D . . . Y.

Yasin's lips moved in and out, and Hal noticed that he had developed a twitch at the corner of his mouth.

Contrary to what some morons have said, the prospect of being hanged does not concentrate the mind, but rather shatters the ability to concentrate.

Hal wriggled in the predawn chill.

The *Adventurer* had pushed away from the dock before dawn, swung round, and, under a reefed mainsail, tacked clumsily down-canal toward the sea.

The story was that the ship was to be put out to sea for re-ballasting, since its master disliked the way it had tacked on the voyage south, and would return later in the day.

Now the sun was well up, and they were following Hal's simple plan exactly.

Just coming up were the two moles at the canal's mouth. The *Adventurer*'s master steered the ship around the jetty, and the bows lifted, meeting the first waves from the open sea.

The *Adventurer* sailed due south until it was out of sight of land, in case anyone on the moles might be watching.

It was good to be awake, to have hastily grabbed some cold cheese and ham on a roll, a glass of tea, and stumbled on deck to make sure Storm had been fed an hour earlier, and was ready to fly.

It was good . . . like in the war.

That was an odd, sudden thought.

Hal jolted, but there was no time for wondering about one's thoughts. He put it away for later, and led Storm down the ramp from the ship to the barge.

He climbed into the double saddle, and Storm quivered, then, at Kailas's rein-tap, staggered forward, wings at full stretch, and striking downward, and again, and the dragon was airborne.

Hal pulled up, and Storm reached for the skies.

Well, he thought, maybe Farren *was* missing something. There was a certain majesty to dragon-flight. Especially with action in the offing.

He glanced back.

The other dragons were on the *Adventurer*'s deck, and one was being led down to the barge.

The monsters would take off within the hour.

Storm climbed high, until the ship was a dot.

There was no need to hurry, for the dragon to strain.

It lacked an hour of midday when Hal turned Storm back toward land.

He thought, at this height, he might fly unnoticed, as perhaps a wild dragon.

He followed the canal's winding, saw Frechin below him, and, on the cliffs above the city, the fortress-prison.

He put Storm in a circling descent, orbiting down, just over the fortress.

Dots appeared, grew, became prisoners in the courtyard, just as on other days.

There were other dots, alert warders on the catwalks. Hal made a face. He'd hoped to find them dozing after the noon meal, should have known that someone like Rospen wouldn't tolerate slackers.

One of the warders glanced up, saw Storm, and yelped in surprise.

Hal could have shot him down, but he wanted the escape to be, if possible, without casualties. If a Sagene guard died, all of the rescuers might face the gallows if captured.

He scanned the prisoners in the yard. Most were running for shelter – Storm was only about fifty feet above them. One stood in the middle of the courtyard, holding his hands clasped above his head.

Yasin.

An arrow whispered past Kailas, but not close enough to worry about.

Storm flared his huge wings, and thudded down on the bricks of the yard. Yasin was running toward him, and two more arrows clacked near him.

Too close.

Yasin pulled himself up behind Hal, who gigged Storm into his staggering takeoff run.

Three other dragons swept down, flying close to the battlements, as Storm's wings flapped, and he was in the air.

The dragons dove and swooped around the fortress, like angry monstrous swallows, their heads darting at warders diving for cover, their tails lashing.

Hal thought of so many crows, savaging an owl.

Another couple of arrows clattered off the dragon's plating, and they were above the castle.

Hal grabbed the trumpet hung on a hook bolted to the dragon's carapace, blatted twice.

Then he turned west, in what was a transparent attempt to delude the Sagene that these four dragons had nothing to do with the four dragons seen above the Derainian ship that had just sailed.

The plan was that when they reached the *Galgorm*, they would sail on south, into the depths of the Southern Sea, before turning west. If they stayed well clear of land, they should be able to reach the great ocean, then turn north to Deraine without being caught.

There might be a stink from Sagene's Council of Barons later, but Hal knew King Asir would hardly turn his Dragonmaster over to them.

Of course, it would be some years, if ever, before Hal could use the apartment he and Khiri had bought during the war in Sagene's capital, Fovant.

But what of that? It had really been Khiri's from the first.

He turned his mind away from that, looked over his shoulder.

Yasin, a grin stapled on his face, clung to his back.

"I owe you a great debt," he said.

"Godsdamned right," Hal agreed.

"What next?"

"Next, we get back to my ship."

Hal brought Storm to a southerly heading, the line of the canal barely visible to the east; used it to find the ocean.

Bodrugan had replicated a spell his master, Limingo, had cast years ago, that acted as a sort of compass to find a ship.

Hal whispered the words, touching the dragon emblem he still wore around his neck:

> *"Beef of old*
> *Covered with mold*
> *We shun thee yet*

> *Your odor set*
> *We turn away*
> *Our stomachs at bay*
> *Protect us all*
> *From your horrid pall."*

The spell had been cast around the salt beef all ships carried as a staple, and which most sailors and all landsmen detested.

Instantly, Hal felt a dislike for a certain direction. There would lie the *Adventurer* – and its barrels of beef.

The aversion was very strong. Hal frowned, then guessed it was his stomach, for he had not eaten any salt beef, thank the heavens, since the war had ended.

"It's nice to be in the air again," Yasin shouted. "Especially without a rope holding me up."

"Very funny," Hal said. "But you're repeating yourself. Now shut up and look for our ship."

"Which will be?"

"The only one around, I hope."

A few moments passed. Hal looked back, and made sure the other four were close behind him.

Yasin jabbed him in the ribs.

"Sail ho, or whatever sailors say," he said. Then, a little worriedly, "In fact, two sails ho."

Hal swung forward.

There were, indeed, two ships, dark dots, ahead. And they were fairly close together, certainly enough for them to have line of sight on the other.

"I guess one is yours," Yasin said. "But the other . . ." He broke off. "I don't have a glass," he said. "But I think the other is a Sagene patrol ship. We saw it often enough bringing supplies out of Frechin."

"Son of a bitch!" Hal swore.

This part of the rescue, after the actual lifting of Yasin from the prison, had always been the weak link. He knew the thin story about re-ballasting wouldn't last beyond the sight of the dragons over the prison walls.

If the *Galgorm* was captured, Sagene's wrath might fall on the sailors, even though the main villains had escaped.

He'd made arrangements for bond money for both the ship and the crew with Sir Jabish Attecoti, and for Bodrugan and the captain to take charge of the vessel if Hal wasn't aboard.

He knew their problems would be worse if Yasin and the dragons were captured with them, and had told Bodrugan the dragon force would try to evade if they saw the *Galgorm* was in trouble. He had also ordered the magician to claim utter ignorance of his plans.

But he'd assumed the worst case would be capture after they'd had a chance to land and change to fresh dragons.

As it was . . .

Hal blew a warning note to the others behind him, pointed down at the two ships.

He turned Storm east, toward where he'd seen, on the ship's charts, small islands.

He reached in a pouch, took out a compass, thought quickly, and devised a heading.

"Look!" Yasin said, pointing again.

Smoke, no, fog was billowing up and around the *Adventurer*. It must be a spell, cast by Bodrugan. A second incantation, a standard confusion casting, drifted up to him.

The *Galgorm Adventurer* might have been a pig, far slower than the coastal patrol ship.

But perhaps magic could save it.

There was nothing Hal could do.

Just when Hal was starting to worry about missing the islands, and being forced to turn toward Sagene, and Storm was starting to tire, they saw them, a pair of dots ahead.

Hal brought his flight in over the islands, saw no sign of habitation, and landed on a rocky plateau.

All of the dragons were trained to a rein tie, and stamped about, panting hard, as their riders, grim and worried, came up to Hal.

"And so this is the ringy-dingy prize?" Farren said. "Doesn't look as if he's been starvin' from worry."

Yasin ignored him.

"I guess," Cabet said, "our best chance will be to wait, then use our spell to head back for the *Adventurer*, although I like that but little."

Calt, very definitely the junior man, said nothing.

"That's not a goer," Farren said. "M'beastie's sore tired, and needs watering and a rest."

Calt nodded.

Hal knew Storm could fly on, but he would be on his reserves.

"I don't think that's best," he said slowly. "I'm afraid we have to go back to Sagene, raid a village or a big farm, then figure what to do next."

"I know where we can go," Yasin said. "There's a big estate we used to resupply from not far from Frechin. That's the bastard who betrayed us.

"He could do with a bit of a lesson."

"Not from us," Hal said. "We're in enough trouble as it is."

Yasin nodded reluctantly.

"But we can *buy* supplies from him, perhaps. Or requisition them, at any rate," Hal went on. "And we'll be gone before the alarm can spread."

"To where?" Farren said. "We can't go a-raidin' hither and thither as we go northward, a song in our heart and a smile on our lips, and hope to get home or even to Paestum without attracting a scowl and a chase.

"I don't think we're the only dragons to be flying over Sagene, and we'll be pursued."

"You're not," Yasin said. "Their Council of Barons still maintains a border watch in the skies. I learned that the hard way."

"And we can't go looking for the *Adventurer*," Hal said. "We don't know if it escaped, or if it's in the hands of . . . of Sagene."

He'd almost said 'the enemy.'

"It seems quite obvious," Yasin said, an ironic smile on his lips. "The only safety we've got is to fly further east, into Roche."

6

They flew north-east, back toward Sagene, and made landfall some distance away from Frechin. They flew about a mile inland and turned due east, Hal following Yasin's instructions.

They grounded where Yasin said to land, in the middle of the palatial estate that Yasin claimed he'd been betrayed at.

Hal and Cabet went to the main house. Yasin grumbled, and wanted to come with them, to wreak a bit of vengeance. Hal flatly said no, and he would have Mariah sit on him if he kept arguing.

The property's owner was supposedly in Fovant, they were told. But the rather nervous major-domo sold them beeves on the hoof, wine, bread, and preserved meats, after hearing the story that the dragons were part of a Sagene border sweep.

The four withdrew to a grove some distance from the estate houses, ate and relaxed. Being former soldiers, they could lie at ease, unworried, with unsheathed swords at their sides, as long as their enemies weren't in sight.

"Now what will we do?" Calt Beoyard wondered.

"As I said, push across the border," Yasin said. "Make for my lands. My family may not be as rich as we were before the war, but there'll always be food and shelter for men I owe my life to."

"Damned well better be," Mariah muttered somewhat darkly.

Yasin stared at him, and Hal saw the stocky man brace for a fight.

Farren Mariah thought about it, then shook his head.

"Naah," he said. "The Dragonmaster said we were to be friends, and that names it."

After an hour's rest, they flew on, toward Roche.

They passed over the ravaged border into Roche near dusk.

Hal thought, wryly, that if anyone had told him, three years before, he'd feel relief at being in Roche, he would have damned that person not only as a false prophet, but a total fool as well.

"Fly east by north-east," Yasin shouted.

Hal turned Storm in that direction.

Near dark, they approached a small town, little more than a village.

"That's Anderida. We can land there," Yasin shouted. "My family is well known."

Hal, not quite trusting Yasin, especially in Roche, made a few orbits before looking for a place to set down.

Anderida appeared quite untouched by the war, and by the civil disorders afterward.

Outside the town were armed horsemen, riding in pairs. One pointed to the sky, then galloped into the town center, where Hal lost sight of him.

Yasin told Kailas to land in the grassy square in the middle of town.

Hal chose an open field on the outskirts, and brought Storm in.

A crowd gathered.

Hal noticed some of them were armed, although they tried to keep their weapons hidden.

Kailas cocked his crossbow, letting a bolt drop down in the trough.

"You won't need that," Yasin said.

Hal didn't believe him. Nor did he disbelieve him.

He kept the crossbow hidden behind Storm's carapace.

The other fliers landed after Storm.

A rather fat man came into the meadow, holding up his empty hands.

"Greetings, strangers." He didn't sound very friendly.

"And greetings to you," Yasin said. "I am *Ky* Bayle Yasin."

There were shouts from the crowd, of welcome and cheers.

"I . . . I greet you, *Ky* Yasin," the fat man said. "But we heard you were in . . . well, desperate straits."

"I was," Yasin said. His command-trained voice, unraised, carried well. "These men . . . Derainians . . . rescued me from a Sagene death cell."

Now there were real cheers. The crowd got bigger, weapons forgotten.

"Then we greet and welcome them, as well," the fat man said. "I am the Town Leader, chosen after your last visit here, during the war, and am named Gavat. All that Anderida has is yours . . . and theirs."

Yasin turned back to Hal.

"You see? Now we own the city. As we shall own the whole of Roche."

Hal didn't know about the whole of Roche, but Anderida took the occasion to have a holiday.

They were given rooms at the best inn in town – there were only three – and payment was horrifiedly refused.

The dragons were put up in the stables behind the inn. The horses there were unceremoniously rousted.

Any time one of the dragon-riders peered out of the window, he was cheered.

They found that embarrassing.

They washed, and went to the taproom for a beer, and then were escorted into the dining room.

The fare was sumptuous.

It began with raw oysters, brought down the River Pettau,

past the ruins of Lanzi. Someone said something about the problem they were having "up north" with barbarian raiders coming in from the east, and that if Lanzi still stood, patrols would have kept them away.

Hal, who'd been responsible for the total destruction of Lanzi, looked innocent. Mariah, who'd also been on the raids, as had Cabet, wasn't nearly so successful.

Yasin asked about Anderida's seeming peacefulness.

Gavat, who was serving as feast-master, nodded.

"Peaceful now, yes," he said. "But not before. There were landless men come on us, and . . . and there was an outrage. An old man was taken prisoner, and his feet held against his own stove, until he told them where his gold had been kept.

"The men fled, after killing their captive.

"But we have a witch, and she sought and found them.

"They were brought back here, and hanged on a gibbet in the square.

"After that, we had our young men – those who'd survived the war – ride guardian around the town's borders, as they ride now.

"Twice, lawless men tried to enter the town, and were driven off. We put their heads on stakes on the roads approaching the town, and since then have had no further problems.

"Not like what we hear from the cities. Merchants, who now travel in convoys, well-armed, have told us of the disaster Roche has fallen into since Carcaor was brought down in ruins and Queen Norcia set aside.

"Fortunately, we need little from the outside.

"But this is hardly a subject for a feasting's conversation," he said. "Try these pasties. But save room. The meal has scarce begun."

The pasties held caviar, also from the north, with soured cream atop them.

Small game birds, stuffed with an exotic fungus and goose liver, came next.

Coins of beef, with fungus atop them, in a rich wine sauce followed.

Hal was starting to founder.

He made it through the fruit soufflé, but caved in before the salad, the cheeses, and the dessert.

Some of his faltering came from the foaming dark wine that was served in profusion.

Some more of it came from his servitor.

Anderida banquet custom evidently dictated that each guest have his own attendant.

Hal's was named Brythnoth. She was nineteen, she had white-blonde hair that Hal thought might be real, a round face and slender body. She also had a soft contralto voice, and firm breasts exposed in an diaphanous loose blouse.

She seemed to think that he was the most fascinating man who'd ever lived, with the possible exception of Yasin, who'd been a family hero during the war, and whose portrait had hung next to the family gods, she said.

Hal wondered if she'd still be so friendly if he told her he'd done his best, through the war years, to kill Yasin at every chance he got.

Hal decided, feeling very comfortable, he'd rather not test those particular waters.

He was very full.

Too full, he thought uncomfortably.

He yawned.

"I am boring you," Brythnoth said, sounding as if she was about to cry.

"No, no," Hal said. "I just need some air."

"Perhaps you'd let me show you our square?"

That sounded like a good idea, Hal said. It also sounded, very vaguely, like a way of getting in trouble.

But he allowed Brythnoth to take his arm, and they left the others still eating, although Mariah gave him a surreptitious thumbs up.

Hal wondered what that was supposed to mean.

The square was quiet, deserted, in the summer dark.

Thank gods the claque had disappeared.

Fireflies flitted here and there, their glow reflected in a winding pool.

It felt quite right for him to put his arm around the girl as they walked.

Just as it felt right, when they stopped to watch a pair of ducks landing in the pond, for him to slip his arms around her waist from the rear.

He felt the warm curve of her buttocks, and his body reacted.

Somehow his hands slid up, cupped her breasts.

She turned in his embrace, and they kissed.

Hal had kissed a few other women since he'd met Khiri. But

nothing more than a single, polite kiss before he stammered about his marriage vows.

He had been unbearably faithful.

And what had it gotten him in return, except, most likely, some women with hurt feelings?

So he kissed Brythnoth again, her tongue flickering in and out of his mouth.

He shouldn't be doing this, he thought.

Why not?

It wasn't like he was married any more.

He woke just at dawn.

His arm was asleep, Brythnoth's head pillowed on it.

He slid out of the covers, walked across the room, took a scrub from his saddlebag, and rubbed at his teeth.

He rinsed his mouth, went back to bed.

Brythnoth was half-covered with only a sheet.

Hal thought of the night before, expecting to feel guilt, indigestion, a hangover.

He felt none of these.

In fact, he felt perfectly damned wonderful.

He considered the sleeping Brythnoth.

She was, indeed, naturally white-blonde.

Thinking of that, he also thought it might be a good idea to kiss her.

She sort of woke, rolled on her back, kissed him back.

As he slid over her, he told his damned ascetic mind to remember what had happened, and stop being so godsdamned self-righteous all the time.

They took off a few hours later.

As Storm climbed, Hal looked back, beyond the town square, at the inn.

The dot that was Brythnoth stood outside, waving frantically.

He wondered if he'd ever see her again, decided it didn't matter, not for her, not for him.

They stopped twice at farmhouses, and, as Yasin had predicted, were the glory of the day.

On the fourth day, they flew over the Yasin grounds. They sprawled for miles, and mostly grew wheat, and table grapes, with the rest of the land given over to self-support.

"It sort of just grew," Yasin had explained, "over generations. Our real land is to the north, almost to the border, and it's said the only thing that can be raised there is sons to grow to be warriors.

"That's very noble, but my great-grandfather also liked to have a full belly, and so he started buying lands down here in the south.

"Little by little, we spent more and more time on these lands, instead of freezing our balls off, making manly poses as we did, up around the border.

"That land had been Roche for only a few generations, and there still were natives who felt they'd been robbed.

"Perhaps they had," he continued. "But we always wondered who they'd stolen the land from in the first place."

The war had cost the Yasin clan dearly.

Bayle's father had died in a duel, "defending Queen Norcia's honor."

Farren had made a wry face, and said, later, to Hal, "So the old man defends the honor, and then that duke, Yasin's brother, proceeds to take it as often as he can get away with."

That brother, Garcao, had been head of the Household Regiments, and rumored to be Norcia's lover. He had then led the group of barons that overthrew Norcia, blaming her for the way the war was going against Roche.

Garcao had died either in the final battle for Carcaor, the capital, or during the interregnum that followed.

Yasin was the only heir.

"Which means, of course," he'd said, "Mother wants me to marry – or, at any rate, breed – as soon as possible, and give up this damned dragon-flying."

Hal had noted that Mother was in capital letters.

He also noted, later, that Yasin never talked about his late brother. He couldn't decide whether Garcao and Bayle had been very close, or not at all.

In any event, Hal, an only child who, as a boy, had often yearned for a brother, thought it very odd.

They landed outside the main house, which was of dark brickwork. The thick walls had been built to withstand a siege, and there were fighting positions in the walls and along the roof.

Low towers dotted the land here and there, to keep off raiders or a full-scale attack.

"My kin, back when we were kids, playing war, would've

peed green for something like that," Mariah said. "Instead, we had to make barricades from crates, and use greengrocers' push-carts for our castles.

"There's no justice in the world."

"What," Cabet asked in astonishment, "ever made you think there was?"

"A man can dream, scheme, can't he?"

Bayle Yasin's mother was, indeed, fearsome. It could well have been her idea to refer to herself in capital letters. She was tall, rigid in her posture, and her gray hair was drawn back in a bun. It was very hard for Hal to imagine her enjoying the marital bed, except as a rather messy way to begin her dynasty.

She actually unbent a little to smile at Farren Mariah, of which he said, later, "Made my damned blood turn to icebergs, thinking she might be crawly jolly into my bedroom. Next time I need to think of somewhat to keep from coming, I'll be sure to let her creep into my mind."

"And lose that soggy erection you've been able to hand-work up?" Cabet asked.

"You're forgetting the war too fast," Mariah said. "Keep to the rigid dignity of a flight commander . . . and in return, I'll not cast a wee spell that'll send the good Lady Yasin into *your* bed."

They were feasted and given their own cottages around the grounds.

Hal busied himself writing a very long letter to Advocate Jabish Attecoti.

He finished, sealed it, found the Yasins' amanuensis, and gave him money to have it sent, via the fastest courier, to Deraine.

Then there was nothing to do but wait.

Until he had word from Attecoti, and found out how much trouble he was in back in Deraine, there was no particular point in planning anything.

There were brick barracks on the estate, and workers trickled in.

It was almost the season for harvesting the wheat, and, before that, bringing in the grapes. Some went on wooden trays, to dry into raisins, but the better reds would be crushed and put in casks, mostly for trading, a little for the estate itself.

Some of the workers came from small local farms, but a lot of them arrived travel-battered, having made the long trek south from the northern lands.

Some, Yasin said, wanted to stay on here, and give up their homes in the north.

Hal, going past the workers' barracks one evening with Yasin, paused, and heard one worker talking.

He, and the rest of his village, had been clearing land for a new settlement. It had almost been a festival, living in tents, with the women and children preparing the meals, while the men cut and burnt the land.

Then the barbarians had struck them.

The worker said he'd hidden in a pile of brush, and they'd overlooked him.

The men had been killed, the children and young women taken off for slaves, and the other women ... The story-teller hesitated, then said that they'd been taken in great cheering orgies by the barbarians.

There'd been half a dozen men who'd lived, all by hiding.

Twice that number of women survived, although three of them "kilt theyselves, outa the shame."

Hal had started to walk on, then noticed the look on Yasin's face.

There was a gleam, as if he'd just heard the call to arms.

That night, Yasin didn't join the other fliers after dinner, but was busy in one of the libraries, writing letters.

Three days later, he left for Carcaor.

A courier brought Hal a letter from Attecoti.

Ironically, it had been brought to Roche's capital, Carcaor, by a commercial dragon-rider, and from there by horse.

I'm sending this by the most rapid method I know of, since I can well understand your desire to be kept current on the events of the day.

First, the matter of your divorce — it is proceeding apace, and, thus far, Lady Carstares and her advocate have presented us with no surprises, or demands that might be deemed outrageous. As per your wishes, I am attempting to keep the entire matter sub rosa, so far with a marked success, although the taletellers have been importuning me for details on your marital dissolution.

I would estimate that the divorcement will be final by the end of this year.

On other matters:

First is the good news. I do not know, nor do I wish to know, the details of your adventure into Sagene. But the ship you purchased, the Galgorm Adventurer, has safely returned, with its entire crew, to Deraine.

I was told, and asked for no details, that the spell proved to be effective. There are some things an advocate should never inquire too fully into.

However, the Sagene ambassador has formally complained to the Royal Court about what he claims to be a wholly illegal act, in that you and some of your friends liberated a criminal, condemned to death, and he wishes all of you to be arrested and returned to Sagene for trial.

This matter I have been unable to keep from the taletellers and, frankly, it's become quite the sensation. I have repeatedly pled ignorance of the entire matter.

However, as I said, the reported involvement of the Dragonmaster in a rather scandulous affair has stayed in the broadsheets, if for no other reason than that there isn't a scandal quite as savory at present.

I have quietly inquired at Court, and been advised that our Royal Highness is not pleased at all. However, it seems that, if there are no further outrages, as he has termed them, the matter will be allowed to die, and it shall not prove necessary to make a response to Sagene.

Unfortunately, it will take some months for that to happen.

My suggestion, based on what I was told, is that you should, and I quote directly from a friend close to King Asir, "remain invisible" at least until the end of the year.

I am most sorry, Lord Kailas, since I assume you wish to return to your lands as soon as possible. But I would suggest the advice should be followed, unless your present situation is completely intolerable. If you must return home, you should be advised of the likelihood of being summoned before the king to answer in this matter, which I cannot recommend against too strongly.

I have taken the liberty of sending a letter of credit to a merchant banker in Carcaor, authorizing him to issue you any specie you may need while in Roche, the sum to be paid by me, from the profits of your estate.

Please stay in touch, and I shall do the same as circumstances develop.

With best wishes,
Jabish Attecoti, Knight

Hal put the letter down thoughtfully. So he was stranded here in Roche for the time being.

He shrugged.

If that was the price he had to pay, so be it.

At least Bodrugan and the men and women of the *Galgorm Adventurer* were safe.

And at least he could now think about being able to stop living off the kindness of strangers.

He guessed that Mariah and the others could return home to Deraine if they wished.

He would be the only expatriate.

And what of that? He couldn't think of anywhere, in Deraine, in Sagene, in Roche, that he regarded as home.

Hal guessed he'd consult that banker in Carcaor for help in finding a place to live.

He'd already, wryly, composed an announcement:

WANTED

By fairly reputable nobleman, if currently somewhat
of a fugitive, a furnished apartment or town house.
Excellent credit and credentials.
Must have room for one companion:
A dragon.
Reply confidentially.

Yasin came back from Carcaor, beaming, as if someone had promised him the moon.

He asked Hal for a moment of his time.

"Lord Kailas," he began, most formally, "I would like to extend an invitation to you, that would involve risk, adventure, and a great deal of flying."

Hal's eyebrows perked.

"After hearing of the depredations the barbarians are making against our northern frontiers, I have spent some time with some friends, and with some of the barons who have holdings in the north.

"I proposed to them, and my plan was quickly approved, that I might be able to do some good in holding back these hordes from the sacred lands of Roche.

"In short, I am going to put together a dragon squadron.

"My idea met with quick approval, since, unknown to me before I met with my friends, several people in the capital had already proposed putting together a military incursion against these savages. As our peace treaty with Deraine forbids increasing the military beyond the paltry garrison units that already exist, this would be paid for and organized by civilians, although run on the strictest rules.

"We will fly north, base ourselves in the city of Trenganu, and provide this armed force with both scouting and fighting potential.

"Since you seem . . . meaning no offense, and considering how much my family and I owe you . . . at, well, a loose end, would you, and any of your friends who feel the same, care to join my enterprise?

"I'll add that, although I'll be commander, you can have my written guarantee that I shall never order or require you or any of your friends to do anything dishonorable."

Hal was jolted out of his own immediate concerns.

"I think," he said, "I could use a brandy to chew on while I mull your offer over."

Yasin hurried Hal to a library, found a decanter of very old brandy, and poured for them both.

Hal took two snifters while he thought, sipping them carefully. Then he nodded.

"Why not?" he said. "Why the hell not?"

7

Hal told his men what he was going to do, said they were free to go, having more than fulfilled their agreement to break Yasin out, and added that he'd give them enough gold to get back to Deraine.

He told them he didn't think the law was after them, in fact most likely didn't even know who they were, but he thought it might be wise to stay out of Sagene for the immediate future.

"I bargained for an adventure," Farren Mariah said. "Plus mayhap a little madness. And chasing wild men about the great northern tundra sounds like both.

"I'll stick with you, Dragonmaster.

"'Sides, you'll need somebody to cover your wrinkly ass."

The other two made the same choice, although it took until

the next day, and Hal thought Calt Beoyard seemed a little hesitant.

But when Hal took him aside, he said he'd made his mind up, and sounded much firmer about his decision.

Yasin was delighted to have them, and said that if Hal knew any other Derainians who might be interested, he'd be proud to add them to the company as well.

Hal thought about writing some letters, but, since he still hadn't heard from Manus, the inquiry agent, he decided not.

He was dimly aware that something was niggling at him, keeping from recruiting any of his ex-fliers, although he didn't think it was the idea of operating with the Roche.

Kailas set the matter aside.

He had more than enough to do, getting ready for another war.

The first step was moving to Carcaor, which Hal looked forward to. Yasin's estate might be luxurious, and his mother assured them they'd always have a home, but it was a bit too far out of the world.

Besides, Hal had to admit to himself that Yasin's mother made him almost as nervous as she did Mariah.

Summer was drawing to an end, and there was a gray drizzle coming down as they overflew Carcaor.

The great Roche capital was a near-total ruin. Here and there were the enormous craters caused by Kailas' and other dragon squadron leaders' sorcerous casting of pebbles that grew into boulders.

Large parts of the city were blackened, fired by either the dragon raids, the final battle, or the crowds rioting in the madness of defeat and despair.

Hal noticed the other fliers were looking at him, couldn't decipher their expressions, looked away.

Even though the remnants of Roche's army were not involved with Yasin, still he'd managed to get permission to use their dragon barracks and handlers.

The terms of the surrender forbade the army to have more than two scouting squadrons of dragons, both deployed on the southern border, and a tiny fliers' school, so there was more than room enough in the half-ruined stables for Storm and the other three dragons.

That done, they set out to look for quarters.

It didn't take long, with Yasin's reputation as a hero.

One of Carcaor's main hotels, the huge Muab, although missing one wing, offered Yasin an entire floor for gratis.

They moved in that afternoon, each man getting a somewhat palatial suite.

The main restaurant maintained its grandeur, even though the city's water system was irregular, and sometimes ran brown.

But that certainly didn't bother any of the fliers, used as they were to privation.

The Roche loved heavy meals, and so it was at the Muab. That night, dinner was a river fish course, a wild boar in some sort of sauce, and a many-layered cake. Side dishes included various noodles and peppery sauces.

Sure that he was about to go under, especially after watching the bottomless pit of Farren Mariah gorge himself, Hal decided to go for a walk.

Yasin swore they were probably in no danger, even being Derainians, but all four carried their service daggers at their waists. Hal thought about carrying a sword as well, decided he was just as good at running as dueling.

Carcaor was even more of a ruin up close. Some of the streets were still blocked with rubble from the stonings, and many of the businesses not burnt out were boarded up.

The people were dressed shabbily, their eyes bare of hope.

A few streets still were lit, but not many.

"Damned good idea, this walky, and all," Mariah said to Hal. "As if I wasn't downcast frowncast enough already."

"I think we should be thinking about a drink," Hal said.

"Excellent thought, fearless leader," Mariah said, bowing toward an entrance.

They heard cheers, laughter as they entered, saw a low circular stage, surrounded by tables. The customers were well-dressed, fat, contented-looking, and their women were young and overdressed, or the age of their companions and laden with jewelry.

Yasin frowned, leaned closer to Hal.

"Black marketeers."

Hal had already recognized them for what they were. Deraine had the same sort of greedyguts.

It shouldn't bother him, here in Roche, once an enemy country. Black marketeers did almost as much to lose a war as a hostile army did to win it.

The entertainment was a rather threadbare magician.

They found seats, ordered drinks, jolted at the price of them.

"One and then we're for the cheapside," Calt Beoyard whispered.

Hal nodded.

The magician noted the four, most unlike the other customers.

"Ah," he said, "fresh blood, so a fresh trick."

He thought a minute, then waved his arms in an elaborate pattern, muttering a spell under his breath.

"Summer's almost gone," he said, more loudly. "And spring is just a memory. But something to think on, something to remember . . ."

He extended his hands, palms up.

There was a breath of a fresh wind in the club, blowing away the fumes of stale beer and musky perfume, growing a bit stronger, with the scent of fresh flowers.

It was as if the floor had become newly turned dirt, and flowers of many hues rose up around the tables. There was the chitter of birdsong, and flashes of bright color.

From nowhere, a butterfly appeared over their table, and darted to a safe landing on Yasin's nose.

There was laughter.

Yasin frowned, not finding this worthy of the dignity of a Roche officer, but kept trying to focus on the butterfly, which clung fast.

Mariah gasped with laughter at the cross-eyed Roche.

At last, Yasin's humor, little as it was, caught up with him, and he laughed more loudly than anyone.

Quite suddenly, the illusion vanished.

There was applause, and people cast money at the stage.

"I thank you," the magician said. "And that last took work, so I'll ask your help in what I am going to do next.

"I'm going to bring forth an animal. Your favorite animal.

"Think hard on its breed, its colors.

"The most powerful thought will carry the day."

"Uh-oh," Mariah said. "Don't anybody think of dragons."

The magician stepped off the stage, and waited.

The air shimmered.

And, quite predictably, especially with Farren Mariah's caution, a huge beast emerged on the stage, overfilling it.

The magician darted away, just as the dragon blatted, its tail sweeping across the club.

Hal ducked as the tail came at them, passed through them harmlessly, and the dragon, its breath quite authentic, screamed again.

"We're for the street!" Cabet shouted, and the four made for the exit.

The dragon-wraith looked after them, and honked in a lonely fashion.

They decided to stay with the street for a time.

Streetwalkers were out ... more than Hal had ever seen before, even in the morally relaxed city of Fovant.

Some were clearly professionals, with a practised patter, and in various costumes, from farm girls to skin-tight black silk.

Others had clearly been driven to whoring by poverty. These women clung to the shadows, and timidly tried to smile when someone caught their eye.

Mariah was the first to notice that the costumed doxies seemed to flock to their own – a street all of milkmaids, another one with female soldiers, a third with garishly painted boys.

"Ah," he said. "The Roche love to be organized in their decadence, don't they?"

Yasin frowned at him.

"I don't understand."

"No," Mariah said. "A man with a butterfiggle on his nose wouldn't."

He started laughing, and Yasin was even more perplexed.

"Now, this should be harmless enough," Cabet said. "A nice puppet theater."

Three schoolgirls went in before them, under the puppets dangling from strings, and Hal wondered what sort of parents would let their daughters out this late, in this part of town.

He quickly found out.

The puppets inside were large, almost lifesize, and their manipulators were hidden behind a curtain.

And they were, for the most part, naked, and performing as lewd a playlet as anything imaginable.

Hal was surprised that he was still capable of being shocked.

His shock grew when he realized that there were many "schoolgirls" sitting around the room, ranging from barely pubescent to in their twenties, all costumed as if for the schoolyard.

The male patrons of the room were mostly middle-aged, many of them with women on their laps.

One girl got up, and sashayed toward the fliers, swinging her hips.

She "accidentally" flipped her skirt up for an instant, revealing that she wore nothing underneath.

"That's enow for me," Mariah said. "I think it's past my bedtime," and he headed back out.

Hal, Cabet and Yasin started to follow him. Hal noticed that Calt Beoyard was staring at the girl as if hypnotized.

"You . . . you go on," he managed. "I'll catch up to you later."

Beoyard seemed to have entered another world. Hal shrugged and left.

Outside, Mariah was shaking his head.

"And I thought nothing could get to me," he said. "Those—"

He broke off, seeing an elderly man, wearing the worn uniform of a high-ranking Roche officer, beribboned and medalled, glowering at them, lips pursed, clearly aware of what the puppet show consisted.

"Disgusting," Mariah said, pretending utter shock. "No wonder they lost the war. There's naught in there but former generals."

Yasin didn't find that funny, but the other three did.

The old man flushed, and strode on as if he had a halberd up his ass.

They went back to their hotel, had a nightcap and went to bed.

After due thought the next day, Hal decided that Carcaor's night-time pleasures were a little rich for his blood, although Beoyard kept returning to the puppet show club night after night.

Hal spent most of his time at the stables, taking care of Storm.

Cabet and Mariah frequently joined him.

The hotel filled with recruits to Yasin's unit, some scarred and most experienced, others not much more than schoolboys who'd somehow learned to fly the monsters.

Eventually there were thirty beasts, and twenty fliers signed on, when Yasin decided they had enough to fight, and, without much ceremony, ordered his troops north.

"Autumn's here, and so, instead of heading south, we fly north," Farren said. "You can easy tell we're about sojering."

8

The long flight north was cold, and grew colder. They stopped at cities along the way, and were greeted with adulation.

Hal wondered if Yasin could be that much of a national hero, then found he'd sent riders north, weeks earlier, advising various city fathers of his route.

It seemed a little dishonest to Hal, but he decided that to feel like that was ludicrous. Didn't kings, after all, send criers in front when they visited the countryside?

Remembering what campaigning was and would be like, Kailas relaxed and enjoyed being made much of.

The Derainians, for some odd reason, seemed especially popular, even though they'd been Roche's enemies.

He didn't much like it, though, when some hero-worshippers, obviously in their cups, mumbled about Deraine finally learning what was right, by helping to keep the less-than-men from their borders.

But again, it really didn't matter.

All that did matter was that he retired at night, very full of choice cookery, to a warm, comfortable bed, and it was seldom empty.

What more could a field soldier want?

Yasin caught Farren Mariah casting a spell to predict the forthcoming weather, and thereafter treated Mariah most cautiously.

"He's even more spooky goosey than you are about wizardry," Farren chortled to Hal.

A week and a half after leaving Carcaor, they landed in Trenganu.

It was the rawest of frontier towns. The streets, such as they were, were unpaved, and turned to mudholes any time there was more than a heavy dew. There was one main street, with meandering alleys debouching from it.

Of course, there were no building restrictions, so a stable was next to a church next to an ironmongery.

They called it a city, but it was no more than a small town, with a population, including the expeditionary force, hunters and trappers, of about four thousand. There were no suburbs – Trenganu just stopped at a perimeter of farms, and then there was half-cut secondary timberland to untouched forest.

The close presence of the "natives," "barbarians," "barbs," here on "the edges of nothing," meant almost everyone went armed at all times.

It wasn't that much of an affectation – the natives were known for daring cross-border raids. Come in, hit hard, and pull back with slaves and loot.

Their warriors could run down a horse, especially one with an armored rider, gut the horse, then slit the rider's throat, and loot and strip him, before the animal stopped screaming.

Their magicians weren't much more than witches, but they had the advantage of numbers, of knowing the local herbs and power concentrations, and the Roche had very few magicians with them.

The natives showed no mercy to anyone. Women were ravaged, and the older ones killed, as were all men. Children of both sexes were made into slaves, the males after being hamstrung, to ensure they'd never be fighters if they were ransomed or freed.

The supposedly civilized Roche took their own slaves on the few occasions they could find a "barb" camp.

Yasin had already hired grooms, groundsmen, guards, servants, and the like, who had made the laborious journey north in clattering wagons, and they'd commandeered a drafty hall that had been a farmers' association for the unit headquarters.

The dragons were housed in sheds that had been intended for livestock shows.

The dragon-fliers themselves, though, were given quarters in inns appropriated by Yasin.

One man, a supply warrant, complained about fliers always having it soft, and Yasin hauled him up in front of the entire formation.

"Yes," he hissed, "the fliers are special. And they'll be treated the same as long as we're fighting.

"Because you'll notice that not only do they get all of the glory and all of the comfort, but they do all of the dying, as well."

He drove the lesson home by having the warrant stripped of his uniform, and literally kicked out of the city.

There were even uniforms for the squadron.

Someone – Hal hoped not Yasin – had found dark gray

uniforms that looked like they'd been intended for ushers. But they wouldn't stand out in the field, and that was more important than gilt and glitter, and better still, they were warm.

Trenganu crawled with uniforms, most of local design. But there were more than enough wearing Roche colors for Hal to realize that whatever military limitations the treaty with Sagene and Deraine had called for, the treaty provisions were dead letters.

Some of these men were volunteers, looking for adventure and blood. Others, particularly the more senior ones, were "observers," sent by the Roche government.

And some of the "volunteers" seemed very much part of assorted formations.

But officially, there was only one expeditionary force, led by a General Arbala.

Yasin said he was one of the better commanders from the war, known for leading from the front, yet without getting himself mired in the trivia of a skirmish and losing the battle.

He was young and scarred, and when Hal first saw him, and heard him speak, he reminded him of his late friend, Bab Cantabri.

The thought made him wonder what was going on with his divorce, and with life in general back in Deraine.

But there were more immediate matters to take care of.

Yasin broke the twenty fliers down into four flights of five, making sure there were at least two inexperienced fliers in each group.

"I know," he told Hal, "you flew in groups of three in the war. Too small to be effective if you got hit, too large to be unobtrusive."

Hal decided he disagreed, but didn't care one way or another. He was willing to try Yasin's tactics, so welcomed two novices to his "flight."

The next step was to figure out just exactly what the squadron's mission would be.

Yasin said the dragons would be used to provide intelligence, and not aerial fighting. There didn't seem to be any dragon-riding natives.

At least, not yet.

Cabet worried about whether the barbarians could also be hiring mercenary fliers – there were certainly enough out-of-work dragon-riders between Roche, Sagene and Deraine.

"Not to worry," Farren said. "The natives don't appear to have gold, and there's naught else to trade, except ox fur or hide or whatever they cover themselves with."

"Young slaves," Beoyard suggested.

"But who'd be the buyer?" Hal wondered. "I don't see anybody rolling in silver who's interested in crippled children around here."

No one had an answer, and so Kailas set out, with Yasin's blessing, to find out what Arbala's headquarters really knew about their enemy, the mysterious forest natives.

Almost nothing was the immediate answer. They were bold, big, and bad, which fit almost all enemies worth fighting.

As far as tactics, size of formation, leadership went . . . nothing seemed known. Yasin's unit was working utterly virgin territory.

Having heard stories about how the barbarians treated their prisoners, Kailas found a witch, had her make up doses of fast-acting poison, and found thin neck chains for them to hang on.

There weren't many takers among the fliers.

Most of them, including Hal himself, were self-assured enough to think that they'd never get taken prisoner, or, if they did, that they could somehow escape before they ended up in the torturers' hands.

He put his team aloft, well behind the "lines," such as they were, practising not the expected formation flying, but observation – learning to search the ground for possible ambush sites, small units of men, camouflaged positions, and the like.

Remembering his own first flights in combat, and how virginal he'd been, he took them east and north of Trenganu, into relatively safe territory, looking for barbarians.

The natives helped at first, by volleying arrows up at any dragons they saw carrying men, then learned they evidently meant no harm.

Little by little, his fliers, and the others being trained by Yasin similarly, got as good as they were able without having flown in a fighting war.

The ground formations having been brought into some kind of shape by General Arbala and his officers, the first operation was planned.

It wasn't very spectacular in design – the expeditionary force was ordered to march north-east, looking for natives.

They should have set off at dawn, but it was mid-morning of a sunny autumnal day before they left Trenganu.

Yasin's dragon squadron was airborne, flying back and forth over the horsemen and infantrymen.

Hal took his own flight ahead of the forward skirmishers.

Yasin had briefed the fliers that Arbala's plan for this day was no more than a shaking-out of the troops. They would march a certain number of leagues, make camp, then return, via a different route, the next day.

While he'd been talking, he kept glancing, worriedly, at Hal, which Hal couldn't figure out.

Then he realized that Yasin was dreadfully worried that he would be angered – how dare Yasin tell anyone of Hal's rank what to do?

He was about to laugh, then realised that Yasin was putting himself in his place, and that if the situation were reversed, Yasin would be most irked. Then the matter became much less humorous.

But ignoring all the fripperies, it was nice to be in the air. Storm honked in pure glee, diving and darting to and fro, and several of the other dragons seemed equally sportive.

Kailas saw his two novices getting into the spirit of the day, and blasted a warning on his trumpet, pointing down, reminding them this wasn't a lark they were on.

The army was closing on a steep bluff. Hal swooped low over it, and saw, crouched behind boulders, at least twenty of the enemy, waiting in ambush.

He circled back, low over the nearest skirmishers, and blew a warning.

Evidently the riders hadn't been told of Hal's purpose, because the scattered formation didn't change, still keeping its flank to the bluff.

Hal cursed, pondered.

Then he swirled Storm down, and down, bringing him in for a landing just in front of the horsemen.

There was a young officer goggling at him.

"You, dammit!" Hal bellowed. "'Ware your front, sir! Archers in ambush!"

The officer gaped at the bluff, which appeared deserted.

"But I've orders—"

"Damn your orders, sir!" Hal shouted, realizing he was sounding very much like Lord Cantabri, and the thought almost made him start laughing.

The officer clearly didn't know what to do.

The situation was resolved by one native, who arched an arrow high that clattered off Storm's armor.

Other bowmen followed suit, and that was enough for the skirmishers.

They rode directly toward the bluff, and three or four were cut down by arrows.

Then the horsemen overrode the archers, who ducked and fled, leaving a couple of bodies behind.

The man leading the skirmishers should have held his troops in place, and sent one man back to the main formation for reinforcements.

That would, should, have meant that no casualties would have been taken.

But the officer would learn that on his own – if he survived the next few encounters.

That evening, Hal was in the stables, burnishing and trimming Storm's talons, when Yasin sought him out.

He had half a smile.

"I have a complaint about you, Lord Kailas."

"From that young idiot."

Young idiot . . . Hal shook his head in amusement. Thinking someone was young, when he was but . . . what? Just turning thirty?

But how old in battle-knowledge?

"Yes," Yasin said. "That young idiot – who happens to be Duke someone's eldest son – went to General Arbala.

"The general told me about it, thinking the matter was a capital jest, and assigned the little duke to ride in the train for a few days to eat dust and learn."

Hal was mildly surprised.

He'd expected Yasin to take him to task, as he'd expected General Arbala to have torn strips off Yasin for letting one of his men dare, dare, to swear at nobility.

This expeditionary force wasn't behaving like a regular army.

Nor did it the next day.

Unfortunately.

Hal had been meandering about the skies, watching the troops move back toward Trenganu, when he saw something interesting.

It was a group of light infantrymen, chasing some barbarian men, killing one here, one there.

It looked, from Kailas's elevation, like men chasing children.

Hal shook his head at the lack of proper perspective, swung lower, and realized, with a sharp shock, that there was nothing wrong with his viewpoint.

The soldiers *were* chasing children, whooping every time they took one down, the attacker pausing to drive a sword into the youngster's back.

Hal should have minded his own business, if for no other reason than that he had certainly killed his share of women and children, stoning cities.

But he didn't, coming in for a skittered landing, and sliding off Storm in front of the pack.

"Halt, you!"

The lead soldier called an obscenity, lifted his sword.

Hal put a crossbow bolt between his feet, and the man slid to a stop.

"We don't kill babies in this army," he shouted.

The men looked at him sullenly.

"They killed Barthus!" one tried.

"Then Barthus must've deserved killing," Hal said. "For not being much of a soldier, letting a child attack him."

"They ain't proper kids, but demons," an older man said. "Learn killing from their mothers' milk."

There was a clamor of agreement.

Hal glanced over his shoulder, to see Farren Mariah orbiting just over his head.

There was no sign of the children.

They seemed to have vanished into a low, brush-covered hillside.

"Get back to the column," he ordered.

There was no point in arguing with a superior officer, who'd already spoiled the game.

Muttering, the men obeyed his order.

Hal, feeling very much the self-righteous do-gooder, climbed back aboard Storm, and prodded him into a takeoff run.

They lifted away over that hillside.

As they did, a stone hurtled up, almost taking Hal in the leg.

That figured.

That evening, they came back to Trenganu.

Yasin gave the squadron the day off.

For the next day, Hal planned a critique of what had happened, which should sit well with a hangover, then time in the stables with the dragons.

But it didn't work out that way.

He was just coming out of the mess tent, trying not to think about the watery eggs, fried bread, and half-cured ham he'd eaten, remembering other, superior meals on the trip north, when he saw smoke rising beyond the city, to the south-west.

He wondered, decided to go see, and, even if it was unimportant, to make his flight aware that nothing in war could ever be planned.

Keeping track of how long it took, Hal ordered his men into the air.

The two new Roche did as best they could – Hal's Derainians were quite used to days that started like this, as were their dragons.

In ten minutes, they were in the air, the last storesman clattering crossbow bolts into the quivers tied to the dragons' carapaces as they waited to take off.

Hal had issued no orders other than to take the five-fingers formation on takeoff that Yasin preferred.

They were out of the pawky outskirts of Trenganu, and over partially cleared forest in minutes, homing on the smoke.

It came from a farming estate – a group of buildings clustered together for mutual protection, their fields spreading on all sides.

Beyond the houses were the barns, and two of these were burning.

There were bodies scattered in the central farmyard, and, even at this height, Hal heard women's screams. He saw half a dozen natives dragging farm women toward a hay rick, which they evidently intended for a bedroom.

Hal remembered that farm worker's story, back on Yasin's estates, and sharply tapped the back of Storm's head.

The dragon obediently went into a dive.

Hal blasted twice on his trumpet for the others to follow him.

He didn't know, didn't care, how many native raiders were down there.

He brought Storm out of the dive just above the ground, and came in over the farmyard.

Storm didn't need orders.

His talons reached out, took a pair of barbarians, and hurled them against the ground, as his fangs shredded another pair.

Hal brought him back in a sharp bank, as Storm's tail lashed across the ground not a dozen feet below.

From an outbuilding ran men, farmers, emboldened by the

dragon strike, attacking the natives with flails, scythes, a sword here and there, pitchforks.

A bearded patriarch was grabbed from behind by a dagger-waving warrior.

Hal put a crossbow bolt neatly into the man's armpit. As he did so, he heard a warning shout, and Cabet, reins clenched in his teeth, crossbow aiming, almost ran into Storm.

The other Derainians had done this sort of thing before. They came in hard, and the battle swirled over the farmyard.

Then the natives broke, running, and Storm went after them, gleefully tearing at them as they went.

It was certain death if they looked back, but they did, terrified of the pursuing horror.

Forest loomed, and Hal pulled Storm up. The dragon whined in protest at losing some of his prey.

They flew back to the farm, and this time, Hal brought Storm down.

Storm folded his wings, and Hal went looking for barbarians.

One broke out of a hut, and fired an arrow at the dragon, which bounced harmlessly off his carapace.

Storm took the man in his jaws, and neatly bit him in half, then spat him out.

A barbarian, wounded, stumbled out, dazed, eyes wide in terror, and one of the farmers spitted him on a pitchfork.

Another was trying to run, and a handful of women were on him, clawing, kicking. He went down, rolled, and a very fat woman dropped a small grinding stone on his head.

Then there was nobody left to kill, and nothing but the moans of the wounded Roche.

Mariah landed his dragon beside Storm, and slid out of the saddle, as one of the two new fliers did the same.

The new man was gazing at Hal with worshipful eyes.

Mariah shattered the mood.

"You're starting again, aren't you?" he said, angrily. "Playing hero . . . and you promised me."

Hal, breathing hard, was still looking for men to kill.

His breathing slowed, and he managed a smile.

"I'm sorry, Farren."

"I remember before," Mariah said. "Got me all speared and bloody and nasty.

"Don't be doing that any more, fearless leader. Or I'll put a spell of . . . of creepy spidgers in your drawers."

Kailas noted the shock on the young flier's face, and started laughing.

"Gods-damned glory-dog," Mariah growled.

9

The rescue of the farmers was made much of in Trenganu. There was talk of medals for Hal's flight.

He wanted none, having more than his share already.

"We could hold out for prize money," suggested Mariah, who also had his share of geegaws.

Hal didn't need any of that, and spent a morose hour wondering what, exactly, he did want.

Of course, the two Roche in the flight were ecstatic about the turn of events.

"Enjoy it now," Mariah said. "The only reason we're being lauded & 'plauded is first it's early in the war, which is always the best time to make your name fame, and second because nothing much is happening right now.

"In theory," he said, "there shouldn't be, either. We should be taking up winter quarters. But five against a goat we'll be parading out on a campaign any day now.

"Why'd you think General Arbarbabarbarala had us fartle out and then back?

"Just because we need a little exercise?

"Believe that, and I'll sell you valuababble real estate in Fovant."

Mariah was right.

Yasin was called in by the general, and told to make his squadron ready for a winter campaign, to march north along the coast, where there were reported barbarian villages to take and hold.

Yasin was passing enthusiastic to Hal.

"That'll push the barbs back to where they're supposed to be, and let our people come in and open up the wilderness."

"Why does Roche need any more land than what it's got?" Hal wondered. "Seems that the war left a lot of the land open, unworked."

"By next generation," Yasin said, "we'll have filled all that up, and be crying for new land for our people."

Hal almost asked if that wasn't the excuse the late Queen Norcia had used for starting the last war, but kept his mouth shut. If Roche decided they wanted all that tundra that lay to the north, let them take it, and contend with the oxen and the wild dragons.

He busied himself making sure that Yasin's supply section was buying winter coats, high boots, stable blankets for the dragons, all the things that generals didn't seem to think of until the first winter storm.

And seasons changed quickly this far to the north.

Which brought the first calamity.

The expeditionary force headquarters had been located in one of the city's few great houses. It was built of wood, and strangely styled after some of the stone mansions Hal had seen the ruins of in Carcaor.

Yasin had been kept late at a planning session, and was still preoccupied when he left, around midnight.

There'd been a rainstorm, turning into hail, and then cold winds.

The water on the wooden steps had frozen.

Yasin was pulling on his coat, a bit off-balance, when he came down the steps.

He slipped, tried to recover, and pinwheeled down the flight.

Soldiers came to help him up, but his scream made them stop.

He was barely conscious, and had Hal sent for.

By the time he arrived, Yasin had been given herbs and a spell, and was fighting to stay awake.

"What a bastardly thing," he growled, pointing at splints on his chest and legs. "They say I'll be wearing these for at least four months, and want me to go back south, for more expert care.

"Afraid I'll lose my leg, they are. Which I surely won't let them take."

Hal waited.

"So I'm out of any campaign until spring, godsdammit!

"Lord Kailas, will you take over the squadron? You're about the only one I really trust. And I'll try to recruit more fliers and dragons for you."

There really wasn't any choice.

No doubt they could find another dragon-flier or, worse yet, put in some cavalry sort. Hal had seen what that produced.

Feeling very unhappy, he nodded.

"Yes. I'll take command."

And that was the last he saw of Yasin.

Later, Hal was very glad to have seen the back of him.

General Arbala was most concerned that Kailas could handle the job. Hal explained, trying not to sound superior, that he had handled squadrons of squadrons in the war, and doubted he'd have any troubles.

All that was necessary was to find the barbarians, and let the general and the forward elements of the expeditionary force know.

The natives hadn't any dragons of their own, and so far their magic wasn't very potent.

Arbala's strategy was quite simple, with no subtleties kept hidden from the common troops – march north-east along the coast, striking at every barbarian camp they encountered. Drive the savages back north, with tales of the valor of the Roche, so they'd never leave their damned wasteland again.

Hal came out of the meeting somewhat less than impressed with the general than before. He might have been a fighter, but he didn't seem much of a thinker.

And battles may be won by fighters.

But intelligence and cunning are what wins wars.

His opinion was reinforced when a light cavalry unit was sent out on a vague patrol to find out "what's out there," without a more concrete plan, or, worse, any troops detailed for their backup.

They encountered a native patrol who, seemingly, panicked at the sight of the brave Roche cavalrymen, and fled, conveniently into broken country.

The cavalry went in hot pursuit.

About four times their strength was lying in wait. The cavalry, hit hard, retreated to the nearest hilltop, and sent a pair of riders for help.

Amazingly, one horseman made it back to Trenganu, and bleated for support.

But it was getting late, and no fool would move out of the city by night.

At first light, a handful of heavy cavalry went out, with banners and bugles.

Corpses need neither, and that was what met the relief

expedition. All of the light horsemen were dead, creatively mutilated.

General Arbala swore, tears in his eyes, on his own sword, that the Roche would revenge the dead.

But that didn't seem to bring any of them back.

Fall brought rains and mud, seldom freezing, over the axles of some of the wagons.

The expeditionary force would have to wait until the first thorough freeze, when the weather would be better suited for modern war.

In the meantime, the scribes descended on Trenganu, entranced with the idea of a Derainian war hero fighting for Roche.

Hal managed to duck most of these awestruck fools.

But there was one he couldn't.

Aimard Quesney, dragon-flier and one-time war objector, showed up at the tiny room Hal used as an office, with a covering letter from Sir Thom Lowess saying Quesney was his representative.

His huge mustaches were larger than ever, and he seemed as morally sure of himself as when Hal had sat over him in a court-martial.

"I convinced Lowess to write that letter," Quesney said, "and I'll write something in the style I know he wants when I get back to Deraine.

"But all that's piffle, and hardly the reason I came east."

Hal waited.

"You did, as you told me at the time, save my life, although being adjudged insane may not be the prettiest way to do it.

"But I still owe you greatly.

"Your man, Manus, found me, just as I was about to enter the priesthood.

"At first, I had no intention of re-establishing contact with you . . . it's very clear our paths aren't meant to be coincidental.

"But I owe you, and, when I heard you'd taken service with Roche, I had to find you, and, perhaps, return a little of the favor.

"First, though, I approached your advocate, and was told your divorce is final, and your estates are doing very well."

"Thank you for taking the time," Hal said.

"I did it because I wasn't sure how I was going to say what I'm intending.

"But what the advocate told me wasn't of any particular help.

"Lord Kailas, have you gone completely off your head?"

Hal was taken aback. No one had talked to the Dragonmaster like that since ... since, well, the last time he'd had a conversation with Farren Mariah.

The situation struck him as funny, and he started laughing.

He got up and went to the sideboard, poured a shot of the raw spirits the people of Trenganu hopefully called brandy, and took it to Quesney.

"Unless you've gotten so pure you don't indulge in anything?"

Quesney took the glass.

"In Roche – and with this abysmal weather – I drink like a watering dragon."

He knocked the glass back, held it out for a refill as Hal filled one for himself.

"I didn't expect that reaction," Quesney said. "I thought you'd be too full of your rank ... sorry, your former rank ... and would have me tossed out of here on my ass."

Hal sat back down.

"All right," he said. "So I'm a fool.

"Explain."

"I think," Quesney said, "that you've gotten so in love with war, with fighting, that you'll take anything that promises excitement.

"That's a good way to get yourself killed, Kailas."

Hal nodded reluctantly.

"Breaking Yasin out of prison – yes, the street stories are very explicit – was bad enough.

"But helping these sorry excuses that call themselves Roche to grab real estate is pretty raw, you know. Hardly worthy of a great war hero and such."

Hal sat up, eyes wide.

"It was my understanding that the *barbarians* are the ones grabbing land."

"Which was theirs in the first place," Quesney said. "Before the war, the Roche were moving north toward the tundra, seizing land the natives had traditionally thought their own, even though it was kept open for hunting, not planted and plowed.

"The Roche stopped their land grab for the most part during the war, but now the old fever for living space has taken them once more."

"I had a letter from a man named Garadice who went north,

looking for dragons," Hal said. "He told me the natives were moving south."

"Probably," Quesney agreed. "It gets cold up there, they tell me. And if the Roche are being their usual lovable selves and grabbing everything they can, why should the natives not try to get back some of the stolen land?

"Don't believe me," he said. "Ask around."

"I shall," Hal said. "Now that you've carried your message of woe and stupidity, would you like to hang around the squadron? It might remind you of the old days."

"It might," Quesney said, finishing his drink. "That's what I'm afraid of.

"No. I've done what I said I would, and given you a warning, not about getting yourself killed, but about losing your soul. I'll get the next fishing smack back west, toward Paestum, and then to Deraine."

"And your priesthood?"

Quesney nodded, started for the door.

"You know," he said, "I'm sort of sorry that I changed, or else that things did around us.

"I might have liked serving under you, on a squadron, at one time."

He shook his head.

"Thereby proving that the first loss you have as a dragon-flier is what little sense the gods gifted you with."

The army might have been waiting for the weather to change, but not Hal or his dragons. He took two flights out a day. Not at regular intervals, remembering the idiocy of a certain, now deceased, squadron commander, who used to send his dragons out like clockwork, so the enemy simply hid under a tree at the appointed hours, then continued on with their tasks.

The flights went out at roughly dawn and dusk.

Each of the new fliers was given a chance to lead a five finger flight – Hal kept Yasin's formations, since the squadron had begun by using them.

When they came back, each flier was mercilessly grilled about what he had seen, and what went unobserved.

Hal frequently sent one flight out after another, then gave the two formations a chance to compare notes.

And he regularly led not only his own flight, but each of the others, evaluating his men carefully.

He wondered why there weren't any women with the dragons, and decided that either the Roche men were stupid in ignoring potential talent, or, more likely, that Roche women had more sense than to want to tootle around on a monster's back when icicles hung from its carapace.

He always tried to approach the enemy in a direction they weren't expecting, such as a dogleg out to sea from Trenganu, turning north-east for a time, then circling back over the lines, such as they were.

He'd barely taken off one dawn when Cabet, who was flying point, blasted a signal at him and pointed down.

They were just over the beach, and the Northern Sea's waves crashed sullenly below.

Rolling in the surf were the bodies of three dragons.

Hal took Storm lower, flew slowly over the corpses.

They'd been dead for a time, and the seabirds had been at them.

Storm bleated unhappily.

Kailas supposed he didn't like being reminded of his mortality any more than a human did.

These dragons had been sorely wounded, torn and gouged, and the wounds looked to be some months old.

Hal remembered dragons, seen from the battlements of Khiri's castle, below on the water with their wings furled over their bodies, heads tucked out of sight, looking like so many paper boats, being carried from the unknown west by the currents.

Many of them were injured, or young, and behaved as if they were fleeing something.

He wondered again what monsters had sent them into flight, monsters worse than the ominous dragons themselves. Demons, perhaps.

But no one had ever offered a clue.

He pulled Storm up, and the flight went on with its mission.

Three days later, as snow stubbornly refused to fall, although it was freezing, and Hal was very glad he'd chivvied the supply sections for proper warm clothing, they saw something quite unbelievable.

He had led a deep penetration out, and was perhaps two days' flight above Trenganu, flying just a bit inland, over rolling scrub forest.

He was looking down, and caught, in the corner of his eye, movement below.

He looked more closely, saw nothing.

He signaled for his flight to fly in a single line, and took them low.

He was in front, Farren Mariah had the rear.

Four dragons passed over the area without incident, then someone below must have been driven to rashness, and three arrows came up, missing Mariah by yards.

Hal was ready to circle back to see exactly what enemy forces lay below, when he saw, on a hilltop, what looked like an encampment, tents of brown cloth, matching the landscape.

Closer, and he saw men, around smokeless fires.

He chanced going lower, and a javelin came up, touched Storm's forward leg, fell back.

Hal took his flight back up, in a circle, while he shouted orders.

Then they dove back down again, ignoring the arrows, counting the enemy.

"How many barbs did you see?" General Arbala's chief of staff asked.

"I'm not sure," Hal said. "I'd guess about a thousand, maybe two.

"And one hill back was another group of them, maybe a little larger.

"We tried a sweep due east, found three more clusters, tribes maybe."

Arbala looked skeptical.

"We've never heard of the natives grouping up like that," he said.

The chief of staff shook his head.

"Not at all."

One of Arbala's officers laughed. "If they are dumb enough to knot up, they'll be all the easier to kill, now won't they?"

Arbala joined his laughter.

"Spoken like a true firebrand. And you're exactly right. And even if they are there, which I frankly doubt, how long, with the winter coming on, will they be able to hold?

"Savages are savages, and that's why we Roche rule the land!

"In less than a week we'll be ready to take them on . . . and if they want to stand around and wait, so much the better!"

Hal kept a frozen smile on his face, got out of Arbala's headquarters.

Back at the hall, he assembled the squadron.

"I want every man prepared to move within an hour's notice. That means packs ready, everything not in use in the wagons.

"Every flier is to keep an emergency pack, with rations, water, spare clothes, and a meal of dried meat for the dragons, at hand at all times."

Calt Beoyard came up to him.

"What are you expecting, sir?"

"Everything. Nothing," Hal answered honestly.

Hal feared that the natives might be laying huge ambushes, waiting for the expeditionary force to move out of Trenganu, and memorized what maps there were that showed what lay immediately beyond the town.

His strategic predictions were quite wrong.

Four days later, the barbarians moved first, and came out of the forests, wave after wave of them, with fire and the ax, intending to destroy Trenganu and everyone in it.

10

They came just at false dawn, having silently moved close to Trenganu in the night, in the rain. The sentries weren't expecting an attack, and it was far easier to crouch by a picket fire than walk the rounds.

The outposts and outer guards died to a man, and the natives pressed their attack.

The first Roche out of their barracks were cut down, and then the shouts of battle and men dying roused the town.

General Arbala's staff ran for their posts.

Which was just what the barbarians wanted.

No one ever knew how they figured out where the command center was: if it was magic, a spy among the "tame" natives, or careful reconnaissance.

But earlier that morning, a hand-picked team of barbarians had slipped through the lines, and hidden in one of Trenganu's abandoned shacks.

Seconds after the general arrived at the center, so did the natives.

They slashed their way through the still half-asleep sentries, killing as they went.

Arbala, his entire staff, and a good percentage of his commanders, as well as more than half of the observers from Roche's army, died in the first few minutes of the battle.

Hal rolled out of his bunk, his mind still asleep, but his well-trained body grabbing for a sword and his pants, wondering with part of his mind why men were so afraid of being naked.

He stuffed his feet into boots, and, bare-chested, ran out of his office, his first thought of the dragons.

They were doing very nicely.

Hal never knew if the natives who went for the dragon stables had been detailed, or were just attacking anything that moved.

It was a very bad mistake.

The barbarians had crashed in the doors of the sheds used for the animals.

Storm, more battle-experienced than most dragons, saw unfriendly men, with weapons.

His long neck snaked out, and he caught two of them in his jaws, and crushed them.

The natives stood frozen in panic at what they'd roused, and Storm's great tail lashed and took three more down.

The rest turned and ran, into the swords of the on-rushing fliers.

There was a brief skirmish, and one flier was down, as were five barbarians.

Somewhere in the mêlée, Hal lost two more fliers, but then his men were strapping saddles on their mounts, and the dragons were thudding in their takeoff run through the door of the barn.

Storm was angry, wanting to stay on the ground, wanting more of these men who'd disturbed his sleep. Hal wouldn't let him, shouted him into the takeoff.

Hal saw running men, both barbarians in their brown, and men in uniform, and screaming women and children. A wedge of Roche broke through to the dragon sheds, just as Storm lifted into the air.

There were lit torches, and hayricks, and then houses on Trenganu's main street caught fire.

Smoke boiled, and Hal banked back, over the town.

There was chaos below, knots of men fighting, other men running, either toward or away from battle.

There were bodies scattered in the mucky streets, and more barbarians surging forward.

Hal saw a formation of natives, and, behind a barn, about a company of Roche, unaware of the natives, wavering, about to break.

He forced Storm down into a slithering landing in a mud-wallow, and was off the dragon.

"You men," he bellowed, "where's your officer?"

"Dead, sir," somebody called back, and Hal noted there was still some discipline left if they could remember to use rank.

"Come on, then," he called, knowing that they wouldn't attack without a leader.

A burly sergeant moved toward him, then another, and then the men were dashing around the barn.

A native screamed when he saw the Roche formation, and then it was a free-for-all. There was a nocked arrow being pointed at Hal, then a spear grew out of the barbarian's chest, bloody point jutting forward.

Hal returned the compliment by blocking an axman aside, spitting him through the ribs, and kicking his sword free.

Another native came in, shouting incoherently, with a spiked club.

Hal knelt, came up as the club started down, and the man's guts spilled over his sword hand, blade buried to the hilt in his attacker's stomach.

He broke free, parried a man's spear thrust with his own spear, finished him off . . . and then there were no natives to kill.

Someone – Hal never remembered who – told him about Arbala's death.

It didn't mean anything. Hal was slipping into battle frenzy.

A woman, screaming, ran toward him, a child in her arms.

An arrowhead spitted her neck, and she splashed down into the mire.

"Let's go," Hal shouted. "Kill them! Kill them all!"

They ran toward the town's center, broke out into Trenganu's main street, saw a column of natives, and attacked.

The barbarians hesitated, volleyed arrows, and ran.

Hal went after them, caught up with one, and brained him with the pommel of his sword.

Other men were coming out of sidestreets, forming on Hal's men, without orders, and they pushed forward.

Hal heard a forlorn blatting, looked up, saw Storm overhead, then three other dragons came from nowhere, Mariah and the other Derainians.

Their dragons, better or more lethally trained than Yasin's, needed little guidance, and swooped low, talons reaching, tails whipping, into the back of the barbarian formation, and scythed through the natives.

This time they broke for good, and ran back toward the forest.

Panic took them, and the Roche were on their heels, killing as they went.

Hal had a moment of hope, thinking they'd driven them out of Trenganu for good, then another wave of natives, screaming defiance, came out of the brush toward them.

Hal, giving a needless order, shouted for his men to fall back, not to go in pursuit.

They were already moving back, back into Trenganu's center.

But, and Hal felt a moment of pride and hope, they weren't running, but retreating grimly, slowly, well-trained, experienced soldiers.

There were other men and women with weapons, or overturning carts to block the streets.

Hal wiped blood – not his own, thankfully – from his forehead, had a few seconds to take stock.

As far as anyone knew, he was the senior officer surviving. If any of the "observers" had greater rank, they knew better than to assume command of a disaster.

Kailas muttered an obscenity, then grinned as he thought of Aimard Quesney, who would probably be doubled up in hysterical laughter if he knew the plight Hal had gotten himself into.

The town around him was in flames, wooden buildings exploding, sending balks of timber spinning.

Across the square, he saw civilians, some wounded, some trying to treat the wounded.

There were others, standing, waiting, hopelessness large in their eyes.

At least, he thought, this godsdamned uniform is so drab nobody's running to me screaming for a solution.

So what are you going to do now, Kailas?

Hal spoke the only answer he knew half-aloud, looking up as a disconsolate Storm swooped overhead.

"All right. If we stay here, we'll die. We're going to fight our way out."

11

Kailas was waiting for the second wave of natives to overwhelm the surviving Roche in Trenganu, but they hesitated for a time, perhaps a little shocked at how many casualties they'd taken in the first assault.

Hal didn't care why. He seized the moment, grabbed armed men who looked like they weren't in the depths of panic, snapped orders.

Find ten men you trust, and go back through the town. Herd all the civilians into the square. Bring dry foodstuffs, blankets, warm clothes.

We'll march out at midday.

He chose other men to try to hold a perimeter against the natives when they attacked again.

Farren Mariah was there, and Hal put him in charge of the remaining fliers. Cabet in theory outranked him, but Hal utterly trusted Mariah, and in the madness he wasn't going to take time to give detailed orders. Besides, he had another mission for the ex-flight leader.

Mariah was to make sure the fliers had their emergency supplies, and the unit's wagons were ready to move.

Dump all supplies except weaponry and what was edible, and have the squadron's wagon-masters pick up the lame, wounded, halt, and elderly.

Other troops were ordered to collect anything on wheels, and anything from mules to oxen to horses to pull them.

He told Cabet to take a Roche flier as companion, take off and head east, toward the ruins of Lanzi, the nearest outpost of the Roche army, and get a rescue in motion.

Quite suddenly it was midday.

He put that burly sergeant, whose name was Aescendas, and that company he'd briefly led, in charge of the rearguard, told him that if the men broke and ran he'd shove his sword up every one of their asses, and then think about serious punishment.

The sergeant started to laugh, saw the cold warrior look in Hal's eyes, nodded, and was gone.

An hour later, the survivors of Trenganu moved off, keeping as close to the coast as possible.

Behind them, the flames of the city rose high.

And then it started snowing.

The retreat on that first day was like wading through quicksand, with a nameless monster at your heels.

The barbarians eventually finished looting Trenganu, and started the pursuit.

The only good things that developed were that the rearguard stood fast, not fleeing, but falling back slowly with the retreat; and the natives now had a superstitious fear of the dragons.

Each time Farren or another dragon-rider sent his mount diving on the barbarians, they scattered and fled.

But Hal knew that wouldn't last very long.

He wished he had a magician who could produce some sort of spell, like his pebble-to-boulder incantation that had ruined the Roche cities. Or firebottles.

But they had no bottles, and Farren said he hadn't the slightest idea how such a spell could be cast, and even if he knew how, he doubted he had powers enough to do any good.

So they marched on, as the light snowfall continued.

In late afternoon Hal ordered the wagons circled, and all able-bodied men, and the armed civilian women, to report to the perimeter.

He wanted to keep his fighters at full alertness, but knew better, and let half his troops sleep at a time.

The natives tried two half-hearted attacks during the night, both easily driven off.

Hal found himself crouched at a tiny warming fire hidden in a fold of the ground, next to an old man who'd armed himself with a native's bow, with a handful of arrows stuck in his belt.

"Y'know," the man said, trying to make some kind of conversation, "tomorrow, about midday, we should pass by my gran'sire's farm."

Hal made a polite noise, not caring.

"I remember growing up on it, right on the fringes of the frontier."

Interest came, as Kailas remembered what Quesney had told him.

"Then more settlers came, pushed past us, built Trenganu, and started letting daylight in the swamp, as they put it.

"And killing off barbs, every time they tried to claim woods back, after we'd rightfully took it with force of arms.

"That was the key marker on Gran's place – we had iron stakes in the ground, with the heads of any barb that we came across.

"Made sure they knew where their place was, and that they wouldn't *dare* mess with any Roche."

So much, Hal thought, for noble causes. The Roche *were* grabbing land, the natives fighting for what had been theirs.

Things like that didn't create heroic ballads, not without time passing and the villainous songwriters victorious, which didn't look like it would happen this time around.

The next dawn, as the column was forming up, Hal took Storm out, flying back the way they'd come.

It had stopped snowing during the night, so the bodies of those who'd fallen in the staggering march were still exposed, lying here and there.

Hal didn't get lower than he had to, not wanting to see how many of them were civilians, women, children.

He flew on, over the ruins of Trenganu.

There were still barbarians looking for something to claim in the smoldering city.

They shouted insults up at Hal, ran to cover when Storm swooped on them.

He flew back along the line of march. Not many people looked up as Storm screamed; they were too busy concentrating on the next step through the slush.

Hal put Storm in the air, unridden, and the dragon took charge of the three monsters whose fliers had been killed in Trenganu.

Hal moved back and forth in the column, chivvying someone here, encouraging an oldster there.

He passed a tiny cart, drawn by a pair of goats, with two children aboard, perhaps five and six.

Hal started to ask where their parents were, saw their tear-runneled cheeks, thought better of it, went on.

*

The natives dogged the line of march, swooping in now and again to take down a straggler who even Sergeant Aescendas couldn't keep on his or her feet.

They laid ambushes in front of the column, but these were spotted by the experienced settlers, or seen from the air.

Hal wondered, not without thanks, why the natives were suddenly behaving like raw recruits.

He guessed maybe their best war leaders had been killed in the initial assault on Trenganu.

"Naw," Sergeant Aescendas explained while the two were sharing a bowl of barley, crudely ground, cooked with a beefbone and some roadside herbs, "people fight best when they're on their own ground."

"But this used to be theirs," Hal said.

"Not for a generation or so," Aescendas said. "Time enough to forget.

"I've been fighting these bastards most of my life, and got no damned illusions about what they can and can't do.

"First time I went scouting with some of our peaceful barbs," he said, "we were camped on a hilltop, and I sent one of them out hunting.

"I watched him go out, zigging here, zagging there.

"He killed something or other that was potworthy, and I spotted him coming back.

"He was on the same damned track, ziggety-zaggety, he'd gone out on, even though he could see our hill and could have come home directly.

"Barbs aren't the stealthy woodsmen city people think they are. They've just got a damned great memory for the terrain.

"And on this ground, they're as blind as we would have been if we'd gone out beyond Trenganu."

The wagons were full.

But the temperature dropped, and people on the wagons died.

Their bodies were unceremoniously cast into the ditch beside the narrow track, and there was room for more to ride.

They had jarred or dried rations, enough to let everyone feel hunger pangs, and hay and what could be grazed for the animals.

Some of those died too, and fed the dragons.

Hal tried to remember how many days they'd been on the march – four, five, more? – couldn't.

Each day started with his morning flight, as much for morale when the Trenganu survivors saw a dragon overhead and felt protected, as anything else.

Then he landed, and walked.

There'd be a rest stop somewhere around the middle of the day, and some sort of tasteless food, then they'd go on until almost dusk, make camp, eat, stand guard, sleep, wake, and march on.

The snow was almost continuous, and twice the column had to retrace its steps to find the narrow dirt road it was following.

Hal tried not to notice the bodies, frozen in the night, or killed by natives slipping close to the perimeter.

This nightmare, he lied to himself, couldn't last for ever.

Hal was treating himself to a whore's bath in a basin full of melted snow, while the column slowly moved past him. He was trying not to think how much he wanted a full-size bath, and then a day's uninterrupted sleep in a feather mattress piled high with down blankets, when a voice spoke beside him.

"Sir? We have a problem."

He turned, saw a small boy and a smaller girl.

"Yes," he said, trying to sound benevolent, and not snarl at having his daydream interrupted.

"One of our goats died," the girl said solemnly.

Then he remembered who they were.

The boy's face wrinkled, as if he was about to cry. He looked at the girl, put on a stiff upper lip, only slightly marred by a loud snuffle.

"We don't know what to do," the boy confessed.

"We tried to make him get up, but he wouldn't," the girl added.

"We've got to take the wagon with us," the boy said. "That's all that's left after our parents . . . went away."

This was absurd. There were perhaps five thousand civilians, and three or four thousand soldiers he'd taken responsibility for on this march.

He didn't have the time, or the energy, to worry about these two children, other than having someone find room for them on a wagon somewhere in the column.

But it suddenly became the most important thing in his world.

He poured the water out, toweled himself dry with his shirt

that no longer made him wrinkle his nose at its filth, and went looking.

He found a pair of very bedraggled donkeys, and paid an absurd amount out of his own pocket for the beasts. The animals' owner swore this was costing him his dinner for the evening.

Hal almost took the beasts at swordpoint, but kept his self-control.

The donkeys were hitched to the wagon, the surviving goat tied to the back, and Hal handed the reins to the boy.

The girl looked at the angle the cart's deck now sat at, considered the donkeys, started to say something.

The boy shook his head.

"Thank you, sir," the girl said, instead of complaining.

"You are very welcome."

From then on, the boy and girl became a talisman for Hal. They had to live to reach the Roche positions.

And if they didn't?

He didn't know.

The column staggered into open country that had been cut, settled and planted.

But the farmhouses were burnt, the barns ruined, and the winter fields barren.

Men and women went out and scavenged the ruins, their need greater than the farmers who'd abandoned the holdings

The sight of what had once been civilization sparked the column to a slightly faster pace, and for once, the natives didn't harry them.

Until late that afternoon, when they crested a rise.

Spread out in the small valley in front of them was rank after rank of the barbarians, waiting for the final battle to be joined.

Someone behind Hal screamed, and a harsh voice reproved her.

The response seemed perfectly reasonable to Hal.

He wished he were braver – if he were, he could just leap on Storm's back, gather the other three Derainians and leave these damned Roche exploiters to their doom.

But he couldn't.

And he wasn't exactly a general who might look at these serried ranks of barbarians, deduce a battle plan, and sweep the field.

The refugees took some kind of formation automatically, with fighters in the front and flanks, and the civilians in the middle.

Everyone was looking to Hal for an idea.

Then shouting came, and a man strode out of the native ranks across the valley. He was very big, very muscled, and wore his hair long, braided behind him.

Behind him came a man with a shield, and a very short, very stout barbarian wearing furry robes.

A wizard?

The big man shouted something.

A challenge.

Maybe.

The man waited for a short time, then shouted again.

It might have been a call to surrender.

The man waved a captured long two-handled sword, and laughed, sneeringly.

A definite challenge.

Or so Hal guessed.

He wished he could jump on Storm's back, take off, and murder the bastard.

But he'd probably dart back into the native ranks the minute he saw the dragon lumber forward.

Hal sighed, walked back to Storm, and took his crossbow and a magazine of bolts from where they were tied to the dragon's carapace.

Keeping the crossbow at his side, he walked out in front of the ragged formation of Roche, and drew his sword.

The great native warrior shouted something, laughed again.

Holding his sword in front of him, as a challenge, Hal walked forward.

"You need some backup?" It was Farren.

"No," Hal said, not turning. "Or, rather, yes. But you don't look like a division of the king's guards.

"Get ready to get the dragons in the air. You'll know when, and what to do."

Operating on the assumption that the man in furs was a magician, Hal advanced on the three natives, forcing his mind into thoughts of swordplay. Wizards couldn't read minds. Or so they claimed piously.

The warrior waiting for him was offered the shield, but disdained it, since Hal wasn't carrying one.

There was about forty feet between the two men.

Hal decided that was far enough.

Moving faster than he thought he ever had in his life, he tossed his sword aside, brought up the crossbow, slid the grip back then forward, dropped a bolt into the track and knelt.

This close, it was a sure shot.

Hal put the bolt into the throat of the magician, who screamed, spun and died.

The warrior shouted, most likely something about Hal's dishonesty, and ran forward, lifting his sword.

He'd never seen a repeating crossbow, and, when planning his great gesture, no doubt figured he'd have more than enough time to cut down any archer, any crossbowman.

Hal slid the grip back, forward, put his second bolt into the warrior's stomach.

He half-turned, dropped to his knees, pulling uselessly at the bolt, which was buried to the fletching.

There was a great cry of outrage from the barbarian ranks.

Hal paid no attention as he reloaded, and shot the shield-bearer in the face.

Another bolt went into the warrior's chest, and he flopped back, dead.

Hal was running back toward his own ranks. He heard the shout of natives behind him, the crack of leathery wings ahead, and Farren Mariah and the other dragon-fliers rose from the knot of Roche and soared toward him, just off the ground.

Third back was Storm, and Farren was shouting at the dragon.

Storm flared his wings, touched down in the muck for an instant, and Hal swung up into the saddle.

Storm took off, and the flight of dragons attacked the natives head-on.

Crossbow bolts spat out, and the dragon claws were reaching.

Arrows came at them, bounced off the carapaces or the dragons' armored faces, and then the beasts struck the barbarian formation, claws rending, tails lashing.

The surprise of their champion's death and the attack by the monsters was too much.

The center of the native formation crumbled, and men were running.

Hal brought Storm up and around, saw the Roche were attacking, and then, once more, the refugees were stumbling forward, a dirty, freezing, unstoppable mass.

*

The next day, they were in still-inhabited land, and armed farmers began joining them, and behind them came servants and women carrying an endless amount of food.

The refugees of the Trenganu massacre gobbled the food, poured home-brewed beer down their throats, and listened to the chatter of victory.

But few of them could smile, and no one loosened his tight grip on his weapon, nor did their eyes stop sweeping the woods around them for an ambush.

Hal sat on Storm, who lay contentedly in the middle of the swarming mass. The triumphant shouting was very dim in his ears.

A few yards away, a small boy, with an even smaller girl, in a cart being pulled by two ragged donkeys with a goat behind it looked at him, then solemnly, not smiling, lifted a fist, with its thumb pointed up.

12

There was a great banquet in Lanzi to celebrate the march west, as it was called, rather than a retreat, with capital letters only a taleteller or two away.

The survival of less than half of the residents of Trenganu, and a few more from the expeditionary force, was being regarded a some kind of victory.

But not by the soldiers or by the Dragonmaster.

One grizzled sergeant spat, "I claim we got our asses beaten like drums, and I don't like it."

The banquet's guest of honor was supposed to have been Lord Kailas of Kalabas, the Dragonmaster, for his brilliance serving a country not his own.

But he wasn't there for the party, nor were the other three Derainians. Those three, with whatever loot they'd been able to acquire, were flying west, planning to make a stop at Paestum, then across the Chicor Straits to home.

Except for Hal Kailas.

He, Storm beside him, sat on a low mountain to the south-east of Lanzi.

It was cold, clear, windy, and both moons were out.

Hal was considering what he should now do with his life.

He decided that not only would he not be flying for the Roche, with their still-grandiose dreams of conquest, but he had no interest in freelance military work.

It occurred to him that good causes – if, in fact, there were any – seldom came to mercenaries.

They were generally stuck with wars that were probably not that honorable, since there were always enough true believers around for the good battles.

He could, he thought for a short flash, possibly go back into the peacetime army of Deraine.

That brought a rather derisive laugh.

Storm stirred and honked what Hal thought might be an echo.

Being quite rich meant he could become a roué in Rozen. But that didn't sit well . . . he'd seen enough parties and partygoers on the flight north to Trenganu and, before that, in ruined Carcaor to make his liver tremble for years.

Hal ruefully realized he didn't make much of a decadent.

He considered.

At one time, his dream would have been to be a dragon-flier, with his own traveling spectacle.

But he doubted there'd be much interest these days, since most people associated dragons with war and death.

Besides, remembering the realities of a dragon show, the catering to stupid people with stupid questions, and giggling schoolgirls, that didn't draw him any more.

He thought, hardly for the first time, that the young wanderer caught up by the war was truly dead.

So the only option left, he thought, was to vegetate on his estates.

Perhaps he should think about drinking himself to death while boring everyone within a day's flight with war stories.

He remembered the words of his first great love: "There won't be any after-the-war for a dragon-flier."

It seemed that he was finding a new illustration of that truth, if not the one that Saslic had meant.

"Oh well," Hal said aloud. "At least I'll never starve."

Storm looked at him, and let go a long burble.

"My friend," Kailas said, "you're going to have to learn people-speak, since nobody's mastered dragon talk."

Storm made a noncommittal noise.

Hal realized the sky had clouded over, just as a spatter of rain hit him in the face.

Storm unfurled one wing, brought it like a tent over Hal.

"Well," Hal said, "at least I've got one friend in the world."

Somehow comforted, he got up, and climbed into the saddle. He pulled a slicker over his shoulders, and tapped Storm with his reins.

The dragon thudded down the slope, wings outspread, and took to the air.

Hal let Storm find his own altitude, then set a course of east-north-east as the storm broke about his shoulders.

Strangely, not at all unhappy, the lone rider flew on through the driving tempest.

13

A month later, Hal sat in one of the drawing rooms of his castle, staring out at the drifting snow.

Beyond that was the long, sloping beach that led to the sea, and which was dotted with small ice growlers.

It was a bleak winter, well suited to brooding hopelessly about the future.

Kailas had returned to Deraine, found nothing for him in the capital, as he'd expected, and flown on north to his lands.

There seemed to be nothing here either, but at least life was quiet, and there were no intrusions, other than the minor noblemen who discovered Lord Kailas was single once more, and threw parties to "get him out of his gloom."

Actually, of course, these parties were intended to introduce said noblemen's excessively eligible daughters.

At the moment, Hal wanted nothing emotional and no one in his life, such as it was, until he figured out what the hells he was going to do next.

At least he hadn't given in to either the joys of the bottle or, worse, falling into some sort of disastrous love affair.

Yet.

He ate, exercised, slept, rode Storm out over the ocean each day, and read many books – the castle's previous tenant had been much of a reader.

He'd sent to Rozen for more volumes, and read indiscriminately – romances, epic verse, history. The only thing he cared little about was writings about the war.

The storm had isolated the castle, which suited Hal quite well. He didn't want or need company, there were enough supplies to last for years, and there was nothing he felt terribly like doing.

About midday, when the weather had broken a bit, he grew bored with the book he was reading, pulled on boots and a heavy coat, and went for a walk down by the shore.

It was far too windy to take Storm out, but he stopped by the stables first, and fed a rather terrified lamb to the dragon.

Frozen sand crunched under his feet, and the wind wailed most attractively as he went.

A gust of wind sent particles of ice into his face, and he blinked them out, thinking he had spotted more bergy bits stranded on the beach.

He had not – the two bulky objects were dragons.

Wild dragons.

One was dead, being rolled by the waves, but the other still lived, and was able to pull himself further up, out of the water.

Hal tried approaching him, and the monster managed a feeble lash of his tail, and a burbling low screech.

The dragon was hurt – a foreleg looked broken, and there was a long tear along his side.

Hal wanted to do something, didn't know what.

A thought came.

He ran back to the castle, shouted up a servant, and told him to saddle a horse – no, two horses – and take a companion, for safety against the storm's rage, to the nearby village and bring back its witch.

"Tell him it's to deal with a dragon," Hal said. "Maybe that'll give him a clue as to what herbs to bring.

"He'll think I've gone mad, but remind him my gold isn't mad."

The man looked puzzled, then ran off.

Hal went to the stables, got Storm, and walked him down to the wounded, probably dying, dragon.

The two creatures exchanged angry hisses, then, proper civilities having been observed, the injured beast lay back down, full length.

Hal didn't approach him more closely.

Within the hour, the witch arrived, a rather rotund, cheerful man, bundled in homespun. Hal's two servants carried big wicker cases.

He spoke in the rather queer dialect native to the district Hal's lands lay in, and Hal had to puzzle his way through the man's words:

"'Tis sad to see any animal, even a monsker like a dragon, in pain, and aye, there's been many of them wash up on our shores this winter.

"Wonder if there's some sort of war going on, almost. Almost like they're as stupid as people with *their* wars.

"Always coming from the west, being washed a bit south to our beaches. Wager there's more on the western approaches."

Hal remembered the dragons that had sailed, wings folded over their bodies, driven by the winds and the currents, past Cayre a Carstares, his ex-wife's citadel, and nodded understanding.

"I spent some time thinking, trying to bring up some spells, or some herbs or poultices that might help, tried 'em, almost got my head tore off for my troubles.

"But two, three, recovered good enough to swim back out and catch the current.

"Seldom saw one hurt as sore as this, but we'll do what we can."

The man cautiously approached the injured beast, who seemed to have lapsed into unconsciousness.

He muttered spells, and took packets of dried herbs from the baskets, packed the dragon's wounds, and loose-splinted his fore-leg. He tried to tighten the splint, and the beast semi-woke, and struck at him with his fangs.

The man ducked away, and laughed.

"Better nor a bull in heat, you are. But I have your measure, I do."

But the witch was sweating in fear.

Hal had a sheep brought down, and killed in front of the dragon, but he showed no interest.

He brought Storm back to the beach, and Storm stared at the wild beast and began a high keening.

Then he picked up the sheep Hal had killed, carried it to the other animal and set it down in front of his nose.

The dragon's eyes opened, and he considered the meal, Storm, and Hal, the witch and several of Hal's curious staffers hovering nearby, then closed his eyes again.

Hal had his retainers pitch a sort of tent for himself, and set watch over the dragon as night closed in.

Storm curled nearby.

Hal didn't sleep that night, or so he thought.

But he dreamed.

Once before, during the war, he'd dreamed of being a dragon, Storm, and that dream had been so real he'd truly believed it.

So was this one, even though it was most strange, and lasted for only moments.

Again, he was a dragon, but one that knew not men.

The sun was warm on his back, and about a hundred feet below him was a savanna, its grasses just beginning to change with fall.

It was a land that Hal had never known, never seen.

He was just beginning to get hungry, scanning the ground below for prey.

Another part of him was watching the skies ... for something.

An enemy?

He looked about, saw nothing except some scattering birds, went back to looking for his meal.

He thought of a full stomach, then quiet digestion atop a crag to the east, near the ocean, and was content.

He saw movement below, under a rocky escarpment, folded his wings and dove silently down toward what must be an antelope.

He was just below the rocks when two other dragons, big, red and black, dove at him.

The dragon felt fear, panic at the ambush, tried to dive out of it.

But the other two were clever, and forced him toward the ground.

He dove at one, struck with his tail, missed.

The other dragon was on him, lashing out.

The sound of his foreleg breaking was very loud, and he keened pain, rolled in midair to escape.

But both dragons were on him, ripping, tearing, and he felt the pain deep in his side. The ground was very close, and—

And Hal woke, sweating, hearing the nearby dragon moan and thrash.

Hal sat, helplessly, listening to the beast's last hours.

The dragon died without opening his eyes, just before dawn.

Hal felt pain greater than he'd known over the death of some men, and wondered at himself.

But at least he had an idea of what he might, perhaps should, do.

Hal left his castle on Storm that day, paying no heed to the dying tempest, and headed for Rozen.

14

Kailas's first stop was at the address that the dragonmaster Garadice had included with his letter.

Garadice's home was just outside Rozen, a large, sprawling, rather unkempt estate.

Hal found him in one of the outbuildings, staring at a large pile of tents, jarred rations, and heavy clothes.

"I'm not looking forward to going back north this spring," Garadice explained. "I hope you've brought something to distract me."

Hal explained his plan – he proposed to fund four or five teams, to be stationed along the west and north shores of Deraine. The teams would be composed of about six men, as many as possible with dragon-handling experience. One of the men would be a wizard, or, failing that, at least a competent witch.

Their job would be to help any wild dragons that beached themselves, first with medical treatment, until they healed enough to be able to fly, or, at the very least, return to the sea and let the currents carry them on.

Garadice made a face.

"Admirable, I suppose, Lord Kailas. But I sense something lacking. Once we – for I'll be delighted to aid you in any way I can – have our dragon all bandaged up, is there going to be any guarantee that it will simply take itself off our hands?

"Suppose the dragon *likes* being cosseted and hand-fed?"

Hal hadn't considered that.

"And the gods know we already have enough half-tame dragons on our hands from the war, with, as yet, no place to keep them or any task to keep them off the public rolls. We've seen how ungrateful the damned people are toward them already.

"Will there be any change in the way the populace feels?

"Remembering, of course, how quickly they've managed to forget the crippled soldiers who fought for them not so very long ago."

Hal was starting to get upset.

Garadice held up his hands.

"Don't get mad, Lord Kailas. You have me on your side, as you should know. I'm merely asking questions that I think we have to answer before riding off on what could be a fool's errand."

Hal, scowling, said he would think on the matter, and left.

After some pondering, he decided his campaign needed a popularizer.

There was none better than Sir Thom Lowess.

Lowess' mansion was, as usual, occupied by half a dozen young women, nobles of the outer provinces who were in the capital seeking excitement and, possibly, a lover or husband, preferably rich.

As far as anyone knew, Lowess merely liked these women's company, and never took advantage of the various offers he'd had.

Lowess, unmarried, wasn't attracted to men, either.

As far as anyone could tell, he seemed perfectly sexless, although no one committed the social breach of asking.

The two men chatted for a while, Sir Thom carefully not bringing up the subject of Hal's ex-wife, then Hal explained what had brought him to the capital, and asked for Lowess' help in promoting his dragon teams.

"I am glad, I suppose," Lowess said, looking out the window, carefully not meeting Hal's eye, "that you consider me some sort of a superman.

"But that would be . . . will be . . . a very hard task.

"People are tired of the war, tired of reading about the war."

"But this isn't about the war," Hal protested.

"In most people's eyes," Sir Thom said, "anything to do with dragons – like anything to do with the Roche or soldiers – reflects back on the war.

"Look at it like this, Lord Hal. How long have dragons been among us?"

"What's that got to do with anything?"

"Perhaps everything. It's been what, a bit over two hundred years since they appeared from the west?

"You know, an awful lot of people had never seen or read about dragons before the war, in spite of the dragon shows and such.

"Dragons equal war equal death. Period."

"That's absurd," Hal said.

"It is," Sir Thom agreed. "But I'll give you an example: a young writer I know asked for help getting a collection of stories about dragons published . . . flying them, caring for them, nothing, other than a brief mention at the beginning, of their war service.

"I tried. I really tried. But all of the people I wrote to came back with about the same response: that no one wants to read about dragons, and for me to suggest to the young man that he find another field of interest. That went from broadsheet publishers, including my own, to those who deal in books.

"I'll give you another example, this one closer to home. The broadsheets wanted ink on your last adventure with the Roche . . . a few months back. Half of that interest, by the way, came from your divorce. Since neither you nor Khiri was willing to talk to the taletellers, there were incredible scandals floating about.

"But now, if I decided to write a piece on your latest crusade . . . I doubt if I'd find a ready market.

"You are, as the saying goes, yesterday's hero."

"Well, the hell with them," Hal said. "I'll go ahead with my teams anyway. I've more than enough money, and don't give a damn about having anything to hand on to the daughters and sons I don't have, don't particularly want, and seem unlikely to have anyway."

"Now, now," Sir Thom soothed. "Getting perturbed about something that does seem to be a fact won't do any good.

"Which brings up another point that just came to me.

"It's admirable – heroic, even – that you want to do something to help dragons.

"But is this it? Is this dragon team scheme the answer? And I'm not sure I know what I meant by that question."

"Answer?" Hal asked, honestly puzzled. "Answer to what?"

"I don't know that either," Sir Thom said. "Look. Let me think on it. There must be a way to do something for these pursued wild dragons.

"But do a stumble-witted man a favor. Think on what I just said."

Again, Hal dreamed he was that sore-wounded dragon. Now he was at sea, a great wind blowing over his tented wings, waves rocking him.

The current bore him steadily away from his homeland. Away from his homeland, but away from those red and black dragons who'd savaged him.

He longed for sleep, for death, but his body denied him.

He would heal, heal and find a new land for a home.

Hal sat in a taphouse, trying to feel sorry for himself, but mostly getting drunk.

Hells, he could have gotten this far staying at home . . . if those vast estates King Asir had granted him were really his home.

He realized he'd never thought of them as such, that in fact he'd really never *had* a home after running away from Caerly.

Kailas grinned, remembering an old sergeant, way the hells back when he was a young cavalryman, before the dragons, shouting, "From now on, th' *army* is your home."

Yes. Right. Of course, Sergeant.

What batshit.

He listened to the laughter and joking at the bar, had no desire to join the roisterers.

Hal realized that, way down deep, he probably didn't like people very much. Noisy, scheming fools who seemed to do nothing but take.

So what, he thought.

That had nothing to do with anything, least of all dragons, which he'd decided would be his main concern for a while, until he thought of something else to do.

Another realization came: he'd probably be better off if he had to struggle for his meals and shelter, like most people.

Maybe there'd be more like him if everything came on golden platters.

Or maybe not.

This, he thought, wasn't getting him much of anywhere.

He glowered at an especially happy drunk, who lifted a glass in his direction, saw the expression on his face, and turned hastily away.

Hal felt a bit better for having ruined, if only for a moment, someone else's evening.

He looked for someone else to glare at.

Maybe it'd make him feel better if he got into a good, serious bar brawl on this night.

Although he'd probably lose, since it had been nearly for ever since he'd been in a fight with anything but killing weapons. He thought the warders of Rozen would hardly approve of him gutting some innocent lush with the dragon-flier's dagger he had at his belt.

His eye was caught by a placard on the wall:

!See!
Real Wild Dragons
!Marvel!
At their Rage
Against Us All
More than 10
Of the World's Most
Dangerous Dragons

There was the address of a local hippodrome.

Hal studied the placard.

After a while, he pushed his half-finished brandy away.

Now, *there* was something he could deal with.

Hal realized he was a deal drunker than he'd thought, navigating slowly and carefully through the snowy streets, having to stop and ask directions twice.

He carefully faced away from the people he questioned, not wanting to paralyze anyone with his breath.

He was in time for the last "show," such as it was.

It consisted of a gravel-voiced man talking about how dangerous the ten dragons were, and how brave their captors had been, without ever specifying exactly how the monsters were trapped.

The dragons themselves, paired, arbitrarily, in thick-barred cages, looked wilted and underfed, hardly a threat to anyone.

But the shill raked a length of steel across the bars, and the dragons obediently screamed, and spat at the man.

Hal paid little attention to the man's blather. He'd done better himself when he was a boy with the dragon-fliers' show. But he did force away his building stupor when the man talked about the hand-forged bars of the cage, and how only the system of locks kept the beasts from breaking free and ravaging Rozen.

After a time, Kailas decided there was nothing more to learn. He went out and found a closet in one of the halls, and crept inside, hoping there wouldn't be any broompushers after the "performance."

He either slept or passed out, but all was quiet and still in the arena when he awoke, except for the rather plaintive roars of the dragons.

Hal slipped out, head already starting to ache from the brandy. He thought he could hold on until he'd finished, then go back to his inn and collapse.

There was a brazier in the central auditorium, giving a bit of light.

Hal stumbled down the steps, looking for something. He found it still lying on the floor – the steel bar the barker had used to demonstrate the strength of the cages.

Hal picked it up, shook it, approved of its weight.

He braced himself, and swung the steel against the rather flimsy-looking lock of one of the cages.

The lock bent, the sound boomed around the arena, and the dozing dragons woke.

He swung again, and the lock sprung open.

Hal moved to the next cage, took a firm grip on the bar, and a voice came from behind him.

"Hi! You! What the blazes are you doing?"

Hal spun.

An old man, wearing what had once been a uniform, stood there.

"Are you out of your mind?" the man, a nightwatchman, shouted.

Hal thought, decided to play the role.

He came out with what he hoped would sound like maniacal laughter, and advanced on the old man.

The man backed up.

Hal laughed again, and drew his dagger.

The old man yelped, found that his legs weren't as old as he'd thought, and fled back out of the arena.

He'll go for the watch, Hal thought.

But he didn't run.

Instead, he went back to the cages, and smashed the other locks.

Then he went to the arena's doors, and opened them wide.

Snowflakes and cold air blew in.

Hal went back to the dragons.

"All right," he shouted. "You're free! Get out! Go north, or . . . or wherever you want!"

None of the dragons moved toward their cage doors.

Instead, they huddled back at the rear of their pens.

Hal swore at them, without results.

He looked about, saw the brazier, had an idea. With his dagger, he ripped one of the stadium seats apart, wrapping the cloth seat back about its frame.

He fired the cloth in the brazier, then went behind the cages.

"Out! Out!" he cried, and waved his torch as it burst into flame.

One of the dragons whimpered, but, fearing fire more than the forgotten outer world, went out of the cage, and up the stairs toward the exit.

Two other dragons followed.

Hal chased the rest of them out of their cages, herding them toward the doors.

He kept the fire in front of his face, and while the dragons struck at him, it was half-hearted.

Only one lashed out with his tail, and Kailas ducked clumsily and drunkenly under the whiplash.

Then the dragons were outside, starting at the cold.

Hal stumbled about, waving his burning cloth.

The dragons broke, one, then two, stumbling forward, wings unfolding with a great cracking like a ship's sails in a high wind, and they were aloft, climbing out and away from the lights of Rozen.

Hal cheered at the top of his lungs, waving his torch as it burnt out.

"Go home! Screw mankind! Don't have anything to do with us!"

A voice came.

"Stand very damned still. You are under arrest."

Hal turned, saw a uniformed warder holding a halberd not a foot from his back.

He dropped the torch.

Behind the warder were a dozen other warders, all armed, some armored.

"I order you to obey my commands, in the name of the king."

15

Hal was unceremoniously tossed into what a warder called a "tank." He explained it was mainly for drunkards who'd also committed some minor felony that didn't hurt anyone.

That made Kailas feel enormously better, a fit compliment on his aptitude as a criminal, to go with his rapidly building hangover.

He took the not particularly clean blanket they handed him, ignored the dozen other wastrels in the cell, found a corner in the large room with its single barred gate, and tried to get some sleep.

He woke late in the morning, with a raging thirst, and sat up.

Leaning against the wall next to him was a huge man, big in every dimension.

"Is there any water about?" Hal croaked, not particularly caring if the monster next to him was intent on robbing him.

"In th' bucket, over there."

Hal wobbled over to it, poured down evil-smelling liquid until his stomach promised it would be sending it all back if he didn't stop.

He went back to his corner and slumped down.

"You th' one they call Dragonmaster?"

"I am . . . I was."

"Before you started flying about and being a lord and all," the hulk said, "was you in the cavalry?"

"I was," Kailas admitted. "Third Light."

"My kid brother was with it, too. He was the good 'un in the family. Wrote letters home. And he was always going on about some Sergeant Kailas. Called him Lucky."

"What was his name?"

"Gachina. Finbo was his first name."

"I remember him," Hal said, telling the truth. "Guidon-bearer."

"That was him," the huge man said. "Got hisself killed in some damnfool battle. One of his mates I wrote to, askin' what happened, told me the godsdamned officers had made 'em ride out with no backup, and the godsdamned Roche heavy cavalry wiped them out."

Hal remembered that battlefield, and its corpses. He'd just

been commissioned, been offered a chance to go to dragon school, had turned the offer down because of the responsibility he felt for his section.

After that battle, they were all corpses, and Hal's responsibility was over.

Hal hauled himself to his feet, stuck out his hand.

"Name's Hal," he said. "Your brother was a good man. I was on the field the day he got killed."

"Too godsdamned good for the godsdamned army," the man said, looking at Hal as if he expected a challenge.

"Most of us were," Hal agreed. The bigger man subsided a little.

"I'm Babil."

They touched palms.

"I'm a thief, normal," Babil said. "Now, since they didn't catch me slittin' any gullets, I'm waitin' trial."

"And I'm head man of this box." He raised his voice, looking about. No one disagreed.

"This is the Dragonmaster," he went on. "Nobody messes with him."

There was a scatter of agreements.

"Not that you've got much to worry about," Babil said. "These is all lightweights. The real felons go to Brightwater.

"Not to mention that you'll be out on bond within the day, even for doing something spectacular stupid like cuttin' those dragons free."

"How'd you know?"

"One of th' warders told.

"But like I say, you'll be bonded out quick. Not like th' rest of us, who'll gentle rot for a time 'til th' judges get off their arses and decide to see about us."

But Hal didn't get out on bond that day.

Or the next.

Or that week.

Babil asked one of the warders, who looked carefully about before telling him that someone, someone "up there," had put the word out that Hal wasn't to be freed.

No explanation.

"I figger," Babil said, "them dragons must've belonged to somebody muckety, or who had a friend who is."

Hal couldn't work out who that could be.

While he waited, he got to know the other felons in the tank, and others as they passed through.

One of them was a man without a name, a small, wizened character with canny eyes, who also happened to be quite mad.

He decided, for some utterly unknown reason, that he hated Hal, and was always muttering when he came within range.

Generally his mutters were something about how if he loved dragons so much, he oughta go live with them, oughta sleep with them, frigging bastardly lord bastard, and on and on.

He made Hal very nervous, even though Babil said there was no worry there.

One day, Babil came to Hal.

"You're either in good – or very bad – shape."

"Why?"

"I just heard, you're for the King's Justice."

"Huh?"

"A warder just told me. Guess that's 'cause you're a lord and all, hey?"

Hal shook his head, having little knowledge of Deraine's convoluted justice system beyond prewar experience of what they could do to a penniless wandering boy.

"Problem is," Babil went on, "King's Justice also means they can geek you if they wants."

Hal blanched.

"Can't understand what's going on," Babil muttered. "And I don't like not knowin'."

The next morning, they came for Hal.

Four warders, two with spears, two with crossbows, took Hal out of the tank.

He wanted to tell them that he was normally quite sober, that he had behaved like somewhat of a damned fool, although he really didn't regret freeing the dragons, but he didn't say anything.

A carriage took him to a public bathhouse, and the lead warder told him to wash the stink off, and put on the clothes he handed him.

He was busily soaping when it came to him.

Both Garadice and Lowess had been right.

He suddenly knew what he should be doing, and it was not running a bandage squad for dragons.

And it had come from the lips of a madman.

The only problem was getting himself free to implement the thought.

Hal had himself shaved by the barber in the bathhouse, and put on the gray striped tunic and breeches he'd been given.

A rather fat, imperious man came in and told Hal to follow him.

Hal thought he recognized the man, but told himself he had to be wrong. All the while his thumbs prickled.

Outside the bathhouse was a dark brown carriage, without windows.

Hal was told to get in, and the carriage started off.

He tried to tell where it was going by the turns, but since he wasn't sure where the prison was, he stayed lost.

It finally passed through two sets of gates – Hal could tell by the warders' self-important shouting of challenge and password – and came to an eventual halt.

Hal got out, and found his fears were quite valid: the carriage was in the royal palace grounds, behind the palace itself.

He had been right in thinking the fat man was one of the king's chamberlains.

King's Justice, indeed.

And what the hells could King Asir want with a common, or fairly common anyway, felon?

"Very good, Kailas," King Asir said in a sarcastic voice.

That was very bad. Hal was, in spite of his civilian wear, at the most rigid attention he'd stood at since . . . since dragon school, after having knelt hastily when the king made his entrance.

Also not good was the king not having used title, either nobility or Dragonmaster.

The king was dressed in dark linen, with short boots, and no crown, not even a circlet.

His face was more worn, and his eyes more tired than Hal remembered them from the war.

There were only the two of them in the tiny audience chamber.

"You know, you've annoyed me quite considerably of late," Asir said. He didn't seem to expect an apology, so Hal remained silent.

"First, you rescue that Roche killer from our ostensible allies in Sagene, which meant that I had to make up some covering story.

"That cost you points, right there.

"Then with this Yasin, you involve yourself in this border war with the northern barbarians, a war I'd as soon see them lose, and turn their attentions to fixing problems in their own homeland, rather than grabbing for more land they don't need.

"Then you take over the retreat when the grab goes sour, which makes all of the taletellers go goosey, and once again you're a hero, this time in a cause that is far less than admirable.

"I was of a mind to let you stew in your wilderness up north for another year, then call you to court and give you some sort of position that would keep you out of mischief.

"But mischief appears to be your goal, and so you get yourself plastered and become some sort of animal liberator.

"Forget everything except this last piece of nonsense, for which I really would like an explanation.

"Assuming you have one."

Hal waited, and the silence stretched.

"I think I do, sire," Hal said.

Asir stayed silent.

"Your Majesty, the way we've been treated since the end of the wars has flatly made me sick. Men, who can know why, is bad enough.

"But dragons . . . poor dumb beasts . . . are nothing but victims."

The king nodded reluctantly.

"It wasn't very wise of me . . . and I had been drinking, which I'm not offering as an excuse . . . but I did what I did, and honestly have few regrets, other than embarrassing you, when you've always been my benefactor."

"Well," the king allowed, "it seems you might have started something. A couple of soft-hearted and soft-headed barons have started an anti-cruelty league. Free the dragons and such.

"That does no harm.

"But I cannot have one of my heroes stumbling around as if he were a law unto himself, as if it were still wartime.

"No. That will not come to pass.

"I had my people inquire about what you were doing, and was told about your rescue groups, or whatever the blazes you were intending to call them."

"I hadn't gotten as far as a name, Your Majesty."

The king humphed.

"Not that it matters," Asir said. "The question is, how shall you be punished? I can't just ignore your depredations, even though all but one of them are technically within the law.

"I can't just throw you in prison for a year or so. The people will, no doubt, hear of your rescue groups, which will never happen if you're in jail, which in turn will hardly reflect well on me.

"I truly wish I was one of those kings of legend I read about when I was a boy, who had convenient islands to which they could dispatch an annoyance they weren't quite ready to behead."

"You do, sire," Hal said quickly.

The king gave him a puzzled look.

"Your Majesty . . . back during the war you once told me you regretted not being curious about the lands beyond, and that maybe that had helped bring on the war."

"I don't remember saying it, but I assume I did," Asir said. "It's certainly true enough."

Hal felt emboldened.

"Sire, I assume you know about the wild dragons that are carried from some unknown land east, to land on our shores, Black Island, or the northern tundra."

"Of course."

"An expert on dragons, a man named Garadice—"

"I know of him as well."

"He's theorized that these wild dragons are the ones that have settled this entire part of the world, since dragons have only been around for a few hundred years."

"You are trying my patience," Asir growled. "I didn't fall off the turnip boat, you know."

"I came up with the idea of dragon teams to help these poor wights that, wounded and exhausted, are carried east to us by the currents and the winds.

"I was ducking the issue.

"Sire, what I propose now is to journey west, using my own resources. I want to find who – or what – is at war with the dragons."

The king goggled.

"And, Your Majesty, if you grant me three or four of your ships, and some of your sailors, who are doing nothing now but sulking at the docks, or sailing up and down eating your rations and collecting your silver, looking for smugglers, I will attempt to end this war that someone is waging against the dragons.

"Or whatever it is," Hal finished, a bit limply.

"Hmm. Interesting." The king went to a sideboard, poured two brandies.

"You may lose that brace, Lord Kailas."

Hal obeyed, relaxing to a still-military, very formal at ease.

The king handed him a snifter.

He stared past Hal, out the window, at the snowy winter.

"Someone once said that if people have enough adventure, either done by themselves or in the vicarious manner, they'll not always be thinking of war, and killing their neighbor.

"I don't believe it, not at all.

"But I am of a mind to test the theory.

"Yes. I think I shall."

King Asir lifted his glass.

"Lord Kailas, it pleases me to set aside your crimes, and grant your request.

"Perhaps saving some dragons, or even trying, will wash our sins against them away.

"So let us drink to . . . to the Royal Exploration West."

16

That was well and good.

But . . .

Hal might have felt like trumpeting about his sudden rise from prisoner to explorer, save for one slight problem:

West was a hellishly general direction to go searching for something he wasn't quite sure of.

He found larger quarters, suitable for an expedition, and pondered the matter for some days.

Then he asked the king for a magician, a very good magician.

"You mean Limingo," Asir said.

"If possible, sire."

"It isn't the loaning for a day or so that I mind," Asir said. "It's the probability that that fey bastard will want to go with you, and good sorcerers are scarce, these days."

Nevertheless, he agreed.

Limingo, as tall, slender and elegant as ever, showed up,

accompanied by a pair of curly-haired, elf-eared acolytes. The magician had always been perfectly open about his sexual preferences, which didn't matter to Hal at all.

Limingo listened to Hal's problem.

"To tell you the truth, not only do I have no idea how to find out where you should seek, but I don't even have an idea on how to start looking.

"I'm sorry. But magic can only do so much."

"I had a thought," Hal said, almost timidly. Magic and magicians mostly terrified him.

"Ah?" Limingo said.

Hal explained about dreaming about being a dragon. Once it had been Storm, but this latest had been of being a foreign dragon, and being attacked by two others, over a strange land.

Limingo stroked his chin.

"I don't know, Lord Kailas—"

"Hal, if you would."

"Hal. I have no idea if that's a way in to our problem. Let me give it some thought."

It was two full days before Limingo returned to him.

"First, what we need is a dying, or very recently dead, wild dragon. Something that has recently tried to make the journey east.

"Do you know," Limingo added, "I almost said someone. Odd, that."

Hal realized that he'd been thinking of dragons as "ones," not "things," for a very long time.

"The only problem," Limingo said, "is that the spell might involve some risk, and certainly some pain, for you."

Hal thought for an instant, then nodded.

"I'm game."

Hal borrowed scouts from the light cavalry, put them out on the western and northern shores of Deraine, with silver as a reward for the first dragon reported.

And they waited.

It took three weeks, and the last of a dying winter's storms, before a dragon, just breathing its last, washed up.

It was far to the west, near the fishing town of Brouwer, which Hal had last seen at the party where he'd met Khiri Carstares, before the disastrous attack on the south of Roche where his first and greatest love, Saslic Dinapur, had died.

The magician and his assistants, plus two dogsbodies, set out immediately by road.

Hal was very grateful for Storm, overflying the mucky and slippery roads west.

They found lodgings in Brouwer, went to where the dragon's corpse lay.

The cavalryman who had found the dragon had been sent back, with three fellows, to guard the body.

It lay on a sandy beach in a cove just north of the long island that protected Brouwer, and was in perfect shape.

"Dunno if anybody uses dead dragons for anything, sir," he reported. "But I thought it well to take care.

"It only died two days ago. Made me uneasy, while it was thrashing about. Couldn't think of anything I – or anybody else – could do."

Hal made arrangements for the man to be rewarded for his forethought . . . and his concern.

Limingo had a tent in his wagon, and ordered the two men with him to pitch it, as close as possible to the green and white body that sprawled just above the high-tide line.

"Now for you, young man," Limingo said briskly, rubbing his hands together like a chirurgeon about to begin an amputation. "If you'll go in that tent, strip down, and rub yourself with this unguent . . . we'll take care of our portion of the ceremony."

Hal obeyed, shivering at the cold. There was nothing inside the tent except a camp cot.

He stuck his head back out, saw Limingo and his two assistants drawing convoluted symbols in the sand. The two laborers stood well back from the scene, near where the land sloped down to the beach.

Evidently Hal wasn't the only one who was a trifle goosey about magic.

The acolytes set up seven torches, on chest-high poles stuck into the sand, waved their hands over them, and they sprang into life. In spite of the onshore winds, the torches burnt steadily, never flickering.

The assistants took scrolls from their cloaks, began reading in unison.

Their chanting was a bit soothing.

Hal yawned.

"Now, you, back inside, and on the cot," Limingo said.

Hal obeyed.

"Now, I want you, as much as you can remember, to feel as you did when you had that dream, that vision."

Hal thought back, tried to obey.

Limingo took a small green leatherbound book from his cloak, started reading, in an unknown tongue.

Hal got sleepy.

Limingo kept reading, and it became a chant, and suddenly he switched to Derainian, or else Hal suddenly and magically understood the language he'd been speaking.

> *"Go in*
> *Go back*
> *Go in*
> *Go back*
> *Into the current*
> *Into the wind."*

All at once, Hal was lying on the beach outside, feeling pain, the long pain that had carried him across the great waters, fading, ebbing, and he knew and welcomed death.

He realized he was now that dragon outside, dying, and he tried feebly to fight against death.

Somehow he knew he was moving backward, still the dragon.

Now he felt the waves wash over him, and whimpered as the pain came back.

Then he was in the surf, the waves crashing at him, at his brutally torn wing, his ripped-away tail, his battered carapace.

He was further out at sea, his wings, such as had been left him, wrapped around his head, a tent against the buffeting winds and waves.

He was alone, no land in sight, the current carrying him.

Part of him was this poor maimed dragon, being swept west by wind and waves, and part of him, a strange part, small, soft-fleshed, lay in some sort of cover on a far-distant beach.

A voice came:

> *"Let it take you*
> *Let it take you*
> *Watch the stars*
> *Watch the stars*
> *Let it take you*
> *Now come back*
> *Come out*

*Slowly
Just a bit."*

He peered out, into the storm's beginnings, up at the sky, as someone, something, had commanded him, saw the night sky, clouds whirling past.

It was day, and the pain was stronger, but so was his strength.

From the depths below rose a snake-headed monster, wide fanged jaws snapping at him, and he found strength, clawed talons striking out, and the surprised snake-head snapped back, hissed, went looking for weaker prey.

He was in the air, tumbling, spinning, crashing down, and for an instant the cold water felt good on his wounds, then it seared, as he came up.

There were strange things in the water, skeins, with fish leaping inside, the skeins being tended by odd, bulky things that were not fish.

He was in the air, floundering, and it was night, and again the voice came:

*"Watch the sky
Watch the sky
Remember the sky."*

He obeyed once more, and then he was flying, barely flying, wing torn, fleeing from those three red and black monsters that had attacked his crag, tearing into his mate and their egg.

Something had told him to fly into the rising sun, and he obeyed, and he saw the sea below fade back, and then there was land—

And there was agony as the three monsters ripped at him, and his mate lay dying, and he fought back, without hope, uselessly—

And something cold dashed into his face, and a voice was shouting:

"Come out now! Come back! Or face the real death!" and it was Limingo, not chanting a spell, and Hal was back on the beach, remembered pain tearing at him, fading down and away as Limingo's spell receded.

He sat up, shaking, his body drenched in sweat.

He threw up suddenly.

Someone was kneeling beside him, holding a hot drink.

He managed to sip it, felt its warmth.

Then he was cold again, and someone draped a cloak over him.

He was one again, Hal Kailas, on a beach beside a dead wild dragon.

But he would never forget those moments of remembered dying agony, as he, the dragon, suddenly without a mate or kit, fled from his home across the ocean, currents and winds taking him west, hoping to see a peaceful land, finding nothing but death.

Hal Kailas remembered what Limingo had shouted, and he looked up at the sky, at the stars.

He shuddered, remembering quite exactly, knowing that he now knew where he must go.

17

!A GRAND ADVENTURE!
INTO THE UNKNOWN
WESTERN LANDS!
JOIN THE DRAGONMASTER
AS HE EXPLORES
LANDS OF MYSTERY
On His Majesty's
Service
HIGHEST PAY
AND SHARES OF ANY PLUNDER
BONUS FOR
THE EXPERIENCED:
Dragon-Fliers
And Handlers
Raiders
And
Officers & Seamen
ALL OF A GOOD HEART
AND BRAVE SOUL
CARRY THE FLAG OF DERAINE
INTO THE WILDS
Apply in person to . . .

18

Hal started putting the pieces of his expedition together.

The poster was nailed up around Deraine. Hal wondered what sort of recruits he'd find, but had other tasks at hand first.

But he did make a call on Sir Thom Lowess. The taleteller was somewhat nervous over not having told Hal about his former wife's peccadilloes, but Hal made no mention of that. Khiri, like many other things, was now in the dead past, and Hal mostly succeeded in not thinking about her.

Hal told Sir Thom that he wanted the maximum amount of publicity, to make sure he got the best in the land.

Lowess said he'd cooperate, but had a suggestion: the campaign was to wait for a bit, until Hal had something concrete to talk about. Also, he was to play utterly mysterious to the other taletellers.

"That'll bring 'em flocking around, sniffing like hounds. Then, later, I'll do my story. Since they'll have been dropping little tidbits until then, there'll be no way the other broadsheets can ignore your crusade, and so they'll go louder and bigger, like hounds baying after their better who's sniffed the prey."

Hal shrugged. He had less than no idea of how the taletellers worked, and even less curiosity.

Now came the ships. He already owned the *Galgorm Adventurer*.

The king gave him a basin to fit out in, and the *Galgorm* was taken into dry dock and given a far more thorough refit than she'd had before Hal set off for Sagene, including new yards, rigging, canvas, her bottom scraped and coppered, and a more seaworthy launching barge built, since they were to be testing the stormy Western Ocean. Also, both the galley and the cabins were made more luxurious. It might be a very wearisome cruise.

The *Galgorm*'s sister ship was given to Hal for a seedling rent, as were two light corvettes, the *Compass Rose* and the *Black Orchid*, as well as two fast dispatch boats.

That was adequate for Hal. He wasn't mounting a battle fleet. If trouble, big trouble, was encountered, the dispatch boats were to flee, and bring the word back to Deraine, while the other four would do what they could to escape.

There were more than enough shipwrights out of work to take care of the rebuilding of the six ships, so Hal turned his attention to the main concern: the dragons, their fliers, and their handlers.

He planned, since he had no idea how long the voyage would take, to take only sixteen dragons, plus replacements, which would give the monsters enough room to be comfortable.

He planned to divide his sixteen into two flights.

His first recruit was Garadice.

The old man came up the gangplank of the *Galgorm*, which Hal had made his headquarters, looked about and nodded approvingly.

"This is more likely a project than you forming groups of bandage experts," he said. "Of course, I'm along."

"Of course," Hal said, although privately wondering if the man would take to his command, since he'd been used to nearly complete independence during the war.

His old dragon doctor, Tupilco, appeared, explaining that no one seemed to need to medicate monsters these days, and signed the articles.

Next were the fliers.

Of course, Farren Mariah, the first he sought out, grumbled, glowered, and accepted the charge of being commander of the first flight.

The second flight went to the man who'd first commanded Hal, back at the start of the war, Lu Miletus. He didn't offer any explanations for why he wasn't content in peacetime Deraine, and Hal didn't ask, grateful for the man's proven ability.

Cabet showed up, which gave Hal an adjutant, and a known replacement as flight leader if there were casualties.

He asked Cabet casually about Calt Beoyard. Cabet grinned. "Remember that bordello in Carcaor? The one with the very young girls?"

Hal did ... and he also remembered Beoyard's fascination with the dive.

"He's gone back into Roche, become the protector of the brothel, and swears he'll never get anywhere higher than a second-story bedroom, or demons can take him."

That was that.

Hal was trying not to lose his temper listening to a carpenter tell him how to reinforce the dragon pens on the *Galgorm* when a wiry man with amazing mustaches came aboard.

Aimard Quesney.

He and Hal stared at each other, then Quesney made a sort of salute.

"Are you coming aboard to tell me how I've found a new and interesting way to make a fool of myself?" Hal asked.

"I thought about it," Quesney said. "Especially after seeing your poster. Tsk. Plunder indeed."

"Unless I'm very mistaken," Hal said, "there'll be no plunder. We're sailing west to try to help the dragons . . . as you, and others, suggested. Or at least to find out what's driving them west, killing them when it can."

Quesney stared at Hal.

"I think I might owe you an apology," he said. "That is truly an honorable, if probably foolish, quest."

"I'm glad of your approval," Hal said sarcastically. "Might I ask what happened to your priesthood? Weren't they quite pure enough for you?"

Quesney flushed, then recovered, and stared out at the harbor.

"I deserve that, I suppose. I've not formally left. I came down to Rozen to see just what you were intending.

"Now I know.

"Is there room for another flier?"

"Are you willing to accept discipline?" Hal asked. "I don't need a doubter always behind me."

"If you'll have me, I'll serve faithfully."

Hal hesitated. Quesney was an extraordinary flier . . . but he'd certainly been a pain in several areas, from his firm opinions to his dissidence.

And yet . . .

"I'll have you," Kailas said, making up his mind. "And don't make me regret it."

A trace of a smile came to Quesney's lips, and he rose, and saluted, a very crisp one this time.

"I won't," he said. "Sir."

The next step was putting Sir Thom Lowess into motion.

His fellow scribes had been frothing at the mouth, trying to get details on this royal expedition into the unknown. But nothing came from either the palace or from Hal.

Then the wave broke, with several long pieces by Sir Thom on the possible danger to the west that might threaten Deraine, the pogrom that was evidently being waged against the dragons. The best and the bravest would sail on a fact-finding mission, he wrote, "and if there's fighting about, there's no readier for it, or braver, than Lord Kailas, the Dragonmaster."

And so on and on.

Sir Thom's fellows had to catch up, with little facts beyond those Lowess had contrived.

Naturally, then, their stories were wilder and more heroic than his.

The second wave of applicants roared in, in person and, in spite of the poster's caution, by post and messenger.

It seemed everyone wanted to go with the Dragonmaster.

Sometimes this was good: there were more than enough applications from combat-experienced rangers, scouts, sailors, dragon-handlers, even clerks who'd spent time in the military.

Sometimes these included faces from the past:

Uluch, Hal's old and taciturn body servant, arrived, announced he wished his old tasks back. Hal asked him what had happened since he was discharged. Uluch said, briefly, "Went back to the greengrocer's. Didn't like it. The boss's wife didn't like me. That was that."

And that *was* that.

Another was Chook, the enormous and lethal cook from Lu Miletus's squadron, whose family had supposedly owned a great restaurant in Deraine.

"I went back, thinking I knew ten ways to steal from the owner. Found out other people, who hadn't bothered to waste time in the army, knew twenty.

"So I beat 'em all up, decided I wanted to lay low for a while, and heard about you."

Hal didn't give much of a hang about Chook's murderousness, remembered how good he was at making gourmet dishes out of ration salt beef, flour, and imagination, and signed him aboard instantly.

Sometimes things were heartbreaking:

No, Hal wouldn't sign someone on because his wife was unfaithful.

No, Hal wouldn't take the romantic student who'd avoided the war, regretted it, and wanted to prove himself.

No, Hal had no idea whether someone's missing wife had signed on under another name, and didn't have time to look.

No – and this was the worst – Hal couldn't accept the schoolboys who sometimes showed up at the docks, with improvised knapsacks, looking for adventure. He couldn't manage to be fatherly and order them back home, remembering himself as a young runaway. But he couldn't take them.

To see the hope in their eyes extinguished like a snuffed candle . . . this sat hard with him, and he took it out on the dockyard workers.

Sometimes it wasn't hard to turn down volunteers at all: men and women with strange, distant looks in their eyes, who wanted something from Hal he couldn't, didn't dare, offer them. Only a few of them were combat veterans, although several lied about their experience.

Sometimes, somebody he'd have liked to have aboard turned him down:

Sir Loren Damien, he of the gentle soul and deadly flying skills, arrived. He listened to Hal's spiel, then smiled.

"First, I'm not going with you. I'm perfectly happy on my farm, raising horses that don't try to tear my leg off, unlike dragons, and tenants who have no interest in anything beyond their plough, a bit of beef, and a pint in the local.

"I came down to test myself, which I suppose is unfair to you, but I wanted to know if I could be wooed by the thought of distant lands and deadly enemies.

"I find I'd rather read about it, later, when Sir Thom writes of your adventures."

He and Hal had a riotous night in the fleshpots, and Hal went back to his work much more cheery, even with an aching head.

Another who wouldn't go, because Hal didn't offer, was Sir Thom. Hal remembered the time the taleteller had gone into the field and found that the whisper of the ax and the whine of the arrow were not for him, except when they were told about at a distance.

Ex-fliers swarmed to him, including a few Sagene, who'd somehow heard of the expedition.

Hal was intrigued that a good percentage of them were women, wondered why, got no volunteered explanations.

He signed fourteen of the very best on, which gave him a few extra bodies to allow for sickness and loss.

He noted, and didn't like noting, a short, slender, Sagene brunette named Kimana Balf. She reminded him of the dead Saslic Dinapur entirely too much, and Hal had forced the past away and wanted nothing romantic in the present.

But she had a great deal more experience than her years and features suggested, and Hal took her on.

One of the last fliers to appear was Hachir. Hal had roughly recruited him at the beginning of the war as a crossbowman, to ride behind him and kill Roche fliers. Hachir had done well, then the ex-teacher had gone back to his infantry regiment.

Later, he'd shown up as a fledgling dragon-flier, explaining that he'd liked flying, and had applied and made it through school. But his return to Deraine had otherwise been a disaster, when he discovered his wife had found a lover.

Seldom smiling, Hachir had done yeoman's work in the final days of the war, managing to survive the vast aerial battles.

But now, he was still mournful-faced.

Farren asked if he was related to a beagle, or had hard times stayed with him after he got out of the military.

"No, the times weren't hard," Hachir said, trying a smile and failing. "I went back to teaching, but couldn't stand nattering little voices and the squeak of chalk."

Farren reported to Hal.

"Too well rehearsed a hoary story." He stopped, made a face. "I guess he's just one of the ones who should've died, maybe getting some kind of medal."

He was silent for a time, then said, very quietly, "Maybe there's more than one with us who that could be said about."

Hal bought Mariah a drink, added Hachir to the roster.

Garadice had found his dragons – mostly the big blacks that did so well, all of them with battle experience. These were in the peak of health, and as well trained as possible. Their riders would be responsible for the finishing touches, and making the beasts lose whatever bad habits their previous owners had given them.

Hal took Storm, even though he was neither huge nor a black, and a second dragon, one of the biggest blacks, which he wryly named Sweetie, after the dragon he'd once ridden that'd been named and raised by a little girl, and that had dumped him into captivity during the war.

Next to arrive were four magicians.

One, as King Asir had feared would happen, was the eminent Limingo. The second was his carefully schooled subordinate, Bodrugan. With them were two acolytes, of course chosen as much for their looks as their sorcerous talent.

"The king isn't going to like this," Hal said.

Limingo shrugged.

"Let him come up with more interesting needs for magic, then."

"What's he going to do, anyway?" Bodrugan asked. "Magicians, even clean-cut sorts such as ourselves, can wreak a terrible vengeance."

Hal nodded nervously, and had Mariah sign them aboard and give them the best staterooms on the *Galgorm*.

With over five hundred men and women, Hal was about ready to sail out.

He was on the deck of the *Galgorm* late one afternoon when he saw a rather large and shabbily dressed man come in the gate of the yard, looking about furtively.

Hal recognized him instantly – the cart-size thug, Babil Gachina, his cellmate.

Hal, half figuring what he wanted, went to the dock to greet him.

"Want to go with you," Gachina announced.

"How much trouble are you in?" Hal asked.

Babil looked surprised.

"How did you know?"

"You didn't exactly have the look of a good, honest working man about you coming through the yard."

"Mmmmh," Babil said. "Got to work on that. Maybe that's what give me away."

"You were doing what at the time?"

"A little robbin'," Gachina said. "Nothin' violent. But the man whose carriage I was rifling's got friends. Friends with other friends who're warders and such. Thought it might be best if I wasn't seen around the usual parts for a while."

Hal thought about what he was going to do and say, thought it would be the worst sort of romanticism.

"You know what happens to thieves aboard ship?" he asked.

Gachina shook his head.

"Sometimes they just get tipped overside," Hal said. "Or sometimes both hands get nailed to an beam, and the thief gets beaten, sometimes so he has trouble walking ever."

Gachina stared at him. Kailas, not flickering, stared back.

"My brother said you was a hard man."

Kailas didn't reply.

"Awright," the crook said. "I give you my family word, which I ain't never broken, that I'll do no harm to nobody or their property, and behave like a good an' proper citizen. At least until I advises you different.

"If you'll have me."

"I'll have you," Hal said. "We can always use a man of muscle. But break your word with me, and I guarantee there'll be no trial or beating.

"I'll deal with you myself."

Gachina looked at the deck, was silent.

Hal stuck out his hand.

"Now . . . welcome aboard."

A smile slowly spread across the big man's face, and he stuck out what had to be a hand, since it was at the end of his arm.

Finally, Hal could find nothing and no one more to require on the ships, and held a final conference for the baying broadsheet scribes, making a mildly revolting but no doubt sonorous speech about the expedition and the most honorable king who'd funded it.

Three days later, the six ships set out.

It appeared as if all of Rozen, and half of Deraine itself, lined the banks of the river leading down to the Chicor Straits, all waving flags and cheering.

King Asir's yacht sat in midstream as they sailed past, and the king was in the bows, holding his scepter, in ceremonial robes.

The adventurers bowed, then gave him a cheer.

Hal stood at the salute until they were past the yacht, then ordered sea watches set.

Everyone except Hal, Mariah, and the king thought the party was headed toward foreign shores.

It would be . . . after one stop.

There would be no room for mistakes beyond the Western Ocean.

19

The secret stop Hal ordered was off the fishing village of Brouwer, about as far west on Deraine as it was possible to be. He'd detached Cabet days earlier, and a detail of twenty men with wagon-loaded supplies.

The supplies were deliberately left in large piles on a dreary, rain-swept moor beyond the village.

Hal's ships were anchored off the port, and all hands brought ashore and marched to the moor.

The order was given to pitch camp, and stand by for further orders.

Everyone set to, after a few moments of surprise that the expedition wasn't well on its way to sea and foreign adventure.

Hal, Limingo and Farren Mariah worked as hard as anyone. Harder, for their eyes and ears were pitched for whiners or malingerers.

There were a few.

They were taken aside, and told they were discharged, effective immediately, from the expedition.

Most of them were astonished.

Hal brought them together, and made a short speech:

"Adventure starts in the shitter, most often. If you women and men can't handle putting up a few tents when it's soggy out, and still manage a laugh, how in the hells do you think you'll stand real hardship?"

They were sent back aboard one of the dispatch boats, which also carried letters to an equal number of the almost-qualified, telling them there were new openings with the Dragonmaster.

Most of the slackers eliminated, Hal called the survivors into a group, and made another short speech:

"You're soldiers, each of you. Now we'll train you to work together. An army, or an expedition, isn't just a group of wild-haired adventurers, in spite of what the taletellers blather."

Each man and woman was required not only to hone old skills and talents, but to learn another trade.

Hal anticipated casualties, with no replacements thousands of leagues from home.

So scouts learned how to clerk, farriers learned how to soldier, and, most importantly, everyone learned about dragons.

The training was, of course, hasty, and probably wouldn't hold together beyond the first encounter with an unknown foe, if there was to be one.

They even played war games, small-size battles.

These were remarkable because casualties were named in mid-problem. Suddenly a private would become a section leader, frequently with no idea of what the battle was about.

Officers and warrants were chosen, tried, and, sometimes,

reduced to the ranks. This was no particular disgrace – the only privileges those in charge had were working harder, longer hours than their underlings, and wearing a dark strip of cloth around their right arm.

The dragons and their fliers were sweated as hard as anyone. Some of them, like the Sagene, didn't know the trumpet calls the Deraine warriors used, so they had to learn. Hal insisted on everyone knowing the signals for a few simple formations: line abreast, column, and a group of vees.

Each flier picked a wing mate, and trained with him or her, flying close company. If they didn't get along, or, more importantly, their dragons hated each other, they found another partner.

Garadice had done an excellent job of making sure the dragons were roughly trained and able to mostly get along with other beasts, so there weren't any major problems when the fliers applied their own finishing touches. There'd be more learning, for both dragon and people, when they finally set sail.

Hal was delighted at the smoothness and rapidity of the training, but gave little sign of his elation, consciously developing a reputation as a man for whom perfection was only passing.

He thought often of Lord Cantabri, and how much he would've liked to have been along, and how much Hal would have appreciated being just a dragon-flier under his command.

He paid little attention to his people's private lives, figuring that anyone who was willing to fight and die should be able to figure out who they wanted to bed or befriend. One rule was that any man lifting a hand against his fellow would be immediately discharged.

He let his men ruminate about what that would mean in practice when they were at sea, and beyond setting someone back on the road for Rozen.

After three weeks, he thought the force had learned as much as it could without stretching the training into months, and had a second shipment of wagons sent for.

When the wagons, filled with delicacies and luxuries, arrived, he told the force they were ready to sail, and would be off duty for two days.

He ordered that anyone found disturbing the peace in Brouwer might be tossed off the expedition, and at least would be given a set of lumps and kitchen detail for the voyage.

To make sure nobody got rowdy in the little fishing port, he detailed two sets of largeish people, including Chook and Babil Gachina, as peacekeepers.

Hal meant this as a final test of Gachina – if he misbehaved, or took advantage, he could walk back to Rozen while the expedition went on without him.

Kailas gave himself a day off as well – he paid for the exclusive use of Brouwer's best café, of the three available, and told them to do their best.

He intended to spend the evening there alone, thinking of anything but dragons, and then have a dreamless, peaceful sleep for at least eight hours.

Spring loomed, but there was still a bite to the air.

Hal left camp, and strolled through Brouwer. Only a few of his team were in the village – the villagers had been neither warm nor cold to the soldiers, something which Hal could have told them was typical of the north-western coast.

They'd already had their sendoff, anyway, back in Rozen, so almost all of the expedition members settled for the delicacies Hal had ordered and the simple joys of being back aboard ship, with a bed off the ground, and a roof overhead against the rain.

Kailas, an hour early for his dinner, went down by the jetty, and watched the fishing smacks tied to the docks for a time.

That was not a life he envied – hard, dangerous, and not terribly well paying. But those who loved it, loved it.

It was chill, a wind coming off the sea, and he pulled his cloak tightly about him, thinking of the warm brandy he'd be having in a few moments.

There was only one other person on the wharf, who was also staring to sea.

After a moment, Hal recognized her:

Kimana Balf, the Sagene dragon-flier.

He was walking toward her, intended to move behind her, without bothering whatever thoughts she was having, but instead wished her "Good morrow."

"And the same to you, sir," she replied.

"A bit chill out."

"I like the cold," she said. "Always have. When I was growing, that meant, unless it came too early, that we'd made it through another year."

Hal had expected some inconsequential reply, and then a good evening.

Instead:

"Why?" he asked. "What odd trade were you in? Fur coats, perhaps?"

Kimana laughed.

"No. I . . . or rather my father was . . . is . . . a vintner. The first freeze, which should mark that all your grapes are off the vine and trampled into the vats, marks the first time you can relax, when the damned gods aren't be able to flood or bake or freeze your crop."

She shook her head.

"A hellish trade."

"I can think of a worse one," Hal said. "Two worse ones, really."

"Which are?"

"Scrabbling underground for coal, keeping one ear always cocked for the crack of a pit timber. Or," and he nodded his head at the docks, "going after fish in a little spitkit in the middle of a storm."

Kimana laughed. "I guess most jobs that you're not in, not part of, aren't attractive."

Hal decided her trace of an accent was delightful.

"True," he said. "I could never stand to be a clerk in a city, for instance."

They walked on, each trying to come up with a worse way to spend a life.

They came to the café that Hal had bought out for the evening, and suddenly the thought of another solitary meal became intolerable.

"Have you eaten yet?" he asked in Sagene.

Kimana shook her head, spoke in the same language. "I hope the mess cooks have saved something."

"A better idea," Hal said, and asked her to dine with him.

She looked surprised.

"We're both off duty," he said. "So tonight I'm just me."

"Which is, Lord Kailas?"

"Hal."

They went in, were greeted by the owner and his wife, and served dinner.

They ate smoked fish on bits of brown bread; oysters on the half-shell; crab on toast with a butter, dessert wine, cream, and spice sauce; great mushrooms, raw, with an oil, vinegar, and spice dressing.

"I didn't plan on drinking," Hal explained. "So I wanted a chilled herb tea."

"I'll have the same."

"And I don't want any dessert," he said. "Not much of a sweet tooth."

"Umm," she said, and so he sent the owner out for a trifle.

He himself had cheeses, and was replete.

During the meal they talked of this and that, but never about the expedition, and Hal realized how very attractive the young woman was.

"I swore I wouldn't bring up anything resembling our work," he said, very apologetically, "but there is a question that's been working at me for some time."

"Ask," Kimana said. "You have only to face a silence if I can't answer."

"I've wondered why we had so many women volunteers," he said.

"May all your questions be so easily answered," she said. "That's easy: men."

"Pardon?"

"Most of us – certainly myself – grew up thinking that men were always in charge of everything, that they always knew best.

"Then the war came along, and they were looking for people who wanted to fly dragons, and almost nobody knew anything about that, particularly in Sagene.

"I'd gone for two flights when a dragon-flier came through, and loved it.

"My father forbade anything as bizarre as joining the army, let alone flying along on a great lizard.

"I was betrothed to the son of a nearby winemaker ... had been since I was born, I guess. It was one of those things that everybody expected I'd do.

"Including me, I suppose.

"But then a recruiter came along. And to my complete astonishment, I found myself going with him. And I loved flying my own dragon more than being a damned passenger. I loved everything about it, including the fighting."

She made a wry face.

"And somehow I lived ... I joined right at the end of the fighting, but saw a fair bit of action.

"Then it was over.

"I thought of going back, marrying Vahx, spending my life

having babies and squishing grapes, and a cold chill went down my spine.

"So I ended up in Fovant, on a small allowance from my father. He was scandalized I wasn't coming home and doing the right thing . . . I can almost hear the capital letters . . . but figured I'd come to my senses, and so didn't disinherit me or anything drastic.

"The gods bless and keep him.

"I studied art, realized I didn't have an inkling, then just hung about.

"Instead of coming to my senses, I heard about your expedition . . . and that was that."

"Interesting," Hal said. "I guess that sort of thing's true for men, as well."

"I think you're missing my point, and where this whole thing started," Kimana said. "You could have gotten out of the service . . . or maybe you did . . . and done whatever you wanted to. So could most of the other men.

"It's different for women. We would've had to go back to things just as they were.

"Mostly, that involved men and marriage."

Kimana shook her head.

"But that wasn't what a lot of us wanted."

"What *did* you want?" Hal asked. "I ask, because it doesn't seem that any of us men know."

Kimana looked forlorn.

"I still don't know. I wish I did."

"When you figure out," Kailas said, "be sure and tell us."

"Interesting," Kimana said. "I wonder why no man ever said that to me . . . or I to him. Godsdamn it, sooner or later men and women have to learn to talk."

Hal thought of telling her about his wonderings about why his marriage had collapsed, about Saslic Dinapur, and her "There won't be any after-the-war for a dragon-flier." But he didn't.

He also thought about taking her hand, and didn't do that, either.

They walked back to the camp without talking much, but were comfortable in each other's company and their own thoughts.

Hal slept well that night, and woke with a smile on his lips, although he couldn't remember what he'd dreamed.

He allowed a day for recovery from hangovers, final

rearrangements of the cargoes, and a chance for last-minute hesitations and resignations.

To his surprise, there were none.

The following day, they set sail on the evening tide, just at twilight.

There was only one person, a small girl, probably a fisherman's daughter, frantically waving goodbye from the jetty.

20

It was very calm for the Western Ocean as they passed beyond the island sheltering Brouwer. But when the ships hit the first long, rolling swells, there were more than a few landsmen, and even sailors who'd been away from the sea for a time, whose stomachs came up.

Hal Kailas was one of them. He kept swallowing, but his guts kept trying to inspect his gums.

He thought he was doing all right; after all, he'd been at sea before, and this was just queasiness.

He put himself amidships, next to a mast . . . and a bucket . . . in case the old adage didn't work.

He was just congratulating himself on his victory when a grizzled sailor went past, loudly chewing a sandwich largely made up of greasy pork.

The bucket came into play then, but Hal felt better afterwards. He went to the scuttle, rinsed his mouth, and concentrated on the watch.

But he didn't go below when the meal was called.

The small fleet set its course west and south, following the directions divined by Hal's vision.

He had ordered the ships' captains to set not only the normal watch, but a second man with a glass at the masthead, to look for anything in the air. That watch was mounted an hour before dawn, lasting, in two-hour shifts, until an hour after dark.

He'd also taken the precaution of having a very heavy crossbow, almost a catapult, mounted high in the rigging of the four larger ships.

He didn't think dragons could see in the dark. At least, none of his civilized monsters could. And since man couldn't, either, there was no point in cutting into the expedition's sleep.

There was little rest for either the innocent or the wicked. Warrants ran troops up and down ramps and ropes, regardless of whether they were expected to fight or forage, keeping them in shape.

Hal kept his fliers in the air for at least half a day, every day that weather permitted, slowly accustoming the dragons and men who hadn't spent time over water to the situation.

He had Limingo recast his spell to the ship's beef, so a lost flier merely had to touch an amulet, think of the salt beef in casks aboard the *Adventurer*s, and the spell would tell him in what direction he did *not* want to go. All the flier then had to do was ignore his stomach, and fly in that direction.

Outside of producing some gastric distress, particularly in Farren Mariah, the spell worked as well as it had earlier.

One thing Kailas did not do, and his officers were strictly ordered to do the same, was waste his people's time with idiotic drills or details.

If you were off duty, you were off duty, and advised to get your head down, Kailas being a firm believer that sleep could and should be accumulated, as could fatigue.

If a soldier or sailor was caught larking about, then the kitchen called, with a loud and clarion voice.

And the passage wore on.

It might have gotten boring if all hands hadn't felt the unknown ahead, which is always a threat.

There were incidents to mark the days:

A huge whale, its back scarred by deep-sea battles with giant squid, passed through the middle of the formation one morning, its odorous spout guaranteeing attention.

Its wise and skeptical eyes considered what it could never have seen before, then it was beyond the expedition, and sounded.

Another time a school of dolphin frolicked around the bows of the ship, playing follow-my-leader, or tag, or who knew what.

Hal had been digesting a meal of the last of the eggs and fried ham and was contemplating feeding Storm and Sweetie, when the dolphin showed up.

They were leaping and cavorting, and Hal was miles away from the expedition, when a voice broke his contemplation:

"I don't believe in any sort of afterlife . . . but if there is, I think I might like to come back as one of them."

It was Kimana Balf.

Hal thought about it for an instant, nodded.

"There's worse," he said, and turned below to feed his monsters.

A storm struck, but one in the air. The sea was relatively calm, although the waves were whipped into froth, and the spray was a third element between air and water.

The ships had all sail struck, and kept a wide berth from their fellows.

Hal lay snug abed, listening to the clatter of the rigging, and the shouts of the seamen on watch.

Alone in his stateroom, he was almost asleep when the thought came that he wouldn't mind a bit of company.

That brought him fully awake, wondering just who his lecherous subconscious was thinking of.

It refused to tell him, and so he bundled back up in his blankets.

But he was not quite as content as he'd been before.

The seas grew warm, and warmer.

Men went on deck without gloves, or even a jacket.

Hal issued orders for any man taking off his jersey to be careful of sunburn, and promised that anyone who put himself in the lazaret for that cause could count on some nice healing saltwater baths to alleviate the pain.

Now a routine came:

Some men, those with little seagoing experience, spent time off watch staring at the horizons, hoping for sign of land, any land.

None came.

Experienced sailors remembered the past. Now, each man and woman had a space, self-assigned and created, only a few square feet. But when he was in it, he was alone, ignored by his neighbors on either side.

Similarly, officers could pace the quarterdeck quite precisely – so many steps toward the rail, turn, so many back, frequently with a fellow, dancing perfect attendance, pacing as he or she paced, turning when they turned. Others were doing the same, completely unaware of anyone else.

Hal felt the men and women could journey for years like that, with never a fight, seldom an argument.

Hal hurried with the others when someone shouted a flying fish was aboard.

He'd never seen such a creature, delicate fins, and light, multicolored body, its colors fading as it died on the wooden planks; had never sailed that far south.

Only the most experienced had, since Deraine was not a seafaring nation, and few of its ships had ever come into these unknown waters.

There was an argument starting about whether the fish flew, or just glided.

One sailor was pointing out, with inescapable logic, that it wouldn't be called a flying fish if it didn't really fly, when the shout came from the masthead.

High overhead, almost lost in the scattered clouds, were a pair of dragons.

Hal found a glass.

They were red and black, and even from this distance they looked huge.

Neither had riders, but they flew together in perfect formation.

Hal, remembering his dreams of murder and pain, felt cold fingers down his spine.

21

The dragons banked, then came down on the fleet as if they were no more than curious creatures who'd never seen man.

But they held to their close formation.

Hal watched, worrying.

Part of his mind reminded him that there were animals in his world that did the same – ducks, geese, the recently seen dolphins – without man's guidance.

Another part muttered, "Bullshit," and tried not to panic.

"All hands to alert," he shouted, and warrants' whistles shrilled.

Hal ran to the dragon stalls.

"I'll have Storm."

"Mine after," called Farren Mariah, checking his crossbow.

The wild dragons lifted from their dive about a thousand feet above the ships.

Storm, even though he was a domestically raised dragon, saw the red and blacks and started hissing like an angry teakettle as he came out of the stable deck, a groom hastily adjusting Hal's saddle.

"Shut up," Hal shouted, foot in a stirrup as he swung into the saddle. An armorer tossed him magazines of bolts, and his crossbow.

The dragon, still looking up at the red and blacks, and moving his head back and forth, thudded down the ramp to the launching barge in a timber-creaking run.

Storm's wings unfurled with a canvas-cracking snap. He took three more steps, was at the edge of the barge, and then he leapt up, and was in the air.

Hal snapped a magazine into place on the crossbow, brought the cocking piece back, then forward, and hung the ready weapon on its hook on Storm's carapace.

Behind him he saw Mariah's dragon climbing, wings slashing for altitude.

The foreign dragons pulled up sharply, and climbed, away from the ships.

They had speed and altitude on the two Derainian dragons, and, at about two thousand feet, converted height to more speed, diving down toward the water, and flying west-south-west.

Storm tried to catch them, but wasn't able.

Hal and Farren Mariah chased the two for a few miles, then broke off the pursuit, their ships still in sight, and turned back for safety, having no idea of what lay ahead.

The rest of the day passed without incident.

At nightfall, lookouts reported two more dragons dogging the fleet.

The dragons – or replacement scouts – were still there when the sun rose.

Hal didn't know what to do: the wild dragons weren't making any hostile moves, and all he knew about them was what he'd seen in his vision.

He didn't want to start a war or take sides in one yet, not

knowing what caused the hatred between the red and blacks and other dragons.

But those two monsters endlessly circling overhead made everyone nervous.

The seas grew yet warmer, and the winds softer, but there was still no sight of land.

However, one of the dispatch boats saw something odd: a huge ring of floats, with nets hanging below them, but never a sight of any boats or men. It was torn, and appeared long abandoned.

Hal had Limingo cast a spell, to see if he could somehow sense the presence and form of the civilization that had made the nets, out there to the west.

Nothing came.

On the fourth day after the dragons had first been seen, lookouts shouted officers to the bridge.

There was nothing, at first, on the horizon.

A very sharp-eyed lookout in the bows, and one of the men at the masthead, were pointing due west.

Hal saw nothing, then slowly quartered the sea with his glass.

At first he thought it was a hair stuck to his lens. Then he saw another one.

There was nothing on his telescope.

He looked again out to sea.

The hair was larger than it had been, and was clearly closing on the fleet.

Hal waited.

In moments, it was clear:

It was some creature's neck, snakelike, sticking up about thirty feet above the water, leaving a purling wake behind it as it came.

"Ain't no seaweed-muncher," a lookout with a glass muttered.

Hal studied the creature. He could make out more of its features now. Atop the snaky neck was a flat, long head, with gaping jaws, and, even at this distance, sharp fangs.

No, it wasn't a vegetarian, not with teeth like that.

"Hands to alert," he called. "All dragon-fliers to their stations. Ready the beasts for takeoff."

Sailors hustled to obey.

The onrushing creature suddenly veered to the side, toward the *Bohol Adventurer*. A sailor was leaning on the rail, gaping at the beast. The beast's neck flashed out, jaws reaching, and Hal heard the scream across the water.

The sea monster had the man by the middle, jaws clenched.

It lifted the sailor clear of the ship. Hal saw his fists drum against the beast's head, to no avail. The creature turned on its side. Hal saw a thick body, fins fore and aft, and then the creature went under, carrying the sailor with it.

Another monster's head snaked out of the wake of the *Compass Rose*, reaching for the helmsman. But someone moved faster, and hurled a marlinspike into the beast's face.

It shrieked, rolled away, and then there was a forest of jaws coming out of the water beside one of the dispatch boats.

The creatures slammed into the side of the small ship, and rolled it hard, its rail almost going under.

The beasts tried again, and Hal realized they must have attacked ships before ... or else they were far more intelligent than any sea creature he had heard of, other than a whale.

The dispatch boat rolled again, almost going over on its beam ends, and then there were dragons in the air.

One, flanked by his partner, dove at one of the monsters, and the rider sent a crossbow bolt into the beast's neck.

Correction ... her partner, as Hal recognized the dragon as Kimana Balf's. Her partner, another Sagene, put his bolt into the beast's body, just at the base of the neck.

The monster screeched, rolled, snapping at itself, and went under.

Hal realized he had more important things to do than gape, and ran down from the bridge of the *Galgorm* to where Storm waited on the launching barge.

Farren Mariah was already orbiting above him, and Hal was airborne in seconds.

Dragons were pinwheeling, diving over the stricken dispatch boat, and Hal found a target, fired, hit the sea beast in its open mouth. It screeched, tucked its head underwater, and dove, Hal not knowing if it was wounded or killed.

He pulled Storm around, looking for another target as he worked the forehand of his crossbow back and forth, reloading it.

A pair of monsters were slamming against the dispatch boat's side, trying to overturn it.

Hal dove on them, and they saw him, and went under.

He looked for another target.

But the monsters had disappeared underwater, as if signaled by a leader.

The dragons patrolled around the ships as the fleet put on full sail.

But none of the sea creatures surfaced again.

After a time, Kailas blew the recall, and the dragons landed, one after the other, and were quickly led up the ramp to their pens.

Soldiers with spears and ready bows lined the rails of the ships.

But they weren't attacked again that day.

The dispatch boat's timbers were cracked, and the ship was leaking.

The crew wove lines through a spare sail, rove it overside as a patch. That would have to hold until they found secure land to careen the small ship and make more permanent repairs.

Hal thought of sending it, or the other dispatch craft, back to Deraine to report the incident.

But he decided there might be more important messages, and more information, to follow.

They sailed on.

Overhead, two more red and black dragons swung through the skies, watching.

22

They sailed on west, doggedly followed by alternating pairs of dragons.

"Clever enough by half," Farren Mariah observed. "Note, they change shift with the glass?"

Hal hadn't . . . it was worrisome enough that the dragons knew enough to replace one another. But now he kept track, and found Farren Mariah right.

Every now and again he ordered dragons into the air against them, but the bigger monsters, having altitude and speed, always avoided interception.

Then he gained another follower . . . or quite possibly more.

One of the snake-headed creatures appeared in their wake.

When one of Hal's dragons swooped on it, it would submerge, then, stubbornly, reappear, never closing, never attacking.

Hal, assuming there were more underwater, posted a watch on the creature, and tried to put it out of his mind, without much luck.

He also noticed that the red and blacks liked these sea monsters as little as men did. One or another of them would occasionally, never with success, try to creep up on the snake-headed beasts, who'd always dive to safety in time.

Hal was starting to get nervous in this utterly unknown and foreign world.

None of the experienced seamen had seen either the red and black dragons or the snaky creatures before in their journeys . . . but then, none of them had been this far west.

The skies were clear and tropical, and temperatures grew still warmer.

But there was nothing on the horizon that suggested land.

Then, Limingo came to him one day and said he'd been having himself mesmerized, and, unconscious, let himself float west.

He'd sensed nothing, and had begun doubting the usefulness of this spell. Then one day, very vaguely, he'd sensed some sort of wizardry, "like a dull glow, before the sun rises, against the clouds," to the south-south-west.

He could nearly indicate the direction on the compass, and so Hal had the fleet's course changed in that direction.

Every day, he put up dragons in predawn darkness, hoping to ambush his followers.

But they figured out his plan, and now were almost on the horizon every dawn, only closing on the tiny fleet when the dragons came back aboard.

Hal gave that up, and put out paired dragons at dawn and dusk, directly on their course, and four more on ten-degree-divergent courses, sweeping ahead of the ships, hoping to see land, or at least whatever had sparked Limingo.

Four days later, they found land.

Of a sort.

The fliers returned to the *Adventurer*s, had themselves boated across to the *Galgorm*, reported, in considerable perplexity.

Hal went out with Limingo behind him, flanked by three other dragons with Bodrugan and the two acolytes as passengers.

It *was* land, about two days' sail distant, and it was quite strange:

It was two islands, the larger about a third of a league in diameter, with reefs surrounded by a huge lagoon.

The main island appeared to be solidly wooded, with no sign of life.

The second island was lightly wooded, also with no signs of settlement.

But beyond the low reefs, which had waves breaking across them, were half a dozen of the net circles they'd seen earlier.

These ones were well-kept, and Hal, looking down on them, understood how cleverly they'd been built. They weren't free-floating, but fixed to stakes. Another net, on the inside of the circle, fastened to booms, extended from one side to the other.

A gate could be opened at either side of the circle, then closed, when fish were penned up.

Then the boom would be worked across, narrowing one of the semi-circles, making it easy to scoop the net's prey out.

But there was no sign of boats or men.

Hal took his dragons lower, but still saw nothing.

He swept over the island, and it looked even stranger – as if it had been roofed, and then the roofing had sprouted branches and leaves.

That made no sense.

"There is magic down there," Limingo shouted over Kailas's shoulder. "Or there has been."

Hal nodded understanding, blew the recall, and they returned to the fleet.

He kept his crews on half-alert all that night and the next day, going to full alert as they closed on the island, even though they'd seen nothing but their constant followers overhead.

Limingo and Bodrugan cast and recast spells.

Nothing.

The snake thing had, thankfully, vanished. At least for the moment.

Hal took half a flight aloft as they approached.

The day before, the lagoon had been deserted, peaceful.

Now, it was a battlefield.

The snake things had swarmed the lagoon, and were tearing at the nets.

But they were not undefended.

Small creatures, smaller than a man, but thicker-bodied, were splashing about, doing their best to drive the snake-heads away.

They weren't animals – they were using sticks, some sharpened at the end, and clubs against the creatures.

But there were too many of the snake-heads.

Hal hesitated for an instant, remembered the old proverb that the "enemy of my enemy is my friend," and grinned to himself.

He blew a note on the trumpet, and Farren swooped close.

"Back to the ship," he ordered. "Bring the others. And spare magazines."

Farren, his reins hanging limply, made a "why are we doing this" gesture, laughed, and dove away.

Hal pointed down, and blew the single note:

"Attack."

And down they went, some on his heels, some hesitating a moment before gigging their dragons downward.

Hal noticed, and was oddly pleased, that Kimana Balf was one of the first to attack, her long dark hair sweeping back behind her.

But the disciplinarian in him made a note to chide her about the hair. It might have been beautiful, and most warrior-like to see, but Hal had known three fliers who had worn their hair long, and were somehow strangled by it, in battle.

He put such nonsense out of his head, loaded his crossbow, and looked for a target.

There were many of them.

He found one, aimed at its head, waited until Storm was very close, killed the beast.

Storm himself was hissing, snarling angry.

His tail lashed around, almost spinning him out of the skies, and caught one of the snake things and tore its head off.

He had another in his talons, tore its chest open as Hal killed his second beast.

Hal expected the snake things to break off, but they were determined to fight, swirling around the nets, striking up at the dragons.

The water creatures had a better chance now, as the snake things ignored them for the moment.

They drove their pathetic spears deep into the monsters' chests and necks, and when the creatures rolled, went for their under-bellies.

Hal took Storm up, around, and back down in a dive, killing two more of the beasts.

He heard a scream, saw a dragon, caught by a snake thing by

a wing, pulled down into the water. Its flier spun off, splashed down, and three snake things tore at him.

Hal kicked Storm around, killed one of the creatures. Then Cabet was coming in from another direction, killing a second.

But where the flier had splashed down, there was nothing but a froth of blood.

Hal brought his forehand grip back, forward, but there was no bolt in the trough.

He swore, pulled the empty magazine free, dropped it in the canvas bag beside him, clipped another magazine in place, and then Farren Mariah, at the head of six other dragons, dove into the fray, a whirlpool of screaming, killing dragons, and their prey.

The snake things seemed to realize then that they were being slaughtered, and broke away, swimming at their best for a gap in the reefs.

Hal's dragons harried them out, and then the monsters vanished into deep water.

Hal took Storm up and around again, and there, just outside the lagoon, was his fleet.

He wondered how the ships could have arrived so quickly, then realized the sun was low in the sky. It was almost dusk.

The barges were in position on the *Adventurer*s, and he signaled for the dragons to land.

He orbited overhead until everyone had landed, then brought Storm in, staggering with fatigue as he came out of the saddle.

He looked out, across the lagoon toward the island.

The water beings had swum to the edge of the reef, and bobbed in the water, only their heads in the air.

They reminded Hal of curious harbor seals.

One of the creatures eeled over the rocks into the open sea, and was swimming toward the *Galgorm*. He reached the landing barge as Storm was led up to the stable deck.

The being was covered with sleek fur, had a pug nose, and intelligent eyes.

It stared for a long time at Hal, as if evaluating him.

Then it lifted both paws – no, hands, with stubby but noticeable fingers – out of the water, palm up.

A sign of peace?

Hal didn't know, but he walked slowly forward, holding his own hands up, weaponless.

23

"Throw him a fish," someone shouted.

Hal glowered back in the direction of the voice. This was no time for japing.

"I'm not jesting," the voice came again, and Hal recognized it as Farren Mariah's. There came a wet-sounding *splot* on the barge deck.

The sea being still trod water close to the barge.

Hal, feeling very much the fool, picked up the fish, and, holding it in both hands, presented it to the creature.

He swore if he heard one laugh from behind him, that person would be sweeping dragon shit for the rest of the voyage.

No one laughed.

The creature lifted out of the water, took the fish, equally ceremoniously, looked up the ramp after the vanished Storm, then dove underwater.

And the watching sea beings disappeared as well.

Hal didn't know what to make of it.

"I s'pose," Farren Mariah said, "we'll now find out if that's a fish that meets their fancy. A fancy fish, as 'twere."

Hal grunted.

"We'll anchor out here," he said. "Put four dragons in the air, and a detail, with crossbows, on each ship to watch for those damned snakes. And man the crossbows at the mastheads."

Two turnings of the glass later, they found out, as sea creatures bobbed up, on the seaward side of the rocks this time, and, not waiting for an invitation, swarmed the ships.

Hal didn't know whether to sound the alarm, but found it was too late, as a wallow of sea creatures buried him.

One was on his lap, another was curiously nuzzling his neck, a third was seemingly fascinated by his smooth skin. All of the creatures were chattering incessantly and loudly, as if sure their listeners understood everything.

"Off me," he growled. "You're too fat to be cute."

But no one paid any attention, until they heard a sharp bark.

One creature – perhaps the one Hal had given the fish to – was splashing for attention about a dozen yards in front of the

Galgorm. Another one motioned at Hal, chattered away, then pointed with a stubby finger at the creature in the water, who swam into the lagoon, turning and beckoning as he did.

Hal had an instant to think.

It would be better inside the lagoon, assuming there weren't any enemies there, than outside, with the snake monsters.

He ordered all six ships to up anchor, and, with a favoring breeze, to sail into the lagoon.

At least, he thought forlornly, we're making our own trap.

As the ships began moving, the creatures dove off them, and swam alongside.

The six anchored in beautifully clear, almost transparent water, and then the creatures came back aboard.

This time, they had fish of their own to present, and various kinds of exotic fruit from the island nearby.

Kailas guessed they'd made friends.

The sea creatures seemed fascinated by the least thing any man or woman did. They even tried to follow, flopping awkwardly on legs that were as much fins as anything, when someone went into the canvas-screened jakes in the ship's bows.

"Like dogs," one flier said.

"No," Quesney said. "Not like dogs at all. Something else. Something I can't put my mind to. But it's unsettling.

"I think."

Limingo was ready with his spell.

He'd taken a bit of fruit peel one of the sea people had cast aside, water from the lagoon, herbs from his chest, and put them into a cotton bag.

He'd dipped the bag in some noxious substance, and surreptitiously rubbed it against the furry back of one of the sea creatures.

He'd touched it to his lips, and then to Hal's, while murmuring foreign phrases, then:

> *"Speak tongue*
> *Ears listen*
> *From them*
> *To us*
> *Bring words*
> *Bring thoughts*

> *Carry them*
> *To us*
> *To our lips."*

After that came a long chant, again in an unknown language.

Quite suddenly, the sea creatures' chatter came clear, many voices talking all at once:

"Big . . . so big . . . could use to pull nets . . . one like us . . . tall naked tree . . . sun higher . . . check nets . . . nets tight . . . new twine . . . fruit good . . . babe has hunger . . . foot scraped . . . watch for wolas . . . like Hnid . . . float well . . ."

"Great gods," Hal managed.

"Now we can talk to them," Limingo said.

"If we want to," he added wryly.

Naturally, once the sea creatures – who called themselves the Hnid – found out that two of the big ones could understand them, their nattering grew louder and quicker.

Hal had to listen to most of it, since Limingo was busy administering the spell to all officers, fliers, and anyone else interested.

"Pour me another brandy," Kailas said.

Limingo obeyed.

"I always thought primitive people – if the Hnid are people – had primitive languages.

"Hah. More fool me. Do you know, they have five different ways to describe how rotten a fish is."

"I'm not surprised," Limingo said. "And they *are* people, if not very advanced. Animals aren't that big a pain. Oh, by the way, those snakes are 'wolas', if you care."

"I'm not sure I do," Hal said. "Not to mention that I'm starting to doubt whether magic is always that useful."

"You and me both."

The dispatch boat the snake monsters had attacked was warped into shallow water near the smaller island, unloaded, then careened.

There was enough dry, seasoned wood in the holds of the ships to make repairs, and the seams were stuffed with oakum and the hull was tarred.

The sailors worked hard, no one taking more than a momentary break.

No one wanted to be stranded on this strange island if any-thing happened.

In two days, when the tide rose, the dispatch boat was righted with levers and rope pulleys taken from the ship's lines and yards, then bodily dragged when the tide was out into deeper water in the lagoon.

Fully afloat, its boats brought its cargo back aboard.

"Seamanlike, that," Farren approved. "Yo ho diddly ho, and have the cabin boy buggered by all hands as a prize reward."

So the sea people *were* on their side.

Except that "scent" of magic that Limingo had felt still needed explanation.

He, Bodrugan, and the two acolytes wanted to explore the islands. There was no objection to them landing on the smaller island and exploring it, which took minutes.

But when it came to the larger, wooded island, the Hnid began whimpering, almost trying physically to stop them.

Limingo halted his investigation for the moment.

It was the enormous brewer's wagon that was Babil Gachina who make the discovery.

The Hnid looked at him with awe, for his size. Chook the cook was similarly regarded.

Why Gachina swam ashore to the wooded island and began exploring was never explained. He claimed he was gathering fruit. Hal wondered if he was looking for something that might be worth looting, but held his tongue.

In any event, after a couple of hours, Gachina reappeared on the beach, looking shaken, and swam back to the *Galgorm*. He sought out Hal.

"There's . . . there's a frigging city under that wood!" he man-aged. "A frigging great city! With carvings everywhere!"

Hal quizzed a couple of the Hnid, got only the vague expla-nation of "dry home," "old home," and "home before," which gave him nothing.

But it was enough.

He collected Limingo, ten men of the expedition with raider experience, plus Gachina, Chook and Farren Mariah, armed them and went ashore. It might have been impolite, but they were too far from home to worry about proper etiquette.

There was more wordless complaining from the Hnid, but they made no move to stop Hal and the others.

"Here," Gachina said. "Here's the way I found to go in."

It looked like the entrance to a fox's burrow. The brush that had been cleverly arranged to hide an entrance hole had been shoved aside to make room for someone of Gachina's bulk.

Gachina went first, Hal behind him, holding back the desire to draw his sword.

He'd expected the burrow to close down, and pushed back his fear of closed spaces, but instead it widened out.

Hal was able to stand, and found himself in what might have been the hall of a forest king.

On either side were great squared stones, carefully trimmed to fit together without a gap.

Here and there were doors and windows, narrow, taller than a man, cut into the stone.

Overhead were the "woods." Hal puzzled, then realized that trees had been grown into saplings, then bent over and tied so they formed an arc over the stones and the streets between them, hiding the city.

He wondered why, thought about the red and black dragons, thought that might be an explanation.

"Here's your magic," Limingo said, almost whispering.

There was no threat, felt or seen, but Kailas felt as if he were in an eerie temple.

"I feel no sense of man's hand working these stones," Limingo said. "But the smell of magic is still very strong, if very old."

There was no point in just gaping.

The men spread out, as if they were on a combat patrol, and they moved through this deserted monolithic city.

It was not unoccupied – Hal saw a Hnid duck back into cover, saw a couple of pups on a higher landing.

But no one came to them, no one spoke to them, and there was none of the Hnid chittering to be heard.

The streets wound around, came back on themselves.

The city felt much larger than it was.

They came to a central square, and saw a ramped passageway leading down, high-ceilinged and wide.

Hal felt a vast reluctance to go down the ramp.

"Don't go down there." Limingo echoed his feeling.

"Why not?"

"I . . . I don't know. But it's not wise."

Hal waited for an explanation, but none came.

They found an avenue away from the entrance to whatever was underground.

The stones on either side, polished ebony, were carefully carved.

They began with beings like the Hnid, swimming in the sea, fishing, fighting battles with fabulous monsters, some of them snake things.

Then stones were shown being carved from a great, looming mountain, shaped, with no mason shown in the carvings, then somehow lifted out to sea and carefully stacked, and the city was born.

There were other islands pictured, other cities built.

Then there were great ships, little more than barges, with twin square sails, sailing away from the cities toward the land beyond.

After that . . . nothing.

There was empty space on the stones to continue the story.

But no one had.

No one knew what to make of it, and so they returned to their ships.

Hal, thinking of that eldritch passage underground, kept men on alert that night.

And, when he finally was able to sleep, he dreamed.

24

All there was, at first, was a soft, diffident voice, amid a roiling sea of gray. The words came haltingly, as if the dream was trying to find a common language with Hal:

I am Malvestin, of the Hnid.

I am but a simple recorder.

But I come from a generation of fisher-leaders, those we call kings, and it is my task to remember from the beginning, when we were but simple animals, living in the shallows, catching our brothers, the fish, with our fangs, as they did, then, later, as our bodies changed, with our fingers.

Hal was now in that street of carvings, of what was the Hnid's history. He saw the carvings, then they came to life, took on the colors of the real world, and moved past him as the voice continued:

That gave us power over our brothers, but we held it wisely, never taking from the sea more than we needed.

But then greed came on us, and we wanted more, and that may be our doom.

Strange creatures came from the depths, and we were their prey.

There had been stories before, about what could happen to those who ventured close to the depths that went down as canyons from our warm, comfortable shallows.

There were many kinds, some huge-winged yet still fish; some like the snakes of the sea that we avoided, but these were huge, and had gross bodies like whales; some were monstrous sharks; others jellyfish larger than any seen, with dangling tentacles that meant death to all who touched them.

We fought back as best we could, with our arms, then with sharpened sticks we found along the shore of the islands we lived near.

We grew more clever, and found our enemies' lairs, and destroyed their eggs, their sprats, just as they found our hatchlings.

Somehow, and this is an art that is now long lost, we learned to have thoughts with the tiny beings that make sea-rocks, and taught them to build in giant circles, around the islands that we chose to live near.

Now we were safer from our enemies, only the snake-headed creatures having sense enough to come in through the small openings in our reefs that we needed for entry and exit, and to work the nets in the outer waters that we had come to use instead of our fingers and spears.

All was good, all was far quieter, and we grew to love the power we had gained.

Now we struck back against the monsters, driving them from our shallow seas into the canyon depths.

Again, our power grew, and some of us learned to work spells, things that could reach for leagues and make changes, or make the fish come to us.

We grew bolder, and, leaning upon our magic as a weapon, we explored the seas, the islands, and found the great island to the west.

Emboldened, we left the water not just for hours, but for days, and our bodies changed, grew legs.

Land and sea were now ours, and we used our sorcery to reach inland.

We found a mountain, then others, who were as sounding boards to our magic, and whose boulders could be worked and transported by wizardry. We carved huge boulders out, and moved them through the water, and then, later, as our powers grew, through the air to our islands.

Fitting stone on stone, we built houses out of the water, then larger buildings we used for gathering places.

Our mother, the sea, was no longer trusted, and we took to the land more and more.

Our cities, our islands, were now outposts to warn against danger.

We built huge rafts, put wind-catchers on them, and sailed west, leaving only the best and bravest on our frontiers.

Now it was time to give up the sea.

We built, on the edges of the western lands, more cities, and, from these, we explored into the land.

There were huge beasts. Some we fought, others were no threat, in spite of their size.

The Hnid stood brave.

Now the world was ours.

Now the elements were ours to worship, but also to serve us.

There was nothing but good around us, and we were the world's masters.

But wise ones thought that we had come too far, too fast, and there was a nameless doom in store.

We laughed at them, but our mirth was hollow.

I wonder.

There was silence, and Hal's dream gave him no images, but in the background, very quietly, was the hiss of breaking waves.

Then another voice came:

Oh Malvestin, you spoke truth, for now is the tale of the downfall of the Hnid.

I am Quarsted, also a recorder, but of the people, not of those who called themselves kings, and ruled with no thought for the morrow and brought our people to grief.

We forsook the sea for the land, and our bodies changed, our lower limbs growing longer and with greater strength.

We settled the edges of the great land, pushed inland. Now our people sought things other than food and shelter.

Now the glitters that mountain streams held became precious, as did other baubles worn by our mates.

We, the Hnid, ruled the world.

Or so we thought.

And then it changed.

There had been dragons, winged snakes, in the skies when we found this new land, and at first we feared them greatly, for we saw them fight against the monsters of the land, and truly they were great warriors.

But they made only a few attempts against us, and so we forgot about them, since there were worse enemies closer at hand, the ferocious beasts of the forests and savannas.

And then it changed.

Our scouts reported a new sort of dragon in the skies. These were red and black, far larger than any we'd seen before.

We saw them attack the other dragons as if they were two different breeds, fighting wars to the death, and driving the older dragons out of the choicer roosting places.

And then they turned against us.

They acted as if they were at least as wise as we were, working in pairs, or trios, or greater forces against us.

They would attack our settlements, fighting from the air until they found an advantage, then landing, as if they were ground beings, and fighting with their deadly claws, fangs and tails.

We could not hold against them.

And so we fell back, from the mountains to the plains, using the rivers to move at night, very grateful that our bodies still held a bit of the scorned water-love.

We fell back and back, to our great towns along the coasts.

Even here these savage dragons attacked us, over and over, even by night.

We drew closer together, and fought as best we could. But that best was not enough, and now the land, and the cities we had built were no longer guardians, but traps for us.

Again, we retreated to the water, and, in time, gave up the mainland.

Our mother, the sea, welcomed us back, although she should have scorned us, and once again, our bodies changed, back to what they were before.

We did not need legs, we did not need deep thoughts, and so the sea took them from us as her price for safety.

Our minds grew torpid, dull, needing little more than the power to feed and shelter ourselves.

We Hnid retreated to our outpost islands, and the tall trees that had grown up on them were woven together to give our cities cover, for the huge dragons still attacked us without mercy.

No one knew why they struck against us, for we meant them no harm, could do little damage to these nightmares from the skies.

No one knew why they fought against what should have been their brothers, attacking without mercy. We saw dragons hard struck, wounded, fleeing to the east, and knew not what shelter they would find.

The snake beings returned from the depths to savage us.

Our mates saw little good in breeding, and so, as the years go past, there are fewer and fewer Hnid born, and fewer of those surviving to become adults.

Now we are as we began.

Woe is ours, woe unto the tenth generation.

All is ended for my people, I fear.

The gods or whatever greater beings there are, if there are any, help us, and those who come and hear our tale take warning for their own lives and the lives of their people.

25

Hal awoke, fighting back tears and rage for the people, the Hnid, of his dreams.

He splashed water on his face from a bucket, opened a port and let the warm dawn wind take away the memories of his dream.

If it was a dream.

He washed, cleaned his teeth, dressed and left his cabin for the deck.

He didn't want to speak to anyone until he'd recovered, but Kimana Balf was at the taffrail, staring down at the ship's wake, her face grim.

"And don't you look cheery," he managed.

"Don't rag me. Sir," she said. "I didn't sleep well."

Hal started to pass by, then stopped.

"You dreamed?"

"And never want to again," she said.

"Tell me about it," he said.

She pursed her lips, said nothing.

Hal took the lead, and told her of his dream, of Malvestin and Quarsted, and the rise and fall of the Hnid.

Balf jolted.

"I, too, dreamed of the Hnid. But my singers were female, and I don't recollect their names."

"I think," Hal said, after considering, "that we had best consult Limingo. This is most odd."

It grew more strange.

Limingo, Bodrugan, and their two assistants had also had the same visions, with small differences.

"Very strange indeed," Limingo said. "And, if it's a vision, the strangest thing is the way the Hnid change – or are changed – in a few generations."

"Not necessarily," Bodrugan said. "I've read of a lizard, in the far south, which can shed its legs and become a snake when it is dry, or grow flippers if the rains are heavy."

"Still . . ." Limingo let his voice trail off while he thought. "It would seem, though, that the Hnid can hardly be considered men."

"I care little of that," Hal said. "But I think we ought to summon the officers of all four ships for a conference. And the fliers."

"I agree," Limingo said, and flags were hoisted, and boats rowed across to the *Galgorm.*

The officers assembled in the huge wardroom, and Hal told of the dream, and Limingo that he believed this was hardly a dream, but a true vision.

There were nervous stirs at that. No one said anything for a few moments, then Guapur Hagi, captain of the *Bohol Adventurer,* looked at Hal and cleared his throat nervously.

"I think . . . without meaning to sound like a poltroon . . . that this dream, assuming the wizards are right and it's the truth . . . means we should turn back to Deraine.

"For I, too, have dreamed this dream of sorrow and punishment of the gods."

There was muttered anger from a few, and agreement about having dreamed as well from others.

Hal held up his hand for silence, then asked, calmly, "Why?"

"Because, well, this sounds like these red and black dragons have some kind of state or something," Hagi said. "I think we might be being foolish, and continuing into what might be a trap.

"Or that we could be outnumbered.

"I think," he said, gaining confidence, "we should advise the king of what we've discovered so far, and see what he wants to do.

"Maybe try to make peace, or fit out some kind of expedition or something."

"We *are* the expedition," Hal said.

"I meant, like a fleet, with a lot more soldiers."

"As yet," Hal said, "we don't have enough information to do that."

"I think we ought to put it to a vote," Hagi said.

"No," Hal said, and his voice carried steel.

"This is not a village conclave. You people put yourselves under my command, which the king himself trusted me to hold.

"There is nothing that gives you the right to question me whenever you want, whenever things go awry. We came on this expedition because we wanted to experience and explore the unknown, and that is what we are facing.

"As you are my officers, I take what you say under advisement, just as I listen to the other men and women, and reach a decision from there.

"No more, no less.

"Now, if no one has anything to add," Hal finished, "this meeting is over. Return to your ships, and we sail on."

There were some mutters, but the officers behaved.

Farren Mariah caught Hal on deck.

"That, maybe, wasn't the brightest thing you've ever done, you know. You maybe should not have held this meeting, and let those dreams go unspoken and remain secret nightmares."

Hal made a face.

"I think you could be right."

"And I think Captain Hagi needs a bit of a watch over," Mariah said. "Or perhaps an anchor stone around his feet before he's given swimming lessons."

"Maybe."

But Hal made no order, and the ships raised their anchors, sailed out of the friendly lagoon, and went on, into the west.

*

Now land rose all around them, but not the solid mass of Hal's dreams.

It was as if they'd entered a river delta, except the water was salt. There were dozens, then hundreds, of tiny islets, growing into larger islands.

Some were swampy, little more than trees whose roots were submerged at high tide, and monstrous serpents, and legged fish that could leave the water inhabited the darkness between them.

Others were grassy hillocks, with tiny deer-like creatures bounding on them, and lithe cats to prey on the deer.

Some of the Hnid swam in the ships' wakes for a time, as if ordered to follow the expedition and report on its fate.

The passages were narrower, sometimes choked with vines, so the men had to kedge back out, and, cursing, find a new way.

Their progress zigged back and forth, and it was hard to hold to that westerly course.

The air was sweet, as the smell of dozens of spices hung around them, spices with no known equal.

"A woman could make a fortune here," Kimana Balf mused. "One cargo of these spices ... whatever they are ... brought back to Deraine, and you'd live in silk."

"True enough," Aimard Quesney said. "If the dragons let you."

The red and blacks were still up there, keeping their post, making no threat to the ships.

Yet.

Hal, a little worried they were off their course to the still-unseen mainland, took Storm up high.

The watching dragons paid little mind to the single monster and its rider, save to move somewhat west.

Hal went as high as he could, until Storm was panting, and he himself sucking for air, and looked west.

Dimly, on the horizon, the "delta" ended, and the seas opened once more.

Spices still hung close as they sailed on.

But now the islands were somewhat kempt, as if a gardener, albeit a careless one, was minding them.

They saw small huts along the water, but they were empty.

Then, one day, a seaman on watch saw the natives: they were like the monkeys men had brought back from the south, tailed, furry.

But they lived in the huts, and were seen with leaf packs.

What was in them was theorized to be spices.

But who, if anyone, they were gathering them for was never known.

Hal ordered boats launched, and tried to make peace with the apes, if apes they were.

But the animals would have nothing to do with men, and so the expedition went on.

Then the islands changed, and were wild and uninhabited once more.

Hal saw the reason: great lizards, almost the length of one of the dispatch boats, that hissed menace when they saw the ships.

Hal sounded an alert, and armed sailors lined the rails, their weapons ready.

But none of these earth-bound dragons did more than menace, and flash their foot-long fangs.

There had been no war so far between the expedition and the red and black dragons.

This changed.

As a pair of dragon-fliers were taking off, just after dawn, one of the wild dragons dove, talons extended.

There were shouts of warning from the ships, but the fliers evidently didn't hear.

The red and black caught one rider by the shoulders, plucked him from his saddle, and threw him into the ocean.

He didn't surface.

The two wild dragons climbed back to their heights, and continued circling.

After the shock subsided, Hal stood on the afterdeck of the *Galgorm Adventurer*, staring up.

Farren Mariah came to him.

"I think," he said grimly, "we ought to think about taking it to the enemy now, for enemy they've proven themselves, for unwarranted liberties."

"Yes," Hal agreed. "Time and time past."

26

The plan was mounted cunningly.

Long before dawn, Hal and Farren Mariah turned out, and moved silently to the *Galgorm*'s landing barge. Handlers brought out their dragons.

Although they wanted to protest, the two dragons were man-handled overside into the water, where they bobbed like cunningly carved corks in the light swells.

They decided they didn't mind the bath in these nice tropical seas as their riders clambered into their saddles.

The ships sailed on past them.

After a time, lights were turned on aboard the ships, almost on the horizon by this time, and sailors began preparing, quite loudly, for an early launch.

As they did, Hal and Mariah gigged their dragons into a splashing run that took them aloft.

Circling, they climbed for altitude, hoping the watching dragons' attention was fixed on what was going on around the fleet.

They climbed very high, gifting themselves with a private sunrise as they ascended.

Below them, in the lightening night, they could make out the dots that were the watching dragons, and below *them*, the ships.

There were trumpet blasts from the fleet below, and Miletus and Quesney, as arranged, made ready to take off.

Hal signaled to Farren Mariah, and the two dragons went into a steep dive.

On the *Bohol Adventurer*, Hachir and his partner also moved their dragons down to the takeoff barge.

The red and blacks were less than five hundred feet below.

Hal cocked his crossbow.

Miletus and Quesney's dragons thundered across their barge, and into the air.

Hal shot the first red and black from above, less than a hundred feet distant, aiming just between the shoulder blades.

The monster contorted, squealed in surprise, as Farren Mariah shot his partner in the wing.

Hal reloaded, fired into the neck of his targeted dragon as Storm dropped past then, on command, flared his wings and braked.

Farren Mariah sent his second bolt into the other wild dragon's throat as he dropped past it.

Below, the other dragons were airborne – but there was nothing for them to do but circle as the two red and blacks, still struggling, seconds apart, crashed into the ocean.

Neither of them came back to the surface.

Farren Mariah yodeled happily.

Hal did not. He swore he'd seen a flash of flame as one dragon hit the water, which made no sense.

It must have been a trick of the rising sun.

He forgot about it.

They'd taken the first step.

The second was soon to follow.

Half a day later, the second trap was set and sprung.

Hal and Farren Mariah had landed, and they and their dragons fed. They waited impatiently until a glass before the now-dead dragons should be relieved, then took off once more.

This time, both dragons carried packs with iron rations and drink for the men, and smoked lamb carcasses for themselves, in case this flight took too long.

There was a high haze, perfect for what Hal wanted.

He and Mariah again climbed high, and flew west and north, until the ships were mere dots almost on the horizon.

They flew in wide circles, waiting.

Hal kept watching the masthead of the *Galgorm Adventurer*. He'd ordered the officer of the deck to signal when his glass showed it was time for the dragon relief to appear.

The banner was finally run up the mast, and, on cue, a pair of red and black dragons appeared from the west.

Hal and Mariah were far above and north of them, mere dots in the sky, hopefully hidden in the haze. But Hal took his partner behind a cloud as the dragons looked for the watch they were to relieve, and saw nothing.

He heard, from below, squawks of what he assumed was surprise, dismay, as the wild dragons saw no fellows awaiting relief.

He flew Storm to the wispy limits of the cloud, saw the dragons below turn back east. Clearly reporting the absence of their fellows was more important than keeping watch on the slow-sailing ships.

Holding altitude, trying to keep between the sun and the red and blacks below, Hal and Mariah followed the wild dragons.

Hal took compass readings as they flew, but the red and blacks held a straight course.

Very unusual – wild dragons, in Hal's experience, zigged across the landscape as they went, distracted by curiosity and appetite.

But not these two.

Ahead of them rose an unknown mass of land from the sea – jagged cliffs here and there, but mostly low coastline.

Unknown to Hal the man . . . but not to his dream-dragon. There was the flashing thrill of home, seen once, never to be more than a reverie in the land between sleeping and waking.

Hal was trying to keep his mind on his mission, but he couldn't suppress a thrill, realizing that he was certainly the first Derainian, perhaps the first man, to see this unexplored land.

He forced that thought aside, concentrated on the job at hand.

The dragons made for one of the cliffs.

Hal took Storm in a wide orbit, to give distance.

The red and blacks flew over the breaker line, and a little inland, then dove sharply, and vanished.

Hal motioned Mariah to dive too, followed suit, and brought Storm out just yards above the low surf.

He had no idea what he was looking for in his pursuit of the red and black dragons, except to find their masters, their home city, and plan a strategy from there.

He knew dragons preferred cliffs and crags for their homes, since flying off was much easier from a height.

So he landed on a low cliff, dismounted, and used a glass to sweep the surrounding cliffs.

He saw no sign of dragons.

Nor did Farren Mariah.

Hal remounted, and they flew on, inland, over a great plain.

Finally, they spotted the dragons, far ahead, mere dots, flying steadily to the west.

Mountains rose from the plain, and the red and blacks flew into them.

Storm was getting tired, but Hal drove him on. Both his and Farren Mariah's beasts still had hours of endurance in them.

The dragons disappeared again into the ridges. Hal assumed the red and blacks couldn't keep in the air much longer than his own dragons. He flew to a high crag, landed, and glassed the rugged range, keeping away from the landward side.

Storm was increasingly nervous, which Hal decided meant

he'd seen and scented the wild dragons, so they couldn't be far distant.

Hal soothed him before creeping to the edge of the crag and glassing the area again.

Still nothing.

He went back to Storm, and he and Farren flew on, this time to the highest peak still on a westerly heading. There was a level spot, almost at the summit, and Hal landed, swept the landscape again.

This time, he found luck.

Of a sort.

In the distance, leagues away, was a fairly large plateau.

On it, he counted ten red and black dragons.

Hal made a face. He'd hoped to find some sort of city that would tell him who and what led the red and blacks.

But there was nothing here except rocks that the wild dragons were using for what could only be a temporary shelter.

That and, here and there, the remains of carcasses that the dragons had fed on.

There was no sign of a civilized building or even crude shelter.

Nor, though he looked for almost an hour, was there any sign of man, or any other being, except the ten dragons.

Hal thought about what he'd seen, then went to Mariah, who'd landed near Storm and was waiting.

He told his partner what he'd found, and not found.

He said he proposed to watch on, and for Farren Mariah to find a shelter, where overhead dragons couldn't spot him, and to return the next day.

Farren Mariah didn't like it, but obeyed.

He took off, and Kailas took his pack from Storm, slapped the dragon's butt, and pointed after Mariah.

The dragon whined, but obeyed.

Hal watched the two dragons disappear, feeling distinctly unhappy, not to mention slightly terrified.

He pulled on a jacket, and returned to his watch.

Two dragons took off, flew toward the sea. Hal guessed it was to resume the watch.

After a time, two others flew off.

It was growing late.

Without any signal that Hal could see, the rest of the dragons took off, and flew in different directions.

Hal tried to record the compass directions each took, but got only five.

He had no idea what they were doing.

But after a time, all returned.

Some bore prey – an antlered animal like a stag, smaller creatures like wild pigs, large birds.

The dragons piled the corpses in a pile, watched while two of them fed.

The two sated monsters left, and then the remaining six fed.

The feeding wasn't like the general chaos Hal was used to with wild dragons, but relatively sedate, with each dragon taking a body and devouring it, and the remaining bodies evenly divided.

Two carcasses were left untouched.

This, again, was new and strange – dragons normally ate everything in sight. But these red and blacks seemed to be saving a meal for the two watching the expedition.

Those returned at full dark, and ate.

Then the dragons curled up, and slept like obedient soldiers.

Hal allowed himself to drowse, woke somewhere in the middle of the night as the watch changed.

Then there was silence.

Before dawn, he heard the new guards going out.

At full light, six dragons took off, and formed a tight, arrowhead-shaped formation. They flew off, to the north-west.

Hal took a compass reading.

In about an hour, six other dragons, in the same sort of formation, appeared from the north-west.

It was as if the guard were changing.

Hal liked none of this.

If there were no handlers below, that could only mean that the dragons were ensorceled by a powerful magician or magicians, who could impel obedience either across a distance, or over a time.

Farren Mariah appeared, flying low.

Hal motioned him in, hurriedly mounted Storm, and set a course back toward the coast.

Once he reached it, he flew south along the shore, but didn't find what he was looking for. He turned north, and found, just out of the sight-line of red and black dragons returning to their base, what he'd been looking for: a deep bay that led inland, sheltered by ridges on either side.

He flew low over it, and it appeared as if the bay was more than deep enough for his ships. Also, there were easy tracks leading inland.

That would give the expedition a base.

He swung Storm back out to sea.

He'd circle around and approach the ships from the east, so the watching dragons wouldn't have a clue what he'd been about.

Then he'd assemble a stronger force, and follow that compass heading.

This time he would be after what appeared to be the *real* dragonmasters.

27

Hal wanted to follow the compass lead, which should take him to the lair of the sorcerers, with all his dragons, plus infantry riders for backup, and all four magicians for support.

But he knew better.

There was no way his tiny expedition could attack what could only be a great city.

The only option he could see was to find the wizards' headquarters, then return to the ships and sail back to Deraine, just as Guapur Hagi of the *Bohol* had wanted.

King Asir would have to take the next step of mounting an invasion force, trying to make peace with the sorcerers, or whatever.

Hal thought, were *he* king, he would try to form an alliance with Sagene and Roche, and then return to this new world, keeping all options open.

But he thought there would be only one option – to destroy or at least render impotent those who were controlling the red and black dragons.

Which would likely mean great magic, which, in spite of Limingo's presence, was far beyond Kailas's abilities. The spells to defeat that unknown city would have to be mounted by corps of wizards, since their magic would surely be stopped, and then a counterattack made.

Hal forced himself to the present.

If he were only to scout the enemy, he would want to be as little visible as possible.

That meant a minimal force of dragons and riders.

Of course his normal flying partner, Farren Mariah, would be one.

He caught himself, realized he'd best consult the man instead of assuming.

Hal found Mariah in his compartment and asked him on deck. He took him to the bow and told the lookout he was relieved for a time, and to go below and have a bite to eat.

"You asked me out here," Farren Mariah said, "in privacy. Assuming you aren't planning to proposition my young sitter, this bodes, modes, not well.

"Or not safety, at any mayhap."

"It's not," Hal said, and told him what he proposed.

"A better bitter way to die," Farren Mariah said. "And I'd be a damned fool to volunteer."

"I agree."

"But if you went bounding off, and got yourself dead, I'd be downcast as all hells," Mariah went on. "So I'm neatly trapped, aren't I?"

Hal didn't answer.

"Aaarh," Farren Mariah said. "All right. You've sprung your trap. Who else are you going to suck in?"

Hal considered.

"Two more fliers, I reckon."

"Who?" Mariah asked. "Every fool aboard'll be volunteering."

Hal grinned.

"Call 'em together, if you would. And have the others come over from the *Bohol*."

While Kailas waited, he went to Limingo, who of course said he would have felt slighted if not given the chance to volunteer, and probably would have cast a spell on the Dragonmaster that would have changed him into, say, a churchmouse.

"Can you do that?" Hal asked in surprise.

"Not at present," Limingo said. "But my wrath would have been such that I would have developed all kinds of new powers."

The dragon-fliers were on board the *Galgorm Adventurer* within an hour, and gathered in the wardroom.

Hal told them what he'd discovered, and what he proposed to do next.

As expected, the fliers all volunteered.

Hal was ready for that one.

He had torn up bits of paper, put them in a flier's hat, and bade everyone to draw one.

Hal barely noticed that Kimana Balf's hand lingered for an instant longer than necessary.

She was the first to announce she'd drawn one of the marked bits.

The second was Aimard Quesney.

That settled that.

Quesney insisted that everyone take adequate survival packs, to include dried rations, a waterproofed blanket, matches, and such.

"We'll not be needing those," Farren said.

"Suppose your dragon goes down?" Quesney asked.

"Then I'll be dead, won't I?"

But he obediently tied a pack to his dragon's carapace.

Hal would take Limingo with him; the others would carry the rations for the dragons and men.

His intentions were to fly to the plateau, which he thought was a way camp, then fly on for a day or two, following the compass bearing he'd taken from the dragons headed further inland, then go to ground and wait for the six dragons being relieved – or so he assumed was what was happening – and follow them to their home city.

"And how how howly will we keep from having those six dragons fly right up our arse?" Farren Mariah asked. "Not to mention if this great city of magicians happens to turn out to be only one day's flying away from where we start tracking the red and blacks, and we suddenly find ourselves shitting bricks and right over the main Palace of the Magicians."

"Then," Kimana said briskly, "we're truly screwed, and you can have my collection of manacles."

"You have a collection of manacles?" Limingo asked interestedly.

Kimana shook her head, didn't answer.

"Both your worries will be taken care of by our colleague's magic," Hal said.

Limingo raised an eyebrow.

"We'll leave an hour before dawn tomorrow," Hal said. "Anyone who wishes to pray has my permission."

But the dragon-fliers weren't a religious lot – not even Aimard Quesney. Which might have explained why he'd failed at attempting the priesthood.

Hal gave his final orders, including what was to be done if there was contact with the red and blacks. If that happened, he said, there was no time for nobility. Any unengaged flier was to flee east, toward the ships, with whatever had been discovered.

He told his fliers to eat, get some sleep, and not think about the morrow, which he knew they would anyway.

Then he went to the captain of the *Galgorm Adventurer*, told him he was in charge of the expedition, and that all remaining would obey his orders.

Hal made a rough sketch of the land they were approaching, told the captain he was to anchor in a bay north of the dragons' flight-line, and wait for four weeks. If no one returned in that time, he was to sail for Deraine, and report everything they'd discovered to King Asir.

The officer told him that Guapur Hagi of the *Bohol* had signaled he wanted to come over to the flagship. It was very important.

Hal grimaced. He didn't have time for Hagi at the moment, told the *Galgorm*'s captain so.

The officer said, skeptically, that he didn't think ignoring Hagi was perhaps the wisest thing.

Kailas was starting to get a little angry. "I'll take care of him . . . and whatever frigging problems he has . . . when we get back. Tell him to put a knot in it for the moment."

Hal ate, slept well, dreaming of what a city of magicians and dragons might look like, and woke ready for action.

He'd reluctantly decided that he was depending too much on Storm, and decided to take his other black dragon, Sweetie.

The four monsters were led, one at a time, down to the barge, mounted, and their fliers took them off.

As the last of the four was airborne, other fliers on the *Bohol Adventurer* started making a grand racket, sure to attract the red and blacks' attention overhead.

Or so Hal hoped.

He led his flight back east, then turned south and then west in a great loop.

He set his compass to bring them over land just south of the compass heading the dragons had taken from the fleet to their first base on the plateau.

When he saw land, he turned south for a dogleg, counted slowly to two hundred, then resumed his course east.

An estimated hour inland, he turned north, and corrected

the dogleg, straightening on the old heading toward the plateau.

It was full light, and the fliers held their dragons to a moderate speed.

Below them were the mountains of the coastal range, slowly becoming foothills, and then the great plain spread before them.

Now Hal took time to observe what lay below him, since he was deliberately holding the formation to a far slower speed than he'd taken before, wanting a bit of warning before they came on something dangerous.

There were strange trees, and the land was torn by deep ravines.

It was hot, but not unbearably so at their altitude.

Hal thought this could be a simple training flight in peacetime, except for the unknown land below them.

It's so damned *big*, he thought.

The horizons seemed as distant as Deraine was to him, even larger than the sweep of the northern tundra he'd seen the fringes of.

There was a strong wind blowing the tall grass, Hal noted. Then he corrected himself with a chill.

The grass was moving in a streak.

There was something hidden under it making the plants move. A snake?

But there couldn't be a snake that large. Hal estimated the creature's length to be well over thirty feet.

He saw Kimana looking down, then at him.

She made a face.

But nothing showed, and they flew on.

Limingo pointed down and to the left.

There was a huge herd – Hal guessed at more than three hundred head – herd of enormous buffalo, or some species of long-horned, shaggy cattle. Hal guessed they would be half as tall as a dragon.

They were huddled in a ring.

Hal saw the reason: there were four tawny predators stalking the herd. They were some species of cat, with mottled coats that made perfect camouflage. Their necks were long, and their heads sported great upswept fangs.

Then he saw something else:

A deep ravine ran beside the herd. In the ravine, creeping, if cattle could ever be said to creep, were a dozen bulls.

The cats hadn't seen them.

It was a case of the stalker being stalked.

Hal marveled at a land like this – cattle having the courage to attack beasts of prey.

Sweetie flew on, before the drama was resolved.

They landed under sheltering trees late that afternoon, not wanting to be in the air at night.

They didn't chance a fire, but ate their iron rations cold, after feeding the dragons.

"Ho for the life of adventure," Farren muttered, tearing at a chunk of hard-smoked and spiced beef. "I hope my godsdamned jaws hold up."

Hal was about to reply when a rustling in the grass outside the clearing made everyone dive for their crossbows.

After a moment, a creature waddled unhurriedly into sight. It was about half again the size of a domestic pig, and had long quills sticking out in all directions.

It went straight to Kimana, who'd dropped the fruit strip she'd been eating, picked it up in its jaws, turned around and trundled back the way it had come.

"So much," Kimana said, "for wild animals' instinctive fear of humans. I think I'll sleep in a tree."

The next morning, at dawn, they flew on, following the compass heading.

Far in the distance, purple mountains rose from the plain.

Just beyond would be that plateau that was the first dragon base.

Again, Kailas led his dragons on a dogleg north, then east, until he calculated he'd passed the plateau camp. He turned back, and started looking for a hiding place.

He spotted a grove of trees that would give them concealment, signaled to the others, and put Sweetie into a gentle dive.

At the last minute, he pulled the dragon up and climbed back for the heights.

The others needed no explanation.

They'd seen the danger.

There were three trees below them.

If they were trees at all.

For all three of them had tentacles instead of branches, tentacles that moved in anticipation of their prey above them.

There were bones scattered on the ground around the trees.

They flew on for a few miles, found another grove that was made up of real trees, landed and made their camp.

Limingo busied himself with spells after dinner, then came to Hal.

"I'm not sure," he said. "I'd know better if I had some kind of relic from the red and blacks. But my magic suggests there are dragons coming, from behind, probably heading toward that plateau."

"We'll wait for them to pass," Hal said. "Or at least until we know whether they're for real."

Limingo nodded, began gathering up his implements.

"You know," he said, without looking up at Hal, "I always wanted to be a soldier. Fun, travel, adventure.

"That sort of thing.

"But when I realized . . . what I am . . . soldiering didn't sound very inviting."

Hal knew what he was talking about.

Supposedly no one was supposed to discriminate in the army against people whose private life was different from the norm. And there were homosexuals in the military, but generally in branches such as medicine or clerking.

Hal had known all too many warriors, who evidently came from some village in a remote area or from one of the more repressive sects, who couldn't tolerate men who preferred other men, or women who liked their own.

He'd always thought those fools had some problem with themselves, some fear that they might be changed by contact with homosexuals, as if it were a communicable disease.

"Then I discovered I had a strong Gift," Limingo went on. "And that decided that."

He didn't seem to want any comment on what he had said, and so the others rolled in their blankets and tried to sleep.

They had to wait for a day, and then six red and blacks appeared, holding to the same northern course Hal had charted.

"Now," Hal said, "we follow them, and they lead us right to their home."

"Not too close," Aimard Quesney said. "I have an aversion to meeting dragons on their own ground."

"That's two votes," Farren Mariah said.

"Not to mention," Kimana said, "not being too quick to go home with them. They might object to uninvited house guests."

Hal made a face.

"You get more like Mariah every day."

"Proof," Farren Mariah said smugly, "that the woman has her wits about her."

They took off, and, keeping low to the ground, followed the red and blacks.

There were clouds in the sky from low to high altitudes, which made it easy to keep concealed as they flew.

The wild dragons began climbing as the mountains drew closer.

Hal held his formation close to the ground, only lifting when he had to.

Suddenly the six dragons ahead dove.

Hal was about to signal his flight to circle when, from a cave on a cliff face, some fifteen red and black dragons dove down at them.

They were well and truly ambushed.

28

Hal barely had time to shout a warning to Limingo to hold on as he turned his dragon into the red and blacks' attack.

They evidently weren't used to sudden aggression from foes they badly outnumbered, and the lead dragons in the attack balked, turning a bit aside.

That gave Hal a target, and he put a bolt into the base of the lead dragon's neck.

He shrilled, and went down, disappearing into the cloud cover.

Hal looked to see if there were riders on any of the beasts, saw none.

Aimard Quesney's dragon had spun, and had a red and black by the foreleg. The wild dragon shrieked in pain, and Quesney fired his crossbow into the monster's gaping jaws.

The dragon curled in agony, and rolled toward the mountainous landscape below.

Kimana Balf's dragon was locked in a face-to-face fight with a red and black, but Hal had no time to watch as a pair of dragons attacked him.

Farren Mariah took one off his back, and Hal fired at the second, wounding it.

There was another wild dragon plunging in from the side, slashing at Hal.

Sweetie ripped at it with a wing claw, and it dove. But there was another red and black tearing at his tail.

Sweetie turned on himself, almost throwing Hal, as a second dragon came in.

Kailas barely sensed Limingo shouting something, then the wild dragon had his mount by the leg, tearing at him.

Limingo screamed, and fell free, spinning down and down to his death.

Kailas shot the second dragon between the shoulder blades, and he contorted and fell away. The first had a death grip on Sweetie, tearing at him.

Hal's dragon clawed at his opponent, paying no attention to his rider's shouts to 'ware his height.

It was too late.

Sweetie hit the ground hard, throwing Hal over his neck, into a thicket.

Hal didn't feel the prickers, but tore himself out of the brush, killed the first dragon, and worked his crossbow's slide.

But Sweetie was writhing in his death throes, ichor spraying, and guts bulging.

Kailas didn't notice. He was transfixed by the red and black's death . . . if that was what it was. Again, as he'd seen once before, and thought it an illusion, the dragon flared into flame, and then there was nothing, not even smoke or ash.

Hal was gaping, then he heard a scream, and saw two red and blacks bearing down on him, exposed on the hillside.

He shot one, ducked behind a boulder as the other struck, almost crashed, but pulled up, turning for another run.

Kimana was there, her dragon striking at the wild dragon's neck, just behind the head. Hal heard the beast's neck snap, and then there was a pair of wild dragons on them.

One went for Kimana's dragon's throat, the second ripped at its wing.

The wing tore, and the dragon spun down.

The beast hit the ground, and Kimana sagged off the dying monster, lying against it, momentarily stunned.

Hal ran toward her, pulled her away from her dragon's body.

Four red and blacks were attacking the hillside.

Farren Mariah and Aimard Quesney came from nowhere, and the four wild dragons veered away.

Kimana was staggering up, recovering consciousness.

Hal pulled her pack from its ties on her dragon's carapace, and a quiver of bolts, threw them to the woman.

She took them numbly, then seemed to come to, saw her crossbow lying nearby, stumbled toward it.

Hal dashed to his own dragon's body, secured pack and quiver.

The red and blacks were coming back.

He sent a bolt in front of them.

These wild dragons evidently weren't used to bows, and climbed away.

Quesney was coming back, Mariah behind him, trying for a pickup. But there wasn't time, wasn't room, and Kailas was shouting them away as other wild dragons bore down on him.

He shouldered into his pack, helped Kimana on with hers.

Aimard and Farren dove down, close along the mountain's cliff, too close for the red and blacks to get them, but Hal had no more time to worry about them.

He shoved Kimana toward the shelter of a nest of boulders. A dragon came in low, snapped at him, missed.

They were momentarily safe.

Hal saw a gap in the rocks ahead, went for it as the wild dragons screamed their rage, circling overhead, looking for the chance to attack.

Then the two fliers were in the open, running downslope toward a vertical face.

Kimana skidded to a halt at the edge, looked down, and shuddered.

Hal did the same, saw treetops forty or so feet below.

"Jump!" he shouted, as a dragon, claws extended, came at them.

She hesitated, obeyed, plummeting down.

Hal went after her.

They smashed into the trees below, crashed through, branches pulling at them.

Somehow neither of them was more than scratched, nor did they lose pack or weapons. They thudded to a halt no more than ten feet above the ground and clambered out of the saving trees, felt solid ground under their feet.

Hal couldn't see the wild dragons above him, through the tree cover, but heard them shrieking rage and hatred.

He pointed at a brushy draw that led on down toward a valley floor, and the pair ran for it.

Kailas was still breathing hard two hours later, as the sun fell.

He and Kimana had found shelter of a sort in a large grove of thorn trees.

The wild dragons had followed them almost to the end, finally losing them in a narrow ravine.

But they continued flying overhead, in ever-widening circles, until dusk.

Finally, Hal's breathing slowed.

Kimana didn't seem, other than her various scrapes, to be out of sorts at all.

"I think," she said drily, "we may have run into a different sort of dragon."

Hal managed a rather feeble smile.

"You noticed."

"I noticed. I always tried to keep track of where the Roche I killed fell. It kept my squadron commander quiet."

"Different sort," Hal said. "If they're even dragons."

"What else could they be?"

"I don't know," Kailas said. "Maybe magical apparitions, created by their masters?"

"Damned powerful magicians, if they can do that. What's for dinner?"

Without waiting for an answer, she moved her pack in front of her, dug into it.

"Naturally, not thinking I was ever going to need anything in this, and that we'd be back at the ships in a day or two, I didn't exactly pack delicacies.

"How about some nice dried vegetable soup?"

"How about," Hal said, "some jerked beef. I'd just as soon not light a fire."

Kimana considered.

"The bastards do fly at night," she said. "And they surely could see a fire, unless we found some sort of cave or something."

"I'm worried that they could sense a fire," Hal said. "Without seeing it."

"You're building these creatures up as something scary."

"They *are* scary," Hal said. "And the only reason I lived through the war was because I always took my enemy seriously."

He thought about his words, grinned wryly.

"I think that was as pompous as it sounded."

Kimana managed a smile, reached out, patted his cheek.

"That's all right. The Dragonmaster is permitted to sound toplofty."

Her hand stayed on his face for just an instant, then withdrew.

"By the way. I don't think I've thanked you for saving me."

"Or you for trying to save me," Hal said. "In spite of orders."

Kimana shrugged.

"I suspect I'm being punished. I never should have rigged the lottery in the first place."

"You did what?"

"Shuffled those bits of paper until I felt the inky one. I always was good with my fingers."

Hal goggled in surprise, couldn't find anything to say.

Kimana chewed jerky, swallowed. "Speaking of which, we'll have to hurry to make the coast before the ships leave. Twenty-four days is all we have left.

"I'm in no mood to play First Woman of the World around here."

Hal took a deep breath.

"Less than that, actually. Because I'm going to find that sorcerers' base first."

Kimana looked at him through the growing dark.

"You're mad."

"I'm mad," Kailas agreed. "But that's what we set out to do."

"*I* didn't," Balf said. "Those weren't my orders . . . and I never volunteer. Too easy a way to get killed."

"Which is why you've got a couple of choices," Kailas said. "We'll find you a cave, and you stay with most of the provisions. Give me three days, and if I'm not back, you strike for the coast.

"Or you can do that right now."

Kimana thought about it.

"I don't like the idea of sitting on my ass and waiting," she said. "And I surely don't like chancing those prairies by myself. Those pussycats didn't look friendly . . . and I don't even want to think about what whatever was shaking the bushes likes for breakfast."

She sighed.

"I always hated heroes," she said. "All the bastards were good for was getting themselves . . . and anybody around them . . . killed."

Hal saw her logic.

"But I can't just turn back. Not this close."

"No," Kimana said, and there was a hint of anger in her voice. "You, being you, can't. And so you're going to get me killed, too."

Without waiting for an answer, she took a blanket from her pack, and wrapped herself in it.

"I guess we'd better get some sleep," she said. "We'll need an early start, and I don't see any point in keeping a watch. Everything we've seen so far could eat us without a fight.

"Goodnight."

She lay down, and gave every appearance of instantly going to sleep.

Hal tried to think of something to say, couldn't find anything logical, rolled in his own blanket.

The next day, they moved out, cautiously, heading toward the peak behind which the fliers had last seen the six dragons disappearing.

There were red and blacks about, snooping like dogs that had lost the scent but knew their prey was still near by.

But the pair weren't seen.

At midday, a gold-colored, unridden dragon flew toward them, keeping low, head snaking back and forth, watchful for enemies.

Its caution didn't do any good.

Three red and blacks came from behind a bluff, and savaged the other dragon out of the sky.

They kept walking

Kimana risked a bolt, and killed a rabbit-looking animal, skinning and dressing it as they moved.

They moved into a near-trot when the terrain let them, always thinking of the sands running, ever faster, through the glass.

Hal stopped before dusk, built a small fire from dry brush he'd collected. They cooked the rabbit hastily, ate it half-raw, went on.

That night, they found another thicket, crept into its midst, and slept, continuing their trek as soon as there was the slightest hint of light in the sky.

The next day, they reached the peak they'd targeted, and found a pass below it.

They started through, but there were dragons overhead, and the land was too open.

A huge bear headed their way, and they pulled aside, into a rocky niche, crossbows ready.

The bear, almost twice the size of any Hal had seen, even in the north of Roche, snuffled at them curiously, evidently didn't much like the way they smelt, went about his business.

There was a creek running downslope, with a pool. Hal saw what looked acceptably like crayfish, snagged a dozen, and they ate well, boiling them in a small pot they carried with them.

There was an overhang large enough to shelter them.

Hal took water from his canteen, scrubbed his teeth carefully, and kissed Kimana goodnight.

It seemed like a good idea.

She looked a bit surprised, then kissed him back.

That was the ninth day.

The next day brought one of the greatest surprises of Hal Kailas's life.

They found the city of magicians.

Hal hadn't been sure of what to expect. Certainly there would be great buildings, standing impossibly high. They would be made of strange materials, and would glitter with gold and gems.

The streets would be thronged with their creations – slaves, bedmates, monsters.

The two had followed the pass around the peak, and, at its highest point, found concealment and looked down on the valley they'd seen the dragons drop into.

Neither of them believed what they saw.

Or, rather, didn't see.

There were dozens, perhaps a hundred, red and black dragons milling about.

But there was no city.

There were great slabs of rock, piled haphazardly to make shelters, not even monolithic construction.

No more.

Hal used the glass he had in his pack, and here and there saw the carcasses of animals, in various stages of decay.

It looked like a bigger version of the dragons' plateau camp.

Nothing that looked human, or like a magician.

"I don't believe it," he muttered inanely.

They watched on.

Perhaps this was just another way station, and their rulers' grand city lay further on, deeper in this continent.

But Hal saw no signs of dragons flying on east, or, indeed, making any flights other than short hops here and there, returning quickly.

They watched until almost dark, expecting something, finding nothing.

Then they went back the way they had come, to the overhang they'd slept under the night before.

"So where are the magicians?" Kimana wondered.

Hal could only shake his head.

"Maybe . . . invisible?" he hazarded. "Or maybe the dragons are controlled by demons?"

"Or maybe," Kimana said, "they *are* the demons."

"Huh?"

"Normal dragons don't explode like a bottle of brandy thrown into a fire," she said.

"I still can't believe it," Hal said. "We'll have to go back tomorrow and make sure."

"And how are we going to do that?"

"I don't know."

They went back up the pass, and found hiding places just at dawn.

The dragons below were waking, stirring about, eating from the scattered carcasses.

About fifty of them were gathered in a circle in an open area.

In the center of the circle was a fire, a ball of flame, as big or bigger than any of the dragons below. But there was no fuel to be seen, and the fire burnt with a steady, high flame.

Then, from the fire's center, a second ball of flame appeared, rolled forward, and began changing.

The flame died, and where it had been was a full-size red and black dragon.

That was enough for Hal. He motioned Kimana back, and once again they went down the hill.

They stopped at their outcropping long enough to grab their packs, then kept going, back the way they'd come.

"What are they?" Kimana said, when they paused at a tiny spring.

"I still don't know. Demons, maybe, like you thought. That sounds good enough for me. Certainly they're not dragons. Maybe the demons came here from some other world, and thought dragons were the best form they could take to conquer, or at least survive.

"Maybe, maybe not.

"But we're headed back for the ships.

"If these things are to be fought, it will have to be with magic. And we don't have much of that with us."

They went down the pass as quickly as they could move.

They had to take shelter regularly.

Red and blacks were flying overhead, again as if they'd scented the man and woman.

The next two days were spent clearing the mountains, and then, on the afternoon of the thirteenth day, they came down to the plains again.

Each night, before they slept, it seemed appropriate for them to kiss.

Their kisses were hardly chaste, but Hal never went further.

He thought he smelt too badly to be acceptable in anyone's bed, barely into his own.

Kimana didn't seem to want him to pursue his romance, and Kailas wondered if she felt equally unwashed.

On the fourteenth day since they'd left the ships, they moved carefully across the plains, wary of encountering one of the great snakes, if that was what they were.

Twice they hid under a tree as red and black dragons passed overhead, but the creatures paid no attention to what was below.

Hal was startled once, seeing what looked like an enormous fat man waddling across the plains.

They hid, and the being approached.

It wasn't a man, although it was almost as large as one, but a furry being with a ringed tail. The fur was black and gray, with a mask-like configuration around its pointed snout.

The animal looked directly at the brush they were hiding in, sniffed, and kept on moving.

Kimana and Hal went on.

They came upon a stretch of burnt-over land, the ground bare, blackened, and still smoking.

Hal couldn't tell what had set the fire, decided it must have been lightning, although they'd seen no storm in their passage.

A confused antelope bumbled across their path, and Kimana shot it down.

Hal gutted it, and they carried the body until they found an idyllic place to camp – just at the edge of the fire zone, the ground hot, and trees a short distance away still smoldering.

Nearby was a bubbling spring, and next to it, a nest of rocks that appeared made for small furless creatures like themselves to hide in.

Hal skinned and butchered the antelope.

"Now, watch my woodsy lore," he told Kimana, and, clutching two haunches, trotted to the smoldering trees.

He used a great leaf to fan the fire to life, and cooked the meat until it was just done.

Hal came back to see no Kimana.

But he heard a splashing from the spring, and peered over a rock.

Kimana, naked, was splashing about in a pool surprisingly deep.

"Dinner," he announced, realizing his throat was a bit dry.

Kimana came out of the water, unashamed.

"I shall drip dry," she said. "Now, you have just enough time to scrape off the worst.

"Here. I found some soap in my pack."

She handed it to him.

"And I'll even wait for you."

Kailas hastily stripped off, and stepped into the cool water. He lathered, submerged, and used some of the soap on his filthy clothes, which were really beyond redemption.

He was about to wash again, when Kimana called:

"My civilized ways are fading. Get your behind out here."

Hal obeyed.

Not quite as brazen as Kimana, he pulled on his wet under-breeches, then went to where their packs lay.

"Sit," Kimana said, her mouth full. "Eat."

He obeyed, and thought no meal he'd eaten had ever tasted as good.

And Kimana, he realized as his stomach filled, was as lovely as any woman he'd ever seen.

She seemed, for the moment, oblivious of his eyes, and he forced himself to look away every time she turned her head toward him.

He was surprised to find his antelope haunch gnawed to the bone.

She had finished her meal, tossed the bone far out on to the plain.

He found a leaf, wiped his greasy, half-grown beard clean, wished he'd brought a razor.

Kimana was staring at him.

Hal had been married, had certainly been with his share of women, but still found himself blushing.

Kimana giggled, got up, went to the spring, and washed out her mouth.

She went back to her bed roll, which Hal realized had been laid out, with his next to it.

She lay back, one knee slightly raised.

Hal thought her the most lovely thing he'd ever seen.

His body agreed.

Kimana gurgled laughter.

"Come here, you silly . . . but clean . . . man."

He obeyed.

Both moons were high in the sky when sleep finally took them.

Hal would have liked to have lazed in Kimana's arms the next day, making love from time to time.

But he was a soldier. Of sorts, at least.

And so, muttering inaudibly, he spanked her awake, thinking of other pastimes that could arrive from such a beginning, and they broke camp.

They moved on, deeper into the plains lands.

They encountered scattered grazing buffalo, saw no sign of the cat-like predators.

The buffalo were even larger than they'd looked from the air, and they made sure not to come close to any of them, especially if they had calves.

The sky was overcast, muttering.

Hal's hair was on end, and then thunder crashed as ball lightning rolled across the sky toward them.

"For those trees," Hal shouted.

They broke into a trot for a distant grove.

Hal saw the buffalo starting to move.

They were walking, then running, massing up into a herd, and charging toward the two humans.

There was no way they could make the trees, even if the spindly things were strong enough to climb.

And Hal remembered what he'd learned about going to a high point, or a high tree, when lightning was about.

He also remembered something a herder boy had told him, forgotten years ago.

"Stop!" he called.

Kimana, just in front of him, obeyed, although she gave him a look as though she thought him utterly mad.

"What are you doing?"

"*We're* going to stand here."

"And get trampled?"

"Cattle won't run over you if you're standing still. They'll run right past us."

"Who told you that?"

Hal lied. "Common knowledge. And I used to herd cows, when I was a boy."

"I don't believe you," Kimana said. But she came close.

She had her eyes closed.

Hal looked at the oncoming herd, their stretching horns, realized the herder hadn't said anything about what stampeding cattle did with their godsdamned horns.

He, too, closed his eyes.

The rush of hoofs became thunder, impossibly loud, louder than what was going on in the skies, and then they were buried by it, roaring on either side.

And then it was gone.

Hal opened his eyes in swirling dust and the overpowering smell of cowshit.

"I'll be dipped," he said, in considerable surprise.

Kimana looked at him.

"You *were* lying."

"Well . . ."

That was the fifteenth day.

It was about midday, and they were moving through tall grass, broken by copses of thorn trees, when Kimana saw movement ahead.

It was what they'd feared most – the grass moving like a long wave.

And it was headed in their direction.

Hal pointed back, toward the closest grove, and they ran hard for it.

He glanced over his shoulder, knowing better, knowing that slowed him down.

The grass was moving faster.

Hal didn't think he could run any harder than he was. He was wrong.

Whatever was chasing them was only a dozen yards behind as

Kimana reached the first tree. Hal threw her up into it bodily and swarmed after her, ignoring the long thorns that ripped at him.

He reached the first crotch, less than a dozen feet above the ground. Kimana was above him.

She was staring past him, at the ground, and suddenly screamed.

Hal had his crossbow off his shoulder, and turned, almost falling, and triggered a bolt down.

He didn't see what he was shooting at, didn't want or need to. He worked the crossbow's action, sent two more bolts down, as Kimana fired too.

There was a hiss, more like a screech, and then the grass was moving away, zigging here, there, and gone.

"What was it?" Hal panted.

"It . . . it *was* a snake," Kimana managed. "I think. But it had stubby arms with claws."

They waited a few minutes, but the monster didn't come back. Kailas thought it might be more dangerous to stay where they were than to keep going.

They came down from the tree, feeling the pain of far more thorns than they'd felt going up.

For the rest of the day, they zigged from grove to grove, ready to flee if the beast, or his friends, came back.

But nothing happened.

They bolted the last of their iron rations just under the tallest tree they could spot, and then climbed as high as they could and wrapped themselves in their blankets, spending an uncomfortable, but safe, night.

The seventeenth day was a day of heartbreak.

They were moving fast, on mostly open ground, and saw a pair of dragons.

Hal glassed them, and saw they weren't the enemy, and, though they were at quite a distance, that both dragons looked to have riders.

They came out into the open, waved, even foolishly shouted.

But the dragons kept on flying away from them.

Hal, in desperation, dug in his pack, found his flint and steel.

He struck them desperately, but the sparks flew into still-live grass, and the fire didn't catch.

He didn't know if that would have turned the dragons in any event, but he sagged in defeat as the two monsters vanished into the afternoon haze.

That night they camped by a small river, and Hal shot a pair of large fish.

But neither of them had much appetite.

They made love in misery, in desperation, finally fell asleep.

The next day, they saw, rising in the distance, the coastal mountains, and allowed themselves a moment of hope.

Then Hal noticed billowing high clouds rolling in from the south, from the ocean. The rain came down in sheets, and they tried to push on through it. But the winds grew stronger, and the rain heavier, and they were forced to find shelter in a thick grove, afraid of what they might encounter in the near-total darkness.

They barely slept, and, still in the dark of the nineteenth day, went on, almost running.

But just after dawn, four pairs of the red and blacks appeared, and they had to hide.

The dragons, as if knowing the humans were somewhere below them, swept back and forth, only flying off in the late afternoon.

Kimana and Hal went on until well after nightfall, moving by moonlight, and were into the foothills when they collapsed from exhaustion.

The twentieth day took them into the mountains.

Hal found a pass leading due east that was smooth, and promised easy traveling.

Then, after two hours, the pass turned north, and ended in a blank wall.

They had to go back for an hour before they could find a scramble to the top of a ridge, and the ridge led on toward the blue glimmer of the ocean.

On the twenty-first day, the last day the ships were to still be waiting, they came down out of the mountains. Below them was the bay the expedition had hidden in, less than an hour's travel distant.

They could barely keep from running, and, well before twilight, crested the last low ridge, the bay fingering out below them.

There was only one ship, and its masts were canted at an angle.

As they grew closer, they recognized the *Compass Rose*, one of their fast corvettes, yards drooping and bowsprit smashed.

The ship was wrecked, dashed against rocky outcroppings at the water's edge.

The bay was otherwise empty, with not another ship to be seen.

They had been abandoned.

29

Illogically, but quite understandably, they ran to the water's edge, not knowing what they hoped to find – a message, a map, a clue, something.

But there was nothing, except marks where boats had been beached, then launched once more.

Further down the beach lay the wreck of the *Compass Rose*. It needed no seaman's eye to tell that it could never be repaired and refloated.

Hal's heart was completely empty, as was his mind.

Kimana raised her eyes, and they were hard, dry.

"The bastards left us here to rot," she said fiercely.

Then the shout came, and they both spun.

Coming out of thick brush up from the water were two men: Hachir, and Hal's longtime orderly, Uluch.

Hal could find nothing more intelligent to say than, "You didn't leave us."

"No," Hachir said. "*We* didn't. But some others did."

"None of us who want to fight ran away," Uluch said. He was looking over his shoulder, up at the skies. "Come on, sir," he said. "Those devils are still about."

Hachir collected himself.

"Yes," he said. "We've only kept this watch out of . . . well, hope that you were still with us . . . and coming."

"What happened?" Hal asked.

Uluch didn't answer, but led them up the beach, taking care to drag his feet so the marks in the sand didn't look like footprints. He took them to solid ground, then, keeping close to brush, to a draw that sloped upward.

The draw widened, and in its center was a small camp,

concealed by scrub brush and low trees. There were camouflaged canvas tents, a small, smokeless fire, and some fifteen men and half a dozen women.

Two men kept watch with crossbows.

Hal saw some of his best: Farren Mariah, Bodrugan, one of his acolytes, four of his fliers, including Hachir, others.

He counted the missing: Garadice, Quesney, Cabet, Miletus, among others.

"Bigods, bigobs," Mariah said. "Now you're here, and the show can begin."

"If someone will tell me what the hells happened . . ." Hal began.

There was a clamor.

The loudest came from Mariah:

"The bartarts went and mutinied on us."

Hal sat down heavily on a log.

"Shit," he said. "Guapur Hagi?"

"At the head," Mariah said. "Other fainthearts."

"I should've hung him before I left," Hal said grimly. "What're the details?"

Hagi had begun plotting even before Hal had left with the others on his long scout, finding sympathetic listeners among watch officers and soldiery.

He had presented his case skillfully – this was not so much a simple mutiny, as a protest against Hal's pigheadedness in not returning to Deraine at once, with the awful news of this land full of danger and the evil, almost sentient, dragons.

King Asir should be warned as soon as possible, so he had time to mount a proper expedition or . . . or whatever he wished to do.

Why Kailas chose to tarry on in this treacherous land was unknown.

Hagi's men passed harsh whispers about Hal's desire to save his own reputation, besmirched as it had been by his adventures with the Roche.

When Quesney and Mariah came back, with word of the ambush, the stories changed a little.

Of course Hal – and that woman with him – must be dead. If not by dragon, then by the horrid monsters of this unknown land.

And with Mariah's report of the dragons that weren't, bursting into flames like nightmare apparitions, that was almost enough.

The capper was the great storm. During the blow, the *Compass Rose* had dragged its anchor, and gone on the rocks. Its captain and half its crew were killed trying to save their ship.

"The muttoneers must've had their plans ready," Farren Mariah said. "Sheep-shaggers that they are."

The mutineers had moved at dawn, and before anyone could do anything, all five ships were in their hands.

Of the missing fliers, Mariah was sure that Cabet, Quesney, Miletus and Garadice must be unwilling prisoners.

That made Hal feel a tiny bit better, that he wasn't a complete fool at judging men.

Those who refused to follow Hagi had had but a single chance to flee into the undergrowth with what they could carry.

"It was only that monster Chook who made them set food, canvas and weapons out for us," Mariah said. "None of the fliers who wanted to stay were listened to.

"And we could hear from the shore Hagi refusing to let us have any of the dragons, the shitheel.

"We could hear our monsters howling, knowing something was wrong."

"So they sailed away, leaving us to die," he finished. "Which thus far, we haven't done, no credit to his worthless ass.

"And we've got what was aboard the *Compass Rose*," Hachir said. "Some dry foodstuffs, and a decent arsenal. Bows, some crossbows, enough spare quarrels for an army. No quartermaster supplies, which is why we're all looking a bit raggedy."

"Probably," one of the rangers said bitterly, "the king'll send somebody back in ten, twenty years, and find our skeletons, all dragon-chewed, and they'll put up a monument to us."

Hal tried not to look at the eager faces who were sure the Dragonmaster would come up with something clever that would save their lives and bring them back, in triumph, to Deraine.

He could think of nothing.

Go to ground and wait? With the creatures of this land stalking them?

Build rafts and sail to the Hnid, the sea people? And what then? Would they somehow help them build some kind of boat capable of the ocean passage? Maybe. That, so far, was the best impossible option.

And if they did build boats, what was to keep the red and blacks from attacking them when they were afloat?

Capture wild dragons and flee on them? The only man really

skilled at taming dragons was Garadice, who was with the mutineers. Hal himself had only long-ago memories of taming
half-wild creatures.

He could think of absolutely nothing that offered salvation.

30

With his worries, Hal thought he'd sleep hardly at all. But just
knowing he was safe . . . or, at any rate safer than he'd been out
on the plains, surrounded by armed, friendly warriors, instead of
being with just Kimana in the wilderness, swept over him like a
welcome comforter, and he slept dreamlessly until just after
dawn.

Kimana was curled next to him, and woke when he did.

They wandered down toward the water.

There was a sentry there, watching for dragons.

They washed, came back.

Kimana took his hand. Hal felt a bit uncomfortable, but no
one made any notice, other than Farren Mariah, who muttered,
"'Bout damned time."

They ate well – some of the soldiers had unstrung clothing for
the threads, and tied gill nets. Others had rocked the rabbit-like
creatures and shot the small antelope.

Hal missed bread, thought himself a sybarite.

He thought more on what they could do to survive.

The first step was easy – get away from the water. The land
was too open, and Kailas thought the red and black dragons
would certainly spot them in time, no matter how careful their
precautions.

And the wreck of the *Compass Rose* would draw the demons'
attention even more strongly.

As far as escape went . . . nothing came.

Nor did he have any ideas about striking back.

So much, he was thinking, for Great, Inspired Leadership,
when two of the sentries gave alarm.

Dragons, approaching from the east.

Everyone found weapons and cover.

There were four of them, three being ridden, two with double riders.

No need to keep guard – red and blacks had no riders.

The men and women burst into the open, shouting, waving, and the dragons circled for a landing.

Hal saw the empty-saddled monster in front, recognized him. Storm.

Somehow . . . but explanations would be for later.

The dragon thudded down, and Hal had his arms around the reeking beast's neck, and it larruped him with its tongue.

Kailas couldn't speak for a moment, then recovered.

The men were Aimard Quesney, Cabet, Lu Miletus, Garadice, and Chook, the cook.

"Thought it was about time for us to come back," Quesney said, trying to be casual as he slid from the saddle.

"Godsdamned well escaped," shouted Chook. "Th' fools went and turned their back, and we were gone."

That, in fact, was just what had happened.

Sort of.

The guard aboard the *Galgorm Adventurer* had gotten careless, and Chook had his cleaver. Once before the massive cook had shown his talents, before Hal had known him, when some attacking Roche had made the mistake of invading his kitchen, and had died to a man.

Now Chook had been biding his time, and saw it.

The guard died, as did his watch mate. Chook bashed open the compartment the still-recalcitrant fliers had been locked in, and they found weapons, and seized the watch.

"There weren't enough of us to take the ship back," Quesney said.

"But we locked the watch below," Cabet added. "And set the dragons loose. Saddled four of them, even though your mount wouldn't let anybody on his back.

"We were trying to decide what to do next, when somebody on the *Bohol* sensed something wrong.

"They had the odds, and so we fled, after grabbing what gear we could."

"None of the other fliers – even those that'd gone along with Hagi – were bold enough to come after us," Lu Miletus said.

"And we thought it was time to see what you were about," Garadice added.

"Poorly," Farren Mariah said. "Poorly-roarly, until just now."

"And now what?" a soldier asked.

"Now," Hal said, "now we can fight back."

It had come to him in a flash, as all the pieces arrived.

At least, so he hoped.

All he needed now was the luck of the gods.

First, he took Garadice aside, asked him how long it would take to train a dragon.

"You mean a yearling, fresh-hatched, or an old, incorrigible sort?"

"Yearling. We don't have time for either a young one or an old fart."

Garadice considered.

"Rideable, unless it's the cantankerous sort, perhaps a month. Fightable . . . twice that. Capable of holding a formation—"

"We won't need that," Hal interrupted. "There's not enough of us to make a formation."

"Now," Garadice asked, "how are we to catch these dragons?"

"A mere piffance," Hal said, waving his hand with an airy manner he didn't feel at all.

Next was Bodrugan. Hal told him everything he knew or suspected about the red and blacks.

"If these dragons aren't dragons—"

"Which I agree with, from what you've said about them bursting into flame," the magician said.

"Then what are they? Demons?"

"I won't use the word demons," Bodrugan said, a bit pedantically. "For, after all, demons are only forces from beyond, from other realms, whom we haven't been able to master, as yet.

"I would choose to use the term elemental spirits, perhaps."

"Elemental?" Hal asked. "Like in earth, wind, water, fire?"

"Just so," Bodrugan said.

"That means they're very powerful?"

"They are that," the wizard agreed. "But also easy – or, rather, relatively easy – to force your will on, since any creature with that innate power will almost certainly be self-confident. Like people are.

"From the elements, back to the elements."

"So you can handle them?"

"I don't know about handling," the magician said cautiously.

"Kill them, then."

"Kill them ... exploding them ... is obviously possible. Wiping them completely out may be almost impossible. Perhaps bringing them under control can be attempted. Or sending them back to whatever realm they came from. Would that be acceptable?"

"If you could devise a spell that would do that ... and keep the bastards from coming back again, hopefully ever, that would be more than enough," Hal said.

"I can attempt to devise such a spell," Bodrugan said. "I'm sure I can come up with something that might be helpful. But whether I can work great magic is another matter entirely."

He looked up at the sky.

"I *do* wish," he said, a bit wistfully, "Limingo hadn't gone and gotten himself killed."

It would take time to create a striking force, time that Hal certainly didn't have.

But he had no other options.

The first step, as he'd figured earlier, was to get away from the coast. There would be nothing to be gained by staying here.

Hagi and the other ships had been well toward the lands of the Hnid when the mutiny against the mutiny had taken place. It would be months before they reached Deraine, and the tale they would have rehearsed by then would certainly prevent another expedition from arriving within a year, if then.

The first stage was cautious scouting for a new base.

It was a pure joy for Hal to be aloft again, especially over land he'd struggled across so recently.

He sent scouts, including himself, to the south, with exact details on what to look for.

Farren Mariah found their new home, and Hal thought, after considering it critically, it was just about perfect.

It took little time to get ready to move. They would make packs of the *Compass Rose*'s supplies, cache what they couldn't carry, and the ground troops would march off toward the new camp.

The dragons would shuttle the men and women from the march to the base, since it was at least four days' journey distant.

There was one more to come.

He arrived in somewhat regal style.

The sentries reported a boat headed toward them.

It was a very small craft, a Hnid net carrier.

This boat carried one human:

Babil Gachina, the thief, Hal's one-time cellmate.

He stood, arms folded like a triumphant prince, in the prow of the tiny boat, very much aware of the impression he was making.

The boat was being towed by a dozen Hnid.

Hal was wondering what the hells had happened, recollected what awe the Hnid had for Gachina's size, when the boat touched bottom, pitching Gachina into the shallows in a most inglorious arrival.

Men helped him up, and he waded to shore, not forgetting to turn and bow to his servants, if servants they were.

He asked for fish, and men hurried to bring them to him.

The fish were pitched to the Hnid, who took them, and without ceremony swam back out to sea, towing the boat with them.

Hal told Gachina to tell his story, and it was quite a tale:

It had been two nights after the mutiny against the mutiny.

"All was quiet, all was still," Babil said, and Hal knew that, if Gachina survived the expedition, he'd never have to live as a thief again, but could make a most comfortable living as a tavern taleteller. "And they struck from nowhere, fiends from all the hells, screaming like damned souls . . ."

To cut through the bar room panoply, the mutineers' five ships had been becalmed, just beyond the skein of tiny islands before the Hnid's lands, when the dragons came out of the night.

Gachina had no idea what had summoned them, but there were "thousands" of them. He admitted to Hal, later, that he hadn't counted exactly, but there'd been at least fifty.

They attacked from out of the larger, waning moon, and there was only a yelp of warning from one sentry before the dragons were on them.

The large crossbows on the masts stupidly weren't manned, and so the dragons were able to swoop along the decks, tearing at men as they stumbled out of their quarters.

One dragon became entangled in the *Bohol*'s sails, and, accidentally, it seemed, brought the ship over on a hard list. Another lit on its foremast, which was standing at an angle, and the top-heavy ship capsized.

Drowning dragons and men screamed into the night, and then the *Galgorm* caught fire.

"Odd that," Gachina said, "because as it flamed up, the

dragons seemed to veer away from it, as though flame was their greatest fear, and tore instead at the other ships."

Babil tried a tale of his heroism, but caught Hal's eye, and told what might have been close to the truth:

He came on deck on the *Bohol* just as it went over, ducked a dragon, saw Hagi ripped in half by a pair of the monsters, and dove overside.

The two frigates were being attacked by the dragons, "bit by bit, the wood ripped off, like peeling a fruit," and Babil stayed low in the water.

He heard more screams, then silence, and he kept down, and then there was silence for a long time.

The sun came up, and there was nothing living and no ships afloat. He was surrounded by bodies and debris, floating dragons and men.

"Then, after a time, the fish people found me, and took me to one of their islands, and gave me food, and then a boat, and brought me here."

Gachina's tale brought the satisfaction of just retribution for most, but Hal saw the expression on Kimana's face, and knew it matched his own:

Now there wasn't even the vaguest possibility of a rescue expedition for years.

He was even more shaken to realize that these demons, fifty or seventy or however many there were, could destroy five ships and several hundred men, and all but wipe out the expedition.

31

Four days' march to their new base equaled a day and a half's leisurely flight, as the dragons carried marchers as they went.

A few chose to stay afoot, Babil Gachina among them, and Hal, having things on his mind, didn't wonder about them.

The valley was, indeed, just about perfect. It jutted off to the west of a deep canyon, and its walls zigged so that it appeared to come to a blind end near its opening.

It was keyhole-shaped, half a league at its widest, two leagues long. The long base of the keyhole was sparsely covered with grass, spare enough that the revolutions of the dragons they hoped to capture and train wouldn't mark the land for overhead observers.

One side of the keyway was a nearly sheer cliff, pocked with caves both small and large, ideal for dragon shelters. The other side was thickly forested.

Hal planned to steal an idea from the Hnid, and have his men bend the trees over, lash them to either their fellows or to the ground, and so roof the area.

All of his women and men were shuttled to the valley without being observed by any dragons, either the red and black spirits or the "real" beasts of the land.

Farren Mariah asked Garadice how they'd go about training the dragons. He grinned wickedly, and said, "I'd tell, but you won't like it, so I'd rather you lived in a bit of suspense."

"Suspense, harness, business," Mariah moaned. "Now I *know* I won't like it."

Hal was about to look for a cave for his quarters when Kimana announced she'd already found their living area.

It was a cave with a small entrance that broadened into three chambers:

"Conference room, living room, bedroom," she named them. "A bend between each of them, so we've a measure of privacy."

Hal could do little but agree.

A tropical storm raged that night, and Hal listened to the rain cascade down outside the cave. He thought of his palaces and mansions back in Deraine, decided he'd rather be here, then called himself a fool for thinking that.

He then considered that it was Kimana's presence that made the difference. Realizing he hadn't gone mad yet, he reached for her, across their bed of piled rushes with blankets atop and below.

Sated, Kimana fell asleep in his arms. Hal was just drifting off as well when a thought came, left him helplessly awake. The thought led to a question that he'd pushed away before, but now it loomed very large.

And better, or worse, he thought he might have a way to find an answer.

A dragon honked below them, and Hal wondered, before he, too, fell asleep, if Storm's presence had sparked his thoughts.

Never mind. He'd consider the matter the next day.

*

Kimana listened to his idea, which he presented without giving a complete explanation, then asked three cogent questions, which Hal was able to answer.

Then she made a face.

"Were we back in civilization, and were I the jealous sort, I'd think you were haring off to see a chippie.

"Why are you so insistent on going solo?"

"Because . . . well, because I don't especially like to be a fool in front of an audience," Hal said. He didn't add that there was a good chance of getting killed answering his question.

"Hmmph," Kimana said. "Playing the hero again."

Hal didn't answer.

"So when are you going to mount this grand expedition of yours?"

"The next big storm," Kailas said. "That blow last night gave me the idea."

"Hmmph again. Who'll command while you're gone?"

"Farren Mariah in charge, Cabet as number two to handle administration, Bodrugan in charge of magic and such."

He called the three together, told them he had a scout to make, refused volunteers and an explanation, told them to keep the expedition in the valley.

"And what about you . . . if you're gone overlong?" Mariah demanded. "Look what happened the last time you saddled up and rode wildly off in all directions."

"That," Hal said smoothly, "is why, this time, I've chosen such obvious leaders as yourselves to keep things going smoothly."

It was three days before the next storm came in from the ocean, from the east.

Each of those nights Hal had slept, rolled in blankets, in the cave with Storm.

Kimana had started to make a joke, saw the haunted expression on Hal's face, decided not to.

For each night, as he'd hoped and dreaded, Hal had dreamed.

Once again, he was that wounded dragon attacked over his homeland by the dreaded red and blacks. Once again he fled east, across the great ocean, to a new land, where he found beings who were not especially friendly, sometimes his active enemies.

But he found a mate, bred, and his kits had spawn of their own.

Hal, waking, wondered if one of them was the dragon who would be named as Storm, realized he would never know.

Besides, this was not the direction his quest took him.

Rather, he tried to force his dreams back, back to the days before, when the dragon was young and adventurous.

Twice, his dreams obeyed him.

When the skies clouded over, and a warm but vicious wind whipped over the valley, Hal Kailas knew well which way he wanted to go.

He took off down-valley, gained height over the flat lands, then turned, set his course into the storm, quartering north.

He didn't need a compass to set his bearing, but used one so that he would be able to give directions to his fliers.

Hopefully, if he survived.

He remembered a cozy hooded laprobe he'd had back in Deraine, and wished for it. The wind might have been tropical, but it still whipped at him, and the rain drenched him to the skin.

He flew on, all that day, then took Storm under the shelter of some great trees at the edge of the plains, where the mountains began their rise.

Over there . . . and he instinctively knew the direction . . . lay the home of the red and black dragons.

Hal's mission was to answer one question:

Was that home the only one the red and black monsters had? Was that the sole point where they could come into this world from their other?

He hoped it was, that his guess, seemingly so long ago, had been right, that there was only the one hellspot, so the ruins of his expedition weren't ridiculously outnumbered.

But he had to know for sure.

He curled up next to Storm again.

He thought, amusedly, that most people would be slightly put off by the dragon's smell.

But then, most people wouldn't be intrigued by his own odor, no matter how much his thorough drenching might have resembled a bath.

Dragonmasters of fable probably weren't supposed to smell like their mounts.

But then, he guessed that noble cavalrymen weren't supposed to smell distinctly horsy either, and he surely remembered his days as a light cavalryman.

On that thought, he slept, smiling.

He woke before dawn, roused Storm, and fed him on two of the smoked "rabbits" he carried with him behind his saddle, ate dried meat from his own pack.

It was still raining, and he wanted a fire to heat water for tea and boil some eggs he carried so carefully, wrapped in a spare set of underbreeches.

But not this close to the red and blacks.

He was just morosely chewing the last bites when he heard the shrill screams from aloft, went to the edge of the grove, looked up.

Through the scudding clouds, he dimly saw a pair of the huge red and blacks pass over.

Had they somehow scented, or otherwise sensed, his and Storm's presence?

If they weren't real dragons, why did they need to call like them?

Were their cries supposed to flush real dragons into the open?

Deciding that was enough questions, he curried Storm, took him to pooled water, and saddled him.

Then he took off, this time flying due north.

To his west would be the red and blacks' sanctuary.

For half the day, he flew along the edge of the plain, then over rolling hills, studded with trees.

Here and there he saw grazing buffalo, once a stalking predator.

But never did he see another dragon.

This was as he expected.

He outran the storm, and it was windy, but clear.

The afternoon grew late, and shadows fell across the land.

The ground below him was familiar, as though it was something he'd passed over as a child, or seen old-time paintings of.

Here the land would climb, and there would be a miniature mountain range, actually a rough circle of peaks around a high, craggy plateau.

That was just what Hal saw now, in reality.

Storm made a noise when he saw the mountains.

Hal wasn't sure what it was, a whimper, a moan.

But the dragon turned, unbidden, toward them, his wings widespread as he reached for altitude.

They crossed between two peaks, and saw the barren valley of the tableland Hal had dreamed of twice.

Storm swerved, as if he had changed his mind, and didn't want to go there.

But Hal forced him to hold his course, and the dragon reluctantly lowered his feet as the land came up at them.

They landed, and Storm folded his wings.

There was silence, except for the whine of the wind, which Hal had thought would be ceaseless.

A few yards away were scattered bones.

Hal walked to them.

They were those of a dragon, long dead, the bones browning, scattered by small creatures.

He couldn't tell what had killed it, or if it had died naturally.

Storm made a strange keening noise.

The shadows were getting longer, and night was coming.

This was a high land that should be haunted.

Not by human ghosts, but by the shades of dragons who'd died long before.

Here, Hal knew, was the home of his dream dragon, his dream dragon and many more.

Then dragons had lived in closer-knit colonies than those they formed in their new world.

Why they'd changed, he had no idea.

He got back on Storm, gigged the dragon into its staggering takeoff, and flew low over the tableland.

There were many bones scattered about.

He spotted a small rocky outcropping, and a bubbling spring nearby, and landed.

He unsaddled Storm, watered and fed him, and found dry wood for a fire.

He didn't fear any red and black dragons in this place.

Storm was restive, curling up, then getting up and sitting, staring out across the plateau, before curling up again.

Hal didn't feel sleepy, but forced himself to roll in his blanket.

He slept, and he dreamed. But this time it wasn't dreams of a single dragon, but of this colony, years and centuries ago.

Four dragons had found the plateau, and made it home.

There was more than sufficient prey on the plains and hills nearby.

The dragons multiplied.

There were other tribes of the monsters, in other parts of the mountains, and they fought their wars of breeding and territory, mostly flash and bluff, although too often the bluff became real, and the great beasts tore at each other and dragons fell to their death before their rage cooled.

Then the red and blacks came into the world, and the wars with them were never bluff.

Every battle was to the death, and the dragons couldn't seem to understand that they were being hunted down like vermin, the red and blacks always choosing their time and odds.

Kits were choice prey to the foreign beasts, as if the red and blacks were intent on exterminating the other dragons.

The dragons fought back, finding the red and blacks' sanctuary, attacking hard. But that single attempt failed to rid them of the red and blacks, and was driven off with many casualties.

Now the world belonged to the invaders.

Then there were far fewer dragons, and many of them flew away, to find other, safer cliffs for homes, or even to join other tribes.

Only half a dozen dragons were left, old creatures, set in their ways.

They were attacked one dawn by the red and blacks, and fought as hard as they could.

But there were too many of the enemy, and the last of the dragons were savaged from the skies.

The land was silent, except for the wind, and the triumphant screams of the red and blacks as they flew over the tableland, then away.

Then there was nothing but the wind, and the passage of empty years.

Hal awoke.

It was still dark, but the horizon was beginning to lighten.

He had the answer to his question, although he didn't know where he'd found it.

There was but the one home for the red and black dragons.

Now it was time to destroy them.

32

The return flight was uneventful, except for one incident: Hal had come out of the mountains, over rolling foothills, and saw another dragon in the distance.

Storm was quickly alert.

The other dragon appeared not to see him, and drew closer.

Hal was about to climb for cover in the high clouds when he saw it was not a red and black, nor one of his own.

Then the wild dragon saw him, and half-rolled in surprise.

It recovered, and, amazingly, neither attacked nor fled, but held its course.

Hal restrained Storm from his attack, and the two flew side by side, about a mile apart, for a few moments, then the other dragon turned away, as if its curiosity was satisfied.

Hal thought that very odd. In this part of the land, he would have thought all dragons felt they had no friends, whether red and black or any other shade.

But he forgot about it when he reached his valley.

His tiny unit was in an uproar.

The commotion had been caused by Garadice, who'd announced that, with Kailas's permission, he intended to make all of them dragon-fliers, from orderly to scout, unless they proved they suffered absolute fear of heights.

Hal was momentarily shocked, like the others, then thought about it.

Why not? After some consideration, he realized that the only thing that "made" a dragon-flier, in his estimation, was a love of being in the air.

Other than that, it was just a hazardous job.

And here, marooned in this alien land, what wasn't?

He announced, to moans, growls and, here and there, some eagerness, that he would go along with Garadice's decision, and that training would begin the next day.

The first stage, as in the famous rabbit-cooking recipe, was to capture their dragon.

Actually, the first step was *finding* a dragon. Or, rather, a cluster of dragons. Hal hoped that what he'd seen in his dreams or visions, that dragons in this land grouped together, still held true, and so he and his handful of fliers went looking.

A long day's flight away, they found a rocky outcropping on the coast that, as Mariah put it, was "friggin' *crawling* with monskers."

Hal refused to let the image grow in his mind, and took his four dragons, Quesney, Cabet, Miletus riding, plus Garadice, Mariah, Hachir and Kimana behind, to an isolated crag of their own, where they spent a day watching the wild dragons.

Garadice passed his time oiling a long, tough rope that had been part of the *Compass Rose*'s rigging.

The others picked two young wild ones, perhaps two or three years old, one male and one female. The next morning, before dawn, the hunters were in the air over the male's pinnacle.

Hal put Storm in a dive past it, and the young beast thought that was a challenge, and rolled out of his nest after him.

The beast didn't notice two other dragons diving on him, one either side, until they crowded close. The young dragon lashed out with his fangs, was pinioned around the neck by Miletus's beast, who didn't fancy having to perform in such a pacifistic manner and started protesting loudly. Garadice, sitting backwards on Miletus's mount, tossed the line around the youngster's neck.

The captive dragon was unceremoniously pulled away from its home rocks, kicking, wings flailing, for about a mile, then Miletus took it to ground.

Waiting men quickly staked the dragon down, helpless, then Garadice ran in, under the monster's tearing claws, and tied a weighted blanket behind its carapace.

It was left to shrill and stew, while the others went back to the crag and did the same to the female dragon.

This time Cabet got raked across his chest, and Garadice nearly had his leg bitten off, before the female was safely grounded a hillock away from its brother.

Next, the men went hunting game from the air, their targets on the ground below.

Four antelope were coursed down and killed.

One each went to the tethered dragons, who showed their gratitude by trying to murder their benefactors.

But, in spite of the rending howls of captivity that night, the next morning, both antelopes' bodies had vanished.

That was a good start.

That afternoon, a pair of the sheeplike grazers were caught, and half a dozen more of the rather stupid creatures driven into a draw and pinned there with brush to provide very fresh meat.

The dragons struck at their warders only half-heartedly when they were fed this time.

Two days later, they were baying for their meals in the afternoon, and paid little mind to the men bringing them.

"Good, good," Garadice said. "These appear to be smarter than the ones I've trained, especially those godsdamned black ones, who just want to kill people."

"Sensible sorts that they are," Mariah said. "Though I believe these are just waiting for their main chance to get us good."

The female almost proved him right, and nearly removed Mariah's ear at the next feeding.

Now the fliers moved their camp close to the dragons, giving them a chance to get used to humans night and day.

This was going very well, so well that Hal made another shuttle to their valley base, and brought back more fliers-to-be.

They captured, tied and mock-saddled two more dragons.

That cost them their first casualty – a scout got careless, taking a dragon his meal, and lost most of his lower arm.

The dragons were now well used to their "saddles," and the time had come to mount them. While they were half-asleep, real saddles replaced the blankets, and then heavy leather hacks, pulled into the beasts' jaws behind their fangs, were used. This last produced blind, lethal rage from the dragons, more than anything since their capture.

"I never thought," Garadice said, "I'd be missing things as basic as chains and bits.

"There's much to be said for civilization."

"You're telling me," a rather pale Farren Mariah, who was scheduled to be the first rider, said.

When the male dragon was familiar with his harness, he was taken aloft on a long lead handled by Garadice, who was sitting facing the rear on a dragon flown by Kimana.

Predictably, the dragon cavorted and twisted, but was too glad to be free of his earthly tethers to fight that much, and, sooner or later, swooped more or less under control at the end of the lead.

Then it got very dangerous.

A third dragon, Aimard Quesney in its saddle, flew close to the young wild dragon, Farren Mariah poised behind the flier.

The third beast veered close, and before the wild dragon could bank away, Mariah jumped, grabbed its carapace, pulled himself firmly into the saddle and hung on.

It was safer, trainers had learned, to make a first mount of a dragon in the air, for a dragon on the ground could roll, and use its great tail as a sweep to tear the rider off.

This one still tried, but the requirements of flying limited his options.

The beast twisted, turned, spun.

Hal, watching on the ground, felt himself pale a little. He'd never had to train a completely wild dragon, and was, at the moment, most grateful.

The question was, who would wear out first?

The wild dragon sagged, held a course, and then Quesney took his monster in close and Mariah leaped again, this time to safety.

"I'm very damned glad," Mariah said, once safely on the ground, "there's no spiritous liquors about, for I'd surely set a bad example.

"As 'tis, I'm grateful I'm wearing my brown breeches."

The next day, Mariah went up again.

The dragon knew what to expect, and so tried some new twisting maneuvers. But Mariah hung on.

This time, he was able to bring the dragon down for a landing, then jump off and run away while the others tied the beast down again.

In normal lands and times, that would've meant Mariah had his dragon, and would now train it.

But these weren't normal times.

Mariah, not having fallen off, would be used as first breaker on each of the wild dragons, to his wild objections.

But no one was listening – they were watching Kimana Balf in her first ride, a spectacular, sky-covering series of leaps by a most aerobatic dragon.

By that evening, there were two slightly saddle-tamed dragons.

Garadice and his team went out and managed to collect two more dragons, both females this time. They almost faced disaster when a third attacked Aimard Quesney, almost dumping Garadice from his perch.

But he hung on, and the two monsters were mock-saddled and pegged down.

"I'm starting to think—" Farren Mariah said.

"Glad of that," Hal interrupted. "About time, and all."

The two were up to their elbows in guts, butchering animals for Chook's ministrations.

"Sharrup," Mariah said. "Before I was so rudely crudely interrupted, I was saying I'm starting to think there's good to be said for armies."

"Like how?" Kimana Balf asked. She was watching the slaughter from a few yards away.

"In armies, bigtime fliers like myself have underlings underlinged to take care of the slops . . . like this one . . . whilst they occupy themselves with sailing yither and hon among the clouds.

"The hells with this equal-opportunity adventuring."

"You want me to make it worse?" Hal asked. "Wait until all of the groundpounders are sailing in the clouds with you.

"Who'll then wash the pots and pans?"

"Quality will out, and all will be chosen for their true talent," Farren Mariah said, in an uncertain tone.

Kimana Balf and Farren Mariah turned their two semi-tamed dragons over to Hachir and Garadice for final training as their own mounts, while they moved on to breaking the second pair.

That went more easily than they'd expected – the two already-ridden monsters seemed to take an interest, and had a honking converse with the new dragons.

"I think they're being told to go along with the course of events," Balf said.

"More like," Farren Mariah said, "being told just when you gets careless and hangs your leg out for an easy nip-off."

Now it would get interesting.

Hal flew back to the valley, brought back more non-fliers, Bod-rugan and, surprisingly, the eagerly volunteering orderly, Uluch.

He'd considered the bruiser Babil Gachina, gotten as far as putting him up behind Storm for the trip back to the pinnacles, then saw the look of complete terror of the air on the man's face, and his clenched eyes.

Another one who would have little of this flying nonsense was Chook, the cook.

Fairly sure of the answer, he thought, Hal asked the enormous man when he wanted to learn to fly.

The man set down the cleaver he'd taken with him on his escape, turned and considered Kailas, who, for an instant, thought of reaching for his dagger.

Or running.

But Chook said and did nothing but turn back to the roast he was preparing.

Garadice himself, strangely, wasn't the best flier Hal had. He seemed to lack confidence in himself, and was jerky with his rein commands, and sometimes too slow to react.

No, there would be some who wouldn't become fliers.

*

They'd taken enough dragons from one tribe, clan, or whatever it should be known as, Garadice decided, so they moved the forward camp further west, to a small mountain range, where there were more dragons.

Also, Hal thought the new fliers were skilled enough for them to start flying patrols, each paired with an experienced flier, and he rotated the pairs from the valley to the forward camp.

"I was just remembering something," Kimana Balf said lazily. She and Hal were in their rather crude tent, made of animal skins.

Outside, a low fog and drizzle kept them from flying.

The dragons were quiet, having been fed an animal apiece, and Hal had named the day a make-and-mend, with no one expected to do much.

"You were remembering what? One of your great victories in the war?" Hal asked.

"Don't be so godsdamned bloodthirsty. There is life beyond slaughter, you know."

"All right. I'm learning." Hal rolled over, put his head on her thigh.

"I remember, one time, after I brought down . . . never mind. Like I said, the point of the story isn't gore.

"Anyway, I did something that somebody of a great rank thought was impressive, and he told me to take a week's leave.

"The war was going slowly, and it was winter and there was not much going on in the air, so I wasn't shorting the war effort.

"I didn't have, as you know, much of a family, or anyway didn't feel like going back to the old winery for a visit, and there wasn't anybody special around that I was sweet on.

"So I convinced my squadron hostler he could spare a couple of horses, and saddled up and rode to Fovant."

"Nice city," Hal said, not mentioning that either he or his ex-wife owned a rather palatial flat there.

"It is, isn't it.

"Anyway," Kimana went on, "I knew of this old hotel, so traditional I don't think they admitted to anyone there was even a war going on.

"It was right in the center of the city.

"I had money, so I took a nice, quiet, huge room that fronted on the back garden, which was looking a little bit bare, since I guess all of the gardeners had been sucked up by the war.

"But I didn't care.

"There was a row of bookstores a block over, and I bought ten or twenty books. Some that I'd sworn I should read, others that didn't matter to anyone.

"Meaningless pliff, in other words.

"And I went to my room, built a fire in the grate and got into this big wooly nightie I'd found, and curled up under some wonderful flannel sheets and feather comforters.

"That was all I did, for the whole week.

"Read, and, every now and then, bathed and dressed and went to find a restaurant, where I kept a book open in front of me.

"Didn't talk to anybody, didn't go anywhere, didn't drink anything.

"Just read.

"And when I went back to my squadron, it was as if I'd been gone for a year or more. I felt like a brand-new person."

She was silent.

"Did you ever do anything like that?" she asked.

Hal thought.

"No. I don't guess I did."

No, he hadn't. He'd always been busy, with his wife, or with friends, or with the war or going somewhere or doing something.

He'd never just sat there and let things pass by.

Not unless he was worrying himself sick, or planning something.

"I wonder if I'd like doing that," he said, a little wistfully.

"Maybe we could try it. I'm sure the Council of Barons has forgotten they want your ass on toast by now."

"Maybe we could."

The training was going better than Hal had expected. But he knew he had only a limited amount of time before the red and black demons discovered him.

Every now and again one of the fliers saw one or two of them, arcing across the skies, as if patrolling their realm.

Sooner or later . . .

There was a great deal to what Farren Mariah had been complaining about – more than just who was to perform the scut details – regarding the virtues of belonging to an organization.

One was the small matter of clothes.

There was wear, there was tear, and there were only four or five needles in the group.

And no cloth, other than canvas that was originally meant to be sails for the *Compass Rose*.

Hal had a dream that they would be marooned in this strange land for years, and that when King Asir finally sent someone to find out what had happened, they'd encounter some stark-naked loons, with beards down to their bellybuttons.

They used animal hides for almost everything, scraping them in running water, then rubbing brains into the hides and stretching and tanning them. Canvas was cut and cursingly sewn into outer garments.

Their technique got better, but Hal still yearned for the feel of fine, clean linen against his skin.

A red and black swooped over the valley, and the men and women scurried for cover.

The dragon came back to take another look.

Hal wondered what it had seen. If anything. He thought he might have gotten careless at having the camouflage detail fine-tune their cover.

But the dragon flew on.

Seeing nothing.

Unless, of course, it planned to come back later.

Hal had no idea how demons thought.

Uluch seemed to have forgotten about his previous life as an orderly, or as anything else.

Now he was a companion to dragons.

When he was assigned his dragon, it was as if the beast, about four years old by Garadice's reckoning, was the only dragon that had ever existed.

As soon as he'd ridden it for the first time, he started spending his nights with the beast.

"Good thing Uluch's feeding him well," Kimana said. "Otherwise we'd come out one morning and find us one dragon-flier short, and that monster picking his teeth."

"Or worse," Farren Mariah said. "I suppose we should be glad Uluch's assigned to a male.

"Otherwise . . ."

He shook his head lasciviously.

"There's something worse," Kimana said. "Or more perverted."

"Both of you can stop, right here, right now," Hal said.

Uluch didn't hear, and if he had, he probably wouldn't have cared about the canards.

Hal realized, to his considerable embarrassment, that he knew nothing about the man, even though Uluch had spent years as his orderly.

It was a little late to be asking for a biography.

If it was possible to dote on a dragon, Uluch doted on his. He'd given it a name, but told no one what it was, for some unknown reason.

He brushed and washed it twice a day, wouldn't let it stale where it slept, flew it to water and bathed it at least every other day.

He'd personally drilled the saddle- and quiver-mounting holes in the dragon's carapace, wincing as he did, using the modified weapons they'd turned into tools.

It didn't hurt the dragon, Garadice swore, but it seemed to pain Uluch to the depths of his soul.

Uluch spent as much time in the air as he was allowed. Climbing high, he would push his mount through maneuvers he'd seen other, more experienced fliers do, and devised ones of his own, getting lower and lower until he ran out of altitude, when he would practise his low-flying skills.

Hal was watching him one day, as he sported with his mount in the open valley of their base.

The day was calm, peaceful. High overhead, Kimana and Quesney fought a mock duel.

Toward the coast, there were a pair of wild dragons. There'd been more of them seen around the valley lately, and Hal was starting to worry about someone not recognizing a red and black until it was too late, and exposing the secrecy of their base.

A pair of just-captured dragons were being taught shouted commands by Garadice and one of the new fliers.

Kailas could smell Chook's kitchen – the aroma of a stew of various animals and wild plants. He thought wistfully of bread, fresh-baked, milk, a glass of charged wine, put those thoughts aside, and went back to watching Uluch.

It took a few minutes to figure what he was doing. He'd put handkerchiefs on the tops of grass stems, not a foot from the ground, and was diving low and having the dragon pluck them away with his talons or jaws.

Hal thought it incredibly dangerous, was deciding how he'd

order Uluch to train more safely without sounding a complete fool, when the red and black dragons appeared.

Hal was on his feet, shouting a warning.

But there was no way Uluch could hear in time.

For an instant, Hal thought the red and blacks had mounted a clever ambush. But there would have been more of them if they'd discovered the valley . . . and then he noted their obvious surprise as the hostile dragons screeched, started to climb, then changed their mind and came in for the easy kill.

Uluch's dragon wasn't there for their fangs. Uluch had had an instant to realize he was being attacked, jerked his animal's bridle, and it had turned sharply into the attack, almost digging in a wingtip.

One red and black overshot Uluch, the other turned with him, striking for the beast's neck. Uluch's dragon reached with a talon, had the red and black's wing by the leading edge, and tore at it.

The dragon screamed in pain, ducked, but ran out of height.

He smashed into the ground, breast first, head and neck futilely lifting as he rolled, over and over, bones smashing.

There was the flash of flame, and then nothing.

The second red and black flew as fast as it could for the valley's mouth.

But Kimana and then Quesney had seen the flurry, and both were diving.

Kimana got there first, her dragon coming down just above the red and black, talons reaching for the monster's head, tearing at its eyes.

The red and black pulled, but was held firm, and Kimana's dragon had it by the neck, ripping upward.

Then it flared into fire, and was gone.

"We're half ready for them," Hal said to the somber group around him. "And I think that's about all we're going to get. We've pushed our luck as far as we can.

"We knew they'd find us, sooner or later. I don't know if they did, or if they just happened on us. I think it was coincidence, but we can't operate on that belief.

"I'm sending two dragons to the forward camp at dawn, and we'll regroup here, and start making battle plans.

"Tonight, I want four fliers on standby, two in the air, and two ready for takeoff. Change over every two hours.

"Fliers, sleep ready to fly, and the dragons will have to spend the night in harness.

"That's all."

It was getting dark.

Hal walked out of the ravine, checking the camouflage over it.

It looked all right.

Then he saw two things:

First were three dragon kits. He guessed them no more than months old, more cute than lethal-looking. They were really too young to have left the nest. Hal wondered if their parents had been killed by other dragons, or by red and black demons, and how and why they'd come to this valley.

They were crouched atop the valley wall, watching everything that happened below very intently.

Wild dragons should have fled, or never have approached the men.

Hal thought, for an instant, that these could be demons.

But they were green, deep orange, and a mottled dark purple, and Hal had never seen demon kits.

At least not yet.

Then he noted Bodrugan, in the middle of the valley, crouching about like he was collecting twigs.

He trotted to him.

The magician looked up.

"Did you see those dragonlets?" Hal pointed.

"I did," Bodrugan said. "I don't think they're hostile. I sense no threat, no danger. I wouldn't worry about them."

"What the hells are they doing?"

"Damned if I know," the wizard said. "Maybe Garadice would have an idea. Ah. Here we go."

Bodrugan knelt, carefully plucked blades of grass.

"Very well then, what are *you* doing?" Hal asked.

"This is where Uluch destroyed one of the dragons today," Bodrugan said. "I'm trying to collect any . . . residue. Perhaps I can develop some kind of spell with it that might help us."

Hal thought that was not a bad idea. Then he had one of his own.

"I want your assistant, Scothi," he said. "I want to put him, with one of my scouts, probably that thug Gorumna, in the mountains, as close as I can get them to the red and black base."

"Why?"

"I don't know, precisely," Kailas said. "I want them to watch those whatever-they-ares, and give me anything they can see.

"We're getting ready to fight them without a plan or a clue.

"And that sounds like guaranteed trouble."

"It does, doesn't it?" Bodrugan agreed, getting up.

"When do you want him?"

"Right now," Hal decided. "I'd like to put them in place tonight. Both moons are rising, and that'll give us enough light to fly by."

"I know two people who are about to become very unhappy," Bodrugan said. "And I suspect if Limingo hadn't gotten himself killed, I'd be one of them."

Hal inclined his head, didn't answer. "Let me know if you find anyone around these parts that *is* happy," he said.

Hal's idea might not have been elaborately planned, but it felt right.

Of course, he'd be one of the fliers who'd put the watchers in place.

He chose two other fliers to accompany him – Farren Mariah and Kimana.

The extra dragon was just in case there were any emergencies.

The two men for the watch, Bodrugan's assistant Scothi, and the former scout, Gorumna, carried heavy packs with food and their bed rolls.

As they were getting ready to take off, Bodrugan came up with two small sticks. "I've ensorceled these two as one," he explained to Scothi. "When you reach your position, put yours on the ground, and don't disturb it. If you have anything to report . . . or if you're discovered . . . wiggle your twig, which my stick'll hopefully echo, and we'll do what we can to rescue you. If you have to run, keep the stick with you, and mine will be drawn to it.

"I wish we could figure some sort of voice-sending," he said.

The two men looked at each other, carefully keeping blank faces, kissed, and it was time to go.

Hal led the other two dragons north and east to the red and blacks' lair.

The mountains rose ahead of him, and he sent Storm low, just over the scrub trees.

The moons were very bright, and he could see almost as if it were daylight.

He brought Storm into a circle just short of the red and blacks' valley, and landed atop a mountain crest.

"The dragons are just over the next ridge," he told Scothi and Gorumna. "I'd suggest you get no closer than that mountaintop there, and find some sort of cover to watch from.

"Good luck."

There wasn't anything more to say.

The three dragons took off, went back the way they'd come.

Hal kept looking back, at the dark bulk of the mountains, hoping he'd been right in his plan, if it could be given that firm a name.

It was false dawn when they returned to their valley base.

The three dragon kits had gotten closer to the valley floor. Two of them were curled in balls, sound asleep, while the other kept watch.

Hal wondered about them once more, then put the matter aside.

There were more important concerns.

33

For five days, about all the Dragonmaster had to do – all that he could manage, beyond the immediate demands of his body and his duty – was stare at Bodrugan's damned stick.

He noticed, but didn't pay much attention to, the fact that the dragon kits were now being fed, first by Chook and Uluch, then in self-appointed shifts by the others.

Uluch also piled dried grass into a mow, and the small monsters found that acceptable bedding.

That made Hal pay more attention, and he asked Garadice if he'd ever seen baby dragons behave like these.

Garadice said he hadn't, except when a dragon had been raised by humans almost from the egg.

Farren Mariah was listening.

He snickered.

"Like that wonderful nightmare you had, back during the

war. Raised by an ickle pretty girl child from the bottle. What did you name it? Sugary?"

"I didn't name it," Hal snarled. "The little girl called it Sweetie."

Garadice looked for an explanation, didn't get one from either flier.

The original Sweetie was not one of Hal's favorite memories, since she'd neatly dumped him into enemy captivity, then vanished.

"Another thing I don't understand," Garadice said, "is why we've been having flyovers by wild dragons in the last few days. I'd like an explanation for that, too."

But no one had one.

Hal had the stick watched around the clock, and, just at dawn of the sixth day, it twitched. Before the flier assigned to it could call an alarm, it slowly started turning.

Hal was shouting for the fliers he'd named for the pickup.

He was taking a very heavy team of six dragons. He would lead three, with the other two fliers being Farren Mariah and Kimana. A second vee was led by Cabet, with Hachir and Aimard Quesney.

Bodrugan wanted to fly as well, but Hal told him no. He wanted the magician to ride behind him, with the stick.

The day was bright with promise, a crisp wind riffling the grasses of the prairies below.

In the distance, five wild dragons saw them, and turned to parallel their flight.

The plains ended, and climbed into foothills and mountains.

Bodrugan leaned over Hal's shoulder.

"The stick is moving . . . so are they. Which probably means they've been seen."

Hal thought for an instant, untied his trumpet, and blasted a note.

The other fliers looked.

He pointed up.

All of them pulled their dragons up into a climb.

If the men on the ground had been discovered, the red and blacks would be attacking them.

And there was no weapon as deadly for a dragon-flier as having height on his enemy.

Hal leaned back, shouted over his shoulder.

"Can you track them?"

"Yes," Bodrugan shouted. "Unless the demons have counter-magic."

Hal took the other five fliers very high, until he would barely be able to make out the men on the ground, depending on the magician to spot the pair.

Now the foothills had grown into cliffs, and they were nearing the demons' base.

And they saw the red and black dragons.

There must have been a dozen of them, swarming around a tree-covered rise, smoke billowing from the ground.

Bodrugan jabbed him in the ribs.

"They're down there. Near the hilltop."

Hal could have guessed as much.

But he nodded thanks, and motioned down, not wanting now to give their presence away with his trumpet.

Two-to-one odds, he thought.

Oh well . . . there'd been worse than that in the war.

He tapped Storm on the neck with his reins.

The dragon didn't need any direction, but instantly ducked his head, and, hissing like a kettle, dove on the red and blacks.

Farren and Kimana were almost beside him, and, about twenty yards above and behind, Cabet and his two companions plunged into battle.

As they closed, a red and black dragon below suddenly rolled over on a wing, and hurtled toward the ground. It exploded into flames, vanished.

So the scouts were fighting back.

Hal heard the angry screams of the dragons below.

He cocked his crossbow, notched a quarrel, looked for a target.

He had no time for more than one.

Two, actually, as he noted Storm's talons reaching for the wing of a red and black. Kailas switched his aim to a second monster, fired, hit fair in the beast's neck. It must have died instantly, for it exploded in midair.

Storm had the second dragon by the wing, tore at it, ripped it almost away, then let go as they plummeted past, Hal pulling at the reins to bring his dragon out of its dive.

Storm came level bare yards from the ground, and, without bidding, climbed for altitude.

Hal chanced a shot at a red and black above him, missed cleanly, ducked as a demon flew close, its wings flailing.

He managed to reload, fired at that dragon, saw no sign of a hit, then there was a large red and black just above him. Storm had it by the throat, tore once, as a bird-killing dog does, and then they were in the middle of the swarming fight.

Hal found a target, and the red and black dove, trying for escape. It almost made it, clearing the ridge crest narrowly, going for the valley. But Hal had a steady shot, and hit it in the body, behind the carapace. The demon screamed, pinwheeled, and then blew up.

The sky was empty of red and blacks. Hal quickly counted his men, and came one short.

"I saw him taken," Bodrugan said from behind, in a shaken voice. Hal had quite forgotten about him. "It was Cabet, I think."

And so it was.

The veteran had been struck from below, torn from his mount, and the demon ripped at his corpse as it fell.

Cabet, Hal thought mournfully, as they landed on the ridge crest, and the acolyte and scout came running from cover. Poor bastard, after going through the war, not being able to find a life, and dying here, in this unknown land.

But then he cheered himself, thinking that everyone had to die, and Cabet, who seemed to have not much of a life beyond dragon flying, couldn't have found a better death.

Maybe.

They flew hard and low, back for their valley.

Hal pulled Storm up and around, in a high bank, making sure they hadn't been followed.

There were no red and blacks to be seen – nor any unridden dragon at all.

They landed.

The others in the expedition could count, and quickly realized who'd gone down.

Possibly the hardest hit was the young woman who'd been Cabet's dragon's handler.

He heard her say, in a very soft voice, "Whatever will I do now?" before starting to dissolve, noiselessly, in tears.

They mourned Cabet . . . but the story the scout and acolyte had to tell made most forget about the flier for the moment.

Besides, fliers and front-line soldiers had learned, in the war, to put their lost aside, or chance having their own souls die with the dead.

Perhaps Hal felt it a bit harder than most, since Cabet was yet another of the old guard who'd finally gone under.

"We moved away from the hill as soon as you'd taken off," Scothi began. "Gorumna took point, since he is the best at wildcraft."

The whole party was huddled around the scouts.

"We'd made it down into the valley by first light, and found shelter in a nest of rocks.

"There were red and black dragons overhead for most of the day, behaving as if they were suspicious of something, but not sure what.

"We didn't move until dusk, then went on, to the hill over-looking the dragons' nest . . . if that's what it's supposed to be called.

"We found a good hide – a rocky thicket. We cleared brush away from close to the ground, so we could watch the valley below.

"We laid out your stick, Bodrugan, like you'd told us, then we waited. I was too excited . . . scared, maybe . . . to sleep.

"At dawn, we could see the dragons, sprawled about, sleeping. They didn't seem to be keeping any watch.

"We counted at least fifty . . . they were piled atop each other, so it was hard to make an accurate count.

"When it was full light, four of them took off, and circled their valley a few times. We stayed still."

"Very still," Gorumna said. "Trying to think like rocks, not people."

"I thought about working up some sort of spell that might make them overlook us," Scothi continued. "But I was afraid of using magic.

"I could scent . . . well, not scent, but *feel* wizardry all around me, but didn't feel like there was any being cast. Maybe the remnants of magic? I'm not sure about this.

"At any rate, we watched on, saw nothing much in particular, except, Lord Kailas, as you thought, there were no more dragons arriving from any other places."

"It was eerie, watching them," Gorumna added. "When they ate, it wasn't with any kind of joy. Like they were just taking on fuel.

"They didn't sleep much, but when they did, they just stopped in their tracks, not trying to make any sort of bed, like real dragons do."

"The next day," Scothi said, "our third in the hide, was when we saw that ring of fire appear that you said you'd seen.

"Four dragons went through the ring, three came back out. Sorry. I meant, three came out. We couldn't tell whether they were the same ones or not.

"Then the ring closed. I didn't see any of the dragons making magic, or any signs of a spell being cast, so if there was one, I'd guess it'd be on the other side.

"The fourth day there was nothing, but the dragons seemed more suspicious, flying close around their home.

"But they didn't come any closer to our hill than they'd done before, so we didn't try to flee.

"Then, the fifth day, the ring appeared again.

"And something strange.

"Something came out of the ring, something that looked like a man."

Hal jerked closer.

"But a crude sort of man, like something a kid would make out of clay," Gorumna said.

"It walked around, stumbling, as if it wasn't used to walking, then went back through the ring, and the ring vanished again."

"We figured that was enough," Scothi said, "and it was time for us to leave."

"We'd no more than twitched the stick, and started backing out of our bush," Gorumna said, "than all of the bastards took off, as if they'd seen us. But there wasn't any way they could've.

"We ran hard, before they got height, figuring on trying for that hilltop you dropped us off on.

"But they were above us, and so we went on down, into a valley.

"They came down after us, flying close, trying to grab us, but we'd go flat when they came in, and warn the other when one of them was trying for us."

"Gorumna shot one down with his bow," Scothi said, "and that made them back off for a bit.

"I had an idea, and used my flint to spark a pile of dry brush into life, remembering how dragons, real dragons, don't seem to like fire much.

"It flared up like we'd thrown brandy on it, and two of the dragons who'd come in low got caught in the flare."

"They took fire like they were tinderwood," Gorumna said

with satisfaction. "Smoke boiled up, and the dragons pulled up, and circled, a little cautious now."

"That gave us time to get to the next ridge," Scothi said. "And then you were coming, and . . . well, that was that.

"I hope we saw some things that'll be useful."

Both the scouts looked at Hal pleadingly.

"What was that thing that looked like a man?" Gorumna asked.

Hal considered, the flicker of an idea just surfacing.

"One of the demons?" Farren Mariah suggested. "Or the main demon himself?"

"No," Hal said, and it came to him.

"The demons that look like dragons came to this land not knowing anything," he said slowly. "Not who or what was the power here, or what form they should take to rule.

"The strongest thing was the dragons. So . . ."

"So that was the form they chose," Bodrugan said.

"Until we came along." Farren Mariah had also gotten it.

"Maybe so," Hal agreed. "I think so."

"So now," Hachir said, "we've seen a baby man. The more they're around us, the more they can learn from us, the more like men they'll look."

"Plus having whatever powers they've got of their own," Hal said.

"Which means we've got to stop them now. Before they get any stronger."

"Or," Farren Mariah said, "figure out some shape that's to man like man is to a dragon."

"All we have to do," Aimard Quesney said, "is work out how."

34

"A minor, minnyscule matter," Farren Mariah said.

"We know they don't like fire," Kimana said.

"I somehow don't think my dragon'll take kindly to my mounting up with a torch between my teeth," Mariah said. "Let alone how I'm to get close enough to the enemy beasties to apply it liberally to their heads and shoulders."

"Magic," a flier suggested, looking hopefully at Bodrugan.

"Magic how?" the wizard said.

"That's your department," Farren Mariah said breezily.

"At which I'm blank, so far. Sorry."

Hal happened to look up, and saw the three young dragons, huddled close together, about halfway down the rise, looking as solemn as young owls.

"This is getting us nowhere quickly," he said. "Let's eat, put our heads down, and be ready to hit them at dawn."

A chill wind was blowing off the ocean as the thirteen dragons flew north before dawn.

Hal wondered if the wind would blow their scent to the red and blacks, decided that was stupid – they were flying faster than any wind.

As the foothills rose, they turned slightly to the west, to come in on the demons' valley from out of the rising sun, and climbed.

Hal didn't want to take them too high, hoping to catch the red and blacks still asleep, and have the advantage of height.

He motioned as the first rays caught them, and the formation obediently closed up.

Hal was about to put Storm into a shallow dive when someone blatted on a trumpet.

It was Kimana, giving the alarm.

The red and blacks were already in the air, high above them and diving, coming in fast.

There was no time for tactics.

Hal kicked Storm into a sharp bank, tried climbing, and a red and black tore past him, talons reaching for Storm and missing.

A ridden dragon flopped past him.

Hal couldn't tell for an instant who the rider was . . . had been, for he was without a head.

Then he recognized the tatters of uniform on the body.

Miletus, his first squadron commander.

But there was no time for the dead.

Two dragons were on Storm's flanks, harrying at him. Storm thrashed his tail, and one dropped back.

Then Kimana was there, on the nearest, wings smashing at the red and black.

It screamed, rolled on its back, and Kimana's dragon ripped its stomach open.

The other dragon closed, and Hal put Storm into a tight turn. The red and black banked as well, and Hal kept his bank, pulling hard on Storm's reins, trying to turn inside the other dragon.

The bank was tight enough for Hal's vision to gray around the edges, and he could feel Storm losing altitude.

The other dragon was turning, turning, and now Storm was behind it, ducking the whisking tail.

The red and black held its turn, and Hal stayed behind it. He was able to force his hands up against the pull of gravity, aim his crossbow and fire a bolt. It hit the red and black near its left wing root, hardly a death blow, and again the turn tightened.

Hal caught a flash of green below him, to his right. They were very close to the ground. He yanked at Storm's reins, and the dragon rolled out of its bank as the red and black, still at a tight angle, scraped the ground with its wing, and bounced and rolled to its death and explosion.

Hal forgot about it, saw another dragon diving down, and cocked and fired. He hit it, he thought, and the demon hurtled on and slammed into a rocky outcropping.

Storm climbed back to the heights. The battle was still a roiling chaos – Hal guessed that all or most of the seventy red and blacks were in the air, and battering at his slender force.

He saw another of his dragons in a long dive, its rider lolling in the saddle. This one was a green and white one, freshly trained, he remembered, though he couldn't recall the rider for the moment.

A red and black was chasing it down, snarling at its rear legs, and Hal put a crossbow bolt through its neck.

The red and blacks were forcing Hal's dragons down toward the ground, and it was time to break free.

Which would have been a neat trick, if he could figure out how to do it.

Hal sent Storm down toward the ground, hoping he could find a defile they could fly into to escape the trap.

He saw something better – a field of waving dry grasses, and the idea struck him.

He drove Storm down, brought his head back to force the dragon to land.

Storm didn't want to, not with enemies in the air, but, whining, he obeyed.

Hal slid out of the saddle, reaching in his belt pouch, found fire-making materials.

Clumsy with haste and fear, not wanting to look up to see the demons diving on him, he struck steel against flint, saw sparks, did it again, and fire glowed in the dry grass. He blew on it, and it flared up, and he fed it more grass, ripping it up with his hands.

Then he had a proper fire, and Storm was screeching at him.

Another rider, Bodrugan, saw what he was doing, and landed clumsily, still not much more than a student.

His arms began waving in a spell, and the flames grew.

Kailas was back in the saddle, and whipping Storm with the reins. The dragon stumbled down the slight slope as the fire built, and they were in the air once again.

Now the battle was at low level, the red and blacks chasing the others around the contours of the hills.

The fire roared higher, and then there was a pillar of smoke.

Hal blew frantically on his trumpet, beckoned, and his fliers saw him, understood, and flew toward the fire, through the smoke. Then they were through, and fleeing west, the fire a backstop, making the red and blacks climb over it.

But Hal's men and women were gone, dots against the plains, heading west until they saw nothing in the skies behind them, before turning for their valley.

One by one, they reached it, exhausted, barely able to stumble from their saddles as the few handlers tried to help.

Now Hal remembered who had ridden the green and white.

Hachir, the one-time teacher and archer, whose life had been shattered.

Three others, including Miletus, had died that day, almost a third of his fliers.

Hal was well and truly defeated.

The day went, handily, to the demons.

35

Hal didn't have much time to mourn his dead as the night closed on them.

The dragons were washed and fed, and then the men. The two low cooking fires permitted before dusk were guttering down as the shadows grew into each other. Hal sat at a distance from the others, staring at the embers.

He'd certainly been defeated before. But he couldn't remember a time when victory had been so important, although there'd been several wartime battles he'd thought vital.

Never before had he faced an enemy who, victorious, would not only dominate this land, but, if his thinking about the new homunculus was correct, might conquer all.

Looking at the dying fires, he chewed and swallowed his tasteless dinner, wondering why the gods hadn't given him a better mind.

He knew what might destroy the demons – the fire that had given them birth – but not how to use it.

And then, in the middle of his agonising, it came to him.

He called Bodrugan over.

The others, hearing the note in his voice, looked up, waiting.

Hal took only a few seconds to explain to the magician.

"It could work," Bodrugan said. "If my spell is as good as it was before."

During the war, Hal had had the idea of dropping boulders on the Roche. The only problem, of course, was that dragons weren't cargo-carrying beasts.

But Hal's idea had been to shatter a great boulder, and have a wizard cast a spell on the pieces, which potentially were the whole, so that when each pebble was thrown by a dragon-flier, it would become the size of its "father."

The spell worked perfectly, and Roche cities were knocked into shambles.

Bodrugan went to work, and in about two hours he had a spell.

"I'd like an assistant," he said.

"Farren," Hal said. "You've a bit of the talent. Help the man, if you would."

"I'm tired of being volunteered," Mariah growled, but obeyed.

Bodrugan had seen some red flowers in the valley, and men were sent to bring them in.

Flint and steel were positioned, and a stack of brushwood was built in front of them, the flowers in odd patterns around it.

Hal didn't like doing this, fearing there'd be red and black dragons about, but saw no other options.

Crossbow bolts were brought, and laid in circles, heads touching, around the brushwood.

Then the fire was touched off.

As it built, Bodrugan began chanting, while Mariah lifted the bolts, as if making an offertory, then set them down.

> *"Remember*
> *What took you*
> *Changed you*
> *Made you elemental*
> *Reaching out*
> *Finding*
> *Base power*
> *Feeling*
> *Building . . ."*

The fire was now roaring, reaching far into the night sky, beyond what the fuel could have given.

Hal looked beyond it. In the darkness, eyes gleamed; the three dragon kits had drawn close to the men and were watching.

> *"Growing*
> *Reaching far to*
> *Change*
> *What you touch*
> *What you hurt*
> *Blood*
> *Or what is used as*
> *Blood*
> *Blood to fire*
> *Blood to fire*
> *Blood to fire*
> *Reach*
> *Remember*
> *And slay."*

Very suddenly, the fire died to embers, and went out.

"Well?" Farren asked.

Bodrugan held out his hands.

"I don't know. The proof will be in the testing."

"And if it doesn't work . . . aarh. My grandfather's spells didn't always sing, either. Sing or singe," Mariah muttered.

But that was the best that could be done.

Hal said stand-to would be three hours before dawn, and gave his simple orders for the next day.

The fliers were told to put their heads down. Rest, if they couldn't sleep.

Hal didn't even try his usual pretense of sleeping soundly and easily, sure of victory on the morrow.

He checked the dragons, starting with Storm.

Babil Gachina found him.

"And what'll *we* do on the morrow, sir?"

"I don't know," Hal said. "Stand by and be ready when we come back . . . those of us who do."

Gachina shook his head.

"Not good enough."

Hal could have gotten angry, but instead was slightly amused.

"Considering your problems with flying, I don't see what you *can* do."

"I can wear a blindfold," Gachina said. "Long enough to put me where I can do some good. And others can do the same . . . or I'll deal with 'em.

"Put us on the ground, sir, in that valley where those damned dragons spawn, and we can surely kill any that come down to us."

Hal considered.

"Yes," he said. "That can be done."

"Good," Gachina growled. "I'll have the rest of my cowards up."

He vanished into the darkness silently.

Hal wandered the small camp, unable to sleep.

He found Uluch with the dragon kits. Two of them were curled, asleep, and the oldest was being crooned to by Hal's once-orderly.

He saw Hal, greeted him without embarrassment. Once he'd been almost servile in the way he talked to Hal. No more. Now it was as if he was an equal.

"They'll be ours, tomorrow."

"I hope so."

"No bare hope, sir. 'Tis a certainty."

Glad that at least one man was sure of himself, Hal went on.

Aimard Quesney was sitting, staring at the remains of the fire.

"You realize," he said, "that all of this is quite damned hopeless. They've got us outnumbered, what, ten to one?"

"Or more," Hal said cheerfully.

"Always good to be following a man who's confident," Quesney said, and stood up. "Oh well. I guess this land without a name's as good a place to die as any other."

He waited to see if Hal had any reply, heard none, so grunted goodnight, and went for his bed roll.

Hal decided that was a way to pass the few hours remaining until they were to fly off, and found his own blankets. Around him, Babil Gachina was rousing the non-fliers, and talking to them in low tones he couldn't make out.

Kimana Balf had her bed roll next to Hal, and was lying on her back, staring up. He saw her eyes were open.

"Well?" she whispered.

"Well what?"

"What of the morrow, fearless leader?"

"I'd rather not be there for it," Hal said. "I'd rather be safe at home, cowering under the bed."

"Would you? Really?"

Her voice was serious.

Hal looked for something else light to say, couldn't find anything.

"No," he said honestly. "No, I wouldn't be anywhere else."

"And that," she said, "is the idiot I've come to love."

She kissed him, and rolled on her side, away from him.

Love? Hal had never heard her use that word before.

He thought about it, and was, suddenly and surprisingly, asleep.

Someone was kicking Hal's foot. He rolled back an eyelid, saw the bulk of Chook standing above him. He was totally awake, sat up.

"There's tea," the cook said. "Anyway, herbs brewed up."

He didn't wait for a reply, but went on.

Hal got up, washed, and had some of the bitter brew Chook had made. There was also fried meat and tubers for those who wanted it. The thought of food roiled Hal's stomach.

Chook paid little attention to his duties, stropping his great cleaver, and stringing his crossbow.

Hal saddled Storm. The dragon was already awake, and seemed eager to go.

Around him the other fliers readied their mounts.

Some, the newly trained, tried to bite, or tail-lash their riders, but no one was struck, the dragons being as sleep-numbed as the men.

Babil Gachina waited nearby with the half a dozen men, non-fliers, who'd be part of his newly created ground force.

Chook joined them, looking somber, with his cleaver and a great butcher knife stuck in his waistband.

Hal tried to think of a noble speech, couldn't come up with one. So he looked at his tiny army, shadows in the darkness, and said, "Let's show them what we're made of," and walked toward Storm.

There was a pointless, ragged cheer, and his men and women followed.

As Hal pulled himself into the saddle, Babil Gachina clambered up behind and wordlessly extended a strip of thick cloth. Kailas bound it around the man's eyes. Gachina winced as if he'd been lashed, but remained silent.

Others of the ground force were already mounted on other dragons.

Hal forgot about his passenger, and gigged Storm into his stumbling takeoff run.

As the dragon cleared the ground, he suddenly screamed, a defiant challenge.

The scream was echoed from the ground, from the biggest of the dragon kits. Hal had an instant to wonder how a beast that small could make that great a noise, and then Storm was in the air, the other dragons following.

Half of Hal's force stayed low, following him toward the hills, the other half, led by Farren Mariah, climbed for the heights.

Hal had learned, in his thousand battles, that no plan survives the first sword-clash. Particularly if the plan is complicated and clever.

He kept his tactics simple:

He would deploy his ground fighters just short of the red and blacks' valley. Then he, and his fliers, would strike the demons at low level, before dawn, when they were still sleeping, or whatever demons did when they were lying down. He'd try to get as many of them on the ground or taking off as possible.

His second element would attack from on high, and wreak as much havoc as they could.

From there . . . from there it was strike where you could, when you could.

Flying low, Hal saw, on either side of him, at a great distance, wild dragons, flying north. He counted more than twenty in one group before he lost track.

He wondered what the hells they were doing about when it was still night.

Then they were in the mountains, climbing, and there wasn't time for anything but war.

Kailas brought Storm down on a hilltop, shrouded in pre-dawn blackness. He turned and pulled the blindfold off Babil Gachina. The hulking thug was pale-faced, and swallowing. But he slid off Storm without hesitating, and called for the others.

Since Hal had considered them skirmishers at the most, he didn't waste time, but kicked Storm into a takeoff.

He looked up as the dragon lurched into the air, and, far above him, saw a flood of dragons, high up, the rising sun just touching them.

There were too many for them to be Farren Mariah's element. He could only hope Mariah had climbed above them.

Hal cocked his crossbow, one of the enchanted quarrels dropping into the firing slot.

Storm was looking down, and saw still-motionless red and blacks below.

Hal kicked him in the ribs, and the dragon tucked his head and wings, and they went into a dive.

Kailas blatted on his trumpet, looked behind him, and saw his element was following.

But the ground was now very close. He pulled Storm up, less than fifty feet above the ground.

Below was a dragon, just rearing.

Hal whispered the fire-spell catchword, fired, spitted it through the neck, and the demon had an instant to scream before it exploded in greasy fire.

Another red and black died to the side from someone else's shot as Hal reloaded and found another target. He shot, missed, had time to recharge his crossbow and put his bolt, its tip just bursting into flame, into the dragon's chest.

He reloaded again, whispered, and killed another demon, and they were past the red and blacks' camp.

He brought Storm up, and back around, this time only a dozen feet above the ground.

There was a red and black fanged head level with his, and he shot at it and flew through the burst of flame.

Other red and blacks were dying, and then, almost beside him, one of his own was caught with a tail-lash, and smashed into the ground, its rider spinning away.

Unbidden, Storm pulled up, and Hal was about to shout a command when he saw the red and blacks that had been in the heights swarming down on them.

Storm hooked one of them with a wing claw, ripped down its neck with his talons, and Hal killed it with his crossbow.

A shadow loomed over him, and he ducked, just as Aimard Quesney's beast gutted the red and black, and it died, screaming.

Storm was climbing, and Hal saw two dragons on Kimana Balf. Storm drove at them, just as Balf brought her dragon in a tight circle, its fangs closing on a demon's throat, then letting go as the red and black screamed and went down.

He came in from the side on the second red and black, had time to shoot it twice before the monster blew up.

All was chaos then, and Hal had no sense of time as he and Storm, one being, one killing machine, tore in and out of the swirl. He almost shot a dragon, realized it was ridden, and swept past Farren Mariah, whose monster's jaws were slathered with a dark ichor.

Kailas saw men trot into the valley, taking time to kneel and shoot carefully into the demons. Babil Gachina and his handful were engaged.

Storm was turning hard, closing on a red and black, and Hal saw Garadice, his dragon with a wing torn away, caught in the jaws of a red and black, going down.

Storm flared his wings, a red and black missed him, and Hal killed it.

There was nothing in front of him, and Hal brought Storm back on the mêlée. There were smoke flares here and there on the ground, and dying, wounded dragons, with human bodies sprawled beside them.

A red and black dove on a standing man. It was Chook. The cook ducked a claw-strike, smashed with his cleaver, and the demon howled pain.

In the center of the slaughter-ground a circle of fire grew from nowhere, its flames gouting out, as if wind-blown.

Red and black dragons poured out of it, almost on top of each other.

Hal realized how few of his own monsters were still in the air, and how many demons were still attacking.

He had an instant to know defeat.

There were too many of them, and as he thought this, he saw

Aimard Quesney caught at the waist in a red and black's jaws, and torn apart.

Storm, as if recognizing doom, screamed, that same great scream he'd unleashed when they took off.

Then he dove on a pair of red and blacks.

His scream was echoed, louder, from both sides, from the sky above, and then three wild dragons swooped in, and tore at the demons.

There were other dragons around them, paying no heed to any of Hal's ridden beasts, but driving into the red and blacks.

The scream was still echoing, as if taken by a hundred hundred other dragons, and the demons were swarmed by wild monsters, torn and butchered.

What had summoned them – Storm's screams, those odd dragon kits – Hal would never know.

The ring of fire flamed higher, and Hal saw, from a thousand feet above him, a ridden dragon diving on it.

It closed, and Hal had an instant to recognize Uluch, standing in his stirrups like a lancer, coolly sending bolt after fiery bolt into the circle.

He smashed into, through it, and the circle flashed into a huge ball of flame.

Then it, Uluch and his dragon were gone, as if they'd never been.

Hal brought Storm around, to see a single flash of flame as the last demon died.

There were no red and blacks in the sky.

There were dragons, wild dragons around him, more than he'd ever seen before, more than he could have imagined.

They swept back over the valley, making sure of the victory, then climbed, like wild geese heading for home, and were flying into the mountains.

That great scream died slowly into silence.

Then there was nothing in that blighted valley but the bodies of dragons and men.

There were fewer than half a dozen dragons still in the air, all with riders.

Storm screamed into the silence, and Hal felt it was a cry of sorrow.

Sorrow and triumph.

36

Storm bobbed happily near the shore of the Hnid's atoll.

Hal sat on the beach, watching him, wishing that men could forget the past as quickly as dragons did.

If that was true.

But at least they didn't show their grief, if they felt it.

Kimana Balf's dragon lifted above the roofed island, splashed in for a landing near the shore.

The last passenger on the shuttle waited dumbly until Kimana undid his blindfold, then Babil Gachina waded to shore, where Chook stood.

A pair of Hnid surfaced, and dove back and forth in happiness, seeing their . . . whatever they thought the giant Gachina was.

All was quiet, all was happiness on the island.

Hal wished he could feel the same, but with few more than a dozen survivors of his expedition, joy came hard.

The survivors of the final battle had returned to their camp, trying to celebrate their victory.

But they knew there was another struggle ahead – somehow reaching Deraine.

They'd begun one step at a time, shuttling supplies, men and women east in single-day hops.

They'd seen no more red and black dragons, and, to Hal, the land seemed cleansed.

Now it would be safe.

Safe for what?

For dragons?

For men to swarm west and colonize, making the creatures of this land their prey, their food, or their tools?

That didn't seem right to Kailas.

He wondered what he should, could do . . . and his rather bleak mood broke as Kimana Balf brought her dragon on to the beach, and a handler led it to where the other surviving monsters were being fed and watered.

"Are you brooding?" she said cheerily as she walked to him, and sat down.

"Nice, soft, warm sand," she said dreamily. "Not moving. I could lie here for a week."

"You'll not be allowed," Hal said. "As soon as Farren Mariah and his crew come back with whatever they've been able to scrounge off the wrecks, we'll all be at work."

"At least we won't be riding dragons," Kimana said. "Or fighting anybody."

"Maybe not," Hal said. "At least, not for a while."

"You really think we'll be able to build boats? Boats that'll make it all the way back home?"

"I don't know," Hal said. "At least some kind of big raft."

"Suddenly, riding the dragons sound like a better idea," she said.

Hal made a face.

That was the other part of his plan.

Those few surviving dragons would fly east as far as they were able. Then they'd land on the sea, and let the current carry them on, as dragons had left this world before.

But this time, they'd have their fliers sheltering on their backs, under their folded wings, as Hal had discovered dragons would do.

At least, the dragons they'd come with. Hal had decided to free the newly tamed creatures before they left.

That is, if they wanted freedom.

Most of them seemed fairly content in the company of man.

The others could join the wild dragons, three or four of whom had followed the remains of the expedition across the coastal waters.

Hal had hoped to see the three dragon kits, who'd vanished when the men had returned from the demons' valley, but without luck.

He wondered if they'd been real dragons, or spirits, and realized he'd never know. Bodrugan had chanced a spell, but found out nothing.

"After we get home," Kimana said confidently, "what do you want?"

"A hot bath," Hal said. "With real soap. A bottle of good wine. Bread. Dripping with butter. A meat pie.

"A nice warm bed, with a roof over it."

"That's all?" Kimana asked, disappointed.

"A bed with you in it."

"That's better." She scooped sand into a pile.

"Do you think we're ever going to come back here?" She caught herself. "Am I allowed to think of us as us?"

"Of course," Hal said, and realized the words came easily. "I mean to the us. As far as coming back here . . . right now, I think I've had enough adventuring.

"A nice quiet mansion, with servants doing all the work," he said.

"I've never had that," Kimana said.

"Past time you try being rich," Hal said, and kissed her.

Three thoughts, none of them spoken, came to him:

It was past time for Hal Kailas to stop being alone.

Maybe it was time to visit that hotel in Fovant with Kimana and a bunch of books.

And maybe it was time for the Dragonmaster to start learning how to master, or at least live with, people.

SEER KING

Book One of the Seer King Trilogy

Chris Bunch

Numantia is a dying empire, the frontier ruled by outlaws, the provinces by rebels, the citizens by discontent. Ancient forces of dark magic grow everywhere, ignored by the Empire's rulers. For two people it is a time of immense possibility and infinite danger.

Hot-headed cavalry officer Damastes and the wizard Tenedos were supposed to die in a mountain ambush. But their enemies underestimated the amazing powers of the seer and the bravery of the soldier. As they begin outwitting usurpers and necromancers, word spreads that theirs is a path of destiny. For Damastes, it will lead to glory and love. For Tenedos, it points to unimaginable heights of ambition. And for Numantia, it shows the way to a renaissance . . . in service to the Goddess of Death.